Haan Moses

Albacore Man
The Moon Women

Manacore Lab   Peterborough   New Hampshire

Manacore Lab

A Division of Plaistow Publications, Inc.
1 Phoenix Place, Peterborough,
New Hampshire 03450

First paperback edition 2016

For information about special discounts for bulk purchases, please contact Manacore Lab Special Sales 1-603-762-7990 or send email to haanmoses@manacorelab.com

Editor Shima Rosenberg
Jacket design by Amaris Bergsen
Logo by Gabe Ringer

Blue Dancers by Edgar Degas 1897

Manufactured in the United States of America

1   3   5   7   9   10   8   6   4   2

Library of Congress Control Number: 2016917430

ISBN 978-0-9982442-0-4 (paperback)

Lyrics from "Tryin' To Set To Seven" by Thomas Milkwood
Used by permission of Spastic Rider Music, copyright 1967

Lyrics from "Four Faces of the Lion" by Thaddaeus
Used by permission of Ravena Studios Singapore, copyright 1970

Table of Contents

The Moon Women

Foreword by Bishop Sargn Ramege

When Haan approached me with the problem, I understood what he was up against yet I felt it was a canyon, which he had chosen to reside within by his own choosing. He and he alone was the one whom these fire gods from hell had picked to eat their waste from the pits of brimstone and belch up their twisted sense of spiriting the good people living under the umbrella of the Beloved. I would have nothing to do with it.

After the first edition appeared on the shelves, most who were brave enough to venture into his word jungles and make sense out of his Rubik's Cube metaphors found an inimical sense of grandeur and grace, but when they came upon the language of the Angels of Abaddon, they were stumped. Although these entities used only simple words, in fact the very words found in the Book of the Revelation the closing gospel of the holy Bible written by Saint John the Divine of Patmos, understanding the content of their statements was yards beyond that with which the normal reader was endowed. In the end, most chose simply to jump over the long chains of Revelate statements and hoped what the Angel had shared wasn't of immediate import upon the story. However, that was an error and so most readers found themselves high and dry on an island of meaningless choices having no manageable exit.

While working with Haan at Manacore Lab and watching how he so deftly put together my own publication soon to be released, I came to reformulate my take on the whole Revelate conundrum. In fact, it was upon my own urging that I stepped up and took a shot at unscrambling a few of the idiomatic quatrains and submitted my take on them to his desk anonymously just to get his reaction. He knew very well it had my signature sewn into the phraseologies, but he played dumb and came to me with such a gaunt face of wonder saying, "Some scribe from the mountains has come forth to produce a marvelous manuscript unwinding the Revelate in such plain Jane terms no one could mistake where things are going in the book." Naturally, I confessed and thus began our undertaking of deciphering the Revelate and laying it all out in plain English for those readers who could benefit the most by our removal of the gauze off their eyes so they could see the new world, which lay beyond the sea of those 1250 words called the Revelate.

Bear in mind, however, that not every stanza has been untangled. We believe the reader should attempt to learn this new way of thinking as it is a mental exercise that will awaken a highly unused part of the brain. Such a process can aid one's understanding as well as disconnect the reader's cerebellum from what Mr. Moses considers is an undeniable abduction lying dormant within their subconsciousness, something that probably occurred at some point in the readers mired past. Therefore, you, dear reader, will come to note that not every word of the Revelate has been translated. What has been remedied is primarily those stanzas which either introduce new information concerning the works of Abaddon or the Khrng as the Angels take on things that may prove untenable to most readers.

Finally, I should like to put in a clarification about a few of the key words, which are repeatedly used by the Angels in the hopes that my preheating of the readers oven shall produce a much better bread in the long run. Very first off the bat is the words that come out the Angel's mouth after he crawls out of his bubble. Well, as you all know at this point it isn't his mouth at all, since the Angel is conversing with Rahm Ibsen via a telepathic connection which the poor boy suffers terribly due to its intensity and its twisted nature.

"UNTO THE ANGEL OF THE CHURCH" is what he says. This salutation is always given to Rahm when the Angel intends to open up a dialogue with their candidate. (Rahm is called the candidate by all of the Angels because

7

he is in fact someone who they are choosing to go forth in a war as their spy so to speak.) This opening statement is both a hello as well as a necessary signal, which the Angel needs to impart so that he can begin to transmit his messages and have them reside within the physical plane so that Rahm may receive them and understand them as well. After Rahm has gained some experience with listening to the Angels dialect, he gets privy to a bit of eavesdropping on some of their conversations, which, surprisingly are much easier to understand than when they speak to Rahm directly, would that they would talk that way with him in the normal course of their encounters with each other. Perhaps, they simply need to maintain their demeanor of big and powerful Angels and not resemble boys on the hood.

The second key word is White. As the Angels explain on numerous occasions, White is two things. First and foremost, it represents the physical plane, this universe, the world of normal molecules and quantum states and forces. It is called White because it represents the universe of White matter as opposed to the many other colors of matter, which make up the universe and which scientists have unknowingly labeled as dark matter. They are all simply other colors of matter. They all resemble the kind of matter that we have but the frequencies of the strings that make up those different matters are all slightly different from ours and therefore we cannot detect them in any way other than we can read the gravity, which they generate. That is the primary reason that we have decided to intuit that there is dark matter such as this in the first place. So, White matter is our matter and the other colors don't matter. That was a joke by the way.

Second we have the keyword of Legion. This and the name of the Time Lord who runs this universe, a god by the name of NIRUNJAN, are words which are neither bolded nor italicized because that is the method Mr. Moses has chosen to delineate these words from true Revelate since they do not appear in the BOR. They are highly indispensable for describing both what the Angels are and also who their boss is. The only other words, which are not jazzed up are the actual names of the Angels themselves, although their home base of Abaddon does connect with what Saint John was given on that day in Patmos. I'm told the whole story was dictated to him by Azrael in the hot sun, which is why the Revelate is the way it is. Nevertheless, their names do come to us from another gospel, a secondary work entitled the Book of Enok. Further study and research into the ancient Aramaic should produce a veritable cornucopia of treasures for the hardcore student who undertakes such a journey.

The third closet to shine a light inside concerns the Khrng and the labels, which the Angels refer to the members of this ultra-race of super attenuated humans. The Angels seem quite gifted in describing these odd characters with some remarkable phraseologies.

FILTHY GLASS DEVILS
THE DEAD REMNANTS
UNCLEAN WORMWOOD OF MAN
THE EVIL LOCUSTS
THE SHAPES OF THE LOCUSTS
THE FILTHY GLASS SCORPIONS
THESE BLACK LOCUSTS
THESE FILTHY SCORPIONS OF MAN
THE SMOKE WIZARDS
THE FILTHY SERPENTS
THE OLIVE EYE DEVILS
THE BLACK PRIESTS
THIS ABOMINATION
THE GLASS HEADED SCORPIONS

We are still loath to meet one. That will come about when Rahm himself sits down and authors his own series of volumes in a valiant attempt to corner the market on these slippery bandits. What they are called intrinsically by the Angels in their world and using Revelate is simply this.

The Moon Women

THE HATED NICOLAITANS

This thing that they hate never leaves the framework of their efforts to quench Mother Earth of this deviance spawned over millions of years ago by a daft and demented individual who wanted only to save his family from certain annihilation. It is almost as if the very existence of the Angels in this world is due only to the presence of this genetic deviance. Due to the fact that the Khrng have built their entire civilization upon an organic foundation and not a corporeal one of steel, cement and the unshifting laws of lift and thermodynamics, they reside outside the weave of normal Time and Space and as such do not disappear at the termination of any particular Time phase as does the rest of normal human civilization. We must suffer that transition while the Khrng continue to thrive and batter against the walls of Time that have imprisoned them within their own enclave of missing Time derivatives. Thus, they are as eternal as the Angels and can neither go home nor taste victory in their war with themselves as well as that of the Angles.

In closing, I should like to once again thank Mr. Moses for his most generous offer to allow me to submit my transcription of what the Angels tried to share with Mr. Ibsen. Someday I hope to meet up with the man and find out what he actually thought about it all himself. However, Haan tells me that may not be possible because apparently the man has chosen to exist within one of the other colored places and not here in the world of the White.

PROLOGUE - **CRYSTAL EVERGREEN**

Summer of '49 was a heaven on fire. Those who expected to vacation in the refreshing balm of the Adirondacks ran headlong into a furnace. Nobody could see any end to it the heat was so bad. What old folks could endure was one thing; the real hurt was the insufferable punishment it placed upon the children. Having little air-conditioning in those days, most people had to be content with an evening breeze blowing through a window. But during the day it was damned hard just to catch a breath.

Most of the residents of Utica, Oneida, and Chittenango had already gone north to enjoy the green forests of Canada and the longer nights of cool forgetfulness. The few of us who stayed behind had little to be thankful for, but what we had was blessed. Looking back on the heat of that summer, I for one felt it was a sign of something deeper. Wayfarers like me, the ones who didn't follow the cross, fell under a different arc, the way of the lonely pilgrim.

When I was a boy, the wheat fields around Cazenovia Lake beckoned with waves of burning gold. A searing white sun had raised them up out of the moist black earth. Having grown to full height, the harvest yearned to be set free like a racehorse straining against its gate. As the wheat twisted in the hot wind, it released a fury which pressed clear down to the lake where it halted against the cold wall of a stone house.

Before anybody was awake, I stole out of that house of granite blocks to explore the world. I called these adventures the Tales of Tim Tim. The pages of my life followed after my imaginary friends back then. Bidding farewell to those windows boxed with red geraniums, I strolled down the gravel lane toward the wheat.

The mallards and geese didn't join me that day. Their craving for snails had taken them over to Grandmother's. At early light, I went along the driveway as pebbles cracked underfoot. The grasses on either side of the road were tall and willowy. Not being able to see beyond the bend made me timid but also curious. I walked on smelling the warm sky.

On a whim, I dove into the waving stalks. It was hard at first as I parted the sharp blades with swipes of my hand. Soon only wheat

11

The Moon Women

surrounded me. Some hit me in the face but I battled onwards against the high stems. I sensed something drawing me towards a connection. Maybe I could find something missing and discover an end to my aimless wandering amongst the big people. I might even get to be a king.

Midway through this sea of wheat, I saw the tops of trees. There was an island thicket amidst these gilded spears. As the sun fed my face, my eyes were narrow slits. Hiding in the heart of the meadow was a glade, dark and beckoning. Approaching as if a cat after its prey, I edged near the tall stand, which contained a wonder unlike this world.

The movement of my breath mixed with an unknown air and I stepped forward. Forgetting I was a five-year-old prisoner controlled by giants, I blended into the shadows as my fears vanished. Then, I heard something. It was not a sound, more like a calling. Something knew my name.

"Rahm," it went.

It did not come from the trees. It did not come from the sky nor the clouds, nor even the sun. The calling came from within the glade.

"Rahm," came my name.

All movement ceased. There was no wind there. The heart of that place rested in mid-beat with its song poised upon the curve of its lip. I leaned in closer watching as the beauty kept unfolding and unfolding. It couldn't have been an hour, but I lived an hour on that fringe.

A hint of happiness came out and propelled me forward. The way in wanted me. On padded feet, I adjusted my angle and entered the glade. There was no question I was welcome here.

"Rahm," it came a third time.

My eyes were now orbs. I breathed in the hemlock and juniper, the oak bark and honeysuckle. And as the quiet engulfed me, it happened!

With a shift, light came. On the game board of my life, just as a chess player moves one piece to reveal pure genius, the cloud moved one piece beyond the sun. A shaft of sunlight exploded into the glade and as it did, it landed upon an infant pine tree. Bedecked with morning dew the man size pine seemed to greet me but it was more than that; way more. Each droplet grew on fire with a gilded sparkle. That single ray of the sun blessed those glowing gems with the power of *Now*. Every moment pulsed with that *Now*. Shining with the light of an enchanted being, the crystal evergreen began to love me. The love went out to surround me. I knew I was home for there were no places to seek, no people to meet, and no words to speak.

Locked in that embrace, the tree infused me with a radiance. And out of it came a still voice. It spoke its word into my being. And its word was this.

HUMAN

Without warning, there was a surge of air as branches and leaves crashed down near me. I looked up. Something punched a hole through the leafy canopy and a window of sunshine opened. A great lifting carried me up and up. And then I flew!

Later on after a long hunt, a venturous Woodie eased down the lane. The crunch of its stiff black tires grabbed at my thoughts as my name was shouted and shouted again.

"R-R-R-Rahm!" my Auntie yelled.

Her speech fluctuated because of a dream, something about two eyes watching from within her closet.

"Your Dad is worried sick! He's as pale as a ghost! Where have you been all morning? It's lunchtime for God sakes!" She yelled as my cousins all piled out of the back of the pickup.

As they took me away, I grabbed for a white feather floating down out of the sky; its edges were charred and black.

The Moon Women

- 1 -

July 1, 1971 - Bangalore, India

Twenty-two years later, I was standing in a private room. Even though the ceiling above me was completely blank, I sensed a familiar presence up there. I looked up. The pull of that force contained an untold desperation daring me to know it. It compelled me to unlock its secrets and release its messages. As I peered into that stretch of unknown peril, I wondered what vistas might blossom out of that void and leak down into my pen and onto the pages you are now reading.

As I stared deeper into that white expanse, it suddenly erupted and overwhelmed me with a fury of confusion and dismay. Out of this gyrating tumult stormed two battling factions. A score of winged warriors chased after a flood of frantic shapes and as this bedlam moved in and out of focus, the retreating forms left trails of crackling sparks spinning off into the darkness. Was I witnessing some conflict from the past or perhaps the future?

With more spinning curls of flame spitting out across the walls, the ceiling folded in on itself and became a gigantic annulus like a wheel having spokes of flame These radiated out and rushed passed me. Spidery explosions of lightning cartwheeled overhead as brilliant convolutions of color washed up passed my face. Screws of blue fire spun by as jagged bands of pearly feathers chased this way and that. Suddenly a pair of pygmy legs skittered passed and disappeared into a gaseous fog. I sensed some kind of invasion had been plunged into my present as if it were an omen.

As the icy bird things wielded scythes of fire and beat their luminous plumage feverishly within the smoky air, I steadied myself against this surge. Silhouetted against currents of throbbing light, a flurry of gray ankles twisted and fled. Seconds later these same legs evaporated within a grand explosion as I witnessed the shavings of a blinding radiance filling my eyes like white-hot rinds being peeled from the core of God.

Then, darkness.

14

What was this insanity? The answer came from a voice within me.

"This is an isolated vision of heaven gone berserk. Take it as a warning signal. See it as a demonstration of a war between beings who hail from a displaced dimension called Abaddon and an ultra-race labeled as the Khrng. Locked in mortal combat for millennia, these two spheres of consciousness known as the White and the Gray fight over the whys and wherefores of man's genetic dynasty. Will humans ever be able to maintain control over their own future? Or will one of these guardian forces gain the upper hand and dominate the universe. No one knows for sure."

From the moment of that eye-opening epiphany, which had descended from on high into my life, a deep knowing burst open within my core. As if breaking out of a trance, the inner knowledge menus of the Khrng awoke from their subliminal vaults buried deep within the recesses of my mind. This reawakening inspired me to tell their story and reveal to the world all of their secret workings as well as their ongoing battle with the Angels of Abaddon.

I blinked and as my numbness withdrew, the flowing dream works condensed into its original state called 'ceiling' to expose a curved bracket jutting out of the bleached surface. Was it an offering come to uplift me? No, it was simply an eyelet so I seized it.

- 2 -

For two days now, I had been looking for a hook or some kind of connection upon which to hang a strange piece of furniture. The offbeat wicker deformity had appeared mysteriously a tick past midnight when thieves are thickest. After I had exhumed it from out of its shipping crate, the light of day revealed its bulimic appearance. I quickly deduced it was a bizarre piece of furniture, which some people call a swing chair. Constructed of rattan and bent into a grand oval shell like an almond eye of bones, it resembled a man-sized wicker basket having a place inside for a rider and an open front for entry.

Strangely, it had my name written on it and something else, a return address that made no sense: The Ora Cable Company, Corabale, Tuscany. Since I hadn't ordered anything remotely like it, I wondered if it was a mistake sent from an Italian shop maker. And

15

The Moon Women

then again, I joked thinking it was masquerading as a quirky postal seat of divinity, a nixie intended for prophesying future mishaps.

Sticking obtrusively out of the ceiling, this iron loop could very well provide me with a means to enjoy my new chair. With hook in hand, I strained to raise it up. Originally intended for a commonplace Asian fan, the metal hook might as well provide an attachment point for my ride rather than serve as another collection device for the detritus floating in the sticky air of South India. After a quick study, I knew the rusted loop would be foolproof.

As chance would have it, there was a length of strong twine attached to the rim of my celestial podium. Pulling my desk over and aligning it underneath the link to the ceiling, I propped the awkward chair upon it. Steadying myself, I climbed onto the desk, hoisted the odd seat into place, and tied a square knot to the steel claw. To make sure the hitch wouldn't come loose, I gave it five hard yanks. This was no time for the meager. I hopped down and slid the desk away.

Voila!

The magical chair was swinging in mid-air. Lawfully suspended in the center of my universe, I knew it would be exceptional for my purposes. Sitting in it, I would no longer be exposed to the all the prying eyes of my friends. I could meditate on my fondest memories and reconstruct the story from the inside out. Floating in pure Space I could disconnect myself from Time. Never more would I have to bear the burdens of worldly strife. From this swinging wicker perch, I could look out over the events of my life as though they were the pages of an unwritten book now being captured before you. But first, it's time for lunch. I put my pen down.

"Oota!" [Let's eat!] Dr. Krishnaswami announced from outside my door.

- 3 -

Dr. Krishnaswami was a Brahmin and represented the quintessential Hindu. A householder with a wife and two children, he maintained a prominent social status in Cooketown, a well-to-do community on the periphery of the largest metropolis in South India, Bangalore. In conjunction with his religious credentials, he had a solid twelve years of post-graduate work in Sociology as well as a doctorate in Education. Most recently, he had secured a most prestigious placement as professor in a Quaker based cosmopolitan institution called Friends World College, which had taken up residence here some three years earlier. Configured as the college's Asian campus, this division had established itself as the primary hub of the school's intellectual endeavors smack dab in the heart of the Dravidian sub-continent.

This impressive post not only granted him a great deal of limelight within his caste but also came with a hefty salary, which provided him and his family with comfortable accommodations within the posh suburban neighborhood of Cooketown. Because of the setup in this western college, he could work out of his household. Furthermore, the faculty handbook permitted him to board one of the students and charge central command rent for that tenant. What could be better for him? And what could be better for me, because I was that student.

"Oota mardi!" [Take your food!] Dr. Krishnaswami exclaimed for a second time.

I had been learning a little Kannada, the language of the Karnataka province of South India.

"Idli vadda, baharla chennahgiday!" [This idli tastes great.] I replied with my Kannada version of 'compliments to the chef.'

The idli, a pure white, sponge-like rice cake, tasted like something between angel food cake and creamy wheat. Idlis have been the staple for South Indian vegetarians for centuries. I broke off a chunk and dipped it into the relish daubed onto the rim of my dish. It was cool to the touch, but spicy to the palate. A dozen flavors oozed across my taste buds. This biconvex muffin has enjoyed a special status in kitchens all across South India as it promises purity and simplicity as well as providing an economical dish for the empty bellies of the poor and wealthy alike. The chutney flavoring of the relish, sambaar, consisted of ground coconut, tomatoes, cilantro, and the hottest chili peppers known to man. Many virgin western palates could not tolerate the heat. Later in life, my tongue will complain bitterly that my enjoyment of this breakfast food was way overdone.

The chef of the house was Mrs. Krishnaswami, a stately Brahmin homemaker. She governed her domestic domain with a firm but loving hand. Aside from her family, she constantly commanded a half a dozen menial servants who received but a token stipend for

The Moon Women

their efforts. Many of the homes surrounding us in this clustered community boarded servants whom many people in the West would probably have considered slaves. Apart from that, the Krishnaswamis prided themselves as members of a more compassionate faction by allowing their workers to have a mind of their own. Yet because of this disparity, the majority of their neighbors considered them too freethinking.

Inasmuch as I had been trying to pick up a few words of Kannada, I couldn't quite keep abreast of her lickety-split pace when she addressed me. Combined with her homegrown catch phrases, her machinegun dialect sounded to me like someone gargling with a mouthful of pebbles. Nevertheless, I could tell she was most pleased that I would ask for more idlis whenever she noticed my empty plate.

"Ramappa heccuya suvira?" [Would Ramappa like more?] Mrs. Krishnaswami offered.

"Haudu. Mattondu dayavittama," [Yes. Another one please.] I requested with a big smile.

She promptly dumped two hot ones onto my stainless steel plate. However, in two shakes of a jiffy, my plate was clean as a whistle once again.

The lavish populace of Karnataka has revered their admirable culture for centuries. Occasionally they have extended its influence by renaming foreigners with quirky eponyms derived from the popular heroes of their mythologies. Consequently, foreigners who had English names, which corresponded to these Hindu namesakes, quite often received Indian versions from the well-meaning inhabitants. Since my given name, Rahm, was most closely like one of the legendary avatars of Hindu mythology, Rama, they called me Ramappa for short (adding the appa makes it respectful according to the protocols of the Canarese language of Kannada).

"Oota ittu!" [I'm done eating.] I announced.

I confirmed with an excitement which implied the idli was so scrumptious I couldn't wait to come back and get some more. You couldn't really conjure up more praise than that. Happy to get a big thumbs-up from Mrs. Krishnaswami, I left with a folded hand nod.

"Ba, Pa!" [Hurry back, Brother!] She replied.

As I mentioned before, in Karnataka everyone is brother, sister, father or mother. You add an appa for a father and anna for a brother, while amma is for a mother and akka is for a sister. If you

18

address someone who is distinguished, you can use the appa even if the person is a younger man. Such was the case with me. It's some form of respectful wishful thinking, I guess. I know, it's oddball ABCs, but that's the way it is in South India; its logic seems to emanate from some other dimension.

I headed to the rear of the Krishnaswami domicile back to my bedroom, which came with a private bath and two closets. A dumpy bed enveloped with a tent of mosquito netting, a dilapidated desk and two well-beaten mini-stools completed my humble abode. And, of course, my neat and nostalgic swing chair. This room will now form an arena upon which the characters of an unusual tale will come forth to unfold a saga many have considered nothing more than a zany outlook on reality. Notwithstanding, I ask you to consider it as an alternative logic with which to model your existence and ultimately reconcile it to be the one thing that will save you in the end. Furthermore, I need to alert you to the presence of what I call furniture Speak, the weak levels of which I must accept as tenuous support for my efforts to begin the story. What is the Speak? You shall come to find out soon enough.

As I hovered calmly in my novel chair, it dominated the inner space with an austere presence. Since this suite in the rear of the Krishnaswami's home was explicitly mine, I decided to call it the K-room in honor of my mentor and ally in the quest for the answers. Dr. Krishnaswami, whom I had also decided to nickname as Dr. K, had become instrumental in unpeeling the onion of passionate discovery; however, as the great Bard once remarked, "Mine eyes smell onions," [1] so even though it may not end well, let's get on with the story.

As the master bedroom to Dr. K's residency, the K-room also came with its own puja chamber, a disjointedly cramped antechamber previously inhabited by prayerful residents for their daily worship of the many Hindu deities. From time to time, I had cooked up some of my own pujas in that claustrophobic hole. What I was doing in those ceremonies requires further explaining, but for now it's time to refine my novel ride.

The Moon Women

The gifted chair came with a few linen cushions of its own. Leaning down, I buried my face into the lumpy cotton. Fragrances from musty closets filled my head. A gray half-pint slithered passed. Startled, I pulled out. Some disguise stared back at me. Was this really the impression of my face imprinted there in the pillow or some other entity staring out from a foreign realm? Perhaps I was simply projecting my own blank look of wonder. What scenes would I glimpse while swinging in this convoluted craft woven by the starfish hands of creatures I would never be able to comprehend? What memories would I awaken by piloting this wicker emissary across the myriad psychic oceans?

To fill out the back, I scavenged a few more pillows from Dr. K's bedroom when the family was down at the local movie theatre. Connecting a frayed hemp rope to the doorknob, I spooled out the slack and hopped back into my swaying cockpit. After pulling the rope taught, I let it go to release it. The momentum carried the swinging settee a foot or so. I absorbed the rocking action in silence. Closing my eyes, I leaned back into the mushy padding. There was a pleasant rhythm pulling me inwards. As I accepted its soothing travel, I sagged into a dream.

The reverie started with an award I received back in 1959. My classmates had elected me president of the Biology Club, an office to which my teacher, Mr. Sands, had added the honorary bonus of a six-week vacation to a popular boys' camp located at the base of Mount Monadnock in New Hampshire. When school was over that year, my parents drove me up to that campsite in the mountains for my stay. As campers, we all lived in spacious army tents with barrack type beds. I had mine heaped up with blankets which created a jumbo throne for sleeping or just kicking back.

With the tent flaps rolled up for the day, I was lying in my bunk while gazing out over the waving grasses. As the pastel confetti of butterflies danced across the meadows riddled with amethyst bursts of phlox, warm breezes caressed my arms embracing me with the hug of summer splendor. I felt like I was floating upon a cloud of genuine peace. At full rest, the needle of my compass pointed towards its true origins. There were no tasks to tackle, no people to confront, and no worries of any kind. What's more, I knew I had had that feeling once before at some point in my younger days, but I could not quite connect to it as yet but felt strongly that some presence would soon emerge.

As my heart embraced the sunlight streaming out from behind the cottony clouds, I drifted off and merged with the azure blue pool of the sky. Off on the horizon, I could barely distinguish the crescent of the Moon as it peaked out from behind a silvery lining. Off its contour twinkled a pinpoint of pink light, which was its heavenly sister, Mars. Counting the few scars on my life, I thanked my lucky stars they were few and far between. At that moment upon the pinnacle of my life, I decided to reflect upon the good chapters and not the bad ones. I valued those auspicious times, but they seemed to have dawned much less frequently than I would have liked.

As I lay there basking in the bounty of that afternoon, I realized this vacation was an unexpected gift. It represented a precious slice of some blessed tranquility because on that fabulous day I felt I had arrived. Right at that point upon the pages of my unfolding biography there were no blemishes or fresh wounds of any kind to muddy this new clarity. In that instant, I understood this poignant peak to be an awakening of sorts. Prior to this renewal, everything had been more or less like the climate of that August: balmy, but occasionally punctuated by unrelenting thunderstorms. But at the crest of that one apollonian moment in summer camp, I came to understand pure happiness.

A white feather came gliding down from somewhere. I caught it and stuck it in my hair. I felt supremely blessed. Besides the dawning when I beheld an enchanted evergreen, this was the only other time I had experienced pure peace and tranquility. I took it to be a rebirth that had burned its image deep into my memory. Over the years, I applied that happiness as a benchmark against which to measure all other experiences. Nevertheless, no matter how sweet it was, that phenomenal vista, my first natural high, did not last.

Now, back in my softly twisting chair, I regained the repetition of a saying. It was a mantra, which I had recently received while wandering high up in the mountains. As I remembered each of the sacred words, my fingers indexed a bead on my mala, a Hindu rosary with which I had also been blessed.

The hand of a Khrng does not contain the dexterity of those potent lines; they are bridled and barren.

The Moon Women

As the palm chair stopped swinging momentarily, I reeled in the slack on the loosely knotted rope to crank myself back up. When I let it go, the curious clock action took up its cadence once again.

The soft maritime flux tuned in the distant cries of a street vender calling out to announce his produce of eggplant and okra. Enhancing those long, drawn out vowels were the pungent aromas of sandalwood and patchouli, intoxicating scents drifting in from the courtyard outside the K-room. My thumb nimbly clicked off another unit of awakening on my mala, a worn Tibetan cord, threaded with 108 rudraksha beads. It was not the fifty or so beads of a Catholic Rosary with the **Our Father** on the large bead and the **Hail Mary** decades done on the smaller ones. My mala used a different set of gods.

These gods ruled a kingdom, which I had uncovered after hitchhiking nearly ten thousand kilometers from the bitter shores of northern France, over the ancient passes of the Hindu Kush, across the baked deserts of Islamic Pakistan and down into the northwestern provinces of India. At the end of that trek, I had landed within a region orbiting the grandest suburb in all Asia, Bangalore.

Over the past six months, this cultural hub of Hindu life had become my homestead and launching pad for many adventures as an FWC student as I had journeyed out upon the Indian sub-continent. While bouncing from one widening populace to the next, my travels carried me through all of Hindustan's major cities, Bombay, Calcutta, New Delhi, and Madras. Between January and June, I had traced the origins of both Hinduism as well as Buddhism in diverse localities including Goa, the Mahayana caves, the temples of Konarak and Khajuraho to the South as well as the Theravada stupas to the North. Augmenting those sites, I had also journeyed to Aurangabad where I had explored the caves of Ajanta and Ellora to survey the ancient artifacts of a religion I renamed as Hindhistain, a combination of Hindu, Buddhist, and Jain.

I had also participated in school outings to the Tibetan Buddhist refugee camps stationed on the outskirts of Mysore, the capital of Karnataka. Twenty years ago, in the course of the invasion of 1950, hordes of Chinese barbarians had driven the Tibetans out of their homeland. By virtue of the altitude and modest climate of

Mysore, these survivors had adopted the Nilgri Hills for their sanctuary. On visiting one of the Tibetan settlements near the village of Kushalanagar, I had the privilege of meeting with His Holiness, the Dalai Lama (head of the Gelugpa or Yellow Hat School). The audience was short but His eyes spoke volumes when he first addressed me.

"Please bring my salutations to my Brother," He laid open His hands in prayerful supplication.

Not knowing to whom His request was to be directed, I was speechless. I felt embarrassed not being able to offer a suitable reply as our guides ushered us out hastily. I could only enshrine His words in my inner chambers not knowing what to do with them. Before we finally departed, He waved me over and added the most unusual thing.

"One day the secrets of the White will be revealed to you."

His parting statement vexed me by uncomfortably exhuming a confusion, which had always lain just out of reach: a haunting presence lurking behind what most people had told me was reality.

- 6 -

My dauntless chair shuddered as if some incoming shaft of ignorance had hit its gyros; an ignorance spawned by those who think they know too much about the world having never challenged its successes, nor accepted its failures. I grappled with my mala and slew the beast by knocking out a decade or two with strenuous repetition on my mantra. Soon I had regained my position over the past and the scenes became clear enough to continue.

Middle of May, the pull of my wandering psyche hauled me northwards along the east coast of India and into Calcutta. Riding a train through the outskirts of this Mount Everest of humanity was such a shocking eye-opener. I lost count of the dead bodies floating in the sewer-like rivers surrounding the ancient city. Parking myself overnight in a shabby hostel, I awoke the following day to flee northward towards Darjeeling where I beheld the vast tea plantations spread out beneath the shadow of the majestic mountains. This hillside resort town was a momentous place for me because it was the last place in my life where I had gotten high with any chemical

The Moon Women

intoxicant. It was to become the first real step towards unraveling the maze leading into the Beyond.

Riding the train further from there into the foothills of the Himalayas, I reached Gangtok, the capital city of an Indian protectorate labeled on the map as Sikkim. While visiting the Enchen Retreat at the heart of Sikkim's capital, I learned about the monastery of Rumtek, the nerve center for the Red Hat sect of Tibetan Buddhism, the other noteworthy denomination of high Lamas.

Nicknamed the Land of High Snows, Tibet is perched north of the towering barrier ridge of Nepal, south of the Mongolian Steppe and west of the border with China. Megalithic Stone Age architectures have peppered the Tibetan Plateau for millenniums and some suspect them to have served as the focus for ancestor adulation back in those prehistoric times. Burial vaults have recently been unearthed; nonetheless, due to altitude limitations and political stickiness, further archaeological study remains stalled. Not surprisingly, some earlier reconnaissance has yielded evidence of archaic humans who traversed the plateau some twenty-five thousand years ago. Nevertheless, some suspect Neolithic populations overran these immigrants and drove them into China four millenniums ago.

This branch (Kagyu School) was presided over by His Holiness, Gaylwa Karmapa, the sixteenth immaculate incarnation of a supreme being named Shakyamuni. Birthed as Rangjung Rigpe Dorje, this powerhouse of spiritual knowledge had been reaching out to westerners for aid in securing survival for His people. By virtue of His benevolent presence, I was most fortunate to have had an audience with Karmapa, a meeting that I hoped might amplify my spiritual saga.

These Tibetans were an incredible bunch. They had cultivated many transcendental yogic practices. From the late nineteenth century, the seat of the Dalai Lama had begun to recognize variant Lamas who had chosen to reincarnate into western civilization. I can't confirm whether or not I was one of them, but Karmapa had been intensely inquisitive of me throughout my interview with His Holiness. So much so, He ordained me as Rinpoche Genga Dorje and welcomed me as a high incarnate being. When I realized it was the Karmapa to whom the Dalai Lama's greetings were to be made known, I relayed the message, which the

Dalai Lama had entrusted me. Upon hearing these cherished words, Karmapa lapsed into a subdued withdrawal. When He returned, He folded His hands and expressed His thanks for such a blessed message from His Brother in the Dharma.

Leaning in with a pinched focus, Karmapa remarked that my jiva (the Indian word for life force) was making tremendous progress on its journey to attain liberation. Via his translator, He further commented that I should shield this fortune from evil. Speaking with a strained emotion, He conveyed a daunting mouthful concerning a shadowy dominance that was about to enter my life through a rift in the wall of Time. And onto that dish he sprinkled the spices of an unexpected outburst.

"Black eyed pygmies plant their seeds within weak dreamers who forsake their treasures for the poverty of a vacant future. Beware their sky craft. These have stolen many peoples and childrens," his translator conveyed.

That power-packed declaration was a precursor to the awakening granted me by the visionary maelstrom, which fell upon me from out of my ceiling four weeks later when the knowledge menus of the Khrng resurfaced into my life from out of the Beyond. In spite of this revealing interview with the chief Tibetan, I would not find out why Karmapa had played such a key role in that metanoia until months later.

Again stymied by having received yet another astounding statement from a High Tibetan Lama, I felt compelled to advance something of my own by impressing Karmapa with my utterance of a venerable Tibetan holy word phrase. I had learned this sacred mantra during a class in college on Tibetan Buddhism. Since I had always been amazed by the things I had learned so far about death, I announced this famous mantra out load in the biggest voice I had.

OM MANI PADME HUNG

It wasn't so much a revelation that I knew this mantra, for it had been printed in many texts including The Tibetan Book Of The Dead, as it was the vibration with which I had infused this incantation and my guttural inflection.

It was in 1909 that German explorers, who were tracking the lost Holy Grail under the guise of botany, first identified this sacred

The Moon Women

word-key as a means to unlock a hidden knowledge via continuous repetition. Later, an American anthropologist, Walter Evans-Wentz, revealed its prominence to spiritual thinkers who at first entirely missed the significance of its providing a channel into the occult strata of modern thought. In 1927 with the publication of this manual on dying, many of the beliefs surrounding the six after-death realms, or Bardos, came to light. Its text explained that only by traversing these otherworldly plateaus could an adept of the science of death, called meditation, be able to stake a claim on the veracity of these inner states of being. Reliving these ultra-phases of sentient animation through which the atma (Indian word for soul) must travel, beginning with its departure from the earth plane at death and ending with its arrival back here at birth, would reaffirm the model of reincarnation as well as underscore a perpetual repetition inherent within the current mode of impermanence called life. Without these Tibetans, we simply would not have learned about any of these pathways, the spooky wormholes into the Beyond.

Sorry to say my utterance of the four charged words was more of an affectation rather than something I had learned. Nevertheless, Karmapa seized upon this unusual rift to offer His uplifting pronouncement concerning my origins, thus setting me up for deeper manipulation. Having no real inclination to become some modern day Columbus driven to discover a new continent or trade route to the heavenly realms of the afterlife, I played along when the renowned Supreme guardian of the Dharma enjoined me to consider his offer of a spiritual boon, seriously and with all good intent.

Karmapa added a further comment regarding the inflection of my utterance. He indicated it might possibly identify me as a reincarnated Lama from the fourteenth century as was He. The translator then mystified me by sharing a remarkable communique, which Karmapa enunciated as if He were chanting a Tibetan prayer.

"Many times at the end of life the light never fades but grows."

Even though I couldn't attest to having transmigrated from the time of the Mongol invasion, I thanked him for his uplifting messages. Finally, he apprised me of His insistence to come back the following day to receive my prize.

As Karmapa's portent trailed off into the background, the gently swinging wicker podium consumed me once more but this time with a pang in my stomach. Having previously suffered the metaphysics of digestion as the root cause for delaying personal progress, I lost my connection to my garden of psychic sprouts and withdrew from my steadfast chair to go grab some lunch.

A couple of idlis and a fried dosa helped to solve the conundrum of mass and light. What has no mass must travel at the speed of light and vice versa. But it is only when the amount of mass is sufficient to create a chrysalis of light like wrapping yarn into a ball that the divine essence of Man gets unraveled.

After assimilating that ball of sulphur and brimstone along with a hot meal, I returned to my dodecahedral chair. The recollection of that time in Sikkim was acting as a gently rising magic carpet pulling me up and out of Bangalore toward those Himalayan peaks once more. My chance audience with Karmapa's distinguished Lama, Ling Po Rinpoche Dadu, was brief but compelling. Karmapa had instructed the Rinpoche to dowse me with acute diligence with the purpose of ascertaining my potential for wielding any number of ancient tools these mystically adept Himalayan yogis had perfected over the centuries.

After this testing phase was over there was a follow-up audience with the great Lama. With a grave oration, Karmapa initially informed me the Kagyu sect were interested in fledging a new line of converts within the West. Because the outcome of Dadu's holy scans had put me at the front of the class, Karmapa divulged most wondrously I might be the lucky one to receive a sacred gift, perchance even a mantra selected from the pantheon of esoteric spheres of Tibetan knowledge. An hour later, Dadu Lama informed me I would receive this unbelievable gift, a power mantra, which, if practiced correctly, could lead to nothing short of a superior knowing.

The final session with Dadu Lama only encompassed a couple of hours but it resulted in my receiving my mala as well as a sacred Tibetan word group. This special mantra came from the ancient predecessors of the Kagyu sect and had not been given out to anybody for over sixty years. Karmapa had ordered his Lama to initiate me into its primal usage and warn me of the consequences should I misuse the powerful saying. Dadu Lama trained me to repeat one word of the phrase with each count of the mala's beads as they passed through my fingers. This utterance was not to be done vocally

The Moon Women

but internally with the tongue of thought. It was a simple feat but its payoff was huge. The Lama confided to me that if I regularly practiced this sacred litany, which he designated as a Siddhi (pronounced "city"), with sweet sincerity and humble devotion, I would acquire a supernatural power. This prowess would enable me to witness the rare emergence of an internal lotus whose opening would bless me with an ability to manipulate Time and its products.

In conjunction to this knowhow of transcending Time, I would also acquire an ability to detect the subcortical vibrations of the people nearest me; I could possibly receive an ability to read the thoughts of weaker people. Lama Dadu explained that if I could complete six hundred thousand iterations, this Siddhi would come to reside within me. Nevertheless, the great Lama warned me not to share it with anybody. Should this hallowed word set get loose and leak out into everyday life of the earth realms, the roots feeding the fabric of Time might get warped and cause an irretrievable spoilage in the world at large possibly even resulting in a catastrophic failure within the coming networks of knowledge. Having had no experience with performing these intimate practices, I was eager for the mantra to blossom within me in spite of the risky drawbacks.

Back in the chair of wicker bones, its gentle oscillations were marking out the sinusoidal beat of a pendulum hanging free from some alien clockworks. I attained one more bead in the count on my mala. As I approached ninety thousand, things were beginning to get particularly juicy.

- 7 -

Somewhere over a forlorn wilderness of dry wheat, flashing scimitars hacked at blueish gray flesh. The Angels made quick work of their enemy, the lowly Khrng, shredding them into a blizzard of flaming confetti. While the battalions of wiry midget soldiers aimed their star cannons at the silver wing-tipped warriors, their commanders ordered banks of fiery red streams to obliterate the Angels as they crisscrossed the skies at frightening speeds. The glory of their light blades of death chased the gray puerile hellions into an invisible tunnel in the air that sucked them up like a solar vacuum. The phosphorescent eyes of the Khrng regulars sealed wide open in horror before winking out. Clusters of obsidian eyeballs swam in an inky blood brine boiling within the twisted seaweed of torn mutant bodies. And the yawning Time funnel floating in the air sucked the mess out of this world.

This transfixion held me under its sway for a moment and then dissolved into a plume of smoke. With my hand jerking back and forth feverishly, something yanked me out of the haze.

"Ramappa!"

Damn it! It was the Krishnaswami's little daughter jarring me out of the Time jump. I leapt up, brushed open a hole in the incense cloudbank, and went to find out what she wanted.

"Ramappa! Bagiloo kudappa!" [Open the door!]

She was struggling to get in but since I had fastened the hawser onto the door cleat when I tied my plucky chair down, she was out there high and dry. When she turned the handle to gain entry, she had shortened the slack held tight in my hand.

"Baratenni, Ama!" [I'm coming, Sister!]

I apologized and dropped the handle to free up the mighty mahogany threshold to my K-room. In she came carrying a plated orange papaya sliced open ripe to eat.

"Oh, Ramappa, Ramappa. You much fruit? And I have my papaya liking best for you, Ramappa," she affirmed politely as she set the thali down.

As quickly as she had arrived, like a pixie she skipped out singing. The golden fruit beckoned to my taste buds with its enriching supply of vitamins and anti-oxidants. As it pledged its commitment to the opulent nature of its growers, I carried it into my wicker throne to relax with the joyous snack.

Just passed half done with the sweet slices of saffron joy, the stalwart chair rewound itself in a psychogenic hic-cup and eructed a nano-fraction of the Time/Space cycle placing me in a Deja vu back track.

As soon as I cranked on the overpowering door, in sprang Rani or Ranakka (the little queen), the Krishnaswami's daughter. This time she let me know the Phone Wallah had come; would I please come and greet him out in the family room.

In India, "Wallah" means worker in the Hindustani language or more commonly simply Hindi. As a direct cousin of Samscrit, Hindi has been in use for centuries and therefore it is the national language. Since many of its words have fewer syllables, Caneresse

The Moon Women

folk often find it much easier to pronounce these Hindi catchwords instead of the equivalent word in Kannada, which in most cases is considerably longer and a bit trickier on the tongue. The Phone Wallah was the guy who would book your phone call if you required contact with someone farther away than across the neighborhood. Since I needed to put a call into my tailor, Mr. Kalazaki, who had his shop down on Commercial Street in the heart of business central, I had sent a shout out over to the Phone Wallah to come and schedule a trunk call.

Inasmuch as we were using the overhead lines in Cooketown, a suburb on the outskirts of the megalopolis, it required the use of these overly worn out channels, which offered no guarantee for success. This was merely one cog in the gear works of doing business in South India, circa the early nineteen seventies. It was a merry-go-round of inverted and dilapidated communications systems. Back in those days, it seemed that it might have been easier to use telepathy rather than technology. Since the get-go, I had suspected the two were cut from the same cloth as the Time/Space fabric, although we mustn't lose sight of just how spooked Albert gets when you toy with his play things.

Again, the Time flip forced me to get up off my butt to go over and open the monumental mahogany portal myself. My God! How does that tiny child manage this thing by herself? As I shuffled down the sterile marble corridor to meet the Phone Wallah, random fears needled me with doubts I had forgotten to pinch out my puja candles. My loose OCD flooded me with manifold imaginings of Dr. Krishnaswami's sanctuary going up in flames. I gritted my teeth against the portent and shook it off only to stumble out into the foyer where a black skinned man, indisputably of authentic South Indian blood, waited impatiently as he nervously strangled his head towel.

"Namaste Ibsen Sahib. You are the one for best business. Ila? Baharla chennahgiday." [No? Very well.]

After claiming he was no miser, he explained in choppy bits of Indianized English and Kannada that some messages might be coming from unexplainable sources. Furthermore, he added that ancient relatives of the Ganges Shudras, low-caste laborers imported from Benares, had done the installation of the telephones wires in Cooketown. By dint of that line clog, they had been experiencing an intermittent degradation of signal strength for some time now.

Nevertheless, the attempt to link up with my tailor would go through with all well-intentioned assurances, although he couldn't necessarily guarantee any response.

Neither could he rule out the possibility of collisions with other transmissions sent from the outer regions. They might generate a rash of troublesome information. Most of what he had to convey was done under his breath as if he was shielding the Krishnaswamis from picking up on his vibes. The whole charade made absolutely no sense. He hesitated for a moment and then inquired why I had greeted him with such an odd appearance. When I demanded what the heck he meant by that he bleated like a lamb and added something about how my body parts were incrusted with icicles. But then, he recanted by mumbling quite conceivably most Americans looked like that anyway. Nevertheless, he convinced me that my call had already been booked so I was all set. I knew that.

Shaking my head, I retired to my K-room. All these off-the-wall hitches were getting stranger by the minute. With a view to relinking with some sanity, I crawled back into my spiraling chair with rope in hand and gave it a sharp tug to restart the fluid locomotion hoping it would clear out all the cobwebs in my attic.

All these out-of-the-chair interruptions that kept popping up in the Krishnaswami homestead were nothing I couldn't handle. Sensing these itinerant personalities coming and going through the Krishnaswami's frontiers wasn't anything to get overly concerned about. I figured these personas deemed it imperative to appear in one segment only to vanish and reappear in a slightly altered fashion in another chapter for the sake of piggybacking a reversal over which they had no control. It was a statement of their maintaining two identities, one within the other.

Undoubtedly, they hungered to impart some ancient treasure or advice carried from neighboring alter-worlds before departing across the warped barriers. There were times, however, when I asked myself if these doppelgängers were even visible to one another, considering the fugacious and non-interacting nature of their appearances. Who knows? Maybe one day all the Saints will arrive and declare me King and I can simply dismiss this trivia as inconsequential. After all, I was becoming a swami of my own merit. Plus, I was quite confident I could conjure up a few dead wizards of my own making.

The Moon Women

Shortly after my return from Sikkim, the news of my travels while up in the land of the high Lamas had become legendary among the FWC community. After having been observed spending long hours alone in my puissant swing chair, the Krishnaswami children as well as several itinerant travelers started a line of gossip encapsulating my stardom. Moreover, some of the borders across the street, namely Dottie, Beth, and even Cathy Rutledge, claimed they were now my disciples. Notwithstanding, my concept of that responsibility was a wee bit mixed at best.

It wasn't long before I had hit upon one of the primary elements of the Siddhi. Not only could I get a 'reading' on what they were thinking, I could also implant suggestions into their heads, which they would treat with an overwhelming urge to follow. I would carefully 'masse' the crux of it over their ego and drop it into the pocket of their need to get, the residence of their greed. I took it to be part of the path I was learning to follow. Twice I had been successful at performing this trick and was pleasantly surprised at the results. As I made another round on the slippery strand, my connection to Time's lost loves, the beads grew wet with a viscid condensation.

- 8 -

As my intrepid chair settled into another entangled depression within the triad of normal dimensions, I cast off the line to its lock in the coming alternate reality. Movement brought it to life and movement drew out the disturbed data from the other times. Whether or not the Khrng had created the chair was not readily apparent at first. But one thing was for sure. The dogged chair was not from this world.

The places the chair was taking me now and the order of things I was remembering were forming a mystical skeleton upon which the audacious chair hung the flesh of my most memorable experiences. These memories were surfacing like bubbles in a pond, as if ornaments hooked onto the boughs of a yuletide evergreen strung up with the electrics of mystery. Churning the mantra while riding this curving rattan capsule, I was hatching a nexus between my memories and an undiscovered dimension. Fervently repeating the mantra while swinging in the resolute chair was unleashing an unknown discordance, a growing psycho-biomagnetic friction, which was melding my energies into an out-of-body vehicle, one that could part the nebulous veils of the mundane and mark a trail into the Beyond. Soon I knew I would forge an unbeatable curvature in truth like warping light.

Not yet fully aware of the possibility of bending Time/Space via a human utterance, I commenced the recitation inwardly. But as the relentless chair moved off its center, another episode unfolded. It was only yesterday the subliminal patterns of some of the gals who bunked in the meetinghouse across the way, were seeping onto my visceral screens. The last time I was over there, one of them, Megan Ross, had invited me to her room to hear about her trekking up in Kathmandu. In the midst of our chat, it was apparent that she not only fancied to have sex with me, but also she considered me something akin to a mediocre incarnation of the elephant deity, Ganesha.

I wasn't particularly enamored unto her overinflated effigy; nevertheless, her fantasy wasn't that far off the mark. As I squared in on her to view her aural persona, she morphed into Durga, a mythic goddess who lapped up the tortured spirits with a bloody tongue. Further, I hit upon a flash that one day while out on a solo trek on the tundra of Kathmandu, the Khrng would unfold their tulip tubes and vacuum her up.

Meg tried her utmost to indoctrinate me with her carnal brand of tantric kundalini prejudice rather than receive any glimmer of the truths the Buddhists have lain down in their scriptures. At any rate, what I did leave her with was a fragment of the tried and true pathway that led step by step to kindness and peace. This was the unmistakable bond between the two of us. It was our calling. I craved no other nor did she.

Since '67 Meg had been an undergrad at Friends World College, or FWC, the moniker its alumni use. This traditional Quaker college had five micro-campuses distributed at prestigious sites all over the globe. She had nearly completed the entire FWC wheel with applicable stops at each facility. After starting in Mitchell Gardens, located on Long Island, for her orientation semester, she ventured onwards to the London campus for six months. Each spoke of the journey could last nearly a year prior to the student traveling onto the next segment of the cultural experience. From London, she had shifted to the pueblo near Mexico City for her third leg of the

The Moon Women

international circuit. Then for some reason, suffering a detour, she had been encouraged to fly back to Mitchell Gardens, conceivably for a tune-up in preparation for continuing onto Hiroshima for her fifth semester. To cinch her sixth phase, she had vaulted the Americas for Nairobi in Africa to reside with the Maasai. For her seventh leg of the degree (ahead of returning to Long Island for the culminating semester of graduation), she had settled in the only FWC site which she had not yet completed, Bangalore.

She was looking forward to receiving her diploma back in Long Island as her final chapter. For many of the matriculating students, the Bangalore campus in Cooketown was the crowning finish to their four-year round-the-world tour. Meg had spent few of her efforts nose to the grindstone performing authentic study within a fifty kilometer radius of Bangalore and the Southeast Asia complex (all two buildings of it). But because of her wide-ranging treks in Nepal she had elected for independent study, which usually meant enjoying an exclusive stash in one's own private Dharamsala.

When I described my adventures in Sikkim, she seemed queerly absorbed and posed questions to corroborate what she had heard from the others. Was I really getting a leg up on manipulating some of the shifty parameters of nuance sex? To the contrary, my tale of the garden variety cobra prompted her to reach over and smear salve on my forehead to ward of some demon or other rakshasa. After the matter of the holy repetition came up, she was slightly vacant. As she leaned back to roll a joint, she inadvertently let her jaw drop when I divulged I was reading her mind. Be that as it may, I could not quite come to tell her about what was going on with the Khrng or where the chair had been taking me. Those secrets can only come forth in the midst of heartfelt intimacy. I ceded the rope another yank and procured one more unit on the Tibetan Time thread.

- 9 -

The next day, I entrusted the vestal wicker chair with its first serious test-drive. Giving the rope a tug, I caught the soft embrace of its swaying pendulum and drifted back to the Tibetan skies over Sikkim during my visit there some months ago. As I visualized an immense blue dome looming over the cosmos, the valiant chair unwrapped the memory: it was not the robin's-egg blue we view in a midday sky, but the rich cobalt blue as seen on the eastern horizon at dusk - deathlike.

Into that blue heaven floated the laziest clouds; as if tufts of a meringue pie, they hung motionlessly set adrift like an armada of whipped cream galleons. Only after sinking their steely anchors into the silt of Tibetan time did their pride right itself under the tutelage of the Buddha.

Directly below this royal vista were the glistening peaks of the Himalayan Mountains. They were not level with the horizon, mind you. They extended thousands of kilometers high into the regions of rarefied air, because they were huge. Really, really huge. The weight of their mountain thoughts fell down all around me like an avalanche of awe. Their prominence issued forth out the bowels of the earth as the frozen secretions of a world too high to breathe.

Upon this dream bed were the valleys stitched together with a patchwork of emerald wedges and fertile paddies, which terraced all the lands below. Mirroring the aerial kingdoms of lore, these glassy shelves spelled out a network, the verdant culture of rice. They were as a haven of living ears listening out over the centuries for any hint of truthfulness, principles, which were lost once, but were now beginning to reclaim their rightful prominence within the framework of history's timeless strata.

Nestled among those paddies, a handful of Tibetan dwellings advertised life. Each one had teak beams inside for structural support and outside, whitewashed plaster walls. Painted upon those ancient exteriors were symbolic masks of blessed beings, the Bodhisattvas. Illusively pictured with cosmic eyes, charcoal curlicues for hair and a distinct line of serenity for lips, these beings starred out over the valley offering protection and promise. For a nose, a Buddhist mystic symbol sat centermost in each ghostly visage.

The gossamer centerpiece to this visual concerto were the thousands of bamboo poles which stood as a vast army of harpoons spiking all the land, each one arrayed with brightly colored prayer flags whipping crazily in the wind. These flags, which proclaimed the spectrum of Tibetan independence, sung out as the wind moved briskly through the high passes. They represented the specters of over sixteen million Lamas long martyred throughout the centuries. Their frenzied flapping unleashed the sanctified Tibetan mantras, which self-chant themselves in humble supplication to the Avalokitesvaras

The Moon Women

and the Padmasambhavas that inhabit the mountain caves. Two hundred yards out across the valley, I noticed a pack of wild dogs chasing a lone mule deer, which was trying its damnedest to gain surer footing on the opposing hillside. It wasn't looking too promising for the deer.

I recalled my departure from Lama Dadu's abode after having received the sacred words, my mantra. Clearly, I had overindulged myself by staying so long in his kampa but he had been so caring and generous. His parting gift had been a cup of Tibetan tea infused with a heady mix of Oolong and bergamot, but instead of the water buffalo milk, which Indians normally stir in to lift the flavor, these highlanders substitute what has been labeled as rancid Yak butter, albeit, not its true origin. Nevertheless, for all intents and purposes, that is indeed what it tastes like. If you are not careful, it can easily cause you to gag. You might even vomit, if you aren't suitably prepared for its impact. For me, the trick was to close off my nose from within my throat so as not to detect the vapors; then give it brisk slurps.

After receiving the instruction and having my farewell tea, I bid my adieu by placing my hands together to bow while bending forward ever so slightly (too much bending is rude.) I spoke the word, Namaste. It is both a greeting and a farewell. It means, "I salute the Godliness within you." Multiple Namastes symbolize an affectionate farewell and mine was nonetheless heartfelt.

After I departed, I cherished Lama Dadu's blessing in my heart deeply, both physically and spiritually. Venturing up the lane from the Lama's hermitage to the gravel roadway, my hand kept nervously caressing the prickly junipers bordering the perimeter of the winding walkway when I came across something fuzzy with a stem. I picked it up.

It was a large white feather lying on the boughs of the low swaying conifers. I wondered what skirmish might have dislodged the shining quill from the wing of some Himalayan owl or at the outset a celestial being traveling overhead. I cradled it in my hands feeling a sense of gratitude that it had come my way. I took it to be a sign that my mantra hadn't come from any concrete realm, more so, from a different dimension, one out of the Beyond. Furthermore, in the forefront of my appreciation lay the unfurled question of why had this gift come my way in the first place? Regardless, I would need to expend more effort before releasing any wind into those lofty sails.

Upon tagging up with the deserted roadway, I looked up. Twilight was rapidly losing ground to nightfall. Had I overstayed my welcome with the Lama? That nagging miscalculation met with a resolute belief that Lama Dadu would not have kept me longer than necessary if he felt my departure was ill timed. As the pale daylight swiftly slipped away, so were my chances for an easy stroll home. Across the way, the yelping of the dog pack reechoed across the valley. It was a cry, which was forecasting the demise of the desperate mule deer.

There were no streetlights in Sikkim. There were no lights of any kind except for the occasional kerosene lanterns, which fed the domestic firesides scattered sparsely throughout the valleys below. Hastily, I made my way in the direction of my bungalow. There was no doubt the nighttime was approaching rapidly. In due course, I came to accept I had misjudged my departure point; the sky had taken on its cast of gathering gloom, the pall of an unavoidable changeover.

Remembering the road would be straight for nearly a hundred or so meters, I pushed onwards. Despite my steady advance, within a short distance, my peripheral eyesight kicked in; staring directly at an object only yielded emptiness. Long ago when I hiked in the forests of my neighborhood, the use of border vision had saved my butt during some sticky situations. Using that technique now, I advanced another twenty meters but then I had to stop. My fears were fighting with my anger. How could I have been so stupid?

When I gazed up into the heavens, the glittering spiral arm of our galaxy, the Milky Way, presented a vertical swath of starlight sweeping over the hillside upon which I crawled like some two-legged strain of ant. Thinking I could ferret out some prescient pheromone markers, which might guide me out of harm's way, I hailed the starry skies above. Riveted to its glory, I beheld the long arm of God pointing homewards. Nevertheless, the dwindling star beams only boosted my visual paralysis.

Little did I know that this particular eventide in Sikkim would be one in which the Moon would be nonexistent. It was an out of phase shift in the lunar cycle, which left only the constellations. With another few meters gained, a nearly lightless domain blossomed in my being. I can truthfully state I have never encountered a more

The Moon Women

sinister night, before or since. The void of that moonlessness was suffocating. I had to stop.

Should I turn back to retrace my steps? Going that way might be more familiar. Certainly, the Lama would put me up for the time being. Every moment of rethinking my efforts was only prolonging my agonies, so I pushed forward.

On my left margin, I could feel a low outcropping having junipers briefly punctuating its run. Edging along hesitantly, I gained another a meter or two against the blackness. My impression of the road ahead recalled a precipitous drop-off existing just beyond those junipers and on the right side loomed the sharp face of the hillside reaching up into the darkness. I pressed my back up against the cold rock to back away from that cliff, which plunged hundreds of meters down. As I heard the barking of the dog pack down there tearing apart their dinner meal, I shuddered thinking I don't want to wind-up like that poor critter.

Here I am, stuck. I've got a tricky chasm on my left border and a vertical shaft of stone on the other leaving only a slim meter wide of dirt upon which to crawl. A slab of rocky ledge jutting out of the bluff was my anchor onto which I clung desperately lost in terror.

Warily I made headway like a human snail. Considering the pitch darkness, I was rapidly evolving into an eyeless newt. After a while, however, my eyes regained some acuity and I grubbed my way along in the dirt strictly from the glowing cast proliferating from the starlight overhead. As I struggled to increase my night vision and regain my visual references amongst the constellations, the next wave of dread overcame me. The Milky Way slowly receded as if the winging arm of some dragon had blotted it out. Slowly but surely came my acceptance of the one inevitability I had been avoiding - the possibility of my end time.

As the mortars of what-ifs exploded with greater frequency, I forced them back and gained another couple of meters against the chilled air. Even a pebble underfoot loomed larger than life. I couldn't quite tell but an opaque fog had descended over the hills. There were only a few visual clues remaining to lock onto. I was as a blind person. Fears simmered on the edge of my thinking. I had lost the Lama's ancient prayer back in the dirt. Being a total novice at engendering the unfamiliar words, I had forgotten each and every syllable of the sacred runesift and its saving graces. Owing to my burning fears, the mantra was now a singed crisp. My breathing was shallow and labored. Though the coolness flooding in after sundown had grown into a dry cold, beads of nervous sweat ran down the back of my neck.

Before I could move, I saw the snake loom up before me. Its militant hiss thrust a fang into my consciousness dragging the air out of my lungs. The indisputable likeness of a cobra rose up with its threatening hood. Its sibilant venom struck out like a dagger. As I froze in fear, it seemed eons were elapsing before I could pull away. I dropped to one knee and gripped the loose gravel of the road as though it were the treasure of Babylon. Was this to be my downfall? The notion of possible safety up ahead enticed me with the sweetness of salvation like the honey of bees. If I could hold out my hand and grasp some freedom, I would be rescued from this foul pit.

As the mogul hissing persisted, the hood of the cobra stabbed in and out at me. In the fever of my desperation, I remembered the feather. Immediately I brandished the slick quill at the dancing serpentine menace. It receded downwards but the hissing continued to pulse with a regular rhythm. I rubbed my eyes to gain more perspective. At last, there was a break in the unpredictable cover. With what little sight I had gained right then, I could find no evidence of the hooded beast. Yet, the reptilian spitting persisted with its dire implications. I zeroed in at the spot from where the repulsive noise stemmed. There, to my astonishment, I could barely make out the bends of a thick hose. Where a metal coupling had joined two hose links together spurts of water were squirting out with a nasty fizzle. I did a double take. How insane! I've just been attacked by a garden hose!

As the fuzz of a weak Moon rose into the dispersing vapors, another myth was lain to rest. Much as I had survived the attack of the venomous rubber hose, the meager temperatures of the high summits had badly depleted my energies. I fought the oncoming weakness and struggled to walk the remaining way back to my bungalow. As I climbed the tired stairs to my loft in the lodge and collapsed onto my bunk, the outline of a Khrng shuttled across the frontiers of my fatigue and consolidated itself into the dust of the lost midnight.

The Moon Women

Things were plainly not what they appeared to be. I would be spending the remainder of my days in the realm of the senses, but from now on I would be unduly mindful with regard to what my senses were telling me as opposed to what I could determine was genuinely based on true knowing. I now realized that not only should you look before you leap, you should really, really look before you even think about leaping, faith or no faith.

Back in my enchanted swing chair, I dug into my rucksack and pulled out my trusty mala. As I moved the rudraksha beads through my thumb and forefinger, one by one, each syllable of my mantra rung true within me with a haunting cadence. My experience in Sikkim would dictate the importance of discovering the truths concerning an inner reality lying just outside the boundaries of what society takes for normal. When I found that place, I would understand the multifarious lesson of the garden variety cobra and the murky deception of that whimsical evening in Sikkim.

- 10 -

A breeze flew in through the window. As my wicker mount swiveled steadfastly in its fixed orbit, I relaxed into its delightful rotation. Acquiescing to its indomitable will, my eyes closed and I drifted off again to a drama, which occurred several months before my inter-visitation in Sikkim.

As I walked down an alley over near Commercial Street in the market district of Bangalore, crowds bombarded me from every direction. As the bullock carts rambled by me, the akimbo drivers spoke softly to keep the wayfaring locomotion in line. While auto-rickshaws buzzed by in a blur, little children jostled at my side demanding baksheesh. The gray crows jumped and cawed out of reach, pecking at garbage in the road, which looked like food but wasn't as if expressing their vain attempts to enforce the rituals of religious pecking would miraculously transform the scraps into something edible.

A figure with wild hair flaring erratically ambled amongst the traffic. As he got a little closer, I determined he was what the locals call a sadhu, an ascetic, who wears ocher colored robes or sometimes no clothes at all. Quite often, these hermits fumble with the ubiquitous icon of an impoverished eremite - a full-length mala of large brown beads. The rare few who have also sworn to a code of silence carry a rat eaten chalk board. Whichever variant you might come across, you will see that all of them carry well-worn bowls to beg for alms from those compassionate donors who provide meals and other benefits. They are barefoot for the most part. They paint their bodies using colors ranging from cadmium yellow to ochre as well as crimson ash to advertise the numerous religious symbols drawn on their foreheads by the priests who feed at the numerous religious watering holes populating the thousands of temples and shrines, which line the highways and byways of Mother India. This one looked uncommonly off the wall.

Swathed in faded orange rags and ambling forward with the gate of a beggar, not only was his hairdo all a muss, but his rizzared skull burned as if he had risen from the pancha agni, the torture of the five fires. This is an austerity in which the contestant spends the entire day plopped down under the inferno of a midday sun while sitting in the center of an area boxed in with four blazing bonfires fuming black smoke, which rises from the four corners of this self-imposed torture chamber. Practicing this penance is common in India and it is called Tapas, a Sanskrit word meaning 'to heat.'

On top of that, he looked like some variety of mountebank, a trickster sadhu. As he approached with his wizened abracadabra, he stared at me with a swelling fury. When he got a little closer, he hoisted his hand and stuck out his thumb. Oh, good, I've got a fan. But, no! He wiggled it.

With a wry smirk, he rotated his wrist and made his thumb wriggle from side to side like a lizard struggling to break free from a snare. In the West, the thumbs-up gesture is the sign of giving admiration and exuberant well wishes. Antithetically within Indian culture, it is equivalent to giving your enemy the middle finger, only much worse. It is akin to proclaiming the individual towards whom this hand-signal points, is both guilty of something disastrously wrong as well as ignorant of the foggy aura surrounding his being - foggy and dense as coal dust. It wasn't so much he was putting forth these encrypted gestures with any maleficence, but rather, he meant it more as a tepid malediction. It was no more than his attempt to straighten me out, more like shouting, "Fire!" in a crowded theatre.

The Moon Women

Running alongside the sadhu was a homeless boy tugging on my sleeve. I figured he was working for a handout, but he began to babble broken English.

"Sahib! Sahib! Maharaji say you no see Paramatma in bazaar. He say you must go back in black water. You no see great white man. You no see Paramatma! [Sir! Sir! The Reverend Sadhu says you will not find God in the bazaar. He says you must go back over the ocean, back to your native place. You will not meet your Maker. You will not find God!]," he stuttered.

"Chelo! Chelo!" [Scram! Get out of here!] I yelled explosively. Thinking he was becoming more of a nuisance than a nuance, I avoided the kid by shooing him away.

"Sadhu Ji say you no go Mukti. You no ride white bus. Mother Kali stop you. Maharaji say Chandra kahlie. No Surya, no Prakash! [The Lord Yogi says you will not find salvation. You will not gain the heavens of light. Goddess Kalima (death) will stop you. The honored reverend says the Moon is empty. There is no sun, no light for you]," he yelled gesticulating furiously like a power puppet.

"Why don't you get lost, you little creep!"

Thinking perhaps tossing him a few coins would discourage his antics and chase him off, I unloaded a few paise, but he kept yammering away like a magpie while the sadhu also persisted with his belittling gestures. Finally, he shoved his caked mug my way, held up his string of earthen beads, and beckoned with them as if he was offering them for sale.

"See Maharaji! See numbers. Is number you stop Kali [See the honored Reverend. See the number of his beads on his rosary. Number is number you must turn Time around]," the boy choked.

I scratched my head. What kind of ludicrous game was this roadside duo running on me? Why are they making such a foofaraw over all this shit? And what's up with the mala? The kid's next invective came out as actual grammar to the tune of some British butler.

"My Dear Sir, you have to reverse Time, otherwise you will never attain your goal. The amount of reversals must be as many as the beads on this mala, one hundred and eight."

Turning his back, the sadhu spat out a glob of brown juice onto the dirty roadway. With betel nut surging in their veins, the two of them wandered off and dissolved into the crowd as if a spent wave fanning out upon the sand. As their memory faded, I was left dazed and confused holding more cold cotton.

I didn't pay much attention to either one of them after that because I viewed this sadhu and his creepy sidekick to be of a social status considerably below mine. Besides, his splattered bleach pigmentation utterly repulsed me. I learned many years later, after I had embraced family life and acquired some responsibilities of my own, it was something diagnosed as vitiligo. But at that time in the early seventies, such was the meter of how much Indian culture had bled into my veins. As it worked out of my system over the years, I was quite lucky that the aversions of my misplaced mindset hadn't eaten all my skin pigments or devoured my colored halo as well.

Having no time for this pair of dimwits, I hurried off to spend some time with my tailor, Mr. Kalazaki, for a most important fitting. He was creating a suit of impeccable glory for me to wear on my travels homeward in August. Regardless, this face-to-face detour with the perplexing sadhu stuck with me like a bad stain that couldn't be cleansed. Later I learned from Dr. K that my coattail-licking sadhu had probably seen me burning spiritually and was simply offering to warn me of an impending doom, something I couldn't register by myself. He was taking a run at jolting my clairvoyant antennae back into service. I will admit due to my hedonistic habits, which were fed by my probing odysseys in the clandestine hideouts down on Brigade Road, my normally ultra-sensitive receptors had become severely anesthetized. Was I going to take this forewarning to heart and avoid the calamity, which was heading my way? And how was I supposed to reverse Time? Dr. K had no answers to those perplexing questions, only his regular terse pattern of advice indicating I should straighten myself up and soon.

Back in the capital of my rotating cosmos, the magnetized wicker chair, I interpreted the figure of that sadhu to be a somber apparition of my baffling destiny spiraling through the back alleys of Time/Space like a dust devil from a future age twisting back on itself with the poise of a telepathic serpent. Yet somehow, messages from enemies of an ultra-race were threatening to seep in much deeper.

The Moon Women

The indomitable chair rotated awkwardly shielding me from the mundane to plunge me deeper into my bizarre histories. Back in January a week or two after I had landed at the center here in Bangalore, Dr. Krishnaswami had accompanied me to a lecture presented by a renowned mystic philosopher by the name of Shri Bhagwan Vingtesh Krishnamurti. Discoursing in both English and Hindi, with occasional emphatic outbursts in other dialects, the Bhagwan created an East-West amalgamation of Vedic and Christian philosophies to narrate his marsupial brand of metaphysics couched within a lumberjack theology. He would extract popular quotations from his traveling bag of Vedic scriptures and then hack them to pieces while unscrambling their hidden meanings using Christian analogies and vice versa. He was an exceptionally charismatic speaker. One of the points he emphasized heavily went a long way in explaining a puzzle, which confronts everyone: the meaning of purpose or the purpose of meaning, whichever you prefer, two sides of the same coin that pays for your future. His talk went something like this.

"Have you ever turned a corner in life to discover the sublime right where you never expected it to be? In the doldrums of everyday tasks, which extend out in front of you as a wide-open sea, have you not, for perhaps only an instant, bumped into an unalloyed tranquility? As you peered out upon a sea alive with sharks from the future and monsters from the past, have you not observed an unexplainable precision living while the movements of snowflakes? As you lay naked upon a drifting raft while praying for survival ever since you could remember, have you not witnessed the emergence of the divine?

"Momentarily, on the fringes of your frail memory, there had been the personification of peace, which visited you once long ago with a sweetness, with a caress from the mother force. Even though your days were riddled with torment and sliced bare by the razors of fear, or you may have found yourself fighting physical pain and losing blood; once, just once, you glimpsed reality as if in a dream.

"I propose to you now that underneath whatever happiness that was stolen from you, whatever warm thrill you felt life cheated you over, there had been a feeling of sovereignty, a feeling of

44

goodness and harmony, if even for a fleeting second. Never mind how ethereal it might have been, on at least one occasion in your life, you have basked in a resplendent sunshine, which smiled down upon you with a loving calm and a smothering care; one that illuminated you with the possibility of endless comfort and well-being as if a benevolence far and above your wildest dreams.

"During this time as you were inspired to overcome the utter banality of your subsistence, hope of the divine began to take root within you and sprout wings in your heart. The birth of that hope is the planting of the seed of spirituality. The sprouting of this seed is the awakening of your true self. And the growing of the tree is the pursuit of the mystic goal, the journey that leads Godward, that which unfolds the mystique of Man."

For me this was an astounding concept, which hit the nail squarely on the head. I knew precisely what he had meant. I could recall that moment back in summer camp when I had viewed a pastoral vista of great beauty. I had experienced that Godward pull firsthand; only I didn't call it that. To me it was more like a force, something, which could lift me out of this realm of death and propel me skyward like flying in a magic bubble at light speed.

When my eyes met with Krishnamurti's I knew that he was fully aware I had tuned in to what he was proposing. And I yearned for him to develop the concept more thoroughly, but he missed that mark and proceeded to march off triumphantly into his own self-created transcendent regions cluttered with his ismistics and his quasi-philosophies. He never visited that tree of paradise a second time. Seems he was weaving an elusive canvas upon which to paint portraits of his own grandeur. Rhetorically, he knit that linen shroud right in front of my eyes and with great expertise; he made me dress in it. Moreover, he invited me to travel through its doorway. Nevertheless, he made no vessel for himself to ride within on that journey. He flew off on a tangent of imagination only to disappear into a vague state like a genie, which had resumed the void of its bottle.

Now back in my pivoting chair, I reviewed the recent chapter in which I had exposed my acceptance of the wily belief that by tirelessly repeating a mantra I could claim a mystical dominance whose tabulation was the mindless turning of muricated beads on an ugly necklace labeled, most ominously, as a mala. This conjoined

The Moon Women

process was necessary for me to climb the steps leading to a promised access into the Beyond. But was it more than that? Was it leveraging a portal into a dimension where only a rare few had dared to venture ahead of me? I knew this awakening had rung my bell, but to what unexplored realms would I be exposing myself and besides that, what unmentionables would I uncage; what monsters might crawl out? In spite of these trepidations, I wanted to know more so I marked off another bead on the ancient mala. Be that as it may, more door battering ratcheted me back.

"Tindi tinnu!" [Snacks to eat!]

Dr. Krishnaswami's son, Ranjanna, announced the next cycle of the dietary regimen.

- 12 -

After the savory pick-me-up, I climbed back onto my Ozymandias pedestal. In the wake of Krishnamurti's waltzing dialectics, the wicker bridge was turning by itself but I regained command to right its wayward tack. Maybe I could detect some residues still fresh from what the gifted speaker had brought me as inspiration to set out across the lone and level sands and dig up some evidence about the unrecorded race. Even though the incense had settled, the glimmer of what he had triggered within me was now a compass pointing me back to the time I met the Ayatollah in Iran. As I looked up, the ceiling showed me the turquoise domes of Islam swimming in a mirage upon the horizon.

After considerable travel across Europe and down into Greece, I had gotten my first big break on my odyssey into the Far East. A fortuitous connection with a band of voyagers who were making their way overland to Delhi had landed in my lap. A spot in their Land Rover had opened up when one of their crew had been laid low with dysentery. Pushing out of Istanbul, the group had roamed the major sights of Turkey and had headed deeper into the holy lands of Islam. After we had crossed the border at Bazargan into Iran, we set up shop in a grimy hotel in the heart of the capital, Tehran.

Shortly after our arrival, my adopted travel buddies acquired the services of a Iranian lad who seemed to have taken an extra liking to me. I suspected he was hitting me up for Americana, transistors and watches mostly. His name was Ramesh Mahdi. My recollection of previous inward callings had led me to believe that by having a deeper understanding of what the Muslim faith could show might gain me a leg up in pursuing my own personal pilgrimage.

Feigning an afterglow from the Woodstock Concert that wouldn't fade, my appearance at the time was quite unusual. I looked like a cross between David Crosby and the scarecrow from the Wizard of Oz. The combination of shoulder length auburn locks and fuzzy sideburns, which traced a curve to the absence of a handlebar moustache, endowed my profile with a clownish rock star look. Unquestionably, it was not the Iranian persona I must assume in order to pierce the thick shield of Islamic culture, which insulates their Mosques against infidels such as myself.

Plus, my attire could have conceivably been tagged as embarrassing. I wore a set of chartreuse trousers and maroon socks. My hiking boots were the customary ones from L.L. Bean, but for my headgear, I donned a cadmium yellow floppy felt hat having a Kelly green band, which trailed down my back. Instead of a shirt, I wore a khaki bush jacket with four oversized pockets and umpteen loops and net sacks. Finally, for amusement, I carried a recorder, a wooden flute like the type played by a someone in grade school.

This woodwind was an important tool. During my travels overland, my habit was to hike my way to the tippity top of whatever summit, which might be easily available. The shout out at the summit would initiate with a homegrown brand of meditation that was essentially a derivative of inverted pranayama. Using a series of brisk breathing exercises, which I augmented with channeling, I concentrated my eyes in my forehead and imagined a pool of swirling blue light surrounding me, the same vibrant blue, which burns within the flame of a pilot light or a Bunsen burner. Occasionally, this meditation would yield extraordinary results. After performing these exercises for a dozen or so hyperventilating laps, I would use my internal senses to reach out into the surrounding territory and send invitations born on hand-sized butterflies which flew out from my core as it grew brighter and brighter with each discharge. The effect might even extend out to a radius of one hundred meters or more.

When I sensed something, I would modulate my vibrations and attempt to contact the entity by initiating some ethereal tweedling on my recorder. This music wasn't really any form of music you could recognize. It was a style of warbling, chirping, and squeaking

The Moon Women

shrieks, which ostensibly came out like nasty noises to the common ear. But it worked for me. I was convinced that I was communicating with beings on the far fringes of sanity. Little did I realize who or what was tuning into this craziness.

When you witness an American peregrinating his way over the thousands of kilometers between the coast of France and the capital of Iran, it's a mind twist that such a wanderer could still be alive and kicking at this late stage of the game. Nevertheless, by reason of the protection afforded me by my international escorts, as well as a hardy pack of travelers who were intent on never letting me out of their sight, I was well buffeted from any possible shocks the environment might throw at me regardless of my eccentric pursuits. As I navigated the homelands of the radical towel heads who burrowed beneath the sands of insurrection fomenting in the bowels of Persia at the time, this was the tenure of my oddball endeavors, the ones I pursued throughout my trek across these ravishing Arabian vistas.

For a lark, I quizzed this lad, Ramesh, if there was any way I could get a peek at the formidable Mosque, the one that was so easily visible from the central trunk road coming into the capital; it seemed to be such a fascinating place. He informed me the Mosques in Tehran were altogether consecrated shrines of holiness and only the Shia Hajjis could worship there.

Historically speaking, there are two branches of Muhammadan theology, the Shia and the Sunni. Each was consumed within a life and death struggle over the validity surrounding the successor of the great prophet, Muhammad, the founder of present Islam. One side (the Sunni) believed it was the father-in-law, Abu Bakr, and the other (the Shia) took the position that it was the grandson, Ali. In either case, they both zealously attacked each other over who deserved to be the rightful successor. To me it seemed both were dubious, but whom I am to judge. At most I'm simply a follower of falderal as far as either one of them is concerned.

In central Iran, where Tehran is located, the Shia was in the majority; therefore, security was tight. There were sentries in the Mosques who guaranteed everybody who got in there was from a genuine Shia tribe. Those on watch would not tolerate anyone inappropriate. In fact, Ramesh indicated if they discovered a non-Shia had penetrated the sanctity of the Mosque, the Mudir would capture the insurgent and might even dole out a severe punishment right on the spot. When I compelled him to explain it in more detail, he drew his finger across his throat. But even that threat did not deter me from pushing onwards against what seemed like martial law.

When I demanded he smuggle me into the Mosque, he looked at me with fearful hesitation. Pursuing the down side proved fruitless; however, after a short pause, he disclosed he could do what I wanted but only for a fee. In addition, I would have to alter my appearance drastically. He narrowed in on me and pestered me with questions tailored to discover my motives. After warding off a few well-aimed prods, I agreed. How tough could it be? With a rolling wrist he made the I'll-be-back signal and disappeared out the door.

A couple hours later, Mr. Mahdi was back toting some native clothing: a pair of trousers made out of a stout woolen fabric like tweed only coarser, an ill-smelling shirt: knock off of its western cousin but with handmade bone buttons, and a ratty ass mat of some kind. In addition to those articles came a pair of weather-beaten shoes dangling tattered shoelaces. He urged me to put this outfit on and then come with him for a little rendezvous. Oh, and don't forget to grab the prayer rug.

We got into one of those dusty yellowish taxis, which have infected the heart of Asia and darted off to have a run at the Grand Mosque living in the city's black hole so
p. 45 . After another roller coaster ride through traffic, we dismounted at the outskirts of the city bazaar. Ramesh latched onto my hand and dragged me into the throngs of shoppers. After a lengthy charge through the leathery crowds, we came to a barbershop, which displayed a weather beaten candy cane pole.

"You cut hair now," he commanded.

Squeamishly, I sagged into the goat hide throne scarred by too many slipshod misses of the blade upon the whiskered throats of misanthropes who had fallen into unlucky whiles. As the humongous Iranian barber leaned over me, the stench of spicy mutton rolled off his tongue and damn near knocked me out. As his buzzing shaver worked its way from temple to temple taking down my side locks, the groggy hair stylist seemed to be complaining to Ramesh over why he was cutting my freaky hair job. After Ramesh handed him some more money, he quickly finished with the buzz cut approach and brought out a beat up pair of scissors to continue with his hacking mission on top. Snip, snip, snip.

The Moon Women

When he flipped out his straight razor, I got a little nervous and jerked back. With a scowl, he yelled at the boy who assured me the whiskers had to go, all them except the dismal shadow on my upper lip; it might pass for an excuse of a moustache. Without using any lather, he hacked off all my facial trappings. And then he encased my entire noggin with a steaming towel. After a stringent soaking, the mad Sufi spun it off and with precise strokes, he carved off what was left of my elaborate frontal trimmings to complete one of the closest shaves I have ever had. There wasn't a single scratch. It was nothing but clean as a whistle Mr. Rahms, all bristled up for a night on the town.

As I stuffed the rolled-up rug under my arm, we bounded back into the waiting taxi. Ramesh furnished the taxi feller with a street name and off we went. To claim that Iranian taxis use body English when they pilot their vehicles through traffic is an understatement. This hair-brained Ali Baba threw his taxi at clogged buses, derelict cars, furtive women cloaked in burkas scurrying to the curb, mangy cows and even policemen performing their calisthenics of directing traffic. Miraculously, by the time we were on them, they'd be gone and our taxi would careen through the vacant hole. I humored myself by imagining how everything might be if I could negotiate life the same way.

Ultimately, we wound up on at the perimeter of what looked to be the jewelry quarter of the marketplace. Shops with bejeweled rings, hanging bangles, and dangling chains of gold in obscene lengths were everywhere. We hopped out of the taxi and dissolved into the shifting crowds. The clamor was shocking. Every shop owner was hawking his wares at the top of his lungs. Sidekick shop mascots were hassling me to come here and there to handle the oodles of jewelry. I was tempted to go and look, but my scout jostled onwards into the crowds dragging me behind him. Down multiple alleys, we trudged. Then, he detoured suddenly and barged slam bang into one of the shops with me in tow.

There was a forest of carpets hanging down at the back of the shop. Shouting expletives at the exasperating crowds, Ramesh shoved the hanging Persian resistance aside and lugged me along after him. After making an abrupt turn in the middle of this jungle of jute, we approached a hidden entranceway, which led down a dim passage distancing us from the racket of the hawkers. At long last, we emerged into a cloistered courtyard facing what looked to be the vast embankment of an ancient building.

Facing a massive metal portal, I knew we had arrived. As the mammoth door creaked back, its crusted facade was as ancient as was the Fire Prince himself. Ramesh grappled with a gnarly claw to shoulder the time worn portal free. With repeated thrusts, it opened enough for us to slip inside. There were piles of shoes everywhere; most had been tied together in long chains, apparently the Persian method of keeping track of them. Towering over a looming counter smothered with a tangle of sandals and cheap flip-flops was the most colossal Iranian in Mustafa's Arabia. My word! The barber guy was big, but this giant was truly a two-eyed cyclops with a turban the size of a beach ball. The boy tugged on my arm and whispered in my ear.

"He guard. He mean. Here, you no talk. If he talk, you say nothing. I talk for you. You are my cousin from North in Kurdistan. I tell him you not speaking our dialect. So you not talk here. He don't know. Now take off shoes!" The moment of truth had come.

As my tour guide conversed at breakneck speed, the Goliath shook his jowls to wave off the repeated incursions of insistence from Ramesh who precipitated more up and down gesticulations like knife work on a butcher's block. Belatedly the Goliath looked over and focused his Islamic psycho-radar on my pea-sized flag of faith. He spat out a bold dictum and then smacked the back of his hand onto his palm. As my high paid go-between flailed this way and that with his explanations, I was afraid the mammoth retard was growing more and more irritated. Fortunately, Ramesh kept applying added applications of monetary liniment. It was looking like touch and go. I verged on fixing to bail but at last Ramesh discovered the open sesame and the giant flinched. When he nodded his approval, the green light winked and we could go in!

Down a crooked corridor that jigged and then jagged, we advanced deeper and deeper into the twisted bowels of the Mosque. As we negotiated a tight hairpin, the way opened into a colossal cavern filled with hundreds of worshippers. The insane babel was deafening. Muslim devotees of every size, shape, and age were kneeling, bowing, and lying down. Some were praying, some were singing, some were hollering at the top of their lungs and all at the same time.

No two practitioners were worshiping in the same way. There

The Moon Women

were families praying together in one direction; there was a bevy of women performing a deliberate, singsong chanting in another. Many more were piously mourning together; death had come to visit. In another vicinity, there were jihadists bowing down and putting their foreheads onto their deep maroon prayer mats in unison. Over in the corner a group of youngsters chanted violently while waving black flags strewn with the burning white emblems of Arabic scrawl. I went to spread mine out but Ramesh stopped me.

"No, not here. Do later. Not with them," he motioned for me to get moving.

I felt drawn to them somehow, but Ramesh's heads-up scared me off. This entire area was jam-packed with pilgrims worshipping in every conceivable way, in every alcove and niche, and in every direction. There was utterly no organization to it whatsoever. It was a mess hall of prayer, a great cacophony of worshipers.

Ramesh led on. We left the orientation hall behind and entered another open space in which all the walls were of alabaster and marble. Into this radius of infinite splendor were inlaid hundreds of phrases quoted from the writings of what I assumed was the Holy Qur'an. Using black agate or perhaps obsidian, the engravers had embedded the inscriptions with line after line across the white shining facades. In that hall, various contingents of pilgrims were also praying in all directions and in all manner of worship, more like an assemblage of absent minds.

"Here we pray," he informed me and spread out the mangy mat in front of me. He himself simply prayed on a geometric dome patterned onto the carpeted floor. I followed his lead and as he repeated some prayers in Arabic I placed my forehead on the mat and made like I, too, was performing the prayers. It felt awkward but also strangely wonderful at the same time, as if I was pledging allegiance to my neighbor's barbeque.

From that assemblage we ventured into another cavernous antechamber entirely plated with gold. The walls exhibited embossed scriptures upon the avenues of mezzotints everywhere. Torches and candles of all sizes reflected their glowing light from the shimmering tabernacles. From that station, we explored another vestibule encased in exquisite silver. Every vertical surface was hand-wrapped in gleaming sterling overlays. Here the scriptures were set with gemstones of topaz, ruby, and vast inlays of turquoise. It was all so breathtaking.

Ramesh pointed the way onwards. We roamed the Mosque from one devout assemblage to the next. The last hall, done entirely in crystal, was supremely the most beautiful of them all. Light from a thousand chandeliers danced from one sparkling facet to the next in an unending phantasmagoria of radiant bliss. This place must have been something very special because only a very few holy men were present to worship. They looked to be eminent clerics of some kind. Each one was clad with rich black robes, as well some of them had grizzled salt and pepper beards. Their worship seemed more like a discussion rather than genuine meditation. When I began to notice they all seemed to be paying considerable attention our way, my chaperon grew nervous and feverishly signaled me to commence an urgent departure. Doubtless we were on borrowed time at that point. We detoured nonstop via a confusion of switchbacks to the front hall in which where we had dropped anchor. We had successfully made the full circuit.

Ramesh asked me to stand pat while he coughed over the brass token, which he had received from the behemoth bouncer. After reclaiming our shoes, he fished out a wad of rial notes to anoint the giant's merciful hand. With our crimes in Islam concluded, we departed those halls of Muhammad Rasul Allah to regain square one on the curbside where we had secretively disembarked. Back out onto the bazaar road, Ramesh flagged down a taxi. As we got going its miniscule wheels wobbled hysterically, being held on by only one good screw.

- 13 -

The following day at breakfast, I was relating all my experiences to my companions, when our rambunctious tour guide, Ramesh Mahdi, burst into the pantry with an announcement. He apologized for interrupting me, but he insisted. After jabbering that he had something of immense importance to tell us, he finally made out with it. Apparently, during our pilgrimage yesterday some influential Shia Mullahs had observed our little stint at the height of our adventures over in Mosque land. They were now demanding to talk with me. In spite of some previous tomfoolery from Ramesh, the seriousness of his insinuations gave me a bad feeling. I suspected

The Moon Women

there could possibly be some considerable backlash coming out of this oligarchy.

"Didn't you tell me we could get beheaded if we were detected in there?" I was thinking it was time to get the heck out of Dodge.

"No. They say you friend of Muhammad. You have mark. They need talk of you." He pleaded.

"Hey. I'm fine with making a move with the Land Rover. We should be heading out for Mashhad in the East and onwards to Herat hidden up in the peaks of Afghanistan. Shouldn't we be getting lost soon, like deep the twisting passes of the Khyber? I'm pretty sure Graham wants us to get going." No sense dawdling I argued but my fellow travelers wanted to hear more from their flunky.

"Oh, Rahm, you should go. It might be totally cool," Evey made with her prayer hands foolishly and frowned.

I had joined up with this crazy bunch of comrades in Athens who had arranged a party of seven travelers a year ago in England and had planned an unrestricted travel log all across Europe, Persia and down into India. While in London, after observing a resident Methodist making proclamations describing what to do when the angels weren't present, instead of waging war with the devils, they should consult something the shepherds had talked over with each other when alone in the wilderness. Seems Evey had overheard one of them in the bathroom mumbling, "Let us now go even unto Bethlehem, and see this thing which is come to pass which the Lord hath made known unto us." [2]

Were these folks orbiting somewhere in the asteroid belt? I put Ramesh and his goofy demands behind me and prepared to enjoy myself over at the Bazaar picking over some of those trinkets. As we all filed down the narrow stairway to find the cantina in the basement of our fleabag stay in Tehran, I got back-doored by another offhand face-to-face. In a tight bottleneck, I squeezed by a tall fellow who presented an American façade under the tussle of a dark mullet. He reminded me of my roommate, Tom Gallager, from back in college days. This was a major brush with fate because I hadn't seen Tom since the forenoon scarcely prior to my frightening confrontation with the Khrng out in the marshes at Bard back in '65. I thought to hazard a guess over what on earth Gallager could be doing here in Iran, but there was no time. For all I know, he was with the State Department. We had to hurry now.

Ramesh was tugging at me incessantly with jabbing bits of English in his attempt to convince me it would be a worthwhile experience, but I was having none of it. I've got to avoid becoming the victim of my own mercy killing.

"Don't you get it, Ramesh? The gang doesn't have a second to spare for me to have an adventure with high Islamic muckety-mucks this late in our travels to India!" I contested argued.

"You say. You fella go for ministry. No Ramadan six days. You go."

The bloody bugger wouldn't quit. Then because he wouldn't let up, I spat out my answer.

"Bite me!"

When we reached the cantina, we plopped ourselves down on the wobbly three legged stools there. Hurriedly our driver from London, Graham Peers, dove in through the door. After paying at the cash register for his tea, he reeled in his wallet which was attached to a dangly chain and stuck it into his back pocket. He must have had all kinds of notes in there from the diverse countries he had been through since France; must have been over a dozen.

"Rahm is going to get knighted by Islams!" Evey let slip as Graham lifted his cup.

"They're not bloody Islams, Evey. They're bloody Muhammadans fer Chrissakes!" Graham was always correcting her and sorely she couldn't stand it.

"Oh! Fuck you, Graham!" She toyed with her stirring spoon. The mudflow out of her yap was heavy at times.

"What's the good word, Rahm?" Graham thrust his gavel fist my way.

As his mannish thumb threaded the teacup's handle, his other fingers supported its pedestal while the rudder of his pinky brought up the rear, Turkish style. Graham took staccato sips of the stiff brew while punctuating the fluid with further inquiry.

"Don't imagine having a sword tapped on yer shoulder by these mad clerics would add anything to your health, Laddy." He had a point but Ramesh butted in with his two cents.

"Imams say he have mark of Muhammad. They give him words from the Holy Qur'an."

"Right. Gimme the lowdown, Boy. Doesn't sound right what the bitch said." He blew on the brew.

The Moon Women

After brushing off another acidic tirade from Evey, Graham leaned in a bit closer for what I had to say. I related to him how, with Ramesh's assistance, I had bootlegged myself into the hallowed sanctums of the grandiose Mosque. I had witnessed unimaginable scenes of celestial splendor. It was like a museum of prayer. Despite my witnessing the pompous glory, some holy ranking Islamic clerics had seen us and now it seems they were demanding a little head to head, so to speak. I didn't like the way it sounded at all. I implored him to confirm the need to push onwards to Kabul. I couldn't feature much of an advantage winding up like that Persian poet manqué, Ali.

"Right. Thing is, we might be here for a fortnight or more, Rahm. The Rover's got a cracked shaft. It's been bangin' like a hammer for quite some time now. I know we're pressed for time, but switching it out East of Meshed is not a lucky prospect. Besides those kippers, I'm not happy on the prospects of finding ourselves stranded out in the frigid bitterness, which haunts these parts. I'm sure you can appreciate what I'm sayin', Rahm." He set his cup to rattle on its saucer and shook out a cigarette.

"I hear you there. So what you're telling me is we're going to be stuck here a while anyway? No use wasting a decent adventure over there with the Islamic big wigs, is that it?"

"Yup. Give it a shot, Bloke. You might save yourself and awaken your inner angel. Blimey! You might push these bloody sods to get off their arses for once. 'We may set forth wheat making the ephah small and the sheki great, but are we falsifying the balances by deceit?'[2] That's plumb ad infinitum come out of the Good Book, Old Boy. My Mum used to quote me on it back in the day."

He blew out an eddy of smoke and crooked his finger for me to come closer.

"When the bloke says you've got a mark of the Muhammad, don't fall for that. It's just a carrot to get you over there, so beware. By all means, go for it and knock 'em dead, Boy, but watch yer back, ma man. Watch yer back." He whispered while shielding his mouth with his hand.

I never figured Graham for a Bible man but it was good advice to be on my guard. He sucked down another penultimate slurp of Turkish manna and took another drag. Graham had seen too many kilometers on the Pakistani highway no doubt.

After we finished off our tea, Graham commandeered the

platoon uptown to the bazaar for a shopping adventure. Having lost the debate, I headed downtown with Ramesh with Graham's warning under my arm.

- 14 -

A Mosque has four minarets, usually one on each corner, but one is central because it is the one from which the muezzin periodically shouts out the call to prayer. Whereas the initial call consists of two words or four syllables, one perceives it as one utterance.

Allah Akbar means God is great. The lah segment of Allah is drawn way out, while the leading syllable is voiced as a clipped shout. The Ak sonant of Akbar is pronounced as Ike; whereas the bar segment is shortened and the r is rolled considerably. Slicing through the chilly fog of midnight or lending relief amidst the suffocating heat of a midday traffic meltdown, this call to prayer quenches the religious thirst of these many Islamic nations. It also serves as a greeting between comrades and friends.

An early frost decorated the bare cobblestones with an icy crust as we approached the Mirador outpost to the ornate Mosque. The Sufi safeguarding the entrance was most bewildered when I saluted him with an exuberant shout.

"Allah Akbar!"

I let loose my salutation and followed it by the brief touching of my chest, forehead, and then the air over my head, the three places of holiness for a Muslim. It was not so much these were employed in the performance of prayers on a mat, but rather they represented the primary arenas wherein God resides: the heart of Man, the third eye and the realms of the Beyond.

We slipped through an ancient portal made from the wood of trees, which might have been alive at the time Muhammad Himself trod these lands. I expected to recover some warmth in there, but essentially, it was more like heading to the vicinity of the polar regions rather than paradise. A spike of chilled disquiet knifed though me.

Ramesh followed the Sufi and I followed Ramesh. The vista of a cumbrous compound, which typically stands as the entryway of the Mosque, rolled by briskly as we turned abruptly down a tight corridor

The Moon Women

and then ascended a steep set of stairs spiraling upwards squarely for four floors. Cascading tapestries from Isfahan lined the walls. Splinters of sunlight ricocheted off the shifting fabrics and caused mesmerizing colors to flood my vision. I realized something was drawing me into another mystical wonderland. Whatever guardian deity had guided me from time to time was seizing my destiny as an unassailable mysterium unfolding in front of my eyes once again. At any moment, I was sure I would confront mysteries from out of the Beyond, things that might bring questions I had not even thought to ask.

As a volley of Allah Akbars resoudned out of the dark hallway, one of the Mullahs marched in. This Mullah was presumably the one who had discovered my subterfuge back in the Mosque. He scrutinized his surroundings as if something devious had presently materialized within his midst. Tattered robes like carbonized feathers cloaked him from top to bottom and emitted a shifting hiss as he paced nervously back and forth. A coal-tar turban wrapped Tartar style dangled its stubby tail down his back. His goat hair beard was only outdone by his menacing eyebrows, which cast storm clouds over his cold, mineral eyes. Seems he was gravely displeased to have to confront me. Tossing quick and mean words at Ramesh, this grave Mullah proceeded with some kind of interrogation. It looked as if Ramesh was confessing to the tune of being a snitch as if to say:

"Well, it wasn't my idea. This idiot kept pestering me to get into the Mosque and wouldn't take no for an answer."

That was what Ramesh seemed to be saying but I had no real idea. In fact, I wasn't sure of anything right then. Like, why the hell did I agree to come back here? The raven black Mullah glared at me and expelled his frustration by gritting his teeth. Then he motioned for us to follow him so in spite of my hesitancy, that's what we did.

After trudging down long hallways and up another set of stairs, we came into an overwhelmingly claustrophobic territory having a reduced topside of a skooch over two of meters; however, the constriction did not add any heat to the place. My breath swirled out in misty columns. Persian carpets not only overlapped the platform on which we stood, but also swung as vertical tapestries disguising vague outlets all along the sidelines. These only seemed to preserve the arctic frigidity of the chamber. Along the backend, there was a slightly elevated tier or Minbar. Prayer mats arranged laterally in two rows divided it uniformly. Slightly rearwards of its midline, a series of sitting pads outlined a potential audience, mini-thrones where pilgrims could sit cross-legged. The chief Mullah enjoined me to sit down on one of those raised seats. I chose the lone one in the corner, which had a miniature demi-roof over it. Slightly distancing itself from the others it could conceivably have been where an honored guest might sit. Somehow, I was connected to it even though I didn't know it was the Mihrab, the stipulated site for the principal cleric. As I nodded my acceptance to this fabled induction, the dark Mullah curled his lip.

One by one, a beatific train of Islamic splendor flowed in from the outer corridors. Each cleric was clad in an elegant kaftan and all in subtle shades of black, gray, or a purplish plumbago and punctuated with a twisted sash. Some had black turbans but most were white. There were a couple dozen of them but I lost count. After they assumed their battle stations they thumbed through whatever missal with which they had been burdened, the Holy Qur'an or the Hadith, I presumed (the two primary holy books of Islam). As the rustling of their Persian palaver abated, in came quite a dapper gentleman who was decked out quite differently than all the others. He wore an impeccably tailored three-piece suit and patent leather shoes. He was a balding chap devoid of any headgear. He deposited some scriptural volumes on his desk and took a gander my way as he peered out over his bifocals.

"Good morning, Mr. Ibsen, my name is Dr. Abdullah Abu Zawari. I am here to act as your Mufti, your translator, and your counsel. We are all most glad to hear you have decided to attend to your responsibilities in this matter. We have learned of your good name through our trusted friend, Mr. Ramesh Mahdi Alwari. We would like you to know that we are all in agreement concerning this business, Mr. Ibsen. Your fate in Tehran impinges upon these crucial matters, which will now be presented before you. Your life depends on it in fact. Only truth and authentic witness can save you, Mr. Ibsen. So, congratulations. Welcome to your trial!"

- 15 -

Occasionally, these shifts leap up and twist the effort to regain the gist of my plight whereas these timeouts only serve to enhance

The Moon Women

the prevalent themes and cement to mix into your mind. So here we go again,

My major effort in FWC was making movies. True, it was only Super 8, also packaged as 8 millimeter (the bulk of photography was metrified), but even as a budding photographer I found I could do a lot with it. I had developed some of my own unique editing techniques and procedures for producing remarkable effects without a formal editing lab. They were even producing a type of the Lilliputian celluloid, which had a magnetic strip on it for recording audio right on the spot. Most of what I had carried from Japan to India was either color or poor man's black and white. Over the past months, I had produced two feature films documenting my unusual travels within the subcontinent. My primary documentary was produced up in the mountains and depicted the Lamas and local color of the remote regions of Sikkim. The second showed the temples of Konarak and Khajuraho in Madurai, Dravidian shrines, which depicted males and females in diverse lockups of sexual union. I couldn't really get into those deep wells with Dr. Krishnaswami. Fate had stitched him up a little too tight for him to venture into those tricky avenues. I wasn't going to mess up on that subject with him, ever. Even after a decade of cryptic cross talk between entities from other dimensions, I'm fairly certain that was a non-event in anyone's book. Most unexpectedly there was a hurried rapping on my door.

"Oota Mardu!" commanded Mrs. Krishnaswami. It was time for lunch.

I headed for the pantry where Dr. K and his little son, Mahadevappa, were awaiting my arrival. I sat down beside my renowned mentor right onto the rigid slate of the langhar, the Hindu eating room. Even the most wealthy of Indian families sit cross legged on the floor for meals. I wondered if furniture had been an invention of the British brought here to intimidate the humble cast of Brahmins. That daydream took me down lanes calculating the relationship between Dravidian histories and the purposes of the Khrng, but because of my recent revelation out of the ceiling, I knew it to be a confounding pursuit so I dropped it. Its implant might have indicated something about my condition but I digressed to juggle more meaningful subjects; namely lunch.

Food was the domain of Mrs. Krishnaswami, the musician of dining. Disklike stainless steel thalis were set down onto the floor in

60

front of each of us. These are the traditional dishes of the South Indian service. The thali is a circular plate approximately sixteen inches in diameter with a perpendicular lip of an inch running its circumference. All the cooking utensils of her Indian kitchen consisted of various alloys of copper, brass, tin, and stainless steel. As preparations commence, these metal implements banged together producing a clanking din, which could pass for primitive music.

First, the server dumps a generous pile of freshly cooked white rice right in the center of the thali. The server dispatches it immediately so it can cool before the arrival of the other staples. White rice has always been preferred in Indian meals. Brown rice is virtually unheard of in India and is a rare commodity, particularly in the South. Even dirt-poor families insist on having white rice for their meals. It is strictly a concern of social status.

We know the rice kernel, which has its bran layer of nutritious vitamins and minerals left intact, is the most trophic type called brown rice. Granted the immense value of those vital amino acids and trace elements are essential for good health, white rice has become supreme. In spite of having its shell ground off with a millstone, white rice has evolved into a greater and greater prominence within the social strata of the Indian diet by virtue of its popularity rather than its nutritional value. Originally, it was available only to the wealthy Brahmins. But as the increased efficacy of the gristmill exploded across the centuries, the white brand became more and more available and thus more economical. Thus, the vast majority of untouchables broadened its popularity and helped raise the hardy staple up the totem pole of the Indian diet to attain the high status, which it enjoys in present-day life.

Adjacent to the rice comes a full-bodied soup of some vegetable boiled to oblivion and laced with all sorts of spices, including coriander, cardamom, ginger and a type of masala consisting of blended chilies, which empowered the dish with a serious kick. Added to these is a rare but crucial component in a true Brahmin kitchen, something termed as asafetida, or hing, an extremely alliaceous condiment, which can augment the meal with a powerful garlicy flavor.

On the upper section of the thali, one after the other, the server places three tin cups each three inches in diameter having a slightly rolled lip. These are filled with helpings of dahl, curd and spinach

The Moon Women

respectively. The dahl comes from lentils, which could either be the masoor (red) lentil from Bombay or, more typically, the channa (yellow) bean from central India. A modicum of sea salt is then trickled onto the other side to mix in for taste.

You are not served with eating utensils when you eat an Indian meal. You have to use your hand and only the right hand. The other hand must be kept discretely out of the way, like a mitt, a dead hand. You can hold it in your lap or even behind your back but you must never handle any food with it. To do so would be interpreted as an extreme sacrilege. Each hand has its own particular function in Indian life. The right one is the one to employ when eating. This can introduce some important microbes into the gut, believe it or not. The left one? Well, let me put it this way. In spite of the Scott Brothers' indispensable invention back in 1890, there are still no toilet paper factories anywhere on the sub-continent, not to mention Asia in general.

You begin by rolling the rice in your hand. Gripping a clump of it between your thumb, index, and third finger, you twist it into a wad, which you then dip into the vegetable curry. You pop this combo-ball freely into your mouth without touching anything else, (that move would be the Indian version of double-dipping despite it's only with yourself). You mix the dahl, the curd, or the spinach into the rice and roll it into a clump, which you then scoop up with a scrap of chapatti, the common flat bread of India. A little touch of sea salt can unlock more of the food's subtlety. Sooner or later, Mrs. Krishnaswami came over to deposit a heaping glob of ghee, or clarified butter onto the rice. This is a greasy puddle of pure fat. Seems mighty horrible, but it adds tremendous flavor to the meal, plus it adds to one's health according to the standards of Ayurveda, the Indian school of medicine.

"Idu baharlah ohlaydiday." [This is so delicious.] I gobbled down another rice ball.

"Methinks Ramappa is the swami of the thali," Dr. Krishnaswami chuckled to himself.

Mrs. Krishnaswami reciprocated a snappy comment in Kannada and snickered.

"Rama is the avatar of the legend. I'm just the legend of Cooketown. Let's eat." I pinched off another gob of rice and tossed it into my gullet.

"Methinks Mr. Rahms should be careful he doesn't explode from overeating so much. Ganesha, the elephant deity, who resides in your nabhi chakra, the belly button, will eat you up if you overindulge in your portions. One should fill one third of the stomach with food, one third with liquids and the decisive third should remain empty," Dr. K coached.

"Well, I've never eaten an elephant, so I think I'm safe in all probability," I pontificated while rebuffing his middling comment.

"Always reaching for the outer edges, Eh? Mr. Rahms?" Dr. K was better than most at spotting the true targets.

As I scraped up the remaining finishing morsels of curried rice and lobbed back the last bite, the finger paintings left over from scooping the dregs off the thali resembled the curvature of celestial wings taking flight. I peered down at this adumbration of my destiny flapping its way out of a temporary prison. What is it going to take for all the dormant seeds of my mantra to sprout and mushroom forth into the white suns, which will raise me out of these black death-planes? And would the shadowy figures always lurking in the background of recollection guide this growth or smother it?

- 16 -

Dr. Krishnaswami had warned me over and over about my divergent activities in the K-room.

"You are not only what you eat, but also what you think. The words, which come out of you, are like fragrances emanating from the heart of a flower. Those words are affecting the listeners with the source energy of whatever thought which generated those words. If you inject them with venom, then you will poison those listeners and their spiritual death will be attributed to you. If you pass onto your friends the words of timeless truths, then a spiritual food having the noblest possible purpose will reinforce them.

"If you are giving these friends of yours any advice, then you will be responsible for the outcome of that advice, no matter how well intentioned it is. I accept your having had many travels and seen many things; howbeit, no matter what you think empowers you, you should know that bringing such a force into this realm entails a grim responsibility the likes of which I doubt you properly understand.

The Moon Women

"No question you are an intuitive seeker who is in tune with many rare energies. It is evident to me you have been hungering for true spiritual nourishment for many lifetimes, more than you can possibly know. Nevertheless, do not sacrifice this heritage by becoming the lender of false truths. That will only lead you to hell."

With a little smirk, he provided that heads-up during a conversation I had with him as he nuzzled my doorjamb while wringing his hands. Sitting cross-legged on my blanket and performing another homegrown puja, I took him to be the patron saint of belligerence. After waving a lit bundle of incense sticks over my head, I made some ugly noises to call Shiva to come forward. As fear gripped Dr. K, over my shoulder a wall-sized poster of the Lord of Living Death, cobra twined round his neck, stared down at the laureate. Behind Shiva, the sliver of a quarter-moon gleamed its ghastly visage in a mulberry sky. Turning the beads in my hand, I threw Dr. K. a cynical leer. Horrified, he retreated to the safe side of the homestead. As he trotted off to leave me alone and forlorn in my K-room, I foresaw one day Dr. K. and his whole family would become the invited guests of the Khrng and take the ride of their lives.

- 17 -

Returning to my amorphous chair, I spotted the bamboozled bone ride had suffered warped gyros causing it to spin down nearly to a halt. I twisted it round more towards the door. I couldn't bear it facing the other direction, but there it was, the ugly window. Clogged with bars and festooned with wrought iron fleurs-de-lis, the deceitful thoroughfare was always kept firmly closed nowadays, ever since the unspeakable theft. Exposed to the outer wilderness, the window only encouraged goblins to inhabit that outer emptiness. Its view stared out onto a barren yard, which led nowhere. On a narrow meridian, only hours after the theft, I observed the shadow of my allergist, Hy Nederman, sliding across that forbidden zone on his way to some undefined subterranean congress with ice princes from the underworld. He had looked at me with a trance-like grimace and declared.

"When will the new Moon be gone that we may set forth wheat?" [3]

I couldn't make much sense of it then. Was there really a connection between the Moon and the wheat? Someone had expressed something like this to me once before but I couldn't get my head to cough it up. And was that phantom lab rat really bartering with ice cubes?

I had never liked that vapid view anyway. Ever since the evening when I had lost my precious silken robe, an artistic creation of iridescent fabrics created by my tailor, Mr. Kalazaki. I had christened it my Maharaja robe and because of its beauty, I always had a great deal of animosity aimed at that void in the K-room. That sinister night something snatched my magical robe in an instant. Hanging in that vile breezeway on a copper hanger like a diaphanous uniform of divinity, the gray hand of some thief had hijacked it. What lowlife could possibly comprehend the depths of beauty and the celestial whim portrayed by that robe as a heritage woven into its threads and transfixed into its glassy iridescence?

But it was more than merely a work of art. I had come to identify it with my destiny. Not necessarily considering myself as an idol worshipper as such, still, I believed the robe was an integral component of my unique psyche, my immortal atma. I had hoped to ascend to never-before-seen heights using that robe, but alas, now it is gone. Nonetheless, I intend to persevere with further discovery concerning not only who took it, but where it has been hidden and who might tell me of its new destination. To be sure, have no doubt that the day I reclaim that divine cloth will be the day that blind sight is put to rest on this suffering planet. That will be the day the Khrng no longer feed; that will be the day the Khrng have finally wrapped-up their work.

-18 -

With a clear will, my wicker vortex kidnaped me once again to place another rare slice of my past life onto the skeleton of Time. Depositing me into a zone, which preceded my birth, my sightline pointed back to that lake in western New York where my story has its roots.

During that wet August in 1943, the Khrng were busy at work within the dense forests of the Adirondacks. This was the second summer my future Mom and Pop had rented a cabin on the shores of

The Moon Women

Big Moose Lake. It had a wooden dock, which jutted out into the lazy waters. Many a sunrise my future Dad would cast his hook out over this haven of mayflies to snag a lake trout and reel him in out of his heaven for dinner. But there were also other mornings in which a dense fog hung over the dock for hours while the Khrng took advantage and scanned the forest for loners. After the sheets of drizzling rain ended, their ships withdrew loaded down with precious cargo. As my boney chair accelerated in rampant circles, I recalled more of my origins.

My Pop to be was a physician and research scientist. My Mom to be was a retired nurse with only one patient, my Dad. She made ample fuss over babying him. It was cute to watch as I viewed them both from the mass hysteria of the fifth Bardo, where the samsari (Indian word for person who is soon to be born), witnesses his future parents engaging in the love act of procreation. I didn't really like pornography and having to watch the fornicating couples from up there was really gross. They all looked like slimy fish calculating the viscosity of chance.

This new Mom to be had grown up in a remarkably tight Catholic community. She had endured many torturous installments of extreme discipline throughout her upbringing within her rigid and truculent ecclesiastical congregation. Maltreated with overbearing emotional control and excessive abuse by all the members of her parochial society, she had persevered bravely to survive her caretaker's scrutiny. There was even some possibility she may have been raped. I came to know of this prospect because she positively hated the Catholic Church and its twisted mores. That is why when she chose medicine, more specifically nursing; she left those traumas behind her. She pined to truly benefit the downtrodden masses and not merely profess weak aid only to screw them over with the ignorance of faith.

My new Dad had been born and bred in Utica, New York. His birthday was a whopping two centuries ago, in 1897. I know that seems ludicrous. It makes me out to be as if I'm Methuselah, whom I might have been in another lifetime, but that's worth another book. Similar to my new Mom's experiences, my new Dad had suffered a parallel treatment under a staunch Episcopalian ministry. He, too, had suffered whippings and beatings from his administrators. Whatever they did to him, he would never discuss it. Not with me, nor have I ever witnessed him discuss anything of the kind with anyone else.

Despite these deficiencies concerning their respective religions, both of my parents had rigid social ties. My Mom had a sister and two brothers I believe: my Aunt Eve, who was a little cuckoo as well as a Christian Scientist; and my Uncle Hank, who was a terrific individual, an outstanding father and an accomplished bowman. Quite often, he hunted deer with a compound bow and usually got one or two every season. I never knew whom the other brother was, I'm afraid.

On my Dad's branch of the tree, there were greater margins of error in the genetic bonds. Dad had two brothers and four sisters. Darkly, before I took birth, both brothers had died. The oldest one, Joe, was a soldier in World War I who died on the battlefields of France. Some claimed he had been a hero, saving over eighty of his comrades in the trenches of Europe amidst the mustard gas and the Krauts. His other brother, Elmer, killed himself with a firearm. Dad didn't have much luck with males on his tree; that's probably why he hovered over me so much and stopped me from doing anything remotely resembling danger. His sisters were Gretchen, Alice, Paulina, and Elizabeth. They all had wealthy smiles, the courage of a man, a go jolly disposition and honored their families above all else.

Gretchen had a harelip and so she never married but maintained her role as a blessed philanthropist to many. The other three had healthy siblings. There was Uncle Mark, the most exuberant one, and Uncle Ted. There was Jake, Paulina's boy, and his brother, Kent, who by dint of some contumacious sensibility, decided to change his name to Alexter McClendon thereby materializing another genetic twist. I don't know. The whole thing seemed a bit off center. But who was I to talk? I was the weirdest of the weird. From my imaginary pursuits to my imaginary friends, I was the black sheep of the crowd.

Last but not least, there was my Cousin Constance. She was the really loopy one on the Ibsen team. She was always chasing me into the bathroom or onto the porch couch or some other out of the way hideout where she could get her hands on me. From the tender age of nine onwards, she was always after me like a banshee. One time she cornered me in the kitchen of the granite cottage situated on

The Moon Women

the lakeshore. Pullout maps amassed from a lifetime subscription to National Geographic wallpapered the plaster acreage exclusively. Being an inquisitive child, I spent many an hour studying the miles and miles of earth's geography glued onto those walls. It might have been where I received repeated injections of wanderlust; a disease designed to inspire its victims to travel the globe searching aimlessly for the promise of an elusive treasure, which could grant immortality.

One morning I was sitting there minding my own business eating some shredded wheat when she waltzed in carrying an armful of gladiolas from the garden. After saving them from certain death by drowning them in a glass pitcher engraved with the intaglio of an M having a stylized French font etched into its virgin glass, she casually inquired, "Hey you, ever heard of a black hole?" and poured herself a glass of water or maybe it was gin. Her latest dalliance from Princeton, a John Wheeler, was always plying her with complicated theories concerning the existence of alternative realities and sundry holes in the fluidics of Time, which she easily thwarted with the pure clear fluid. Most likely hailing from the same gene pool as my father, she was always pushing the envelope of her chemical boundaries.

She was wearing a terry cloth robe having a loose sash. Out of the blue, she threw her leg up onto the counter exposing her private parts and asked with a lurid grin.

"Wanna touch?"

I was so utterly horrified with my spoon frozen in midcourse. But I could hardly take my eyes off that hairy mess with the bloody stripe slicing vertically up and down through its central furry axis. I was yanked back to a time when I had been molested with a similar vision but back then it's occurrence came upon me with more of a pleasant sensation, whereas this time it was sheer terror. It was as if she had uncovered some chthonic chuckhole, whose magnetism was sucking me in like the proverbial blackest pit in the cosmos. Who said a black hole has no hair? That dude should have seen this one! In the eleventh hour, I was able to tear myself away from its gravitonic suck by yelling my own pet theorem.

"Yikes!"

Spoon flying, I bolted as fast as I could. I will always remember her witchy cackling stalking me down the crooked hallways. It brought back the time I was hauled by my ankles down the long dank corridors while being conscripted by the spidery hands of the Khrng.

Far and away, my mother and father came to love me a great deal. They demonstrated their love in many ways. All the physical contact was normal. They were always affectionate even to the extreme degree of making me embarrassed. They hugged and kissed me as if it was a contact sport. But to them it wasn't their affection and parental consideration which was paramount, it was religion.

Borne out of their mutual indoctrination was the one facet of living for which they had come to the same conclusion, eliminate all trace of religious dogmatism and the venom of biblical truths. Throughout the formative period of their youth, they had witnessed the devastating effects of hard-hearted church regulations and the lacerating toxins of Bible thumping prognostications. When they came together under the bonds of matrimony, they agreed they would save their children from that evil, permanently. Above all incertitude and providence, the foul diseases of theistic beliefs would never, never, ever, ever touch their children. No matter what happened, they would protect whatever offspring they produced from the ravages of any form of worship, repentance, and especially prayers. They proposed to create an insular shell with which to surround their progeny and thus spare them the vicious needles of blind faith and the rulings delivered by false deities.

Together they represented the twin obelisks of a fierce contempt, which defended the sensitive zones within my life and that of my sister, when she came along. Their formidability and their mantrums of unremitting persuasion entombed me in a veritable sarcophagus of unspoiled ignorance until the day I was enticed out of that cave, bit by bit, by an unsuspected hero in the sociology of knowledge. By imitating the lessons of one of America's great free thinkers, I began to change. Who was this modern day Plato? He was a philosopher who pioneered a school of sectarian spontaneity, which has not been previously spouted upon these shores, that of the American Cowboy. His name was Mr. William Boyd.

William Boyd was my first Guru. I spent many afterschool sittings studying his philosophy and listening to him narrate the epic tales of man's significance to the cosmos, as well as, propound man's equality with man, to his favorite companion and disciple, Buster Crab. Even to this day, I have his photograph mounted in a frame in

The Moon Women

my bedroom. It is one of the Life magazine covers, the June 12, 1950 issue, if you're lucky enough to track one down. Outfitted with the traditional uniform regarded by a majority of the country as noteworthy for a Cowboy as well as his regal headgear, he represented his profoundly respected stature in American culture with his ten-gallon hat, or Stetson, depending on which sect of Americanism you follow, Eastern or Texan.

The process of Mr. Boyd happened all on its own. One Sunday morning as my parents were upstairs performing their devotional practices, sleeping, I had inclined into my favorite armchair having brass appointments, which held a cocked adjacency to the fireplace in our laundry area in Wellesley. That was where the Andrea television was located, where I watched his many exciting episodes. I had scarcely eaten my way through a string of Fluffernutter sandwiches while waiting for the show to begin when I drifted off into a dream.

In my reverie, I was traveling on the outskirts of a tribal city somewhere in the holy lands like Bethlehem. A despicable king ruled all the surrounding regions from his demonic palace. Like the barbed tails of many dragons, the lances of his soldiers were piercing the children and killing them. The rays of these monsters were reaching out into all the land with a venomous vibration. Armies of midget bloodless beings were preying upon the young, unwrapping their thoughts and incising their brains with microscopic sickles. The only protection the children had was a handful of white feathered warriors who flew on glistening wings of unearthly metal. Annihilating the vile vermin with crescents of brilliant light, the Seven of Abaddon had been pursuing the Khrng for millions of years, but the babies continued to die. I knew my time had come so I woke up. This is how the mechanics of Mr. William Boyd's theories came into me, as dreams instilled by the sagas of Hopalong Cassidy.

As yet, unbeknownst to my parents, my life, as created by them, was an unusual experiment. It demonstrated the premise that even in the sterile environment of an impotent non-religious nurture, the genes of pure conscious experience could eventually come out and blossom into a tree of radiance. Even though my theological enthusiasm in those early years was non-existent, it was not hopeless. Into this utter vacuum of ideals, concepts, and transcendental beliefs, a seed was planted. If you suggest it unfolded because of the way my

70

parents cared for me using their essential loving nature, I would have to rebuff your proposal with a passionate denial.

"No. Absolutely not."

Their constant drinking, smoking and cursing could not be adjudicated to be an invective manure out of which a kernel of flawless truthfulness could sprout and grow. Not even close. Their full-blown alcoholism was in its rawest and most invasive form: the drunk couple. It was a poison, venomous enough to eviscerate all the delicate threads of unadulterated spirit, which must be present to prepare the foundation that will don the fabric of a super conscious life. Adding to that pollution was the constant smoking of Benson & Hedges cigarettes. As I write this at the age of sixty-six, I must acknowledge that undoubtedly it must be by the good graces of some celestial deity I don't have lung cancer from all the secondary smoke I had to inhale in the course of my formative years. My mother even sucked down two packs per day when I was in her womb. Nevertheless, in spite of these drawbacks, witnesses from the Beyond had unquestionably preordained my outcome.

The frosting on this triple layer cake of spiritual torture was their constant swearing. Both of my parents spent hours and hours perfecting their one-upmanship upon the ladder of tears (eyes) and tears (rips), as they disassembled each other's arguments, revamped the frontiers of their beliefs, and reshuffled the concepts of their chemically altered realities. Let loose to explore the wilderness of authentic cussing, they produced a full-fledged line of profanity and backed it up with a bill of materials explosion list of expletives second to none. Their mastery over these superhuman feats of devil worship laced with the arsenic of vitriolic superlatives was undeniable. They frosted it with a sickly coating of sexual overtones, which was without reproach. They could have catholicized their own religion with it if they had been so inclined. As a couple, they could have received the label of the mho unit of crystalized acrimony.

My emergence from this cocoon of ineptitude and absence of Godly thinking was a long and arduous one of serendipitous discovery extracted via pure providence. This writing is essentially its saga. Alone in a prison underworld of incongruities, I was granted the vision and the gift to create a tiny reflection in a dark puddle of my cramped cell, which became on fire with gratitude.

The Moon Women

The journey taken by the pneuma who inhabits the body sometimes referred to by names such as Rahm Progegas Ibsen, Rinpoche Genga Dorje or Muhammad Mehdi Abdullah depicts a fresh slant for thinkers to digest in the craw of their examination into being. It invites them to proceed diligently with their investigation into the possibility of the divine as well as the probable reasons for the elimination of dour evil. What the Khrng might have injected into this equation will undoubtedly alter all possible outcomes. And this alteration will be further amplified by the advent of the Seven Angels of Abaddon. How much those two factors will complicate the traditionally accepted views that comprise the basic knowledge pools depends entirely on your capacity for engendering quantum faith - not exactly the standard viewpoint.

Learning how the Khrng maintain a strangle hold over the bulk of human consciousness is not only an alarming prospect but it is also a frightening forewarning, which can result in a squirrelly confusion as far as the well-rooted concepts of humankind are concerned. The one redeeming feature in this entangled stratagem is the fury of the White, which proceeds out of that realm as its warriors, the Seven Angels of Abaddon. As you read on, you will eventually come to the proposal that these two, the Khrng and the Angels, are in fact the same thing or at least two sides of the same coin. What you do with that finding is up to you. It's your choice. I know you will choose well. I did.

I got out of the entranced swing chair and spun it counter-clockwise hoping the spinning would reset its psycho-magnetic core and cause it to search in a more favorable direction. No matter how many times I twisted the ropes, the swinging wicker basket came back to the same unsettled direction. Was the chair's inner wizardry reaching out to communicate something in relation to the theft of my robe and the loss of its prophetic effect on my life? On the other hand, was its proxy usurping my gender charged stance on life? Eventually I got back in. As the timeless chair merged with my timeless chant, scenes from my most recent romance fluttered in my face like the wings of a frightened dove.

CHAPTER 2 - **TIAMI BROWN**

- 1 -

February 6, 1971 - Panjim, Goa

Tiami Brown was not my girlfriend. She was my friend, no doubt about that. And the part about her being a girl couldn't be argued by anybody. But it was the combination I couldn't pledge allegiance to at first.

Tiami was born in a posh neighborhood on Long Island by caring and protective parents. Her Papa represented the second generation from Italy and as a talented insurance salesman he had achieved appreciable success promoting longevity amongst the elderly. Her Mamma taught phys-ed at the local elementary and came from a mixed background of Irish and Negro extracts from the Gold Coast. Tiami was, beyond all shadow of a doubt, the most attractive black woman I have ever had the good fortune of confronting head on. She had the complexion of a milk chocolate supermodel, the features of a Farrah Fawcett, and the presence of a Cleopatra. Her enamels sung with a sparkle spawned from the Moon itself and her smile was so infectious she could command her every wish and whim over any male on the planet. And for some damn reason she totally dug me.

It was Miss Tiami Brown with whom I had chosen to travel the many hot spots in this enchanted land of the rebellious Hindu. Tagged as a sweetheart couple who gallivanted through Banglore's Brigade Road, or its bazaars, or its shopping marts and discos, the two of us never missed a beat. Many an eventide we had shown off dancing like a King and Queen from contrary wonderlands; we were the Maharaja and Maharani of Cooketown. It hadn't taken us long to partner up and amplify the city's popular cheer as support for our relationship. Furthermore, we had sealed the deal by inventing nicknames for each other. Not having much aptitude as a word sleuth, I had christened her as Brownie. Mostly though, she just called me Asshole, or Hey you.

In spite of this gravitas of intimate familiarity, the most bizarre feature of our relationship was that we were both devoutly celibate.

73

The Moon Women

Even though we would hang on each other out on the dancing arena or neck while hidden in a murky corner of the disco, we never got down to business and hooked up. Hiding no lack of any affection, we kissed and we hugged. I can truly say neither one of us had any good reason for not doing it other than competition. I can't count the times we had been ushered out of the dance derby over at the 77 Club, Brigade Road's raciest dance hall, because of our provocative moves, some of which were so steamy everyone present had to stand back and watch; we were often black listed for weeks. Yet our relationship was purely platonic.

Once while we were flying from Bombay to Goa on holiday we played a little kissing game. Notwithstanding the incongruity, it wasn't just any kissing game. It was a kissing game with some unusual parameters.

"Brownie, what's my dental count today? Pick a number and guess?" I nagged.

"Well, if the average male has 32 including all four wisdoms, I would say 32. But, wait, since I know you really don't have any wisdom and I know it's you, let's not forget the wild card factor, the answer's not going to be so obvious. Why don't you give me a clue and smile!" She dared raising her eyebrow ever so slightly with devil-may-care spunk.

"M-m-m. Not so easy." I retorted. "Let's ask the stewardess."

Indian Airlines flight 719, scheduled for routine transit from Sahar airport into Sao Vicente aerodrome, was due to touch down in thirty minutes. Typical for domestic routes our first-class tickets didn't afford us much privacy on the compact DC-9 jet cruiser. At any rate, the reduced cabin space forced me to enlist the aid of the crew.

"Ek minute! Bhai Ji?" [One minute! Young lady?]

As orange and green silks flashed by me, I hailed the stewardess. Acknowledging my shout-out, she adjusted her unibraid and gracefully folded her hands with her utmost to serve.

"Yes, yes. Werdy helpful for you, Maharaji. Vhat iz your vishes? I yam especking English?" The airline specialist offered her cultured cheer while repositioning the clump of jasmine punctuating her pleasantries.

"Achaa. Namaste." I revered. [Very good. Hello, how you doin'?]

74

"You have toothpick?"

"Tooth? Pick?" She replayed my request.

As she attempted to decipher the words using her tongue as some organic prototype of oral abacus, I put out my index finger and thumb to show her about two inches worth.

"Shandis."

That's what I thought was the word for wood; regardless, it seems my Hindi was not measuring up. My pronunciation was nearing the fringe of another word which was considerably more descriptive than what I had intended. The flight aide twittered awkwardly, hid her embarrassment with her hand, and fled back down the aisle.

"Quit harassing the flight crew, Rahm! What's that circle?" Brownie sparked pointing at the pattern of a wheel on the woman's flowing scarf.

"I'm not. She's helping. Oh, that. It's the lions of India. State emblem I think."

"They don't have lions in India. They're all dead. I gotta pee." She pushed up the mini-table and twitched her finger at me to vacate her route.

"That's why they have it. Have fun."

"Jerk! Scooch over, I've gotta go."

She rose awkwardly pretending to catch herself with her forearm. Why do women always do this? They're fully dressed. There is really no way their breasts are going to spill out all over the place. Is it something akin to a polite gesture, which is attempting to apologize for their overdeveloped superstructures or an unintended accident that might result in gross embarrassment? Modesty might be another word for it. I had no other word for wood so I added this.

"Sandaas."

But that simply meant toilet which brought another outburst from the retreating aviation specialist.

"Hey! You stay put!" Brownie spouted.

After she teased me with a wink, she made a beeline for the rear of the cabin.

"Khanna is corning," I beamed back while making the Indian eating signal with my pinched fingers tapping towards my chops.

I humped the armrest and peered out the oval bubble. Five thousand meters below, the countryside rolled lazily along. The

The Moon Women

herringbone patterns of washed out greens from the dried out farmlands merged with the fresh beiges of the eroding deserts to form a tapestry older than most of the other villatic acres in Asia. As the dead yellows of the squalid villages were swept aside by the shadow of our jet blotting them out like some incongruous hand, the rural panoramas flashed by to leave a spate of smudged streaks across the eroded death mask of Mother India.

Despite all the cold water thrown onto the gaiety in the galley, the fuse from Brownie's wink finally lit a spark of intrigue. Its incendiary track converged on a monorail, which led nonstop back to the lavatory. The thought of "What the heck is going on back there?" got wiped off the windshield of my brain like a splattered fly and I was out of my seat in milliseconds.

"Keejiye!" [Sorry!]

I brushed passed an elderly Brahmin woman. In my slow-motion hurry, I realized why married Indian women are so rotund. It is because their communities worship them much in the same manner the natives worship Brahma bulls as they eat anything and everything while roaming freely from street to street throughout the motherland. Empowered as the mark of eminent status and the result of competent pleasure yielding progeny, these women of the sub-continent are the true Hindu deities.

"Excuse me!"

As I raced rearwards, my proclivity for recognizing true talent when presented with the artifacts of divine intervention was no more evident at that moment than in succeeding instances of facing Indian piety. For instance, when I observed an Indian teenager adjusting her headphones as the Bee Gees wailed "Stayin' Alive" into her ears, I contemplated the frailty of her longevity unfolding even in the face of her cultural odds. I forced myself to withdraw from that bollixed affirmation and flapped my way rearward. Doubtlessly the cellular memories, which had been barely disconnected from the aromas of Papadums steaming up in the jet's galley, were the cause of my interruption. Got wings on my shoes and I'm . . .

"Coming through!" I made public my intent.

Fighting in the chill air against oblong trays loaded with hot meals, I negotiated the flipsy-dipsy aisles as the pilot administered the prologue to landing. Was I in deep Space with the aliens, or were the little bastards cleverly infringing upon my innermost headroom?

76

Even though I didn't really know if she was in this one or not, I clutched at the circular handle, which read "Occupied." After I applied an encouraging tug to get the handle to give, the sound inside said it all. My response was to pound fiercely on the wafer thin door.

"Brownie?" I exhaled my anticipation with puffs of a latent after-breath.

When the "Vacant" sign popped up, I lifted the latch with a lurch and looked out for any spies or CIA operatives before levering myself into the lavatory. As a fallback intervention to ward off possible invasion from future cold mauls, I decided to look the other way. The extreme altitude was wreaking havoc with my mumania, thereby reducing it down a notch into the lamda zone. I gave myself repeated slaps to come out of it.

"You shrew!"

My entrance into the theatre of Shakespearean comedy would not come easily; nevertheless, I was not going to put up with any of her stinking monkey business. As soon as I got in there she jumped me and our lips locked. As we initiated an oral dialectic of residual flavors and mandibular massage, I thought, "What the hell is she up to?" Belatedly, I realized she's using her tongue to count my teeth while at the same time she's getting her licks in, stinger and all.

At this chapter in the saga, I must alert you to a condition, which you will be tempted to avert yourself away from but it will be in vain. It is my deep-seated obsession with M words, a psychological condition my shrink has diagnosed as mumania. This infernal syndrome comes from an infection of Khrng magiophags implanted within my cerebrum at the time of my abduction back in Cazenovia when I was but a boy. Please bear with me when it occurs.

- 2 -

Tiami Brown had been after me for weeks. Prior to arriving at Friends World Collage as an honor student from Oceanside High, she had made applications to over a dozen liberal arts institutions throughout New England. She had singled-out FWC over all the others because what she really craved was travel. Over and above her traveling bug, she craved the unattainable - bumping up against the savage frontiers of the unknown as often as possible.

My excuse was I had most recently reconnected with the FWC

The Moon Women

campus, namely my suite at the chez Krishnaswami, ala the K-room. After smashing a few barriers of my own making while traveling in the Himalayan mountains, I had returned carrying a magnificent treasure, which I had won, not by climbing Everest, but by climbing the steep cliffs of the lost kingdom of Tibetan Buddhism.

After she came to learn I carried with me the most exciting batch of tales from the fringes of civilization, Brownie decided to target me as the most likely choice for securing viable inroads leading to outlandish adventure. Plus, these stories of mine, drenched with the doggedness of the Tibetans, were staunchly documented with actual celluloid proof of my escapades. Since I had dutifully captured all of my travels on film, she was even more driven to corral me with her charms.

Shortly after I had returned to Cooketown from the great peaks, I released my movie entitled, "Land of the Lamas," a thirty-minute documentary revealing exquisite views of the snow frosted peaks as well as the pinnacles of a world filled with Tibetan Lamas. I compiled all of my footage taken at the highpoint of my stay in the Tibetan Buddhist monastery of Rumtek in Sikkim and produced a full feature celluloid statement of a day in their life. Having captured the gaiety and joy of these high-rise pioneers in the stratospheres of religion, I offered viewers a rare peak into the Rinpoches' celebrations of the Buddha's birthday in early June. The reigning Lama had no problem with my forwardness as I joined right in the midst of the dancing monks while they celebrated the first sunrise of Siddhartha. Tantalizing close-ups of their emotionless faces inspired me to portray their tortuous ballet of mesmerizing cartwheels over my head as dozens of red robed Lamas whirled and twirled all around me like a whirlwind of euphoria. Using double and triple exposures, I created a visual experience the likes of which there was no equal comparison. Furthermore, I manufactured a striking audial sphere of other worldly musica and baritone narration, which added an ethereal depth. I had taped those recordings within my sound studio, which was none other than the bathroom in the Krishnaswami's headquarters, ala the K-Room, only it wasn't really his bathroom. It was mine.

Annexed to the honored K-room was a twelve-foot cube of set stones having a normal Asian toilet, the kind I prefer but can never get nowadays. This bathroom also had a walled off stall in which to shower with a bucket and a dubha (small can) as there was no shower spout or hose of any kind. Impressive slabs of sawn granite paneled all the perimeters in this bathing ovum. These unforgiving surfaces provided a startling acoustic resonance for my music.

Over the course of these extravagant travels to many ethnic environs, I had purchased samples of rustic instruments ranging from woodwinds to fiddles, mandolins to tablas and other percussion devises of catholic genesis. During the recordings, I occasionally fingered the mbria, an African wooden resonating instrument having irregular tin strips, which vibrate with plunking tones when plucked with the thumb. There was also my trusty recorder, which supplied the aerial registers of a peeling vibrato. After playing all of these musical contraptions in tutti myself, I then remastered the separate excerpts by weaving them together into an ethereal soundtrack via my mixing board. When this audio was married to the staggering exposures of the Lamas dancing in front the breathtaking scenes of the Himalayas, the result was spellbinding. It displayed the alpenglow of the mountains juxtaposed with an unusual sensuality inherent within the graceful pirouetting of the intoxicated Lamas. No one could have suspected such uncorked passion could have been extracted from these regimented and grimly austere monks of Buddhist purity.

When Tiami Brown viewed that documentary, which I featured in a showing performed at the end of her midyear phase, she was so impressed with it deep down she convinced herself of the notion I was a budding cinematographic genius who was really going places regardless of which continent I might land. Come what may, she was not going to lose out on that ride. Additionally, in a private screening I had shown her my other movie entitled, "Khajuraho: Temple Of Divine Sex." That one was none other than a point-blank graphic depicting the carved reliefs which pictured couples in a million different positions of intercourse covering every square meter of the vast extremities of half a dozen classic temples. I had accompanied these steaming visuals with some typical Indian sitar augmented with some rudimentary voiceovers, which provided historical perspective. It was a flat and linear flick without any true artistic flair, but she took it to be a statement of my interests in women and sex in general.

Nothing could have been further from the truth. Nevertheless, it took her quite some time to realize that. Coming close one day, I

79

The Moon Women

explained my theories about meditation; how accessing the subtler planes would not happen for a newcomer who was prone to follow his "other" brain. This seemed to intrigue her more and more, yet she never really caught onto its significance. Moreover, she was firmly couched in the mundane. Despite the drawback, I was determined to uplift her prospects via psychic osmosis.

Besides the more glaring angles, she had never even had a marginal brush with anyone her own age who was crazy enough to express a null desire to be with her sexually. If she had the inclination, her boy toy would only be Johnny-on-the-spot to perform the needed prerequisites. Notice I implied *null* desire and not *no* desire, because I would have had to be bona fide eunuch not to have sensed the animalistic sexual aura exuding from Miss Tiami Brown. My external genitalia were not only intact; they were in perfect working order most astoundingly on numerous occasions, especially in college. However, no matter how much I explained my concepts of telepathy and meditation, she would listen for a second and then flat-out change the subject.

Aside from all that, she was such a pleasant gal to be with. I loved the way she laughed, so open and nonjudgmental. Her whit was not as sharp as one might think from talking with her but she possessed incredible instincts for locating the heart of the magic. I have never run into anyone who ever got over on her with cute words or clever tactics. Moreover, she was one of the limited few who not only understood my humor but also savored it. Tiami seemed to intertwine with it while encouraging me to evolve with every challenging polemic we had together. Whether it involved the anatomy of being or the existence of which flavored high hid on which FWC campus, our contemporaries saw us as inseparable and even though the Krishnaswamis didn't consider us a literal part of their family, they were clueless as to how to get rid of us.

Much as his sheepishness had prevailed, Dr. Krishnaswami was convinced that high Ritjiv priests had scheduled an exclusive Brahmin hell solely for him, one designed for opportunistic professors who concoct ways of improperly awarding themselves with salary and social status by permitting a heathen mixture of evils to carry-on within the confines of their pious domiciles. Considering the constant fuss and some of the pungent aromas, I think he knew very well what Brownie and I were doing back there. Yet for the time being, he was copacetic.

- 3 -

Back to the kiss that wasn't a kiss. As our mentholated mouths mingled, an exodus of diverse passions fired up and down our spines to reach the supreme top and the sickest bottom simultaneously. I relaxed into it as her roving tongue clicked off my dental units like some newfangled system of Braille.

"Twenty-nine." She purred.

Her warm breath had the flavors of strawberries and almonds backed up with a hint of vodka. As we unlocked finally, she smeared a mist on my glasses.

"Close, but no cigar." I moderated.

I had begun to notice the triple dings of the prelude to arrival notifications.

"The Captain wishes to announce we will be over Goa shortly. We will be landing in Sao Vicente momentarily." The familiar attendant's air gab came in over the PA.

"Is this some rubric of a mnemonic code, which you've put together so you can divest me of my treasure?" I pondered.

"I know it's twenty-nine and I'm not counting them again. Doesn't matter I know that's what you want me to do." She declared as she tried to smudge my lenses a second time with her nose.

The superficial sexual tensions between us were only surpassed by the motivation to one-up the other, because when it came right down to it, we enjoyed the competition of our relationship more than in any sexual or romantic overtones.

"Okay. You win, this time, but one day, it's going to be thirty because I'm tired of looking like Captain Hook." I confessed my Adler alley-dog syndrome.

"You'll never look like Captain Hook to me. You'll always be my Peter Pan." Her hand moved passed the margin of my back to release the lav's lever.

"Wait! I'll be stuck in here. Lemme out!"

As unplanned humble embarrassment washed over me, my hand lunged forward to unhook the latch but the thin hatch was already on its way to Zanzibar. She had ducked under my arm. As she promptly resumed her nest by the fleet lookout over Goa, all I

The Moon Women

could do was follow: an outcome symptomatic of what we had going. As I discreetly made my way to retake imperial guard over my queen, the occupants of the jet-powered transit grew unsettled. Flitting eyes bird-dogged me down the aisle as I regained my seat over the wings. As the aircraft shuddered and bobbled, I plunked down behind the upright vinyl backing and took cover. When the wheels made that little screeching noise as the rubber kissed the tarmac, everyone applauded, but I knew it wasn't for my performance.

Why do passengers always clap when their flight achieves touchdown? You would think it was a big championship and our team had clinched the crucial score. On one hand, I knew Brownie had captured another victory in her heart, but on the other, I wasn't quite sure how the final competition would be played out. I didn't know how blind I might be to its true worth or even what kind of scars these sex wars would leave on me or on her.

- 4 -

That evening I viewed Tiaimi Brown as the personification of muliebrity. Lying comfortably in our suite on the coast just south of Panjim, she was partially eclipsed by a haze of mosquito netting as its soft malines weft articulated a tented pyramid, which outlined her sleeping area. Was I beholding the profile of a goddess slumbering against the muslins or a demon in distress? Not caring for any such pillow talk, she had drifted off into a fabulous dreamscape concealed only by a swash of peacock silk. At six meters, this cut would have been draped by an Indian woman for normal use as a Sari. But Tiami liked it for her sleeping attire. She was clad with nothing else.

Goa was hot and moist with explosive scents of jasmine and hyacinth, which battled with devilish curlicues of incense for the conquest of my nostrils. These scents taunted me from the outer limits of the twin windows, which insulated our sleeping quarters from the rambling purr of the auto rickshaws down below. As the heady mixture of the Goan airs came to inspissate the long night's stillness, I marveled at my luck to be here with Tiami in this removed paradise. Gone were the underarm funk of humanity and the putrid sewers of the slums. Here in Goa we were to find a slower life, one of careless abandon and yet, a greater appreciation of each other. A harbor community, this Portuguese colony promised rich living and bountiful produce from the ocean. Fortunately, for us now there were no dead fish chasing us.

With my head drooping in the predawn shadows, the soft bubbling of my hookah offered the steady comfort of a warm friend. Working the glowing ember of a marijuana bud, which topped up the bowl of its main stem, it had done its job well. A laden volume titled <u>The Bhagavad Gita</u> lay in my lap. I had barely unraveled the excerpt in which Shri Krishna was explaining to his keen disciple, Arjuna, how to thread the shaft of his light-arrow onto his bowstring and put it through a kite, a falcon-like bird, perched three furlongs away. That's friggin' six hundred meters out, I calculated. That's absolutely mind numbing. As I questioned the authenticity of this ancient treatise, plumes of smoke flowed out of my nose. The hooting of the Patanjali Express far off in the distance wailed like a loon and jarred me out of my dream. The business of the day had not yet begun.

Nuzzling her pillow Tiami Brown shifted to face in my direction. Why could she not fathom the inner way? What precluded her from duplicating my steps? These and other questions circled my thoughts like vultures. Was she to be a vehicle or a hindrance in my search for the inimical?

I looked at her nose: so refined. It was not the typical squat nose of an Ethiopian runner built for maximum stamina and endurance. Hers was the aquiline nose artists seek to immortalize with oils. Her ears, one of which was now visible and wreathed with ebony tendrils of her latest coiffure, were superb. I have been an aficionado of ears ever since I was a toddler admiring the ears of my nanny, Mimi. Classic ears have a thinly spooled peripheral curvature, rounding down to a well-formed lobe having a teardrop contour, but impeccable ears portray a supreme balance, and are pristine and Godlike. But what do they hear? That is the question. Are they there simply for focusing sound waves? Or are they tools necessary to glimpse the stars and unlock the secrets of the universe whose answers belong to creators of the untold song?

However, no artist could ever duplicate her eyes. Under those amber lumps of eyelid, Tiami had the greenest eyes I'd ever seen. Alien green I'd call them, for they could launch me into outer space dimensions I would not have believed existed. Yet even in the presence of these cosmic attractions, I resisted her magnetic visuals, both because of the just-too-good-to-be-true factor and also because

The Moon Women

I believed myself to be the product of racism.

- 5 -

My father was a Gemini and eleven years older than my mother, a Libran. He hailed from the late nineteenth century, 1897, a date not so much removed from the conflict, which nearly tore America in two - color. Having come from a bloodline spanning generations back to the Mayflower pilgrims, he owned a strong pedigree. His forefather was a doctor and his grandfather, a minister. This hand slapping play of medicine and religion was a swapping match, which reached its roots a dozen cars rearward on the Ibsen train. Healing bodies and paving the road to heaven was respected work for Ibsens of all centuries, clear back to the Magna Carta. Black Death was not only the threshold into white life for those Ibsens who could trap it in a bottle, but also a conveyance, which led to another mansion of the Father, the one of repentance.

Never no mind, regardless of this lineage, my Pop was a rare bird. He threw a twist into the familial braid and altered what would have been the logical choice for his road in life, the one that bent in the undergrowth - religion. But it was not to be, or at a minimum, seriously avoided. Selecting neither of the two roads, which diverged in the yellow wood, he took the one that belched fire and brimstone, the one, which was worn out completely - high finance in the blast furnaces of pig-iron. Despite this interruption, the kink in the Ibsen chain of command was but a brief respite; nonetheless, it exposed an indelible stigma within his genetic markers, one that never left.

After my father died, I had to tally his personal effects for the attorneys when I came across a bundle of filing cards with cryptic notations listing the commodities he had purchased daily and their costs, together with calculations showing how he could get a more economical stretch out of them over the long run. Oddly enough, I have this same compulsion along with another queer OCD condition I have decided to label as furniture Speak, or more directly the Speak. It is a neurosis demonstrated by the ritualistic identification with furniture or various generic objects of investiture, which never resist associating themselves with my presence. I have often worried if these oddities originated in my indigenous DNA or perhaps were put there by the Khrng during their little house party while hovering over

84

the wheat in Cazenovia.

When I was five, I made a colossal mess in the pantry over on Stern Street, my father's first owned residence as a doctor. I had managed to draw Grandma Ibsen with peanut butter and strawberry jam on the enamel surfaces of the kitchen. Her portrait looked to be a masterpiece plastered over that bland expanse, never mind it presented a disparaging affidavit she was of brown extract. Her glistening lips were without equal, as splendid as a Dairy Queen kiss. What accentuated the contrast between the red and the white was the wallpaper, which was dotted with a periodicity of blue forget-me-nots. It was a genius statement of not only my patriotism but also my conspiracy to defeat my bombastic parents.

Her hairdo wasn't too neat, but her lipstick sure was red. That's what did it. I loved that big red kiss which lit up the kitchen with an unreal red power. It made me realize the flames of God can erupt with brimstone and hellfire boiling out of those hallowed outlets any minute. My Mom got so enraged she beat me with a wire coat hanger after she had ripped off the paper backing, which had a clever moto printed on it: Finklestein Cleaners - We clean up your mess. It left bruises on my forearms, back and shoulders, which didn't fade for weeks; some never have. So where was my savior then?

As punishment for this dastardly deed upon my body, at the crack of daybreak shortly after I had risen, God electrocuted her on the spot. At the time, I was hard at work building empires with hand-me-down blocks in my bedroom. Little did I know at that age when you wash silverware in the sink you ought not to turn on the lights. While clutching a handful of silver spoons in the washtub, she reached over with her other hand to flick the switch so she could brighten up the picture; something no more than simple muscle memory taking over. In due course, seems when she did that, God sent a walloping surge of electric current flowing through her body jolting her clean out of her shoes. He then proceeded to slam her across the kitchen and smash her neck smartly into the refrigerator right on its handle nicely rupturing three of her vertebral discs.

Smashing, I say! Just smashing! Serves her right for beating me. I was convinced it would have been better if my peanut butter portrait had been framed, not washed off. Instead, my Mom was the one who wound up having to carry a framed badge of shame, a clinical collar, which elevated her neck to reduce the pain. No

85

The Moon Women

different from a dog wearing a cone collar to prevent it from licking its wounds, she ambulated the downstairs like an invalid in a wheelchair. But she never whupped me with a wire hanger ever again. She was the one who was framed up now. Don't matter none the wounds of her ordeal would lead to scar tissue, which would one day wind up to be my destiny.

By dint of similar fortuities, every so often in the formative phases of my childhood, my mother was out of the picture. She was out of commission as instructors of poor language are apt to comment. Enter stage right our hired nanny, May Whitaker.

May was of pure African extract. Her people allegedly came over on a ship lined with slaves registered with miscellaneous catchall names. Her mainline had not been the progeny of mixed marriages. May was as black as they come. She exuded Negro history from her boiled knuckles down to her bowl-legged walk, from her faded do-rag down to her high-laced shoes whose thick leather soles echoed dull thuds on the oak flooring as she laboriously lugged the overloaded food trays up the back staircase to my sick mother's sleeping quarters. A hundred bobby pins were nested in her hair to clamp down her heritage from the coasts of Ghana and Ashanti land. She buttered hot toast with her index finger so as not to filthy up another knife, and muzzled over a dozen clothespins in her teeth to peg down fresh laundry ferried in not one, but two, heavy wicker baskets to hang out in the white air of Wellesley, suburb to Boston's corporate digs and the polestar of bleached, white America.

For years, May cared for both my sister and me. She made our meals, did our dirty laundry, scrubbed the floors, cleaned the counters, and made our beds. May was our Mammy. She was super Mom to my ailing Mom, who was in and out of hospitals for over a decade. May rode the bus to and from her apartment to her place of work, our home. My father paid her two bucks a day plus carfare. Sometimes, but only rarely, he would offer her a ride back to her dowdy cold-water flat in south Boston. Generally, he didn't like venturing into that part of the city where those people cohabitated.

Why my father was a racist, I don't know. No similar bigotries lurked in the depths of any of my aunts, uncles or other limbs on the genealogical tree. Notwithstanding, he must have had a problem with May because every time he interacted with her she was humiliated.

My father was a drinker. Upon rising, he always had his coffee and toast. And yes, he liked to have a beer every so often. Coffee and beer were the primary avenues for H2O to hydrate his bodily machinery. But there was another fluid he could never refuse, his best buddy, Jack Daniels, good ole No. 7. I have a subliminal snapshot of the bottle it lived inside. Labeled with the stygian insignia of the devil and inscribed with searing letters proclaiming the road to hell, it always advertised its insistence for evil with a Gothic font of gleaming white capitals and lower case dominions, which grinned back out at you like the toothless jaw of a recently interred skull. Fresh from the foundry, the dark amber liquid granted abstinence from pain having embraced its origins in Hades. I call it a foundry and not a distillery because evidently its incarnation, in all likelihood, begins with fire and brimstone, sparks flying everywhere. All I know is it sure created the flames of hellfire and brimstone within my father because every time he hoisted that black bottle to his lips, verbal magma spewed out of him like hell sauce from a dragon.

The target of those eruptions was more often than not, May Whitaker, except whenever she raised her do-rag to stand obediently at attention right in front of him. Most of the time when she was taking care of the needs of his children, myself and my sister, he would behave as the well-adjusted martinet everyone preferred him to be. Barring those limited occurrences, when she was not within shouting distance, he would let loose his flaming oral vomit denouncing every fiber of her being. He appeared to be psyching himself up for M-day on the bloody beaches of Normandy. Needless to say, I've got to avoid quoting any of his ranting because it's way too scalding for my inept fingers to deal with on this antiquated typewriter which would, dollars to doughnuts, disintegrate underneath me should I actually put those words to paper. But it was (and these are his words) God awful!

In part, I am writing this book in the hopes that in some way my humble talents will mitigate his burdens weighing heavily upon him in the second Bardo where he awaits my arrival and the magnanimous pardon, which I will present for his liberation. Not for any disservice done to me, but more so, for those foul words he uttered at the expense of my Mom's nurse and caretaker, May Whitaker.

Words can be powerful weapons. And nothing corrupts quite

The Moon Women

as much as absolute power. I forget which Saint who flamboyantly uttered that witticism. Notwithstanding, my father had never come across any of the great saints even though he might have been contemporary to most of them. By the age of thirty-two, he had adopted the hat of a renowned businessman and rose to a vice-presidential desk holding down the books of the Bethlehem Steel Corporation. His marriage to Cynthia Mueller, sole daughter of William Mueller, emperor of the sheet metal empire, had unrolled euphoric stepping-stones to grandeur and exuberant wealth. Having aspired to the throne of a dynasty of steel and flatfooting for profit, my Dad did well as he climbed rung after rung up the corporate ladder. Eventually, he probably would have wound up a multi-billionaire. But after coming face-to-face with the unavoidable banality of a flavor of daily living, which was not only suffocating but numbed his inner fires completely, he woke up out of that head trip one morning and realized he desperately craved to take on a role no different than his paternal elders, that of the physician. And he threw it all away to become a doctor.

Perhaps it was in his genes because it wasn't just some whim or fluke, mind that. Unquestionably, something had invoked its power over him. His familial specter had gripped him with a passion to save suffering humanity from itself. It was his métier, his calling. What importance the role of saving of his own spiritual assets figured into this epiphany was patently immaterial to him. As fortune would have it, this eye-opening vision came to him merely months prior to the stock market crash of 1929 in which the majority of the wealth that would have come to him as VP of the steel company imploded and was swept away.

He divorced that woman and her two sons, both of whom were born mentally stunted. One had his cranium crushed at the end of a botched delivery. The other forcibly collided with a surgical pan at birth, a ploy attributed to a physician who was in too much of a hurry to get to the golf range; net result, brain damage. Both of those events so enraged my father over medical incompetency that he vowed such bumble-brained activity would never stain the fabric of his Hippocratic prayer cloth.

As it turned out he had no stomach for the real-life practice of medicine upon living patients who were about to die. The kickback of having his history label him as a social misfit countermanded this aberrant aversion by leading him out of the hospital and into the laboratory. On top of that, the result of his confrontations during World War I (particularly the astronomical quantity of bombs which exploded so close to his proximity they not only blew out his eardrums but also destroyed all trust in himself) caused him to suffer a serious psychological dysfunction - fear of people. This further barred him from facing the intolerable halls of healing head-on, so he transferred into research.

What in the human body comes the closest to molten steel running into ingots? You guessed it: blood. He surmised the blood cell to be the end all and be all of the human stockpile. But blood should not be inferred to be merely a fluid; it is an organ. And like any other organ and it should be treated as such. There are chemicals and nutrients, which are beneficial for the blood and there are ones, which are mortally deleterious. There is healthy blood and there is sick blood. My father was damned and determined to track down the thousands of systemic diseases attacking the blood. This was his war.

In the same token, blood is not only an organ but also a commodity. Red blood can be collected and shared amongst humans of all colors. It can also be disassembled and its individual components can be injected intravenously to heal the manifold dysfunctionalities, which can occur within the holistic cross-section of a human being's constitution. My father was one of only a handful of trailblazing doctors to recognize this concept and act on it. He was the one who created a practical solution in which erythrocytes could effectively be stored for a significantly useful time - 21 days. That work led to the largest percentage of whole blood to retain a sufficient viability necessary for the rejuvenation of a dying body. His CPD, or Citrate Dextrose Phosphate solution, serves even today as the most effective way of maintaining the correct pH balance in human blood.

Lastly, even though his business was blood, I must state categorically my father was not a vampire. Let's just get that straight and not have it hanging out there. Over and above all else, even though his peers might not have considered him an egalitarian hero, he was a humanitarian of the highest order. Unfortunately, for his heirs, he abandoned his business hat, which he had worn in the steel mills. Year after year with every new discovery he made, his humanitarian ideals prevented him from ever patenting or in any way

The Moon Women

laying commercial claim to a single element of this great work. He gave it all away freely and the only thing he desired deeply was recognition, which he did receive in abundance, no doubt about that. Unfortunately, I must confess, as a sour after note, many of his colleagues attempted to usurp claim to his great service after he died.

During his career, thousands lauded him for his scientific contributions. The entire medical community awarded him prize after prize for making extraordinary strides in preventative medicine. Furthermore, by reason of his pioneering work of providing the very first plasma bottles directly out on the battlefields, the President of the United States, Harry Truman, decorated him for preventing the deaths of over one hundred and thirty thousand wounded soldiers who fought during the invasions of Europe at the conclusion of the Second World War. To this day, I have those medallions, which Truman presented to him at that ceremony. I keep them very close to me in a secure place.

Nonetheless, in the end, the evil, which took him out, wasn't boisterous vanity or feigned hubris, neither was it his drinking nor his cussing. No. The culprit, which finally did him in, was tobacco. Having spent his every waking hour since puberty inhaling cigarette smoke, he died in the intensive care ward of the Deaconess Hospital in Boston sucking down terminal gasps of oxygen to sustain his pneumonia-filled lungs, which were failing under the devastating effects of emphysema. He was four months clear of his seventieth birthday. That noon in October when I went to the hospital to gather his things, a Jamaican nurse sympathetically apprised me he had expired at a minute to ten. She shared with me that before my father had lapsed into an unconscious state, she had spent a few minutes with him. They had repeated the Lord's Prayer together, Psalm 23. She emphasized even at that late stage in the game he was able to say it by heart.

The Lord is my shepherd, I shall not want. [1]

She added my father had beseeched her to share something with me, "Tell him to remember the second line."

He maketh me to lie down in green pastures;
He leadeth me beside the still waters.

He restoreth my soul. [1]

I thanked her for taking care of him in the end of life as well as sharing those sentiments from my father. Those two places mentioned in the prayer were the two habitats, the pastures of waving wheat and the calm waters of reflection, where I had always enjoyed what some say is the meditator's duality, the one of suffering and the one of peace. More poignantly, I reminisced it was indeed classic he had forgotten the next verse, the line on righteousness, but that figured, knowing him. It was also most ironic that the last human being my father got to be with on this earth was black.

- 6 -

His anger died with him, but his song lived on within me. Squarely like the dog, the bark was worse than the bite. When his yelling came out of me, it didn't necessarily mean I was angry. It was merely an expression to indicate sometimes enhanced emphasis is necessary to clear up the fog of war, but nobody got that except Tiami Brown. She had always claimed my tongue was a blade, which would blunt itself on her beauty.

Whether it remains in the genes stained with failure or in the retrofitted scenes witnessed in stale repetition, the mind has a way of re-enacting the events of childhood. Mixing the flavors of one emotional dessert with the spices of intellectual condiments, life produces a range of correlations with the people we love. This soup, married with the input of fast servings, sometimes comes out as sweet candy or bitter acid. The sweetness lends a hand in the fabrication of love objects of exquisite beauty whereas the acid etches hate objects of ghoulish horror. Truly, it is a double-edged sword hanging over the Damocles of one's destiny. All the same, Tiami rejected both of these viewpoints.

The shifting airs repositioned the shimmering silks across her mulatto abdomen as the da Vinci in me sketched her exquisite features upon my imaginary canvas. As though a sleight-of-hand artist performing incognito, he captured her exposed belly button and painted the subtle crease as it inched across her buttery skin; its detail pointed both north to her breast region as well as nether wards to the lady's palace. Being respectful, he followed the upward trail towards

The Moon Women

the twin hillocks of perfection.

The fullness of those peaks appeared from time to time as the poorly covering fabrics sluffed up and down lightly kissing the curvature of those heavenly mounds, which could put an Athenian goddess to shame. Upon the pinnacle of each was poached a circular areola. The art of his admiration embraced those peaks of feminine idealism upon which rested a sweetly domed raisin whose tint was darker than the rich mocha chocolate of its base camp. Searching for their equals anywhere in the free world would be futile.

He witnessed the nipple protruding ever so slightly as it seemed to grow in minute increments whenever the peacock silks licked at it in the balmy air. An indentation alluded to the font, which would one day nourish copies of her serpentine figure. In the faint light, my surrogate da Vinci detected the microscopic droplets of a milky substance highlighting the lip of that duct. Using a tiny brush of only one camel hair, my Leonardo reached over to capture this pristine detail but his oils had gelled.

A bell from a Portuguese church across the bay tolled its wakeup call jarring me back out of my renaissance reverie.

Bam!

It hit me.

As the epic goes, the legendary avatar, Lord Krishna, had entreated his prime disciple, Arjuna, to assume his stance and focus upon his intended target, a large bird of prey perched on a branch a considerable distance away.

"But Lord, how can I strike such a target? It is barely visible," Arjuna propounded in confusion.

The young archer seated one light-arrow and drew his bow to the jut of his jaw to make ready.

"Can you see the goal clean and true my Sisha?" Lord Krishna inquired.

"Yes, my Lord. It is now in full view," Arjuna responded.

"Now, with all your might, concentrate on the neck and beak of the bird. Inform me when you are picturing only this," Shri Krishna decreed the subsequent steps of the training.

"I am beholding nothing but the neck and the beak, your Lordship," The faithful follower of the Dharma delivered his reply after a moment of strong scrutiny.

"Using the Holy Will, which you have learned to summon from

your innermost center, focus solely on the beak of the bird. See the beak as the only object in your mind," The Avatar commanded his trusting disciple with firm resolve.

Several moments passed before Arjuna could comply with his Guru's command. Ultimately, he assumed a victorious hold.

"The beak is all I behold, Maharaji." The immense tension set into the bowstring stunned all the surrounding cosmos with a hum, which reverberated in Arjuna's trembling reply.

"Hear me now, my obedient one. Know the eye of the bird to be the only item existing in this entire creation. See it as the zenith of God consciousness itself. Believe the eye of the bird to be the goal of Maha Samadhj; the eye is your veritable liberation. Declare to the downtrodden when you have collected this depth of concentration, my fearless one," The Avatar administered his supreme command.

Time balanced on one leg. All air movement upon the plain ceased. The Guru waited. There was not a single muscle moving in Arjuna's entire body. Even his pulse slowed to a little over sixteen beats per minute. His breath was but a thought riding the wind.

"I am the eye, Guru Ji!"

"Release!" Lord Krishna ordered.

The light-arrow surged ahead unaffected by the wind, nor acted upon by the laws of nature, nor even the terrors of Lord Time. The light-arrow flew flawlessly heading for its mark. But what was the bird seeing?

My gaze reversed to anticipate the valley of pleasure. The subtle crease dissolved into the periphery her lower harbor. The peacock silks had flown the coop. There she was as her entire palace yawned wide beneath the vanishing starry skies. Her distinctly carved labials were slightly ajar curving away to the vestibule of her vagina, hidden from view yet continuing to entice the hungers of my hindsight to probe its depths. The waking reflex of her leg and the shifting of her arm brought an abrupt curtain call to my wandering odyssey. The hookah stopped bubbling. Quarrelsome Hindi noises clashed out in the hallway. Was I slipping into the slough of despond? Insomuch as I was not a respected Christian, who would come to my rescue now?

Wake up!

The bird saw it all. It saw the practicing young disciple. It saw the Avatar gleaming with the thousand hues of the spectrum. And, it

The Moon Women

saw the light-arrow streaming towards it to take out its eye. The light-arrow struck its mark. Straight through the neck, and through the beck, and through the eye, and through the brain it plunged.

"I have won the target, Kishan!" Arjuna shouted joyously.

"You have won nothing, my Son. The bird's destiny has simply been revealed. The succeeding phase of its karma has been put into action. One day, the atmani within that kite will be reborn as your daughter. In a fit of rage, she will tear out both your eyes and you will be forsaken as a sightless man to wander lost in an unknowable universe. This is the Great Will. This is the Mauj. As an unalterable result, you will come to realize your true rank in this kingdom of Saints and wander the jungles as a blind man. But from this loss you will rise above all earthly delights with a flawless vision which will reconnect you with your source, the infinite oneness of the One. But that was then and this is now. On today's tide, you must stand at attention. War has come upon us. Speak to me no more on this kite or this eye." With this renunciation, Shri Krishna mounted his giant Arabian stallion and galloped off towards his home in Giri Dara Nagara.

- 7 -

"Hey."

Tiami whispered softly, gathered the iridescent silks around herself modestly, and sat up.

"What time is it? Can you toss me something to wear?"

I laid a juba lightly on her arm and remained silent as I took my seat while returning a faint smile. After a pause, I cut through the awkward stillness.

"This book is fantastic." I licked my thumb to turn the page.

"Have you been up long? Can we get some Chai, maybe some idli waddah?" She was gradually reclaiming her perspectives with little concern for literature.

"I don't think they have idlis in Goa. No matter. I have Chai and something they call dumplings on the way. Have you ever felt like a bird, Brownie?" My question was aimed at peeling back some of the riddle.

"Rahm, don't act like an ass. I'm real thirsty and I don't need this silliness." She was bordering on crotchety. "I need some Chai or something."

"Well, this fellow killed an eagle by shooting a light-arrow at its eye from over six clicks away which is so remarkable I can't even fathom it. Oh, and I saw you naked when you were sleeping. Do you want sugar with that?" I gushed.

We had a little coded joke we would always add to whatever we had going. It was simply, "Do you want sugar with that?" It was a blasé kind of word game, which I dreamt up to reduce the pressures while ratcheting up our dialectic with some iconoclastic humor. The comeback was, "Yeah. Two lumps."

"What the hell are you talking about, Rahm? Mind telling me what time it is please? Why do I have to ask twice?" She was becoming way too irritable.

Okay. So she wasn't going to play. Gotta get my Mr. Butler costume on and serve her up some sanity and some sugary cerebral donuts here.

"Seven nineteen, Your Holiness." I was the finest manservant ever.

"Yeah. Two lumps up yer ass." Jabs Miss Brown
Bam!

It hit me smack in the gut. I was going to be other people. I would act out a smorgasbord of distinctive personalities to alleviate her fluctuating moods. I could invent a complete persona and put together a neat disguise for the taking. I could be anybody she might imagine me to be. I would be peeling away the unread shells of different psyches lurking just below my skin.

"Say, I've got an idea." As I explained the genius gambit of my plan and all its ramifications, her face took on a distorted look.

"You off your rocker? How much shit you already do this morning? You outta your ever loving mind, Rahm? Gimme that!" She clawed at the juba with her talons.

Just then, a fumbling click came from the doorknob, the signal it was time for Chai. As the matronly Indian woman deposited the tea service on the dresser, she held out her hand, which I paved with a ten-rupee note. As she smiled warmly, I noticed her nose had sundry piercings from which clusters of expensive 24-karat gold ringlets drooped. She also had a multiple saris, which had gift-wrapped her to perfection. That or she was really plump. I swear, the population of Indian women is going to possess the entire cosmos

The Moon Women

what with all the gold they carry screwed into their noses and stapled onto their ears. After I handed her the rupees, she departed with a tasteful Namaste and folded hands. I Namasteed back.

By now, Tiami Brown had finished dressing. As she displayed an impressive amalgamation of fabrics including Kashi silk swathing her shoulders, maco cotton in a juba normally worn by a man, and purple slippers inherited from her grandmother, she projected an aloof untouchability, although I knew otherwise. As she sat quietly sipping her ginger Chai, she resisted the impulse to comment on my intrusive stare as I measured the quantum index of her bewitching ratios plotted against the normal lines of her incredibly exotic fires, as I'm sure you can recall from the recent scene I was reporting sans the gilded scissors.

Brownie and I carried our Chai to the seats out on the balcony overlooking the sea. Goa's tides had retreated from their high water mark. Exhaling the brackish air of discarded seaweed, the swooshing of the curling breakers out in the harbor blended with the slur of sleepy traffic going by on the streets below our bungalow. Goa certainly was a paradise for bourgeois tourists. We took slow, tight sips of the hot Chai.

"What do you mean by what you want to be?" She confessed some confusion about my scheme.

"How 'bout a blind man? I could get all spruced up like a rich Brahmin or even better an Englishman, but I would be holding a blind man's cane to tap my way along. Here, take my arm. You'll be my underling. Let's waltz from shop to shop and see what happens." I was proposing the basis for my half-baked plan.

"That sounds loopy, Rahm. What's it supposed to accomplish? Seems to me you could be demonstrating a premature mid-life crisis." She was not so easily persuaded to join in on this lark.

"Don't be so quick to throw a monkey wrench into the nitty-gritty of my creative genius," I spouted egregiously.

I kept explaining the outlines of my prefabricated adventure, which I was hatching as fast as the words came out of my mouth. Fortunately for me, Tiami was not the sharpest tack in the carpet so I didn't have to go overboard that much before she was chiming in with her own versions of the preflight scenarios.

"Where are we going to get a blind man's cane? That's not so easy, you know." She was wary but no longer suspicious.

"Let's find out if there are any schoolhouses for the blind near here?"

That seemed to me to be the most logical move in pursuing the logarithms of our matriculation with the visually challenged. After we settled up with breakfast, in no time we were out in the lobby asking the manager where the indigenous blind blokes resided. A Mr. Patel overheard us interrogating the baffled receptionist and stood to acknowledge our quest with his curveball psittacism,

"They have sown wheat but shall reap thorns. They have put themselves to pain but shall not profit." [2]

With that rampant Christian declaration, he apologized only to inform us he knew of one establishment named The Institution For The Hard Of Hearing And Visually Impaired. Purportedly you don't merely refer to them as blind folks. After he jotted down the address and handed it over, we were off and running.

We took the elevator down to the street and flagged an auto. I handed the rickshaw wallah the address and we buzzed off making our way down the clogged narrow alleyways. As we zigzagged through a bustling community of coconut vendors, I happened to look down at Tiami's breasts nestled so nonchalantly in the twin envelopes of her silk sari and tried desperately to resist the flip-back to this morning's reveal. She looked back with a cocked head and a squinted eye.

"When you a blind man, are you gonna get to see me at long last, Rahm?" She was targeting my funny bone but I steered her off course.

"I can see you quite fine, Brownie. Why just this morning I…"

"Oh, buzz off!"

Confessing my scandalous daybreak skin patrol would not come to bear so readily a third time, so I kept quiet. As the auto drew to a snappy halt with a lurch, her hand landed in my lap from the impact.

"Hey, if you're itchin' to meet Mr. Johnson, you should have phoned ahead for an appointment." I was nasty.

"Can I get two lumps with that?" She hopped out of the auto with a chuckle. I knew we were clicking now, Boy!

As we entered the institute, I introduced myself as Sir Jonathan Pugsley III from Devonshire, England. We were on holiday for the fortnight from our encampment in Old Delhi, where I taught the

The Moon Women

history of religion. At this juncture in our travels we were conducting research on the Indian Saint by the name of Sarmad who was not only a Jew but also a Muslim. Furthermore, biblical scholars of Persian history also traced the possibility this Saint was also blind from birth, save a two-month lapse, during which time, using miraculous faculties, he had endowed himself with blindless sight as proof of his divinity, only to be thrown into prison.

It was at that time Sarmad orated his famous misinterpretation of the most holy saying in all of Islam. "There is no God but God and Muhammad is the prophet of God" is the classical prayer said by all devoted Muhammadans. However, to his great detriment, Sarmad spouted only the first four words and stopped abruptly.

"There is no God."

Sarmad stated most humbly and categorically this was the fullest extent of his experience and progress with regard to the matter.

For this heinous insurrection, the local Imams beheaded him right on the spot. Miraculously however, this horror did not curtail his indubitable dominance. He simply picked up his detached head, ran up the stairs to the top of the Mosque, and while his head dangled precipitously over the courtyard he spouted a few poems illustrating the need for compassion and love, and then he promptly disappeared.

I explained how we were hard pressed to locate a facsimile of the segmented cane that Sarmad carried; we needed to determine both the extent of these inexplicable side effects as well as ascertain the likelihood Sarmad had brought said cane with him on his walks from Benares to Calcutta when he could see with spotless clarity.

If you're having trouble with this tale, you can imagine the embarrassed disenchantment of these workers at the institute who had been devout Brahmins from birth. They retreated into an adjacent coat closet to either inform the authorities or prepare themselves for the Indian version of Armageddon. But since this intermission had been rehearsed somehow, astonishingly they reappeared instantaneously with an exact replica of the red and white folding cane and handed it over. I thanked them profusely in my thick Scottish brogue as we dashed madly out the door and hopped back into our rickshaw, which had been faithfully cooling its jets expecting our reappearance and also ten more rupees.

Immensely liking the English gent who I had invented (his only discrepancy being proper attire), I reckoned the completion of the costume required a pair of leather English wingtips and some tweed slacks if we could have laid our mitts on them. I already had a decent button down dress shirt but had always preferred the ones with French cuffs having those stitched fissures for cuff links, so innuendo, as well as a set of yellow topaz ones in my toiletries. What's more, the finale must be a genuine English silk topper so off we zoomed to the marketplace. Man for man, Brownie and I were on a roll.

She truly loved to shop. She chatted up a storm with her smattering of Hindi. She also threw in all flavors and bits of French and even some Portuguese. I don't know how she did it, frankly, but she was way cool to be with. In the long run, we completed the short bucket list except for the topi. So off we shot to the Topi Wallah. After purchasing the bowler from the milliner, we raced back to our spacious purple suite in the Magistrate Arms and buried ourselves in our bayside window. I ordered two thalis with a full complement of chutney and four mango lassis, a pot of Chai and a plate of jalebis, which Miss Brown loved so much. It was time I learned how to be a blind man.

- 8 -

The wicker works had slowed or lost steam. Its dynamic seemed to adhere to the darker tempos or presumably negative Time if there is such a thing. I think they have discovered anti-matter but I've never come across the status of anti-Time. All the same, I suspect it must be the way in which someone might wrench wide a pit in the cosmos, a tunnel that could conceivably lead to an unending nothingness, an ultimate reduction in the gravitational soup, or merely the likeliness of a paler shade of white. By the same token, my mala was adding a crucial component to the chair's windings. In nothing flat, it had regained its energies and off I went, deeper and darker than ever like a dream within a dream.

It was the nice nighttime, August 1953. I was nine. It was a question of man's best friend. As all the dogs slept, the crickets were keeping perfect track of the temperature. Crickets don't give a hoot for the properties of Time and Space. Their scientists do not inhabit a timeline estimated by the ticks of a clock. Their equipment

The Moon Women

measures a timeline based on chirrups. They carry on within a realm of mirages, heat domes, and thermal inversions all of which require them to count each piddling fluctuation of the temperature with their knees. And they do it out loud with a chorus of chirps as they celebrate their supreme deity with a most enchanting music.

Whereas we count the minutes and seconds, crickets count the imperceptible changes in the vibrations of atoms. Since they exist in a microcosm of heat, they measure their surroundings with an entirely different time dilation principle, the one of divine thermodynamics.

"Let me turn down your sheets," offered my imaginary friend, Jane, quite courteously.

When she pealed the soft blanket down from my pillow, a bug hopped out and made a beeline for my ear. It was a baby cricket. I shrieked at the sight of it.

"Ahh-ohh-uhh-ehh-ihh!" It was a piercing howl.

"Oh, quit it! Don't be such a big baby!" Jane snatched the horrible beastie and popped it into her gullet.

"Crunch, crunch, gulp!" Came the gnashing of her molars.

"Eewww! Jane, that's disgusting." The sounds of her mashing plumb grossed me out.

"What? Take a lesson here. You have to learn to control your thoughts and modulate your principles. Then, you'll be getting somewhere and maybe even amount to something. What you should learn is that there is a difference between the things we see and the things, which really are there. All the stuff we see and hear is like the raisins. The real items are the grapes. That creepy bug for instance, do you really think I ate it?" She offered her empty hand.

"Yup. You snagged it up and swallowed it down. I saw you do it." I peered over the hem of my sheets to see more.

"Then what's this?" She opened her other hand and there was the baby cricket alive and happy.

"How'd you do that?"

"Listen here. The world of the crickets doesn't flow through Time. It jumps from ring to ring like the mythical characters of a weird book in which the chapters seem to randomly occur and then disappear accordingly to whims of an invisible author. The crickets are creating their own unfathomable calculations within the mathematics of heat. It doesn't seem to make any sense to us at first, but when we look at these episodes through the lens of absurdity, we begin to see a sharper picture unfolding." She snugged the sheets up tight.

Jane was always making similar absurd declarations and enunciating all sorts of hypothesis detailing the living creatures in the sky and the wheels of fortune breathing in the jade crystals forming behind the wall of Time.

"Someday you are going to write a book about your life. You are going to write it the same way you play Jacks where you bounce a small rubber ball off the bumpy concrete and catch it no matter where it lands. Whatever number of jacks you pick up will decide the person you are at any given moment. Whichever hand you use to catch the ball will determine whether the Moon or Mars is before you or behind you. A righty Moon may make you laugh; a lefty Mars may make you cry but the wall will always be the same. The wall is a place from where an invisible hand moves at the speed of light to shine its glory on the universe and color it with chance. It functions like the math of the future, like the march of the lemmings into the seas of dead religions. And you will become the Pied Piper of poetry who will stave off an encephalic virus from enslaving all mankind. Yours will be a book read by humans but written by crickets." She discontinued from conducting the crystals of micaceous pixie dust to monitor to her job, me.

"But, Jane. I'm not a cricket. I'm a human being." I insisted halfheartedly.

"That you are, my boy. Now, go to sleep. Have pleasant dreams and carry the chirping of your brethren into the land of cotton candy and sugar plum mountains," She mused.

With that, I drifted off to somewhere else where there aren't any crickets I hope.

- 9 -

Dr. Krishnaswami was sitting at his official desk working the mechanics of an unproven genius. His black Little Orphan Annie hair vibrated slightly and seemed to strengthen his His illusive two-dimensional framework propped up on a stress-tested ottoman, which displayed the leather of executive privilege. His son,

The Moon Women

Ramujappa, had insisted I pay the good doctor with the currency of two earlobes.

"So sorry, Sir. Mr. Rahms, I must speak with you concerning some matters." He proposed apologetically.

He was so efficient at performing his job as the main man of his world.

"Sure. What is it, Dr. K?"

I loved calling him that. He mistakenly construed it to mean I was poking fun at him whereas I simply meant it to be a mild compliment inferring he was fine and dandy; he should dig it. No matter how strenuously I assured him of my good intentions, he was ridiculously lost in the dust whenever I poked fun at his sore spots.

"It seems the police are requesting to meet with you. You must go down to the Cantonment this very day itself and as soon as you are able to go. I'm going to accompany you to verify it is all done properly." He was trying his darnedest to comfort me as well as preventing the petty officers from plying their skills at charging me any unnecessary fees.

"It's probably about my Maharaja robe. I wouldn't worry yourself over it. There's no sense in getting your good self all wound up by going all the way down there for no reason." I assured him while throwing in a twist of Brindian (Indianized British English), which always made me whince whenever the locals spat it out at me.

Furthermore, I wasn't having any of his matronizing, since I had already been down to the police Cantonment last week, right after the theft had occurred. The cops insisted I jot down my blow-by-blow and donate my John Hancock onto the bottom of umpteen forms. All the officers were quite nice and offered me Chai and biscuits from the galley. They thought it was quite prestigious to have a young American visiting their troop barracks, notwithstanding I wasn't qualified as a man on horseback.

The good doctor was explaining the details of the afternoon's itinerary, when his son, Rajudeva, popped his beak in the door and said the Missus was having some trouble negotiating a bill, something the resident street hoods had left at the back door. I'll bet it was more like one of those cryptic missiles the Phone Wallah had precipitated but there were too many words in Kannada I didn't know yet. Either way I was glad it didn't wind up to be one of those off the cuff lectures on the meaning of warped Time factors or which wormhole in the fabric of being lead to overbearing boredom.

"Just a minute, Mr. Rahms. Let's continue this inquisition down in the alley."

With that parapraxis, Dr. K. excused himself and disappeared into the bowels of the household proper.

Left alone to pursue further exploits of woolgathering I gave way to a tangent inclination. I'm not waiting here forever, came the pressured wind from the outer margins of my inner megacosm. I bombed upstairs to see if Meg was home. Inasmuch as she had completed all of the FWC campuses as well as tucking some industrious trekking in Kathmandu up under her skirt, I figured she had the credentials to decipher one of my most pressing enigmas, the underlying devil of the tooth gap. I knocked politely on her door.

"Come on in. I don't bite!" She spared me with fair warning.

Attired in garish combinations of Tibetan garments spiced up with a dash of Varanasi silks and the weavings of a mad Kabir, Meg was always knitting something. As she lounged in a worn Hathaway armchair, I grabbed an adjacent plot on a fine Italian quilt protecting the core of her sleeping quarters.

"How you doin', Meg?" I dallied upon the open playground as I triangulated on my elbow.

"Hey! Not so fast, Cowboy! Who said you could stake a claim in my bed?" She threw another stitch and smiled.

Meg was sorely bullying me, but we both knew if I hankered for it, I could park myself there all day 'til the hounds came home and all night for that matter.

"Claim? You and I both know what the true stakes are, Meg. But really; what can you tell me about Cancer women?" I was trying my level best not to let my mean Moon bleed through my thin skin.

"What? You're interested in my kith and kin? Do you think I have a degree or better still a doctorate on Cancer sisters? Do you think I have some vaccine, some Mantoux test, that I can slip underneath their skins and peal back all their secrets? Takes me two months to get you into bed and you're chatting up some other Cancer bitch. You dog!" Since she was approaching the snappy zone, she put her ball of blue yarn down.

"Anytime you wanna go, Meg, just lemme know." I said tongue in cheek. "No, really. What are the pertinent issues that I

The Moon Women

should know with regard to these Moon children?" I was baiting more hooks than I could reel in.

"Okay, then. Well, as you already know, Cancers are ruled by the Moon, which means they have the Moon controlling their outer Crab selves, but what most folks don't know is they have its opposite, Mars, controlling their inner selves. That's what gets them so loopy. Their antipodes, the Lamb women, or Aries, are more stable because outside they have the hard shell of Ram under Mars, but the softer insides of the Moon. Whereas classy broads like me seem to be all flexible and a little fluky on the outer banks but within we're burning at war with something. It's usually a negative goal, which, more than not, gets represented or personified by a love interest. You understand. The Cancer symbol is said to be a crab but to you and me it looks more like a tipped over sixty-nine. That stir up any memories for you, Bunky?" She shot me another one of her lavish devil smirks as she twirled away with her needles.

"And the rest is," I rolled my hand for further details.

"Fuckin' hard nut you are. Cancer gals have rounded faces, moon-like. Get it? Whereas, Aries chicks have noses like lambs, faces like sheep. The Cancer child is also marked by one other surprising feature." She paused with her hook dangling out in front of her grinning puss. Help! Help! Don't eat me! Worm and all.

"Yeah? What's that?" I took a nibble.

"Why don't you move in, and I'll let you know." Her grin increased.

"Quick! I'm on hiatus with the Maharani from Brunei. Give!"

"Shit! Can't blame a sister for trying. Cancer women, by and large, have a slit between their two incisors."

Right when she divulged that shocker, she smiled and lo and behold, there it was, the little gap set there like a postage stamp declaring - Priority mail. Open at your own risk.

"What did you say?" I had to get a replay to make sure. "You mean to say Moon children always have a tiny slot there?"

"Pretty much. Some women who have orthodontic work done maybe in their teenage years also get other corrections as well. Dentists usually fix all those traditional screw-ups when Daddy's licking the tab. What say you and I get down to some serious fucking?" She leered at me with that wide-body, tooth-gap grin.

"Thanks, Meg. I think Dr. K is calling me." I squirmed out of the brainy Nelson hold she had tried to place on me and darted for the door.

When I got back to the Doc's office, its emptiness prompted me to reclaim my nexus with a Brahmin's terminal reality. I plunked myself down on the wooden bench, which was canted solitarily away from the doorway, and got my yogi mojo going. I looked this way and that to size up any items of consequence in case I might require some reference, some fulcrum for future invasions. I discovered a filing cabinet eclipsed by the K-man's desk. Wonder what's in there?

Upfront it posed a pushbutton lock, but the tumbler was sticking out which meant it was unlocked. "Hey, Doc, you get a friggin' F for security," I thought. Gliding out on its ball-bearing main shafts the drawer coasted free to a public viewing. An assortment of manila folders and loose papers filled it to the brim. Each of the folders had the name of an FWC registrant captured under a blue cellophane tab.

I located my own in there. I also came across ones for the students currently enrolled here in the Asian campus. Then, I came across a name, which I didn't recognize: Ilene Ireland. I had never before come across anyone by that name on the roster of fwikdom. Who could it be? I yanked it out.

When I pealed back the ID photo, my mind spiraled into a giant corkscrew. It was Brownie! Why the heck was Brownie's photograph stuck in this other chick's folder? In a twinkling I scanned over miscellaneous tidbits of old news and more recent circulars, when I fell smack dab upon a hot bulletin. Brownie's birth name was Ilene Ireland. Seems she had been assigned this other name of Tiami Brown to protect her because of a sexual assault, which she had suffered some five years back on Long Island. It stated something, which implied her old boyfriend had grossly maltreated her; perhaps it was even rape.

It did not indicate Ireland was her maiden name or that she had been married or anything of the kind. It looked as though her guardians had selected FWC as a reputable hideout for her to seek some anonymity. I also came across an information sheet, which disclosed her birthday as July 16, 1945. Wow! I knew the significance of that day because of a report that I had compiled back in the halls of ivy in the Bard library. Brownie was born on the

The Moon Women

precise instant Robert Oppenheimer had tested his atomic bomb, Trinity, out in the desert of Alamogordo. Brownie was not only a Moonchild; she was a bona-fide Atomic child! She was not only a Cancer sign; she was born under the sign of the mushroom cloud! I slid the drawer back tightly into its closed state in the cabinet.

"Holy cow!" I stammered aloud.

That was a brain load! How could she keep that hidden from me for so long? Did we even know each other? Then, it struck me. Why would she share something so personal and so intimate with me, a guy who would not even hook up with her? That moment we had together after she watched my movie was one beautiful experience, but it wasn't sex and it wasn't long. I'll never know now bearing in mind the unlikelihood of her doing the Bangalore phase of her degree again. Patently, she will more than likely move onto the Nairobi or my luck, the Hiroshima campus. I fawned an awkward anticipation of bumping into her at Mitchell Gardens at the tail end of some alumni get-together. Who knows? Ilene Ireland? Wow! Maybe I should have nicknamed her Trinity?

I got bored hanging out idly for Dr. Krishnaswami to jump-start our get-together. It was like so many other troublesome rendezvous with Indians. Their concept of two minutes or simply a single second could wind up consuming anywhere from a week to an arm and a leg. On the way back to central K, I nearly bumped into the pesky Phone Wallah who was loitering in the middle of the road looking lost and yearning for an incoming call. Regrettably, I couldn't help the feller; I was on a mission. I overheard him muttering back at his outpost something about the vagaries on the angel of the Lord who had come upon him and the comet tail floating over its belfry. But I had to go. As I indexed my mala with a steady grip, he simply dissolved into thin air.

An ashen sickle of the quarter-moon crawled higher and higher to slice an incision into the vault of heaven. Spilling out of this wound in the rib of God was a waterfall of angel quills, which fell onto the horizon leaving faint white stars.

- 10 -

Intent on regenerating the psycho-magnetic strands humming on the edges of my boney ride, I settled within the Time padding and plunked my magic chain to encourage some lift. As the transformation loomed up within me, in no time I was back on the beach in Goa. There would be many more excursions out and about this quaint Portuguese province to test our hypothesis of avoiding karmic accidents. As if sacrificial lambs lying upon the altar of pantomime, we pushed into the irregular realms of further rib-tickling travel.

After acting out the American blind goof for a couple more days, we also did a blind Brahmin spoof using all my Bombay Pundit apparel. The best thing was we were getting fantastic mileage out of the cane. I had little recollection if the clan back at the institute had indicated we should surrender the cane or not. When we moved on, I abandoned it in the lodging underneath the twin beds never fearing its true owner would draw forth to locate the rare pole jack as it cohabitated with the dust bunnies.

At one point, I proposed to Brownie I play the role of a blind matador. She took one look at me and cracked up.

"Not only are you going to get gored to death in two seconds, but you'll be disrespecting every Brahma bull in the country. You get an A for effort though, Moron!" She shook her head.

"I guess I'll pass on that one." I spoofed. "Pass. Get it. I'll pass."

"Oh, shut up!" She quipped. "Pass me a mineral water, would you please?"

Once I mimed a Yogi and Brownie was my assistant. We meandered from market to market begging for food. It was surprising how many shop owners offered us food to eat which was all remarkably tasty. In one shop, the owner presented us with thalis loaded with bitter gourd, a dish I adore. After masquerading with this clowning routine for some time, Brownie was growing tired of it all. I sensed that shortly my whacky experiment was about to crash and burn.

On the train back to Bangalore, I assumed the charisma of a wealthy Arabian Sheikh. (Pronounced "Shake.") Don't ask me how I pulled that one off. I happened to have a gingham duster and a wreath of thick blackened hemp to serve as my Igal, with which I crowned myself the necessary sultanic powers. I had an extravagant pair of Milano sunglasses, which I slapped over my baby blues. The flowing robes of sheikhdom were easy to muster up. Brownie also

The Moon Women

got all gussied up to look like an enticing Arabian princess with a meshwork veil. The taxing feat was simulating Arabic, which neither one of us had any idea of how to speak. I developed an offbeat system of guttural clicks and intensely sibilant phrases. Somehow, we were able to muddle through it all to get our intensions across and remain anonymous. The cockamamie aspect of it all was we openly smoked hashish!

As is the case with all Indian first-class compartments, we were riding with other travelers. One was a couple from Bombay. They had been vacationing down South in Kerala at a Christian cooperative. After the train got rolling, the woman abruptly rose and announced her portent with a Dravidian drawl.

"He sent it and signified it by his angel unto his servant." [3]

She proceeded to sit down in double-time and never divulged anything more. There were bastions of obsequious Christians traveling throughout the countryside. I chalked it up to another episodic anomaly.

The other was a businessman, a Mr. Menon, from Bangalore who was returning to his village in Davengere. All well-educated Indians always introduce themselves to you as they put forth their spiel to sell you something or interview you for a membership in their particular devotional society or Bhakti as they call it. This one represented a rare sect of Hinduism branded as the Radha Soami Punth. He described it as a way to avoid death by dying daily or it could be I was flummoxed not reading him properly. It sounded a little like buying a life insurance policy after you had died. But everyone is entitled to his own form of insanity. Hey, I'm no one to argue against someone else's religious anarchy.

On whim while passing a roadside kiosk I had purchased a delicately carved hash pipe fashioned entirely out of ivory. Constant use had blessed it with a jubilant taffy yellow. As we discreetly imbibed our pleasure fumes and sipped our Chai serenely, the portly rail carriage shuttled violently along its route southwards. Our smiles certified the misaligned righteousness hidden in this biblical act of innocence. And it made little difference to our fellow travelers who watched blankly out the curtained portal at the dusty terrain sweeping by as we hurdled crazily towards our destination in midtown Banglaore. Fortunately, there were only a handful of depots listed for this express line. In no time, we were pulling into the railway station near the Mysore Road.

When Dr. Krishnaswami bumped into us as we toppled head over heels into his main divide, he gave a start and bobbled his pitcher of Chai like a fumbled football from a bad snap.

"Who the hell are these ragamuffins?" he thought, only it was probably in Kannada.

After we identified ourselves, he tittered hysterically with a warbling burble, which reminded me of gargling only with tadpoles not pebbles. He hollered for his wife, Shanni, to come out and witness our wily costumes. In the bat of an eye, we quickly ducked into the backroom of basecamp to retire within the K-room, my off-limits shelter. We were pretty pooped and quickly shed our garments, which grew into a pile at the foot of the bed. Brownie plunked herself down in my Time chair. With my foot, I gave her a push. She really loved my heavenly chair.

- 11 -

As we drift in lazy sleep in our cozy beds, whales are working hard at sea. They inflate their lives within mental oceans and deposit their treasures on the shorelines of prolonged recognition. Though their lungs are compressed at tremendous depths, they rip unbounded symphonies out of their hearts. The orchestral Humpback whale calls earth her home. Hunted practically into extinction, the majesty of this leviathan continues to expand its claim on history. Is she calling out for the Medic? Or is she calling out for the Messiah? We have much to learn from the whale.

As she glides through the deep, her songs go out into dimensions of water like metaphysical megaphones. As pressure waves moving through the ocean, these maestoso raptures travel across vast ranges underneath the silvery surfaces. These melodies originate in the white spectrums of frequency, but they also modulate in and out of inter-dimensional regions. The songs filter off in one chasm of the ocean, only to reappear off another shore after passing through a transitory shift. The same whale, which created these orchestral passages within one sphere of Time/Space, can rehear her songs many thousands of kilometers away and even many years

The Moon Women

away. Moreover, she can retrieve these sub-sonic morsels at will like marinated memories.

Occasionally after I had hiked to the summit of some mammoth hill or mound in England or a towering peak in Turkey or after scaling the foothills at the base of the Himalayas, I let loose with my ethereal recorder. I was obliged to proclaim the sum total of my previous lifetimes had condensed into light like a beacon, only some devious entity was using me and manipulating me like a puppet. It was making me go through these dramas by playing out the haphazard conclusions no different from the whales retrieving their projected memoirs.

The times with Brownie and the occurrences which evolved amidst our time in Goa, were also like the songs of the whales, like a tuba player pushing the keys in a clear-cut fashion to create the melodies of the future. Brownie and I had been making cosmic music together for quite some time. Whether or not we were finalizing the residues of quondam incarnations or inventing the birthplaces for new ones was not entirely apparent to me yet. Nevertheless, in whatever way we had harmonized within these interludes, I was certain that momentarily, I would have the answers to some highly perplexing incongruities. Likewise, I knew the final solution would lay within something, which had already been shown to me even if I hadn't yet devised a distinct picture of what it could be yet. Where this news would eventually bring me wasn't written in stone but it was undeniable. Barring any drawbacks, I knew I was ready; I was one hundred percent ready.

The wheat fields lay like virgins pining for their husband, the sun, to marry them erstwhile praying to be saved from the molestations of Time. With their sizzling light blades, the Angels hunted over those waving oceans of grain like White legionnaires swimming barely below the belly of the Beyond. Hungrily, they sought out their prey, the vile locusts of doom, the unknown shadows of humanity, the vile and treacherous Khrng.

- 12 -

Back in my bold swing chair, I had the occasion to reflect on what Dr. Krishnaswami had told me concerning what the Vedas have divulged concerning karma.

110

"Karma is not only mundane, karma is the munition for the mundane. Karma is what fires the universe with life. It is what actuates all sentient beings and allows them to engage the reduction of their regularity." He described the repulsive thermodynamics of life and death.

"There are three kinds or weights of karma: the Present, that which must be carried and burned up during our current life; the Past, that which is stored for later dispersal; and the Active, that which we generate within this life itself." He outlined the basics of it.

"You create karma when you are driven by desire. If you had no desire you would have no karma, you would have no body. This, in essence, is one of the central threads in spiritual thought whose nucleus centers on the most primal desires of all - eating. The requirement of sustenance is not imaginary. It was not something simply dreamt up on the remote fringes of our imagination. It is an undeniable law of survival. Failure to act on it only brings degradation and the eventual end of our trail of breaths. The important factor to realize here is there are degrees to which you can fulfill this desire. There is a full range of possibilities. You can ingest anything from a morsel of bread to a two hundred-course dinner. There are some sloths capable of eating in one sitting what an ascetic would not eat in a year's time. This is an example of the accelerator of desire. The harsher and more violently we push down on that pedal, the more karma we are revving up.

"When we act we cause energy to be expended into the cosmos at large. This energy puts a mark upon Time similar to a warm breath, which forms a haze on cool glass. Transforming thought into action scars the purity of Time/Space in the same way your boots leave footprints in the snow. When you toss a pebble just right, it skips across the surface of the pond and generates ripples, which go out to the shores. In the same manner, the resultant impressions from our thoughts, our words, and our actions inscribe a trail upon the subtle psychic lenses resident in an alternative upper world; the impacts from such imprinting creates our karma. This alter reality cited is designated as the Akash which means 'Sky.' It is similarly labeled as the Astral plane, or the Beyond.

"Recognizing that it is not connected to our terrene existence isn't necessary in order to comprehend that it is real and that it is not conceptual. It is an authentic realm existing entirely with its own

The Moon Women

unique makeup having a ratio of matter to mind to spirit slightly different from here. The ratios for those three primal constituents are proportioned with an altered gradient as compared to the sphere of our day-to-day origins.

"On the Astral plane there is more spirit and more mind but less matter than here on the earth plane. Or rather, the matter is finer, more subtle than here, and the mental energies are stronger and the spiritual juice is much more powerful. This ratio is a key factor in the basic laws, which govern the nuts and bolts of each plane. These laws have been stipulated for the purpose of maintaining a series of higher realities which define not only the existence of a perspective hovering outside what we all call the everyday norm, but also lead to an unimaginable expansion into many more transcendent worlds as well.

"In our universe, this place we call the grand macrocosm, or Pinda as the Hindu pundits have been known to label the physical universe, substances are constructed in a trickle down matrix. All matter consists of clumps of chemicals, which in turn are composed of different molecules. Subsequently, those molecules are made of atoms further fabricated from particles arranged from subordinate units termed as quarks, which in like manner came into being from vibrating entities the quantum soccer players have termed as strings. Most leading physicists have come to accept this tree-branch-leaf master plan to be our model as the agreed upon structure of all matter.

"The vibratory rates or frequencies of these strings determine how the entire system spills out from its central origins into its diverse complexity. When this frequency is altered even in the minutest degree, the accordion skeleton inherent within the building blocks of our corporeality also gets substantially changed. These altered vibratory rates demand everything that was spawned according to initial laws, will then be transformed into an updated status, a different state. One unique set of building blocks can only recognize another set via a dual dovetailing between both systems, which substantiates the compatibility of both rule sets. Others, which are discordant, are invisible and therefore unknown. These limitations form a boundary or a divide between one reality and the other. This is known as Vedic Dharma, the other side of the karmic coin.

"Karma is also multi-dimensional. Actions go out. They also

go up.

"There is a curious Russian toy some call a Matryoshka doll that looks like a bulbous little man who has a surprise inside. Along his midsection is inscribed a delicate incision or joint which cleanly allows a division between the upper portion and the lower one. If you apply a tugging pull to both the top with one hand and the bottom with the other, you will hit upon a divergence and the two halves will separate. Within the outer man is another one exactly like the first inside, only a tad smaller. It is reduced in size such that it can be enclosed within the primary one. This slightly smaller man also has a matching joint circumscribing its midsection, and he, too, can be separated into two halves exposing a third man within. This segmentation continues inward until a miniature fifth man is unveiled from out of the fourth. In comparable fashion, there are multiple planes of existence as well as multiple levels of increased consciousness, one contained within the other. You could add an insight to this metaphor: we live in the smallest one, the one in the center.

"Each of these levels of reality demonstrates its own unique vibratory rate and arises from a sympathetic set of laws which guarantees its exclusiveness. Consequently, the arrangement of the building blocks of our universe, this realm of frail impermanence, exemplifies the relationship the laws of karma have between one plane and its neighbor. It is similar to that toy man which dictates its mold to its outer cousins by perpetuating the design of its heart seed. In a similar fashion, the multiple planes of conscious subsistence replicate themselves; moreover, what goes up is stored, what comes down is unleashed.

"An action performed in the lowest realm has an effect on what is allotted for that jiva when it crosses into any adjoining realms. And so on, and so on. Nothing escapes the boundaries of this set-up. There are no actions, which have no reverberating effects. The effect of every action is marked down in its respective slot among the upper planes and remains there until the time comes for it to be collected and consummated.

"Please understand that the entirety of karma truly lies outside normal human comprehension because it is not only multi-dimensional, it is a recondite element to the normal human brain, and as such it is unusable information. Any form of previously measured

The Moon Women

organics currently at our disposal can't perceive the truth about it. Even if there were extraterrestrial visitors from another planet, these things would be unreachable by them as well.

"Quite surprisingly, recent scholars have revealed the Vedic scriptures have cited the possibility for a number of rare individuals who might exist outside these norms. These insinuations form the basis for the advent of prophets, messiahs, and seers from the Beyond, rare individuals who can manifest extraordinary abilities of knowing things, which are outside the range of the run of the mill population. These upstarts are the ones who from time to time alter the normal perspectives of the human populace as a whole. And it is disturbing to have to admit most of the important structures of human intelligence and knowledge have come from ideas proliferating from this small collection of oddball thinkers.

"If every action of every human being who has ever existed or now inhabits the earth could be input into a computer as digital information, you can imagine how large that number cruncher would have to be. It would be so far outside the range of human possibility to build such a mechanism, never mind completing the job of entering the vast wealth of data involved. On top of that, if you were to add into that construct the actions of every organism alive now plus all the ones which have ever been alive on this blue marble (not to mention the possibility of other planetary organisms), it would amount to a figure that would extend all the way to the Moon and off into the wild blue yonder! Such as it is with karma.

"Karma is the fuel and the machine which burns that fuel is the incarnation, the body. The atma inhabits a body in the same manner as energy inhabits oil. When certain hydrocarbons are cracked and burned, energy is released in the form of light, heat and torque or twist. It pushes out like a demon trying to circumvent its cage. The form of light is the attention, for the attention is the expression of the jiva's atma. The tongue of thought goes on licking its way through life depositing a trail, which determines much of the blueprint for its future encounters, its karma to be. The heat is that measure of the jiva, which directs the machinery of the corporeal form, the manifestation of desire through thought, word and action. And for the thrust we must consider these determiners: how the nutrients are used, how the breaths are consumed, how the heart beats and how often and how long. All of these represent the twisting dynamic of the will of man. Seemingly his own and seemingly boundless, it is a direct result of the jiva's allotment which is rooted upon prior actions and recorded as its karma. You getting the picture here, Mr. Rahms? Stop the burning. Maximize the spirit's power by uncovering the truth.

"Now that we have defined the width and breadth of karma and its trickle down mathematics, let us get back to the flavors of karma. One type, the present type of karma, is that which prescribes the blueprint for the experiences we are now undergoing. These must be endured by us daily and include all the major considerations for one's corporeal circumstances. How much wealth we are going to have, how much health we are going to enjoy or suffer, how much fame and fortune will come our way, how much employment or unemployment we will receive, how much pain and how much pleasure we are going to experience. All these things are pre-determined; moreover, we resolutely confirmed them prior to our entrance into the bodies, which we now inhabit. This is the script of our current existence mapped out on the palms of our hands, on the soles of our feet and on the breadth of our foreheads. Only a true clairvoyant artist can interpret those maps effectively. An artist who reads and fathoms the Akashic records well enough to do it with justice in the light and knowledge of the Beyond. And that person, my Friend, is very, very rare. Furthermore, you should know this. I'm not one of them. And neither are you.

"This type of karma, which we have been discussing, is termed present karma. The Vedic pundits call it by the name of Prahlabda. With every thoughtful construct, spoken utterance, and manifested deed, we have been making these karmas for eons and eons. With every lifetime we terminate, whether it be that of a human or any other species, all those events of that lifespan have been recorded and tallied up. When the map or blueprint of our forthcoming lifetime is to be made, many of the karmas from our preceding incarnation are used, but only a partial allotment of those karmas are utilized to form the upcoming corporeal vehicle. The remainder is not undergone immediately. This slice of the karmic pie is shifted into a virtual storage bin or warehouse to be let out at a later time, in a later body, when the proper time arrives for its usage. These warehoused karmas are doled out as they are required. Unfortunately, they are never exhausted. These stored karmas are the Past karmas and the Pundits

The Moon Women

have documented them with the term of Sanchit.

"As we continue to generate karmic events from all the events in our present life, we create the karmas, which are the freshest and the most current. These are our active karmas and bear the label of Kriyaman in the Vedic Dharma. Only a moderate slice of them are rerouted and woven back into our active karmic load in this life itself. These less substantial events are reconciled in this fashion. The bulk of the iceberg of karma is resolved from the present type, those debts, which demand payment in this life itself. These karmas are static and will only finish up in this lifetime. The active karmas that have not been touched at all in this life move into the repository for availability for use in future lifetimes. When we have burned through all our present karmas chiseled into this life unit's blueprint, we die. Our atman moves into the after-death planes, the six Bardos, and we receive the polar judgment concerning the positives and the negatives. Depending upon the outcome of that battle, our future life unfolds.

"What we will receive for our forthcoming turn on the wheel of transmigration will depend primarily on what we have done during our present turn on the wheel. The process is endless, measureless, and unavoidable. What's more, it is next to impossible to get the human body in successive lifetimes, unless at some point in our present life we contact the one and only force or entity, which has extricated itself from this entangled net of karma via persevering a path of self-discovery. That one is immensely difficult to track down, Mr. Rahms. I am sure you will have quite a time searching for it." Dr. Krishnaswami ended the lesson.

Searching for and finding this rare and illusive force, whatever it might be, is the story you are about to read. The jolts which you will encounter during this odyssey may shake up much of what you have learned is common knowledge. Venturing deeper into the eye-openers in this book is not advisable for the faint of heart or for those who are not prepared to witness true visions from the Beyond. It's my job to water down the dismay of this jarring news by entwining it with scenarios, which evoke love interests. It is only from having been persecuted by the Khrng and thus having a full understanding of whom and what they are that this author has come to realize this is the most successful method for unlinking most readers from the lethal grasp of these parasites. So take a moment and prepare yourself for what you are about to learn.

- 13 -

It was sixteen years earlier, back in '55, when it all started, the thing with the windows. Bear with me because divulging this secret is downright painful. This might not have been the first time, but it was the first time I can recollect now after my opening gambit with the ceiling, which was further confirmed by the arrival of the guiding swing chair.

As I twisted in my vortex Time basket, the images of my childhood back on that day in Marshfield repainted themselves on the underside of my eyelids. Out of this kaleidoscope of neural unlacing, the north shore of Massachusetts came into view and, more specifically, a private beach. Running the entire coastline, this waterway is the only beach, which can claim the true status of being completely private. Even the National Seashore Parks on Cape Cod and all the swimming areas surrounding Truro are open to the public. This four hundred meter stretch of sand in Marshfield is the prime yardage of a remarkable community known by the local residents as Rexhame Terrace.

Originally, fourteen summer accommodations were built at the close of the nineteenth century; back in the day, they were the "spec" houses of their generation. Each one was a two story built upon stone pilings having no cellar. A roofed porch encircled the perimeter of the ground level. Put together by the hands of stewards and the sweat of oarsmen hailing from the whalers, each home was sided with rough, cedar shakes requiring constant maintenance. These periodic upgrades brought about varying shades of tan and gray as the hard winters beat against the raw wood. Numerous double-hung bays had hurricane shutters for further protection against the ocean's maelstroms, which blew in off the outer banks. The fascinating aspect of each one of these dwellings was its "widows walk," a miniature railed porch atop the peak of the mansard roof where the wives of the whalers would wait and watch for their men to return from waging war on the leviathans of the deep.

Presumably looking out for his family, my Dad bought ours for a meager twelve thousand big ones back in '52. He figured it would save him the expense of providing exciting summer vacations

The Moon Women

for his offspring by serving as (his words) an in-house faraway paradise every year. In mid-June, we would all pile into the big station wagon and head off to Marshfield as we abandoned whichever suburb of Boston we might have been residing within at the time. We enjoyed this vacationland until the end of August or even the after Labor Day, if classes had not yet begun. This was both exciting as well as exceedingly boring: exciting because it was an astonishing environment to spend the summer, what with the ocean and all the surrounding activities; boring because it was always the same neighbors and the same scenes every single day of every single summer. It would grow on you like barnacles on a boulder.

Once in August 1954, at the ripe old age of 10, I cranked out my first Einsteinian move, which I hatched to break up the monotony of summer life much in the same way Albert played with his trains I hear. I invented what I decided to advertise as "The Carnival of the Century." After planning the layout for over a dozen arcades, I proposed to entertain all the vacationers living in Rexhame with devilish games of fun. In the primary booth, run by Peter Hartman, my co-partner in crime, there was an overturned bicycle with playing cards clothes-pinned at an angle to the spokes of the rear wheel. As he cranked the big wheel round and round using one of the pedals as a handle, it didn't take long before it was rapidly whirling and the clickety-clack of the playing cards slapping against the spokes let loose with carnival gaiety. Since I had painted one of the forks white, when the wheel stopped it would signal the winning number.

When Hartman got a taker, the bet was a buck on whichever card it might stop. Nailing it correctly was the only way to win, which (compared to some of the other games) was considerably difficult. The big prize was my Dad's portal television set. Fortunately, Dad never showed up for any of the fun. He was too busy commiserating with his best pal, Jack Daniels, over the Red Sox and why they had lost with such humiliating ineptness.

In this way, there were no payouts and the whole shebang progressed quite successfully. The prizes, consisting mostly of things I had stolen from my sister's room, were rarely, if ever, actually won, but everyone had a terrific time pissing away their hard-earned cash at the games. Sometimes they would keep working the wheel for hours to win a prize before giving up and moving onto an adjacent scheme of super pilfering.

I, myself, manned the plate smashing booth. This one was the most popular. I had spent weeks going door to door throughout the Terrace asking the neighbors if they wanted to contribute something for the Rexhame Grand Carnival coming soon to a neighborhood near them. It was a worthy cause. They loved this con so much that when I inquired if they wouldn't mind donating any unused plates or any other china or dishes with which they could part for the plate smashing arcade, they were only too happy to drag out armloads of old China and dishes. To my astonishment, I amassed a mountain of worn out crockery, enough to choke a horse.

The beachhead stocked all the stones needed for smashing the crockery. All I had to do was persuade a handful of the bigger kids to go down and cart as many wheelbarrows of baseball sized rocks up the long path to my back porch. Boy, were they stupid. I could have ordered them to haul the rocks back down to the dunes, dump them off and then drag the same rocks back over the cobbled footpath ad on infinitum; the same way a legendary muscle bound chap hauled a huge boulder to the top of a hill only to have it roll back down over and over like a fool. But I was a kinder, gentler type of devil. I was a man of destiny, you might say.

In the back of our house, there was a dilapidated carriage stable for horses. And in between the primary framework and the stable there was a little shed, which originally served as an outhouse. In the early sixties, Dad converted it into a bathroom. Its original eighty-year plus door remained where it had begun life. Even though he safeguarded the wood, he removed the useless hardware and tossed the ancient doorknob into the garbage. Eliminating the need for a key, he substituted the lockset with a manual levered latch for easy access. Thus, the dismissed device left behind a dilapidated keyhole, which now presented an indisputable invitation for youthful adventures.

I spent many rain-soaked afternoons planning my marauding raids on that dismantled bunch of tumblers to peek through its pleasure tunnel. Depending on whom the occupants were, my adolescence was rapidly catching up to me. I was occasionally transfixed counting how many wipes the neighborhood gals had to expend before ungluing their derrieres from the yawning oval. One rainy noontime when I was feeling particularly adventuresome, Phyllis Wallace busted me as I spied on her through that sinister

The Moon Women

keyhole. After taking a shot at poking my eye out with her nail file, she screamed out her fix for my ogling syndrome sending me fleeing off the screened porch and down toward the dark dunes.

"Mary said unto the angel, how can this be, seeing I know not this scoundrel?" [4]

Even though I couldn't mistake her swear words chasing me off from that frowzy hole, her threats didn't stop me the next time. It wasn't until many moons later when I discovered why I was so drawn to the compulsion of starring into small holes or investigating openings into the unknown. Inexplicably, it was the principle reason I was able to escape from the Khrng that day while floating over the fields.

One redolent summer, I spent all my time assembling model airplanes in my bedroom. Whatever ventilation that bottled-up space provided didn't do much for positive life. Since it abutted the rear porch there wasn't sufficient air movement. Quite regularly, the fumes from the modeling glues succeeded in getting the better of me. Many a time after banging on my door and receiving dead silence, my parents would pry it open only to find me collapsed onto the linoleum after an exhaustive dogfight. As a fitting sendoff right after Labor Day that summer, I crawled out onto the barn roof and enacted a titanic battle in which the Japs destroyed every winged fighter before I tumbled off onto the porch. No broken bones though.

I wasn't quite sure whom the Japs were, but I knew they were badass. They were as bad as bad could be. I knew this because my father would rant and rave over them 'til the cows came home while imbibing heated inspiration from his bottle of Jack No. 7. The following summer I got into racing hot cars. I was convinced super cars would not be as dangerous as fighter planes. Plus surprisingly, the Old Man could drive quite well when he was drunk. In spite of not having any challenging road enemies I knew of, he was constantly on his guard. On numerous occasions, he acted as though the mafia were tailing him.

The plate smashing continued throughout the weekend and the wherewithal from this lollapalooza kept rolling in. I was absolutely massacring them. At sundown, I split the profits with Peter, who didn't know any better. He bought the reasons I had enumerated in a handwritten list of expenses and after stuffing my excuses down his throat, I walked off with most of the cash. It was a hefty sum, which totaled to well over eighty-seven and change. I was going to spend it all on a bow and arrow set, but Dad put his foot down with a big "No" to that. This led to a catfight fight at the dinner table between him and my Mom who was always arguing in my favor.

"Look, Jack, the boy's on the verge of a manic depressive mess. Let him have the damn thing. What the hell do you think can happen? That he's going to shoot you in the back? If that was ever going to be the death of you, I would have done it years ago!" She not only had a good point; she had also won the battle.

I stapled the paper target onto a pyramid of hay bales. On its background, there was an outermost blue circle, then an orange one followed by a thinner yellow band ending with the crimson bulls-eye at the center. I had some ten meters of lawn on our border of the house, which abutted the O'Donahue's. I drew the string back and let the arrow fly off in the approximate vicinity of my intended striking point. I considered it the optimum trajectory for success. The arrow flew over the bales by a good meter barely missing the little blonde O'Donahue girl.

"Yikes!"

I bellowed as I looked here and there to determine if anyone had noticed my miscalculation. As she picked dandelions amidst the yellow melilot clover, she was oblivious to the danger overhead, which prompted my life saving measures.

"Sarah! Oh, Sarah." I yelled. "Your Mommy's calling you. You might head home and find out what she wants." I was only protecting her from herself. I feared she might fall out like Memnon.

As her screen door slammed behind her, I plucked another arrow from my trusty quiver. This one was going to be a winner. I just knew it. I definitely had no idea what the hell I was doing. I had no training, nor had I really ever seen anybody get instructions on how to do this. Something was driving me via innate instinct and I loved it. I suspected it was some order of medieval manual training.

"Release!" I shouted aloud to myself.

The arrow flew out of my hands with a twangy singsong. It stabbed the hay bale nicely kissing the fringe of the blue circle, right on the target's periphery. At least I was on the paper. As I declared myself marksman extraordinaire, unbeknownst to me riding high on

The Moon Women

the widows-walk stood a little blue man with a peacock feather in his hat.

. These and other fun activities rounded out the pastimes in the course of our eleven to twelve week vacations. We also got to frequent our beachside residence on the weekends or the holidays throughout the year.

I'm sorry if it seems like it is taking forever to explain the heart of the matter, what I intended to tell you in the first place, the openings out of hell, or whatever. It's just that the whole thing is rather difficult for me to deal with at times. One never knows if finally confessing it will cause it (and this would be the worst possibility) to continue forever; or (and this would be the less gruesome outcome) cause it to never repeat, which might be preferable, just not particularly news worthy.

Both of my parents chose this vacation spot to be what the Old Man branded as "The Last Stop." She had her fifth and terminal coronary there the summer of 1967. And he was sent from the Terrace to the Deaconess Hospital to have his intestines fixed, an operation which drained him of more energy than he could have afforded. While he languished in the recovery ward of the Deaconess, I was with him prior to the bitter end. We shared an awkward and disjointed one-way conversation during which he disclosed a significant and sinister element of doom. The fifth floor of that hospital was rampant with pneumonia germs. If they put him over there to recuperate, he wasn't going to get out alive. Sure enough, that's where they stuck him after his operation and he died in October of 1977.

It was late in the year because in 1972, he had the domicile winterized for year-round occupation, but he only got five years out of it before he expired. All in all though, he got reasonably decent mileage from the little summer spot. It figures out to a tad over $25 per day over the 25 years that he got to use it. After he was gone, my sister and I couldn't agree on what to do with it, so in 1978 we sold it for $98,000. Twenty-five years later, it was my understanding it was on the market for well over one point two million. In the last hour, its location as the only private seaside in the Massachusetts caught up with it. Its memorability was at last memorialized.

Sorry. More M words from my syndrome of mumania. It's unavoidable. You'll get used to it. Be glad you can't catch it from reading this book. It's something you can only get after having been abducted by the ultra-race and stuck in a phrenic oven for what seemed days, but was really only minutes. The significant factor with regard to the Marshfield connection was that I was never visited by the Khrng there; only in the other environs like the Adirondacks and the Hudson River valley. However, it was the first place where I knowingly confronted the vents in the fabric of Time/Space, the openings of horror and what came out from the Beyond. As far as I can tell at this fragile point in the process, these experiences have changed me considerably.

- 14 -

As I've already said that's when it came to me initially, my problem with the windows. It was the summer of '56. I was preparing to go into the seventh grade at Wellesley Junior High School that coming fall. One day in late August due to a special invitation from two of my summertime friends, George Marsh and Carl Beauchesne, I spent nearly eight hours swimming way out in the ocean off a jetty in Brant Rock. Carl's Dad had offered to take us out on his trawler for the day to do some diving with snorkels. I was pretending that I was a manatee or, when others weren't looking, a merman chasing mermaids.

I swam for the entire afternoon out on that breakwater deeply immersed in the cold currents without ever leaving to acclimate. Even though on board ship they had outfitted me with a wet suit on my uppers for protection, everything below the belt had been severely overexposed to the frigid temperatures of the lower depths as I investigated the murky haunts of lobsters and sand crabs. This oversight had allowed all of the warmth to drain out of me to such an extent that when I finally climbed out of the ocean, I was the color of the underbelly of a starfish - deathly white. Nonetheless, even after I got home I didn't detect anything unusual or out of the ordinary right away.

That evening I enjoyed my regular activities of dinner with the family followed by an hour of Huntley-Brinkley with the Old Man and then I turned in. Following a decent night's sleep right after breakfast, I hoofed it down to the waterfront and had a good swim as usual. But when I came out after surfing the waves my body was

The Moon Women

coated with an ugly rash. It looked like some manifestation of a marine maculation, like a leopard with the measles; plus it itched. I showed it to my Dad as well as to his associate, Frank Wallace, who was staying with us that summer. Dad always had one or two couples over at some point during the summer months to partake with the liquid refreshments and provide sparing partners for his fiery brand of conversation.

Uncle Frank, as we came to call him, suggested that quite possibly I had tangled with some jellyfish. He'd seen them floating in the waves when he took his dip that day. Since these jellyfish frequented the shoreline in the late summer, he surmised it was probably that. Patiently he suggested I should wash without using any soap and then lightly pat dry with a soft towel. He assured me the rash would quickly disappear. I did this and just as he had claimed, the rash faded away overnight.

The next day directly after my morning chores I hiked down the sandy footway for my swim. Since it was low tide, I waded way out and dove into the breakers. Sure enough after I came out of the waves, the same ruby red rash besieged me all over my extremities. It was beginning to annoy me, moreover, this time I was also feeling a little woozy. So I called it a day and jogged back to the house. Upon disrobing, I followed the suggestion of my Dad's colleague, had a quick shower, and patted dry. Like before, the rash disappeared in an hour or so.

At dinner, everyone was commenting on what the heck could have attacked me because no one had seen any jellyfish in the ocean that day. They told me which food not to eat. They told me which stuff not to do. Above all question, if it was up to them they would have barred me from certain television programming because of its obvious toxic effects on the thinking of young people.

When I dove into the breakers on the morrow, I didn't get in too deep before I was rapidly overcome with the agonizing welts a third time. In a flash, I attempted to reverse my direction in the waves but I lost count of which way was which. Somehow, I managed to reach the shore and when I came out, I had to bend down, and put my hands on my knees for a minute.

Aunt Phyllis saw me having trouble and sprinted over to give me a hand. The world had started to spin slightly and I felt like heaving up my guts onto the sand. I told my Aunt I wasn't feeling all

124

that well and then I collapsed onto the sandy shore. She called for her husband and then made one of her off the wall conclusions. She claimed she could see the angels of the Lord hovering above me as if they were waiting for something. I had always surmised she needed to have her cerebral digits logged more effectively but she insisted the angel had come down and proclaimed:

"He shall receive power only after the Holy Ghost has come upon him." [5]

I was getting quite dizzy and could no longer sit up so I lay out flat on the warm sand. My swim trunks were all sandy underneath and I didn't like the itchy feeling in there. I turned sideways to view my legs, which were all blotchy with upraised lumps of bloodshot flesh ringed with milky borders and I hatched my parting thought.

"This can't be good."

I looked up at the spinning clouds and then totally conked out.

When Uncle Frank and Aunt Phyllis got together, they watched me lying there passed out on the sand for a few seconds before making their diagnosis. Since I was all covered with blotches, which had caused my unconscious state, they made several remarkably keen decisions at lightning speed. One of them made a beeline for home base to get my Dad and the other one stayed to protect me from drowning as the tides advanced in the interim. I regained consciousness momentarily and watched the sky and the sea exchange places. When I uttered a comment on the local color, I realized something was going on that I couldn't get my head around and then I too coughed up a postphrenic turdball:

"Stand in the gate of the Lord and hear his word." [6]

Then I blacked out for good as the spirit of the highest came over me.

Back at home base, Uncle Frank informed my father of what had happened. My Old Man deduced the situation was critical. In a flash, he jumped into the family's Detroit wonder and drove all the way down the narrow track through the huckleberry shrubs and the beach grass, over the dunes, across the band of stones and right onto the beach a few meters from where my lifeless body lay helpless baking in the sun. He threw me into the back of the gas-guzzler and took off for Marshfield Heights like a hot load out of rifle.

The Moon Women

Ahead of my Dad's manful assault of the beachhead, back at the house Uncle Frank had phoned over to a Dr. Cohen who was standing by in emergency mode bracing for our arrival. Like Joseph, who was afraid to be the father of the Messiah, this Cohen guy was amped to the hilt. Two naps back he had seen this nightmare unfolding on his office floor like a vision of bad blood on a lintel. After having kissed his mezuzah piously, he paced to and fro wringing his hands and swearing a blue streak awaiting the coming of the devil.

"Baruk Ator Adonai. God help me with this one." Dr. Cohen muttered to himself.

One score I'll concede with regard to the Old Man was that should a clutch play come at him he was always on his toes and solid as a rock. Even if he had had some highballs in him or the shit had the fan, my father was like a stone cold bulldozer. He was not only as cool as a cucumber but also articulate and decisive. Furthermore, he employed extra-ordinary precision in the fulfillment of any goal he set his mind on. And that included driving. As Uncle Frank proceeded to imitate Roger Ward on the Indie racetrack as he strained to keep up with the Old Man on his jet-fired plunge down Route 139 toward Marshfield center, it was useless. Uncle Frank later updated me how my father was nowhere on the radar.

"Jack must have been busting the century mark on his race to save your life, Kiddo." Frank reconnoitered in advance of running it public.

The Old Man backed the rocket fueled Chevy straight up to the main entrance of the doctor's office knocking over a little statue of a black guy in a gaudy red riding outfit. Dad hopped out and with the aid of this obese doctor, they both jockeyed me into the lobby littered with brochures and pamphlets explaining every malady from pregnancy to peritonitis. As my world went white once more, I keeled over onto the braided rug, belly up. And then the strangest thing happened.

Instantly I was viewing the room below me from a raw and divergent perspective. Apparently, I had popped out of my body like a pea out of its pod. Somehow, unbelievably the waves of gravity had split themselves into two poles, because my Dad and the bald doctor were pacing on my ceiling, which used to be the floor. Glued to my old ceiling, which was now my new floor, I was shocked to find my plane of existence was all topsy-turvy. When I looked up at what should have been down, I saw my father and the dumpling doctor scuffling back and forth kicking at a ragged rug, which tugged at their feet unawares its worn threads flapped away while twirling in the winds of a sickly inverted world. They kept arguing over what to do with me and whether or not I was dead or alive. As they parted ways with fists drawn, lo and behold, there was Rahm Ibsen, lying on his deathbed! Well, if that was me, who the hell was I?

It was so strange to see this. Moreover, clear as a bell I could understand everything they were saying. My Old Man was rabid and foaming at the bit with his usual ejaculatory vomit. Stomping on the crisscross chevrons of the carpet's geometrics, the pudgy doctor was flapping his arms like an albatross attempting to gain some lift and claim authority over my father. A handful of white feathers fluttered down onto my dead body below me. I wasn't sure if the feathers were from him or some other gravitational drift.

Not only could I clearly examine this other place, but there was something else going on here. With the two Einsteins above me battling over my wellbeing, another hook from this altered realm dug its claws into me. Manifesting next to a Norman Rockwell painting of a boy with his pants down something troubling crawled out. Swaying sideways on the doctor's paneling and right above Norman's national treasure was a shining metallic rectangle. It seemed odd to find such a weird thing in a doctor's office because it looked like it should belong in an amusement park. As the pantomime in the pits bogged down like molasses, the argent frame gradually came into focus. It gained an undeniable permanence within the other dimension into which I had been vaulted when I died.

When I shifted my head into its imaginary wind, my cerebral glide caused its door to open. Unfolding itself like Venetian shades, the electroplated matrix unzipped its lower seam to divulge a ghastly field of utter blackness. Presently it began to harvest a crop of stars. I peered into that diamond studded tunnel to discern anything at all which might resemble a planet or even a moon, something recognizable, something to tell me I might be watching through a hole in a planetarium, but no such luck.

From out of the darkened recess, a streak of intense light rocketed from one brink to the other and then balled itself on the insides of the orifice. The erratic floating rectangle had a wet filmy covering on its entrance like the membrane of a bubble. As I reached out to touch it, without warning it bulged out at me as if something from the other side was intent on coming through the blockage. I waited and to my horror, the balled up bottom of a pot pushed out or what seemed to be a metal globe maybe. As this elongated projection proceeded to enter my topsy-turvy universe from the other side, I tried to run but I was upside down on an inverted ceiling, so I couldn't move an inch. And then something terrifying issued forth out of that threshold!

Pushing passed the placental film, which shielded my perception from that other region, as if some invading energy, the thing manifested itself by appropriating a humanoid shape, one body part after the other. After the bubble covering shredded, I was horrified to witness a hand at first followed by its two arms. But then its leg came in as well as a torso and finally a chromium head which resembled a flattened football. It rose to a staggering height and when the Klatubaratu turned to confront me, I could see its entire body was covered with teeny burning feathers like flaming tinsel.

As the entity blossomed into tangibility, its fire flakes revved up and I had to shield my eyes. My mind told me it must be hot but I could sense no actual heat from it, only a radiating energy. Two oblong circles materialized in its nickel-plated mask like miniature wheels turning within wheels. As the metallic lights of the two outer wheels revolved, so did the inner wheels gradually rotate the other way like sparks within glassy marbles. These were its eyes, I guessed, spheres of bice green crystals spinning like miniscule moons. When fully opened, they burned as if piercing turquoise egg-shaped eyes. As my vision connected with the being's laser gaze, a rising buzz saw of crackling chimes burned its mentis flares into the pulse of my brain frames with an indescribable pain. And then I received its words, its message, like blinding scalpels slicing into my cortical tissues.

UNTO THE ANGEL OF THE CHURCH [7]

SALUTATION OF AN ANGEL
OH, HELLO TO YOU SIR
CITIZEN OF HUMANITY

BE NOT DEAD
BUT OF LIFE   PAY ATTENTION TO ME

128

THESE ARE THE THINGS
WHICH ARE THE FIRST
AND THE LAST   THIS IS IMPORTANT

AS THE ALPHA AND THE OMEGA
THIS WITNESS HATH NEED TO HONOUR
                         I HAVE EXPERIENCE

AND PLACE YOUR PRESENCE
                         I WILL ENLIGHTEN YOU

WITHIN THE WORLD OF THE WHITE
                    WITH THAT WHICH LIVES
                    IN REALMS OF WHITE MATTER

AS LEGION *TO ABADDON*
                         I SERVE ABADDON

COUNSEL OF PHILADELPHIA
                    AS COUNSEL UNDER PHILADELPHIA

AND THE SON OF MAN
                    AND CARRY THE SEEDS OF MAN

I CARRY THE MARK OF AZRAEL
                    MY NAME IS AZRAEL
                    AND MY TITLE IS

KING OF THE ANGELS

I COME TO YOUR PLACE OF LIFE
                         AS I VISIT WITH YOU

I KNOW YOUR WORKS
                         I EMPATHIZE WITH ALL

AND YOUR TRIBULATIONS AND POVERTY
                         OF YOUR PROBLEMS.

I KNOW YOUR BLASPHEMY [8]
                    I KNOW ABOUT YOUR DIFFICULTIES

FEAR NONE OF THOSE THINGS
                    BUT DON'T WORRY

WHICH YOU SUFFER
                    ABOUT ANY OF THAT.

129

The Moon Women

BEHOLD THE FILTHY GLASS DEVILS

THE HORRID MUTANTS

MAY ONE DAY CAST YOU INTO A PRISON

WILL PUT YOU IN PRISON

THAT YOU MAY BE TRIED

YOU MAY BE CONVICTED

AND YOU SHALL HAVE TRIBULATIONS

AND SUFFER THE CONSEQUENCES

TEN DAYS, NAY TEN YEARS

FOR 10 DAYS AND THEN FOR 10 YEARS

BUT BE FAITHFUL UNTO DEATH

BUT DON'T LOSE HEART

AND I WILL GIVE YOU

AND I WILL TEACH YOU

A CROWN OF LIFE [9]

A SPECIAL SECRET FEW KNOW

Azrael stepped forward and placed his hand upon his chest.

A DOOR WAS OPENED IN HEAVEN

THIS IS A DESCRIPTION

AND THE FIRST VOICE OF AN ANGEL
WAS AS IT WERE A TRUMPET SPEAKING TO AB
CALLING YOU TO COME UP HITHER

TELLING HIM TO LISTEN

AND I WILL SHOW YOU THINGS

AGAIN THIS IS AN ANGEL

WHICH WILL BE HEREAFTER [10]

SAYING HE WILL SHARE THINGS

IN THESE THINGS I HAVE WITNESS

OF WHICH HE HAS KNOWLEDGE

A VACUUM OF DEATH THE ANGEL DESCRIBES
DWELLS IN THE AIR WHAT HAPPENS WHEN
OVER A VAST PLAIN THE ANGELS FIGHT WITH

OF GOLDEN WHEAT

THE KHRNG OVER THE WHEAT

AT THE MOUTH

AT THE OPENING

OF THIS OPENING

THERE IS A LOUD SOUND

BUGLES AT THE THROAT

THAT PULLS THE DEFEATED

LIKE TWO HORNS WHICH

INSIDE AND COMPRESSES IT

SOUND OUT THE SINS FOR

INTO VIBRATIONS THAT CAN BE

THE UNJUST VOICE OF SATAN

SUCKED INTO ANOTHER WORLD

THE LORD OF DEATH BORE WITNESS

THIS PROCESS WAS DESIGNED

TO THIS PLATFORM OF DEEDS

BY THE ONE WHO CREATED THIS WORLD

AS THE LOYAL RECEIVER

THE ANGELS ABIDE BY THESE RULES

OF HIS MESSAGE LIKE RED CRYSTAL

THEY APPLY THE REGAL GUIDELINES

AND ORANGE CARNELIAN AND

THEY ENLIST THE NOBLE TRUTHS

BRIGHT GREEN CUBES ADORNED

THEY UNDERTAKE THE RESULTS

WITH THE SHAPES OF EYES

AND EXTINGUISH THE MUTANTS

HAVE LENT TRUE KNOWLEDGE

VIA THEIR KNOWHOW THEY PAY TRIBUTE

TO THE SUFFERING ONES

TO THOSE WHO HAVE BEEN ABUSED

THE THRONE WAS SURROUNDED

SOMETHING LIKE FUNERAL RIGHTS

BY A VESTURE OF COLOURED LIFE

ARE ARRANGED FOR THE DEAD

A RAINBOW WHEEL OF BLISS

MANY JOYFUL COLORS

AND FOUR AND TWENTY VIALS

SURROUNDS THE 24 VIALS THAT HOLD

131

The Moon Women

WILL CONTAIN THE DEAD REMNANTS

WHAT IS LEFT OF THE MUTANTS

SOON TO BE TRODDEN TO DUST

TO BE PLANTED INTO THE PAST

IN THE WALL OF THE ALL TIME

AND CEMENTED INTO TIME

FOR EVER AND EVER   FOREVER

The champion angel resettled his enormous wings and continued with his bluster.

AS THE SEED OF YOUR WINGS

IMAGINE HOW MUCH

ARE TO BE ADDED UNTO THE

THIS FEAT WILL ADD

BEGINNING OF YOUR END

TO WHAT WILL COME

I AZRAEL LEGION *OF ABADDON*
SON OF MAN AND FROM THE
DOMINION OF PHILADELPHIA
I DO HEREBY   STALWARTLY
GIVE YOU THIS NEWS   I GIVE YOU THIS NEWS

I COME FROM THE SEED OF LIFE   AS AN ANGEL
GIVER OF THE DIVINE TREE   I HAVE THE SAME DESIGN
I HAVE NEED OF WITNESS   AS YOU AND EXPERIENCE
FROM THE UNWRITTEN PAGES

THE SAME THINGS AS YOU LIVE

LIVING IN THE WHITE BOOK

IN YOUR REALM OF WHITE MATTER

YOU ARE WORTHY TO TAKE THIS BOOK   I AM CONFIDENT
AND TO OPEN THE SEALS THEREOF

THAT YOU WILL TAKE THESE IDEAS

FOR YOU WERE SLAIN TRUE

AND OVERCOME ALL DIFFICULTIES

AND HAVE REDEEMED YOUR SOUL

132

BECAUSE OF YOUR HEART

BY THE BLOOD AND BY THE WIND [11]

DRIVEN BY HISTORY AND FATE

YOU MUST MEASURE YOURSELVES

IN THE SAME WAY

IN THE SAME MANNER

TRUST IN US AS WELL

PASS THIS TREASURE THROUGH
THE DOOR OF YOUR PLEASURE
AND FIRM WILL   SERIOUSLY CONSIDER THESE IDEAS
AS MY MASK IS MY TASK

MY INSISTENCE IS AS MY MISSION

AS LOVE WILL CONQUER TIME

(STATEMENT OF THE LAW OF PINDA)

FOR I AM AZRAEL   I AM AZRAEL

     It looked like the Time messenger might be turning down its flame jacket since it stalled for a bit, a hesitation in preparation for its departure I trusted. After the demon bars ceased hammering into my consciousness, the blazing anodized flames subsided and the flaring tinsel flakes first dimmed and then died out altogether. The agonal sentient compacted its contour nearing the split in Time and before the titan could draw out any added deliverances it abruptly projected itself in through the burnished frame and was gone.

     The ribbon of silky foil descended closing off the shifting fairyland from my view, thus restricting all further access to this experience. That is, until the knowledge menus were awakened within me when I beheld the vision of the White cast down from the lofty limits of my divided spaces in Cooketown where the enraptured chair became instrumental in reconstructing the entire prophecy like a white book handed down from out of the ceiling.

     After this interruption upon my anguished plight, I peered down upon this deviant clinic and noticed the recalcitrant physician was angling to protect his insurance premiums by lowering the boom on my father.

     "Get him out of here! Get him the hell out of my office, now! The little bastard's slipped into anaphylaxis! He's not going to die

133

The Moon Women

here! I'm not insured for that! Get him the fuck outa here!" The fat doctor's expletives befouled all the clinical appliances with more scathing blather and other more outrageous sullied expressions.

My father was screaming for him to give me an injection of epinephrine, but the draggy pants doctor was yanking me by the malleolus of my ankles unsuccessfully endeavoring to drag me back out through the door. As my noggin bumpitty-bumped over the sill plate, I saw some stars and wondered if astronomy would be in my future.

The reason the Khrng do not display any malleoli is because they have genetically reengineered much of their skeletal appendages in favor of complying with the increased demands of weightless longevity.

- 15 -

As I watched this ruckus in frozen silence, an ambulance with a big red cross finalized its port of call. The frazzled paramedics unfolded their gurney and hoisted me onto it. This act of total benevolence caused the bilateral laws of the cloned duality to collapse. Flat on my back on the thin bed, I looked up at my father from a more normal perspective. Dad was waiting patiently on the same ground upon which I would walk again soon. He squeezed my hand as they carried me over to the yawning mouth of the ambulance and fed me inside.

The Old Man rode with me all the way over to the Plymouth Hospital. By the time we approached the emergency entrance, I was as right as rain. Nevertheless, in spite my personal evaluation that my condition was completely normal, they triple folded the gurney back out onto the tarmac and trundled me in through the disorienting glass doors which revolved like a merry-go-round.

"Can you walk, Son?" He inquired timidly. He had scaled down his assiduity rate of due diligence.

"Sure, Dad. I'm okay now." I felt my response was measured and fitting, but they put me into a wheelchair anyway and stuck me in the hospital. With swiveling hips, the candy stripper escorted me upstairs to a private ward and smiled her hearty welcome. I thought perhaps further introductions were in order but my father's close doctor friend, Dr. Hymen Nederman, came into the room instead.

134

"We're going to do some tests, young man. I assure you, we're going to get to the bottom of this. I think I know what it is, but first I'm going to perform one or two tests to be certain; to eliminate those possibilities which are outside the norm, if that's okay with you."

He seemed nice and what's more, he seemed unusually attentive to the details. He pointed out my forearm persisted in displaying trace remnants of the rash. To this day, I still present a subtle marbling there. I don't think the mark was caused by anything else, especially not from my one abduction with the Khrng, although, I can't be totally positive of that. Two shakes of a jiffy later, he came back for my appointment for him to take a look at my arm and find out what had happened to me.

"Do you have any pets?" He welcomed me while fondling the triangular rubber end of a miniature mallet, something to test how much pain I could take no doubt.

"No. Not really. What's that?" Always finish with a question if you're lying.

"Doctor's call this a plexor, but you can call it my toy hammer. In point of fact, it's harmless. I use it to test a patient's reflexes. It works like this. Here let me show you." As he gently held the malleolus of my ankle, he tapped the joint on my knee with the prong end of the tool. My leg jerked up when he unlocked its spring.

"It's not broken so why fix it? My Dad says."

"Very well. No problem. It looks fine there. Sure no pets, no fuzzy creatures in the household?"

"Nope. Nothing fuzzy but my sister." Glaring smile on that one.

That was my statement on all the facts, though I knew otherwise. It had only been a few weeks earlier when I had trapped a baby Kestrel in my butterfly net. I had been training her in my screened-in porch to be my pet falcon and my friend; I called her Monami. Many of our neighbors including the O'Donahues and the Marshalls voted to liberate the bird. Even the Wallaces demanded I should let her go to fly free while professing this macaronic.

"Be it unto him *secundum* with the word. The *falcon* should depart from here." [12]

The Moon Women

"If you could kindly go over and sit in the exam chair over there, I'll be with you in a minute or two." His bedside manner continued to be assuring.

The day on which I had set my beloved pet flacon free my Mom had her first cardiac moment and I knew why. You can't unlock the ones who become captured by your love. Nederman came back after only fifteen minutes with a tray containing something hidden under a towel.

"We are going to test you with this rare and unusual substance. So, please do not be alarmed." He was making me acutely anxious now.

After gently grasping my forearm and turning it over, he plucked out a cotton ball with his tweezers, dipped it in a cup, and swabbed my arm with it. A whiff of a horrible smell nearly gagged me and I twitched back.

"Don't despair. It's only isopropyl alcohol. It won't hurt you."

"Yeah? I'll bet that's what they told my Old Man right before they hooked him on their devil juice."

"What's that? Listen. Don't worry about that. Your father has more stresses on his mind than Tesla had wires."

He removed the cloth and exposed the mystery substance. Ice cubes! He's got ice cubes. He chose the largest one and set it firmly down on my arm, which he swaddled with sterile gauze finally wrapping the combo in a napkin.

"Surprised? This won't hurt you either. Let's see what happens with it. It's my experience it will tell us what the culprit is." He advised with a twitch of his moustache.

"Couldn't be worse than the beachfront on which I died." I knew I had been born during the Normandy invasion but couldn't remember it right then.

"Yes, well, please sit quietly for ten minutes. Then, we will resume the operation by uncovering your arm. Then we'll find out what's what." I could tell he was pleased as punch it was all going so well.

By the way, the Khrng don't have any malleoli on their shins, but you already knew that, didn't you? If you don't, it is an indication your brain has also been eaten once, if not more often, depending on your memory loss graphics.

- 16 -

Dr. Nederman returned to his office. He must be handling numerous patients at the same time. Either that or sickly people were appearing in one waiting room after disappearing from another without any respect to the walls. He unraveled the towel and only a little piece of the ice slid off my arm onto the tray. Where the ice cube had perched for what seemed hours was an ugly welt twice the size of the original cube.

"It appears you are allergic to cold, Raynam." He mispronounced my name with his obscure Lithuanian accent. "This is truly an unfortunate malady. There is presently no proper diagnosis for this infirmity. I will advise your father to call my travel agent, Dottie Ambrewster, to arrange your ticket to the Caribbean. There you can behold the angel of tropical delights and perpetual sunshine." He showcased his Baltic hilarity and hit the bricks for the petrol pumps.

There would be no magic bullet for me. From that day onwards, they labeled me as the "Human Muffin" because every time I had to venture into the arctic regions of the winter months I was swathed in assorted layers of wool shirts, sweaters, and coats. So much so, I could hardly walk. I had a Russian trapper hat, which had flaps you could fold down to cover your ears. My sister attached the male and female counterparts of snaps, which you install with a little tool and bang with a hammer. She got them in the five and dime store. After she installed a row of them on both the hat and on the collar of my winter coat, she gave it to me for a test drive. The package had the word, "Grommet," printed on it; however, my sister pronounced the word as "Grow-Met." When I was all pimped out and waddling down the road with my earmuffs fully engaged like a Raggedy Ann Frankenstein, she would announce to the neighborhood, "Here comes little Grow-Met," and crack herself up. My sister was a twit like that. I bet the Khrng ate her out on a regular basis.

I put my Cossack cap back on and stumbled along the lonely road home not even noticing the bruised underbellies hiding in the low-slung strata.

The Moon Women

Can you expel future lifetimes by acting them out on the muddled surfaces of conscious play? Or could it be the acting is what jacks up the karmas which must eventually be fulfilled? Back in the rotating chair, I unwound the episode of the second coming down in Goa while a murder of crows out in the courtyard dissected their decomposing lunch.

Tiami Brown and I had ventured into a heuristic laboratory moving in and out of the first of the inverted Bardos, or quasi-states of being. We were frontiersmen foraging our way through unknown caverns of psychogenic confrontation. But, where would it lead us? Would the future discoveries we bumped into extemporaneously become solutions that would short circuit past events under which we had struggled in the interest of uncovering mysteries out of the Beyond? Or would the things we exposed prove the entire hypothesis to be off the wall? Would the characters we impersonated today reverse the characters scheduled for us to become tomorrow? On the flip side, would we be tempting these experimental folks to perpetuate a reality which we could never shake off? And more pertinent to the situation, did Tiami Brown even give a damn? Or was she simply dreaming up more devious ways to jump my bones?

Thinking I couldn't get more juiced up with metaphysical moonshine than that, I jotted down a last-minute entry into my journal. I reread the new lines I had penned.

> *Would the taste of Brownie's body be the poison*
> *that would consume me and terminate my trip?*
> *Or would the blind man I was about to become*
> *locate with his walking stick that which*
> *could not be found by men with mortal sight?*

We were having lunch in an out of the way Chai shop out near the inlet where the fishing trawlers launch. As the gulls cawed overhead, the lazy surf lapped softly against the flat sand. But I was blind so I couldn't see a thing. I could not see the azure skies. I could not see the boiling clouds, nor the half-naked Hippies frolicking underneath their volleyball nets all along the main drag on this coastal paradise. What's more, I could not see the loveliness of Miss

Tiami Brown perched on my arm.

"Not so close, Brownie. I'm not an invalid. I'm just blind is all. I'm supposed to see everything with my magic cane. Remember?" I scolded her softly.

"You gonna direct this like some movie producer establishing fame and fortune? My job is to help you see what you can't see. So don't I need some proximity?" Miss Brown overruled my orchestrating.

Tapping myrmecologically like a lobster having only one antenna, I had spent quite some time feeling my way over to the set of driftwood benches stationed on the remote frontier of a rattan hinterland. With my sixteen-megabit crab cane, I had at last tasted some success in the late stages of my adventure. I caught her soft slurping Chai and decided to feel her out.

"Brownie, you done with that yet?"

"What the hell? How you know what I'm drinking? You supposed to be blind."

She was always correcting me.

"I can hear the noises you've been making with those cups. How many so far? Four?" I assured her of my gradual headway.

"Look! You a blind man. I know you got them real dark glasses all wadded up on your nose, but believe me, you ain't got no idea what it is to be blind. You tapping that cane like a busted chop stick. You sure ain't no Ginger Baker and youse ain't even goin' anywhere."

She was pick, pick, pick.

"Oh, I be goin' somewhere, Ma cane be goin' up your leg like a hound dog after the bunny wabbit."

I choked back the tears.

"Ain't you supposed to be a damn Englishman? You like Sonny Bono putting on an impersonation of Ray Charles and a sick one at that."

She underscored my actor guy was not working out.

"Okay. Okay. Okay. My lady. Shall we be off?"

So I brought back the thick brogue of my English agent, put my tweed hat back on and set off tapping out Morse code to whichever beings would receive it and respond. We spent the entire afternoon in this continuous pantomime. The more I tapped to get everybody to jump out of my way, the tighter she clenched my arm

The Moon Women

gleefully blowing into my ear and whispering her incessant exuberance. She was so in love with the utterly insane magic, which I created routinely. Never mind there was no guarantee it would persist, she was along for the ride for as long as it would erupt out of me. I was the fire and she had the fuel. It was a marriage made in the underworlds. I was the never-ending machine. And she was lightning in a bottle.

Needing to answer the call of nature, I wandered off the beachfront shivering riskily as a unusual squall of cold rain descended upon my shoulders. Brownie had already retreated to our suite in the hotel. I guess her indifference towards my blind talents had succumbed to her certitude concerning my ineptness.

With my blindness in one hand and my tapping cane in the other, I headed for some warmth in the smelly bathroom. The shuddering escalated as I zigzagged my way into the sandaas. To add to my druthers it was pitch black inside the urine-drenched cave, although that didn't matter much since I was blind. Remember?

In the fraud of my sightless corner of shadow and rimy death, I stumbled forward searching with my cane for the lone drainage trough in the corner of the lavatory. When I found it over in the corner of the dingy darkness, I made the man maneuver to urinate but something caught my attention. A cluster of jagged fragments in the enclosure put there by age shifted me off balance but an inner reserve righted it: that common patterning software took over; the one, which the brain uses to formulate random shapes into rectangles or faces. As I fixated intensely upon the pixelate signal, it acquired definite relief. As it swelled out from the side of the long tube, it evolved into something concrete and began to glow as well. I had the unmistakable déjà vu feeling of recognition but it was only faint and fleeting.

After striving to recoup this bit harder, I was convinced I had witnessed this type of thing somewhere in the depths of antiquity. The silvery aperture surfaced on the clammy yellow barricade, which crawled with the meager leftovers of society. The sardine can then unpeeled itself and something other than dead fish slithered out. An excessively tall man-thing draped in a flaming chromium jump suit squeezed itself out of the lucent funnel like some weird version of an occult gymnast. Its cultivated crop of frilly aluminum petals, or were they fire feathers, bristled fiercely as it unwound its joints and prepared to do a devil dance. Swimming in the saucer of its featureless aspect were two marbles swirling with the blue and white clots of our celestial home, like miniature earths, which became its eyes blazing at me like beacons. Where ever his oral cavity might have been didn't matter because his radial curtain of coin sized bells seared into my frontal lobes with a surgical nastiness. I held up my cane to protect myself and bit into to it with all my strength to overcome the searing pain as the thing drove its daggers of electric juices into my consciousness.

UNTO THE ANGEL OF THE CHURCH [13]

SALUTATIONS AND GOOD DAY
MY CHURCHES ARE YOUR CHANNELS.

THE FAITHFUL AND TRUE WITNESS
IS MY OFFER BEFORE YOU

BEHOLD
I STAND AT THE DOOR AND KNOCK

THIS IS MORE OF A DESCRIPTION

IF ANY MAN HEAR MY VOICE OF WHAT THE ANGELS DO
AND OPEN THE DOOR AND HOW THEY PREPARE
I WILL COME INTO HIM TO CONVERSE WITH THEIR
AND WILL SUP WITH HIM SUBJECT AND EDUCATE THEM
AND HE WITH ME [14] ABOUT WHAT THEY NEED TO KNOW

TO HIM THAT OVERCOMES HATE
I WILL GRANT TO SIT WITH ME
ON MY THRONE EVEN AS
I ALSO OVERCAME [15]

HE THAT HATH AN EAR
LET HIM HEAR ME [16]

I COUNSEL YOU TO BUY ME GOLD

MY ADVICE TO YOU IS THAT YOU

TRIED IN THE FIRE

The Moon Women

SHOULD BE GENUINE IN YOUR EFFORTS

THAT YOU MAY BE RICH [17]
AND INCREASED WITH GOODS

AND BE CONFIDENT IN KNOWING

AND HAVE NEED OF NOTHING

THAT WHAT YOU ARE IS GREATER

AND KNOW NOT THAT

THAN ALL OF YOUR PROBLEMS

YOU ARE WRETCHED

NO MATTER WHAT THEY ARE

AND MISERABLE AND POOR
AND NAKED AND BLIND [18]

As the mercurial being shook his chromium flakes at me like a metallic burning broomstick, the bandages on my mind, lesions that hid the most recent nutty messenger, hadn't even worn off yet. Scars from that confrontation had barely sealed over. The hollowness in my noodle promptly filled with more of the biblical psychobabble like brain razors.

FOR YOU I HAVE HONOR
FROM THE DOMINION
OF SMYRNA
LEGION *OF ABADDON*
AND SON OF MAN
I AM RAMAEL   I REPRESENT THE COUNCIL OF SMYRNA
AND I SAY AMEN   AS RAMAEL

FEAR NOT THE FOUL SMOKE DON'T BE AFRAID OF THE MUTANTS
CREATURES OF PALE FLESH   KNOWN AS THE KHRNG
FOR THEIR WORKS ARE
NEITHER COLD NOR HOT
BECAUSE THEY ARE LUKEWARM

THEIR TYPE IS BOTH VERY OLD

AND NEITHER COLD NOR HOT

AND EXCEPTIONALLY TWISTED

142

I WILL SPUE THEM OUT OF MY MOUTH [19]

THIS IS A DESCRIPTION OF WHAT THE ANGELS

OVER THE PILLAR OF AMETHYST

DO TO THE MUTANTS DURING BATTLE

OUR HANDS SHALL BE LOOSED AND

AS THEY SUBDUE THE KHRNG

THIS UNCLEAN WORMWOOD OF MAN

AND FEED THEM INTO THE VORTEX

SHALL PASS THROUGH

THAT WILL EMULSIFY THEIR EXISTENCE

THE MOUTH OF TIME

AND REMOVE IT FROM THE NOW

DOORS THAT GO NOWHERE
THAT LEAD TO THE WORLD
OF THE UNJUST
AND THE UNTIMELY WILL

OUR POWER SHALL SEND THEM
WITHOUT ANY BOND OR PLACE
FULFILLED ONLY
BY THE WHITE LIGHT
AND IN THAT WHITE
COMES A NEW NAME
THAT WILL BE WRITTEN
SO THAT NO MAN KNOWS
SAVE HE THAT CAN RECEIVE IT

I WILL COME INTO THEM
WITH QUICK FIRE
AND WILL FIGHT
AGAINST THEM
WITH THE SWORDS
OF MY MOUTH
AND MY FIRE

The Moon Women

HE THAT OVERCOMES
　　　　　IF YOU UNDERSTAND WHAT I AM TELLING YOU
WILL I GIVE TO EAT
　　　　THEN YOU WILL PROFIT GREATLY
OF THE HIDDEN MANNA [20]
　　　　BECAUSE YOU NOW KNOW OF MY POWER TO HELP YOU

Ramael spun round and came at me with a sleek fire sword the size of an oar to brandish its impulse wing in front of my eyes. Howbeit, frozen in fear, I leaned back away from the terrifying colossus.

THIS BATTLE COMES　　RAMAEL NOW SPEAKS ABOUT THE RUSH
AS A RED HORSE　　　AND HIS POWER THAT HE EMPLOYS
TO BE PASSED OUT　　TO OVERCOME THE KHRNG
AS A RED HORSE　　　AT THE SPLIT SECOND
WHILE THE WHEAT DOTH REST
　　　　OF CONFLICT OVER THE WHEAT

GREAT ABOMINATIONS
BATTLE OVER
THE TRODDEN HEAT
IN THE GRASS
AND LEAVE THE SIGN
OF A GREAT SWORD
LAID DOWN UPON
THE WILDERNESS THE RESULT OF BATTLE WITH THE KHRNG

AS THE LEAVES
OF THE WHEAT REJOICE
THE BRIDE OF VIRGINS
HAS GIVEN HER BLOOD
AND THE COURT OF MAN
WILL SEE THE RISE
OF THE BLOOD SUN WAILING

144

FOR THE WAY OF MAN IS TO LEARN
OF THE WAY OF WOMAN   The superiority of women
                      lies in a paramount position with regard
                      to the angels of abaddon

THE CITY HAD NO NEED OF THE SUN
FOR THE MOON DID SHINE IN IT FULLY
FOR THE GLORY OF GOD DID LIGHTEN IT
AS THE LAMB IS THE LIGHT THEREOF
                      The way of righteousness must prevail

THERE CAME UNTO ME THE ANGEL
WHO SAID COME HITHER
AND I WILL SHOW THEE THE BRIDE
THE LAMBS WIFE AS TEN WOMEN
                  The ten women are the message of the mission

FIRST COMES THE FIVE WOMEN OF THE MOON
AS RAMAEL I MEASURE THE WALL
ACCORDING TO THE MEASURE OF A WOMAN
TRUE AND GREAT AND RIGHTEOUS
                  In this half of the saga come the moon women

THE FOUNDATIONS OF THE WALL
WERE GARNISHED WITH ALL MANNER
OF PRECIOUS STONES EACH BURNING
WITH HER FAITH AND HER LIGHT
THE FIFTH WAS SARDONYX
              The fifth Moon woman's psychic element is sardonyx

NOW COMES THE WOMAN OF SARDONYX
ARRAYED IN PURPLE AND SCARLET COLOURS
SHE WAS DECKED WITH A SILVER ROSE
AND PEARLS HAVING A GOLDEN CUP
IN HER HAND FULL OF ABOMBINATIONS

145

The Moon Women

SPEAKING OF FILTHINESS AND FORNICATION
HER PURPOSE IS PUT FORTH VIA SEDUCTION

CARRY HER SPIRIT INTO THE WILDERNESS
AND SEE HER FLY WITH WINGS OF HIM
HAVING THE NAME OF BLASPHEMY
WITH THE SEVEN HEADS AND TEN HORNS
WHEREIN HER SLAVES HEART BURNETH
AS THE FRUITS OF HER SOUL
LUSTED AFTER THE DEPARTED
REALIZE WHO AND WHAT SHE IS AND SUCCEED

KNOW THIS WOMAN TO BE THE WAY
TO KEEP THE ALTAR BRIGHT
AND YOUR MIND ALIVE THERE IS NO SHAME IN INDULGING
AS LONG AS YOU REALIZE IT IS FOR THE MISSION

ANNOINT YOUR EYES
WITH EYESALVE
SO YOU CAN SEE [21]
HE WHO IS CHOSEN FIRST
TO WITNESS THE BATTLE
AND WRITE THE THINGS
WHICH HE HAS SEEN TRUE
AND THE THINGS WHICH ARE
AND THE THINGS WHICH
SHALL BE HEREAFTER [22]
KNOW THAT YOU ARE THE FIRST OF MANY
AND AS SUCH WE HONOR YOU

THAT YOU MAY PROPHESY
BEFORE MANY PEOPLES
AND NATIONS AND TONGUES
AND PRINCES AND KINGS [23]
FOR THE TIME IS AT HAND [24]

UNDERSTAND YOUR MISSION TO BE A GREAT ONE

In the midst of the bells, Ramael withdrew his octopus entity back in through his nickel-plated star portal as it yawned a sleepy close. And the scroll of heaven shut down.

- 18 -

The remarkable chair had stirred the pits of pious magic and the let loose the ropes of branding fears which push up against the works of merciless men who feed on the carrion of fools. The rope in my hand was as a rudder, which unleashed the apocalypse of futility upon the sheet of the lost nights.

That March Brownie and I were getting to know one another. It wasn't long before we were undertaking wild and exciting forays out across the sub-continent, one of which was standing squarely on the crossroads of planning a night on the town while running low on cash.

"How you fixed for baksheesh, Bro?"

Kenny rarely came to visit. He was a mix of Korean and Columbian parents, but deep down, he was nothing less than thoroughbred American chowder.

"Down to the baby notes, Man. Micro-paisa, if there is such a thing. How 'bout chu?" Dad's antecedent injection of greenbacks was gathering dust over in my lockbox in the puja cave. It hadn't yet undergone its transformation into Indian rupees.

"Yeah, that's ripe. Some of the others are low on rupees, too," he reported. "You up for a nifty trip?"

"What did you have in mind?" I knew full well what he had in mind and I knew exactly how nifty it would be, or not, but I hoped my part in it might be avoided altogether.

"Bop over to my pad, Man. We'll have a go at it. Say, fifteen minutes?"

Kenny always seemed to be reasonable but I got the feeling more prescient enchiladas were headed my way.

In India, the national currency is the rupee. You can submit your cash or your Travelers checks to a bank or to a Thomas Cook's office where they will gladly exchange your coin for Indian currency. Not surprisingly, they will charge you a fee for each transaction. That

The Moon Women

fee coupled with the differential between the rates on the black market and what of the banks charged was what prompted our actions. The international exchange set periodically by a league of bigwig Arabs over in Dubai doesn't provide the most lucrative rates you can find. You can get a much better rate dabbling in the under-the-table market; so much better, in fact, sometimes it's a seventy to ninety per cent increase. So if you know where to go, you can magnify the value of your traveler's checks significantly.

Kenny knew the correct places to go. He was his own self-appointed micro-manager. He knew the high-class connections whom he could rely on for the choicest deals. Whether it was for rupees or dope or any other thing his heart desired, he knew where all the righteous connections lay. So we all got together to hatch a plan over in the meetinghouse located contrariwise to the Krishnaswami residence.

Compared with most other buildings in Cooketown, this homestead wore a mask. On the surface it was an unusually large, three story residency. But internally it was a nest of hippy caves surrounded by Grateful Dead paraphernalia, lined with exotic batiks, and permeated with heady smoke fuming out of meter high hookahs. Referred to as the penthouse, Kenny's pad was the top tier of this so-called guesthouse. He and his current heartthrob, Beth Stevenson, hung out up there as a couple and rarely did anything to cause anyone hassles. In fact, Kenny never did anything, except do dope and fuck Beth. But today he had serious business to attend to - procuring rupees for us gang of fwiks.

There was Kenny and his main squeeze, Beth. There was Jeff Finklestein and Cathy Rutledge, not a couple, merely friends. There was Megan Ross and Dottie Ambrewster. Can't say much for those two; they could be bi. And bringing up the rear guard was Brownie and me; everybody considered us a couple but Brownie and I knew better.

As we reported how many rupees we would be changing, Kenny indexed the customer base ticking off a tally with his finger to tabulate the final sum.

"We've got over eight thousand smackers in total," Kenny looked disappointed.

Someone was struggling to push the door free but Beth had secured the bolt latches when she sealed us into this papal conclave.

"Who's there?" Dottie demanded.

"What's a girl gotta do in this town to get a ticket to ride?"

"Eew! Lemme get that!" I sprinted over and released the two latches but only freed up the door a crack.

"Do you want sugar with that?" I anticipated the return code.

"Yeah. Two lumps," came the honeyed reply.

As Brownie gently scooched passed me, I caught the brunt of her manslayer perfume. No weakling, she could have knocked me over if she had felt so inclined.

"I've only got three hundreds," she volunteered while flashing the triad of Benjamins.

"Well, if we could get to ten large, we could get a much better deal, but it looks like this is as much as we're gonna have," Kenny reported.

"Guess we'll have to go with it." I offered. "I anticipate a little more later, but for now that's my entire stash."

As the others concurred their stock status, I concluded the Old Man had been regular but never premature.

"Now, we are going to draw straws to decide who will do the leg work," Kenny always liked to create his angles. "Short stick flies."

We each drew our respective straws out of his hand. I drew third and sure enough, out popped the short one meaning I got the green light to fly.

"Balls!" I spat.

"No problem, Mate. Listen, the pool will cover all your expenses, so don't sweat it. Whatever your expenses you incur will be way balanced by the inflated exchange rate. So, no worries, Jack. Merely ferry the dough and do the deed, Man. Whatever you lug back here, we'll split according to the shares of whatever we put in. Trust me. We'll clean up like bandits!"

I calculated it was more like a mixed bag at worst. Kenny seemed to be on top of it all. And I was his main musketeer.

The clay plume of the half-moon played tricks with the profit line, which the international bankers had inscribed upon the monetary rule of the night's inner vaults.

The Moon Women

The following morning as I poised for departure on Dr. Krishnaswami's porch by paying my farewells to the Missus and her little son, Ramu, or whatever his name is when in walks Brownie.

"Come to offer your bon voyage?" I egged.

"Nope." She had her spunky look as she avowed categorically. "I'm going with you."

"Hurray!" Dr. Krishnaswami roared. The two of them would be gone at last he thought surely.

"Er, wait a minute. I don't think so," I raised a finger.

"Rahm, please? Pretty please?" She pleaded with me.

Mrs. Krishnaswami interrupted the logical enforcement of Ibsen's statues and annotated bylaws with a stream of Kannada.

"Shanni says your woman has served you all this time and has asked you for very little. You must indulge her this one request." Dr. Krishnaswami paraphrased her lingo.

"Come on, Rahm. Nobody said the two of us couldn't go. Didn't Kenny tell you the expenses would come out of the exchange rate and we'd be way ahead no matter what?" She was becoming her own litigator.

"Yeah, and I suppose you want sugar with that?" I caved in.

I really couldn't argue with those emerald eyes and especially with her arm riding my shoulder, like a mariposa lily.

"Two lumps." She lavished me with a quick peck on the cheek and Mrs. Krishnaswami folded her hands in support to seal the deal.

The airport was old hat to us. We had been there many times escorting our companion FWC buddies to and from the many displaced ports of call. Not long after, Brownie and I were airborne and making our way en route to New Delhi on Indian Airlines. Regrettably because of my late-notice attempt they had no accommodations in first-class. We had to go coach. Nonetheless, coach was tolerable back in those days. You could order a wholesome Hindu meal with Chai and mosala dosa. It was really quite convenient to get pure vegetarian food wherever you traveled. That was one of the comforting advantages of touring South India, land of the genuine Hindu.

As I watched out the window, the mesa of Madya Pradesh swam by underneath the belly of our plane. Occasional uplifted massifs clogged with monticules of boulders split the land below in two. The ailerons of our macropterous aluminum eagle expanded backwards as we landed with cheery applaud from the passengers. As we taxied off the runway to the unloading zone, the standard mockup, it was always a shock to disembark through the oval conduit and go forward into the atmosphere of an untried territory. The stench of it was always so overpowering.

In short order, we made our way to the mini-motel, the Parkway, which was an excuse of an annex to the big and bold Chandi Chowk Bhuvan, which was fully booked. We threw open our one suitcase and collapsed onto the bed together. After lighting some incense sticks we hit the hay. Tomorrow promised to be quite fortunate. We had to get this job done rapido and get back to Bangalore with all the loot.

Next day after sunup we got up, did our showering thing, separately of course. Brownie and I had come to accept our mutual independence. We considered ourselves consecrated platonic lovers. Each of us granted the other a great deal of respect and space to breathe. That in itself made it immensely difficult for either one of us to dislike to other one. In fact, it amplified our mutual tenderness, which was pretty neat.

We had developed another minor custom besides the "two lumps" thing. Whenever we got ready to go somewhere together, we would plant a hot smooch directly on each other's oral bulls-eye. It wasn't a sexual thing, or at least I thought it wasn't. It was our primary method of mobilization. This time, preceding our departure into the sphere of smog and terror, which was New Delhi, we hung there after the heated kiss.

"I always thought your teeth were so spectacular, Brownie. What's the deal with that space there?" I needled thoughtlessly.

"Oh, that. Didn't I tell you I had braces when I was a kid? Since I've been over here that little gap has opened back up some. I'll have to get it fixed when I get back to the States. What the hell are you checking out my dental rack for anyway Rahm? You some kinda weirdo?"   Women always get so defensive when you shine a spotlight on their foibles.

151

The Moon Women

"Sorry, but it's quite a rack, I must say. Hey, you never know. They always say the perfect ones can only be detected because they have a hidden flaw. And only their Prince Charmings can know what it is." I was walking on water.

"Yeah, what? A vagina?"

Off we ventured to downtown Ma'Gog.

- 20 -

The capital of India was hotter than I remembered it. Limp grease coated every marly meter of the city. Everywhere legions of combustion engines cranked out foul black soot as they drank from the diesel fountains. As thick plumes of oily soot vomited out of every rusted orifice connected to a moving vehicle in the land, I gasped at the sight of it. There was little color in the surrounding sights of this slime pit of rampant humanistic waste. Unlike Bangalore, where so many waving strands of vibrant lavender bougainvillea climbed the bricked borders amongst the umbrella-like vermillion poinsettia trees dangling five-fingered clusters of bleeding stars, Delhi looked incredibly dead.

We pitched our tent in a corner booth at the dank terminus of a shabby fryer joint. I didn't like the spot but this is where our taxi had dropped us when I requested a straight shot for money laundering. After I had done a quick once over in an attempt to locate our promised rupee vendors, my alarm registers got triggered by the juicy sizzling of papadums aspiring unsuccessfully to breakout of the boiling oil. Tuning into that clue, I was on the verge of grabbing Brownie and bolting when three hirsute gentlemen with neon turbans the size of basketballs tramped in through the slipshod doorway.

Introducing themselves as Mr. Singh, they joined us at the booth by plugging all the escape outlets. They were all Mr. Singh. A Mr. Such-and-such Singh, a Mr. You-know-who Singh and another dim bulb who didn't say much. The big cheese with the most rowdy headgear explained the rate would be close to 28 rupees, which was considerable because it was only 15 back in Bangalore.

"How much dollars you be having your good same self, Sir?" The greasy bearded one sandwiched in the middle inquired with his curried Indian accent.

152

"Eight thousand," I replied firmly. I thought I would keep it simple in case math wasn't his strong suit.

Brownie's token role was moot. Uh oh - M words. You know what that means. Best to wrap this up before all hell breaks out, but the bearded Sikh's mealy complexion pushed up against my territory.

"That much two hundred lakhs rupiah," he slurred his words hurriedly.

I did some perfunctory calculations in my head.

"You give two thirty lakhs, please," I was not going to be shorted.

"Okay. For you, my rate 29. I yam givingk two ten, best," The Sadarji rebutted.

"That's okay, but two twenty-five is even better. We will be pleased to take two twenty-five," I countered. Appearing meddlesome might be seem as a weak selling point.

"No, no. I yam give berry best rate for you, Maharaji. You no get 30 rate Aaj nowheres. You take two sau fifteen. Final offer." [Great Sir. Today. Hundred...]

The moneyman was getting pushy and quite perturbed. I knew I was walking on eggshells balancing his whit with his anger. If I toppled him over the edge, he might decide to cut me with the gruesome knife those turbaned Sikhs pack in their waistbands. Putting Brownie in harm's way was not my idea of a healthy move.

"Listen. You give me two twenty and I'll throw in an extra hundred under the table," I flashed the Ben Franklin I was holding up my sleeve.

The jumbo Sikh leaned over and grabbed my collar. There was a creamy froth starting to congeal in the corners of his mouth. Beneath the table, I felt a hand glomming onto my knee. He narrowed his eyes to slits and sputtered.

"You werry, werry hard man, Mr. Green. Eh? You no shut up. Give!"

His hand squeezed my knee a second time. With a flick of my wrist, the whole ball of wax came together as the blood returned to my brainstem. I jammed the Benjamin into his hand. With a shit-eating grin, he unearthed two missing bicuspids on the bottom ledge of his jaw, the prize for my genius marketing play.

"Tum daal raen!" [You stay put!]

The Moon Women

He ordered us to sit tight as the other two remained staring us down. As the raunchy Sikh money Mafioso departed, the saloon doors swished back and forth high fiving each other.

"Chai karo?" [Got any Chai?] I whimpered smiling at the masthead.

The dirty one looked at me and grunted. Then, he waved his hand at his sidekick parked by the hostess desk. His head wobble was the uptick for some drinks.

"Rahm, how long is this going to take? I'd like to get out of this measly shit hole. Like today!" Moment to moment, Brownie was edging into nervous city.

"It's cool. The big dude will be back in a jiffy with a heavy bag of rupees, or the two of us are going to be their saucy entertainment for the evening," I made a pearly grin her way.

"On, great!" Her cheek squinched up. "I gotta pee."

"Not now, Brownie. This is all about timing. Give it a minute more," It was a juggling act.

"Rahm, I said I gotta pee. Get out of my way!"

Her biologicals were not going to be orchestrated by anybody. I bounded off the bench but the shadow covering home base shot out his hand as if to say nobody is going anywhere.

"Ladaki. Sandaas." [Woman. Toilet.]

I employed some Hindi to inform the sidekick gangbanger to make way as I aimed my thumb at Brownie. The thumb gesture was an infinitely derogatory one, which showed my superiority over the woman. In this culture, it was not only accepted, but well understood to be a statement or show of authority. The guy grunted and let her pass. Brownie made a move for a crucial pit-stop in the men's room. Hey! It's India. As she passed by me, I noticed the macule of her vaccination mark on her deltoid. Why I had never seen that before?

In the meantime, Chai showed up. Our attending soldier at arms poured out five steaming cups. I blew on mine as the two grunts chug-a-lugged theirs. Those maggots have probably burned off their taste buds from so many years of downing the volcanic brew.

Presently Brownie rejoined the round-table. I rose to let her in which alarmed the guardian suitor who unshielded his kirpan. Fortunately, the chief macromancer reappeared at the appropriate sequence in the Time stream with a moldy shoebox. He shoved the warring faction out of the way and dropped his full weight into our booth. With a smug leer, he slipped the lid off the stained container and tipped it slightly to display its contents – multi-colored money bearing the Ashoka lions.

One by one, he dealt out two rows of bundled bank notes onto the table. There were eleven of them. Each one must have totaled twenty thousand rupees for the total to come to the agreed upon sum of two hundred and twenty lakhs. I tapped on a bundle and demanded in my finest Hindi.

"Kitna?" [How much?]

"Doh."

The main dude raised his 2 fingers, meaning there were two hundred, one hundred rupee notes in each pack.

Each one was wrapped tightly with colored paper bands having Hindi markings stamped onto them with purple inks. Undeniably, I beheld hot cheddar scraped up in a bank heist from God knows where. Common sense said I mustn't rain on this market order. Even so, I picked one up and rifled through it with my thumb. I didn't intend to get gypped no matter what. I flagged it with a passing grade.

"Tik." [Good.]

I was feeling mighty fat jus then.

"Tum dolar ab dena." [You give dollars now.]

I unloosed my rucksack from my shoulder and dumped the contents out onto the table. Chunks of US currency tumbled out. With a single scoop of his arm, the mealy Sikh shoveled the entire pile into a burlap sack he brought out from underneath his bench, strapped it tight with a drawstring and tossed it to his second lieutenant. The whole thing shocked me since he never even attempted to count it or anything. How the hell did he have even the slightest clue as to its value? Money changing via predestination came the response from the peanut gallery.

"Tum Chandi Chowk Bhuvan, Nambar saat, ek, nau, heina?" [You Chandi Chowk Bhuvan, number 719, isn't it?]

With a finger he drew out the three numbers in the greasy film on the tabletop and smiled one of the most confident smiles I have ever seen. Even though I knew he had missed the mark, I decided just to go with it and deal with the consequences should they arise.

The Moon Women

"Hanh, Ji. Problem? Tum mere pass aao. [Yes, Sir. Problem? You come to me.]

I raised my cup to salute him. The leer plastered on his mug never departed its displacement. But by that time, my Chai was nearing room temperature. I had lost faith in its purpose anyway. I drank it down and tabled the cup. Brownie had but only touched hers.

"Bus." [We're done.]

I did my spry hand folding gesture and double-tapped my bald spot towards the sunshine, the uptick for our exodus.

"We're leaving now, Dear. Come, let's run along, tout de suite," I made like I was giving her the covert code word conveying all is well in Marrakech.

"Namaste!"

I aimed my stern sendoff at the primo Sikh gentleman. He also returned his Namaste and swiftly extended an arm awarding us permission to seek our permanent withdrawal. I took a step closer to him and mustered my enhanced adieu with a curried gumption.

"Sat Shri Akal!"

He looked flabbergasted, but then he closed his eyes, folded his hands, and with a warm bow reciprocated with his own response.

"Sat Shri Akal, Ji."

Unlike previously when he was throwing bar bells at me, he now had a genuine smile. The words, "Sat Shri Akal," are the salutary greeting, which all Sikhs give one another, particularly when within the Gurdwara, the temple or place of worship for those devotees who follow the Sikh religion. At heart, it means, "Go with the One, True God."

I had been privy to that lesson while in Kashmir but that story is a far cry from this one. Feeling we had escaped certain doom, which had been only alleviated by my coded farewell gesture, I secured the shoebox, grabbed Brownie, and made a beeline for the doorway. We were back in our rooming house in no time. I arranged for meals with room service and booked a call with the concierge for Indian Airlines to get us a flight out ASAP. I had hoped for first-class but confessed to the agent I would take whatever straw she threw at me. That only caused more bollixed feedback so I just spat out my, "Just-do-it, Okay?" into the bituminous handset and declined back onto the lumpy bed.

Seeing the ocean of lettuce covering the king size sleeping tarpaulin buggered my caution button. Snatching a bundle I began to thumb through it to determine if each bill exemplified genuine currency as well as insuring if each was a hundred rupee note or not. Suffering a miscount was out. Brownie had engaged her own bundle with similar uneasiness. As usual, we were both on the same wavelength. Then, the phone rang. I concluded it must be Indian Airlines getting back to me about our flight so I picked it up.

"Yeah? Whadai get?" My greeting wasn't formal, but neither did it smack of my usual intimidation .

"Is it the room of Miss Tiami Brown?" It was a female asking.

"Sure. You got the right number. What is it?" I felt no remorse.

"A telegram has come for Miss Brown," The marginally concerned woman informed me.

"Could you please send it up right away? We're busy." I proposed, engendering the need for some expediency, and hung up the phone.

- 21 -

There was no knock on the door. There was no one requesting an entry. I was expecting some form of delivery, but none came. As I was having a plate of parpadoms and melon cubes, Brownie had drifted off into nappy pastures on the one bed. She had claimed the entire thing. A number of times she had offered me a place in it. She was never coquettish or winsome and never made seductive advances with lurid hints or lavish appearances. She was always straightforward and honest.

"Rahm," she would say. "If you want me, you should just say so. In fact, don't even use words. Just use your lips. I can tell the difference between a love peck and the fuck of love. You can have either one but just know this offer might not sit on the bed simply for the taking forever. It's up to you. I'm not chasing you all over the barnyard like some over-estrogenated mama chicken. If you can't smell the roses then get the hell out of the garden."

The manila envelope caught my eye finally. Looks like the receptionist had slipped the tattered folder under the sill quite surreptitiously. I walked over and picked it up. It was heavier than it

The Moon Women

looked. It had those funny looking telegraphic cutouts pasted down so no one could remove them or change whatever they had to say. Just two scraps stating: TIAMI BROWN ROOM 719. It was stuck together with glue from somebody's trembling hand. A rubbery whiff leaked out giving an unwanted clue to its contents. Yet there was no denying it, I was the loser in this match. I wondered if I should open it. At this juncture, the score was definitely a love forty game. Brownie yawned herself awake.

"Did the thalis come?" she rotated her body in my direction on the bed.

"There's a telegram for you, Brownie," I felt like I was pronouncing a sentence.

She opened her hand and I inserted the telegram into it. She received it like a child receiving a gift on her birthday. Oddly, she had never even hinted at what her birthday might be. She always avoided the subject and kept it from me as if its mention was a dark incantation, which would destroy both our friendships simultaneously. But I knew better.

I handed her a dull pencil from the bedside table to get the thing open. She inserted it clumsily into the throat of the envelope but the dull green stick couldn't cut it so I unhanded the telegram from her and buggered the seal myself. A paper fell out. We looked at each other stymied. My inaction prompted her to bend down and retrieve it.

It was an agonizing moment watching her struggle to unlock its contents. Repeated study of it only twisted her insides further. With tears in her eyes, she looked over at me and simply stuttered, "No."

I knew it was something akin to what a whale must experience when it gets harpooned. Watching her collapse was like watching a pristine rose wilt via a time lapsed slowdown in one second. Her forehead crinkled up. Her eyes squinted tight from the pang of the news. The corners of her mouth bent downwards and her bottom lip protruded with a wet quivering.

"My Mom died. She died," she sobbed and looked at me for forgiveness.

Her pronouncement shot through me like the proverbial arrow. Now, I knew I was the falcon and the archer at the same time.

"Oh, Brownie, I'm so sorry," it was all I could say.

She cried into my abdomen for a long, long time. I remained hugging her tightly to comfort her sobs, seeking to absorb her pain with all my might. As I stroked her soft, dark hair and smoothed her heaving shoulders, I tried to dissociate the agonizing weight from her heart, but it was a bone crushing weight, which would not lift easily. I lost my grip and the telegram fell to her feet. Delicately I picked it up to see.

> METOO STOP
> THERE HAS BEEN AN ACCIDENT STOP
> MOM WAS PINNED BY A CAR STOP
> SHE DIED IN ACCIDENT STOP
> PLEASE COME HOME STOP
> WE NEED YOU HERE STOP

Down below there was another pasted-on farewell bit.

> SALLY STOP

It was a total mail bomb. I joined her bedside, put my arm on her shoulder, and hugged her tightly. After some moments, her sobbing calmed down and she started to gather her wits a bit. She reached out for my hand as her mainstay.

"Who's Metoo?" I quizzed to meliorate the situation.

"Oh," she sniffled. "That's me. They used to call me that name when I was little because I would always answer them with, "Me, too!" whenever they were fixin' to do something or go somewheres. So, they made it into a nickname; they named me that, Metoo. They put it there so I would know it's them and not someone messing with me. I've had problems before," she broke down and cried some more.

I made like it might be helpful to lie down together and get under the covers and hug a while. She was mum, but, she got the idea. By and by, we were hugging and holding on beneath the waves. I kissed her on her forehead and put all my heart into her. I think she knew I was reaching out to comfort her. She looked at me and into my eyes. I knew she wanted me to kiss her. I looked at her a while and then closed my eyes. I connected and gave her the deepest tongue-swallowing kiss that I had.

159

The Moon Women

The whales would have been proud of me during that moment. The most compassionate and melodious harmonies came out of my being and was spoken through my lips into the being of that woman. Our bodies melted into paragons of celestial splendor and the emotional fluids of our beings mingled in an orchestra, which played crescendo after crescendo and pianissimo after pianissimo. Even the degrees of minute pianississississimo filtered out into the night.

Whether we had sex or not I am not yet prepared to acknowledge but I would not really consider anything we did upon those sheets to be concerned with the lower chakras. I would even go to the extent of saying notwithstanding the count on my belt or my share of climaxes, what Brownie and I shared should not fall under that gate in any way imaginable.

The whales were certainly singing then. Whatever the future reemergence of those songs will initiate, I don't know, but it will be one in which this man receives the treasures from the hereafter and from the hereafter of hereafters, like the whales and like those happy Babushka dolls who are smiling within their multiple dimensions of sadness five times over.

- 22 -

The jaunt to the airport was one of the most unsettling rides I have ever tackled. Every screaming peddler in the city battered us with cries; every odor choked us and every bump in the road slammed into our viscera. The honking cars and the grinding rasps of their brakes caused seething migraines of pain to shoot through our mental cavities like bad peyote.

Brownie was in a total daze having contracted a bout of diarrhea during her most recent outing in the loo, which had left her a little green around the gills. I hesitated to say anything further for fear of upsetting her on top of the merry-go-round ride. I looked at her with an intense gaze and emitted an encouraging remark.

"Whales don't have gills, Brownie."

Squinting behind her Foster Grants, all she could do was shrink back away from me.

"Rahm, don't do that. I need you here, Okay?"

160

I had remitted the three Benjamins she had committed to the pot earlier. Plus, I added another five hundred rupees for travel coin. I suggested maybe she buy something nice for her sister and her folks back in the States. She said she would; it was the mature thing to do.

Since my departure was only a half hour after hers, we had to walk gingerly to reach the international gate on time. I had managed to get her into first-class with a direct connection into JFK. Only hours earlier back in the renta-room, I had socked down the bread to pay for a one-way ticket. Since the Parkway had afforded us Five Star status, the service rep from the airlines had dropped by to collect payment. She was aghast when I produced a bushel of hundred rupee notes. The ticket price was well over $3300.00, but because I was paying in the rupees, which we exchanged at cut-rate prices, I got it for over forty-five per cent off.

I watched Brownie amble down the aisle. As she neared the entrance to her transport, she looked so frail and helpless. Be that as it may, I was comforted by knowing whatever higher forces had guided me across the twelve thousand kilometers of hostile terrain from Europe into Asia; over the Khyber Pass and down across the deserts of Pakistan into India, would also carry her safely back to Oceanside, Long Island, where she would once again be with her loving family and friends. But I would be long gone and long forgotten.

"Why?" I beseeched the Man upstairs who had elected me to be her man of sorrows.

- 23 -

"Ciao."

She waved and then disappeared into the barren conduit, which led to the innards of her ride home. I bowed to the probability I would never see her again. That thought sent a shiver of shame down my back. I let her down; let her hanging. I wasn't her man.

I turned feebly hunched over like the Man of Calais and trudged off towards my departure gate. It was true I had done the sacrifice of her charms but that had only led me inadvertently to this insipid grief in my gut. Had I earned any progress on the path towards recognition? I couldn't say. At least I had won some modicum of freedom for whatever that was worth.

161

The Moon Women

Since I had already heard the announcement of my boarding call, I was on a tear to get to my own gate. What I didn't know yet was there had been an emergency notification over at the central office in the control tower. Having come in two shakes after sunrise, it was the worst possible collision of unlikely events - a bomb scare. As a consequence, certified staff were conducting a detailed search of each passenger and principally their carry-ons. That was a snag – a snag that would not be advantageous.

All I was transporting that morning was a miniature duffle bag. Besides having a pair of socks, underwear and a fresh shirt, there were only two other items in there, which might present the slightest stickler. One was the one hundred and sixty thousand rupees wrapped in tight bundles decorated with purple notations and telltale Hindi cryptograms. The other was, (you guessed it), my stash of dope.

It contained some choice nuggets of hashish and assorted clumps of some outrageously potent marijuana all nicely sequestered and well cloaked in its plastic hiding place, and all right in plain sight. My soap dish was going to be the first hot topic out of my bag. Considering I didn't know they were going to undertake this in-depth search, sadly I was unprepared.

Never having my bags examined on any preceding Indian Airlines trips, I approached check-in feeling confident I would come away clean. I sauntered over to the gate, which consisted of a folding table pitched in front of a cubicle segment, which blocked any visual access to the entrance onto the Boeing 727. Anticipating what phase of Murphy's Law would manifest from around the corner, I dumped my bag down on the counter with a firm confidence.

"Good morning." I greeted the woman who was accepting boarding passes.

Standing beside her was a tall lanky gentleman dressed in military garb topped with an olive beret. With his police stick, he tapped on my bag for me to open it. I knew right then and there I was going to have a problem but prayed maybe I could fake it.

"Be glad to." I fired back.

I figured a display of supreme daring could not hurt at this point. Unavoidably, the initial object to come out was my soap dish. I displayed it proudly.

"What is this?" The military inspector challenged.

"Soap? It's soap, Dude!" I stated my self-evident gospel with supreme indifference.

Infected with an epidemic of salutariness, I was hoping he would realize it was, for all intents and purposes, simply a soap dish. Obviously, he was hunting for bombs, mind you. Big bombs!

"What is this?"

He commenced his third degree once more as his snake eyes darted in and out at me.

"Soap! It's soap, my Man." I reiterated.

I made hand washing signals and underarm scrubbing motions in a futile attempt at pantomime to underscore this endemic trend. He looked at me and then he looked back at the innocently appearing soap dish, which was like two boxes in one. The top fit over the bottom to keep the soap from escaping the confines of its universe and especially to keep the drippings from leaking out. The clincher right now was that all my drippings were leaking out all over the place.

"Please open, Sir." He ordered.

He was not going to be deterred so easily. I distinctly detected moldy scales on his hide. So, I surrendered and slipped off the upper half to show him what was inside.

"Peekaboo!" I clowned but he didn't get it.

Sitting innocently naked in front of his glaring eyeballs were awesome chunks of hashish and one or two sticky buds of my favorite playmate, Mary Jane. The stoically uninitiated might conceivably view these miniature wads of heaven as some curious brand of soap bars, as insignificant dark and ugly soap cubes, that's all. I was loath to admit maybe not your typical floral essences molded like Valentine hearts, but I was hoping past all hope he would accept this testimony and move on. Bombs, Buddy. You're hound dogging for big bombs! But, no! He has to add further allegations regarding my baggage.

"Soap? This not soap!" He stated furiously.

He had to resay it to just to be sure I understood his soured skepticism. Beat up the English, Man, but buy my soap.

"You sure, Dude? Sniff it up your nose why don't you?"

I offered my reasonable proposition for an ingratiating conclusion to his abuse. Feeling comfortably insulated by the cultural

The Moon Women

downwind, I allowed myself a decent range of mockery and rattled with his frogger some more.

"Really Man, it's just bubble bath. Can't you tell that?"

"What this? This what I say?" He persevered with his demands.

By now, the coils of his constriction were intent on bulging my eyes straight out of my noodle. Perhaps I should alter my approach slightly with a modified upgrade to the stratagem.

"Smoke, Dude. It's smoke, that's all. Can you dig it?" I encouraged him to get with my self-effacing routine and move on.

Keeping the same O sound, I thought if I repeated it slowly just as he had grilled me so fervently a second previous with his railing invective, he might go along with this updated version of my skedaddle tactics. Skip to the rope ma Lou. I was hoping he might possibly buy into this idea as some new persuasion of smoking tobacco. It's possible, no? The decorated security agent looked at it once or twice and grasped the container out of my hand to put it up to his McCarthyite nose.

"This not smoke! No, not tobacco. What this is Sir?"

He looked me square on with his reptilian brain radar probing the throes of my foxy American drift. Okay, I'm "2" and "0" here. I've got one more pitch headed my way. If I don't knock it out of the park I'm in deep shit.

"Blow. It's blow. You know, just blow. What more do you want from me?"

I immortalized my stance on the matter as I bellowed straightforwardly sticking to my guns with another long emphasized O vowel to embody added candor. Nevertheless, staring back at him and knowing that any wavering in my voice or in my stealthy glance would expose the quantum evils lurking in my heart, I transmitted my strongest hypno-spasm visual laser penetrating eyeball.

Well, guess what? That one flew directly over the plate too: he wasn't buying it. Unfortunately, it appeared as though my up-and-coming investment campaign was going to be fouled to left field. Back to the dugout for me. Damn it! Now, I'll have to trudge all the way back to Delhi, get another reservation in Ratville and rebook an overnight red-eye back to my sock in the wall in Cooketown.

"No. Not blow. This ganja. This is offense!" He stated eagerly like labeling a newfangled specimen for his museum.

164

"Ek minute." [One minute.] He held up his finger.

He trotted off to the rear of a makeshift cube stand. When he came back, he had two other officers with him, one of whom was a much more of official looking ripper who was now carrying my soap dish Hitler style as if it were toxic.

"Sir. This is ganja or what you hipsters call pot. This is illegal substances to be having on the aircraft or within the airport limits. Do you understand?"

Hipsters? Was that his idea of Miranda, I pondered? Or, was it simply you're allowed to have this stuff, just not in the places where we perform our jobs, places where we can actually see you with it outright as in the middle of the terminal?

"I'm terribly sorry. I didn't know. Please excuse my error." I apologized.

When everything else fails, what's the birdbrain move a novice crook makes? You go it. Plead ignorance to the law. Yeah, that always works well.

"I'm sorry too, Mr. Ibsen. I'm afraid to inform you that you are under arrest. You are being arrested for transporting illicit substances upon airport property." He demanded I put my hands behind my back because he was going to handcuff me.

"What? Are you kidding? I've got to board my flight! I've got to get back to Bangalore!" I pleaded as though I was late for the christening of the Ark.

By this time, the other rodent had dug passed my underpants and socks and was extracting the umpteen bundles of rupees. There was virtually more scratch in my satchel than the mealy-mouthed private made in his last ten years on the job. When he came over with the bundles of hundred rupee notes and showed them to his boss, the look on the big Honshu was one of sheer mortification.

"What is this, Mr. Ibsen? Why are you transporting this large quantity of rupees?" He drew out the E for what seemed like an eternity.

At the end of his canyon, the Sundance Kid tossed in the towel instead of eating his gun, although I didn't have one at the moment. I opted for telling the truth, another novice move on my part.

"Changing money with my pals over at the Kasbah."

The Moon Women

My confession might have saved me a bucket of grief when everything was said and done. Open-and-shut case they look the other way when it comes to the black market but for the dope market they pounce on your ass. Otherwise they could have impounded the whole mess and even confiscate the currency. Tell you the truth, I was surprised they didn't simply run off with it. After grilling me repeatedly, all he got was more of the same alibi.

"Just changing some moola into rupees at one of your local establishments, Boss." Merely sticking to my candid deposition, Detective.

They manhandled me, the smoke, and the pile of dinero over to a claustrophobic holding station. I had to sit there for the quite a while. Over a period of too many hours, sundry Wallahs bobbed in and out of the revolving door of permission offering to ring up a tab for Chai, masala dosa, chapatti, fried chilies, a Thumbs Up or, on rare occasions, a Fanta, which is an orangeade soda. I plead guilty to all those charges. Time passed by in quadrants of Asian sludge.

Sometime in the late afternoon, they unlocked the door, handcuffed me a second time, and escorted me out of the holding cell to voyage forth across the traffic in a ramshackle jeep. Two jigs later, I was the proud occupant of the Delhi Cantonment, a jailhouse of sprawling units lined up end to end like railroad cars. My hosts enjoyed flagstaff accommodations in an administration office across the avenue.

In keeping with my international status, they had reserved the one cell on the end of the block, saying with a giggle they were granting me plush Five Star status; I should be most pleased to get the stockade, which contained only one other prisoner and not five. The dumpy guy curled up there in a skittish huddle looked like a Muslim brother in his thirties and reminded me strangely of Sambath Kyew, in spite of the fact I knew that wasn't possible. He was dead. But this one did have those same nasty dirty clothes. Plus, he looked really, really scared just like Sambath did right before he was shot. But that comes later. You'll just have to excuse me because I'm suffering from the discombobulating disassociations coming off the random chapter effect.

- 24 -

The cell was the filthiest shit hole I have ever seen in my life. The icy concrete floor displayed a rat's nest of prisoner aftermath. Littered with twisted scraps of brown stained paper, foul detritus, and scatterings of incrusted waste set adrift upon these concrete sheets from the endless procession of its previous residents, the place sucked. All along the crumbling interiors there were haphazard frescos created by former captors locked in state as they wiped their hands to rid themselves of unwanted filth. A more complete engorgement of human crud and debris I have never witnessed. Moreover, this piss hole in a shit box was a torturously cramped pigpen; call it three meters square with a low-slung concrete slab for a ceiling to give its guests the true feeling of slammer life.

There were two contaminated mattress pads thrown lengthwise for sleeping, each one defining the margins of secular life. My prisoner buddy had already bedded down on the one farthest from the drain and the smell. Cheerfully now I could call the other one home. Over in the squatter's lowlands, away from the raunchy mats, lines of squashed excrement orbited a solitary turd like rings circumscribing Saturn. And daren't I forget the flies enjoying themselves everywhere. The stench was like living death.

My first major bummer occurred after lying down for a while to get some shut-eye. It had been a trying day and I couldn't imagine what I was going to be up against come sunrise in this dungeon. But it looked bad. Rolling up my khaki army jacket, I made a pillow by tucking the wad under my head. I stretched out to get some long due unwinding. In no time, something was biting my calves. Hiking up my pants, I discovered a horde of bed bugs digging into my flesh. Flicking them off didn't minify their onslaught. Indisputably, they were Hindustani bed bugs because after they had ceased tumbling, they obediently righted themselves and reinitiated their march in supplication to their deity, the blood sources resident in my legs. Sleeping here was going to be futile.

I hobbled over to the vertical slab of rotten brass that was the dungeon's door. There was a pitiful looking rectangle of sky up there, the outlet to freedom, from where I might get a shot at registering my future prospects. It had wrought iron bars running vertically every few inches. I clung to them desperately watching dusk slide into the

The Moon Women

city. It was fixing to replace the muscle of daylight with its boney darkness.

As I hung there moaning over how the heck I was going to get myself out of this mess, I witnessed the gray crows caw to one another quibbling over dried mango skins. The murmur of traffic in the distance uplifted me with some expectation of meaningful calculations. As I stared into the soft twilight, I could observe a single star hanging just over the vague tree line. The Khrng could not usurp my privileges now. I had taken refuge outside their locator shields. In some ways, their company would have been preferable to this wasteland; the featured sights of barren alien territories might have offered perverse entertainment, except that notion would be misleading; there really aren't any alien habitats to fret over.

- 25 -

I spent midnight with Montezuma's revenge, but this strain was more like the Maharaja's revenge thanks to the burning hot geysers, which shot out of my ass. Knowing I desperately needed some milk of magnesia, I contemplated chewing on the buttons of my bush jacket for some relief but the threads wouldn't give.

This decrepit hoosegow had no heat of any kind except for the captured bodies. Insomuch as there were only the two of us and we weren't going to be snuggling up, that's for sure, by the wee hours of pre-dawn, the cold sleuth had granted its blessings in quantum buckets. The previous evening I had forced myself to swallow some of the slop they put into the wretched feed pan, which the guards had tossed into the cell like a hockey puck. It was akin to slurping battery acid. It had burned going down as well as squirting out my rear. At best, I was lucky the discharge of yellow chyle had carried all the other turds and excrement down and out the two-inch gullet in the corner, which was our toilet. Clean up was clean up.

Occasionally one has to feel blessed with the little things in life, those silver linings, which everyone keeps harping on. You know; the ones which go by really, really fast. So fast, it's hopeless to recognize them successfully; the ones that are proof of alternative realities, which we are always running away from; running and howling from the far-flung pranks we pulled back in days gone by.

168

From a shallow snooze, what little there was of it in the sit up sleeping state, I had a wicked case of myalgia tightening up my thighs. The nasty vampire cooties had kept me on my toes until the bleeding rays of sunrise. Exhausted, I drifted off as I shivered in the freezing lockup. Leaning against the gritty façade, my back had become a slab of dead meat.

Desperately I pondered the crumbling frescos facing me, the ones, which portrayed the pitiable histories of previous clientele who had scraped their declarations of plebeian vanity by grinding their fingernails down to the bone. Perchance some of these Paleolithic visitors even sparked some pride as they recorded the underlying meanings of their putrid banalities upon the crumbling extremities.

Besides my two complaints concerning the lack of sleep and the results of bad food, I was undeniably suffering under the annoying malady of muscae voliantes: I kept seeing floaters whenever I blinked my eyes. It was as if I was visualizing a mist of gnats floating a short distance away from my nose, a malady having as its cause loose cells and cell fragments, which float in the vitreous humor of the eyeball.

Incidentally, I had two phantasms while in that hallmark of claustrophobia. One occurred as I was staring out the barred vent, which earmarked the jailhouse door yielding the only path for transcendence. It was a bulky slab of bruised iron posing as the main deterrent to random outbreaks of lunacy. This time I wasn't struggling with the bars like a hopeless hostage or tank drunk lunatic. Squatted down with my back against the cold concrete, I was imagining the pastures of flowing wheat and racehorses wound up with delirium as my body temps sank.

When the iron bars changed somehow, I knew shortly it would be upon me, the window again. The vertical shafts of steel were no longer made of a dead metal. Instead, they had become alive with intense heat. They proceeded to emit burning colors, like an ingot, which had been extracted from a crucible. As the bars continued to glow, they also initiated a slight rotation. It wasn't long before the set of bars were spinning furiously. Their pin wheeling action created a solid mass of incandescent light, which forged itself into the now familiar rectangle, the threshold from out of the Beyond.

As it stabilized, I focused more intently on the sheen of its rippling metal skin. Soon the edge of its shade rose eerily to manifest

The Moon Women

an inky unknown, which exploded with pinpricks of light and I just gave in. And out of this starry void came the appendages and then the torso of another off-world being whose makeup was sheathed with those chromium tinsel flakes. Sparkling with its cold-fired insanity, it came through and thrust its ghastly presence into my space. It ignored my partner in crime who slumbered conked out on his mat enjoying his little death with the bugs and the offering made as a precursor for blessed life.

As the alter-demon strode towards me, it cranked up the lumens on its tinseled glitter to whiter than white. I was surprised the intense brilliance of the thing's flame suit didn't wake the officers in the Cantonment office across the way. I hesitated not knowing if I should strike out or back off. As the angeloid advanced with determination, its azure eyes were horrifically intense as it unfurled its wings forming a canopy of whiteness over our territory. Seeing its molten feet sparking on the grimy floor, I could clearly discern faint Arthur Murray footprints creating a glowing trail behind it as the fire being progressed in my direction. Then with seething rage, the burning chimes rained down and bisected the back streets of my mental apparatus with a vengeance.

UNTO THE ANGEL OF THE CHURCH [25]

THESE THINGS SAITH
HE WHO IS THE FAITHFUL
AND TRUE WITNESS.

IF ANY MAN HAVE AN EAR
LET HIM HEAR [26]

AS DOCTRINE FROM EPHESUS
LEGION *TO ABADDON*
AND SON OF MAN
THIS SERVANT DOETH HOLD

I SERVE THE COUNCIL OF EPHESUS

THE PILLAR OF KOKABEL

I AM KOKABEL

HE THAT LEADS US
INTO CAPTIVITY

170

Haan Moses

SHALL GO INTO CAPTIVITY

HE THAT KILLS WITH THE SWORD
MUST BE KILLED BY THE SWORD

HERE IS THE PATIENCE AND
THE FAITH OF THE SAINTS [27]

I HEARD A VOICE FROM HEAVEN

The sounds of water

AS THE VOICE OF MANY WATERS

And thunder are the

AND THE VOICE

Initial Astral sounds

OF A GREAT THUNDER

I HEARD THE VOICE OF THE
HARPING OF HARPS [28]
AND THEY SUNG AS IT WERE
NEW SONG BEFORE THE THRONE
BEFORE THE ELDERS
THAT NO MAN COULD LEARN
BUT HIM WHO WAS
REDEEMED FROM EARTH [29]

ONE OF THE CRUCIAL INNER SOUNDS
INDICATING INNER TRANSCENDENT KNOWLEDGE

AND I SAW ANOTHER ANGEL
FLY IN THE MIDST OF HEAVEN
HAVING THE EVERLASTING
GOSPEL TO PREACH TO THEM
THAT DWELL ON THE EARTH [30]
AND TO SAY WITH A LOUD VOICE
FEAR NOT
FOR HIS JUDGMENT IS COME [31]

The Moon Women

Kokabel took a knee and assumed the posture of a praying man in confession.

WE HAVE PUT DOWN
THE EVIL LOCUSTS
THE SMOKE OF THEIR TORMENT
ASCENDS FOR EVER AND EVER
THEY HAVE NO REST
BY DAY OR BY NIGHT

THE KHRNG ARE HARD TO RECKON WITH

BEHOLD A WHITE CLOUD AND

THIS IS A STATEMENT

UPON THE CLOUD SITS ONE   OF THE PRIMARY PURPOSE
LIKE UNTO THE SON OF MAN   WITH REGARD TO WHY
HAVING ON HIS HEAD   THE ANGELS APPEAR
A GOLDEN CROWN   AND PERSEVERE IN THEIR PLAN
AND IN HIS HAND   TO ENSNARE THEIR TARGET
A SHARP SICKLE [32]   USING PSYCHIC WEAPONRY

SUCH A ONE IS YOU   FOR INSURING THE FUTURE OF MAN

The majestic angel stood up and extended his paw thing in my direction.

THE SEVEN ANGELS HAVE COME
OUT OF THE TEMPLE HAVING
BEEN GIVEN THE SEVEN PLAGUES

THE SEVEN PLAGUES ARE GATES

CLOTHED IN PURE
AND WHITE LINEN AND
HAVING THEIR BREASTS
GIRDED WITH
GOLDEN GIRDLES [33]

THE GIRDLES ARE KEYS

172

AND A GREAT VOICE
CAME OUT OF THE TEMPLE
SAYING TO THE SEVEN ANGELS
GO YOUR WAYS AND
POUR OUT THE VIALS T‍HE VIALS ARE TOOLS
OF THE WRATH OF GOD
THE NIRUNJAN *THE BURNING GOD*
UPON THE EARTH AND UPON [34]
THE SHAPES OF THE LOCUSTS T‍HE LOCUSTS ARE THE KHRNG
THAT WERE LIKE UNTO HORSES
PREPARED FOR BATTLE AND ON
THEIR HEADS WERE AS CROWNS
OF GOLD AND THEIR FACES WERE

HORSES WITH FACES OF MEN
AS THE FACES OF MEN [35] A‍RE THE SUPERMEN

THEY HAD HAIR
AS THE HAIR OF WOMEN
AND THEIR TEETH WERE
AS THE TEETH OF LIONS [36]
THEY HAD BREASTPLATES
AS IT WERE BREASTPLATES
OF IRON AND THE SOUND
OF THEIR COMING
WAS AS THE SOUND
OF CHARIOTS AND
OF MANY HORSES RUNNING
TO BATTLE [37] T‍HESE ARE THE MACHINES OF WAR

The great angel held up his burning hand as if proclaiming a Faustian prophecy.

THESE ARE THE THIRD
PART OF MEN LIKE UNTO
SERPENTS THAT COME

The Moon Women

AS A PLAGUE
UPON THE EARTH   Which are a genetic component

AFTER THESE THINGS
I SAW ANOTHER ANGEL
COME DOWN FROM HEAVEN
HAVING GREAT POWER
AND THE EARTH WAS LIGHTED
WITH HIS GLORY AND HE CRIED
MIGHTILY WITH A STRONG VOICE
SAYING BABYLON THE GREAT
IS FALLEN AND HAS BECOME
THE HABITATION OF DEVILS
AND THE HOLD OF EVERY FOUL
SPIRIT AND A CAGE OF EVERY
UNCLEAN AND HATEFUL BIRD
              Something is about to occur in the world
              which will enable this transformation

THEREFORE SHALL THE PLAGUES
COME IN ONE DAY WITH DEATH
AND MOURNING AND FAMINE
              This is the calling of the John

SHE SHALL BE UTTERLY
BURNED WITH FIRE
FOR STRONG IS THE LORD GOD
              Mother Earth shall burn
THE NIRUNJAN *WHO JUDGES HER* [38]
              As the martyr of Man

SUCH IS THE PROPHESY
THAT WILL BE BEEN GIVEN
UNTO YOU BY THE PROPHETS
TO GATHER THE SEEDS OF MEN

174

FOR THE GARNISH OF THE WHEAT
HOLDS THE KEY FOR ALL
THE MANY PEOPLES AND NATIONS

This prophetic statement from

AND TONGUES AND KINGS [39]

Kokabel must be well understood

Kokabel gathered himself into a fetal bundle and withdrew back through the crack in Time and the aluminum escarpment settled down confirming its schedule. It reclaimed its original stature as the bars of my cooler. And the gate to heaven sealed up its wind.

The second catalepsis occurred later on after an oddball noise woke me some time before midnight. I had slumped over and was aimed dead ahead at the shit hole delta of this tawdry slice of Hades. Since it was well before dawn, my cellmate had been motivated to secure what he trusted would be some privacy. He had squatted down with his back facing me. All I remember was that dripping appendage hanging down from his rectum. That's all I'm going to say concerning that caudate vision.

They came to get me at a hair passed seven shortly after the guards had downed their fix of Chai. They manacled me hand and foot and hauled me off into the back of an olive-drab van crammed with all the other hoodlums. The stench in there was horrid. As we vacated the Cantonment, there was another prison unit pulling in which had a black logo of the Ashoka Chakra or the Wheel of India on its side. Inside I glimpsed someone who was a dead ringer of my former partner in crime, Sean Gregor. That doppelgänger keeps showing up in the weirdest spots. What if the poor bastard gets himself trapped in the morgue. To help him, I pronounced a solemn prayer I made up myself.

"And it came to pass, as the angels were gone away into heaven, be safe and be toward God." [40]

- 26 -

It was a twenty-minute outing through the maniacal streets of Delhi. Miracles of life and death never cease on the streets of this Asian sub-continent. After our rusted caboose had run over one or two homeless beggars who couldn't get out of the way in time, they

175

The Moon Women

dumped us all out onto the gutted run siding a walled-in quadrangle, which looked to be nearly forty meters along its edge. The lag-wall was open ended at the entrance but nowhere else. Even in the early morning, the climate was hot and muggy with stale humanity. The motley exterior of the Court of the High Commission, anointed with the life and death sagas spanning five centuries or more, posed its barricade to justice and freedom.

Caked onto the pealed and gouged plaster was an organic mural of pain and suffering. A Jackson Pollok coating of sloppy fixes and the legal vomit of pained verdicts inveigled the viewer to ante up more of his sanity or else go all in. Encrusted with the barnacled wounds of agonies the viewer could hardly fathom nor empathize over, these were the walls, which were smeared with the pathos of lowbred humanity. Just as the crop of barnacles grows on the backs of the elder whale to shield him from the harsh realities of his world as he searches the ocean's depths for his misplaced love songs, these walls have provided a barrier against the harbored grief of lost battles, and the buried lies of purged witnesses. But I suspected that entombed within their core was the real essence of life captured like a crystal of truth that the world would never see or gape in awe of its misaligned magnificence. These were the walls, on which you wouldn't want to land your fly especially if they could talk. These were the maculate ramparts, which had overseen an army of legal palette knives fillet the flesh of felons who had lain manacled in legless forlorn over the last four hundred and ninety thousand days, these were the walls which deserved complete avoidance, if you could help it.

Punctuating the mid-border of the exterior stockade were recessed embrasures. Each one had a greasy brass ring the size of a dinner plate mortised onto its stone lip. Two of the body snatchers lugged me over to one of these harnessing stalls and hooked me up like a cow soon to be slaughtered. By undoing one of the imposing manacles on my wrists and then threading the loose handcuff and its adjoining chain through the tarnished loop to again clasp it back onto my wrist was how they set me free in my playpen of torture. I felt like a Mameluke slam tethered to a slave post.

My eye wandered the landscape for any hint of budding foliage, which might grant me temporary relaxation simply by observing it. After practicing this exercise for several moments, the

176

lowing of my sightline landed on an impoverished mimosa splattered with droppings from the jack crows. Their street gang operated a justice system of their own waging mock legal battles over scraps of rotten fruit. I wondered what savior would redeem their useless efforts. It wasn't hard to see my own desperate plight locked up in that reach. Where is my Mordecai now? Who is going to get me out of this mess? My prayers were frantic and saturated with a waxing desperation.

It wasn't long before I caught sight of a mammoth Sikh walking my way. He looked like a barbarian down from the hinterlands. With his tangled grizzle of a beard and his flaming yellow turban, he drew a jagged bead on my downtrodden status. As the fuselage of his headgear flapped like the prehensile tail of a moon tiger, his flabby jowls jutted out when he growled his welcome.

"Sahib Iggyson is it?" The rancid stench of neglected mutton leaked out through the porridge of his Hindi accent.

"Yup. That's me, I guess." Any greeting would do.

"Yeshir, Iggyson, I read here you be suffer from bad charges of this ganja. Is it not?" He was barely comprehensible.

"That's what they tell me." I wasn't really sure what the charge was.

"Iyam lawyer, Mr. Iggyson. I can lawyer for you and get you bery okay deal, Sir. I remedy these charges for your same self. For you two hundred rupees only. You be liking it in prison so much and it be exciting in there after all. Five years maximum for you. So no worry for you not more." He brushed his spatulate hand over the moth-eaten woolens of his horsehair jacket, which paraded more of a bear costume from last Halloween than any barrister attire.

"Well, thanks, but no thanks. I think I'll wait for a quicker deal to come by. Sorry." Since the whole shebang looked like a bazaar, I thought I might as well treat it like one so I waved the wingnut off.

"Achaa! Apka pagal hey! You a crazy fella. No?" [Okay, fine! You're crazy.]

The gormless weasel sauntered off lazily mumbling more Hindi expletives to himself. His mad-brain locomotions kicked out a scud of dust in his wake. I gathered the loose shreds of my life up close like some ensnared marine proteus wrangling to grow an

The Moon Women

appendage of emancipation. Was I too cavalier with him? Only time would tell.

Presently, I spied the second turban on the horizon. This one was a bright Martin red. The stout Sikh underneath it was a tad smaller than the other one, but he looked to be better dressed to a certain degree. Although he wore sandals unlike the last Sadar Ji who was barefoot, this one's demeanor was way smoother than the other hump. Unfortunately, when he came closer I was appalled his complexion had excessive pockmarks like the netted tracings of the rind on a cantaloupe. "What brand of malarkey is this one going to feed me?" I wondered.

"Namaste Ji. My name is Mr. Singh. Have you a binding contract with the other barrister? If no for that I shall begin with some proposals." He introduced himself and laid into me with his Marshall plan.

"No. Not at all. What's your deal?" I figured let's get on with it already.

"Well, Mr. Ibsen, this is quite a grave charge, you follow me? The court will not accede to less than a four-year sentence, I'm afraid. It is your great and esteemed fortune that should you accept my services. I believe I could get such bad sentences cut cheap for you only. Let's agree to five hundred rupees, Sir; if you would so kindly sign here, please." He handed me an enormously fat pen along with a batch of messy crumpled up sheets of paper with rudimentary type on it.

"Not so fast, Buddy. Ah, what did you say your name was? Mr. Singh? Well, I think I'd be able to get out sooner with your successor. Thanks a lot anyway." I resisted his Machiavellian stranglehold.

"No, no, no, no. There will no be any others. I assure for you. My offer is most last and most best offer, which I will be get for you today. If you no accept it, you gonna wind-up staying in prison many, many years. It not a nice place our prison, Mr. Ibsen. You feel for me?" He was tenacious. I'll give him that.

"Yeah, I do feel for you, Man. But no is no. I said no thank you and I mean no thank you. No thank you ever so much." He wasn't buying it frankly.

"Listen here, Mr. Ibsen. Don't be a malcontent. I must insist you agree with me this offer most fast and double-up or else. It is the only one you have Aaj, Maharaji." [Today, Sir.]

"Chello, Bhai! Chello!" [Piss off, Buddy! Get lost!]

Taking a dim view of his connection to the Indian Mafia, if even there was such a thing, I cut him off in mid-sentence and flicked my hand to dust him off. Over and above the notion that this gesture is an extreme token of disrespect and derision, it is irrefutable in India. You don't argue against the insult of that move. Angrily he departed swearing beneath his breath in garbled Hindi or Urdu or some other native dialect. All Indians are a multi-lingual bunch. At a minimum, they all speak three languages. Muttering he made his maddened retreat.

While lingering for my succeeding benefactor to arrive, and I was moderately sure there would be one; I corralled one of the road hawkers over to me thinking maybe I could buy some sambaar chutney or perchance a couple of dosas. My unforeseen lurch caused all the soldier dudes to freak out. All askitter, one hoisted his Garand at me. And with his finger on the trigger, mind you! Dumb move on my part, I guess.

In due time, a further divergent law understudy waddled my way. This one had a spinach colored turban wrapped much more cleanly and with some flair. He had a business suit and actual shoes.

"Good day. Mr. Ibsen, is it? I am Harvinder Singh at your service." He wobbled his mustachioed hairnet. Sikh gentlemen always have fully grown beards, which they bundle behind tightly wrapped netting strapped into their turbans.

"I am understanding prior negotiations for your clemency have not been satisfactory, Sir. I should like to grant you one time my package arrangement offer one thousand rupees only. That guarantees you a max stay of but six to nine months in jail. It also guarantees my malpractice insurance, which one cannot do without these days. You can pass on this arrangement, more likely, should you do so, I cannot come back. Time is money, you see, Mr. Ibsen. Time is money." He glowered with a fishy hand offering.

"I never refuse to shake a man's hand. But your offer seems to be a little lite. I would simply like this misunderstanding to be over and done with. Now! You get what I mean?" I was just cut and dry. Please release me from this shithole!

179

The Moon Women

"I don't think you be thinking well of some importance from a situation of yours. You charged with some capital offenses requires much of a mandatory term in prison today, which must, must, must be served. There is no way round about on this, I am assurance for you, Sir. I have been the district councilor six years to tell you quite honestly and most mentionable, you must accept this arrangement; otherwise, your days will become much disturbed for the dire consequentials quite a while until your end. Do you hear me?"

As the turbaned windbag concluded his bumptious assertions, spicules of sweat mixed with the oral foam whipped up from his flapping tongue started to gag me. I summed up his service by starring at the fading mimosa lining the streets. With another flick of my hand, he, too, faded into the boondocks.

As the noonday sun beat down upon the million pulsing hearts threatening to crush me with the gravity of desperation, I had no choice but to release these futile tensions and allow the flatness of fatigue to creep into my bones. Admittedly, many have claimed I have scads of patience coursing through my veins but lately it was waning thin. I realized it's only genetic and, more romantically, unavoidable, but I reserve the right to resist classifying it as any kind of link to immortality. Granted it came from my mother's tree. The Old Man was a time bomb.

It wasn't more than thrice the twinkling of an eye before a broken down taxi swung by and out jumped the fourth dapper law sleuth. He was quite younger than the other three. He sashayed straight over to me and performed the prerequisite indoctrinations. His name was also Mr. Singh. However, this paralegal's deal involved a cute twist, one thousand now, and one thousand later when I was out of prison. I would only have to be in jail for one or two months at the most. Out came a bunch of papers for me to sign. Pleading avidly for me to drop my signature on the dotted line he trotted out his ballpoint, which he waved imitating the conductor of an orchestra. His demeanor was hypnotic. I must say I was tempted.

"Mr. Singh, I realize you are most generously providing me with the choicest plan that has come across my desk today, it's just that unfortunately I've got to be back in Bangalore no later than tomorrow at the outset. If you can do that, then we can talk. Otherwise, it's a no-go." I was using colloquialisms, which were over this chum's academics.

His attempts proved to be futile as well just like the other cadre of Sikh lawyers. He trudged over to his wrecked taxi and departed leaving a sooty brume of exhaust. As he drove off, I watched an overgrown pachyderm lumber down the alley all by itself twirling its trunk and cleaving mimosa limbs on which to munch. You can witness these surreal events almost every day as you live and breathe in India.

Fighting off hunger, I was making book on when the ensuing legal beagle might show. If I had a watch on, I'd be checking it periodically, but they stole all my toys when they put me into that pigsty of a jail. I would approximate the sun had crossed the yardarm with grace as empires lapsed since they hitched me to this watering trough, which, by the way, was bone dry.

"Hey! Can I get a Chai?" I tried to catch the attention of the daffy prison shepherd, but it was to no avail.

These jailors get heavy duty training to look elsewhere. As I was wasting away at the hitching post and mopping the sweat off my brow with my sleeve, a spotless graphite Mercedes lumbered in. Its glass was fully tinted so I couldn't really tell who was in there. It sat there ominously on the tarmac for a moment and then the rear door swung clear and out came the slickest Sikh businessman I have ever seen. This one looked like the real deal. He had a white turban, whereas the previous Sikh's was turquoise. The proud Sikh who stood at the ready had a three-piece suit and sharply creased trousers. He was fitted to the nines, as they say. He was even wearing sunglasses, Ray Bans, if I'm not mistaken. His strapped beard shone like glacier ice. He came over and suavely introduced himself as Mr. Singh, of course, but I had a feeling this Mr. Singh was the genuine item.

"I see you have been quite beleaguered by my esteemed associates so far today, is it not? Have no fears, Mr. Ibsen. I am here to assist you. There are some prominent people who are seriously concerned over your whereabouts. We don't need to mention any names, to the contrary; but they must not be disappointed." He calmly postulated his motives.

"I'm all set to fly like a bird. Drop me a line and I'll buzz off." I was also in quite a dehydrated condition in spite of there still being considerable cosmic paste left on the toothbrush.

The Moon Women

"You Americans; always so clever. Would you care for some Chai?" He smirked. This chap was a true benefactor and a godsend. I could tell from his spit polished wingtips and his grill of gold caps.

"Dyin' of thirst, Dude."

He retired for a brief pause at the window of his big Merc and snapped his fingers. After which the driver handed him a thermos and he sauntered back to my place in the sun and unscrewed the cap. With a deft flip, he righted the cup and filled it with some fine smelling Indian Chai which he handed over along with two biscuits to boot.

"That should square away some of your needs for the forthcoming whiles. Now, I propose to have you out of this den of iniquity within the hour. How do you like those sounds, Mr. Ibsen?"

I took the Chai and his proposal and downed both.

"Excellent. Your sounds are excellent, Man. What do I have to do?" I was eager to get this show on the road; work to do, places to go, people to see. I handed him back the empty. He put the cap back on the thermos and gave it a stiff tap.

"Before you hear what I have to say with regard to your exoneration, Mr. Ibsen, you must pay earnest attention to my words and deliberate upon my remuneration. It is a flat fee. It covers all the exigent payments, which must to be made to the court as well as my fee." He bobbled his head in teeter-totter fashion, as Indians do when they are squarely leveling with you.

"In view of some importunate circumstances and the ineptness of the prosecutor who has overlooked the salient facts of this case, one of which being the arresting detective has since deceased antithetical to your confinement, your case poses weak prosecution at best. Thus, the court's attorney now has to face the onerous hurdle of tracking down another one, another detective with the wherewithal to overlay the confiscation of your property. I am most confident concerning our strategy of a genuine Latches defense, which will avoid any irksome prospects for the most part. Trust me, Mr. Ibsen, I shall have this matter resolved straightaway. And thereafter, by reason of a special card, which I plane to procure at the proper moment, your record will be cleanly expunged of any and all recorded charges as well as possible connections to your municipal files and links to external ones including Interpol. Are you with me?" He was exceptionally thorough. Of that, I was categorically certain.

"Well, all righty then, King Daddy. Let's hop right on that pony   and   ride."

"Oh, you giddy Americans! Always so clever. When you are discharged from this dungeon, and you will be, Mr. Ibsen, have no fears about it, I will escort you from the courthouse. Forthwith I shall deliver you to some appropriate Five Star accommodations guaranteed, where you will be booked into a penthouse suite with all the amenities so that you may unwind at your leisure and reestablish some modicum of sanity after all this mess. What say you to these plans?" Upon his humble vest, he pressed his palms together in prayer.

"I say bully for your plans and bully for your esteemed presence, ma Man! I say let's go for it! Get me the hell out of here! Please!" I was ecstatic.

"Oh, wery good, Sir. So wery good. I shall commence my efforts immediately."

"Oh, by the way, how much is it going to be? Er, you know, the cost?"

"The fee for this service is typically seven to eight thousand rupees. But not to hassle for your same self, Sir. Thanks to some inopportune circumstances, for you, Mr. Ibsen, the fee will be a mere five thousands. Is that acceptable to your kind self?" His professional mannerisms were second to none.

"Fine and dandy, Chief!" I didn't care if my knight in shining armor hadn't a clue to what I just bonked on my forehead. "Let's get movin' and go, Daddy 0!"

"Such genuinely upliftment on your part, Sir. Very well. I am to begin direct off with your New York minutes. Please to you for a courtesy and seem to wait here on the spot." He was ever so polite but his trips on feigning back home cheer were not making tremendous strides with me quite yet.

"I ain't goin' anywhere, Ole Buddy. Donchu fret a wink. I'll be here fending off all the rivals who might be running some game to steal my favorite brass coupling here. It's a betrothal for Samson, I believe." I don't think he followed any of my maximalist logic.

"You Americans! I can't help it! Always so ingenious. Let's hush up. Well, one moment, I shall just now go and come." He trotted over to his luxurious German ride and crawled into the back seat. The car rolled out proudly with the winning composure of victory.

The Moon Women

Two shakes of a jig later, I was escorted into the High Court, a squalid sweat pit crammed with detainees all hollering and screaming from every platform and hollowed cage and even from the balconies. The guards shepherded me over and made me wait at a slatted gate. I was so conspicuous like an overgrown macrocyte loitering in the platelet zone. Way up on his bench the Judge was engaged in a hushed chat with two slicker'n-shit attorneys.

"Excuse me, Your Honor! Jawaharlal Singh here. I wish to plead an urgent Doctrine of Latches Estoppel, Your Honor. Henceforth, if it please this court it is attested inclusive of a suitable appendix accompanied by all the legitimate writs of Mutatis Mutandis motions to wit, Sir. If it please this most honorable court." He was putting everyone else on hold with his inflated insouciance.

The Judge made a smug scowl and looked down at me as if he was observing some hairy insect harboring a lethal stinger.

"There will be no suchlike occurrences in my court I'll have you know. Who is this derelict?" The Judge was attempting to disperse us with a salvo of rancid mouthwash.

"If it please the court, may I approach the bench?" Mr. Singh sure knew his stuff.

The Judge, whose name, not surprisingly, was the Honorable Judge Bindranath Singh (said so on the plaque), waved my Mr. Singh over with that hand flapping gesticulation where the forefingers appear to pat the air. As is the custom within Indian courts, they discussed the matter, not with Hindi, but using their bastardized curried English.

I overheard my attorney state most categorically the charges didn't carry any true malfeasance because the indictment cited an outdated and void statute. Without delay, they talked feverishly and then that chattering escalated into a fist pummeling argument, which languished with a lengthy pause. Yet, little did I know the dismissal of my case would pose an embarrassing black mark upon the face of the court. The only remedy for this legal lesion on the Judge's tribunal coattails was to override my attorney's efforts directly with a shocking conclusion - I would have to go to prison on the spot!

Nonetheless, hand it to my Mr. Singh to unearth a loophole within which you could park a jumbo jet. With a graduated cleverness and the winsome persistence, he unraveled a cinch in the Judge's background, which involved some young ladies whom ole

Jawaharlal had dangling on his expense sheet. I hung on an eternity of desperation, which was abruptly cut short by His Honor's shaking his head miserably in defeat. Ole Bindi made his head wiggle of acceptance and I knew we were in! Jambalaya! Sock it to me! Then the Judge waved his white flag with this declaration.

"Hear yea! Hear yea! This honorable court must insist and declare the following verdict: the defendant, in an attempt to offset his indictment of contraband and thus, mitigate his sentence, has pleaded that he had recently, and quite unexpectedly, been searched upon boarding one of our domestic airline carriers, that his journey [Indian Airlines flight 719] was delayed due to a bomb scare search, which, unbeknownst to him, had been declared for the purposes of public safety and the security of our ports and aerodromes, to wit, the Sahar International facilities, which, incidentally, has been seen to provide significant discounts to customers who have been enrolled in the Janata Samaj; said search having been conducted under the auspices of a proper bench warrant, which nevertheless, and most confusing for this foreigner's plight, was lacking the certified seal and stamp of a sitting magistrate, the one being out of station during the indoctrination of his jurisdiction; is hereby released without prejudice."

They dilly-dallied in and out with some more mumbo jumbo. For his conclusion, my Mr. Singh handed over some papers to the Judge. After shuffling through them, he signed them on the bottom line and my Mr. Singh waved them over his head in victory.

Holy Toledo! Get me the fuck outa here, Cisco! Now! I was feeling quite giddy.

With a crowning nod, my Mr. Singh came over to me and busied his finger at my shackles and handcuffs to indicate their removal to which the bailiff complied with earnest haste. I was so happy I hugged my Mr. Singh with a big double armful. He got all flustered and waved me off, but I did it anyway. I never want to go through anything like that ever again. I was elated at the pas de deux the Judge had with my Mr. Singh and how the whole strategy played out so lickety-split. I thought wouldn't it be a miracle if the justice system in America could work in this same manner. Boy, would that save the American taxpayers a bundle of cash.

Whilst exiting Delhi's rookery of justice, I picked up on two curveballs. Although I was no vexillologist, I had noticed the Indian

The Moon Women

flag queerly askew on a crooked staff. Menacing wires had drooped down out of a breach in the vaulted dome of the ceiling and were strangling it. At the hand of this wicked brute of anarchy, the patriotism of the land was having its honor mercilessly choked out of it. And it was tilted over and touching the floor as well. It looked all wrong, that's all. For this to be the sovereignty where justice and the laws of the land were dispensed, it sure seemed they should have put more true grit into the display of their flag. The second oddity, which kept flashing alarms, was all the mossy green upholstery; it was everywhere. I took it to be a dismal omen of misaligned furniture Speak and so I split from that place forever. I birddogged my Mr. Singh out through the mangy crowd and joined him in his limo.

"Hot damn! Where we going now, Boss?" I was overjoyed to be free after all the drudgery.

"I am so very and most joyously touched to have been meeting to you, Mr. Rahm. I can only say most other Americans I have counseled did not prove to be, well, so very cordial and uplifting; I must say. So in proper answer for you, Sir, we will now proceed to the Cantonment itself to retrieve your personal effects. I am going to request the recovery of your satchel, your funds, your wardrobe, and your hygiene as well. And, if I am lucky, perhaps I will even be able to retrieve your ganja. We shall see, isn't it?" My Mr. Singh was a man of unwavering commitment.

"Thanks, Perry, ma Man. Do lead on."

We arrived back at my memorable homestead, the Cantonment barracks, and parked opposite to the jail.

"You wait here. I'll see what to do for your same self." My Mr. Singh got out and deftly ascended the crumbling steps. In no time, he emerged with my satchel under his arm.

"I regret to inform you, Mr. Ibsen, but the officer would not relinquish the ganja. Not for mentioning, Sir, I was able to retrieve your rupees, your personal effects, as well as the soap dish itself, Mr. Ibsen. I hope this is satisfactory for you, Sir? Conceivably you might replenish it with some other types of soap." He chuckled. He had certainly gone the extra mile, er, kilometer. This has to be acceptable for continental glamor.

"I'm fine with it, Mr. Singh. Home James!" I offered this cliché thinking he would have no idea what it meant, but instead he split his ribs and slapped his knee. Professedly they get reruns of Perry Mason way out here.

Off we tootled to my new palace, the swank Taj Mahal in New Delhi. They checked me in and then escorted me to the elevator. As I was thanking Mr. Singh profusely, he bowed humbly but then reminded me there was one nagging detail, which I had neglected to do yet.

"If you would be so kind as to remit my fee, it would be so fabulously appreciated." He swiftly entwined his fingers and bowed slightly.

"Oh, my God. I totally blew it. I haven't paid you yet. Man! Please forgive me. Come up and we will have some Chai and I'll be glad to pay you your fees." It might possibly be a little awkward to be seen rifling through my dirty laundry down in the lobby.

With an acquiescing hand folding he most humbly concurred with my suggestion as we both climbed into the elevator. We got off even though the lit seven overhead didn't come on. After accompanying me to room 719, he slid the key in to the slot and ushered me in with his outstretched arm. The suite had a large central chamber enveloping a massive cathedral sleeping quarters. Perched on either side of the uprights as if life-size twin dolls were two of the most gorgeous Indian women whom I have ever seen. Their smiles radiated the special stardom of Bollywood.

"And what do we have here, Mr. Singh? Is this my bonus package?" I was a little in disbelief.

"Why, yes, Sir. We have taken the liberty of providing you with some much needed relaxation and enjoyment, if it is permitted to do so. This is Shakuntala and Bindi. They can also speak a little English. Should they not live up to your standards, Mr. Ibsen, we can request some other suitable styles." He was trying to be most gracious.

"Oh, I like their styles mighty fine." I dug into my satchel and hauled out one of the bundles of rupees. I counted out the fifty one hundred rupee notes onto the nightstand. Then I tossed in ten more. When I did this, Mr. Singh offered his hands in a most hospitable manner. He accepted the wad of dough and graciously bowed out with more prayer hands. The women also bowed.

"And them?" I highlighted the young ladies.

The Moon Women

"All set, Sir. Your pleasure awaits you." He intimated with a wave of his arm. He namested his hands with one more picturesque flash and ushered himself out the door.

"Ladies, can you say masala dosa?" I was famished.

They grinned and pulled down the covers on the super-cloud mattress having a fluffy maxwellian canopy and mastoid bedposts. Yeah. You get it.

Over a wide sweep of flowing wheat south of the Flaming Cliffs in the remote province of Omnogovi, Mongolia, the pearl tooth of the quarter-moon bit down on the golden kernels as they danced in unison beneath a steel gray sky. Glinting shafts of silvered wings raced by the blind voids thrusting in and out like the breathing of prayers, which once had suffered the mystical weight of an unrecognizable dimension. Tucked within the chains of knotted stalks, five Angels garnered their energies and sealed in their promises to Abaddon as they teetered on the verge of a biblical challenge. The burning gospel bells intercepted me as Azrael announced his herald.

UNTO THE SERVANTS OF LEGION

AS ABADDON IS MY LIFE AND WILL
I HAVE HEARD BEHIND ME
THE GREAT VOICE OF A TRUMPET
TO THRUST ME WITH MIGHT
INTO THE FACE OF TIME

BEHOLD I WILL COME QUICKLY
AND HOLD FAST THAT WHICH
NO EVIL MAN THING CAN DO
AGAINST ME OR AGAINST
MY FAITH IN HIM
OUR LORD NIRUNJAN
THE BURNING GOD
TO TAKE MY CROWN
OR MY SOUL

Haan Moses

UP UP AND AWAY MY FRIENDS
TODAY WE SHALL SLAY
THE EVIL NICOLAITANS
AND REMOVE THIS EVIL
FROM ALL THIS LAND

As another chapter of intrigue and collusion unwound, the beads in my hand moved steadily towards the terminus of a worn and altered reality. And as the chimerical chair twisted on its pivot of evil, the secondary passages of lust unbounded came upon me.

The Moon Women

- 1 -

March 9, 1967 – Mission Hill, Massachusetts

Some four years prior to my stint in the Delhi lockup, I was cohabiting with three women in an opulent crash pad located inconspicuously on a quiet spot on Cherokee Street just across from The Home for Little Wanderers in Brookline. One was a Jewish princess by the name of Jackie Rubenstein. She was the arm candy of my longtime pal, Davey Marshall. Davey was going with Jackie and Mickey, his twin brother, was going with Jackie's underling at the Harvard Coop , Carol Nelson. She was the daughter of Theodore Nelson, the movie magnet. He had produced similar series as Magnum PI and other shows. The third woman, Alena Philpott, was my seasonal bed partner. In spite of that status, it did seem to me I was merely performing some service for rent deal because neither did I have a job, nor did I pay them the wherewithal to stay there. Outside odds, they considered me the communal mindless mascot. However, if that were the case, you would think more sexual favors should have been required. In any case, there I was with the three of them.

One day the subject of Madame Devareaux came up over a casual cup of coffee.

"You should go see the grand Madame. She can tell your future from the stars." Alena claimed while pouring me some of her brew.

Back then, I didn't think much of astrology, neither did I have much of an inkling of what truths it could tell me, since I had always relied on my own self-styled semblance of the predictive sciences ever since I was six years old. You might say it was a combination of Ouija and Tarot, only I performed it much like present day prognosticators like to do with a replica of an eight-ball, which they shake furiously and then turn over to peer into a magical aperture. With not even a scintilla of a drumroll, a cube floats to the top and displays a caption proclaiming its divine guidance - Come Tomorrow, or Your Worst Fears or even You Win!

In my version of the game, I put the King James Version of the

190

Bible up for grins instead. I would close my eyes and randomly open the Good Book to any page, put my finger down somewhere, and read what it had to say. Look, I'll do it for you presently, no joke. Let's find out if it works. I let the Bible fall free and placed my finger down on Nehemiah 5:09:

> Also I said, It is not good that ye do;
> ought ye not to walk in the fear of our God
> because of the reproach of the heathens our enemies?

This excerpt calls into question the present dilemma. It is stating because of the wrongful doings of our enemies, the buggers who do not agree with our faith, we need to be protected by the Almighty so our methods can be strengthened. Not that I'm preaching things about God because I'm no believer. It's merely this pericope meshes perfectly as an example of my prognosticative abilities.

I split the Good Book a second time with my third digit pointing to Nehemiah 7:01:

> Now it came to pass, when the wall was built,
> and I had set up the doors,
> and the porters and the singers,
> and the Levites were appointed.
> That I gave my brother, the ruler of the palace,
> charge over Jerusalem: for he was a
> faithful man, and feared God above all.

Here we have the prime importance of the wall as pietistical significance. For without the wall, you cannot have the porters, the singers, and mainly the doors, without which you cannot pass. Nor can you have those who shall administer and rule. The complete structure of your life depends entirely on the wall. Everything impinges upon the presence of the wall. Additionally, the brother who maintains all dictation and control over the wall, that is to say, the one who can explain and redeem the wall, will prevail. He will be a man of faith and a man of God, if you can follow that train of thought.

Recognizing these quotations from the Bible as advice and, furthermore, prophecy on whatever subject was in front of me, was

The Moon Women

my methodology for speculating on the future as well as adding significant meaning to any particular enhanced historical perspectives which might arise. When applied in conjunction with one another, these two biblical quotes allow for a lens-like view to the subtle workings of the subject at hand, whether it is myself or some other fool. The prophetic words also have a dynamic two-fold quality in that they mark an assertion, which encompasses the subject's overall disposition as well as the direction of one's primary motives, not to mention one's imminent prospects.

For me, these interpretations were a litmus paper, a telltale that provides invaluable aid in divining the magnitude of the psychic juices flowing within the words and chapters, which turn on the spinning wheel of transmigration, the dancing juggernaut of e pluribus unum - out of many, one.

This craft of divining the prophecies required an immense amount of skill in making a legitimate interpretation of the words from the Bible. I came to recognize myself as the one who could do the best justice with this notably significant post-apocalyptic work. I had never gone wrong with any of the readings, which I had made for myself. They were always true and they always came true. I never did it for anyone else because doing so would amount to none other than the prostitution of my precious inner self. Ergo, I knew deep down this Madam Dumbo, or whatever her name was, could only be grandstanding as an impersonator, a pseudo-mystagogue; so I decided to foil her disguise.

"Oh, sure," says I. "Let's give it a whirl. Who knows? Could be I'm going to be a king or even win the lottery. I could use the cash."

The following week, moving in tow with Alena's complimentary appointment encircling my neck like an albatross, I knocked on the celebrated Madam's door. It was an imposing rampart with many iron studs sticking out of it. The metal looked worn as if from hordes of mismanaged clients drumming with their fists to reclaim their hard earned paychecks lost to this feeble fortune-teller.

There was no answer right away. The sickly silence given in response to my apprehensive woodpecker rapping awakened further doubts. Poor man's bet, nobody's in there and I can detour this labyrinth of mysterious misery. But when I decided to test its resistance with a with a hefty shove, the mammoth gateway eased back a fraction to lay bare a slice of darkness. Not to be deterred, I applied more violence to encourage it to retreat or else. After receiving sufficient success, I slipped inside.

At the finish line of a cumbersome hallway hung a dim lightbulb. Feeling awkward over the possibility some rare fortune may await me, I ventured forth to find out what the obscure light source was hiding. As my cowboy boots echoed on the slate runway, I came to a set of French doors, which I parted like a gunslinger barging into a saloon. I wasn't expecting the O.K. Corral, but I did think I might find a witch's haven or perhaps even the Fairy Godmother's clubhouse, but it was neither.

I found myself in the middle of a large chamber overrun with the ornate trappings of seventeenth century French paintings, furniture, and objet d'art. So much so it was suffocating. Instantaneously, my infuriating syndrome of furniture Speak jumped out from the background of my thoughts. I had been afflicted with this perversion from the time ever since I was a child. So far I hadn't been able to track down from where it had come, but I had an idea it had something to do with the eye-opening trek I had made once into the wheat one Sunday morning when I was only a tyke. No matter what I had done to unravel the piqued duplicity, I had always been powerless to defend myself against its moronic intrusions. The kicker was any arrival of furniture Speak was also an alert of the presence of a strangeness I had come to call the "other people."

Beyond a shimmering curtain of petite crystal globes, I detected the willingness of two Prie-dieu Vesper chairs with stitched edges, cardinal satin upholstery, and tight silk gimping. A bevy of walnut Victorian Lady Sit-downs with horsehair waddings added their solid consequence while waiting patiently adjacent to the pair of Vespers. As the Speak surged forth into the framework, I tried to push it back but it overcame me hands down. Even though it was a harbinger of something ominous, I struggled to conquer its duplicitous annoyance and pressed forward against all odds. In the adjacent chamber, a lengthy Victorian chaise lounge topped with a lurid purple damask presented an evil presence. It could be she did clairvoyant scans for her patsies as they unwound their pocketbooks while lying down - not any prospect I would envy. A confusing mixture of lavender and mushrooms infused the stale air with something ominous.

The Moon Women

Moving through the glass-beaded portal, a strikingly large woman emerged with a lilac manteaux riding upon her shoulders.

"Iyam Madame Devareaux." Her European voice boomed with a fearful saturation of baritone. Was it a woman or a man thing in drag?

"Are you Monsieur Ibosen?" The knell of her N seemed to hang in the air. I presumed the message I had deposited with her electric secretary had not been lost. Hey, not so telepathic after all, is she?

"Yup. That's me." I accepted the identification; nonetheless, she had mispronounced my name with her extra syllabic nuance.

"Merci, Monsieur. Merci. Votre hand, s'il vous plait." [Thank you, Sir. Your hand if you please.]

Her guttural tones washed over me like Beethoven's fourth note soured to the hilt. As she peered at me with her Manx cat eyes, her breath carried the funk of martinis and marzipan.

"Huh? You wanna see my hand? Thought you was a starlady."

I was really scratching for straws here. What on earth had I gotten myself into? She narrowed her eyes, eyes heavily accentuated with eye-liner.

"Oui, oui, Monsieur. Yours hand. Ze palm, please!"

The gargantuan woman glared down upon me from her well over two meter perch amongst the chandeliers and brocaded fonts. An ovoid pendant of moss agate swam on her mountainous chest; its spidery veins had the earmarks of a pentagram and within its satanic core hid a Tantric swastika. With an outthrust arm, she demanded my allegiance for the second time. I offered my hand palm up making sure it betrayed not a scintilla of hesitation or trembling fear.

"Excusez moi. The other 'and, Monsieur. Ze right 'and. Droite, s'il vous plait." [Excuse me. Right, if you please.]

She apologized as she bridged her landfall shunting the two Vespers.

"Oh, sorry. Here's the other right."

" Hmmph. Merci, Monsieur." [Thank you, Sir.]

As she grunted her dismay, she snagged the Victorian Lady and sat down somewhat disturbingly on it while still firmly gripping my hand.

"Etrange. Mal de tete? Have you ze head-pains, Monsieur?" [Strange. Headache?]

She looked up at me with her wizened face.

"No. I feel fine. Just get on with it please."

It wasn't the response I expected right off the bat. As she traced the histories hidden in my hand, a chill wave rippled up my spine. Scratching with her purplish index finger, crowned with a malachite sparkler inlaid in high karat gold, she scrutinized my palm while marking off a strange set of squiggles on her pad with her free working limb. Her shorthand made me think of Arabic even though logic told me it must be French.

My thoughts raced back to my senior year at Huntington Prep and my tutor, a Monsieur Leveignor. During a word contest in my French III class, he had marveled over my pronunciation of "droit du seigneur." It had amused him I had done so well with my word. Most of his students had trouble pronouncing phrases with that level of difficulty. This had led him to conclude my success with it had only been a freak accident. Later in the day after my homework, I had looked it up to unwind its meaning which was somewhat ghastly: it signified the customary right of a feudal lord to have sexual relations with a vassal's bride on the eve of her wedding.

As the grand Madame's sooth digit plotted the tomorrows in my hand, those perverted back patterns were having a crack at meddling with my mind. While she moved her gaze from my palm to my forehead and then back to my palm, I tossed in the white towel for any possibility for escape. After analyzing these two cellular poles on my wrinkle map for a few jigs, she looked up again and aligned both our eyes to pierce my inner depths with an edgy frown.

"Please sit down, Monsieur. Vhat you 'ave is of Lanus Albanus. It is ze seventh sphere of ze exaltation of Venus, Monsieur. Unfortunately, to your detriment a fallen star too often accompanies its promise. For zhat, Monsieur, ve need to plot ze chart."

"Well, oaky. Now we're getting somewhere." I took my place on the other Victorian Lady Sit-down.

She arose from her queenly perch pushing aside the Prie-dieu to once more inhabit the stratosphere of her stodgy narthex and made man-sized strides toward an expansive bookcase. As my gaze followed her withdrawal, I detected an unusual specimen hidden tenebrously in the secluded catacombs of her cathedral. It was an Edwardian music stool, a mid-Victorian dining chair having a buttoned pop-up seat cushion. She selected one or two compact

The Moon Women

volumes, which I took to be references intended for use during the occult surgeries she performed upon her referent victims. Then, with her legs splayed like starfish, she clumsily reclaimed her perch atop her Victorian semi-throne.

"Albacore, Monsieur? Does any of zhat seem familiar?" She thumbed the pages of the miniature book, yellowed from accessing monotonous futures. A stately Mobier grandfather clock having exceptional oak carvings and a manly brass pendulum towered over her shoulder conducting its concerto of sullen thumps along the far end.

"I'm tuna fish?" I chortled while dragging on my earlobe.

With a doughty sneer, she blew air through her pursed lips as the V of her mouth hooked backwards. The wiry brass turnings of her hairdo reminded me of the paralysis of Medusa. As I imagined her reptilian bonnet start to come alive, I knew she was beginning to have a memorable effect on me. She licked her thumb and settled on the page she had been hunting for all along. I glanced over at it. It was festooned with myriad columns of numbers and arcane symbols, the planets I surmised, maybe the mean sun too. And the minute hand slipped passed the half way mark.

"You are Taurean, is it not?" She hadn't even inquired on my birthdate yet. I presumed it was something speaking for her credentials.

"Yup, May sixth at daybreak or so my Mom let on once." I was professing my effete originality.

"A quelle heure, Monsieur?" [At what hour, Sir?]

"Huh? Oh, yeah. Heure. Six I believe. Yeah, six at dawn. Six am, Madame Devareaux."

"Oui. I 'ave ze page ici, Monsieur." [Yes. I have the page here, Sir.]

Fumbling her hand in a drawer located below her writing tablet, kitty corner to a Versailles provincial Three-post having satinwood veneer and cabriole peg-legs, she withdrew a handful of tools from the Bronze ages: a thin metal ruler, some kind of etch-a-sketch apparatus, and another one which looked a little like a protractor. She also had a compass, which went round with two spiked points.

In a jiffy, she had gone through the mechanics of stenciling the map of my horoscope. Marked out were the twelve pie-shaped wedges of the houses, each one with its relative glyph of the Zodiac,

196

plus the Sun, Moon and the eight celestial bodies, as well as all the contingencies showing the planetary aspects. Once as a sophomore at Bard College, I had studied this science myself as well as palmistry but had found them both loosely cryptic at best.

Taking in a lungful of the tomblike atmosphere, she settled back and closed her eyes. For a time and a half time her guttural wheezing matched the pointless clicking coming from the Edwardian grandfather timepiece. The duet of her measured snores combined with the regularity of the gravity devise intruded onto the horizon of my brainstorming like the prow of a shipwrecked dream. Time was not standing still, but it was indubitably taking a noticeable break. Suddenly she belched forth with a colossal statement of my worth.

"Ze Albacore Man is never exhausted in his quest for ze self. 'e is both within himself and also escaping his own self a thousands of times over. With every newfound definition of his self, he destroys all foregoing forms of his image only to realize zhat history amplifies one's position in ze universe. No other man can realize ze full impact of zhis creative force other zhan ze Albacore Man, Monsieur." Her brutal monotones reverberated off the swinging ballast of the massive bell ringer forcing her nodus deeper into my presence.

"In your case, Monsieur, Venus is exalted in Taurus and has no other prominences except zhat it is in ze twelfth house. Zhis is ze house of imprisonment and secret cults and societies. You are forever in danger of becoming captured by ze negative energies, Monsieur. You must ensure for yourself a place of honor and status within some protective community. Venturing away from zhese forms can expose you to grave vulnerability. Use every effort to center yourself within zhese protective hubs of secular life.

"Be not afraid of wealth and beauty, for zhese, alzough they appear to be of ze shallow material vorld, vill afford you solace and vill prove to be your support for all things spiritual. Always look to ze spiritual, Monsieur, for in truth, zhere is nothing else.

"Numbers are at your command. Zhey are at your beck and call and vill always serve you well. If you look to ze numbers, you will have all your goals met face to face.

"Your Moon is in Libra, ze one who holds the scales. Balancing those of the Moon and those from Mars, you will weave a web of intrigue and mystery. Upon this cocoon of double-dealing you vill balance your fates like a juggler performing circus. Your true friends

The Moon Women

vill all be Librans. And Libra is guiding ze sixth house, ze house of service and devotion. Zhese tools are at your command and vill aid you in ze composition of your life.

"For most people ze vords are something to learn and to use for communication. But for you, ze vords carry a divine power. Ze power of ze vords is for you a veapon or a miracle cure against evil. Ze zhoughts, written or spoken, can build castles or tear down ze empires, Monsieur. A single vord for you can terminate life or grant life. Zherefores, Monsieur, always choose your vords tres carefully and know zhat you carry zhis great power vhenever you direct zhem vith your great life forces.

"Find service to ze highest Lord. Vorship in ze house of service glorifies vhatever Supreme Being you may elect to follow. Choose vell the Deity zhat you place in ze temple of your heart. Once you have chosen, zhere is no looking back."

Madame Devareaux was having trouble drawing in the necessary air to continue. She looked like some cabalistic bellows wheezing out astral progeny. I could feel puffs of vapor seeping from her soggy lungs as her eyelids blinked repeatedly unleashing the fluttering protracted concepts.

"On the outside, you vill wear many costumes. Some vill be like uniforms, others, like manacles. But in your within, ze Albacore Man must have success in ze discovery of ze super seed. He must secure ze highest principles of living for his self. His within shall be as ze garden and ze orchard of ze spirit. He must produce ze divine crop as ze fruit of his vorship of ze one true God. This is ze true vork of ze Albacore Man. Notwithstanding, zhis vork can be and usually is marred and detoured by soured events."

With her prophesies spreading into my heart like a fungus, I was gagging on the thickness of her perfume no doubt worn since her last crucifixion. I winced knowing it surely must be eating through the sagging flesh of her underarms when she started to gasp. Perhaps she will catch her death and my future prospects will be left to rot as a heap of adiopocere dying on her vermillion carpet. Off on the margins of the séance a phone rang. It had that passé princess phone clang to it as it radioed a divergent signal and then fell dead.

"Excusez moi, Monsieur. Iyam being called a vay." Two petals from a wilted carnation fluttered from her neckline like scarlet scales off a dragon as she elevated herself up and out of my sight. I saved the vespers Prie-dieu as it fell back from her launch.

Was I getting all this? You're fucking right I was! This was most astounding! Incroyable, [Incredible] as the French would say. But, how could she know all this bugaboo; not simply from that little book of numerals, signs and symbols? It seemed unlikely what she was preparing to forecast for me was calculated from those asinine runes. It must be coming from something other than ordinary reality. But what?

Her hulk reunited with her present disease dragging a burgundy velour Fauteuils armchair behind her like a wounded soldier. She collapsed onto it off my flank.

"Pardonnez-moi, Monsieur. [Excuse me, Sir.] It has come to my notice zhat zhere are zum childrens who need me to drive zhem to ze jardin d'enfants, er, how do say, ze kindersschula [Kindergarten]. If you prefer, ve could return to zhis vorks later in a day or two. Or we could have it be all fini [finished] today tout de suite [right away] if you vish. Ve could finish here and now. Vhat is your vishes?"

Wait! She had baited the hook in front of my eyes, called a fish, a fish, and reeled me in with it. Now, she wants to play throw back? I don't think so.

"Now, please. Finish now if you don't mind, Madame." That was all I had.

From underneath her over-hooked nose came another chapter of unlinkage from her quivering lips, lips caked with layer upon layer of mercurochrome lipstick.

"As you vish, Monsieur." She thumbed her nose lifting it slightly as she proceeded to index my chart once again.

"It is vital, Monsieur, to inform you zhat your line of Albanus has one vul-ner-a-bil-it-y." She drew out each one of the six syllables, which slid out with their own separate reverberation, like marooned bubbles in a millstream.

"At the utmost bottom of your chart, Monsieur, you 'ave vhat is ze name of ze fallen star, Monsieur, one zhat is, how do you say, demented?" Her eyes constricted their focus upon the lump in my throat.

"Have you ever 'ad zee breathing disease, Monsieur?" Her interrogative re-infected an extinct wound.

I drew back. What breathing disease, I asked myself? Asthma?

199

The Moon Women

"Asthma, Lady Devareaux? Do you mean asthma?" I put it quite bluntly. Her medium-ship had inexorably landed a gold star. Impressive.

"Oui, oui. As-sa-ma." She wheezed her way through it.

"Oh yeah. I had that when I was a boy. But I'm over it now." I coughed.

"Alors, absolument!" [So, absolutely!]

"You must avoid ze Cancer child at all costs. Since your Mars resides in Cancer, it is considered fallen, n'est-ce pas?" [Isn't it?]

"Et plusment [And furthermore], she lies at zee bottom, ze le plus [most] bottom of ze chart, Monsieur."

"At all costs you must guard against ze Cancer child as vell as zhose from ze Red side, Mars. Zhese two are for your downfall only. Ze one of ze Moon vill drain you and ze other of Mars vill burn you. Avoid zhese two at all costs." Her cautioning finger sketched an insignia in the air as though she was mathematically tabulating some diabolic.

"En outre, Monsieur [Furthermore, Sir], zhis danger vill also present itself in a most unpredictable manner by forming lumps in your brain channels. Savez vous [You know]? Bulbs of dangerre, Monsieur." She jammed her finger at me like a dagger, thrusting it for emphasis.

I jerked back. The stubborn uprights of the vespers stuttered on the chipped stone flooring.

"I don't get it. You're saying my innards have growths? What? How can that be? I thought I was pretty healthy." I was thoroughly bemused as well as unamused to boot. This whole dizzy charade was thoroughly going downhill now. Was she merely fixing to get rid of me so she could pick those brats at the bus stop?

"Ecoutez moi, Monsieur! [Listen to me, Sir!] This is tres important. Balls of confusing and chaotic energies vill cause you to go off track at times. Zhey are like ze shooting stars, no? Like the comets or ze meteors zhat rain down in ze nighttimes. Zhey bring ze little people with ze large black eyes und zhare large oval ships. Zhey are violent and vill occur with devastating results. Zhey are sometimes unavoidable and many times rare, but vhen zhey do occur, you vill also be guarded by another force, Monsieur. I can only tell you zhat zhis force comes from ze White, a region of timeless mind zhat shelter ze secrets of ze origins of our universe. Vhen you are attacked by one, ze other vill remove you and you vill be taken to a different place and yet you can begin again. And zhese new beginnings vill be for your benefit in ze longer run.

"As you find ze worship of higher and higher deities, more of zhese trusts, zhese demons vill attack. Toutefois [However], you vill survive. Should you eventually find ze very highest of all ze gods, Monsieur, zhen your rebirth from zis turbulence vill place you in ze most exalted palace. Even as it may appear to be like a prison or it may even be as ze dungeon itself, you should know in your heart of hearts, zhat ze Vill of ze Great One whom you choose to serve and vorship vill protect you and carry you through all ze hell vorlds into vhich you may have fallen. One day you vill return to ze most sublime of all universes, vhere you vill be a king and you vill enjoy all ze kingdoms of heaven.

"Now, I must go. Here is your chart stapled to my card. You can send vhatever token of your appreciation to zhis most honorable and charitable organization, ze name of which is on ze back." She let it go for the taking.

With that sticky closing point, she disappeared beneath the dripping veil of strung beads. Behind it, I picked up on an instant flash of a Khrng moving off into the depths of the subterranean obscurity but then lost it in a flash of altered Time splinters.

Alas entrusted to my druthers, alone and discomfited, I chose to exit the Madame's den of transmundane masquerade. As I scrambled out to manhandle the unwieldly entry portal, which was preparing to imprison me within the French inquisition, I forced it back and stumbled out onto Beacon Street in a daze. As I pocketed her card, I noticed the key word tagged for my reference and donation: The Baman Oracle. With a sickly minimalistic feeling, I wandered off to the apartment. How many times has it come upon us: something sinister reveals our inner selves only to pursue us with the shadow of death?

The impact of this encounter with the frightening Madame instilled a density that would sink into my depths like a rare earth element, illusive but undeniably present in my every effort to secure the truth. Yet many moons would need to pass before these seeds planted from out of the Beyond would ripen and bring forth the being whom the grand Madame had christened as the Albacore Man.

The Moon Women

A little bit after my clairvoyant affair with Madame Devareaux, I was hard-pressed to succeed in a new entrepreneurship in sales while cruising westward on Route 90, also tagged on maps as the Massachusetts Turnpike. My ride was a fresh, off-the-line Chevrolet Impala. Even though it was a rental, my calfskin boot was hard on the plate of the accelerator. It was nearly midnight.

As I shot passed the wastelands of yesterday's snow spotting the landscape, I had come across very few cars on the road between Boston and Bard College, my intended target. Along with it being a magnific evening, cool and crisp, Maia, the brightest star in the Pleiades, was smiling down on me. Since I was enjoying nothing but keying in on my driving, the radio was mute.

I was doing a neat 90 mph. The weather was pleasant and the road dry. "90 on 90" I mused to myself. I should be arriving on campus in a little over two plus hours. Right then the microscopic glint of distant headlights came up on my rear mirror. When I say distant, I mean my pursuer was a good two kilometers back. Nonetheless, I could pick him out because the road only had a one or two turns in it. As I watched the dancing high beams come and go as the rearward portion of my travels meandered here and there, I kept my eyes peeled to detect his possible advancement. Figuring it wiser to cut some speed, I eased back with my foot's pressure on the accelerator: a little over seventy is safe. The meandering roadway threaded its way through a series of rolling undulations as I approached a hilly countryside. After I exited the run of hills, the frogger's beams were way closer. This guy is onto me.

It was only few more road markers before the flashing blue lights upended my glassy excursion. Pulling my four-door over onto the shoulder, I came to a halt as a scud of road dust caught up with me. After fumbling to get the electric window button prepped for discharge, I waited nonchalantly expecting a visit from the Man. It's funny how these unpredictable inconveniences serve to sharpen the wider scope of one's life. A shaft of blinding light smashed into my rearview as fearful thoughts ripped through me like micro-meteorites driving the millibars of my blood pressure up several notches. As the Trooper advanced towards my car, I lowered the edge of my freedom a fraction unable to prevent the frigid air from invading my cabin.

"Good morning, Sir. License and registration, if you would."
The Statie was going by the book.

Frosty sheaths of his breath spilled in through my cleaved
defenses as I thrashed my hand every which way in the glove
compartment to locate the yellow paper of my rental agreement, the
stand-in for my registration. I dug my wallet out with the other hand,
fished out my license, and handed the legal sandwich to the lawman.

"Here you go. It's a rental." I confirmed.

Not knowing the mustachioed State Trooper had been on
patrol since three the preceding afternoon or that he had elected a
double shift in order to buy his new wife a birthday present, I waited
patiently for his opening move. He rubbed his eyes warily as he
studied my papers while angry winter continued to fill my cabin with
its seething frigidity.

"I didn't realize it was so late." I replied to cut the chill
between us.

Shivering in the snappy air, I found my bad stab at breaking
the ice had landed flat. His "Good morning" had thrown me. He
flashed his light in my face while his vocals or lack thereof broadcast
zip. As I anticipated his probable responses, a quick regression shot
passed the playback channels.

At that juncture in my life, I was in transition. I had moved
out of my father's domicile in Newton. Even with the good graces of
scoring straight As in my geology classes at BU, I had opted for a
life of crime. It didn't matter so much my years at Bard had come to
a crashing halt. Rather it had lead me to assume the guise of a
traveling Wilbury spreading elation and cheer to all the lads and
lassies on my bygone campus.

I had equipped my salesman's sample case, a medium sized
Samsonite suitcase, with four kilos of Acapulco gold, an ounce of
cocaine, and an assortment of uppers and downers, including five
hundred hits of acid, a quarter ounce of PCB and an eighth of DMT,
two thousand Black Beauties and sixteen dyno-mite Peyote buttons.
It was unlocked.

The muscle bound Trooper strolled over to my front bumper
and checked out my license plate. He shined his torch onto the
windshield and tallied up the corresponding info on the inspection
sticker, the decal on the plate, and what was stipulated on the
registration. Well, that's not my job, I thought to myself. I hoped

The Moon Women

Avis hadn't rented me a typo. Then my designated Massachusetts silverback returned to blast me with his searchlight again while clearing the backseat and cabin, a proper verification it was free of terrorists I presumed.

"Suppose you'd like to know why I pulled you over?" He commenced first contact finally.

I wasn't sure if this was a statement or a question.

"It's your road," I fired back unsuccessfully falling short of mortally wounding him with no good gun.

"Couple of clicks back I clocked you at over 85, right after you crossed the Great Barrington exit. Then you caught my lights and backed off, didn't you?"

He was cagey. Most likely, he figured I would spill the beans and wrap up his work for him.

"Look. It's pretty late. I've been going hard at it since early today, er, I mean happenstance, er, yesterday. Hi there. I'm on a hiatus from heavy studying, you know, humanities and hubris over at Harvard yahd so I'm gonna hang out this weekend with my homeboys on the Hudson near Bard College. I might have let my speed hasten some but it's been such halcyon weather, don't you think?"

I was spinning the tallest yarn I could with my H words. My mumania had degraded to minus 5 degrees of M. I hoped it wouldn't lead me to the other one, you know - hell.

"Your homeboys at Bard, huh? What's in the trunk?"

His breath shot out at me as he targeted my throat with his gaze.

"Not much. One bag is all."

Play dumb was my line of thinking. His underscore of my alma mater had gotten my guard up.

"Mind if we take a look?" He queried with a smirk.

Queen to queen 8, check. That specter in the back of my brain chimed in. You know, the one who always knows all the moves right before they emerge into the limelight.

"Sure. No problem."

I was figuring some additional nonchalance would save my king and stave off his middle game. As I got out of the car slowly, the Trooper made way. He took two steps back with his spit-and-polished State boots crunching on the road ice. With his outstretched palm, he made a subtle move toward a triangular patent leather pouch hanging on his hip. Who is checking whom, I thought?

I bobbled with my handful of keys, inserted the correct one, and the trunk lid popped open like a jack-in-the-box. The only clownish poltergeist to slither out was what remained of my car's warmth. As it collided with the inverted temperatures of the frost zone, there was a gradual lift pulling me upwards as my heart sunk.

The rear compartment was spacious and devoid of any items with one exception, my professionally insulated, graphite, multi-pocketed, fiberglass, hard-shell, Samsonite suitcase. Even as I now proclaim myself none other than a novice logophile, I figured if I kept stringing dumb adjectives together, the inevitable would not come to pass. Naturally, I was wrong on that score as well.

"What's in the suitcase?" he imposed his prying hook.

"Just my clothes plus some memorabilia. Want me to open it?" I responded in a calm and matter-of-fact manner.

This was a sacrifice play put forth by Mr. Cool. This was an eyeball-to-eyeball bluff direct from the Texas Hold 'Em tables of Las Vegas. Even though I had never been down on the strip, I was betting with it big time. The tall lawman looked at me, then down at the suitcase. And then his gaze landed back on me. He attempted to pierce my forebrain with the needles of his eyes. As the abacus of his phrenic divining rod clicked off the plausible units of my future, the biting cold enlarged its grip on my insides. It didn't take him long to reach critical mass.

"Memorables, eh? Open it!"

Damn! Wrong M word. I leaned forward into the cavern of the trunk, two handed the suitcase, put my thumbs on the releasing tabs, and prepared to meet Achilles head-on. At that precise instant, a bunch of squawking came out of his patrol car. As I stopped in mid-motion, the Trooper jerked erect hesitantly. His cruiser flashed its giddy lights staining the snow electric turquoise. After he caught the gist of the scanner's transmission, he yanked me back and aimed his gloved finger at a bump in the road.

"Stand here and don't move!"

I stepped back once or twice as his directive gelled forcing me to remain motionless. My jaw clenched in preparation for the oncoming twist of fate, which looked imminent. I crossed my arms

The Moon Women

and futilely applied warm-up motions on my arms. Only a threadbare shirt separated me from the raw down-east air.

The Trooper hurried back to his cruiser, unstrapped his Brown Round from the back of his head, and dove behind his wheel with the slam of his door. The finality of that thud brought an uncanny calmness to my within as if I had been drained of all my energy. I thought it might possibly be due to the increased weakness from the frigid temperatures but since I hadn't been visited by the condition of death by cold in many years due to my ripe old age of 23, I took it to be merely the result of fatigue from too much driving that day. In the crevices of my cephalic back pocket, however, I came across a flashback of a similar shortcoming, which had resulted in an uncomfortable split with the norms positioned by the hands of those wiser than myself.

Soon, an icy grip from an alternative dimension dug into me initiating the premeditated severing of the flow of ordinary Time/Space relationships leaving me frightened to the gills. Shivering in the late winter air, I came upon one of those book 'em Danno scenarios. What else could it be? Here I was caught dead to rights, standing nearly naked with my proverbial pants down around my ankles. All the Master Sergeant had to do was take a peak in my traveling kit of goodies and I'd be soon serving hard time in the slammer. Yet I wondered - had I depleted all my Hail Mary plays? I delved down into my empty and untrained heart to squeak out my hopeless request to the Big Man upstairs. It is often in ridiculous situations such as these in which weak-minded people resort to desperate moves in the form of prayers more often with no worthwhile results other than another Benjamin left in the tithing plate.

As the stifling chill, which precedes twilight, continued to deplete my energies, I blinked my eyes. I could make out a cut in the air as if something had made an incision into the wall of Time ripping it apart and allowing a sweaty terror to dominate my mind just as once in the far distant past it had dissected the day-to-day outlooks on measured life. Horrified it would spring upon me once again and dig its tiger claw into my brain again, I stiffened as I prepared for the coming collision with my displaced astral cousin.

Equidistant between the Trooper's squad car and my rented Chevy, a filmy rectangle of a silvery glimmer gradually unrolled itself out of the carbon backdrop like a diaphanous satin shade. Its mirrored surface widened out with an unworldly glow. From within this floating vent of shinning liquid mercury, I sensed something powerful - powerful and awful.

After the base of the rippling shade lifted up, a witless starry welkin presented its unknown. A streaking gob of firelight shot passed and then narrowed in on the loose crack in the solidity of the normal Time/Space medium commoners have mistaken for reality for eons. This glob of supreme consciousness compressed itself into a man shape and made like a thief climbing in through a levered breech housing an unclaimed treasure, me. Stepping through the floating vortex in the continuum came a jumbo humanoid swathed entirely with itty-bitty silverish flames; flames or it could have been glowing feathers; I couldn't tell which. The thing was super tall like some three meters, which was friggin' colossal. I thought I had lost it.

Rubbing my eyes to clear away the confusion, I considered a call out to the Trooper but he appeared to be frozen as a plume of whiteness hung stationary between his mouth and his handheld microphone. Was I facing one of those bulbs of danger, which the Madame had warned me about? Succumbing to the impact of the creature's arrival, the memory segments containing all former visits from these monsters snapped back into focus and I had to delineate what might be coming at me next. Although, I couldn't quite figure out why these tinsel dudes kept blowing in from the outer ice dominions only to show up here to protect me from my enemies. Then again, perhaps they were my enemies?

As the creature's head trained its tractor beam my way, revolving craters on his planetoid frontage opened and commenced to melt into turquoise spheres resembling tiny versions of the third rock from the sun while trapped in a timeless abyss. They melted into turquoise pools and formed themselves into eyes having no pupils or any irises, simply inhuman, egg-like eyes. With no other features which I could discern, only those megaloid humanesque spheres of evil, the thing came at me with its terrorizing will. Its whole body seemed to be shining with a brilliance out of which brain crushing icicles of a high-pitched electric buzzing stabbed into my thoughts. Like a hundred telepathic hyper-dermic needles, a transmission

The Moon Women

painfully injected its force into my thalamic grid work. I had to clamp my hands over my ears, but it was no use.

UNTO THE ANGEL OF THE CHURCH [1]

I AM COME TO SAY THAT
ALL MY CHANNELS ARE OPEN.
ARE YOUR CHANNEL OPEN?

COME INTO THE WHITE

JOIN WITH ME AS I VISIT
WITH YOU IN YOUR WORLD

AS I AM MATARAEL
HONOUR OF THYATIRA
LEGION *OF ABADDON*
AND SON OF MAN

I AM MATAREL

I GIVE YOU WORD

AND I BRING YOU UPDATES

YOUR BALANCES ARE NOW

ANY PUNISHMENT FOR THESE CRIMES

CLEAR WITH THESE DEEDS

HAS NOW BEEN ERASED

BUT KNOW YOU SHOULD NOT

BUT PLEASE UNDERSTAND THAT YOU

WORSHIP THE BLACK DEVILS [2]

SHOULD NOT SIDE WITH THE KHRNG

I GIVE YOU THE MYSTERY

LET ME EXPLAIN TO YOU WHY

OF THE SEVEN STARS [3]

THESE THINGS HAVE HAPPENED TO YOU

I SAW A NEW HEAVEN
AND A NEW EARTH
FOR THE FIRST HEAVEN
AND THE FIRST EARTH
WERE PASSED AWAY

THE PASSING FROM KALI INTO SAT YUGA

THE NEW CITY HAD NO NEED
OF THE SUN NOR OF THE MOON

Haan Moses

FOR THE GLORY OF GOD
DID LIGHTEN IT AS THE LAMB
IS THE LIGHT THEREOF ONE MUST LOOK INSIDE FOR TRUTH

THERE CAME UNTO ME
MY ANGEL WHO SAID
COME HITHER
I WILL SHOW THEE THE BRIDE
THE LAMBS WIFE
AS TEN WOMEN THE PROPHESY OF THE TEN WOMEN

FROM THE FIVE WOMEN OF THE MOON
AS MATAREL I MEASURE
THE WALL ACCORDING
TO THE MEASURE OF WOMAN THE YARDSTICK OF HUMANITY
IS NOT MALE BUT FEMALE

THE FOUNDATIONS OF THE WALL
WERE GARNISHED WITH ALL MANNER
OF PRECIOUS STONES EACH BURNING
IN HER FAITH WITH HER LIGHT
THE FIRST WAS JASPER HER PSYCHIC ELEMENT IS JASPER

NOW COMES THE MOON WOMAN
OF THE FIRST PLACE ARRAYED
IN WASHED TOPAZ AND WOOLEN
HONEY RUNNING WITH A HIDDEN HARVEST

SHE WAS DECKED WITH AN IVORY ROSE
AND RIPE OLIVES HAVING A PALE CUP
IN HER HAND FULL OF ABOMINATIONS
SPEAKING OF FILTHINESS AND FORNICATION
INTRODUCES THE FIRST OF THE MOON WOMEN
WHOSE INTENTIONS COME VIA SEDUCTION

209

The Moon Women

BEHOLD
THE NEW CITY OF GOD
COMING DOWN OUT OF THE SKY
PREPARED A BRIDE FOR YOU
ADORNED FOR HER HUSBAND
WITH A SHINING HEART
AND JASPER STARS   HER LIGHT IS HER SONG

I KNOW YOUR WORKS   I KNOW WHAT YOU HAVE DONE
AND YOUR LABOUR   AND WHAT HAS HAPPENED TO YOU
AND YOUR PATIENCE AND HOW
          BUT BECAUSE OF YOUR PATIENCE
YOU CAN NOT BEAR THEM
          BY REFUSING THOSE YOU DON'T TRUST
WHICH ARE EVIL   THOSE WHO SAID THEY WERE
YOU HAVE TRIED THEM FOLLOWING THE SAME PATH AS YOU
WHICH SAY THEY ARE APOSTLES   YOU CALLED THEM OUT
AND ARE NOT AND HAVE   AS LIARS AND CHEATS
FOUND THEM TO BE LIARS [4]

KNOW YOUR PRAYERS
WILL BE ANSWERED
FOR THIS IS NOT YOUR TIME

EVEN AS MY PART IN THE BOOK
HAS NOT YET COME FORTH
DO NOT PUT THE REVELATION
           DON'T WRITE THE BOOK UNTIL
OF MY PRESENCE INTO THE LIGHT
         YOU HAVE RECEIVED THE WHOLE STORY
AND SOUND OF THE WORLD
         OF THE WHITE AND OF THE DARKNESS
UNTIL YOU HAVE FOUND
         THE STORY OF THE ANGELS AND HOW
THE KEY TO MY DOOR
         THEY WILL ONE DAY DEFEAT THE KHRNG

Cleanly and without any extraneous obstructions, his messages zoomed into my cranium and branded its purpose there. There was only the acutely painful tinkling of the microscopic bells, which reverberated either inside me or in the elevated perimeters of the etheric sphere hovering round about me, the item traditionally referred to as an aura. The entity reentered its mirrored threshold and the window proceeded to roll itself back out into the stygian night.

With the realignment of my true self came the reinforcement of a brief confirmation of the other visits from these visionary surgeons who attempt to rearrange my cerebral furniture as they deposit their warped dreams only to retake their internal fire beds like cowards out of the fog of insanity. The message was as if another stanza in the epic saga of their outer battles with mutants from another world as well as something concerning my own prominence in the process. That and their infernal insistence that women are the better half of the gender spectrum. However, this time the ole Rasputin brought me a jot of forgiveness as it seemed I was spared my penance of putting fire to the butt end of my joint, quite literally. But then, painful though it was, the remembrance dissolved in a wash of amnesia like the retreat of a lost wave, which left only a dim nostalgia touching the surfaces of recognition to leave me exhausted but somehow renewed.

Again, the closing of the cruiser door redoubled through the Time/Space registers as if it had done a contra-flip to replay the interval of the Trooper entering his cruiser. For a split second, I toyed with the thought perhaps I could make a run for it. The border was only fifteen kilometers away. Doubtless, I could reach that. By the time he got up to speed, I might be able to have outrun him and made it to the New York border. I looked at my Impala and then over to his Crown Victoria. Little chance he has anything less than a 429 under his hood; I'd probably be toast in less than a dozen kilometers.

In the whirling blue lights, the Trooper's door swung open and out he came at a gallop while still holding my papers as if an Olympian torch.

"Close your trunk, Mr. Ibsen."

Holy Jesus! I had feared the next words would be, "You're under arrest!" But, blessed Mary, they weren't.

211

The Moon Women

"In the future, Mr. Ibsen, try to keep it down. Speed kills. My gut tells me you're hiding something in that suitcase of yours, but I've got to responded to this emergency call over in East Chatham. My name is Sergeant John Benton; here is my card. If you have any questions regarding this traffic stop, you can contact me at my extension, or put in a word with dispatch. Have a good morning, Sir, and please obey the speed limits."

He palmed my identity sandwich with a wink and trotted back to his patrol car. Soon after he had sped off with some considerable rear wheel spin, the inertia of the highway returned.

"Queen to King's Bishop 6. Checkmate. Limits be damned; I've won!"

I yelled out addressing the infinity of the cosmos. I was so relieved! Still, the foggy reflection of a celestial spirit who might have visited me from out the realm of the dead pharaohs continued to hang on the horizon of my cortical mirage. I looked up. I could only perceive one star shining in the black velvet overhead.

- 3 -

I made all my deliveries over at Albee Hall on the main drag next to Stone Row and was out of there within my grace period calculated to avoid detection. Lickety-split, I made the over four hundred fifty kilometer trek back to Brookline, dropped off the rental at Avis, and flagged down a taxi back to the apartment. When I inserted the key into the lock, I heard the shower. The only way to know who was in there was to knock and simply plunge ahead inside.

"Are you decent?" I grilled the occupant with a devastating preliminary move prior to my entrance.

There was Alena standing naked while peering into the bathroom mirror - maraschino cherries perched atop two gorgeous mammee apples. She was flossing her teeth. As the tiny filament indexed one impeccable dental unit after the other, she performed her job meticulously. As she headed down the homestretch, I observed she had a significant gap between her two incisors. Then, she turned face forward, nipples perky.

"You're back early. Nobody's here now. Wanna fuck?" She tossed the floss into the toilet.

"Glad to see you too!" I blushed.

"How much did we rake in?" She was planning a whirl over at the Ark.

"Three grand; everything was perfect. I even beat a cop on the highway. And I then I think I bumped into another one of those angel creeps. Not really sure about all that though. Sometimes that stuff gets real fuzzy on me." I was saving the best for last. After all, I was the man of the house.

"Decent. But angels, huh? You're not supposed to smoke that shit when you're driving. Whaditha cop do?" She glossed over the particulars and squashed the toothpaste.

"Standard play. My bluff was a beaut, though. You missed a spot." I put the focus back where it belonged - on her body.

To say my Alena was not exactly ugly was a complete litotes. Her naturally blonde hair styled in a rave pixie cut, lapis eyes and perfect belly bulge added to the splendor of her petite body, which was wrapped with the most beautifully tanned skin I have ever seen. It betrayed not even a hint of tan lines. I don't know how she accomplished this feat because she never participated in any skinny dipping sessions that I knew of and they didn't have tanning salons back in those days.

"The apartment's empty." She raised one eyebrow and clasped her arms about my neck like a python.

"Are you making a pass at bribing me?" Two could play this game.

"I don't call it bribing." She said mashing her knee into my crotch and holding it there with relish.

"I need a shower." I reached in and cranked on the large dial to change the subject. The warm spray hydrated my arm.

"You need me!" She planted one on me to set me straight.

In a flesh grabbing frenzy, we hopped into the shower as a single bundle of lust. I let my drenched sweats slide off onto the bottom of the tub and we got down to business. In no time, the tangle of my wet pants plugged up the drain hole. As the buildup inched higher, my wet socks kept slipping on the smooth porcelain. Pulling them off in a split second, I ratcheted the faucet open some more while simultaneously ratcheting up the beat of Alena's back dimples as they slapped against the steaming tiles.

The Moon Women

Owing to Alena's connections at the bookstore, come fall, a remarkable opportunity for self-improvement cropped up. One of them began with seven men who convened across an oval table, a triple-leaf model, which exhibited a gaudy cross grain. You could call it a mensal meeting of the minds. Minds, which were going to formulate a rocket ride to riches. It would require cunning; it would require timing and it would require cojones the size of basketballs.

Sean Gregor was an MIT post-grad. He had won entrance to this Olympus of the intellectual community by nonchalantly solving a brainteaser in under a hundred seconds. That accomplishment put his IQ somewhere north of the 170 mark. Sean had also scored off the charts on the Minnesota Multi-phase Personality Inventory or the MMPI. Haplessly that meant Sean's OCD was OTFT, (Over the Fucking Top)!

All the same, Sean had some deep-seated issues. Don't we all? Every day of his life, he madly labored to dig up a way to shut off his mind. With each tormented moment, his mission in life was to turn off the banshee roaming his brain. He needed to be free of it. Having gone through one oblivion after another, he was driven to more and more radical solutions. When heroin failed, it was looking pretty grim for Sean. Then, when he never expected it, I came along.

Seam found I had a way of sparring with a unique brand of cerebral tennis he so loved. Using twists of humor and the spices of a wanton lifestyle, I created an elusive paradise of thought provoking riddles while throwing out perplexing arrays of confusion, which begged the question, "Was life worth dying for?" He loved these types of vexing absurdities and other similar ironic paradoxes, which I tossed out at him constantly.

"What's a Marxian Marde Gras?" Or "What would Heidegger do if being a Nazi meant approaching interstellar infinity?" He loved it when I coined extensive quasi-technical phases to indicate absurd notions of unthinkable science such as an Advanced Logistical Brain Anomaly Capable Of Radical Events. So far as possible he became manageable. It would take his mind off his mind. See, there's another one.

When Larry "Mitch" Mitchum reminisced about his latest junket to Nebraska and described the acres of pot growing by the side of the road we thought he was joking. Mitch had seen it while touring the back roads of central Nebraska, visiting his comrades in-country. Supposedly, at the peak of World War II, the government subsidized thousands of farmers to grow hemp for the purpose of producing rope needed to harness the machinery of war. They cultivated enormous quantities of it, various strengths necessary to secure everything from a horse to a battleship in the harbor. After the war was over, without further financial push, the growers abandoned these tracts of farmland and let them fallow in preparation for the economic boom.

As an offshoot of Roosevelt's New Deal, further aid encouraged the replanting of these fields with corn for feeding the masses as America boomeranged into its new job as the world's breadbasket. Bigger and bigger machines maintained the vast corn beds, but the perimeters of the rectangular sectors were uncultivated borders in which weeds of all sizes and denominations took root and flourished quite successfully. One of these remontants were the plentiful variants of the hemp plant, originally cultivated for war, now discarded and forgotten to waste away peacefully all on its own, which naturally enough, it never did.

"There were plants in there over three meters high, Dude!" Mitch expounded. "It's mind blowing there's so much of it."

"Sure it wasn't you that was high, Bud?" Sean fell on him like a starving vulture.

"No way, Man. The shit is large out there. It's all over the place. Trust me."

This award winning declaration occurred during the midst of a heated brainstorming session, which Sean conducted to generate the means to get enough cabbage to start a legit business. A discotheque sounded profitable. We were spoiling to engender a place where the hip tribe could get together and enjoy the latest disco beats. The Ark was immensely popular at the time and we were scheming to get over on the owners with bigger and better bands. Plus, we could rake in piles of coinage selling booze over the counter while at the same time dealing dope under the table.

"Iron Butterfly is a terrific band, but what if we could deliver the likes of Hendrix or Joplin. That would be super." The Marshall twins asserted as they high-fived each other.

I had another sip of my mint julep and then blurted out from the axis of nowhere, "Why don't we fly out to Omaha, rent a U-Haul,

The Moon Women

fill it with grass and then drive it back here and sell it. Not many expenses and we could clean up totally! I bet you we could net thirty thousand in one trip."

I blurted out that pipe dream more as an absurd proposal to get a laugh from Sean rather than taking a serious stab at a meaningful investment. Everyone had a raucous chuckle over it after which we tried to get back on track with some probing conversation, which offered cleverly concocted, harebrained schemes. Sean was withdrawn for a minute or two when all at once he came out of his fog.

"What the hell did you just say, Rahm?" He grunted as though he were suffering beneath the handicap of a 30-second time lag. "Run that by me one more time please?"

"I was only messing with your mind, Dude, manufacturing a mailbag of mantic fan mail from Manitoba. Get it?"

"Naw, that wasn't it. Back the truck up, Man. It was something more like a convoy on a dope run. No?"

Feeling perhaps a recap might calm his devils briefly, I regurgitated my half-baked ploy for profits.

"Fill a five-ton rent-a-truck with the bogus weed and haul ass it back here to sell it as though it were the real McCoy. Forget about it. It's hemp, Boss, not real pot, only duck weed, swamp grass." I was recanting my tribute.

"Yeah, that's true, but it's cannabis. One's sativa and the other's indica, if I remember my herb class 101 correctly which is usually the case. I think one has a higher cannabinoid ratio than the other but I forget which is which. It might be I'm wrong and then again we could smoke our way to the answers. But since hemp is a cannabis cousin or something like that, I'll bet it's a carbon copy of the real one when it's wild, plus I'll bet you it a million it will smell flat out like Mary Jane when it's smoked." He was gaining speed.

"Mitch, you didn't happen to smuggle any of it back here, did you?" He was striving to placate with variable in-roads.

After Larry Mitchum responded in the negative, Sean was off and running.

"Come on!" He spouted. "We're going to Kansas, Dorothy."

"Oh, Tom! You can't be serious? That's ridiculous." His moll screamed.

216

"I said pack your shit, Todo. We're off to see the lizard!" He screamed.

"I have a feeling we weren't ever anywhere other than Kansas." She tossed him the suitcase.

The uptick played out with Sean and company flying to Omaha, renting a large Mercedes and driving the more than two hundred kilometers out into central Podunk Nebraska.

Surrounded by an ocean of corn silk, they detoured the well-beaten trail and plunked themselves down right in the heart of corn country. Everywhere they looked, silos, cows, and unending rows of corn told them this must be the place. They deplaned and made their way down into the widest canyon they could find, a clogged gully of hemp. After they had waded in hip high into the brackish slime and come out on the other bank, they spied the most beautiful two meter plus pot plants, which were in their harvest bloom with sticky clusters of buds all over them. With their machetes, they went to work hacking down dozens of the towering plants. After an hour or so, they hauled them back out to the Merc, and threw them into the trunk. They drove back to their travel lodge and hung them in the bathroom over the shower curtain to dry them out overnight. Then they packaged them into plastic trash bags, which they stuffed into their luggage leaving just enough time to flag a redeye and make a beeline back to Cambridge. On the flight home, their sole activity was sleeping.

When I got a call from Tom, I was waking from a nap on the Danish Fan Back. Whatever phantom that was chasing me back into this realm had stamped its imprint on my residual thought waves, which were floating in my freshly unloaded cerebral cartridges. The squeeze on my temples was intense.

"You won't believe what I have here?" Sean stated emphatically. "You have to come over and try some of his shit." He hung up.

I got myself together and advised Alena I was heading over to Cambridge to hang out with Sean and his ladylove for a while.

"It better be business or you're dead."

Happily she was agreeable with it. Couple of rowdy moves later I was trudging up the stairs to his apartment on the third floor. Carolyn answered the door.

The Moon Women

"This is all your fault, you know. I hope you're pleased with yourself. Now I have to put up with this bullshit!"

I could tell she was glad to see me. After passing her security check and saluting the twin statues of Osiris, which guarded the hallway, I plunked myself down adjacent to Sean as he hailed the executive place at the head of the monolithic oak plank. Sean handed me a blunt the size of cucumber. While not knowing where this was all going, I stared vaguely at an expansive Mollweide projection of the world fanned out before me, made ready, and sucked in a lungful. After holding it the measured mile, I blew it out. Nothing. So I ponied up my best college try with another deep lung full. And then, a third time.

"This shit is crap!" I exhaled.

"Yeah, I know, but who's gonna notice? These days Boston is totally dry, Dude. They would smoke their grandmother's underwear if they thought it would get them stoned." Sean was prophesying all on his own.

"I know, but Sean, once they realize this is crap, we are going to be black listed for life."

"I don't think so. They need this shit. Bad!" He was nodding his head in emphasis. "Five trucks minimum." He held up the five fingers of a man. He was way ahead of everybody.

"Okay, but I say we start with one and see what happens." I didn't feel the need to get caught with our pants down.

On Saturday, the seven demons from Dallas had a crucial head-to-head: Sean, the Marshall twins, Larry Mitchum (the instigator), Corey Bernard, Hange Brimer and myself sat together at the oval table. Brimer volunteered himself for piloting the wheelhouse. He would wear his minister outfit to take the heat off any possible interference from the police. He stood and started to preach some of his prayer words.

"Verily, verily, I say unto you, except a kernel of wheat fall into the ground and die, it abideth alone, but if it die, it bringeth forth much fruit [5]. Plus, listen to this one. This is the bomb. Doth he not cast out the fitches but cast in the principal wheat? [6] We're all going to be rich! Methinks we're all going to be feelthy rich, Sean. Did you know fitches is a genus of sativa? That's dope, my friends, biblical dope."

Carolyn screamed at him to sit down and to stop yapping Bible shit. She loathed sermons and she unconditionally despised religions even more. My parents would have knighted her with sainthood.

The outline for the plan unwound smoothly. We would all fly out there, stay in a lavish tavern in Omaha, harvest grass from midnight to dawn, fill up trash bags, and deposit them along the border of the road so Brimer could come along with a hauler to scoop them up as if collecting the garbage, only we were going to be collecting a grand per bag. I would direct the loaded truck down to my Dad's property in Marshfield where I was to coordinate the drying and pressing routines. Sean would be the one to divvy up the profits based on the percentages calculated in direct proportion to efforts spent in the weeds. This was the plan. Question was what would the results be?

That week we were all set to go in no time. Point-blank, the plan was unmitigated genius. Thank you. Thank you very much. Every stitch of the plan worked flawlessly, except for one screwy happening. When I was out buried in the triple meter weeds and not able to discern much other than the panorama of vegetation and the starry firmament above me, something unexplainable happened. As I was slicing and dicing through those unforgiving stalks with my scythe, I witnessed the intrusion of a gargantuan gray tube, which seemed to be dangling inexplicably from some unobservable platform floating a considerable distance up in the murky heights. It simulated the trunk of some monster elephant sweeping down through the corn stalks a dozen meters off my starboard flank. This tube thing looked to be nearly two meters in diameter. As mysteriously as it had come down from out of the aerial regions, it sucked itself back up into the moonless skies and disappeared. I have never beheld anything like it since that I can remember. When I inquired about it later, no one else working in the weeds that night had witnessed anything like the gigantic proboscis coming down to scan through the corn stalks as if it were searching for something or someone.

Several months afterward, I learned of an inordinate peculiarity, which occurred simultaneously to my observation of the gray tube out in the cornfields. It was an incident over at Malmstrom Air Force Base in Montana some three thousand kilometers away, at

The Moon Women

which time dozens of military personnel stated in a hearing (convened later at the behest of several senators), ten Minute Men missiles went off alert status and were essentially reduced to fluff for almost a complete day. And most importantly, this malfunction occurred after the staff had observed multiple saucer shaped air craft coming and going over several different missile silos. Not a single one of their personnel could get the controlling software for the missiles to respond. At one point, they had to notify President Johnson things were on the verge of Armageddon. This coincidence dissolved into the hazy vacuum of mindless pushups activating a null domination.

One month later, I was a whopping fifty Benjamins richer. Sean was extraordinarily happy, as was everyone on the team. But like most things in life, some player's eyes were bigger than their hindsight. Minister Money Bags, Hange Brimer, opted to be his own mutineer and broke off by himself. The core flank had another go-for-broke discussion. We annexed some justified modifications into the plan to greenlight a smoother run. We then tackled another trip. On the second visit, we stayed for a week. We pumped out three overburdened truckloads! We had to shift our target sectors because the neighboring farmers wondered why all the hit and miss flashlights had been seen surveying here and there on the habitually deserted roads. Many a midnight as we moiled away in the hemp swamps up to our hips like a pack of mudders running the Derby, dogs bayed into the empty sky.

Once we had resumed the homestead, no ifs and or buts, we were humbled by the mountain of pot spread out in the attic of my Dad's barn. He, of course, had retired quite comfortably in Needham because Marshfield was the summer cottage, which slept undisturbed in Rexhame. We were more or less non compos mentis as far as our encephalopathic delirium running solo by the sea goes. We did all this work in October and November. We were exceedingly lucky to have had a warm and quite a dry autumn that year which was ideal for curing pot. I hatched plans to undertake a second pasture picnic out with a convoy of recreational vehicles but it never panned out. When all the dust had settled, I was doing quite well with a signed lease listing a $1200 per month suite on Beacon Hill, plus in my driveway sat a brand new Ford Shelby GT-500, which was one of the most breathtakingly awesome automobiles which I have ever owned and I've owned a few nice ones over the years.

The inability for anyone to get off on the crap didn't really deflate the sales. Some molecular modifier had ruined the tetrahydrocannabinol maturation cycle reducing it to muck. The feature of looking authentic and putting out the correct odor made it possible to sell it quite easily. The rest was hype. I had a welding shop down in Brant Rock build me a kilo press armed with a thirty-ton hydraulic jack, enough steam to press the kilo bricks into tight blocks in no time.

Since it was Halloween, circumstance deposited me down at the local five and dime named "Ducas." I snapped up all the cutesy prizes kids go nuts over like orange wax whistles, plastic spiders and miniature gray haired witches. I put one of those kiddy toys into each kilo I pressed. After sales mounted swiftly, there was a spooky legend, which sprung up surrounding the so-called "Trick-or-Treat" kilos. Because of the widespread dope drought in Boston that fall, all our keys sold out by Veteran's Day. At one point, the Mafia butted in and usurped all the mark up. Unfortunately, a couple of dead heads got wacked. But by that time I was long gone. As a dismal outcome, Hange Brimer got busted after he set off on his fourth voyage. His greed ultimately eclipsed his priest frock.

Along a lonely sweep of waving grain in north Whales, sparks discharged across the secluded depository of stalks for an instant. Later at dawn, perplexing markings delineating sharp diamonds stamped out onto the expanse of wheat. When viewed from the nearby cliffs, the diagram closely resembled a pair of balances put there as a scrambled message from Beyond the stars.

- 5 -

Just as the dead leaves were gathering in the gutters around town, I doubled up on my luck while hanging with Alena. I was tracking down places to park some of my proceeds from the Omaha circuit. No spring chicken, I hustled to tie down an ad I had clipped out of an automotive flyer. It brought me over to an out of the way section of town. That sparkling day in early November, I was on a quest for the true muscle car.

The Moon Women

The garage door was out of kilter. Weston wrestled with it to get it to relinquish its dominion over his illusive prize. As the vinyl slab yawned back, his open-sesame uncovered the blunt-force of a Shelby. An expansive cobalt hood gleamed with its domination of sheer power. In its center, a monumental air scoop rose out of the gloom like the resurrected skull of some extinct reptile. Once the unbroken light of day had probed its fingers into that seclusion, once we had swept away all the cobwebs from its hibernation, the Mesolithic beast shone in all its glory.

In defiance of sitting in this dusty and oppressive garage for the entire summer, the sultry vehicle presented an overall condition of excellent to supreme. Its cobalt finish sucked in my hungry attention. It had a racy white stripe, which ran down its central divide, bumper to bumper, as if it had been licked by the tongue of God. Multiple intakes scopes adorned both its flanks, eighteen-inch wheels advertised superiority over the road and with the exception of the windshield, every inch of glass had been resurfaced with opaquely tinted security film to underscore its incognito persona. The impressive auto projected the aura of pure muscle. This was definitely a bona fide GT-500 as was certified by the logo stripe laminated to the running board.

"Wanna take 'er for a ride?" Weston asked. "Be but a minute or two to fire 'er up."

"Sure. That would be dandy." I was feigning the smokescreen of aloofness, instead of jumping out of my gourd with excitement and screaming, "It's a fucking Shelby fer Chrissakes! Damn straight I wanna ride her!"

He tidied miscellaneous odds and ends out of the way of the grill and repositioned a carton of motor oil, which was stacked way too damn near in my estimation. With the rear of the behemoth unfettered, he skirted the fender and snapped the button on the pilot wheel. It popped open and he got in.

"Cross your fingers she starts on the first crank. Sometimes she's a bit sluggish. It's tricky. Here goes." His confidence played dodgeball with his prospects.

He cranked the starter once and or twice. Out came the dead zing of the starter motor winding over on itself followed by the lonesome whir of the spin off when it disengaged.

"Can you hand me that can over there?" He thumbed at his bench. "I think she needs a little coaxing."

As I reached to get it, something clicked as he undid the hood latch. After whipping passed me to the driver's side, he knelt down at the grill and cocked his head to get a lock on pulling out the hood pins. Extracting a cotter pin clamped onto a stud, which protruded through the hood was how you got into the engine compartment. There was one on the other corner as well.

"These are racing pins." He proclaimed proudly. "They ensure the hood won't come loose no matter what the speed or what you might run into."

"That's comforting." I mumbled curtly feigning a blasé façade to dampen the bottom line all the while fixing my gaze on the cobra logo buttoned into the hubs of her outrageous mag-wheels.

"It won't be but a second now." He was posing to mount an offensive but came off facing the eight ball.

He lifted the hood up where by means of an obedient hydraulic arm it poised like a Doberman waiting for a command. With a twist, he unfurled the central wing nut, which clamped down the lid on the air filter dome over the carburetors. Tugging at the donut, he removed it from its perch over the Olympian quad array of down stacks. It unsealed with a gradual pealing pop. After placing it to the side, he sprayed a mist of the ether over each of the four silvery down-stacks.

"That should do it. The timing's set at a crisp eleven point three degrees so you will get the most horsepower when she's warmed up. But sometimes to get her going you need to use the ether to coax her over the hump and wake her up, so to speak." he validated after he reset the air dome, dropped the hood back into position, and relinked the pins.

He crawled over and squeezed back into the cockpit. I detected a crunch as the clutch pedal spring distended as the spanners released. He only had to turn the starter once. There was a snuff as the ether fired down into the four barrel. Then, she roared into life with an incredible rumble. This was the mother of all muscle cars!

I can't really describe the shivers and the goose bumps I got when I beheld that 7 liter V8 regain its grip on the lives of mortal men. A gust of stale exhaust blew out the back of the garage. The raw growling rumble you can only get from an authentic Ford 428

The Moon Women

cubic inch monster surged through my solar plexus. I had to step back. The thunderous, mellow note of the exhaust only amplified the impact. Then, Weston juiced a full tap on the accelerator and caused dominions of sheer power to rattle the spaces between my teeth. Then mercifully, he let her fall back to an intermittent idle.

"See. She's almost warmed up. Hop in!" He hailed.

Weston Perkins had been one of the head grease monkeys over at Homestead Ford for over eight years. After having digested all the manuals for the entire herd of Ford models, he then graduated to chief mechanical engineer. The cherry on his pie was being selected as one of the best muscle car jockeys in New England to go down to Texas and work with Carol Shelby and his crew of well-known technicians. From then on Weston was the only one who did all the servicing and troubleshooting on each of the high-performance Shelbys, which came into the dealership from Texas.

Later, out on the road, he explained this particular car had been a demo model, which customers could try out. They had only put a shy 3000 kilometers on it. After some braggadocian idiot had accidentally over revved the cams topping its fixed 6200 rpm redline, she had come up lame and had to be stowed in the pits. After purchasing the car for a song, Weston was the one who broke the engine down to its basics and then rebuilt it from scratch. When he did that, he put in a list of custom upgrades including superior performance camshafts, lifters, pistons, rods, and what not as to boost the stock specs from 430 HP to well over 500!

"This thing is an animal," he barked out over the growl of the muffler or lack thereof. He maneuvered it out of the garage gracefully and onto the highway as he methodically shifted the stick into second.

"The only advice I have to give you is don't baby her. She needs to have the ever lovin' shit kicked out of her."

With that streetcar dictum, he got her rolling down the garage ramp and out onto the road towards the Pike. Straight off, he was easy on the car making gentle and deliberate shifts from gear to gear at ranges that didn't seem to ask much from the mammoth engine. He wasn't revving it much over 2500 before grabbing another gear in the shift gate.

"I thought you said it needs to be kicked?" I was expecting some exhilaration.

"Well, there's a few cops in the vicinity I'd rather avoid. We need to get down by the turnpike entrance. Then, I'll show you something of what she can do."

Now, that's the ticket.

Dancing across the undulating road pitted with potholes, the MacPherson struts imparted a nimble feel smack dab to my derriere. After negotiating some side streets, we came to the entrance for the Route 9 bypass. Since he had cleared the traffic, he zipped a rev, downshifted into second from fourth and came on with the power band at around 3500 rpm, which sure as hell smoked the rear tires as the fearsome beast launched itself down the ramp and out onto the expressway. As my head snapped back mercilessly whacking against the headrest, my stomach got deposited back in the road somewhere.

Immediately, he pulled her into the fast lane and from there it was a moonshot into oblivion. We rocketed up over 160 kph in seconds. Weston threw a speed shift into third, sped up to a steady 220, and then shifted it into fourth to cruise. She hummed along as if she was on a Sunday errand to the mall. For a showstopper, he dropped back into third and goosed it causing the tail to kick out in a mad fashion. He was positively correct. This thing was an animal, a total beast. And she was going to be my beast!

"One guideline you should take home with you is this. Whatever happens, do not take her over six grand. In fact, it's mandatory to shift at 56 or even 57 hundred if you can nail that. If you get up over six K, the valves are going to start to float and she could seize on you. Could be expensive: not impossible, but definitely expensive. Got it?" He was downright stern with it, no minced words, just the facts.

"Okay, but one thing though, what's the final number?" I had my own ideas of figures buffeting the upper registers of three grand but I lay back to get it from him first.

"You can have this car for twenty-eight and not a penny less." He was adamant.

At first, I scratched my head but then I looked him straight on and said, "Done! When can I pick her up?"

"Really?"

"Yeah. You had me on racing pins."

"Great. Spare me two days for the prep. If you come down to the dealership on Saturday she'll be all systems go: pink slip, registration, the works." He added he could use his office to negotiate some of the papers, the title, and what not.

"I'll be there." We shook hands and exchanged good-byes. In the same way I had predicted from within the wheat back when I was just a boy, on the morrow, I would be King.

- 6 -

The unwinding chair reversed its coil upon my thoughts as it trapped me within a tangent vector and vomited me out into another era of my prepubescent youth. Why the erratic chair had chosen to thrash me so violently from one framework into its alternative state was no less disconcerting than mixing mayonnaise with mustard. It's not my choice but undoubtedly there is more going on here than simple horse play.

When I was six, because of the exploits with my fictitious sidekick, Little Boy, as well as my Red River bike, I was getting to be a big deal in the neighborhood with all the kids. One day tossing marbles out back they asked me what my religion was. I knew last summer while on vacation at the lake, I had the pleasure of meeting with a talking Christmas tree but that was my secret. I did not ever intend to divulge that treasure so I told them I didn't know what they meant by the word, religion.

"You know, you're religion. What are your parents? Are they Catholics or are they Protestants?" Corey Faucet and Ralph Bernard bullied me for the answer.

I didn't know what my parents were and confessing they were keen worshippers of the brown bottle faith made me queasy.

"I do not have this thing, religion." I contested emptily.

"Joseph is the Son of David and Mary is his wife," said Ralph. "And Mary had the baby Jesus in her belly. He was conceived by the Holy Ghost."

I did not like this talk of ghosts and bellies.

"I'm a good boy. I've never ever heard of all that stuff before." I disputed sheepishly.

They claimed their religion had books called Mathew, John, and Luke. I never heard of a book having a boy's name. If I had a book with a name, I would call it, Two Gun Jack.

"Well, why don't you come with us to our church? You can see if you like it." They were encouraging me to get ahead in life.

"What do I have to do?" I dithered not perceiving the poisonous fruit dangling two hairs away from falling into my hand.

"Be here tomorrow at seven sharp. We'll pick you up and drive you over to our church. Then you can know where it is and worship there whenever you like. Just remember. Wear your best clothes." They listed their requirements for the mission.

Two clicks after sunrise I greeted them alongside the vacant lot down on the corner just the way they had suggested. I was wearing the nicest outfit I had. When they met me there they were all smiles and carrying on. I thought this was going to be a fun time because I had never seen anybody fussing so much over showing up with fancy duds.

After only a short joyride, we neared the Cathedral of Saint Mary. The bunch of us hiked the granite steps, which led into an enormous hall. Choir music was cranking out of their phonograph. Each of the members filed in and crossed over. I was a bit hesitant to go because it seemed so overwhelming to be facing a living church tribe after all these years. After a while, they lured me to the doorway of the mountainous church with a Tootsie Roll.

As I approached the edifice of this terrifying abyss, there was a man standing on something like a podium or pulpit as if he were floating high above all the other churchgoers. All decked out in his priest digs with a purple scarf strung round his neck, he was right on the verge of speaking when he stopped short. He stared me down face-to-face frozen with a bad puss. I thought it was stupid. What's the idea of showing up here to get some religion if the instructor doesn't know what to say?

One by one, the parishioners rotated their heads and looked back at me. Like popcorn going off in a fryer, they began to giggle and laugh and then they broke out and roared. One by one and two by two, their laughter doubled and tripled. Soon the entire crowd was balling and slapping their thighs. You would have thought they had seen some goofy clown or even worse, a ghost. I didn't have a clue as to why. I stood there all alone turning all red.

"Pssst. Take your hat off!" My neighbor advised me sternly.

With my trained western humility, I removed my ten-gallon hat. It was emblematic of my outfit. I had my Hopalong Cassidy shirt

The Moon Women

with the carmine tassels. I had my Hopalong Cassidy chaps with the leather fringes on the sides. I had my Hopalong Cassidy vest with the four deep pockets. Encircling my midriff was my patent leather Hopalong Cassidy belt, which held the forty fake shiny silver bullets. And on each hip hung my two holsters housing my genuine Hopalong Cassidy pearl handled revolvers in dazzling chrome. For my finale, I had my Hopalong Cassidy boots on which I had strapped my starry five-point spurs, which made a little jingle when I walked. I had worn virtually the finest clothes I owned. And I was damn proud of it.

Needless to say, that was the last time I visited church as a youngster. Later in the day, after my friends dropped me off back at the corner, and the registers were set back to a clean slate, I came to meet someone new. Jane had arrived. Why the Khrng had delayed her admittance was not revealed to me until after she introduced me to Midge. Romance was to be the king pin of this game.

- 7 -

When I was eight was when I discovered sex. Midge Levy was my first Jewish girlfriend. She had side-parted, brunette hair, which flipped up nicely on the ends. Her face was peachy not patchy. Her laugh was provocative, as well as rambunctious. Her Mom put a pink ribbon in her bonnet every day. She liked to do things she was not supposed to do. Her dresses were always spotless and well ironed but her breasts had not pushed out yet. She liked Pepsi not Coke. She was faster than spit on her Elgin Bluebird and she always won at Hopscotch. Plus, she could write her name in cursive. She was my age and yummy.

She lived in the same neighborhood in Wellesley in which I did back in 1950 only four streets over. Midge's house was a two story, which had shutters embossed with those vertical clefts reminding me of Hostess cupcakes. The panes themselves had mullion inserts, which enhanced its Hansel and Gretel look. And even nicer, it was painted a chocolate brown with cream trim which made it look more and more like a yummy Hostess treat.

Her parents were usually not at home. When the home front belonged to Midge, she sometimes led me into the pantry to feed me. There, she plied me with an unusual delight, which she began as a regular peanut butter and fluff sandwich, but in between the layers, she sprinkled rows of M&Ms and raisins smothered with strawberry jam. It was the greatest sandwich I have ever eaten. This was ostensibly when I got hooked on PB & J most likely. I couldn't get enough of it. The hooked nut in the shell was basically one day that fetish would lead to dire consequences when I was a sophomore in college. Be that as it may, I was hooked on Midge. too.

After that delectable experience, she led me upstairs and into her parent's bedroom. The place was cavernous and smelled like dead roses. A smaller side room, which served as their closet had a series of vertical mirrors granting a wraparound view all the way to the back and from the sides as well. Midge snatched my hand and pointed me into the bank of mirrors. Then, she got behind me with her back towards mine and hooked her hands back to seize mine.

"See. Now you are me and I am you." As she repeated this singsong phrase over and over while spinning us both in circles, a cascade of snowy feathers spilled out from the rafters as if snow falling down. I checked on what genus of angelic dove had made its nest up there or might had lost its way seeking refuge in the bleakness hovering over Midge.

After my dizzying experience in the spiral closet, she led me by the hand down a stuffy hallway to a hard-to-see back staircase, which led up into the attic. When we got up there, it was scary as hell like midnight all over the place. To this day, I have an appalling reminiscence of detecting the profile of a Khrng peeking out from the wooden undercarriage of the roof flashing. It was only a foggy image so I buried my eyes in my hands and only peeked when I had to follow closely behind Midge. And the thought faded away.

Then I saw a beaded chain dangling down from a naked bulb overhead. The obscenity of its grotesque protuberance hung down out of the crusty plasterboard like a dead turnip. After Midge tugged on it, its click manifested an apron of dull light on the filthy floor. Only two pieces of bad furniture were up there: a twin frame with a worn mattress, but no linens or blankets for it anywhere, and one ratty Fauteuils with dimpled buttons, stained pink upholstery, and mouse eaten kick posts, which stuck out like spigots. Those two and an orange crate sans the fruit made up only a smattering of the Speak, which took the edge off a tad. Even at that early stage I had was aware of it but hadn't yet connected to its inevitable outcomes.

The Moon Women

Midge escorted me over to the cheesy citrus hamper and ordered me to sit down. Time shifted and I regressed back to some cage or containment vessel in which once upon a time the Khrng had trapped me on board their ship. It came to me as a foggy yarn Little Boy had unraveled back then as if an ancient doubloon buried in the folds of my youth but then it was gone.

As I snapped back, Midge shuffled over to the bed and squared her back to face me. Then she put on a painted scowl and began wiggling her hips. It was as if she was performing the dance of the Mau Maus. As she was gyrating there with her butt going side to side like a little devil, she shimmied her hands up under her dress and hiked her underpants down. She took them off one leg at a time and threw them onto the armchair with a risqué twirl. Then, she jumped backwards onto the naked mattress. Inching excitedly so her back was flat to the headboard, she smiled her hundred-watt smile straight at me. This maneuver put her into a squatting pose with her private parts exposed and aimed directly at me. Alarmingly she simply reached down and opened the thing up.

"This is my peepee," she bragged quite confidently as though she was displaying some fossil, which had never before been exhibited to any suitable audience.

"You can come and look, but you can't touch."

I was warned.

I had no idea what the hell was going on. Since I was a slow developer, I thought females were pretty much like Barbie dolls, flat, barren, and gender-neutral. What was all that strangeness going on down there? There were a few hairs growing on it and some little folded fleshy parts with a pink hole in the middle. I got up off the shoddy crate, took a step over to the edge of the mattress, and bent down. I had to get a closer look. It was the most anatomically twisted thing I had ever seen. I looked away and frowned with confusing shock. When I looked up Midge beamed and pointed down at the mess in her middle. I looked back at it. Even though it looked so weird, I kind of liked it.

"Does it hurt?" I imagined it would because of some ruddy clots here and there.

"No. It's my peepee and I love it. My Mommy says it's my candy," she boasted proudly.

I made a grimacing facial expression as I thought. What? Eat that? Are you kidding? That's gross! But then, something equally shocking hit me: my penis had grown to nearly three times its normal size. That totally freaked me out. What witchery was this? I jumped back. Midge could see that between my legs, my peepee had become my hot dog. I was embarrassed as well as mystified. Would she make fun of me?

"That's your cock," Midge pointed out matter-of-factly. "Mama says the cock goes into the hole in my peepee when I'm a big girl," she vocalized the words but it didn't seem to me that she was a true convert yet.

"Are you sure, Midge, because that sounds really gross." I was becoming thoroughly disgusted with this adventure into bizarro land. I just begged to get this over with.

"Can I go now? Billy wants me to trade cards with him this after." I had to invent something, anything, just to get out of there.

Even if the Son of man shall send forth his angels, I couldn't get out of that flesh trap fast enough. I am pretty sure Little Boy would stand with me on that score. I bolted down the stairs, blasted out the door, and made a beeline for home turf as fast as I could go. I was not going to have her flap-dragon eat me up on that afternoon in fair-skinned suburbia.

Midge and I went to the same school and we were in the same grade. It was third grade. Our teacher's name was Miss Devlin but she was a substitute. Both of us looked up to Miss Devlin in spite of her cruelty, mainly because she was a very tall and pleasantly attractive older woman, perhaps, twenty-two, or even as much as twenty-four. She always wore colorful velvet dresses. Or at a minimum I thought they we velvet. They were always really soft and plushy whenever I rubbed up against her.

Miss Devlin was the strictest substitute I ever had, but she would always smile. That was her alarming curve ball. No matter how hopping mad she might get with you, or how loud she screamed, she always had a clown-like smirk plastered on her kisser.

On class day Miss Devlin was instructing us on the adding tables I so liked. Midge and her bevy of friends were all twittering and shushing over in the elite block of the classroom. It wasn't long before a bubble of snickering caught everyone's attention, including Miss Devlin's.

The Moon Women

"Is there something you would like to share with the rest of the class Midge?" Miss Devlin was narrowing in on it.

Oh, my heavens! She's going to tell on me!

"No, Ma'am." Midge announced calmly as she stared at me.

"Now, children, we're going out on a fieldtrip after lunch." Miss Devlin always had surprises for us.

We had our milk and our cheesy peanut butter crackers. Then, we lay down on our mats for our usual fifteen-minute nap. While we were resting, Miss Devlin explained we were going out for a walk in nature on this beautiful day in early June. We were going to go out through the parking lot and then hike down the footpath, which led over to the base of the sledding hill. The walk would curve by some unusual plants, which Miss Devlin was going to educate us on all their names. I was excited we would be coming to know some of the nature in the neighborhood. Then Manny Lopez farted. Miss Devlin outright ignored him but not the entire mimicry of the class. She simply kept on with her process.

"Okay everyone. Let's go."

On cue at noontime, Miss Devlin got us up and out the door. We marched off Indian file in the direction of the mammoth hillock, which made for terrific sledding during the winter months. On the way, we had to march through a patch of forested vegetation. Here, her shortcut was thin. We came to some bushes and tall waving grasses lapping at our feet. All of a sudden, Miss Devlin yelled out a command.

"Stop children! Please stop and come over here. Gather round me, please." Miss Devlin was ordering us with her constriction.

In seclusion, she hovered near a lonely little plant in the ground.

"Children!" She commanded reverently. "Take a look at this plant here by my shoe. This plant is extremely dangerous! Its name is poison ivy. You can always tell if it is poison ivy because the leaves are always in bunches of three. The leaves are always this Kelly green color and always real shiny. That's the main thing: a three-leaf Shamrock that's super shiny. You must never, never, ever touch this plant. It contains a poison and once it gets onto you, it will cause you to get sick as a dog. In no time, you will be itching all over your body. Then, you will become nauseous and you might even throw up. One time I got some on my body and it was so awful, I can't even tell you how disgusting it was. So, please, be on your best behavior and please be very careful when you run into this plant. Stay as far away from it as you can get. Whatever you do, never, never, ever, ever touch this plant, its leaves, or any piece of it. Let this be an important lesson for you." Miss Devlin then announced if anybody had any questions.

Most everyone was devastated and in shock. There was righteous dead silence.

Like pie in the sky, I had the most dingbat urge pop into my yet undeveloped brain. I strolled over to where Miss Devlin was shielding the children from the vile and evil danger of this charlatan, three-fingered menace. With a trace of malefactor gleam in my eye, I proudly glared at the spotlighted specimen and grinned. As Miss Devlin looked down on me unapprovingly, I smiled nonchalantly and announced with considerable defiance.

"Watch."

I bent over, pinched off one of the leaves, wadded it up between my fingers, and held up to Miss Devlin.

"Time fer lunch!"

I jammed the juicy green morsel into my mouth and commenced with some serious chewing. I was fixing to manducate her annoying ridiculousness straight the hell out of my life.

Miss Devlin went fully ballistic spouting unbelievably foul curses of impending doom.

"What are you doing, you nasty child? That's a poisonous plant! You cannot eat that! Stop! What are you thinking? Spit it out right now!" She commenced to slapping me hard upon my shoulder and arm.

I merely kept chewing.

The instant I plopped the wild salad into my choppers all the children shrieked with out-and-out terror. Beth Stevenson and Cathy Rutledge fainted dead away. The ones still standing broke formation and skedaddled back to the classroom. All except Midge, who kept watching me with the calmness of a cat stalking its prey in the grass.

I chewed on.

At that point, Miss Devlin realized she had lost all control of her pupils. She attempted to corral some of her straggling brats, the ones she could get her hands on, and herd them into the playground. The others were nowhere to be found. When I finished with my

The Moon Women

chewing it was time for my big finale. I marched over to Miss Devlin, snatched hold of her arm, and swallowed. Then I showed her my fully wide and freshly emptied oral cavity.

"Look!" I had devoured the entire poison ivy leaf all by myself!

"Oh, you horrid little creep. Get away from me!" She bolted towards the back entrance of the schoolhouse.

Could it be eating the poison ivy had become my own personal mithridate for Miss Devlin's poisonous leer and quite possibly the Khrng's organic locators as well? Notwithstanding, I'm not quite sure how a poison can be a cure, but without that head start I would have inadvertently shown up as an item on their knowledge menus at some point in their process. I'd would have been hopelessly lost.

- 8 -

Back on the Hill with Alena, I awoke from the previous round of sacraments to the sweetness of bananas. I like bananas but there was something more to it. It was bacon. I like bacon, too, but together?

I looked up and beheld the tiny body of Jesus impaled on a bloody cross. If He had taken the sins of all mankind onto his shoulders, why did they have to complicate the whole thing by making a trillion copies in the form of miniature crucifixions? Wouldn't the normal one have covered all the bases? Give me a break. Wouldn't a man-size nailing have done the job? And what's up with all those beads, the rose beads and the silver? Or would it have been as a dead mallemuck wreathing the neck of the Pope?

Out the corner of my eye, I caught Alena entering from apartment central. She was wearing a sheer silk robe, which allowed the backlight to filter through the crack between her legs. It perked me up some to realize she had doffed her panties that morning. She was carrying a tray plated with her banana bacon combo and one drooping daffodil, plus something shiny encircling her neck so I hit her with the 64 thousand dollar question.

"Why do you leave your rosary on the bedpost overnight?"

"I've brought your wake-up meal so get up you lazy oaf!" She deposited her breakfast creation.

234

Alena was not avoiding me, she simply needed to have her needs met. This prompted me to acknowledge her selfless services of bringing me toast and flowers to eat.

"Thanks, Love. You're the greatest. I've never had bananas and bacon sandwiches for breakfast. So, what's up with the rosary? Do you do it or not?"

Two prongs on the fork, or was it the forked tongue? Could it be I was Jackie Gleason sending Alice to the moon or was she simply morphing into Alice in Wonderland since I was the Mad Hatter evidently?

"Pipe down and eat! I got that rosary from my Mom. At bedtime, I use it to say my prayers with it. What do you use?" She was going to launch me to the Moon, but soon she realized what she was asking and to whom, so she quit her bitching and said, "Never mind. What was I thinking?"

"Nuttin' honey. No, really, I'd like to learn how to do prayers. What's the secret in this sandwich? It's yummy. I like it. It's marmalade, isn't it?" I was betting on making breakthroughs on both levels of this mystical milk shake.

"What do mean? You need lessons for prayers? Haven't you ever prayed in church? Where were your parents?" She was ripping my plan to pieces, but on the shy side, her approach was mildly sympathetic of my midrashic mess.

"I've never been to church, except once when I was a kid. I'll have to admit it was a bit weird but that wasn't my fault." I declared embarrassingly having confessed it to someone after such a long dead stretch.

"You've never been to church? You've never, never, ever, ever, in your whole life, gone to church?"

She deliberately flipped her question upside down. She was the head majorette of the righteous mambo.

"I'm telling you that, no, I haven't really gone to one as a practitioner, that is." I was adamant, but it wasn't working. Not wanting to appear mean spirited, I let it go.

"Would you like to? It's not like it's something you have to join. You don't even have to be a member and it won't cost you a thing. You just go." She was running conversion plays on me already as she bent over to reclaim the empty tableware.

The Moon Women

"Yeah, only you have to pay with your inner spirit." I made the throat gagging sign. "Then they raise you up you to heaven to get your ticket punched." I pantomimed the meteoric ascension while noticing she was braless.

"You should not joke about it, you know. It's a sin to denounce the Ten Commandments." She moralized. She was becoming a product of her own dogma and a hot one at that.

"I don't mean anything by it. I'd like to know what it's like, that's all. I'm not the mailman. I'm the male man. Get it? Male man?"

She batted me one. Admittedly, I was volunteering although not with the best intentions. I just needed to get laid.

"Okay. You can come with me when I go to church this Sunday." She promised.

"That's friggin' tomorrow. Can't I have some time to get organized? What if I haven't finished my bucket list?" Now I was getting cold feet.

"You're going and you're going tomorrow, with me and my Mom. And that's final." Alena was communicating four shells deep as she applied ample layers of her morello lipstick.

"What's the payback?"

"You'll find out later. Now it's time to finish your breakfast."

"What if I've got to find out now? Someone told me once; if you've got an itch, scratch it."

"Is that anything like I'll scratch your back if you scratch mine?" She put the plates down and pouted.

"More or less. But my scratcher's on the fritz, so instead I'll have to use this."

I got up and jammed my hips out toward her. My half-flaccid cock swung out of my crotch hatch and into the wind. With a squeal of excitement, she knelt down and ate me up. As I reggaed in place to get fully loaded, she massaged the family jewels bringing me up to the busting point.

"Roll over, Doll. Lemme work your dimples."

One of Alena's favorite things was to have the Venus dimples in her back poked methodically while taking me in doggy style. From that little move alone, she was able to climax multiple times while I searched for the one mountain peak orgasm. In no time, we had resurfaced the linoleum with a sweaty sheen. The emergence of

236

natural spontaneity was one of Alena's most enduring features, that and her perky breasts.

We killed the remainder of the day, which was short enough as it was since I had only surfaced from out of the cotton jungle after my catnap late that noon. We enjoyed a movie over in Cleveland Circle. Whatever the movie was I could tell you it wasn't the Ten Commandments. Charlton Heston was not gracing us for Christmas, but one day I knew I would find him heading an army of militia and plotting to overrun the White House on a platform of "Equal Votes, Equal Guns."

Smells of coffee and hot jam weren't the same as bananas and bacon sandwiches; nevertheless, I woke the same way the following day, only it wasn't passed noon. I wasn't being molly coddled with her hot toast, merely placated for no reason. Tasty toast, though. I had five slices, three with cinnamon. That rosary stood fast hanging where it had been nailed since yesterday onto her bedpost. I hadn't observed any prayers during the preceding bed down. Could be she performs it when I'm going to the bathroom. I thought that was a little selfish of her. She gets to talk to God and I get to have a bowel movement.

As I nosed the car into the one-way entrance of the church's parking area, the headstone spelled it all out in incendiary letters, "Church of the Sacred Heart." I confirmed my vote on neutrality by underscoring I had maintained first-rate behavior while driving. I'm sure her mother appreciated it but I hadn't received my chalice yet. I threw out a high-five to Alena but only received a dumb comeback.

"It's not like that, Rahm."

As we approached the towering cathedral guarded by a congregation of pink flowering crab trees, there was a billboard out front offering announcements. It broadcast info for up-and-coming events with oversized letters inserted into peg holes. The caption-of-the-day declared, "He anoints you with life everlasting."

Man! That has to be the most out-of-sight advertising in the country. It wasn't like the usual banal adage:

Try our mattresses and you'll sleep like you're on Cloud nine!

Or the worn out axiom:

Our televisions have the biggest brightest picture in town!

Theirs broadcast its disclaimer as:

The Moon Women

If you come and visit us in here
And take home a sampling of our monism,
It will ward off all the evils,
Which have resulted from your otherwise
Dismal and Godless subsistence.

What's more, if you hit the jackpot you can even win a blessed life which promises to go on and on with no alba-cross to gag you. In my opinion, that could be a good thing, or, it might be very, very bad if it had to transpire in this dump.

We entered in through the big doors, which had wide heavenly wings unfurled for all the parishioners. It reminded me of Noah's Ark, although I can't say I had much draw down on that score, most of the animals had gotten lost apparently. I was happy simply going in. A schoolgirl by the door handed me the program for the performance. We landed midway down in the sparser sector; conceivably, where all the newbies go. Alena insinuated it made no difference but that came out like a maid's tale.

After I played fumble finger with myself a while waiting for all the worshippers to finish filing in, a hush fell over the bunch. Then singing weakly seeped out of them after they dug out their so-called songbooks that they found in a dwarf shelf nailed onto the seatback bracing off their knees. Alena had hers in hand and had hitched her star to the choir. She turned her head briefly to share with me it was a Roman Missal.

I looked at it and asked how fast it could go and where it might land. I didn't want wind up as collateral damage. She jabbed me in the ribs with her elbow and then aimed the page straight at me. Then she pulled the trigger by nodding towards it. I simpered I was saving myself for Jesus and my tonsils for the Opera, although I had no tonsils ever since I was eleven. I listened intently to try to pick up on some of the words from the hymns book and maybe sing along lamely:

> He should have fed them
> also with the finest of wheat,
> and with honey out of the rocks
> should I have satisfied thee. [7]

It sounded like a bit of an exaggeration to get honey out of a rock, yet the finest of wheat was a fond memory of my time as a boy out by Cazenovia Lake. I wondered if perhaps another baby pine tree was going to appear and anoint me with everlasting jaundice like it did before.

There came a glimmer of hope that, quite possibly, the thoughts of the wheat might mend the heavy scars on my heart. And was there really an Angel flying above me always ? Were the events of my life simply his shadow, cast down upon this physical drama stage of impermanence while using me to justify his ways and his works as he flew across the dreamlands battling amidst a war I knew nothing about? Was I really a platonic plaything in his heaven of horror?

The stained glass in this place sure was an eyeful to look at. I liked unraveling the oddball wedges to formulate the figurines of all the Bible folks. I was making it into a neat game. I had the thought that possibly they could put together a religion based on that trick alone. It might be easier to sell, easier than God anyways. God always seemed to me to be such a tall order.

Alena had encouraged me to adopt a well-mannered demeanor but eventually I reached my melting point. Wriggling with nervous anxiety, my alter ego flowed out into the pews like a pilgrim gaging with cholera. As Alena elbowed me in the stomach, I got yanked back real fast. The smiling globe of her countenance was unduly present. I was secure in spite of the possibility of suffering possible molestation from these displaced Christian preacher devils.

After the speaker conducted a series of hand washings (apparently the dish soap in his kitchen wasn't sufficient), he resorted to shaking a humungous lantern of smoke from side to side. It fumed up the place something fierce like a bobbing hookah.

"He's stoned on that thing. Right?"

"Noaaah! Shush up! He's the Father. Pay attention. This is important."

I thought she was going to whack me with her book but she would have lost her place so I got saved by the word of God.

"Who's father? I thought those guys were eunuchs or some other mutant dick. Father of whom I'd like to know?"

The Moon Women

"You're impossible. Why did I even bother bringin' you here if you're gonna poke fun at it all. Can't you be civil and behave yourself just for once so you can benefit from the blessings?"

"I guess. Don't cost me nuttin'."

After the Father man with the purple polyps bagged his medicine dance, some of the audience stood and formed a queue outside the pews. One by one, they tread towards the preacher man who dropped a biscuit onto their protruding tongues. Alena corralled my arm and encouraged me to go and get one.

"It's the Eucharist. The body and blood of Christ." She pronounced its purpose solemnly.

"I didn't realize you people were cannibals." I received another correctional jab in my shoulder.

"Well, what's it taste like?" I felt it only fair to request some indication of what I was ingesting.

"It's not about that. It's to save yourself from your sins. You have to be loyal." She was becoming wildly patriotic, toward the church team anyway.

"For sure? They flattened the guy out? Was it really two thousand years? So did they put preservatives in that?" There was a plethora of inquiries lining up in my head to receive a decent chance at making penance with the source of their aggravations.

"Shut! Up!"

Alena whispered while enunciating each word like a cleaver. With brute force, she dragged me off to get our church tickets punched. When it came round for my turn, I shot out my hand to receive the biscuit because I wanted to examine it prior to committing it to my digestive altar of the acidic apostles. The man looked down at me as if I were a show dog, which had missed its mark. He made a motion with his hand, which reminded me of a stripper I had bedded once, who compassionately advised me in a similar fashion.

"Okay, but you need a redo; somethin's not workin' with your fryer, Buddy."

I frowned back.

"Is it vanilla or coconut?" It looked like it could have been either one.

Alena slammed me in the gut hard this time and twisted my arm.

"Shouldn't I get a choice? That's only fair, isn't it?"

"Oh Rahm quit it! Just put it in your mouth."

As I scanned the ecumenical magistrate's donation, I was going to reply with, "I'll bet that's what he says to all the kids." But I kept mum just as she had advised. I let the papery wafer fall free like an abandoned feather from some angel who had overtaken the building. It landed in the middle of my tongue. It tasted like stale flattened out rice. At least it's not like chicken; that would have been alarming. But it wasn't something I would make a steady diet of, that's for sure.

"M-m-m-m, yummy. Thanks a bunch."

Alena hauled me away choking.

"You're impossible. I'm so peeved." She crabbed.

"You'll get over it later tonight." I winked.

She wound up her arm to belt me one in the kisser but then she laid her hammer down and re-holstered the weapon.

When everybody had received their scrumptious treats like proper little doggies, they all resumed their seats and sung some more songs. I tried out my a-capella, which seemed to crank down Alena's jitters, enough to be more satisfied, peaceful almost.

The priest fella raised this puny baseball bat made from a brassy alloy all decked out with a filigree of micro toys glued onto it. He came down the aisle as all the recruits came out of their pews and waited alongside in rows. As he proceeded towards them, he waved this bronzed dildo in the air as though he was flicking something on them. I didn't get a righteous feeling from it right then and ducked to seek cover by holding my hand over my eyes but Alena caught me and stabbed me in the gut again.

Violent spurts of a viscous fluid shot out the end of his nozzle and drenched everybody like a feral fountain. It might have been water but that really wasn't clear to me yet. I wanted to see it better but I was having some trouble with the whole deal, frankly, so I took cover behind my seat back. The horrendous devise wasn't connected to a hose or any faucet that I could tell which made it much worse. Most of the parishioners were waving their hands over their heads and then collapsing back onto the hard oaken benches after he had done his dirty work. One woman even keeled straight over onto the floor!

"Aren't they going to help her?" I pleaded.

241

The Moon Women

Alena shushed me. As the Father man kept knocking them dead with his stick, I began to see the need for prayers. Then, he eyeballed another woman who wasn't getting into the proper mood. Using the flat of his palm, he plopped it right down onto her forehead with a gentle slap. Soon as shit, she keeled over in a heap. Some of her relatives helped her be comfortable down there, but they didn't pick her up or revive her in any way. Droves of proselytes were falling left and right. Eventually, he got to us.

When her mother went down for the count, I rigged my lines to get whacked with the worst of it as the pontiff threatened to bless us. Poor Alena joyfully accepted the brunt of his devil juice and went down on his second splash, then he turned to me. Heaven help me, I thought.

The Malthusian macromancer paused, studied me for a moment while drilling his loosely configured lasers my way, and shook his head. At last, he dosed me with his splash potion. Its cardinal contact was like a cooling rain. But then, with a grim deliberateness, the warmth drained out of my midsection and as it did, an iciness replaced it deep into my abdomen like a zingy peppermint Slurpee. Its tentacles plunged into my chest and spread throughout my body like an icy octopus all the way to my back. It was an odd but pleasurable sensation that was dissolving a presence into my core like the promise of a malignant gospel. I tried to speak out but I could not. It ensnared me within the mutistic grip of its mutinous dominion. It didn't seem right to me. Slaphappy, I fell backward into a weird obscurity. I gripped the wooden pew back with all my might. But then, it came to me, something I had just had a flashback about a moment before - my one saving encounter from the Beyond. I thought back to my childhood when I had experienced something which was extraordinary for me, something, which I had always valued as a divine revelation. I remembered my tree, my crystal evergreen.

Instantly the kidnaping entity fled apparently intent on chewing on its next victim. I was immensely overjoyed as the mad devil doling out the blessings moved on. When it was finally all over, no one had anything more to say so we filed out of the church. The Father man who had done all the damage was standing at the exit thanking all the fans for putting up with his nonsense. I thanked him graciously but I kept my distance. He seemed pleased I had come to his church but coldly diffident thanks to my success in hindering the application of his satanic lemonade.

As Alena and I exited the church grounds, we promenaded hand in hand. She instilled some confidence that my accompanying her was worth some reward later on, which did warm me up some inside. At least it might lead to some righteous work in the white, the white sheets, that is. That was religious wasn't it? When she politely inquired how I liked it, I told her I'd let her know as soon as I had figured out what the hell had just happened. I insinuated it might take me some time, however. And then I punctuated my statement with a sour puss.

This time I lit up the tires and got us spinning down the road towards home, fast. The Moon's bony antler tore up the star-gate as all the seraphim scattered to the heavens and released ball bearings of flaming hail, which cascaded across the northern frontiers leaving a residue of cold prayers.

- 9 -

Back at the home front, my chair of Christian purity spun wildly with the notion of the Christ bearing witness to an illegal transformation and a wry prejudice for which the hated ones could no longer answer. Calls from a bothersome disservice rained fast and hard upon the refuge of a heated song and a withering style. As I snuggled deeper into the chair's vast innards, an unflinching pulse took up its beat of pounding reverence once again.

Today was inventory day at the bookstore and Alena and I were going to be teammates. Our job was to finish the east section, and then go out back to the warehouse and finish counting all those books as well trying our best to complete the task without dying in the process; updates to the master files had been way overdue. In short order, we got down to the business right after our coffee break. If Alena didn't have three cups of java in her belly, she was useless. I loved her belly. On occasion, I would put my mug down on it and tongue her button. Tracing the crease, which ran down to the valley of the shadow could entice me for hours on end. It made me confidant in knowing I was entitled to her trust. But on that morning we were doing books.

The Moon Women

After a solid hour, we were up to Camus or maybe Canby. This constriction caused me to have a flashback of my crash pad at Bard in which I had the vision of the melting volumes. Why I had scribbled so many oddball sayings there on the wall next to my bed was a placement I couldn't place. The recollection gave me an eerie feeling, like a Déjà vu, but slightly off; more like a recurring repression stuck in a loop. But that was now and this is then or maybe it's later. Sometimes all of these prescient hiccups foul me up some.

After we had catalogued all the books over at headquarters, we went back out into the warehouse to inventory the dusty stacks of books piled in endless rows back there. The remoteness proved to be an enticing prospect when coupled with our separation from store central provided the unexpected liberty of being all alone. Alena managed to unfold her scheme so our trail would wind through the G section out back. After a few hours, we had cleared a path all the way over to Goremykin, Goring, and Gorky. A Nazi sandwich on Russian rye came to mind. As I high stepped my way towards the vaulted shelves, my tongue picked the caraway seeds out of my teeth like the crumbs of lost gold stripped from the Juden.

Alena unbuttoned her blouse with a spunky cat leer stapled onto her puss. In the dimness of the warehouse corridors, she appeared to me as a stained glass angel moving in cubes. As I lifted her onto a pallet, I anticipated the possibility of some serious inventory work. But then, it all switched. Like a bolt from nowhere, I stuck my hand out and selected a promising edition from the shelf. I let it fall open. Was this another episode of Biblical Ouija unfolding out of the blue, or was it the White? I quoted directly off the page:

> He came and he walked among us. On the mead,
> He talked to us about our sorrows. By the stream,
> He showed us that the cause of those sorrows
> Was our own doing. He gathered our prayers
> In front of our faces that we might see our need.

"Hey. This is right on."
But Alena really didn't want to get into it.
"Yeah. Well, if it's so excellent why don't you take it to bed later tonight since I'll be having a holiday?" She was tit for tat.

"Okay. If you want to be that way," I disclosed with undue vim and vigor:

> He also showed us that there is a silver lining
> In that grief. He taught us how to convert the pain
> And turn it into understanding and joy.
> He taught us that through that understanding
> Would come empowerment like roots
> That can support a tree of great height.

"Are you hearing this?" I needed her vote.
"I hear you knocking, but you ain't gettin' in."
Whose test was this?
"Very funny. Just for that." I made further public to the walls:

> Through the suffering will come a greater
> Knowledge of what it means to be a Man.
> Seeing that knowledge take root and
> Sprout forth in our hearts, gives us
> Great compassion and great gratitude.
> It gives us ourselves. It is called virtue.

"My! That is truly moving. Who wrote that?" Alena aspired to know but I suspected she was simply a sectarian mole.

"Lemme see. It says, Edward Taylor. Seems he's a clergyman or perchance a seer."

I was so impressed with my selection from the racks of telepathic intimidation.

"Well, why don't you take ole Edward there over to the backroom and find out if you gonna get as hot a blow job as I might give you if you weren't such a jerk!" She jabbed me in the stomach with her finger.

"Nice! Real nice."

I returned her service. There was a muffled shout from outside.

"Alena!"

The fire exit opened and a cry came out from the office.

"Jackie's on the phone. Says she's got a burning snag."

Alena's sidekick had butted into our little bivouac.

The Moon Women

"You wait here. I'm not through with you yet, Buster!"

She got up and stomped back into the store. Without Alena's guidance, I had to take a load off. I scaled my finger down the spines and targeted another selection - a sixth century Christian monk by the name of Exiquus Dionysius who authored one titled <u>Caelorum Regnum</u> (Kingdom of Heaven). Whew! That's quite a mouthful. I couldn't wait to find out what this bloke had to say. I let the binding spread wide in to induce the work. The book fell open and I reported to my imaginary audience:

> It is in the human heart,
> Where the warmth of God shines.
> It is in the human mind,
> Where the footprints of God walks.
> It is in the human eye,
> Where the laughter of God echoes.
> And it is in the temple of the human forehead,
> Where the stairway to God's home begins.
> Your home. Go there and climb it.

The elevation of that passage repeated within me like an unending stream of prayerful thoughts seeking to come home. I wondered why this was always happening to me. Surely, there is something trying to save me from an unavoidable calamity or perhaps the answer might be more to the truth I'm simply another pawn in the game of life. I jettisoned those enigmas and wondered when Alena would come back and provide me with continuing distractions to mislead the long arm of destiny from dragging me off again. It was becoming more and more evident that I required some connection to stave off those grappling hooks, which were always hovering just outside my sanity.

While I wandered in and out of the empty aisles amidst tall stacks of cardboard cartons and broken crates, I speculated on why there was an excessive accumulation of straw back here. Even though Spring had sprung and the Lilies of the valley were reminding me of another candle on my cake, I knew we weren't stocking a barn or some livestock corral. I hiked myself up onto a low riding palette to get a grip. It afforded me a decent angle to the door, in case Alena came back. When she resumed our schedule, we would need to make hay to get back on track.

A scruffy homeless guy sauntered by; he had emerged from a bend only to hurriedly transition behind a large mound of cardboard crates. I readjusted my position with regard to the wall and fiddled with a loose piece of straw while contemplating what Alena's return policy might entail. Then, he reappeared again dragging an unwieldy wooden plank behind him. It had a battered look, decrepit and dirty, and was that blood I saw there clotted to its side? His dessert aura sparkled with sweat.

With bits of straw clotting his tangled locks, which welled down atop his grungy shoulders, he was struggling to get a better hold on the awkward log. Flagged with filth, he must have slept with the goat herders last night because he was spattered with forsaken reeds. His garments weren't even the workaday garb of the warehouse; they were just disheveled rags. His windblown merle tunic was stained crimson on the cuffs. Across his forehead, he wore a bandanna with a pattern on it, what looked to be the imprint of curling waves: it made me think of a surf bum. Finally, in exhaustion, the withered vagrant dumped the beefy log down at my feet with a smash.

"You want some help with that, Guy?"

I felt obligated in some detached way.

"This burden is mine. Do not wish away another's burden unless you are certain it is not his treasure," he said as he caught his breath.

"It looks like your boss has you up against the wall with that thing. How far do you have to drag it?"

From his rebuke, I wasn't sure if he was correct in the head. It looked like he might have been bouncing off walls for quite some time.

"Look around, Brother. Many walls surround us here in this world. Pass them by, Brother; don't make them your home. If you meet the wall with force, it will lay you down. If you meet the wall with love, it will bow before you and its door will open. The way in is through love, Brother. Know my words to be true."

There was a flash in his eye and a thunder in his voice.

"Yeah. Sorry. Thought I would offer some help is all."

I didn't feature knocking myself out.

The Moon Women

"I don't think I've ever seen you here before."

I drummed my pen on the back of my hand.

"If a child is enjoying his candy, would you spoil him in the name of his health?"

He wiped away the sweat under his eye.

"I'm not sure I follow you."

"The lamb which has lost its mother shall gain the stars for its succor," he said as he squatted down near his log of wood.

"Well, have a nice day with that. I've got to get back to my counting."

"The man who counts his coins is a fool. The man who counts his breaths has taken the first step on the path toward home." The derelict plucked at the dried stalks adhering to his tunic and collected them into a bunch.

"No. It's books. We're out here counting the books. It's for the inventory."

I leaned a little backwards on my crate to regain my composure.

"Those who build their knowledge from books are building castles of sand. A strong wave shall one day wash them away. Those who build castles of knowledge from waves of love will outlast the centuries." The stumblebum threw the handful of straw onto the floor.

I got ready to jump down and run. This guy was heading off into the land of goofballs.

"What is your good name, Brother?"

That's when my ear spotted the slight lilt of Australia in his accent.

"Rahm. My name is Rahm Ibsen. Nice to meet you. I have to get back to work now," I replied glibly.

This little offhanded run-in was beginning to go a little maverick on me.

"Rahm is a good name, Brother. It means, 'He who will be fulfilled.'"

"Well, merciful thanks. I'm always glad to get some good news," I proclaimed.

My gratitude was there; maybe the understanding would come later.

"I thank you for lending me a kind hand. Mercy only comes to the merciful. Good news comes from above."

"Yeah heard that one before, done that one before. Whatever."

"The knowledge that doesn't die is as a treasure hidden in a field of wheat - its design fulfills its purpose." [8]

"I'm not sure what that has to do with anything? What do you know about wheat? You look like you barely know how to dress? I'd like to get back to my book, it's a whale of a tale and I need to finish it, if you don't mind." I retorted on edge. He had touched upon something I felt was none of his business.

"Jonas was deep in the whale's belly; so shall the pilgrim suffer in the heart of Time." [9]

"You're throwing too many catchy terms at me as if you're trying to sell me some new world principle, some perversion of all the stuff I learned in school once upon a time. What do you know about pilgrims or the heart of Time?"

"Be not amazed to learn about the four quarters of the universe [10] and how its city lies foursquare [11] in the face of Time."

"Okay, that's it. I've had quite enough of this. I've got a good mind to shut you down, Buddy. What gives you the right to lecture me on all this shit?"

"When you went into the wilderness of wheat to see, what did you expect to find – a reed shaken by the wind, or the coming of the Son of man?" [12]

"Wait. How did you know about that? Nobody knows about that. I've never told anybody about that day, not even my mother."

"Do not refuse the preparation of the end of the world and the coming of the reapers, the angels." [13]

"So you know about them too. What else do you think you know that will break open my bankbook? I don't have much money in it but that's where I'm sure you're headed, isn't it?"

"Be also as the bridegroom who went forth to meet his ten virgins that they should light him with their lamps. They are as the winds, who direct the path of his ship upon the sea." [14]

"Gotta go there too, eh? I'm not surprised. You're something else, isn't it? Didn't realize that I was so lucky as to have that many more girlfriends though. Ten, Huh? Suppose you hang out with that ole broad, what's her name, Devermore or something?"

The Moon Women

"He that has ears, let him hear, Brother. Are you with me?" [15]

"I don't know. You're too much. I gotta think about all this shit. Right now, I'm just not up for it, you hear me? This is some heavy shit, Bro."

"My yoke is easy but my burden is light." [16]

"Yeah, that's what you say. I'm not fallin' for all this crap. I'll have you know that. It's not in the cards right now. Besides, how do I know you've even got the right guy for this stuff. I mean, you could deal this stuff out to most anybody. Why don't you go get them?"

"Many are called. Few are chosen, Brother." [17]

"Oh great. Now there's something I've never heard before. Sorry. I'm just not buying it. Do you even work here?"

This wayward book stacker was on a longer than usual coffee break I thought.

"My work is the mending of hearts. I am come to spread the fire of peace and the flames of love upon the brothers and sisters who hold it their hearts, but know it not. The limb of this tree is but a boat on which my boss has commanded me to sail."

"Who's your boss, Mr. Ripple?"

I had to ask. Ripple was a ballbreaker from the get-go.

"The Great One over in the office of Time. I think you call him by the name of King."

The pitch of his words first gained and then fell.

"Oh, yes. Mr. King. Good man," I confirmed.

"A good man is but a child of Peace. With a strong right hand, he knows the way of the morning star."

"Okay, then. Well, you have a nice day with all that."

I had to get him moving because Alena would be coming back any minute.

"Remember Brother, the prophets have taught us two things. One is about Love. The other is about Time. God is Love and Love is God. Time is but the complete and utter absence of Love. Those are the two truths, which wind themselves round the central pole of whom you are - the rest is Boring Dung."

He put his hand upon my shoulder and burned his eyes into mine. I crouched down to get away from this freaky dude but his sermonizing was evidently cranking up some more as he preached his crazy words from his cardboard pulpit. Who was this lost soothsayer? And why is it I always have to be bombarded with all this God talk?

"The mountain of Love, Brother, is the light which flows from eye to eye. Those who come to me, come through the glory of this fire, which burns firm like the sun. Those are the flames of the Father, which burn through the ashes of Time to breathe the life force of Love and Truth and into the dead carcass of eternity. That is worth the trip, Brother, that one."

I thought this vagabond had plumb fallen over the edge with all his loopy talk of burning eyes and dead bodies.

"What time is it? Have you got a clock on, Brother?"

I consulted my timepiece.

"Yes, it's 3:16."

"Bless you, Brother. Mind that. There are men who speak of what heaven knows, but this beggar must learn with his feet. Please accept this fig. It comes from the tree of life to offer protection from the specter of death. As well it may show you a road not worn down by the boots of the weary."

He tore a matchstick from the cross member and handed it to me. Then, he hoisted the Golgathan trunk back onto his shoulders. As he was placing the six-foot crossbar back upon its perch, I could see something had sliced across both his palms causing them to bleed. The enormous weight of the beam and its sharp edges must have made a wound there like a simian line. As the impoverished outcast trudged off passed the mounds of pallets, trickles of blood followed him for his bare feet had been torturously worn through. At last as the outspoken drifter crossed his final bridge, Alena emerged from the business end of the facility.

"Oh, good. You've got your pencil ready. Pencil dick that is! Let's get down with this inventory."

She squirmed against my chest while unbuttoning her blouse.

"I don't know. I think I just met someone really far-out, only he might have been only a beach bum from what I could tell," I whispered into the confessional of her ear.

"What the hell! I'm away for two seconds and you're doing someone else? Bastard!"

She grabbed me by the crotch and squeezed.

"Ow! Why'd ja do that? Whadidaydo? Peavey bitch!"

The Moon Women

"It's called your just deserts. You're gonna die of thirst along with your wimpy sand hog."

"Ah! Wait a minute. Something just happened here. That homeless feller, he was. Wait. Is there a worker here who wears a bandanna with waves on his head? Wait a minute! Those weren't waves. Those were thorns! Not waves, but thorns!"

Then I got the slap shot.

"I don't believe it! I think I just had a heads-up with Jesus!"

I was dumbfounded.

"What? Okay, listen to me! You are not only admitting straight to my face you're getting head back there, but from the sounds of it you were probably getting high as well and all without me, you snake. I'm outa here!"

Alena threw down her clipboard and stormed off.

- 10 -

Once when I was two years old, my Ma had a little book with pictures of all the presidents in it. I used to sit in her lap, point to the pictures, and say the names one by one.

"Who's this, Rahm?" Ma would ask.

"Abu Hammad Link-In." I offered my answer with a proud giggle.

I could name all 33 of them back in 1946. I had a sense of winning, like completing a Rubik's Cube nine shells deep. Three years later after I had grown up more, I got my first imaginary friend after my visit upstairs with the Khrng. His name was Little Boy. Little Boy was instantly my buddy. They installed him permanently into my brain. He called when you came to him and he went where you weren't. There wasn't a thing he couldn't undo and everything he did was unraveled immediately. To say he was my best friend would be calling him the inverse of an angel even though he had nothing to do with good or bad. He was just there when he knew he needed you.

When this roulette wheel called life flipped into random mode, it was he, Little Boy, who was there to insure it clicked off the integral chapters properly and at an even rate satisfactorily by degrees. Little Boy made sure the goodness would be metered out at a rate which was both comforting and frustrating at the same time.

The clincher was you could talk to Little Boy. He looked a lot like me, only better. He didn't have any of those annoying failures in life, which keep making everything a trying bore. He always had an agreeable way with most things. He made pretty good sense on any particular topic and he was always right there on the spot with it. Nobody could ever stop him from helping me. In fact, nobody even knew he was there.

One day, My Mom yelled at me to tell me not to turn on the stove when she wasn't home. We had a gas stove and the pilot went out sometimes. On that auspicious day, Little Boy told me sometimes it wasn't necessarily wrong to turn the stove on after Mom left to get her groceries. Leaving kids alone back in the forties wasn't much of a big deal back then. So I cranked open the knob on the stove to get it ready because Little Boy had announced we were going to roast some crickets. We had captured them the day before underneath the porch. Unluckily, the pilot had blown out only moments previous when a wintry gust rushed in as my Mom headed off to the market.

By and by the place started filling up with gas. The methane was choking. Little Boy wasn't at all affected. He kept poking at the crickets to see if they were still alive. He was preparing them for their pilgrimage to heaven, the blue flames on the stove. He figured since crickets spend all their devotional practices in pursuit of the temperature, they must worship heat and therefore the holy flames must be their after-place.

As the gases accumulated in the kitchen, I grew groggy. After a brief passing, the thick gaseous brew knocked me flat on my back. Mom came back to the apartment and when she saw me collapsed there what a shriek she let out. I knew this because later on Little Boy told me so. After dropping all her packages, Mom threw open all the windows and doors and tugged me by my heels out of there so fast. For me it was a miracle my Mom was a registered nurse because she knew what to do. Otherwise, I'd be dead now and in all likelihood, so would you. You don't kid me for a minute. I know exactly who you are so stop pretending.

In two slaps, I was sucking oxygen and had come back into this world. When she demanded why I had done such a nutsy thing, I confessed it was Little Boy's idea and it wasn't like that. He was smart and funny. But she scolded me like a mad woman claiming it was wicked to fabricate such wrongful ideas; she claimed I could have blown up the whole apartment. Right there and then I knew what I had done was the exact correct move to have taken. It was as a sign from God.

Listening to Little Boy was my goal in life. There wasn't a single idea he could cook up which I wasn't gung-ho to carry out. I can't begin to recollect the dozens of experiences I had while acting on the instructions of Little Boy.

- 11 –

On one occasion a year later when we lived off Route 9 in Newton, Little Boy and I had one big adventure. There was a bridge over Elliot Street where we lived, only it was a flat bridge; the highway dipped down under the east side of this level run of the horizontal span and came up on the far end. This railway bridge had serviced the Central Massachusetts Railroad into Blue Hill Station for over 60 years. The train trestle ran straight for nearly fifty meters, but the place was wicked scary. Only a tight and frighteningly narrow overpass, barely the width of a railcar itself, provided next to nothing for a walkway. There wasn't even anything remotely resembling a catwalk on either border. A sign reading danger sat at the entrance declared pedestrians were forbidden to cross - failure to obey would chance disaster.

Early on that fateful day right after sunrise, George Marsh, Carl Beauchesne and I made a gamble with Little Boy. He had a secret about a neat place out on the bridge where there was a nice patch of sand, enough for us to play Cotton Robin, a game in which you blow up the enemy right in its tracks; but he doubted we would go. He said we were chicken. But I knew better. We took his dare and the four of us headed off.

We had been out there on the overpass for only the span of two dead robins when I looked up. Way down the tracks, a jumbo-sized locomotive was bearing down on us like a rampaging rhino. Even though I could tell it was still a ways down the tracks, I knew it would be on us in no time because it was barreling along like a boiling steam chimney outa hell. I got freaked to the hilt. I couldn't see any place to hide. Because there wasn't any shelter on either rim of the railway for me duck into, I was frozen with fear. The other boys all ran quick as a wink to the other end of the tracks for safety but I was too little to make it there without getting run over from what it looked like, so I had to make-do.

When the Engineer of the locomotive stuck his head out his cabin and identified some poor fool crouched down in the center of the tracks, he hauled on the train whistle with all his might pumping it like a judge calling for order with his gavel. By the time the train was on me, the Engineer had set the brake lever full force. The huge, iron wheels stuttered on the tracks sending out sparks everywhere. I was transfixed as the volcanic behemoth loomed larger and larger on my dwindling horizon. As it bore down on me pumping out gray donuts of smoke and throwing out twin sheets of yellow flame on either side, its diabolical density seemed to challenge the very laws of gravity. I sensed a desperate prayer enabling a suitable lift, enough to raise it up off the tracks and propel it hell bent for threatening the boundaries of heaven; but in reality, no such luck.

I turned to Little Boy and made a silly grimace. "What now?" I pleaded desperately. He put his two arms together and cupped his hands over as if he were a praying mantis. I thought to myself, "Little Boy wants me to pray now? Pray now. Go to heaven. That's it."

He shook his head, and made the motion a second time and pointed to the rim of the bridge abutment. Suddenly, it occurred to me he wants me to hang onto the edge. With the igneous beast threatening to crush me, I calmly walked over to the bridge's frame and hoisted myself onto the sidewall. With my biggest muscles, I mashed myself against the brim of the riveted steelworks.

Two seconds later as I clung there like a bedraggled rat, the monster train swooshed by me. I can remember it even to this day. The feel of the loud belching steam vents blasting over me and the shower of sparks chilled me to the bone. And following that was the scream of metal grating upon metal which charred my nerves to the core. As the steel hulk shot passed me, the edges of its rusty claws ripped at my shirttails.

In the midst of facing that avalanche of crashing steel and belching flame, I saw something for which I had no explanation. Hanging out in midair some ten meters above the turnpike below was a little door. It was like the one I had seen once on the tele in a program named <u>Alice in Wonderland</u>. It made me quite happy to see it for I had in mind I might be taking a quick peekaboo down that descending tunnel one day to tangle with the Queen of Hearts. I was

The Moon Women

prepared to put her to shame. But such types of fantasy were not to be. This door was not an actual door because its sill was now a slithery shade, which rolled itself up to show me the total blacknesses of the outer spaces. It seemed demented but wonderful at the same time. And then it swam with stars!

As I clung to the gridiron abutment, the train and the world surrounding me froze up solid as a rock; pulled up dead like a dog on a leash it was. I kept staring at the gaping cavity chock-full of stars. Because my thoughts had been clean severed from the explosion of the locomotive, I was now riveted upon this smarmy balcony viewpoint. The glass in the windowpane changed into an elastic film like saran wrap in Mom's kitchen only stretchy and as it bulged outward, a golden light on the inside of it got much brighter.

As the pearly glowing gunk grew outwards, it expanded into a big tangly clump and then it blossomed into something with octopus arms or maybe legs like a person, only not a regular person but really, really big person, like a frosted aluminum giant. Its appearance could have been something like a snowman, a gargantuan snowman but I can't say for sure because I was so scared out my head at the time. Its shell or whatever suit the thing was wearing was coated with peewee icicles, which were also on fire somehow. Its head, which was nothing more than an overblown steel football, had two large eyes in the shape of ovals, like big blue eggs bulging out.

When I peered into its Time tunnel and into those piercing turquoise eyes, I started to hear an indescribable whining. I thought it might be the train's gigantic wheels still screeching on the rails or perhaps its whistle screaming full blast, but then it wasn't because the train world remained in block form. The screeching nails-on-the-blackboard sound was coming at me like what Little Boy could do. A pack of thoughts, which I knew weren't mine but were being sent to me from Little Boy's insides. That's how we talked. But this was more like an older person yelling at me as if my erecter set had acquired an invisible voice. I didn't like it much but it wasn't up to me. I could only hang on as these jabberwockies came at me with their digging needles of fire.

UNTO THE ANGEL OF THE CHURCH [18]HELLO AND GREETINGS
IT HAS NOT YET COME TIME

YOU MAY NOT YET BE READY

BUT FOR YOU AS YOURS IS NOW
> BUT I HAVE BEEN SENT

KNOWN FOR ALL IN ABADDON
> TO TELL YOU ABOUT YOUR PURPOSE

I AM AZRAEL LEGION *OF ABADDON*
> AS COUNCIL FROM PHILADELPHIA

SON OF MAN AND COUNSEL
> I AM AZRAEL

FROM THE THRONE OF PHILADELPHIA

I AM NOT THE SUN NOR THE STARS
BUT HAVE COME TO TELL YOU
YOU ARE NEITHER THE SAME NOR
> THE GREAT ONE IS WITHIN YOU

DIVIDED FROM THE ONE WHO KNOWS
> THOUGH YOU KNOW IT NOT

THERE WILL COME A KEY
> ONE DAY SOON YOU WILL KNOW

UNTO TO YOU TO HOLD AND MAKE
> THAT YOU ARE TO PERFORM

THE WORKS OF THE FATHER
> A GREAT WORK IN THE NAME

TO HEAR OF THE WORD
> OF THE GREAT ONE AND

AND TAKE UP THE CRY OF BATTLE
> FIGHT A GREAT FIGHT

TILL THEN I REMAIN
> IN THE NAME OF TRUTH

YOUR TRUE SERVANT
> TIL THEN I GRANT YOU FAREWELL

AND GIVE YOU GOODLY LEAVE

The tin giant shouldered its way back in through the waxen portal and disappeared. As the heel of its foot cleared the lip of the portal there was a popping noise like a cork being extracted from a wine bottle like what my folks used to make at dinnertime. The

The Moon Women

curtain came down and the square of sliding mercury faded away. As it evaporated out of sight, it removed all of its essence including all cognizance of the visit, that is, until my wake-up call from out of the ceiling in the K-room when everything regarding both the Seven as well as the Khrng snapped back into focus like a whippet after a rabbit.

The gnashing scream of steel on steel erupted back into my frame of dual possibilities as the fire belching, hundred-ton torpedo locked up all its hubs. Most likely, if I hadn't been so malnourished back in those days I would have become ground chuck by the locomotive's bone-crushing wheel teeth. Perhaps my emaciated condition also might have added to why I had no recollection of this sighting from the other places until many years later when I was grown up.

Subsequently the train came to a screeching halt. Riders poured out of every exit. A burly, red-capped Engineer came bolting out of the locomotive's headquarters and as he hit the gravel, his steel-toed boots clicked on the iron rails. Huffing and puffing he came over to me.

"Blue Satan! My God! Thought you was hamburga little fella!" He spouted choking back his sweat.

While the slurry in his throat shifted to a lesser degree, all the passengers surrounded me in a stew and felt me all over to confirm I was still all in one piece. It was shocking. Eventually, the crowds calmed down. The Engineer and his novice conductor guided me by the hand and led me back home. Since it was Sunday morning and nearly noon, my Mom and Pop were asleep as usual. After considerable delay and a ton of pummeling by the big conductor man, my Mom resurrected herself out of her doldrums and came to the door. Ten years later to the day, she would have to have a mastectomy to save her from certain collapse. It was so pleasantly fortunate Little Boy had persuaded me never to eat any animals or anything, which was blood red or dead black for that matter.

"Captain Albanus, Maam. Pleased to mee' cha. Found your boy up on the trestle, we did," the Conductor tipped his cap.

"What do you mean? That's impossible."

"Not a nice place fer playin' games, Ma'am! We damn near run him over, we did. Pardon." He jabbered.

"My son? How could that be? He's upstairs!" She betrayed the weak purposes lining her hairnet.

"Wouldn't make much sense if he were dog meat unda ma wheels, Ma'am. Be like Satan siftin' his wheat. No use at all, Ma'am." He bowed respectfully with a phlegmy cough.

My Mom did not like Bible talk and all the mentioning of Satan and suchlike bad language, particularly so ungodly early before her sunup booze. Nevertheless, she thanked my grimy escort and reclaimed her sovereignty over her offspring, albeit, dismally vacant. I had excused myself to go to my room to be with Little Boy to check on my mud turtle. That was when I realized Little Boy was not only my pal, he was even better. He had bestowed me with a guardian angel come to bolster me with an armored cape like Superman.

But the memory faded. Back in my supernumerary chair, I overturned a doubt: had anyone ever suggested my fictional companion might have been camouflaged as my visiting angel, an angel who might be the protector from the Khrng, as well as the knower of the ways of the wheat? The answer was orbiting right outside the rings of my gyrating chair.

- 12 -

Casting off my time machine, I blew out the candles and tore down the hall to see what all the excitement was. Early May in Cooketown had blossomed with full festivities raging within the Krishnaswami headquarters. Shri Bhagwan Krishnamurti Maharaj had come to pay his former classmate a visit. Dr. Krishnaswami was exceedingly overjoyed his esteemed colleague, the Bhagwan, had come by for this surprise Darshan.

Dr. K promptly ordered Shanni to prepare thali meals for everyone, but Krishnamurti would not permit the taking of meals until he had conducted Satsang, the discourse of the enlightened One as presented to his followers. Krishnamurti had come with his entire entourage. The Krishnaswami's abode was flooded with practitioners from all over the neighborhood. Brownie and I were awfully lucky to attend, as well as all of the other fwiks from the Big House across the way. Brownie's yoga trainer, Vingtesh Ganapati, also arrived accompanied by a blind man who wandered in tapping

The Moon Women

his cane. The fellow portrayed the semblance of an itinerant castaway who had an uncanny likeness to, well, ah, myself! Brownie and I looked at each other with a giggle.

Krishnamurti's lady attendant, Monica, began the service with a prayer from Luke 2:10:

> And the angel said unto them,
> fear not: for, behold,
> I bring you good tidings
> of great joy, which
> shall be to all people.

The crowd quickly settled down as Krishnamurti began his magniloquent monologue. He selected a chapter from the Gospel according to the apostle John. He loved to discourse from the New Testament to Dravidian audiences, because a major portion of his message concerned how all religions essentially provided the same teachings. Many thought he was discoursing on the far side of his normal milieu, but he would always object by telling his audience to heed what he was really giving out.

"Pay attention," he would say. "I am not sharing anything new. You simply haven't been listening to my predecessors."

His mercurial powers were second to none. As well as mixing religious delicacies, he created a mitosis between the ala carte nuances taken from the yoga of the Gita with the main service of Christian dogma to produce a unique amalgamation of spiritual thought. The adherents to these diverse religions should understand an important view: don't regard your brothers and sisters as different from yourselves merely because of some secular disagreements. All religions come from the same seed, as Krishnamurti put it.

"Once there was a man who was notably influential. He also sustained a genuine piety. His name was Nicodemus. He was the Pharisee ruler of the Jewish tribes at the time of Christ. One day he decided to have an interview with this Jesus. He was so impressed with the Man. Despite not having seen any of the miracles in person, which would have attributed to the possible divinity of Jesus, Nicodemus was undeniably convinced these transfigurations had happened. He related to Jesus due to the many tales of these miraculous performances of Jesus, even as Nicodemus was purveyor of the tribes, he understood deeply that Jesus was a man from God. And that the spirit of the Lord could be working in such a person, working through Jesus. The Disciple John now relates the response of Jesus in this gospel."

Monica then shared the passage from The Gospel According to St. John, namely 3:13:

> Except a man be born again,
> he cannot see the Kingdom of God.

"This is not a monition. This is a prophecy!

"There is an inner world. This world can only be contacted after one's consciousness travels through the third eye, or the threshold in the forehead where the Manit dissolves into the Menat. This Kingdom of God can only be attained via the process of inverting our thoughts, our consciousness. This turning of our attention inwards, this inversion of our mind, is the same thing, which happens to a voyager when he dies. At death, the consciousness abandons the body for all time. It travels through this gateway never to return to the physical body. Using the instructions of a proven pilot of the Over-self, a Guru, this portal can be crossed at will while alive. This is what is meant by "born again." What one sees on the other side is the alluring threshold to the divergence of the Beyond, which is so beautiful it can only be referred to as the Kingdom of God. There is no other way in which to describe what the traveler sees there and no other way in which to experience this holy palace, other than by sincerely following the teachings of an accomplished religious scholar, a Guru of spirituality.

"Nicodemus then asks the minister from Galilee, 'How can this be possible? Can a man be born when he is old? Can he enter into his mother's womb a second time? Surely, this is a joke.' John relates the subsequent response from Jesus."

Monica divulged the verse from John 3:05:

> Except a man be born of water
> and of the Spirit, he can not
> enter into the Kingdom of God.

The Moon Women

"If you have ever practiced genuine meditation, you will recognize the description in the foregoing line. It's because one of the internal sounds is the sound of gurgling water. The bubbling of water and the rushing of water are different mystical sounds, which herald the advent of an inner tunnel leading upwards during strongly concentrated meditation. These water sounds are examples of the sounds, which the novice aspirant detects on his way within. Jesus is toying with Nicodemus, since He is giving him only a tidbit and no more. Now listen as Jesus continues to elaborate on this important subject."

Monica continued the Gospel from John 3:08:

> The wind blows where it listeth,
> and thou hearest the sound thereof,
> but canst not tell whence it cometh,
> and whither it goeth: so is every one

that is born of the Spirit.

"The wind sound is also another one of the internal sounds, which one hears during the experience of going into the Astral plane. But neither the water sounds, nor the wind sounds, are the special sound, which will have a magnetic influence upon the spirit and pull it deeper into the region of the holy lights. Jesus is holding onto this jewel in the ointment, the one sound, which manifests the genuine pulling. He will only share that clue with his closest disciples. Jesus underscores Nicodemus is merely a proverbial seeker scrounging for tastes.

"Then, Nicodemus and Jesus have a little tete-a-tete, in which Nicodemus says, 'How can all these claims be true? It's preposterous!' And Jesus exposes the logical outcome, 'Well you're a big man in this town. Why haven't you come across anything like this beforehand? The Pharisees are telling you all sorts of bogus plots all the time in which you invest. So why not this?' And Jesus continues by declaring something quite remarkable. John records his quantum leap forward."

Monica submitted the next quote taken from John 3:13:

> And no man hath ascended up to heaven,
> but he that came down from heaven,

even the Son of man which is in heaven.

"What is Jesus saying here? Simply this: unless you are a human being and do the practices as instructed by a track-proven mystic voyager, someone who has himself mastered these innermost oceans, you cannot and will never rise into the Kingdom of God. Further, He states not even Jesus Himself can bypass this requirement of God's law. You cannot enter into His paradise unless you have the mark of the One who came down from that Kingdom. Unless your anima reincarnates into the body of a man, you cannot perform the technique of rising into the midlevel of these heavenly regions. You can only be awarded this inner knowledge from the One who has acquired it from his overlord, his Father in Life Everlasting. Jesus says even was Moses lifted up by the serpent in the wilderness before beholding the burning bush. So must Jesus, Himself, be lifted, by some agent from the Beyond, never mind He is the Son of man, the perfected guide of those internal forests. Thus is such for the advent of John the Baptist. Then, Jesus begins to orate the wholly classical reference. John has recorded it thus."

Monica qualified the verse from the Good Book at John 3:15:

> That whosoever believeth in him
> should not perish, but have eternal life.

"When you follow the instructions of a certifiable instructor of the spirit and attain the prowess to forsake the body and travel into the divine regions of light and sound at will, then, you do not ever have to be reincarnated ever more. You can follow this teacher, the Son of man, back home to your final destination, where you will remain forever and ever. Undivided faith and utter devotion to your guru are the cornerstones for successfully performing this art. Now, John records the most quoted verse in the entire Bible."

Monica spoke the famous lines from John 3:16:

> For God so loved the world,
> that he gave his only begotten Son,
> that whosoever believeth in him
> should not perish, but have everlasting life.

The Moon Women

"My Dear Ones, what this verse does NOT mean is that Jesus came to save all the sinners of the world for all time - for then, for now, and for all eternity. Claiming that absurdity would be synonymous with telling the analogy of the Chinaman who drank in all the oceans so his brothers could go and collect all the fish living in the sea. Jesus came only for those converts whom He touched personally with His hands and with His body and with the Words, which emanated from His actual larynx. Actual sound waves, ladies and gentlemen. You cannot get the correct medicinal cure from dead pharaohs!

"The 'only begotten Son' is the one mentor who comes to us as the 'knower' in many changing bodies, over and over. He is the 'only begotten Son' because this true docent is so rare and exists only singularly as the human pole through which this divine force of God consciousness acts throughout all eternity. There is always a genuine Godman, or Sat Guru, alive, walking, and talking on this planet for us to contact.

"That is why Jesus talked as the Son of man because the Son of man is the only true guru. He did not refer to Himself as some glorified reiteration but only as the Son of man because it was the generic 'Son of man,' the universal adept, to which Jesus was referring. It is a tangible, organic, and breathing doctor of today from whom you will get the curative potions and the medicinal remedies not from a dead one. Unswerving faith is crucial to be sure, in fact, it's mandatory. But the formula for success is the same. It is the true deliverer who comes in a new clothing, a new body, that's all. Jesus had stated in the preceding verse, 'If you have this faith and perform the practices as I have instructed you to do, then you will go back to your true origins. You will not ever have to come to this horrible place again.'

"The very fact that this lesson exists is an understatement of God's love for all of suffering mankind. God's love makes it possible for there to even be a Son of man, the ultimate pacifier. The existence of this truism within the lineage of the true prophet, the Sagittarius, is proof of the love of God and the proof of the spark of infinite consciousness, the burning of the Lord. It is the pure drop of the Christ man, as is this.

"All those ears, the ones which heard the words of Jesus and who were with him physically, are the ones whom Jesus helped with

264

their spiritual progress homewards. Far and above all others, His story was one of the greatest stories of all Time. Recording that story was equally important. Nonetheless, the story's recording cannot render life to the perpetual power of a Jesus unbounded. One must have intimate proximity to the teacher for acquiring any comprehension of what the true teachings are. Otherwise, we are riding on the reach of our imaginations and the rush of our emotions, not to mention the confusion of banal interpretations from so-called priests and Popes.

"Jesus cannot help anybody who was born after He departed from this world of atoms and molecules. Jesus was only one figure in a long lineage of celestial visitors who all fall under the corporeal slant of doing the work of the savior, the Christ - men who come to help seekers learn the techniques of dying while alive, an inner practice which enables them to go within and visit the Kingdom of God."

Krishnamurti raised his folded hands in prayer to his gathering. He then motioned to Monica to pass out Prashad amongst all those gathered along the prestigious borders of the Krishnaswami abode. I was immensely uplifted from hearing his discourse. I knew now the one who would escort my torn spirit into the sublime regions of the Beyond would be making an appearance any moment. Krishnamurti was some kind of a mobilizer for me in the same way John the Baptist was for Jesus. Of this much, I was doubly certain.

As the Moon's pearl climbed the empyrean trellis, which led cloud wards out into the grandeur of the wild blue yonder, the tertiary ribbon of romance was about to be untied in short order.

The Moon Women

CHAPTER 4 - EVEY NATHANSON

- 1 -

December 12, 1970 - New Delhi, India

The streets of Connaught Place were crawling with people like ants on a corpse. The cacophony of auto rickshaws, mopeds, and diesel monster trucks mixed chaotically with the punishing clamor of the shouting produce vendors, yammering cloth hawkers, and children balling for handouts. Amidst this tornado of confusion, a shrill shout cut through all the smoke.

"Hey Rahm! Come over here and look at this!"

It was Evey Nathanson, the woman with whom I had come overland into Iran. She was demanding my presence tout de suite. I leapt up and peered through the bars of a bifurcated fencing, which separated the two of us from the bullpen.

A pair of cobras was weaving back and forth bobbing their heads to follow the upraised palm of an Indian lad. He was baiting the cobras with the tranquilizing motion of his swaying hand. Every time either one of the cobras lurched to strike he would instantly jerk his hand out of harm's way. On the periphery of the snake charmer's dancing hand movements, an elderly man squatted while holding a dirty cloth bag, which wriggled like a tortured beast. There was something visibly menacing inside that sack, something large. The toying scamp never ceased his hypnotic wrist dance as he continued to distract the two ferocious serpents. After a moment, with a flick of his wrist, the man snapped the bag and a wiry, brown animal spat out.

"A mongoose!" I informed Evey with a harsh whisper. "Look! He's got a mongoose."

"What's he gonna do with it, Rahm?" She was astonished.

"That mongoose is going to rip those two slimers to shreds, that's what." I prophesied the gruesome outcome.

In spite of being married, Evey seemed to have a penchant for accompanying me whenever she could. She was the second woman in our wandering cavalcade riding from Athens to Delhi who was fixing to get into my pants. As the mongoose and the two cobras dallied, she pressed into my shoulder to get a closer view.

266

"Do tell, Rahm. Is it gonna eat 'em?"

"Probably. Where's Ron?" I felt responsible enough to ask.

"Oh, he's over at the Embassy having our visas renewed. Tell me more about these snakes. You seem to have a leg up on this snake thing." She flirted while running her shifty con to take the emphasis off her husband.

"You mean the Office of the High Commission? That's where you extend your visa." I was not in total agreement and felt it necessary to identify the proper perspectives at that point.

"No. It's the American Embassy. I think Ron is doing something regarding our passports. I wanna hear some more about your take on those snakes, the hot snakes, Rahm." She licked her lips once again.

With a lightning flash, the sleek rodent lunged for the throat of one of the cobras after it had discharged its strike. The mongoose caught the spent snake tight in its needle teeth and shook violently. The masochism of the moment was purely a matter of course.

"One cobra down." I whispered in Evey's ear.

"Rahm! You coming onto to me with your wispy snake charmer in my ear? Your little snake tactic?" She ran her eyes down to my groin.

"Why, not at all!" I backhanded her volley. "Check out the mongoose. It's about to kill the other one."

"But it looks like it's dead already, Rahm. It's barely alive. Why can't the snakes ever win? I'll bet your snake is a winner."

"Evey, you're not seeing it correctly. Just wait and watch."

Leaving snake numero uno lying in marcescent tatters of a bloody pool draining into the ashen dust of the New Delhi alleyway, the mongoose made three energetic steps one way and then swung violently to the other and backhanded the second cobra with a blinding surgical strike. As the sleek mongoose made its marque, the poor cobra had no chance whatsoever. The entire fight lasted less than five seconds. After the skirmish had ended, the elder street hawker collected the little carnivore and crammed it back into the blood stained canvas sack to suggest the murder had never happened.

"It's all over." I conceded frowning at Evey. "Let's go."

"Look's like it was over before it began I'm afraid. There's only one snake sneaking around here." She poked me in my belly again.

The Moon Women

"I guess we should blow this joint." I grimaced.

"Yeah. No snakes left now. I told Ronny we'd meet him back at the room. Come on."

As she slipped me another one of her creepy leers, the siesta sun made an angle off her pearly whites. Even the little gap between her buckteeth seemed to sparkle. The four useless buttons trolling down from her neckline seemed sadly not to have done their job. I nabbed an auto-rickshaw and with a gust of wind, we were off down the bad brown road.

"Rahm, why don't you come up? We'll have a pot of Chai and you could tell me all about your exploits like when you climb up to the tops of those hills with that wooden wand of yours, your little rod." She almost had me convinced but then she didn't.

"I don't think that's such a good idea, Evey. What if Ron gets back? He seems to be an intensely passionate guy. I'd hate to wind-up like that strung out devil in Istanbul. You know, the one who latched onto you after I did the belly dance with the dancer. Ron decked that fool idiot with one fist." I was dancing desperately to evade her advances.

The rickshaw drew to an abrupt terminus with a stuttering noise at the drop-off for our Islamic roadhouse, the Jahangir Mahal. You remember. The one, which was my initial landing zone in India after completing my endless trek over the Hindu Kush and the Pakistani deserts with the Land Rover crew.

Considering it to be the gentlemanly thing to do, I escorted Evey upstairs to her floor where I proceeded to trot out my excuses to get going. She insisted I step inside if only for a second just to see if there were any burglars or clandestine kidnappers lurking in the closets or hiding behind the furniture, which included a pair of bare bones cots sheeted with yesterday's linens. A red and black rug hung on the wall as a first class presentation from the leading experts of haute couture and guarded its post next to a flimsy Luann satellite closet, which faced a cracked wall mirror spidered with dead veins of inlaid filigree. I couldn't imagine what the bathroom had to offer from the glancing blow that it had given me as Evey approached its decrepit interior.

Before closing the door on her privacy, she pointed to a teapot on the end table and indicated I could get some tea ready if I wanted.

Then she did a presto-pronto and with an expeditious twist, she tiptoed into the sandaas as if to pee or do some other lady-like thing.

Hoisting the piping hot pot of Chai, I poured out two cups of steaming amber into the tin cups. I should have been on alert for the rising of the Speak but it was too late. When I looked over, there was Evey fully exposed with the dying light of the afternoon falling on her alabaster body. She had shed every stitch of clothing. The contrast between her bleach blonde hairstyle and her raven pubic triangle was altogether ghastly. What the hell was she thinking?

"Come on Rahm. We only have twenty minutes but I won't let you down, Baby." She hissed.

She leapt across the quilts like a militaristic matchmaker and attacked me. Ripping my shirt off, she rubbed her breasts over the masculinity of my chest. Not even making advances as if she intended to seduce me in the normal way by attempting to turn me on with kissing and embracing, she began her carnal advances.

"Your hairy ass drives me nuts, Rahm. I can't get enough of it. Ronny's a hairless scumbag. I hate Ronny. He's an ass." She was frothing.

I didn't really want to get into it, but I also did not want to taunt her or cause her any hurt. I kept pleading with her to quit.

"Evey! Evey, stop it! What's going on here?" I was afraid she on the verge of executing her martial plan.

"You know what's going on, Rahm. I want your ass."

She clutched at my groin with one claw while ripping open my drawstring with the other. I had to push her away. It wasn't that I couldn't get it up, or that I didn't find her attractive. She had killer looks as well as a feverish sexual vibration, which was consuming her with a wanton lust. But this was only my second day in India, the land which I had pursued forever, the land which hid the treasure of all treasures. I had been saving my spinal prowess and sexual stamina for something a wee bit farther higher up on the old Jacob's ladder and Evey Nathanson was not it.

"Please don't!" I forced her back but her clawing hysteria wouldn't stop. It was more than simply a minor penalty.

It is devastating to a woman when she gets this far and receives a cold rejection. Whether it is a planned dynamic or merely a chance collision, the impact of refusal can be overwhelming. Embarrassed, she drew back in shock. She could not say the actual

The Moon Women

words. Her naked body said it all. There was a telltale scarlet line on her thigh. I had avoided her menstrual headache.

Escaping without even finishing my Chai, I shunted the door to her chambers. Behind the closed doors, there was a crisp hissing like water striking fire. The organic lances of the Khrng had located their intended target.

The opaque disk of Earth's shadow inched its way across the chalky visage of its cousin, the Moon. As this occlusion slowly consumed the horseshoe of frail light, its dominance died out as a blank lining of emptiness. Only those functioning in the paradise of the Angels could fathom to where the Moon had fled. They were the ones who had command over the formless lines of the future driven into the wheat day after day.

- 2 -

The wicker zone abandoned the normal lines and as it triangulated a passed vector, I was back in my predicament two months earlier with the Ayatollah in Tehran. It was no wonder now what was going on with the Angels of Abaddon and the Khrng, but here is how the central theory of the Islamic connection ties into the scheme of things. Let's continue with what the supreme chair has unfolded with respect to that sticky issue.

While awaiting the arrival of God knows what, I stared unabashedly at the micaceous dust particles, which were spinning in circles within the lofty regions of the claustrophobic den, which lived deep in the bowels of the Mosque. Trapped within this minimal atmosphere like mentally disabled insurgents for whom there was no escape, the indefatigable cosmic raiders became on fire from a ray of the morning sun, which had seeped in through a fissure in the mortise work. They seemed to portray a mordant astral battle, micro angels with hair thin lasers confronting a masked enemy over the fate of the Milky Way galaxy. The M words of my mumania resounded through the backyards of my mental machinery like a pounding hangover. It was indeed more evident than usual.

As I peered into this mini-drama unfolding behind the swirling rugs of Islam, I couldn't help but notice my cerebral virus had been bumped up a notch. Implanted by the Khrng many years ago while I was strapped down onto a bench of rotting flesh which

270

had grown itself up out of the oozing floor of their cargo ship, it had been with me ever since like some psychogenetic parasite lurking in the back of my brain. Grabbing onto any loose straw, I yearned to go back to the astounding halls of the Mosque and the mania growing there. I needed to lose myself in that melting pot of prayer and claim my harem of hibernating virgins; however, fresh announcements from Dr. Zawari dragged me back in.

"Presently, Mr. Ibsen, we are waiting for the arrival of the Imam. He should be with us shortly."

He set his bifocals down onto an exquisitely engraved desk. The facing barricade harbored lengths of hung fabrics hiding an additional entrance into the hall. I sensed a commotion going on behind the twisting rugs. Presently two clerics emerged manhandling an elaborate demi-throne, which they set down halfway between the befuddled clerics and the orderly rows of cushions. Plastered with Arabic engravings on its edges, this venerable appliance was surely going to become the sitting place for some major player in this whacky charade. I unbuttoned my bush jacket, crossed my arms and sat back to relax. Quite bluntly, from the looks of this deal, I thought come noontide I'd be digging my way out of some serious camel kaka.

Hastily the Dark Mullah batted back and forth behind the flapping fabrics while preparing his papers and citations. After bulldozing the Persian rugs angrily, he proceeded to announce act one with thunderous intent. Dr. Zawari came forward and relayed the fuming gerent's directives concerning my future probabilities for incarceration. First, he introduced this menace as Abu Bakr Abdullah al-Alami, chief lieutenant to the Ayatollah. And after depositing that nastiness in my midst, Zawari unburdened himself of his list of overinflated indictments. The nefarious khan smiled, flipped his back, and withdrew his rancor and his heat. After a moderately awkward pause, he returned and broadcast another horrific announcement, which Dr. Zawari reduced via a trailing voiceover.

"His Holiness, Prophet of the Sixth Imam, Ayatollah Milani."

Into the compressed chambers strode the figure of a tall and stately elder. He was dressed completely in black: his silks, his turban, and his robes, all except his beard, which was a snowy white. He had sharply chiseled facial features and steely blue eyes, which seemed to cleave me in two. Taking his seat on the mini-backed

The Moon Women

throne, he smoothed his beard down his chest. Then, he made his blessing and looked over at me with a faint smile.

"Good deal," I thought. I've got a fan rooting for my team for a change. Little did I know how true this was to be in the end.

Urged by the Dark Mullah, a discussion flared up amongst the central clerics. Spouting off their charges of how I had defamed the holy Masjid by parading myself throughout every nook and cranny in their holy domicile, thus contaminating the devout prayer rugs of the Hajjis, this cloister of angry parishioners was on the brink of convicting me. While the crow flapping of the Mullah's kaftan rallied the faction to bring my death knell, the Ayatollah gravitated towards a secular peace calmly observing as if from a lofty height. Soon enough it was crystal clear this Mullah was to be my prosecutor as well as my henchman, while the clerics posed as the witnesses pressing in with their slicing slander. Surely the Ayatollah would see beyond the vituperate tactics of my executioner.

Dr. Zawari spelled this all out to me in no short order. After the Dark Mullah had wrapped-up with his scorched earth policies, the Ayatollah broke his silence. His speech was serene and dignified as he shifted the discussion my way.

"Sir, what is your purpose here in Tehran? There are now very serious charges against you. What say you?" Dr. Zawari aimed the Ayatollah's remarks in my direction with a bony finger.

I thought for a moment and closed my eyes. So much of my quest flashed in front of me. Holding up one finger pointing heavenwards, I encapsulated it all in one quantum leap.

"For many years I have been searching for the answer to one nagging question, what is true religion? I thought I might come upon it here in your Mosque."

To which the Ayatolla unleashed a forceful fusillade of oratory against my pitiful declaration.

"Please pay close attention, Mr. Ibsen. Our way is a stern way. There is no place here for sightseers. We honor the Ka'bah and honor Mecca five times a day with the purity of our hearts, our minds and the jewel of our immortal selves which we surrender to Allah. From dawn, Fahr, unto the eventide, Isha, we pray to Allah the merciful. Those who interrupt that river of holiness stand in error. Tell me why I should not consider you guilty of these transgressions." Dr. Zawari made clear the Ayatollah's intentions.

272

As the Imam was talking, I surreptitiously consulted a miniature notebook from under my jacket: what I had learned of Islam from a borrowed encyclopedia dug up in the dank basement one afternoon back in Mitchell Gardens. Doubtless, it would offset less than one jot of the toy log. Yet, within it lay the jewels of the Prophets, so I took a shot.

"Can anyone under Allah's command be detoured or prevented from tracing the lines of divine inheritance laid out in front of him? Was that not how Muhammad himself found God?"

"So you say Allah himself has lead you here even though you are not of our faith, you are not the proper bearer of Allah's word? This is blasphemy. This is punishable by the laws of our Hadith."

Zawari handed me further indictments from the Ayatollah: seems I was digging myself in deeper, so I doubled down with one or two more catch phrases from my notebook.

"I heard a voice which said, go into the Mosque and you will have the Sahada and the Salaat. How could I know this if it was not from Allah himself?"

I hoped some of those sketchy words in my logbook, which I had copied from those moldy pages, were about to pay off. The Ayatollah paused and after angling a thin finger crossed his lips, he motioned for the Dark Mullah to step closer. After an animated dialogue, Dr. Zawari relayed the Mullah's insidious counterclaim.

"My Ulama, Abu Bakr, sees you as an infidel of the worst order. He says Satan has sent you here to spy on us. What say you to this additional charge of espionage?"

At this point, I went for the long shot. I changed my posture and rotated slightly. Instead of being cross-legged, I swiveled my legs underneath me, bent my left foot beneath the other one, and flattened it from toe to heel onto the rug. A sketch in my scribbled notes showed this was the orthodox position that an Islamic pilgrim, a Hajji, must take when doing prayer to Allah. Turning my head the other way to engage the Ayatollah I replied with a plucky self-assertive brogue.

"Lah Ilahah Illah Allah. Wa Muhammad Rahsul Allah." [There is no God but Allah. Muhammad is the undeniable voice of God.]

As I bowed my head and touched my forehead with my handkerchief for what reason I had no idea at the time, I proclaimed in my native tongue.

The Moon Women

"The angel, Mikhail, who speaks to me from the right says the pure one praises Allah while the false one decries the infidels. Should I not trust this angel? Allah Akbar!"

When the Dark Mullah heard my words as imputed by Dr. Zawari in Arabic, he squished his malthic turban in desperation and bridged his forehead with his fingers in a viselike grip fixing to explode. As a flush of confidence warmed across my face, conversely a wave of bewilderment swept over the Ayatollah's continence.

"How does this angel call to you, Mr. Ibsen? With what does the angel salute your being?"

"With only one salutation, O Great Imam."

UNTO THE ANGEL OF THE CHURCH [1]

In retrospect, the Arabic Dr. Zawari used to convey my response to the Ayatolla has been stamped upon my inner mirror for all eternity. The Islamic academician repeated the words with a fixed emphasis as if he himself was overwhelmed to a point surpassing all bona fide reason.

"Iilaah Malak Al-khan-isha [Unto the angel of the church]."

When the Ayatollah received this pronouncement, he drew back with a gasp. As his eyes dilated, he upheld his hand and motioned for his chief right hand man to bow down. The Dark Mullah froze in place. Destroyed, he slumped to his knees. Then the Ayatollah looked over at me and reiterated with signature agitation.

"Again, Mr. Ibsen, for what purpose have you come to us?"

"I am looking for the Great One who leads me from sigh to sigh." I looked the Ayatollah squarely in the eye.

The Ayatollah gripped his arm, dropped his eyes for a second, and then closed them altogether. I thought the dimension of Time/Space might disappear into that unbroken rift of silence. Gradually with a wrenching anguish or it could have been a yearning which broached eons, he gained back his wits. As the Dark Mullah crumbled downwards, the Ayatollah commenced to forgive me of my crimes with a gracious pardon, which Dr. Zawari shared with me directly.

"We regard Prophet Muhammad to be the One for whom you are searching, Mr. Ibsen. For this reason, we offer you safe refuge. If

274

you share with us today your beliefs in our Great Imam, the Divine Prophet Abdul Ali Reza, we shall absolve you of your sins of sacrilege, which have insulted our sacred place of worship. We shall accept you as our Brother in faith. What say you to this membership?" The Ayatollah proposed his truce.

I knew within I had the mongrel dog by the throat but I needed to be free of all these fools and get on with my real pilgrimage into India. Nevertheless, some congratulations were in order.

"I accept the great Prophet of Muhammad as the freshest Prince of the Eastern star and with no question, His Grace has led me to this most sacred place so I could come to properly know Him and be with Him."

To this, full astonishment overcame the Ayatollah. He nodded reverently and reciprocated would I desire to be welcomed into the Shia, the true Islam? Could I accept the Holiness of the twelve Imams and the divinity of the family of the Ali?

"Most devotedly I swear by that oath and ask only that I be shown a copy of the Qur'an so I may place my hand and my head upon it."

This curveball utterly confounded the bank of twenty-four menfolk who proceeded to converse freely with one another. Many of them appeared to be arguing in my favor. It was something I could determine because I could tell they were referring to me as "Yank."

The Ayatollah then leaned in and talked to me in a hushed tone. Dr. Zawari translated automatically as if a voice band of altered consciousness.

"My dear Mr. Ibsen, I too have been visited by this angel, Mikhail, only for me his name is Ataah al-Alma, otherwise referred to in your Bible as Apollyon. For many years now, he has come to me with the messages from heaven. This news concerns the arrival of such a one who will prove immeasurably valuable in combating a turbulence, which has erupted out of heaven. It has been made given to me now, Mr. Ibsen, it is possible this savior quite possibly might be you. From that perspective, I am blown open to share with you this warning as been just given to me from the Ataah.

"There is a great war taking place in heaven. Light is the food base within that region. Its commerce is what gives life to all those who reside there. The forces of that purity are being bombarded by the goblins of a spiritual famine, which perpetuate a blindness of

275

The Moon Women

faith. As they continue to consume the light food, these demons also seek to devour the very backbone of truth by proposing to repudiate our honored ideals, which have guided us for millenniums. They are demanding sole discretion over the words of death and its targets, to whom it may touch and to whom it may grant immunity. This we cannot have.

"Now these demons have infiltrated our religion and represent a splinter faith, which professes the spine of Islam but is itself boneless and devoid of any virtue. These defilers are an expanding revolutionary faction, which persists in the bowels of our religion like a cancer, like a virus of unprecedented proportions. The elders here, our spiritual leaders, dissent to this rebellion but are having tremendous difficulty in guarding the younger generation from falling prey to this evil. We are bound by the White forces of Allah and do not wish to speak aloud of the ignorance, which has come upon our homeland and the fear bubbling in our people, which perpetuates this evil and allows it to fester unchecked. Please try to understand this, Mr. Ibsen."

As the Ayatollah pronounced his judgments, Dr. Zawari construed to relay the bulk of it with an unusual surgical precision. What's more, it was apparent the holy Imam was becoming gravely drained. Settling into a reserved and withdrawn manner, he clasped both his hands together under the loose sheathings of his tunic and remained motionless for some time, apparently meditating or at a minimum trying to gain more energy and sensibility with regard to the proper judgments concerning my future.

At long last, words from an agony years removed from the diurnal fading of the lunar disk seeped out of his nucleus like a radioactive warning. As the Ayatollah's advice spun up, the chill in the cloistered chamber inched downwards toward the death registers.

"I am now recognizing a special aural cast in your spirit, which I have only witnessed once previously and, as such, I am most shocked and surprised as that time was with my minister, the Mawla of Tabriz. Your acceptance of our faith is also tenderly heartwarming and renews our sympathy for the Americans who have not treated our lands well lately. It is from my Mawla's blessing I now pronounce you, Muhammad Mehdi Abdullah, Most Praised, and Guided Servant.

"You are on the verge of witnessing a colossal struggle, both

276

spiritually and within your nation. You and you alone have been gifted with knowing the true stations in this conflict, those of the White as the Omega, those of the Root as the Alpha who are us and yet not us, and those who promote faith in mankind, the Prime as the founders of faith. These will award you a vantage point unlike all others; furthermore, they will ask you to make a unique contribution. You can accept this decree, presently in fact, but know that sometime in the not too far away future, they will present you with a disclaimer under contract. Please know what I and what these twenty-four Imams gathered together here for your witness are praying for you to accept your responsibility regarding your placement within this task the same way you have now accepted your guilt in the sacrilege of our Great Mosque."

As he concluded, he unintentionally released an avalanche of ebullient dialogue within the cloisters of the upset clerics while the ice-cold crept deeper into my veins. All the mullahs and clerics were enswathed with layers of worsted textiles to ward off possibilities of being invaded by any scrambled evils lurking in the frigid depths of this cloister. Their chattering flew up like pigeons fleeing in fear. A thin growth of ice grew out across the laminated surfaces of Zawari's desk, a nice Dutch marquetry corner table, preserved with a pair of woven Jaquard coverlets on either rim. As the shiver of this rapid rush of backdoor furniture Speak abated, the Ayatollah proclaimed His retreat.

"Allah Akbar!"

The Ayatollah put out his hand and terminated all further discussion. Speaking in monosyllabic tones his words were as a soothing balm calming his jittery audience. Dr. Zawari conveyed this with one all-encompassing announcement.

"His Holiness has given the instruction."

This magnificent beacon of Islam stood abruptly and made a wave of his arm across the throngs of rising clerics who bowed. He then left his dais and departed into the hidden after dark of the great Mosque from which he had originated. Dr. Zawari motioned for me to follow. The Dark Mullah also removed himself from the proceedings without receiving orders to do so.

Daggers of false truths coiled in his eyes like feral serpents, but I was immune to his venom at that point. He brushed me aside as he exited the conclave to get into the antechamber first where the

The Moon Women

Ayatollah had withdrawn himself. As I got ready to go, Mullah Abu Bakr continued to argue his militant hysterics with the Ayatollah who was patiently listening. As the angry Mullah was concluding his scathing diatribe, the Imam interrupted and ever so lovingly looked down upon the stunted Mullah. He articulated several emphatic phrases one after the other, which I presumed must have come from the holy Qur'an. They seemed to carry all the wisdom and scented truths of this desert kingdom. His punctuated his bywords with the familiar "Allah Akbar."

Dr. Zawari touched my shoulder and whispered the essence of it.

"Even as the Abu al-Alami had demanded your punishment, Ayatollah Milani has reiterated the way of the true Hajji is not of revenge, but of forgiveness. He recapitulated to his Mullah that although this foreigner has defiled our sanctuary in a most grievous manner, you must allowed yourself to assume a more pleasing stand in the eyes of Allah by forgiving him his many sins, rather than by inflicting punishments upon him for transgressions he did not even understand. Now, he is your brother. Accompany him to the place of worship and help him to know the five prayers and the Sajdah. The time will come to rain vengeance upon the heathens, who have viciously defiled our holy lands, but it is not today, and it is not this man. Now go!"

The stigmatized Mullah bowed in front of the Ayatollah. Moving swiftly out of the Imam's audience, the Dark Mullah seized hold of my sleeve and schlepped me down the dim underpasses into places no heat had reached for days. I marshaled my energies to defeat the oncoming inevitability. With all my might, I got my own rhythm going in spite of the camel packing Mullah.

As the black comet of the Islamic underground spewed his acidic gases of a trailing after cast, Dr. Zawari and two of the other clerics pursued this confusion of bumbling somersaults all the while double-timing it to file out through the back tunnels of an immense series of frigid chambers and icy connecting crosswalks. At one point without warning, the Dark Mullah checked me sideways like a linebacker with a breakaway tactic. As I bounced off the glacial till, his ominous shadow disappeared down an adjacent corridor into the lightless bowels of the Grand Mosque to combust further inunctions of ill action against the presumed infidels defiling his land who he would undoubtedly capture and ransom off for political gold. Plainly, he had no intention of having anything more to do with me, never mind demonstrating the elementary prayers of Shia.

Jostling along the slippery ramparts, I lost sight of the Mullah's dirty laundry flapping in the hoar frosts as I headed deeper into the tortuous underpasses. As the dimly lit tunnels twisted away from me, I flung myself headlong towards what I hoped would be my exit out of this nightmare. However, the rolling gyre of the haunting shafts was more of a maze than I recollected since coming in here. As these depths tightened their grip on my guts so did the arctic blast dig into my bones. Its crush discharged the unused air out of my lungs in foggy puffs. All this confusion kept doubling over on me as one rugged panel rotated into another one, which unfolded still another.

As the dwindling twilight drew me into a sharp cul-de-sac, which offered no way out except one slim crevasse, I grew more claustrophobic. Squeezing myself passed its ragged edges; I snagged my army jacket on a nail strategically angled at my belly. While wrestling with the annoying barb, I lost touch with the hall of unending lineups, which replaced itself with quivering shutters, which threw its corrupt geometry of a stroboscopic light wheel onto my efforts. The blades all shifted one way and then another. As the speed of their flip-flopping revved higher and higher, it reached a point of a steady blur to become a radiant curtain, which formed some kind of rectangle.

The window was again upon me. It scrolled upwards leaving a vacuous pocket, which led to the innocuous sky works permeated with stars and shooting comets. Having only a dismal recall of one or two other times whereupon similar mechanized hallucinations had occurred with such obvious evil, I loaded up for an unavoidable collision with some voyager from a cosmos I would rather not have to withstand.

Out of that breach in Time, loomed a markedly tall being having the appearance of a synthetic humanoid giant whose casing was composed entirely of liquid feathers or conceivably silverish flames. The sockdolager waved its flipper at me as if to bow. How odd I felt. As it rose, its entire sheathing, ensconced with tinsel chips projecting a diamondy crystal dimension, raged forth with a boiling light. When it moved towards me, a fever pitched tinkling buzz also seemed to emanate from out of the entity. Its bright turquoise eyes

The Moon Women

elongated like egg-loids. These were the only features, which swam upon the being's chromium globe floating free above its shoulders like a levitating ball. As its hell fired skin bristled, the razor sharp chimes chiseled through me like a buzz saw. Had the Dark Mullah sent this angeloid demon after to me to finalize his slash and burn tactics or was it an emissary sent by the Ayatollah to educate me further on the status of the war in heaven?

Admittedly, I thought it to be some terror demon come to accost me of any possible spiritual treasure I might have accumulated on my helter-skelter odyssey across Asia. But one thing was for sure. This angel dude was sending out some seriously heavy vibes. This was a far cry from any mark of pantomime or theatrics. Its command came into me with a piercing injection of head splitting pain, which caused me to fall back defenseless and alone.

UNTO THE ANGEL OF THE CHURCH [1]

RECEIVE THIS SALUTATION
OF AN ANGEL AS GOOD TIDINGS
AND PEACE, CITIZEN HUMAN

BEHOLD I WILL MAKE THEM
OF THE SYNAGOGUE OF SATAN

THE ANGEL BEGINS TO UNWIND

WHICH SAY THEY ARE JEWS

A STORY OF THE THIEVES OF TRUTH

AND ARE NOT BUT DO LIE [2]

WHO PLOT TO DISABLE KARMIC LAW

IMMEDIATELY A THRONE WAS SET
IN HEAVEN AND ONE SAT ON IT [3]
HE THAT SAT WAS TO LOOK UPON
LIKE JASPER AND SARDINE STONE
AND THERE WAS A RAINBOW
ROUND ABOUT THE THRONE

DESCRIBES THE NIRUNJAN

IN SIGHT LIKE AN EMERALD [4]

THE BURNING GOD

ROUND ABOUT THE THRONE

Haan Moses

WERE FOUR AND TWENTY SEATS
AND IN THOSE SEATS SAT
FOUR AND TWENTY ELDERS
SITTING CLOTHED IN WHITE RAIMENT
AND ON THEIR HEADS   DESCRIBES THE ELDERS
THEY HAD CROWNS OF GOLD [5]

                            THOSE WHO HONOR THESE LAWS

OUT OF THE THRONE PROCEEDED
LIGHTNINGS AND THUNDERINGS
AND VOICES THERE WERE
SEVEN LAMPS OF FIRE
BURNING BEFORE THE THRONE
                    DESCRIBES THE SEVEN CHAKRAS
WHICH ARE THE SEVEN SPIRITS [6]
                    OF SPIRITUAL CONSCIOUSNESS

BEFORE THE THRONE THERE WAS
A SEA OF GLASS LIKE UNTO CRYSTAL
AND IN THE MIDST OF THE THRONE
AND ROUND ABOUT THE THRONE
THERE WERE FOUR BEASTS
                        THESE FOUR BEASTS ARE THE
FULL OF EYES BEFORE AND BEHIND [7]
                        SIDDHIS WHICH DISTORT POWER

THESE COME FOR MEN
BUT ARE NOT MEN
THESE HOLD ONTO DEATH
THESE COME TO GIVE MEN
OF THEMSELVES BUT TAKE
THE LIVES OF THE PRECIOUS
AND TURN THE LEAVES   THESE SIDDHIS TRICK MEN
OF PRAYERS INTO THE IRON
                    INTO BELIEVING THEY CAN MAKE THEM

281

The Moon Women

The titanium Angel then bowed deeply and proceeded with his Revelate rhapsody.

AS I AM OF THE LEGION *OF*
OF ABADDON AND SON OF MAN
I CAST THE TRUE MARK
OF LAODICEA AS TURIEL
SON OF GOD THE NIRUNJAN
THE BURNING GOD
HATH EYES LIKE UNTO
A FLAME OF FIRE
AND HIS FEET
ARE LIKE FINE BRASS [8]

BEHOLD I WILL MAKE THEM
TO COME AND WORSHIP
BEFORE HIS FEET
TO KNOW THAT I HAVE LOVED
AS OUR SET OF SEVEN ANGELS
FIGHT THE ARMIES
OF THE LONG DARKNESS
KNOWN TO YOU AS THE UNCLEAN
THE FILTHY GLASS SCORPIONS
WHICH HAVE DEFILED THE WORLD
WITH THEIR ABOMINATION OF EVIL

Taking a knee, the great Angel opened his arms and in a somewhat pleading manner seemed to insist that what he was about to transmit should bare greater weight than the usual Revelate chatter.

I WILL GIVE HIM
THE FOUNTAIN OF LIFE

THE ONE THAT FLOWS FROM
BETWEEN THE LEGS OF WOMAN
<small>BIRTH IS A VALIDATION OF SUPREME ACHIEVEMENT</small>

FROM THE FIVE BELOVED OF THE MOON
AS TURIEL I MEASURE
THE WALL ACCORDING
TO THE MEASURE OF WOMAN <small>THE YARDSTICK OF HUMANITY</small>
<small>IS NOT MALE BUT FEMALE</small>
THE FOUNDATIONS OF THE WALL
WERE GARNISHED WITH ALL MANNER
OF PRECIOUS STONES EACH BURNING
IN HER FAITH WITH HER LIGHT
THE FOURTH WAS EMERALD
<small>HER PSYCHIC ELEMENT IS EMERALD</small>

NOW COMES THE MOON
WOMAN OF THE FOURTH PLACE
ARRAYED IN A RAIMENT OF RAIN GRASS
AND GREEN LIONS IN BATTLE OVER SHEEP
WEARING THE PENNY FROGS OF FALSE GODS
NOT THE GARMENTS OF RICH SEA GREEN
KNOWN TO HER PLACE

SHE WAS DECKED WITH AN EMERALD ROSE
ADORNED WITH VINES OF HAIL
AND IN HER HAND A TRUMPET OF DEATH
CALLING FORTH THE ABOMBINATIONS
SPEAKING OF FILTHINESS AND FORNICATION
<small>INTRODUCES THE FOURTH OF THE MOON WOMEN</small>

HE THAT SAT UPON THE THRONE SAID
BEHOLD
I MAKE ALL THINGS ANEW
AND HE SAID UNTO ME

283

The Moon Women

WRITE
FOR THESE WORDS
ARE TRUE AND FAITHFUL

AGAIN THE DICTATE TO WRITE A BOOK
AND ENCAPSULATE THE WORKINGS
PROFESSED BY THE ANGELS OF ABADDON

SHE THAT OVERCOMETH
SHALL INHERIT ALL THINGS
I WILL BE HER GOD
AND SHE SHALL BE MY FACE
AND HOLD THE EYES OF MY MIND
AND HE SAID UNTO ME
IT IS DONE

THE MOON WOMEN COME TO LEAVE THEIR MARK
AND THEN RETURN FROM WHERE THEY CAME

WE PUT FORTH THE ANSWERED CRY
YET THESE BLACK LOCUSTS
CONTINUE JUST AS THE WHEAT
IS LAID DOWN WHENEVER
THE LIGHT STANDS HIGH
OVER THE PURE AIR
WE HELP THEM THAT DWELL
UPON THE EARTH

WE PURSUE THE KHRNG AS BEST WE CAN
ALAS, THEY ARE WITHOUT NUMBER
AND TAKE TIME AS THEIR MOTHER

BECAUSE YOU HAVE KEPT
THE SILENCE WELL
I WILL ALSO KEEP YOU FROM
THE CURSE OF TEMPTATION
WHICH WILL COME UPON
ALL THE WORLD

THESE FILTHY SCORPIONS OF MAN
284

MUST BE SENT
INTO THE LONG NIGHT
FROM WHICH THEY FIRST CAME
TO US FROM BITTER WORMWOOD
AND BLASPHEMY AND WITH
POOR UNDERSTANDING
BRING LOOSE WATER AS WITNESS
TO THE WEIGHT AND WISDOM OF MAN

Unfurling his ten-meter wingspan of dazzling mercurial feathers, the Angel pointed his fire finger at me.

AS TURIEL *AND* LEGION
TO ABADDON
SON OF MAN
AND LION OF LAODICEA
I GIVE YOU WORD
OF LIGHT AND SOUND FROM
THE WALL OF THE ALL TIME

With the shutdown of its cerebral fire drizzle, the astral bandit telescoped its residual warpage back into his tin-can Time tunnel, which zipped itself shut to resume the aforementioned pit of the hollow underpass.

As I reversed my detoured route and regained my line of sight with the fleeing mob, Dr. Zawari, the two faceless clerics and I raced down the winding corridors and then out into the light of day. We wove our way across the flat rooftops dodging laundry and the crazily whipping black and white flags of turbulent Islam.

Scaling staircases up through obscure flights, I made a firm resolution not to be disappointed this hasty departure had postponed my initiation into the prayer routines perchance forever. Could I now even consider myself converted into the Shia or was the whole show merely an anagogic abortion? No matter, I'm going to get to heaven one day before they close off all the doors from intruders. Of that much I was certain. If I was convinced of anything these past few days, it was that.

The Moon Women

Somewhere along the way, Ramesh joined back with us. When we got to the final gateway, Dr. Zawari and I parted company with cordial sendoffs. I salaamed my parting, "Allah Akbar!"

Ramesh and I popped out onto the street at dusk and flagged down a taxi. A while later I was back in the cantina of our funny little Muslim hospice with its drab tearoom. My travels in Muslim land were winding down but not so much with Evey. Her hooks were poised to dig in much, much deeper.

As I readjusted my bearing in the floating chair, I reflected on my saga in the Grand Mosque and the encounter with the puzzling chromium birdman. Why was it that I seemed to be chosen to evolve spiritually via successive relationships with some unimaginable lineage of feminine magnificence? Was I only uncovering a much, much bigger mystery that the world needed to hear about? That might be the case and then again, it might just be a ticket into the Beyond. I was more certain than ever that when those plums fell, I would be more than ready and willing to grab them.

Again, my mala moved like an emerald snake between my fingers numb from the endless repetitions.

- 3 -

One of the events, which happened some time prior to my entering Afghanistan in route to India also involved Evey. During an overland expedition from Athens to New Delhi, the conniving cabal with whom I was lucky to be riding had taken an aggressive tour of Turkey. After heading about three hundred kilometers southeast of Ankara, we had reached our destination and bedded our Land Rover down in a dusty canyon in central Turkey alongside the village of Goreme. A honeycomb of cave dwellings surrounded us. Selecting one, which was prominent, we set up our encampment on the frontier of this quaint village.

The township itself perched on a hilly mound roughly the size of Fenway Park. Curls of Turkish hookahs floated out from the heated cookeries to cover the lion's share of the western horizon. Dusk had begun to filter its indigo wash over the skyline and dissolve away all residues of light left by the retreating sun.

This area was once a vast outcropping of volcanic lava flows, which had occurred over a hundred thousand years ago. Sediments of pumice and ash had settled here to accumulate well over a hundred meters thick from the pyroclastic flows spilling out of a series of volcanoes. Over the millenniums that followed, powerful rivers had carved conical formations out of the ashy silts. These floodwaters must have flowed quite rapidly because the spires, which emerged looked like chiseled, upside down ice cream cones. Insanely slender spires pointed skyward like an army of crocodile teeth armed and ready to march forth into battle. Ranging in height from eight to well over sixty meters, they stood rocket-like, frozen against the energized dome of the upper firmament. Many were arranged into multiple clusters. Whereas here and there two of them were mated together like husband and wife facing off in some century sensitive debate others were grouped together like bandits waiting for ambush. Occasionally, a lone ashen spire could be seen silhouetted against the suffering vault of the blue hereafter, like a rebellious soldier preparing for battle.

It wasn't evident whether the shadowy movements hiding within those sandy fangs were or were not residues from the Khrng. However, I reminded myself to be on the alert for possible unwanted solicitations from the bastards. Out of the East a grotesque, orangey-gray Moon emerged over the emaciated mandibles of pumice. As it crept higher over the maxillary brim of the world, it was as a vast pumpkin showering its Halloween, Trick-or-Treat grin over the fertile acres.

Evey, Ron, Graham and I gawked at the sight of it and watched as its pterodactyl cusp swept a tangerine blaze of squashed horror into our framework to obliterate the dim possibility of true peace. They say that if you are able to discern the Moon's minute movement in relation to where you are on the Earth, then you are really in tune with the cosmos. I thought I could, but then I wasn't sure I had.

Everything on this desert backdrop seemed frozen. As the muezzins kicked off their calls to prayer upon the canopy of little Islam, their shouts echoed over the moonscape, which was floating above us like a gloomy prelude to some poor confidence. "Allah Akbar!" I stiffened as the calling poured out to awaken the sand demons rattling in the cold, hard air.

During the second and third centuries after the Christ had resurrected Himself, the early Christians had come to this place and

The Moon Women

transformed it into a consecrated community. Using sharp axes and the spaded tongue of the martel, these early Christian neophytes dug into the soft pumice of the looming spires to carve out miniature residences in which to thrive and worship. Over the decades, they put together an entire technology for constructing these remarkable places. Some of the rooms were only a couple of meters wide, but others were truly cavernous sizing up as ten by twelve meters and more. The founding fathers also lugged in beams to support the ashen ceilings. There were even some two-story dwellings but we were not supposed to go into those because the weak structures might prove dangerous.

These volcanic spires must have seen their share of cruel fighting in the day. There seemed to be bushels of straw, wheat chaff, and bloodied feathers strewn in patches within the dirt staging. Many of the chambers were also tombs. The mastaba-like coffins honeycombed the flooring of many of the spired domiciles. Naturally, there were no bones because the coffins had fallen victim to grave robbers many, many centuries ago. Some even had the tops to the sarcophaguses thrown aside. These early architects also hollowed out some of the larger spaces into chapels. In these they had presented frescos and other crude paintings of early Christian portrayals, which evoked the apostles, the Madonna and the poignant parables of Jesus including the most majestic one, His transformation into the Anointed Christ.

Some scholars believed this settlement in Goreme was one of the birthplaces of the second century Gnostics. They were the ones who preserved the esoteric teachings of Jesus, the ones, which concerned the hidden knowledge of the seven chakras (often referred to as the seven candlesticks, especially in the Revelation) and the secret practices needed to acquire proper entrance into the aerial kingdoms. One of the side rooms displayed an excerpt of the Old Testament, Jeremiah, chiseled out in ancient Aramaean. Our Turkish advisor translated the paragraph for Evey and I.

> I am the root and
> The offspring of David,
> And the bright
> And morning star. [9]

A few well-known scholars favored the idea that Jesus studied with a guru in India who extended down from the origins of Supach Sudarshan Sahib, a practitioner initiated by Karunamai (a former personage of Kabir Sahib who was an Indian mystic poet from the fifteenth century.) Over the millennia, this lineage of Saints has preserved the teachings of a form of yoga known as Surat Shabd Marg, maintaining it well the same way it was taught some two hundred and twenty thousand years ago. It was intrinsically a path of Bhakti, or devotion back then.

After our troop had established their personal digs for general bivouac and sleeping, Graham announced our new neighbors had invited us over to a local watering hole for sup and merriment. Who could resist that? When mealtime swung near a little after seven, we all got going on our trek over to the nearby village of Goreme. The plan was to hike over there on foot because it was only a few kilometers away. Why waste petrol?

As we headed out, a fog had begun to collect in the basin of the flat valley within which we had set our camp. Surrounding us were the hundreds of spires and pointed monuments, which looked like the conical bones of dragons. After we had traveled some hundred meters out from our campsite, the fog had grown quite thick. As we waded deeper and deeper into its midst, we lost sight of our mobile halves, the loss of which prompted us to pick up the pace. To counteract our growing fears we gleefully scooped handfuls of the glowing soup and tossed it at one another like slushy snowballs on a late winter's day. Joyfully we kept on truckin' and made our way towards the fringes of the town and the happy flickering lights as the muezzins offered their calls up to Allah into the chill air.

Either the terra firma had subsided or the fog had grown thick as witch's brew because eventually it lapped on the edges of our shoulders. After a while, only our heads could be seen gliding along over the swirling curds as though we were flying through a low-lying fogbank after growing wings. For only a moment, I thought I spied a pair of inky eyes swimming along beside me just below the crests of the billowing, liquid clumps of cotton. As we approached the village, funky Turkish folksongs filled the air. As we crawled out of the milky sea like cosmic crustaceans, we came across a bar sunken in the cellar of a crumbling building.

The Moon Women

I was sporting my overland costume, which consisted of the sundry trappings of cultured wizardry. If you missed that chapter, its list ran like this: safari jacket, hiking boots, olive trousers, yellow floppy hat having a chartreuse headband, which trailed down my back. Taking no chances, tonight I wore a terrycloth towel like a garland circling my neck displaying a Mae West trick in case it got bitter cold later on. I also always carried my recorder for some musical accompaniment, although I never claimed I could maintain anything close to harmony with it.

The fluky feature with my outfit was I didn't have even a single stitch of blue anywhere. Blue is the color, which Muslims regard to be the most religious color. The few times I had questioned the locals concerning the possibility of there ever being such a belief, I always got the same answer – "Who knows?" Nevertheless, the absence of my having any blue clothes made me appear as a renegade demon to the all the regional Hajjis. Since I didn't know that then, I continued to razzle-dazzle them with my clownish mannerisms. I know - bad idea.

As we entered the basement establishment, there was as much tobacco vapor down in that eatery as there was fog outdoors on the plains. Turkish tribesmen have a predilection for smoking the hookah, a pedestal style water pipe. There was a cadre of them situated in various haunts of the underground hovel. The presiding MC directed us to a booth over on the fringe of the festivities.

There were also two other non-Turkish partygoers whooping it up twisting in the other spiral arm of the cantina. They had emerged out of the corpse-like fog to join the party some time prior to our arrival. A Mrs. Amandama introduced herself. She was vexed with a hypnotic observation that her partner, Bob, had gone off the reservation. He was in the throes of performing wild hoochy-koochy maneuvers with a herculean Turkish herdsman who was brandishing his musket in one hand and a bottle of anise in the other. The stout woman informed us that the graying escort was her esteemed traveling companion, a Mr. Robert Hines, I believe, a geology professor from Arizona. She didn't feature losing him to the Turk. They had come to study the volcanic spires and stupas of Goreme. When Bob had inadvertently tuned his radio to the Bible channel coming in over the aurora borealis from Athens, he had found this.

And thy wife, Elizabeth
Shall bear thee a son,
And thou shall call
His name, John. [10]

"Jeezum Crow!" He jumped up. "How'd they know that?" He twisted the knob on the AM radio to bring in clearer reception but only got snap, crackle and fizz (not necessarily the background noise of the universe).

We had a sumptuous meal washed down with a deluge of wine and Ouzo, a colorless anise flavored liquor having quite a nasty kick to it. We all got rapidly plowed which led to some hectic dancing with some of the more inebriated Turkish camel jocks. I was carrying on with my own wild syncopated beat using my recorder. They couldn't keep up with me, or vice versa. Evey got totally loaded. The perplexing factor in the whole party time affair was the Turks were more interested in me than they were in Evey or Martha.

The cyclops over in the basement humping the hookah had pupils the size of walnuts. His dim core sucked the tender heartedness out of me replacing it with a heady mixture of varicose confusion tinged with an Ouzo induced lust. It was as a gravity forged beyond the dark matter of an unknown Time/Space drift.

As time would have it, I had to venture into the privy to expel the products of excess Ouzo. Needing to shift my path away off from the intractable whirling devils smoking up the place, I stumbled off in the direction of the piss pot. As I leaned against the stained tiles, which abutted the urinal, the biblical mania of the psychical surgeons over took me once again. Slipping through the quantum gates of a dilated gravity, I came upon the obvious, yet something was different. This time I wasn't going head to head with my Angel visitor but somehow peering down on their existence from higher up. Maybe the Ouzo had propelled me into this unpredictable distortion without any suitable introductions. Strains of an overheard conference ensued couched in the sanctified Revelate of Angelese. Had I become a surrogate angel eavesdropping on two of the appointed ones? Only the cerebral colander bleeding its waste into my rear quadrants could tell me anything to prod these upstarts.

MATAREL *I'M WORRIED*

The Moon Women

AZRAEL *HAS TAKEN ON*
A HEAVY BURDEN

THE SERPENTS HAVE PROVEN
TO BE MUCH STRONGER
THAN WE FIRST THOUGHT
THIS GO ABOUT

NOW HE HAS BEEN GONE
FORTY AND TWO MONTHS
TO FULFIL THE FIRST WORKS
UPON THE HOLY CITY

NEITHER DO THE THRONE
OF THE TWO OLIVE TREES
NOR THE CANDLESTICKS
THAT STAND BEFORE
THE LORD GOD
OF THE EARTH
THE NIRUNJAN
THE BURNING GOD
BRING ANY NEWS OF HIM

THE THRONE OF THE TWO OLIVES REPRESENTS THE TWIN POWERS RESIDENT WITHIN THE REALM OF WHITE MATTER THAT OF GOOD AND EVIL WHICH PERSONIFY THE PRIMARY NATURE OF OUR WORLD THAT OF DUALITY

IF ANY EVIL WILL HURT HIM
FIRE COMETH OUT
OF MY MOUTH AND
I SHALL DEVOUR THIS ENEMY
AND IF ANY MUTANT OF MAN
WILL HURT HIM IT MUST
IN THIS MANNER BE KILLED [11]

After Shamshiel got his two cents in, Matarel carried forth the duologue.

SHAMSHIEL *THESE HAVE POWER*

TO SHUT HEAVEN THAT IT RAIN
NOT IN THE DAYS OF THE PROPHECY
AND HAVE POWER OVER THE WATERS
TO TURN IT TO BLOOD AND SMITE
THE EARTH WITH ALL PLAGUES
AS OFTEN AS THEY WILL [12]

THIS MAN WE ARE WATCHING OVER
AS AZRAEL *SPEAKS TO WHIT*
SUCH A COMMANDED PROPHECY
IS NOT KNOWN TO ME
IN A CLEAR AND JUST WAY

AZRAEL *SAYS HE IS OF THE WHITE*
HE HAS KNOWLEDGE OF THE KEY
TO THE BOTTOMLESS PIT
BUT I CAN NOT AGREE THAT
HE IS STRONG OR WORTHY
NOR THAT HIS INDIGNATION
IS RIGHTEOUS AND
IS NOT DARK LIKE THE
BLACK EYED ONES
WHO PREY UPON
THE SON OF MAN

I AM GIVEN TO OFFER HIM   OFFERING A BLACK STONE
A BLACK STONE WHEREIN   IS SYNONYMOUS WITH
A NEW NAME WILL TURN   PROCLAIMING A THUMBS
HIS WILL AND HIS WAYS   DOWN TO AN OPPONENT

After Matarel turned to end his Revelate philippic, Shamshiel added more to the homily.

MATAREL *WHEN THE ELDERS*

The Moon Women

HAVE FINISHED THEIR TESTIMONY
THE BEASTS WILL ASCEND
OUT OF THE BOTTOMLESS PIT
AND SHALL MAKE WAR AGAINST US
AS THE HATED NICOLAITANS
AND WE SHALL OVERCOME THEM
AND KILL THEM [13]

AND WE SHALL TAKE THE REED
LIKE UNTO A ROD AND OUR ANGELS
SHALL STAND SAYING RISE
AND MEASURE THE TEMPEL OF GOD
THE NIRUNJAN *THE BURNING GOD*
AND UPON THE ALTAR
AND ALL THEM THAT
WORSHIP THEREIN [14]
AT THAT TIME
WITH THIS WORK
WE SHALL KNOW HIM MATAREL
AND HIS DARKNESS SHALL KNOW
OUR LIGHT AND OUR PROMISE

I WILL GIVE ALL   SHAMSHIEL REITERATES
POWER OF THE WHITE   THAT IT IS INEVITABLE
UNTO MY TWO WITNESSES   THAT THEY SHALL LEARN
AND THEY SHALL PROPHESY   THE TRUTH ABOUT THEIR
A THOUSAND TWO HUNDRED   NEW CANDIDATE AND NOT
AND THREE SCORE DAYS   BE CLOUDED BY DOUBTS
NO MORE TO BE   NOR LOSE THEIR WAY
CLOTHED IN SACKCLOTH [15]   IN THE DARKNESS OF FEARS

    With this awakening pronouncement, the funnel of my vision collapsed and I found myself swimming in a thick Turkish effluvium while lying prone on an unforgiving bar pew. I had to fight off several of those drunken Turkish mokes with my trusty high mileage

294

recorder. He wouldn't listen to "No" until I beat furiously on his thick head with my unforgiving musical Billy club. Eventually he retreated to his bunk in the smoke pit. Forthwith, the maddening affair wound down and we paid our farewells.

The stroll back was worlds apart from our incoming trek. The fog had completely cleared. The Moon had taken its perch upon the nebulous edge of Time bathed in velvet onyx. Even though it promised to be an incredibly august evening, it was quite brisk by reason of the radiational cooling of the still night, a dry chill which cut to the bone. We had to juice it up with a cheery jog just to keep our selves mobilized and warm.

As I looked up I beheld the magnificently bright Moon. Right off its periphery, I could also see the sister planet, Mars. I had the thought that these two celestial bodies of polar matter were the ones, which had generated the most interest for humanity over the centuries. Yet their dualities were as the Yin and the Yang of our earthen analog. One is large and surprisingly close while its energies are subtle and innate; the other is far away and unduly small while its energies are demonstrative and violent. Smiling, I knew the swapping back and forth of these two cosmic vertebrae had become the backbone of my spiritual quest.

As we advanced through the growing chill, the dragonesque spires of our campsite grew closer. Way above us, hovering in a moderate geosynchronous orbit was a scouting party of Khrng who were intent on nailing down the probabilities for each of our lives. Their probes would reveal whether or not we would eventually become entangled within the cerebral webbing of their viral software long ago deposited anonymously within us during our adolescence just as with most other people on the planet. Oddly their proximity to and from the Ouzo pit hadn't spared me my visit from the Siberian madman. Further praxis from the Khrng's calculations would dictate all the outcomes. Auspiciously for me, my baseline was the only one not registering a green trail on their organic screens.

- 4 -

Shortly after I had crossed the border at Wagah to arrive within the motherland of India despite the inimical delays, I had my closing encounter with Evey. After conducting my complaisant visit

The Moon Women

over at the Office of the High Commission, I reclaimed my place back at the boardinghouse. A traditionally clothed ethnic woman presented me with a complimentary Chai, which I gratefully accepted. She also handed me a Catholic prayer card with a resurrected Jesus on it. It was out of place for two reasons: one, it was a Mogul whorehouse, and two, the blood looked fresh. On the back it read:

> And the angel answered
> And said to the women,
> Fear not: For I know
> That ye seek Jesus,
> Which was crucified. [16]

Why do these cards always have such atrocious grammar and punctuation? I had learned the 'who versus which' rule way back in high school. Moreover, colons should come only after complete sentences and contain something of equal meaning or a list. It wouldn't be that impractical to correct these errors. I'd offer to do it; however, I would never reach the promised land. Furthermore, since the woman presented with such a raucous strawberry red sari, she reminded me a little of my beloved fifth grade teacher, Mrs. Sweet.

I was parched from putting up with the procrastinating bureaucrats since daybreak, plus the visitation from the thaumaturgic brain-trust. Why did those voyagers from that bizarre realm keep appearing to brainwash me with their propaganda of heaven gone berserk? Didn't I have enough to deal with just getting to India where I belonged? There didn't seem to be any rhyme or reason to their fanaticism or even whom or what had put them up to pestering me so much with all their Bible speak. Moreover, I had to avoid the seething knowledge menus of the Khrng as well as having my clinical case of OCD washout my mind with outbursts of furniture Speak, not to mention the incurable craziness of my M word obsession, mumania, a periodicity which always occurred under insufferable circumstances. Jeesh, why do I even bother to get up in the morning?

One time in Delhi soon after I had come through Amritsar on the way to the capital, I got the idea I should attempt to prolong my visa for as much time as possible. I figured I was saving myself some time but what I was really doing was setting myself up for a ride, the likes of which I would never witness again; only it wasn't going to come from the direction I thought it would.

Typical for this tribe of left-brain challenged dim wits; the management had indicated there had been a mix up with my accommodations. From what I could tell, one of their staff had muffed the clean up on aisle 3. When I inquired for my key, a Mr. Singh at the reception desk shocked me with the news that the hotel staff had transferred all my packings to another suite in the establishment. He was quite apologetic. Because of this screw up and because no standard rental configurations were currently available, they had reserved one of their Five Star penthouse suites. Naturally, I was dumbfounded, but I accepted his expressions of regretful gratuity and proceeded to my new room, er, palace.

Right on cue, the elevator didn't work. When I looked at my key fob, up came the primary problem. Stewed by the continuation of more coded abuse, I found it was 719. As I marched up the stairs two at a time, I vowed to do something to reroute this unapproved change when I came back down later on. I was not going to have my conveniences reeved away so promptly. As I approached the fourth landing, a sickly wooziness churned forth from my lower quadrant. I thought the Chai was safe in these parts. How could they screw up Chai?

At last, I was on the terminal climb but the stairs seemed taller at each stage. When I cleared the top, a distorted panel greeted me. Bracketed with posts, it contrasted significantly from all the other doors in this dive. After a couple of misapplications with the fob, I managed to get the troglodytic entryway to swing open. Facing a cramped vestibule I believed might lead to the treasure cave of Ali Baba, I moved forward groggily.

The failing temperatures were alarming. That in itself set me on edge. After I exited the rear of the hallway, I entered a quaint sitting room replete with a sumptuously upholstered Sheridan sofa flanked by Thomasville armchairs, which surrounded a handsomely carved coffee table presenting ostentatiously inlaid ivory. The cheap Indian kind if you can truly claim there could ever be a cheap category of ivory, which could remotely be judged as cheap considering the large-scale loss of elephant life. On the other side, lying in wait to kidnap my vision was an enormous Hepplewhite settee with cabriole legs. It had Moroccan goat-hide leathers and

The Moon Women

matching messaline silk braids. A convoy of Portland Tub cathedras with stippled show wood having hammered brass nails gathered themselves to counter three Barcelona rockers having chromium frames. The contrast was painfully alarming. I should have realized the strong presence of furniture Speak was forecasting the gloom of an unavoidable prospect, not to mention the uncomfortably freezing air. This was nearing the nastiness of a two edged sword of insanity.

On the far side of the room, there were two doors leading to other rooms, or so far as possible, I imagined there might be other rooms. At first, I didn't know which one to choose. I had a mild Deja vu feeling of Daniel and the lion's den, although, actual replay of the lions was coming in a little hazy; it didn't haunt me like it had previously.

Lackadaisically, I chose the one on the right and slipped through. As it widened out into a cavernous closet, which swallowed me up like Jonah's great fish, a substantial emptiness engulfed me. In spite of my release from possible detention, I truly do have to scold that Mr. Singh at the reception desk and declare him the demon he must assuredly be, not to mention scold him for the advance of an uncomfortable chill.

This is dismal, I thought.

Encased with ugly walnut paneling showing spooky masks, which starred out at me like inverted visages of feral Khrng zombies, the vacant closet surrounded me. On the center of the far side hung a mirror framed with triple scalloped molding fringed with cyma curves. As the chilliness bit into my bones, the facets of glass shrank away to patches of frost, which crept in on its periphery. The glass itself was the century old type having wavy distortions in it. As I studied this bygone artifact, rectangles of spectacular luminosity spun up inside the mirror - a picture within a picture within a picture. Where have I seen that before?

The self-reflecting mirrors telescoped out and out twisting themselves into a column of radiance, which sucked me in visually. As it reversed violently, it was as though I was peering through a pair of binoculars backwards because the landscape seemed really far away. Once more, it reversed itself and slammed back upon itself to become the solitary sunshade. Up slid the billowing film disclosing a colossal vista of stars strewn across the infinity of empty Time/Space derivatives.

Pushing against an invisible film, which lapped the perimeter of the blank cavity, some fingers, a hand thing, and then an elongated arm began to push in. After the limbs came through, an entire physique sprung in to form its occupancy before me. Its glowing feather scales burned like fire ice all over its body. The only jumbled curveball was this one was only a little over a meter and a half tall, like my size, but it replicated those same oversized Robins egg eyes, which rotated with a blue electric aura. At short notice, the screaming rip of its crowning bells plunged into my central lobes as its revolving turquoise eyeballs bore into mine with fried thought daggers.

UNTO THE ANGEL OF THE CHURCH [17]

SALUTATION OF AN ANGEL
CITIZEN KNOW THIS
MY WORKS ARE SUCH

BE NOT AFFRIGHTED
WALK WITH ME IN WHITE

WALK IN WHITE REFERS TO THE

FOR YOU ARE WORTHY [18]

WHITE MATTER OF THIS UNIVERSE

AS THE SMALL
AND LIGHTENED FORM
OF HERMONI **AND AS**
LEGION **OF ABADDON**
AND SON OF MAN
I AM ELVINHAMMERAX

HE IS SAYING THAT HE IS A

BONDMAN OF PERGAMOS

REDUCED FORM OF HIS SELF

I COME TO YOU UNDER TRUTH

AS HERMONI FROM PERGAMOS

AS MY FULL CREATION
DOETH NOT PASS
THROUGH THE GATE OF

The Moon Women

THE WALL OF THE ALL TIME
          The materialization of the Angel

AT THIS TIME I FEAR YOU
          Was perhaps hindered by the

TO PLEASURE ME AS I AM
          Poison dissolved within the tea

YOUR FELLOW SERVANT
          Thereby restricting his entry

THE SIXTH SEAL
WAS GIVEN TO FIGHT THE EVILS
          The sixth seal is a weapon

OF THE SMOKE WIZARDS
          Used against the Khrng

AS THE GREAT SHAKEN MOUNTAIN
WHICH COMES AS A LAKE OF FIRE
AND AS AN EARTHQUAKE OF FEAR
FOR THE SEVEN OF ABADDON
WHO BATTLE WAR
          To subdue them and

FOR MANY OF YOUR YEARS
          Cage them in Time

Hermoni swiveled quickly and pointed up to the bright sky as the sun retreated behind a cloud to hide.

A GREAT EARTHQUAKE FOLLOWED
BY THE BLIND DAY
IN WHICH THE SUN
BECAME AS BLACK
AS A SACKCLOTH OF HAIR
AND BY THE BLIND NIGHT
IN WHICH THE MOON
BECAME AS BLOOD [19]   One day during an eclipse
FLYING IN THE AIR   Of the sun while the Moon
LIKE A RED FIG TO FALL   Bleeds as if it were on fire

300

INTO THE SEA LIKE THE WRATH

THE GREAT SHIPS OF THE KHRNG

OF THE FILTHY SERPENTS

WILL PLUNGE INTO THE OCEAN

AND THE BITTER WATER LIKE FLAMING METEORS

OF THE UNBELIEVING KINGS NEVERMORE TO SAVAGE MEN

THE STARS OF HEAVEN
SHALL FALL TO THE EARTH
EVEN AS A FIG TREE CASTS OFF
UNTIMELY FIGS WHEN SHAKEN
BY A MIGHT WIND [20]

AS THE CORRUPT DUST CLOUDS
SPUE OUT OVER THE STAR CLUSTERS
EATEN EDGES OF DEPARTED HEAVEN

HERE WE HAVE A DESCRIPTION

WILL OFTEN BE AS A ROLLED

OF THE MERGING OF THE TWO

SILVER SCROLL OPENED

REALMS OF ABADDON AND THE

ON A LAKE OF TRANSPARENT SPACE

REALM OF WHITE MATTER

FURTHER EVERY MOUNTAIN
AND ISLAND WILL BE MOVED
OUT OF THEIR PLACES [21]
AND YOUR MEN OF STONE
MEASURES AND MIND

THE ANGEL WARNS HOW THE

WILL TELL THE MULTITUDES

SCIENTISTS SHALL PREDICT

ABOUT HOW THE BURNING BED

THE MOVEMENTS OF THE

UNDER THE EARTH'S BREASTPLATES

TECTONIC PLATES AND WHAT

301

The Moon Women

Hermoni, as Elvinhammerax, hurriedly departed through the mirrored portal and Time uncollapsed into a reinvention of the traditional continuum. I pondered how symbolic his description of the scrolling of heaven, which resulted when the Seven suffered defeat in battle with the Khrng, also simulated how each one of the Angels launched their appearance out of the metered star-fields. There was always that same aluminum shade going up and down to produce the Angel's magical entrance and departure. It might be this was symptomatic of their crusade to connect with me as some cathartic treatment from their loss in warfare, their failures in defeating the Khrng over the millenniums. I wasn't truly worthy to be evaluated as any kind of aid or antiseptic fix to their falling down. But I was honored to be permitted a chance to do whatever I could do.

As the closet vomited me back out of its claustrophobic occupancy like a belching whale, I sensed the missionary position coming on. The door on the left wouldn't open right away. Was it the hesitancy of my hand or the loss of friction with the doorknob? These and other doubts were swirling in my head like a tornado on salvage patrol. What was I saying? Or, rather, what sin was I going to fulfill? Then the door opened.

When I got into the room, wait. Let me rephrase that. After stumbling into the room, I lost my balance, catapulted into the opposing room divider, and at the same time slammed my noggin on the disgustingly flat hand of one agonizing thought: I've been dosed. Rubbing my eyes to reclaim some perspective, I concluded I was facing the city of Bortion.

There, lying comfortably on a gigantic mid-Victorian sleeping throne with their backs against a floral headboard, were, not one, but two naked women. Initially I surmised one of them might have been a maid. Then the floor went a little fluid on me a second or two, after which my upper mind started to play do-si-do with my lower mind. My left-brain was waltzing with my right-brain. And unmistakably Tommy Milkwood was wailing from the belly of a yellow plastic radio perched nostalgically off the end table facing the twins.

The place is goin' sideways.
There's a rambling I donno why.
I been out walkin' the slippery highways
With two black birds flappin' in my pie. [23]

"Hi, Rahm! We've been thinkin' 'bout chu Man. Why doncha mosey on over here and sit your sweet ass down," came the mellow tones.

"Evey, is that you?" I rubbed my eyes. "What the hell are you doing here? And who the hell is she?"

Tommy droned on and as he did, it was evident they had been visiting with him as well.

From everywhere I'm on a major bummer
But can't say I've done this ere before.
No doubt been balancin' my balls higher,
I been tryin' to set to seven
Them junkies at my door. [23]

Maladroitly, I crash-landed on the brink of the ample Cannonball dream platform. The two flesh mongers eyed me and then they eyed each other. It seemed to be the advent of a ménage a trois was unfolding in front of my eyes. Little did I realize Evey was the machinator of seduction.

They attacked me and they attacked each other. Fabric and flesh flew everywhere. Whatever had doped me up had also rendered me an eight armed quadriplegic. I tried to scream out. I tried to ward off their clawing hands. Pretty soon, they had me down to my briefs. They didn't wear briefs that day. In the crowning hour on the beachhead of bravery the languished man of Calais hunched over with his loathsome burden. Undaunted, he finally had to put his weapons down. Tommy beefed up the pixie pie.

One time over in New Jersey
I got into bad company.
I dusted off the silver mercy.
I only heard what I couldn't see. [23]

The Moon Women

The alabaster body of Evey and the ochre one of the whore encircled me as if a pair of serpents entangled in a lust knot. As something lowered me into the trance constriction of the love itch, my member shot out like a red-hot poker. They both took turns riding it like bobbing for unicorns at the carnival. The masses of flesh moved everywhere. There were no places to hide. The lamplights on the dome of heaven were the only friends I had to confide any news of the one I truly loved. I lost her in the chandeliers, which rode the realms of gypsum bliss floating above our flesh rant. I couldn't stop her screams from coming into my ears. I imparted the secrets of my love. Yo, Tommy, don't forget me.

> Slit ma throat an' hook a clue
> He been scratchin' a dead arm that he once knew
> Was only the end of a hard black rope,
> Tryin' to set to seven
> Them junkies at my door. [23]

The sex was incredible. What the hell had I ingested for me to stay so erect and for such an eternity? I had climax after climax. It seemed like these two wenches were determined to drain me of every ounce of bodily fluid until they had satiated themselves in this orgy. In these frantic hemorrhaging spits, they forced me to relinquish my hold on chastity. It was all gone except for a parting flag, which flew o'er the lonesome pole of my weakened faith. I rekindled memories of my time with the Ayatollah and the ones who had ordained me as a follower in the Shia Mosque of Islam. Their swirling tar-feathered robes flew over our lurching naked bodies like the winds of Islam magically transforming the mushy cotton landscape into the carpets of glory and retribution. Tommy witnessed no holiness that day, only the laughing lust of doom.

> Folks way down in Birdland,
> Playing with their brains.
> Why not steal the plastic banker's blood
> Cause their backs are breakin' from the strain. [23]

The Imams had endured their sacrifices of messianism. They all had shed blood in some way. They had poured their vital energies out into the market places of mankind to save the suffering ones from the plagues of hell. Now I was reeling from the weight of these two women who were obsessed with cramming pleasure into my writhing torso like needles of heroin pumping the searing milk of madness into the psychogenic marrow of my heart. There were no riddles in the twenty-one carbon atoms, which they had collected. Connected with the twenty-three of their sister, hydrogen, they had only smoked some hash to help them with their backs. A lone little nitrogen hero was holding his banner high. Bonded with tomorrow they married the five oxygen angels of Immaculate Conception. Tommy continued with his chant.

> Then you lose what you want to see
> Because they can't show you any better metaphor.
> Headed to Adolf's, git my wager on,
> Tryin' to set to seven
> Them junkies at my door. [23]

Up to that segment in the timeline, I had only made love to one woman at a time; I could count the sum on one hand and maybe half the other. The sex I had that day on the nadir of the Continental Hotel outdid all the sex, which I had had in my meager two point five decades of sucking wind; it surpassed it unquestionably by sixteen candle light years. It was ungodly and unending. With every orgasm, I feared further I had lost more and more of my precious spiritual essence. Abandoned in the dirt like a smudge of chalky powder, my goal of chastity was gone. I flowed out into the rivers of carnal doom like the ebb and flow of the cosmic tides. I didn't know to what extent this broken bliss would carry me, nor could I halt the pounding of my thrusting hips.

The tattooed whore from Delhi knew all the kinky moves. She even educated Evey on how to do it and when. They slew me like a turkey buzzard. But then, they crawled into my corpse and made it dance like a zombie. I did the St. Vitus dance on the sheets of Verdun licking the mustard gas off their cracks. They tossed me on the rubbish pile to steam in the heat of wanton lust and die all over again. And after they had culminated with their custard, they came back to inject me with another highball. This ménage was meshing with the membranous labyrinth of my mental porridge, edacious

305

The Moon Women

meal worms chewing on the dying melodies of my hollow mellophones and the biological media of endless exchange. Tommy relayed the inner tunes.

> I'm holdin' down ma wonker,
> Up to New London.
> Say it ain't so bad Jack
> Find me in the blinding light.
> All I can say is nothing good is done alone. [23]

Then, they invented a new ploy. Evey kissed the whore who resisted at the inaugural lock up, but the hash must have coaxed her on. In due time they were sixty-nining each other, while I had been elected to cork the one on top and have her taste my fine wine. As each one rolled over, I maintained my persistence with the dorsal orifice. The whole show was a Time sandwich of ecstasy. The flavors mingled in my nether jaw. My knee was in some other vestibule. As my thumb dug its eager purchase into the bowling ball of the clef of one game plan, my tongue was in the tail of the other shrew. I heard the rolling thunder. I saw the pins fall away. My jackpot was in sight but there would be no end to this delirium. Tommy knew where to take it from here.

> I be jammin' on my wee bunky
> Missed the talkin' man.
> Mr. Blue K gonna put me on the floor,
> I'm loaded on the real world, gals,
> I'm tryin' to set to seven
> Them junkies at my door. [23]

In my ghastly separation there was a clanging going on. It was the message I needed to hear. It was not coming from the traffic. It was not coming from the pavement. But it was coming from somewhere very close and very near. Even with it being but a fluke passed the yardarm, I knew my watch was over. I felt my vital forces expanding in all the directions under the sun. I dug into my pocket and drew out the Alpha. I hankered desperately to open the locket I gifted to the mother of my son. I hungered to get to the summit of my hike through the fog of grief. Even after circumnavigating this terraqueous globe like the Omega sign of remorse, I alone was the one who had bitten the apple. When I climbed out on that branch, the prime fruit had begun to dance with delight. It bit my head off when the cracking slapped its horse and galloped off with the wind. It made a motion like a curtsy and then it investigated my groin. I choked my somber pride down. I made the albino horn dance. I flew to Denver with the preacher. I returned with Ginsberg's moldy poems. He published my toilet paper novels and then unfolded like a ghost holding his magic lantern. Some romantic killed the President in the corner of God's eye right underneath the ropes. Tommy unwound more of the glamour.

> Gotta hook up in the harbor,
> And shake off the memes.
> I drift off slow and blunder,
> Blowing out the yellow candles on my schemes. [23]

The carnal delights of the two whirling sex dervishes were winding down, but the armies of the five horsemen were still on the prowl. I was reminded of the drama of Queen Draupadi and how Duryodhana and his wrathful twin, Dushasana assaulted her virgin beauty. They had whored her out as a prize after a gambling match with Beeshma and Arjuna who had lost her. The two dastardly cousins were tearing off her clothes in an attempt at rape. Normally, a sari is six or seven meters maximum. As they unfurled her dress in gleeful anticipation of their reward, she prayed in desperation and sent her plea to Lord Krishna.

"Please save me, Oh, Great One, Lord of this Universe and the Cosmic Beyond," she pleaded as she readied her frail form to be unraveled in front of the entire establishment.

"Have no fear. Your prayers will be answered, my daughter." From his place in Vrindavan, Lord Krishna soothed her suffering in due course.

"Hurry, my Lord. My garments are practically depleted." She cried out in unequivocal anguish.

"My sweet disciple, I am racing with the wind on the hooves of my most trusted steed." Krishna was not sparing a second to reach her. The more she prayed, the more the satanic twins shed handfuls of cloth, but the sari seemed endless. The charade was that Krishna

The Moon Women

was miraculously causing the sari to go on doubling itself, as the two devils unwound its lengths.

"My tears are my only covering, my Lord. If you don't come fast and put an end to this humiliation, I must surely expire." Draupadi was emptying of all her fervent hopes.

"Have full faith, my Siksha. Your trust has saved you." Upon his gigantic stallion, the Prince of Giri Dara Nagara flew over the landscape to console his consort.

"At last my Lord, I am but extinguished."

Like a fire deity, Krishna galloped up and lifted Draupadi into his arms to save her from the pillaging being done by the two dastardly rascals. She embraced Him with all her devotion and supplication, although in hindsight she had one item on her mind.

"Oh, my dear Lord, why did you take so long to save me? I was in dire peril." She begged of his pardon.

"Flesh of my flesh, jiva of my life. You hailed me thinking I was in Vrindavan. If you had realized my true abode lays within your exquisite being, I would not have had to ride my stallion over such a treacherous distance. I would have come to you instantly. Place this jewel in your heart for all time." Krishna enlightened his disciple as Tommy enlightened the dance going on between the sheets.

> Some games don't pull no bloopers,
> No midrash gamblers like they did before.
> I been to Bulgar town.
> I sucked the blue balls down.
> Now I'm tryin' to set to seven
> Them junkies at my door. [23]

They purged all vitality from my body. The marasmic beating of my heart was on the verge of quitting. Fortunately, with whatever poison my veins had been laced was wearing off. The spasms of salacious frenzy had waned to their lowest since the inaugural uptick of this wanton arbitrage. I had to dig down deep into my livid sinews and pluck the chord of my Over-self. I had to expose the silver thread, the one, which anchors me to something more than I thought I was. I knew it was in me somewhere. I merely had to search faithfully until I got my hands on its pulse. I knew it was going to bring the house down. I collected the remaining units of my stamina sucking it out of those diploid strands of my DNA, the double twisting pairs of the two sides of life, which have been carried from heaven's door. I let it out. I let it toll. I let it have its salvation once more!

"Allah Akbar!" The sound erupted out of the pit of my core.

"ALLAH AKBARA!" Out it came a second time and it plunged through the heart of the whore.

"AL-AA-HHH! AK-BARRR!" I roared forth to the heavens of Islam.

All evil flew from that place instantaneously. She wasn't a Hindu prostitute! She was an Islamic whore! She came from a Mussalman's home. When she absorbed my utterance bellowed as authentically as I could from my time in Tehran, a bolt of horror, amazement, and repentance wrenched through her. It yanked her attention back into the Mosque where she had once bowed down to the East to face Mecca from where she had wandered long ago as a child. Darkly, she saw her true mission.

She collected her garments and shirked back. Now exposed as the carnal wraith that she was, she knew I had executed her with my thaumaturgic shotel. Slack jawed doesn't even come close. The meperidine of the Mickey had begun to wear off but the muddle-headedness lingered with its draining spigot leaking out my vital forces. As I stumbled out onto the balcony overlooking a landscape, which was retaking its shape from a dazed disturbance, I found three feathers lying on the marble handrail, vestigial flowers from the Beyond. Nevertheless, the Khrng were able to come away with yet another prize, a potential future fetal seedpod.

The crooked finger of the new Moon pointed down from its perch over Delhi. Its spine of pale light spun the wheels of an unavoidable collision with star bred humanity.

- 5 -

After checking out, I was gathering my bags in preparation for my departure from Delhi. I had figured arriving from out of the clouds wouldn't be an appropriate move for a boarding student so I pursued my adventure overland by riding the train all the way into the switching deck in Bangalore. Even though I hankered to substantiate my place in FWC with my actual presence for once, I could only secure regular passage in the back end of a cattle car.

309

The Moon Women

The one remaining task was to relieve the concierge of my valuables in the downstairs vault. Some precursor consternation had inspired me to deposit them there prior to my initial voyage across the satin sheets with Evey and her carnal doppelgänger, the twins of vernal lust who befriended me with no regrets and a bon vivant au-revoir. Leaving the important trivia of a withered existence unattended in one's room even while sleeping was the equivalent of inviting all the rascals of sloth and greed to come and visit. Little did I know that soon another prophet from the Beyond was about to drop by unannounced.

Again, I climbed the miserable stairs back to my rookery in the eagles nest. As I gazed at the number it seemed vaguely familiar - 719. Somehow, that value contained some extraordinary significance but I hadn't a clue as to what yet. Infinitely glad I had avoided a marital headache not to mention my love sleuth who had accomplished the unthinkable, spiritual suicide, I would be traveling onwards to Bangalore posthaste.

After finishing my trek back to my suite, I ordered some Chai and biscuits from room service. While passing time as I anticipated the arrival of my snack, I organized my notebook by jotting down the major points of my day for future reference. As I scanned an overview of the city, the early evening muezzins announced their signals to Allah.

The approaching dusk swam in over New Delhi signaling a swarm of pigeons to perform their spectacular marathons looping round the minarets of several nearby mosques. They flew as though they were competing in a vertiginous aerial tournament. Perhaps, they were the reincarnated ghosts of our boys who flew sorties over the airspaces of our enemies during the last big war. The muezzins reechoed with their competition as well, calling out the reminders to the lost ones to come back to prayer; come back to Allah and be consumed with His burning Love. I had often questioned why each mosque had its own muezzin and why those muezzins all announced their prayer calls at the same time. With over a dozen mosques in Delhi, one prayer call soared up to greet the evening one after the other, and so on, and so on.

There came five firm raps on the flimsy door to my quarters. Before I could even get to it, in flew a tall desert rider robed immaculately in flowing pearly satin. A coal-tar igal tamped down

310

his sun washed headgear, the ghutra, which framed his aeolian features and tented his shoulders like a Bedouin pilgrim. He didn't look like the normal bellhops who had arranged room service previously. He had the appearance of an Arabian Sheikh.

"Oh, yes. Please, do come in. You can set that down right over there." I felt obliged to give the Maulvi my commands.

The mysterious visitor strode straight into the large foyer. He made a beeline over to the coffee stand, which squared its presence with a hoary Broyhill camelback sofa projecting a genuine Persian flare. After placing the slender necked Turkish teapot soberly onto the parquet surface flaunting some exquisite wooden inlays, he sat down. With three fingers, he deposited two demitasse teacups ornamented with pearl and turquoise. Then, he took his august station on the domed sofa.

"This is not the Chai which you ordered previously. This is Turkish coffee. It is both positively hot and powerfully strong. Please come and sit." He patted the sofa with his sun kissed hand.

I stepped back in temporary shock unable to respond with my usual blistered excuses and then he hit me with his intro.

"My name is Abu Abd Allah Muhammad al-Qasim. You can call me The Abu if you wish, or simply Abu; whatever you prefer. I am only His humble servant." His English was impeccable with a dash of British sourness.

"Ah, so good to meet you. What's up? I'm on the way to go out. I've no time for solicitors." I offered more of an apology than I felt was necessary, but he needed to hear it.

With his flattened hand, he shoved at the air in the direction of the large mahogany door to 719, which he had left wide open. The movement closed the thick portal with a thud as if his push had caused a potent pressure wave to move through the air and remove any possibility for my escape.

"Please sit." He reiterated more firmly this time.

Timidly I joined him on the empty place on the wisdom-laden sofa. His stature was overpowering. It projected me to a place high atop a sand dune somewhere in ancient Persia.

"Originally, I came from the Manichaean lineage. The angels, Jibril and Mikhail, have advised me of your need for my services. Therefore, I have come to unfold the secret of the Dubing Norg, that of the Hejaz and the Nejd, that which comes from the Alif and the

311

The Moon Women

Ya. Their power is to add unending meaning to some endeavor by way of marrying it to the moving threads of God's divine sounds, the sounds of ethereal prayers issuing from the celestial spheres, which portray a different light, a different language or altered reasoning.

"When you identify a work, which lends true meaning to life, then, by all means, play that music loudly. Dance to that music. Dance to that tune. Spin and whirl in the ten ecstasies and be consumed in that song. It is the Song of the Moons and of the Planets and of the Stars. It is the sound of God, the sound of Allah, heralded by the glowing love, which burns within the hearts of the lovers of Allah. We eat with Allah. We eat of Allah. We burn in Allah's Love. We burn with Allah. We are the burning of Allah, now and forever more." He concluded with his hands flapping high in the air over his headdress.

I was afraid he might be going into dance mode and whirl about but he calmed himself down and forged ahead by sipping a bit more of his tea, an inordinately hot taffy liquid. What was in that stuff I wondered?

"The Norg, or the Nejd, is a way of providing nourishment vital for promoting mystical growth. When combined with the exaltation of the Dubing, its entirety simply means to evolve into an exalted state, to attain God consciousness, to be the intoxicated whirling dervish, to evolve into the divine Mussulman, the twisting snake of Love, to be the true Sufi." He put his empty cup down.

He lifted the consecrated teapot and poured himself another cup. I was convinced it constituted something more than coffee. I nursed mine having only swallowed a tiny sip to insulate myself from whatever the hell he was on.

"Deep in the core of your world of the West and lying within your own mosques of knowledge, your clerics and mullahs, labeled misleadingly as scientists, have unscrambled the building blocks of life. They have deciphered these keys of procreation by duplicating the sleeping serpent of being. You call it by the letters DNA. Yet, you know not what its message truly is. You have studied it longer than the cycles of the celestial bodies encircling our mother the sun, yet, you know not its principle. The code of the twin snakes cannot be read like a book. It has to be sung like a prayer. It is the melic prayer of Allah born within the cosmic lotus, which humbly begs the inception of life. The markings on the twin snakes are the score to a magnificent concerto. Played as a celestial orchestra and sung by an astral chorus, only the one Allah who knows the opera of the spheres can reveal its solo duets. See it as a cellular overture, which lends itself to all the celestial instruments. Shams 'ud-din-Muhammed, more popularly ascribed to us as Hafiz, the Persian poet, once reminded us thus:

> I am a hole in a flute
> That Christ's breath
> Moves through.
> Listen to his music! [24]

"The music of these dynamic ligatures is an infinite series of vibrations. These vibrations, these frequencies, are as numbers, and, as such, they are quantifiable. They are the steps of a dance, which results in the creation of life, no matter what species emerges. One has but to dance to the music to know the reality, to know the truth." He polished off his second cup of Mohamed Atta's beloved brew.

"But how do I know you're telling me the truth?" I leveled with him.

"My laws are established to the wall. My visions are written in the sky. By that Allah in whose hands rests all life, hug the tree that mourns the death of life in order that the sobbing of the saddened be surrendered unto the darkness and the light of the tree of life reach out onto all the hearts across this land just as the Father on high pervades all times, all creatures and all things. See the God of man burning brightly in the hearts of clean men; men who have come to the mosque of purity and surrender.

> Make thoust body
> A temple unto the Lord.
> Give to Allah.
> Give to His temple.
> Into the realm of your body.
> Do not put filthy things
> And the ways of death
> Into that holy place.
> Do not drink
> Any alcoholic fluids.

313

The Moon Women

> Do not take
> From the tobacco plant.
> Do not ingest
> The spirits from bulbs
> Of the white sap.
> Do not participate
> In the slaughter
> Of the little
> Brethren of Allah.
> Do not place
> Your joint
> Into the womb
> Of any woman
> Except your wife." [25]

Again, his cup landed on the table where it paused for a moment before he engaged the minaret of the teapot. I had another couple of sips thinking it might help me to follow him. It was most assuredly a knock out cup of Turkish coffee.

"On the holy day of Muharram when over the earth, a flaming star sings from the heavens the message of the end of Time and the death of all decent men, you must listen. Is it not? No one should ignore that call. It is the consuming wrath of Allah coming down to decimate the world. But, when that fireball lands to only lightly kiss Mother Earth with a Goodness and a Mercy, then, all men know it to be a sign that Allah, the Merciful, has shown His divine graces upon all men.

"The ones who revere that heavenly rock and glorify it in its rightful place of reverence as a reminder of the death and misery, which they were spared by His Heavenly Graces, do the work of Allah. Those who worship a rock in and of itself are not worthy of Allah. But, to give thanks of His Great Blessings which go out unto the multitudes, that is worthy of His remembrance and His prayer. That is the true Mihrab of Mecca.

"It was so, unto that place I surrendered my time of cheer and uphill meditation. It was when I drifted off onto the downside of many slumbers I came upon a place of comfort and plenty. Both the angels, Jibril and Mikhail, opened my body and removed all the filth and impurities from my heart. They removed all traces of error,

314

doubt, idolatry, paganism, and disbelief. In their places, they infused me with wisdom and faith. They raised me into the lowest paradise. The beauty of that region was indescribable. From there we traveled from the seat of the Ka'baah to Jerusalem and then hence with their wings of fire, I ascended through the seven circles of the Kingdom of Allah. Whereupon, Moses, the patriarch of the Saints, greeted me, not as the Mufti, but as the Messenger. Through Moses, Allah commanded the brethren to harken to the words of the Lord. In the lineage of Adam, Abraham, Aaron, Joseph, Jesus and John, Moses declared my placement upon the ladder to be its headstone. A joyous tribulation came unto me saying formless be the One who requires so many to pray for so few. Thus, the demand of prayer was set as the fingers on one hand: dawn, morning, noon, dust, and finally the one of night. So, said Allah. So sayeth the One True God. Thus, my name was set in their way. The lips of Allah were freed within me. And I came as the Abu, aflame with the Love of Allah." He set his cup back down onto the shellacked surface.

As the fourth and all-consuming minaret assumed its corner in the diamond known as the keystone of the Great Mosque of Islam, Muhammad, the Abu, rose up, bowed graciously, and walked majestically out of the room.

Two minutes later, the Chai Wallah knocked. I had him come in and put his pot down. As I handed him a two-rupee note for his efforts, he extended two hands of gratitude and a quick pour.

"I'm good." I returned a minced head wobble and let the young fellow out.

- 6 -

Back in my gyrating pleasure dome, Dr. K. floated in as if he was born on a carpet surfing the billowing airs. I'm not sure if levitating in the K-room qualified as not actually being in the K-room.

"Mr. Rahms, I have the most astonishing thing in all the world to tell you. From our prior conversation, you know how my life was a misery. After so many years of examination and profound study, I had debunked the popular Indian Saints once and for all, as well as the histories of their teachings. Initially I had traced their lines back to the pyramids but after persistent study, I discovered they go all the

315

The Moon Women

way back to the Vedas themselves. Subsequently, one day when I received the news of this special academy, Friends World College, I thought I could come on board and elevate my ability to pursue this proposal as well as my role with my cast. What I required at the time was more resources to investigate my theories and so I knew my chance to use you students from America in my research was the answer. That is why I have put up with all these shenanigans for so long.

"Notwithstanding, I could not have possibly imagined the stresses it would put upon my poor family. Never no mind, these years have redoubled my ability to gain a leg with regard to my search for the answers to life's questions. Unfortunately, it was when you decided to reside in my home I became aware of things from the other places; things which Shanni and I are not comfortable facing. We fear they could be coming from Kalima and the devils of Time. It is my sincere request that whatever it is that you are hatching back there stays there. If at all possible please don't let it out under any circumstances."

Like a wounded ferret, Dr. K retraced his route back to his side of the divided territories and enlisted the protection of the woman holding the pots. I returned to my orbiting chair as it widened out the circles of my sagas, which continued to rain down into my headspace. The quaternary session of loves lost was on the verge of offering up its secrets.

CHAPTER 5 - **CHHUMPAR KYEW**

- 1 -

February 4, 1970 - Siem Reap, Cambodia

My two-bit room in the Auberge Inn was bare bones. Sometimes the moments of rich life are dressed with poverty. A beat up Coxtail cot, pitched in pitiable obscurity, flared its exiguity against the far corner. Flanked by an oddly configured Hutch hunched over in fear of ambidextrous mishandling, was a rickety nightstand needing a shim. Its devoted slant bore its polygamous marriage to two dilapidated low-backs having lathed walnut stumps limping in an adjacent recess.

I didn't like sitting on either one and the bed was atrocious. This smack of austerity lined with but a trace of the Speak propelled me back out onto the dirt pathways surrounding my cottage early enough to catch a glimpse of a saffron trail of Buddhist monks tracing their matutinal parade along the edges of this shrinking town. The monks displayed a cautious charm all the while proceeding to claim what breakfast the Buddha had intended for them on this radiant sunrise in Angkor Wat.

With the twisting of a hungry serpent, the brothers wound single-file along a delicate arc of mendicancy as their detachment guided their stomachs towards a fulfillment, which lay hidden within the fringes of this sleepy village. Step by step, this mélange of apricot wedges shifted rhythmically in time to the singular drum beat being rung out by the hatted monk at the rear of the line. As their empty begging bowls glinted in the angled light, a haunting presence cut through the groggy haze, which tugged at their dancing feet while the waving palm fronds conducted a chorus of Sisiphon tree frogs.

As their curiosity betrayed a repressed riddle hiding under the cloak of their meditation, the saturation of their prayers masked the statement of their hunger. As they looked my way, envy leaked out of them like the fetor of beached whales drifting downwind on a nameless beachfront. Unknowingly they ignored my folded hands directed toward them in respect. Since moments earlier, I had detoured the greasy eggs set out at the hostel and had hit the road to

317

The Moon Women

hail a taxi instead; I hungered to feast on a different vision, the temple.

Angkor Wat was a manifold monster. The main compound was nearly half a kilometer on its outer run. After twentieth century surveyors had checked the boundary, surprisingly, they determined it was off by only 3 millimeters all the way down its full flank. It was an absolute megalopolis. What artisans of architecture could have mapped out and built such a thing?

Surrounded by detailed escarpments on its perimeter, the bulwarks delineated representations of all the mythical devotees of the many Hindu deities as well as many Buddhas. These tokens of worship were not the direct deities themselves but only their devotees pictured on some of the outer verandas. With statues of relief chiseled into the stone, the embankments also depicted the many fabled players and the tales of their worship and devotion towards the prime triad of deities, Brahma, Vishnu and Shiva. A moat preceded this bridgework and signified the oceans of Meru. Pairs of apsaras, alluring celestial dancers, who served as messengers between the priests and the deities, gathered in festive gaiety along unequal runs in the containments.

Observing the stunning grace of these statues sparked a flashback to something, which occurred while en route to the sprawling complex. My taxi had detoured down a circuitous dirt road along a stream, which bordered a sparse Cambodian community. It was plain to see its inhabitants had been eking out their livelihood for generations within this removed region. Haphazardly, I caught sight of a village girl lowering her watering can into the lazy current of a weak creek bed bordering her birthright. As she performed her domestic duties, she was unaware of a colorless hand parting the blades of club grass a few meters away. A moment later, she was gone. The work of the Khrng is ever eager.

As the temple surrendered its acreage to the portrayals of the Chaitanya figureheads of both religions, I continued my study of its Cambodian heritage. The carved frescos depicted the many travels and adventures of these historic heroes during both the creation of this world as well as its day-to-day maintenance. While observing this colossal army of figurines, I noticed within the architecture of each one of these concentric temples were window-like formations, which coincided with one another: rectangular indentures paralleling open channels of emptiness and thus enabling an unchecked viewpoint. At odd periods squarely in the midpoint of these fissures, a statue of one of the primary Hindu deities arose silhouetted in a provocative pose.

During the sixteenth century, Zhou Daguan, a Chinese diplomat, spent a year in residence within the territory of Angkor. He wrote an account of all the temples with meticulous descriptions. Hidden in the shade of giant Ficus with their gnarled strangler fig cousins, row after row of circular bumps had lain submerged in the foaming waters of a lazy creek for centuries. Each bump was nearly a foot in diameter and carved out of a dirty sandstone. These were lingam stones worn down to near stubs by the flowing waters. The cylindrical egg-like sculptures resembled the male phallus, symbol of the deity, Shiva. Row after row of lingams led like an abraded road to another formation in the riverbed, that of a chubby low-walled depression having a narrow inlet. This discontinuity represented the Yoni, the Hindu symbol of the source of all life, the vagina.

I had picked an interesting angle in which to set my camera for some photos when a young Cambodian lad greeted me with his small-town cheer.

"Zhhyum reaup soua?" He lowered a gangly leg to steady himself on his turn-of-the-century bicycle.

"What's that? Reap what you sow?" I didn't get it.

"No, no, no." He burst out in grins.

"Zhhyum reaup soua. Means how are you?"

He reaffirmed and waited. Back at the hostel I had made contact with a little of the Mon Khmer language which is spoken in this region of Southeast Asia. At length I clicked with it.

"Zhhyum reaup soua."

I also greeted him with traditional respect.

"You wan gurl? Yum, yum berry good."

These guys don't waste any time.

"I'm Okay. I'm looking at the temple at the moment. Time for you to run along." I turned away to change the subject.

"What hotel you?" Super gamester, he got directly to the point.

"Siem Reap Auberge." Doubtlessly mesmerized by the spectacular wonder of this magical place, I let it slip out as I was checking up on my job.

The Moon Women

"You good GI. I bring gurl you room." He wasn't letting go of it.

"That's Okay. I'm quite Okay." I replied.

I was having none of his mass-marketing strategies. Hopping onto his monstrous bicycle manufactured at the time of the Civil War no doubt, the cunning lad wobbled off down the road. As his dust rose with his departure, I realized that by responding with "Okay" repeatedly, I had rubberstamped his pyramid scheme with perhaps too many affirmative nods. Well, if he shows up I'll put my foot down. I may not be a man of the cloth but I am most assuredly master of my inner self.

Cloistered inside the fourth structure were all the Buddhas themselves, including the one who gained liberation twenty-five hundred years ago, Siddhartha Gautama. The writings of Buddhism mention many incarnations of Buddha consciousness. These sacred partitions were rampant with the reliefs, statues, and carvings of so many of these dedicated figures of devotional thought. Bear in mind the tunnelways themselves were embrasures created within each of the mendicant structures marbled with the patina of centuries. Built from thousands of enormous stone blocks, the temple stood as a testament to a colossal figure of Asian lore. It was unimaginable how King Suryavarman, the monarch in power during the twelfth century, could have constructed the entire thing in less than thirty years.

The igneous blocks, which made up the five enclosed structures, were the size of cars and even buses. At the time of their inception, they were morticed together with a tight precision, which would have been highly difficult to repeat even with modern day techniques. Over the centuries, seed-lets of jungle vegetation had taken root between the cracks and developed into gargantuan Ficus trees, some measuring over four meters in diameter at their base. In out-of-the-way places, these shoots grew to ungodly dimensions, which now towered over the eroding architecture after having lifted the cubic weights into the air; some were cantilevered almost vertically, as the yawning webs of the Ficus trunks hoisted the mammoth sandstone blocks into dizzying angles.

A deity, Vishnu, was set into one of the watery triangles with his many-armed pose, Catherine-wheeling across the entrance. I was flabbergasted at the quantity of visually shifting realities, which collided within the twisting patterns of worked stone strangled within the grip of the ravenous vegetation, which had invaded from out of this jungle paradise. Its beauty seemed to choke one's equilibrium for level life.

The primary complex in the middle was a superlative creation containing five stories of advancing platforms, which you could get to only by hiking hair-raising stairways. An astoundingly beautiful dome capped off the final complex, the one, which is most popular and heavily photographed as the quintessential representation of Angkor Wat. The quarter cones rose over eighty meters whereas the primary one rose over a staggering hundred meters into the skies. Angkor Wat was an exquisite marvel.

- 2 -

On the second day of my exploration, my rickshaw dropped me off in the middle of nowhere on one of the avenues, which bordered the southern rim of the temple. As I peered out over the mammillary landscape spawned from the dozens of Buddhist stupas, which mother true religious sustenance to the thirsting Cambodian hearts, I zoned in on the millenarian enclosures, which seemed to hide a supreme mystification.

After I prepped the tripod for my Nikormat with which I digested some primary wide angles, I traced out several moving pans with my Canon Super 8 movie camera by augmenting a dichotomous shift to document various uncommon perspectives of the grand structure. All of these long shots I planned to edit with some of the artistically cropped moving footage taken the day before. Finishing up with the full scope material, I took a little walk to get closer to the preliminary outer wall of the mammoth temple structure. Soon afterward I located something, which needed further examination, an artfully laid-out portal built directly into the face of the grand wall.

As I stood to confront this transitional vacancy, a large window spanning the continuity of the stone, I detected something unusual. Peering through the opening, I could tell it lined up with another one connected to its inward temple structure. There was a second window displaying a common center to the one, which was right in front on me.

"What flavor of Maha Maya is this?" I wondered.

The Moon Women

As I focused further upon this unusual noumenon, on its fringes another one popped up. It seemed the multiple temples were rotating to align their congruent hollows within each of the separate temples, one within the other, to create a hollow tube spanning a great depth all the way through the grand structures. However, my conception of these probabilities was outmaneuvering the basic laws of the universe and the normal mental states of all the prescient minstrels known to history. Even though previously I hadn't noticed them all to be so concentrically arranged, that failure didn't deter me from deducing the obvious, perhaps it was something I had drunk back at the Auberge. Nevertheless, still bent on celebrating possible future discoveries, which could potentially obviate the normal lines of humanity, I seriously considered the inexorable placement of these openings with the stone. Furthermore, I don't remember anybody ever describing any witness of this tunnel-thon because if they had, I would have been so severely impressed by it I would have made some relevant notations in my journal so that I could film it should it ever materialize in front of me. As I kept staring into the endless chain of tunnels, a picture within a picture within a picture, I was jarred out my trance by an explosive uproar.

Slap!

As the crack of a hand landing upon someone's cheek came from behind me, I shifted my immersion with the vortex telescope to locate the source of that terrible act. Across the streambed, which wound alongside the road, was a billet of thatched shanties, living places elevated high up on pylons. Below these stilted homesteads, bands of chickens roamed the ground searching for peckable table scraps. Underneath one of them, I discovered the cause of all the ruckus - some creep was beating the shit out of a young girl. He was repeatedly landing blow after blow upon a defenseless female. Inflamed I screamed across the missing water for him not to do that.

"Demons fear to tread where angels walk!" [1] I yelled.

Across the mud-caked depression where the vital waters once abounded, the scoundrel still continued to rain his abuse upon the young girl. Apparently, my remake of Pope hadn't found its mark; for all intents and purposes, it had fallen on deaf ears. So I unleashed the big guns.

"Hey, you, asshole! Quit it!"

He looked at me angrily and sputtered something in his dialect, which seemed pretty close to curses. At least he stopped slapping the girl and stormed off in a huff. Proudly I had terminated his malicious mischief and put a stop to his evil tactics once and for all.

The shy thing looked back at me with an embarrassing glance and then smiled with a twinge of appreciation. I waved back. She bolted up the shoddy stairs, which led up into the shanty causing chickens to explode out of the every outlet, down the gangplank, and into the rain soaked yard. Pecking madly for their next garnish, the birds hung out with a bunch of kids who were playing a common game of spanking the old bicycle tire. As they chased after the withered rubber O, their blows impelled it across the dusty yard into the hands of another kid who struck at it and sent it rolling back. As they kept up with this Third World ping-pong, I turned back to ground zero to locate the unorthodox cavity hiding in the long stones.

Assuming I had put a stop to the abuse of the young girl, I resumed my place, which I had occupied prior to all the ruckus. I centered myself with the initial entryway and then adjusted my alignment to secure its parent innermost airway and angle it correctly with the one after that one as well. After I had juggled four of them into view, an additional bewildering sensation came over me. As the fourth wall element came clearly into focus, it seemed as if all the sounds around me dissolved away leaving only a dull echo bonging in my ears. The sound was like the sloshing sounds of water softly lapping against the insides of a sonorous cavern buried deep underground.

As I kept staring into the hollow shaft in which all the duplicated cavities aligned equally, miraculously the fifth complex spun into place. There was now a whole series of void portals springing concentrically one within the other, one rift within the other and another and so on, and so on extending now into the heart of the temple. After a short while, zoom! There were also counterpart discontinuities in the stones, which expanded out through the far layers of each of the coaxial compounds. A full-blown tunnel had exponentiated itself out through the conjoined windows eleven replications deep!

I was utterly transfixed. With the sloshing water tune repeating in the background, the whole thing became a mystical

The Moon Women

meatus. If I had known any better, I would have taken some meclizine to counteract this Asiatic vertigo for I had no idea what telepathic macrocode I had unraveled in order to generate this attenuation, this reduction of the regularities normally present within the stones.

"I've got to get this one on the record," I thought. I raced back over to grab my bag, tripod and 35mm camera, and hustled back to my sanctuary facing the odd tunnels. Quickly setting my tripod, focusing my camera, and aiming towards on the wall, I was shocked. It was gone! Wait a minute. I could not believe what I was seeing. Was I not in the correct spot? Previously I had dug my heel into the soft red clay in the open meat of the road to mark my placement. I had found my heel print. As I scanned the hardened mud of this village road, I could find no other marks anywhere near me. This was where it was. I was somewhat puzzled. The hollow sound of artesian petrification was gone as well; the only sounds surrounding me now were coming from the jungle.

"Eliminate what has changed since you experienced the wonderment," came the words from the upper registers of my think tank.

In attempting to backtrack the steps leading to the strange vista, I replayed my movements and the altercation with the thug over in the village. But it was to no avail at first. So I pretended in my mind to yell at the cruel handed attacker and envisioned myself sending care packages of aid to the young girl in a pantomimed effort to provide her with freedom. Still nothing. So I picked up my gear and abandoned my intentions of recording the phenomenon. I just wanted to see it again.

I peered ahead and concentrated using every ounce of focus I had. I bore straightforwardly into the precise axis of where the missing link had once materialized amidst the openings. Then it began to happen again. I let it. At first, only three of the openings came into focus, but after a little bit of staring and concentrating, the other three locked onto the game. Then, whoosh, the back five sprang into place as if they were magnetic. As well that hollow stuck in the well melody came back to haunt me as it did before. I listened to it intently.

In the multiplex hub of the shifting windowed tunnels, a figure sprang up, that is, a near naked body bounded into the middle of this telescopic mirage as if a marionette jumping onto a theatre stage. Because of my previous encounters with Asian cultures, I recognized who the figure was. It was the persona of Shiva, the deity of destruction and regeneration. Now fully alive and performing in front of me, he manifested all the transformative powers in one hand. His skin was a teal colored manganese and his hair, dreadlocks. His eyes were tiny glowing pumpkins. As he yawned, something came out.

Right up front I figured it was his tongue sticking out at me, but the tongue had grown into the head of a tiny cobra. As Shiva curled back his oral perimeter menacingly, the cranny between his two front teeth seemed to grow wider and wider until it was splitting his head into two halves. As the two shells of his head sloughed off, his body unpeeled like a banana. And out of the divided coils of this unwrapped body the cobra extended its length until it adopted the abnormal size of nearly two meters. By that time, the snake stood cantilevered on its tail eye to eye with me. I watched the squirming needle of its forked tongue flicking in and out. As it did so, I detected the piercing stab of a thought dagger driving into me like a telepathic juggernaut. A blasting neuronal unit deployed in my cortex with the zing of a lightning bolt. When I claimed my place in the road, the thought bud had blossomed yielding the following prediction.

"Step closer and prepare to greet many more prophets from future's past. They will come to you to unfold the radius of your destiny and your place in the design of Man. Listen well to their words."

Instantly the divination vanished like throwing a rock into a pond. I don't know how many frogs had fallen before I noticed it was raining. All I could do was stand there staring at the now dead vortex as the pouring rain drenched the surrounding jungle. What the hell had just happened? I caught my wits and jogged over to rescue my photographic gear from the torrential downpour. I packed my gear, loaded it all into the travel bags, and headed back to the Auberge.

This was a key confrontation in which I had run into a true paranormal phenomenon, which hadn't been launched by psychedelics or magic mushrooms. Besides that, I was just glad it was something out of the Beyond, which wasn't initiated from the polar hoar frosts involving those star spangled snowmen. I knew I had to find out more about Lord Shiva.

The Moon Women

Dripping wet, I regained the weak comforts of my broken down hostel. Dropping my two duffels to relieve my back, I didn't notice anything unusual at first. My only thoughts concerned the hot bath I needed to scrounge up in that infernal hole called a bathroom. However, hiding barely visible within the dark bulkhead of an unlit corner was a tall Cambodian woman. I rubbed my eyes for some clarification and threw off my backpack, which hit the deck with a thwap. Had they put something in my lunch over at the temple? Because from dawn till dusk this day was turning out to be way too spooky.

I looked over and there she was smiling back at me sheepishly. A shock of black hair unfurled all the way to her hips; a Luna moth green chemise topped her cream pajamas and tucked over her ear was a clump of jasmine punctuating her innocence. She was barefoot.

"Yum yum?" She posed with embarrassment.

It all came back to me with a full head of steam: the kid back at the temple and his proposal. What a doofus I am! I should have chased after him and put a stop to all this right then and there. Now what? Dejected I slumped into the swallowing settee. The slender female came over and knelt down in front of me. She tried to press in between my legs. Her hands nervously tugged at my belt.

"Whoa! Whoa there, Sweetie. I haven't gone through the experience of a lifetime only to come back to this dump for a blow job," I spat crossly.

She gazed at me with a start and fluttered her enormous eyelashes.

"You no like? I Khammi. I yum yum for you," she seemed insistent.

"Que lest votre nom [What's your name]?" I spat without realizing I couldn't speak French.

It was not a prohibited question. Since it was easier for her not to understand me, I got no answer. I sensed the wheels grinding away slowly in her head. Soon enough, a glimmer of courage arose to overcome the preprogrammed subliminal machinery. Her eyes came up off her toes and into mine with the muted measurement of trust.

"Je suis m'appelle Chhumpar." [My name is Chhumpar.]

The fragrance of her essence was like a combination of root beer and vinegar with a hint of whiskey: root beer for incentive, vinegar for the douche, and two fingers of backbone. With virgin apprehension, she unbuttoned the pearl buttons of her tunic. It was beautifully woven, just as she was. Underneath this gown, or Bupok in Khmer, she had a pale chemise of faint muslin.

"Rose," she whispered delicately with embarrassment, only with her sulky pronunciation it resonated more like Rhhooursh.

I got hold of her shoulders, stood her up and as I gathered my balance, I rotated her one-eighty. As I gently lowered her down into a sitting position on the worn fabric, I smiled and placing my hand on her shoulder I said, "You. Stay. Here." As I patted the air in front of her face while firmly enunciating each word to get her to stay put, I made a move towards the establishment. Seeking to untangle this mixed up ball of misplaced lovelorn fancy, I ran down the hall to the reception desk where I collided with the balding manager.

He seemed creepy. Outcroppings of facial maculations made him look as though he had the guise of a monkey. He was chattering into the horn of an elephantine dialing devise. Finally, when he came across me languishing there, he put the weapon onto his chest, leaned over at me, and said, "Oui, Monsieur?"

His Cambodian French would have had him marched off to the guillotine in Paris, but my French was even worse. And if you speak English in this country, straight away they assume you are military and you need to get laid immediately.

"Une fille dans ma chamber? Dites-lui de partir. Allez." [In my room, a girl? You tell her to go. You go.]

I did my damnedest to rack my brains on what the hell to say about my predicament. Much as I had been proud of my solid performances on French tests back in Huntington prep, I was fourteen thousand kilometers from any possible reinforcements at this point. The squat imp looked at me with a horrifying grimace. His mal-occluded incisors protruded passed his upper lip like a macaque.

"Bonjour, Monsieur, bonjour. Comment allez-vous aujourd'hui? C'est une femme de chambre. Non? C'est une femme de coeur, Monsieur. A votre service. Eh?" [Good day, Sir. How are you today? She is a chamber maid. No? She is a woman of the heart, Sir. Whatever pleases you.]

The Moon Women

He said as he picked a curl of tobacco off his lip and flicked it passed my nose. I drew a complete blank. Attempting to spit out something further to encourage the chiseling monkey to help me, I cranked on my withered brain banks to address him with some more of my faltering French idioms.

"Je suis un homme honnete, Monsieur. Je ne suis pas de la gauche!" [I am an honest man, Sir. I am not a pervert!]

I ate the "au" and swallowed the "ch" shushing him to fermez his bouche. [Shut his mouth.]

"Mais, non. Peut-etre avez-vous la folie des grandeur. C'est tout!" he replied smugly. [But, no. Perhaps you suffer from a delusion of grandeur. That's all.]

He resumed his monkey chat on his oversized ripe banana. As chance would have it, from out of the thick layers of mundungus tobacco vapors hovering behind me came a rescuing interruption.

"Excusez moi, Monsieur [Excuse me, Sir.] Can I be of some assistance? My name is Jean Devereux. And your good name, Monsieur?"

A Frenchman who had witnessed my plight suddenly chimed in. In no short order, I shared with him who I was and that I was visiting the majestic temples to create my idea of some artful photography. Then I recounted the saga of the fellow on the reptilian bicycle out by the roadside, which must have resulted in the appearance of the little woman in my room. I admitted there must have been some misunderstanding because I was now dealing with a mud hen in a swan dance. I was tired and I simply wanted to get a bath and go to sleep. Could he help me excuse the young damsel? I wouldn't be needing her services, ever. He confirmed his deep understanding by whole heartedly concurring with my wishes.

"Merde [Shit]! Everyday these monkey bastards go on sucking us dry. Will it never end? Merde! Mongoose in a manger, Monsieur. Mongoose in a manger. Merde! Maintenant juste me regarder [Now watch me.]. I will now slay this rodent."

He charged forward as my middleman with my banner of defiance riding proudly as he unfolded his searing directive.

"Qu'avez-vous a dire pour votre defence de cette intrusion , Monsieur?" [What is your defense for this intrusion, Sir?]

The Monkey Man guarding basecamp pretended to ignore him right up front, but my French comrade in arms repeatedly blew rank pipe smoke into the Monkey Man's direction until he had encased the mingy monkey within a nebulous soup. Monkey hung up the phone and opened with an unceremonious pawn to e4.

"Monsieur?" the Monkey Man confronted his opponent.

Reputably they must have had similar duels in times immemorial. There were phrases like "A bon chat, a bon rat," from the Monkey Man. A rapier phrase meaning: A good cat, a good rat.

My French stand-in countered with "Le coeur a ses raisons que les raison ignore."[The heart has its reasons that reason knows nothing of.]

Quite an appropriate appraisal of my standpoint I thought.

The Monkey Man of malice came back with a resounding, "Il faut cultiver notre jardin et ont tendance a nos propres affaires." [We must cultivate our garden and tend to our own affairs.]

The finale for the Monkey Man was, "Peut-être que cela aussi sera un plaisir de s'en rappeler un jour." [Perhaps this too will be a pleasure to look back on one day.]

As the two dueling gendarmes continued to rip each other to pieces like the proverbial snake and mongoose, I was somewhat in awe their rhetoric was sometimes so ferocious their closing summations were in Latin! The concluding jab from Monsieur Devereux was, "Experto credite." [Believe one who has the experience.]

Wow! A more engaging tangle I haven't run up against in quite a while. I was shocked to have witnessed this melodrama in the heart of this miniscule village in Podunk Cambodia!

As Devereux and the Monkey Man went at it, the extreme difficulties of the day and the complete depletion of my energies found me dropping off the edges into a slight dream place. During this naptime, I found myself once again facing the temple.

The formal layout of the place went something like this. The outer run was a good four meters thick outside of which ran a wide mote, which encircled the entire complex. This primary wall structure had a walkway, which encompassed its topmost level. In between this separation and its cousin there was a span of vacant sod envisioned to be a public parcel to separate and insulate each individual edifice of the pentad. The architects envisioned it to be a beautiful concourse with pathways lined with benches upon which visitors could sit and enjoy the gorgeous surroundings.

The Moon Women

Constructed as though it were an endless mansion encircling the periphery of this palace of divinity, the first temple was twelve meters thick. That would figure out to be a clean five hundred and seventy meters on one side. Are you picking up on the idea of the utter magnificence of this place? Moreover, there was a separation of some nine meters or more, which entertained a garden populated with a multiflorous species of flowers and trees.

The second temple was a good fifteen meters having two entire tiers each one containing all sorts of statues and carvings and pictorial representations. It had a solid roof on it like the others and it sported numerous domes and turrets. That temple compound was followed by a thirty-foot garden, with another distinguished collection of floral bushes and miniature trees. The third temple was over twenty-five meters and extended three stories circumnavigating the perimeter. I can't imagine how many of these enormous stone blocks it took to build these structures.

The third innermost structure increased to three stories and embodied all the Boddhisattvas and Apsaras who were essentially the faithful devotees to the Buddha. There are also numerable divergent Buddhas who have incarnated in previous millenniums. All their mystical tales are portrayed in relief upon the vestibules of this gargantuan temple. Cloistered inside the fourth structure were all the Buddhas themselves, including the one who gained liberation twenty-five hundred years ago, Siddhartha Gautama. You will encounter within the writings of Buddhism itself there exist many incarnations of Buddha consciousness. These sacred partitions were rampant with the reliefs, statues, and carvings of so many of these dedicated figures of devotional thought. Bear in mind the tunnelways themselves were embrasures created within each rung of the mendicant steps of the temple and marbled with the mystique of centuries.

The hulking dominance of the fourth inner temple was followed by a twelve-meter floral section, which was magnificently breathtaking. Not only did it house rambling gardens, but it had large trees, not only the smaller shrub-like ones as existed along the other insular borders. Again, don't lose sight of the concentric voids sequenced at regular intervals throughout the base perimeters of the entire building.

The last temple plateau was a majestic thirty-five meters thick. It extended a towering four stories into the air. You could travel the sprawling staircases higher and higher to view out into the surrounding jungles. This boundless temple was a staggering three hundred eighty meters on its front side. That's supremely mindboggling. It also maintained the same squarish crawl-ways on its ground stage. This pyramid also had hundred foot margins containing every imaginable flower, bush, and tree available within Cambodia. Forming an introduction to the courtyard, it yielded a breathtaking architecture dedicated to the ultra-pinnacles of Buddhism. This superlative creation was a full five stories advancing platforms, which you could get to only by hiking hair-raising stairways. The three astoundingly beautiful domes, which everyone photographs to capture and represent traditional Angkor Wat capped off the complex. The quarter cones rise over a forty meters and the primary one in the center rose a staggering sixty meters into the skies. That's besides the five stories! This temple was a two hundred meter cubic colossus. It was an exquisite marvel.

When I awoke, Devereux and the Monkey Man had concluded their exhaustive analysis of the situation.

- 4 -

And now for the rest of the story. [2]

What the aftermath of the trifling debate disclosed was I now faced a dilemma. The woman in my room arrived for only one reason - to have sex with me. Even though I had not yet paid for her, on the day of my departure from the Augerge, I would find the expense affixed to my tab whether or not I enjoyed her services. It was only four hundred rials (the Cambodian monetary unit) or roughly seven US. If I chose to dispute the charge, no big deal, the Monkey Man would unfortunately be unable to locate my passport when it came time for me to travel (big Cheshire smile on that one I bet).

The other twist of the blade was the girl was a virgin. Her sponsors authenticated this condition prior to her being all gussied up and sent over to my chambre dans le hotel [room in the hotel]. If she returned to her place of origin with her maidenhood intact, they would brand her with a molten iron rod on both cheeks. From then onwards, her entire subsistence would be a pitiful pall of misery.

The Moon Women

When he unfolded this news, I looked at the Frenchman with horror. My eyes wandered his features like a navigator searching for a place to ditch with only fumes in the petrol tank. What the hell was I to do?

Devereux sucked in a plentiful draw on his Meerschaum and blew out a swirling trail of turbid smoke. The job of facial cartography on his worn features uncovered a jagged scar, which circumscribed a line from over his eyebrow, which ran down below his chin. He had that perturbing gap between his front two teeth as well.

I had a cleft between two of mine as well but my void was from a missing bicuspid on the upper rack. It made me look like a pirate. How am I going to snatch this treasure out from beneath the decks of this revolting French frigate? I stared at the Monkey Man and he returned a wily smirk. I got up and shook the hand of my accomplice while thanking him profusely.

Heading back to my room to deal with Thursday's child, I played a brainy shell game on what the chances might be for me to pull this one off without losing a few digits or worse, the main digit. When I got there, the dear girl was all the more trapped in that whale of a settee which seemed to be devouring her. I knew she wouldn't be eaten like Jonah. She was a female.

I sat down on the extremity of its cousin, the soiled mattress, with my elbows on my knees and my crumpled knuckles on my chin. I looked at the nervous woman and then down at the bed. I had never quite been in a situation quite like this one before.

Yet I knew there must be some deeper meaning here. Over the years, I had learned that all experiences have many levels. Since this episode now unfolding in Cambodia was taking place on my voyage west towards India, the land of promise and mystery, I felt this impediment was perhaps an introductory step up on a Jacob's ladder of discovery promising to lead me towards the many mansions of a new kingdom, the Dravidian sub-continent. I concluded as well it might just be the onset of a transition into something of the Beyond, something big. So I turned it over very carefully in my mind.

My thoughts spanned back over the moments of the day: the melting heat, the illusive discontinuities in the stones, and the mystic well into which I had metaphorically fallen. Could the solution to this stickler be lying in there? The terrific photos I had taken that day at the Khmer temples would later show a clue. Angkor Wat was such a magnificent place. Knowing all about it was adding an indescribable dimension. But what was I doing there at the time of the windows? I remembered my heel mark, which I had left in the clay road on the border of the dry streambed and the impoverished village. Like a flash, the spectacle of the maniac striking the underprivileged Kampuchean female came back to me. Instantly I knew I had the key so I scrambled back out to the reception desk to face my antagonist.

On the double, I scoured the darkness for my pal and confidant, Monsieur Devereux. After locating him stashed in an abandoned stall while feverishly nursing his clay calabash, I excused myself and asked to join him to share something about the girl. Much to my joy, he was happy as pie to assist me further. I submitted my proposal: could he double up on another conversation with the Monkey Man and retrieve the name of the village, which resides on the southern bank of the pagoda superstructure, the one directly across from the riverbed. Devereux admitted he had no idea what significance that might prove in the final act but it would be his pleasure to attempt to do so. He charged out to intercept the Monkey Man amidships.

I overheard phrases like, "A grand frais," meaning: At grand expense. And, "A huis clos," like: With closed doors. And then, in conclusion from the Monkey Man: "Aide-toi et le ciel t'aidera." [Help yourself and heaven will help you.]

They had quite a go of it, which was well suited by my absence. After round one, my gentleman arbitrator retired to his corner of the coliseum.

"Mon Dieu! Ze man est impossible. Pommes et des oranges, Monsieur! [My God! Apples and oranges, Sir!] Mais [But], I 'ave zee name. C'est Svey Park [It is Svey Park]. It is not a place into which you should venture alone, Monsieur. It is a den of iniquity."

My French gendarme disclosed.

"I don't follow, Devereux. What's that mean?" What could be so repugnant I surmised?

"Whores, Monsieur. Whores and child whores. It is a most vile and terrible place, Monsieur. A sewer really. A human sewer!" He squinted his eyes and cocked his cranium.

"Merci, Mon ami." I sped off back to confront the origins of my dilemma.

The Moon Women

Excitedly, I charged into the dimly lit hermitage and knelt down on the neglected settee beside her.

"Vous yum yum maintenant? Oui?" [You yum yum now? Yes?]

She barely managed to get it out. I could tell she was terrified.

"Quelle est votre village?" [What is your village?]

I could not think of the French word for village. Dumbfounded she looked at me and whimpered, "Yum yum?"

"Non, non. Ecoutez-moi! Votre mere? Votre pere? Ou sont-ils? Ou es la maison? Votre maison?" [No, no. Listen to me! Your mother? Your father? Where are they? Where is your home? Your house?]

I spat it all out like ball ratcheting ferret and demanded in the best French I could put together; I needed to find out where she lived. She looked at me and looked back at the door. Was she thinking of giving me the slip? As she teetered on the rim of whatever sanity she had left, a tear rolled down her un-cosmetically upgraded cheek. Perhaps she was on the verge of losing it and spilling all her yum-yum out onto the grimy floor.

"Votre village? Votre mere? Votre pere? Vos enfants? Les Enfants? En famille. Les enfants perdus? Le jour des enfants?" [Your village? Your mother? Your father? Any children? The lost children. Children's day?]

I was babbling French idiotically.

"Ma famille? Voulez-vous connaitre ma famille?" [My family? You want to know my family?]

She exploded in tears. I had uncannily come upon the right combination of twists and coded numerals to cause her lock to miraculously pop open.

"Oui, oui, Madamoiselle. Quelle est votre famille?" I redoubled my efforts. [Yes, yes, young lady. Where is your family?]

"Svey Park. C'est Svey Park. Mais pourquoi, Monsieur?" [Svey Park. It is Svey Park. But why, Mister?]

At last she had released the precious clue, my key to solving this conundrum was now in hand.

"Pas maintenant [Not now]." I raced out.

Down the dwindling corridor and back over to Devereux's cage, I galloped. He had been treading water in my absence. In a mix of lightning English and disturbing French sub-titles, I explained the episode of my inner research with the vortex shift back at the site and how when photographing the prep scenes near there, I had inadvertently witnessed a villager violently striking a young woman over and over. I surmised the young woman who was now waiting in my room was the same one whom I had witnessed getting assaulted out by the shrine as I set up for my shoot. I inferred perhaps Devereux could inform the Monkey Man of this battery and ask him how I could go about pressing charges against the criminal who had perpetrated this humiliating offense against the young woman who is now residing in my room. Should we go to the police or strictly speaking how do we begin to properly deal with this case of molestation?

Devereux backed me up one hundred per cent; however, he cautioned me against falling into a dangerous trench now exposed in the depths of this gutter of human trafficking – I would be bargaining with the girl's life. Even if I played all of my cards in the correct order, there was no guarantee my plan would not backfire; I could get her killed if I wasn't careful.

Again, his rapier clashed with the foil of the Monkey Man. After Devereux had let loose with his volley of ammunition, the Monkey Man quit flapping his jaw for a moment and looked over at me with grim caution punctuated with a lurid leer. He then engaged Devereux with a deliberate and methodical harangue, which often times referenced my person as he repeatedly fingered me. The shooting match concluded with, "Vive la difference!" [Long live the difference!]

Even I knew what that meant from way over here. Devereux came back and divulged the weighted verdict.

"He says he understands your opinion in this matter. He says not to bother further. The authorities will punish this abuser accordingly. Besides, he says because of this clever trick, he will make sure your account is not charged. Plus, he assures you his man will escort your visitor home safely. No one will punish her in any way. In spite of that, he wants you to know, come the morrow she will most likely be sent out on the same quest to some other establishment and to some other customer who, in all likelihood, will not refuse her services." Devereux tapped out the bowl of his pipe on his heel.

The Moon Women

My French litigator suggested I could invest in his services such that he would visit the local police headquarters and inquire about the possibility for effective prosecution of the scoundrel, her uncle. However, he advised that might not be the best defense. Nevertheless, I was adamant and sent him on his way.

Match point I thought. I looked over at the Monkey Man who was now glowering at me through the smoky atmosphere. I realized somehow the motherfucker had won.

- 5 -

With my trembling hand, I swept away the glistening black strands of Chhumpar's hair like obsidian silk from a porcelain doll's cheek. The ambiance from a brocaded lampshade bestowed an opalescent quality upon her skin. After she loosened the drawstring on her pajama bottoms, which fell to her feet, she collected them and laid them gently on the foot of the crumpled bed.

"Et tu?" [And you?]

She was pointing out I wasn't keeping up with the procession of fabrics. For the second time tonight, she undid the clasp of my buckle. She got onto the bed in a kneeling pose and helped me off with my shirt exposing my notably hairy chest. Releasing a start at the experience of it, she blew a little air through her pursed lips and exhaled something in Cambodian. Then she softly roamed her fingers through the waving stalks of my Basque heritage. Inexplicably no one else on my limb of the family tree had received such a voluminous gift. I don't think it was because I was adopted; more so it was the result of selective genes and the luck of the draw, or more likely my selection from the couples proposing their matrimonial intentions in the fourth Bardo.

As her delicate fingers tugged at my pants, even though my permissive approach was an experiment in cultural perspectives, she was turning me on slightly. Was she bluffing? Did the technology of zipper evolution really surpass her comprehension? She playfully put her hand into one of my pockets and fumbled nervously in search of a memento. The coinage, the penknife, and the nail clippers were amongst her choices. After pulling out the clippers, she fondled it inquisitively attempting to figure out how it worked. Soon she undid its secret and squealed with excitement at its simplicity. I was on the

336

verge of getting fully aroused, to lay it on the line candidly. At any rate, since going side-street wasn't my plan, I felt certain my safety was behind strong enough fences when abruptly there came a soft knocking on the doorframe.

"Monsieur Ibsen? It is Devereux. May I come in, Sir?" He had discharged his inquiry with law enforcement.

"Oui, oui. Come in, Mon Ami." [Yes, yes... My friend.]

As I pulled over the one chair hesitantly, I proposed things were not the way they looked.

"I was merely offering to indulge her inquisitiveness. You know, to kill some time until your arrival. She's a curious creature, indeed!" I bandied my defense poorly.

"Oui, oui. Or perhaps your indulgence, Monsieur. N'est-ce pas? Le coeur a ses raisons que les raisons ignore [The heart has reasons which reason doesn't know.] Eh?" His favorite phrase came floating out.

"Possibly. What have you learned, Monsieur?" I was eager to receive any and all the important updates.

"There is a worthwhile prospect at zhe garrison, Monsieur, Inspector Lee. I know this fellow and I trust him. He has helped me with some situations, how you say, of discomfort. I related your experience of the young woman and the man who beat her mercilessly. Unfortunately, Monsieur, this sort of thing is not such a problem for local female property. The Inspector knew of whom I was referring and added there was little he could do about it. That fellow, as it turns out, is her uncle. She has no other family or connections in life, Monsieur. That is why her uncle has enlisted her in this sickly business. Fortunately for you, she is seventeen according to the paperwork, which was document there at the office." He stated.

"No luck, eh? But wait. What do you mean by fortunate for me? What do I have to do with it?" I interrupted. Wasn't it merely a matter of record?

"Only should you decide to have her, Monsieur, she is of legal age in Cambodia." He mythicized.

"Look Man, I'm simply offering to save the poor girl, not fuck her! Get it?" I was flailing my hands miming Don's windmill.

The Moon Women

"Je comprends [I understand] completely, Monsieur. I am giving you all the information I can. No more, no less," he was being up-front with me so there would be no disconnect on the matchup.

"In any case, Monsieur, zee prospects are tres mal [very bad]. Not so good. The police are not interested in entertaining a case having to do with foreigners. That is as far as it will go. I apologize, Monsieur. I was hoping for something more, how do you say, 'positif?'" He hung his head to his marrowbones.

"Listen, you claim to know that inspector pretty well? Do you think he would help us?" I was not only altering my plan, but also enhancing it at the same time.

"Oui. Je pense, Monsieur [Yes. I think so, Sir]. What did you 'ave in mind?" He brought out his meerschaum and made ready to load it.

"Since he probably speaks the Khmer dialect do you think he would be willing to translate for us?" I was setting the stage. Would he be our messenger of mercy? Or our mastermind of misdirection?

"Oui, mais [Yes, but], 'e does not speak any English, Monsieur. How do you make for that?" He pumped wads of Mars brown tobacco into the burnished bowl of his masonic pipe. Devereux was becoming the mastic, the glue, which would bind Chhumpar's future with her autonomy.

"Yes, but you do," I stated bluntly.

Devereux instantly connected with my train of thought charging into the station on a brimming head of steam.

"Two translators are better than one. Go get him," I launched my preemptive strike.

And Mother Mary said, "Behold the handmaid of the Lord."

3

The china saucer of the Moon worked its way up into the onyx palace of the sky and bathed the Auberge with its glow. It cast a thorn of moonlight across my dingy crash site in Siem Reap and struck an uncanny shadow as it lit up another stick of useless furniture tossed into a hollow in my crypt. Skulking like a haunted tree with splintery branches, the lopsided coat catcher was radically out of place because no one in this country wore hats and if they did they never removed them. On top of that, it blocked all view of a typical cover up in the art world, a cheap copy of a French gem.

Chhumpar had keeled over lost in sleep after her trying day. As Devereux and I talked in somber tones, some species of beetle crawled over her toes. The bone-weary lass did not even stir. She was dog-tired having had her fill of all these shenanigans. As I drew the cotton blanket over her midriff and shoulders, I admired the perimeter of her lustrous ebony hairline inscribing the rearward portion of her neck. It was clean like the edge on the horizon at dusk. Her cheek snuggled into the pillow. This was the best place for her.

- 6 -

The following sunup I had decided to relocate the coat rack with the idea of throwing more light upon my French proof of life.

The print hiding behind it delineated a bushy bearded gent with a pipe in one hand and a palette in the other. His thumb and forefingers were caked with the vivid colors of a painter's oils, which he artfully worked with a slender brush onto the canvas. On the surface of things, the scene demonstrated a clear-cut commonality, simply an itinerant artist involved with his craft. Yet lying beneath that platitude was another simplicity, which chilled his audience to the bone. This unobtrusive painter was staring precariously into the eye of the viewer to place possible voyeurs on notice concerning the error of their ways. In other words, he was presenting them with an important alert – "Qui fait cela, vous?" [Who's doing this, you?]

The subject of his artwork appeared candidly behind him, a bevy of ballerinas rendered exquisitely in their blue marquisette leotards. Captured in the midst of ballet pregnant with the delicate movements of pirouettes, demi-lies, and what not, were the dancers, some wearing marabous round their waists as well. The style of the artwork was of the French Impressionist painters; you could differentiate the choppy marks of the brush strokes. It had a messy look to it until you backed up a bit. The added ingredient of distance clarified its effect. It wasn't one of those paint by number jobs, that's for sure. I reflected the odd painter guy looked a good deal like Devereux. When he came in, he found me lamely studying the framed masterpiece with inquisitive gravity.

The Moon Women

"Do you know what that is, Monsieur? It is, how you say, ironic such a thing exists in zhis place." He seemed obliged to inform me of some historical trivia.

"I don't know. Looks like you." My response unveiled my aberrant ignorance.

"Ah! Mon Dieu, Monsieur. Plus improbable. [My God, Sir. Most unlikely.] It is a portrait of Edgar Degas. He was a tres importante [very important] and influential French artiste of the nineteenth century. Do you know what is so highly unusual for this painting, Monsieur Ibsen?" He was unfolding the lesson while using all his professional wiles.

"Not a clue. Sorry." I was beginning to get a wee bit irritated, but this bloke had done so much for me so I indulged him a tad more with a hand roll.

"He 'as painted himself as solicitor on ze grounds he is sampling the products of whoredom, Monsieur." Devereux twisted his moustache with a lifted eyebrow.

He explained at that time in Paris, all the marriageable ladies who were training to be ballerinas, were also obligated to be prostitutes. Gentlemen suitors would come to watch the ballet, which was all quite classical and decent, but then they would select one or more of the ballet dancers to retire to secluded antechambers backstage where the women would administer additional services, as it were. Social mores of the decade allowed for such practices as the commoner on the street universally accepted this custom. Be that as it may, it was not something to dally about loosely in the corners of daily culture. In fact, there were staunch religious elements, which sought to eradicate this practice.

This painting, done by the French realist, Edgar Degas, was an utterly outrageous demonstration exposing the vile social aberrations of the times. The public was asked to focus in on this hideous behavior since it was illuminated right up front via the lens of Degas' works. It magnified the practice to such an extent that his paintings on this subject grew to be a motivating factor in repealing most of these acts from the public forum. Nonetheless, it did not remove its enormity entirely, for it crept into the manure of society, the back alleys of prostitution. Nevertheless, Degas was not mincing words with his oil on canvas amalgam of accusations exposing the crudity cloaked behind the titillating choreography. Although society regarded him as a manner less worker of the cobblestones who had simply made light of the much-valued materialism of his comrades, in the end his pointed ridicule tagging these immoral acts as heinous and unwanted became a battering ram, which toppled the citadel of immorality all across Europe.

"Good for him. I feel Mr. Degas and I are on parallel wavelengths. Let's burn the bastards!" I was ripped.

"I 'ave zee Inspector, Monsieur. He is waiting in the lobby, in case you had a mind to speak to him beforehand. What should we do?" He was prompt and he had a real "can-do" attitude, which I appreciated no end.

"Tres bien [Very well]!" I knew that much. I laid bare the main point of my plan.

"I want to buy the girl. Permanently!" I engaged him head on.

"Merde! Qui va la!" [Shit! How is that?]

"J'achete une fille. Okay?" [I buy one girl.]

"Zis is not possible, Monsieur. Comment cela est-ce possible? She is not furniture." [How it is this possible?]

He was babbling away like a tipsy Elmer Fudd.

"Listen, Monsieur. Try to follow my logic. Watch. Let's do the math," I initiated my strategy with one of my favorite phrases. Encapsulating my theories into the timely duration of two frappes, I put forth my button-down approach.

"Look, she's seventeen years old. They can only lend her out as a prostitute for two or three years. By then, she is bound to get pregnant because of the lousy birth control methods they use or else she is going to die from some pandemic or other mishap. The Monkey Man specified she was going to cost four hundred rials for her services and that's my price. Don't tell me his daily customers pay that much. Even if the pimp keeps a quarter of the profits when all is said and done, I think he'd be quite well off. If her health doesn't suffer any setbacks all week, I would estimate she could service, let's say, an average of fifteen johns. If she is able to maintain that track record for forty weeks out of the year, which is a comfortable range allowing for moderate time off for menstruations and other interruptions, it multiplies out to approximately sixty thousand rials per year.

"Now, you have to figure into the picture an amount for her room and board, clothing and laundry. Presumably, there's

The Moon Women

significant overhead involved in keeping her alive. At a minimum, business averages would calculate out to a third at the most. That comes to forty thousand rials times three years, which is approximately a hundred and twenty thousand. We've got to tell the Monkey Man to explain to her pimp I'm willing to save him all that bother and headache and offer him one hundred thousand rials right now!" I put the finishing touchups on my dissertation.

"That's a little over two thousand US." I proclaimed.

"You are undoubtedly crazy, Monsieur. But I like your style. Your heart is positively in ze right place, Monsieur, but do you have zhat much money?" Even though he was initiating his acceptance to the full arbitrage, he speared some question towards my banking protocols.

"Well, I've got some five hundred on me. Maybe I could sell one of my cameras?" I was willing to go the extra mile to put the Monkey Man and the pimp where they belonged.

"You realize, Monsieur, that inevitably it is not ze Monkey Man with whom you 'ave to negotiate. It is ze pimp, the Uncle. I am told his name is Sambath Kyew." Devereux had done his homework.

"Okay. Whatever. Whomever. What do you think of my plan?" I needed his feedback. I needed to know I was going in the proper direction.

"How much do you prefer for zee camera Monsieur? I was thinking of buying one of those when I got to Singapore, n'est-ce pas?" Even he was plotting an avenue to get in on the action; nevertheless, it contributed to his merchantability.

"We'll see. Let's get the Inspector in here. Run the plan by him and feel him out." With the opportunity to snag my Nikormat, Devereux was unequivocally on board. Plus, he'll be an excellent moderator.

When the two of them came in, Chhumpar woke up and saw the policeman. As soon as she got whiff of him she leapt up off the sheets to duck out the door. I caught her and yelled for Devereux to ask the Inspector to calm her down using Cambodian. We are not going to lose anything in translation from now on. The Monkey Man was hanging close just outside the door, listening. Not without precedent, the Inspector had attracted a lot of lookie loos, forasmuch as he was the local long arm of the law.

I yanked the door back and spat at him, "Allez-vous en! Partez!" [Go away! Leave!]

Devereux yelled some expletives at him as well. He stumbled back down the hallway to crawl back into his cage. Inspector Lee had begun to settle Chhumpar. As she sunk down into the eclectic settee, I watched her expression as Devereux negotiated with the Inspector. It appeared she could comprehend the French quite rapidly because she looked terrified when Devereux repeated the words, "Il veut acheter la fille." [He wants to buy the girl.]

She nearly tripped over herself making another beeline for the exit. I caught her and gently settled her back down on the shattered boneyard of a bed.

After Inspector Lee gushed with astonishment over my revolutionary ideas, Devereux gesticulated the finer points. He finished with the main crux of the plan as the two of them hem and hawed for the better part of the day it seemed. Lots more hand gesturing added to the deal. Plus, both of them were twisting their fingers frantically in the midst of an intense session of the mustachio game.

When they seemed to be nearing the end of it all, Devereux showed me his upturned finger.

"There is a probleme, Mon Ami. Zee Inspector says for zis idea to work, you must marry the girl. It is as I had you believe previously, Monsieur, em—poss—see—bla."

"What kind of impossible? What kind of a marriage? Is it a civil marriage, which must be performed?" I was exploring all the possibilities.

Devereux dallied back and forth with the Inspector. As round after round of strategically timed Ouis rung true, I was getting a righteous feeling surrounding it all and thinking quite possibly, we could arrange a marriage of convenience.

Devereux came back. "If you go in front of the magistrate and submit all the legitimate papers and suitable bribes, it can be, Monsieur. Mon Dieu. Pas mal, Non?" [My God! Not bad, no?]

To be sure, Devereux was kindling a nice shine as he earned his medals of merit with appreciated subterfuge.

"What about the girl? The Inspector has got to explain the entire proposal to her to get her reaction. But please be sure you explain I am buying her sovereignty not her body. Apart from that, I

The Moon Women

know I can dole out enough of the green stuff for her to go wherever she needs. I will even accompany her back to Phnom Penh if that's what she wants. I am not going to harm her or take advantage of her in any way. Please be clear on that point when you tell her, Monsieur," I stressed the humanitarian motives forming the basis of what I was attempting to do.

Inspector Lee and Chhumpar batted back and forth at each other for quite some time. Their tete-a-tete got woefully daffy when the Inspector grew angry with her and began yelling with frenzied up and down hands. Eventually, she seemed to get it and looked over at me with the most inquisitive expression as if she couldn't quite unravel why I would entrust her with such a miraculous gift. Even though she was unsure of what it would do to her or to what extent she might be able to take it, she never rejected it completely. In spite of looking quite baffled, her smile showed me the feral terror had at last fled from her face.

While Lee was asking Chhumpar if she had anybody to accompany her to freedom or would she go with Monsieur Ibsen to Phnom Penh, Devereux and I discussed the Nikormat.

"I can spend the two thousand if you will throw in the tripod, the lenses, and some of your Kodaks. How many rolls are you now having, Monsieur?" He was calculating his options.

"I came with twenty. I think I've shot six or seven max. So, fourteen, I would say." We were narrowing in closer to a deal. This was advantageous because then I could bankroll the rest to bargain with officials.

"If you don't mind I may need that in rials, Mon Ami." I plotted the outcome, but he was quite well with it.

'Pas de problem, Monsieur." [No problem, Sir.]

"So, that's settled. What do we do now? Do we confront the uncle or go to the magistrate?" I stood awaiting the dawn of the one, two punch.

"Monsieur, the Inspector advised if we don't have an agreement with the uncle, then we are in no position to approach the magistrate. Ca va? [Okay?]"

"How much will the magistrate require by the way?" I fixated on getting all the Ts crossed as soon as possible.

"Maybe five thousands." Devereux relayed from the Inspector.

"Any other bribes? Mr. Lee for instance?" I posted to Devereux he must ply this inquiry in the most tactful way.

When the Inspector responded, he was overwhelmed. "Mais non, Monsieur. [But no, Sir.]" He shook his hand at me waving off the compliment.

"What about the Monkey Man? I don't plan on any trouble from him either." I was attempting to crossmatch everything in its correct place.

"You could offer him a tip, but no more than fifteen hundred to two thousand." Devereux delivered.

"Okay. Done; twelve hundred for the Monkey Man. I've got to keep as much as possible for Chhumpar. How much will be needed to keep her safe and ensure a decent start in Phnom Penh?" I urged Devereux to be careful this was all going to land in the right place.

Devereux and the Inspector tore into it by and by. They arrived at the figure of twenty-five thousand, but they confessed I could get a much higher rate out for my dollars out on the city streets. It might run me close to $375 all told when everything was said and done. That seemed like a bargain for me at this juncture.

"Oh, okay. That will allow me sufficient funds for my expenses in Phnom Penh until the Old Man wires me more bread." I polished off my drink as I twitched my fingers to display the sign for coin of the realm, which drew a nod from le Monsieur.

"Have Lee go inform the Monkey Man and find out how we can contact the uncle. We need to get this project rolling as soon as possible. I've got a plane to catch in a day or two." I could afford a short detour but my scheduled journey to Kuala Lumpur could not be offset by anything further than that.

Ten minutes later, Inspector Lee returned with the needed directions. Devereux relayed the hairless dwarf was so blown away by our valiant attempt to help a low-life from his own country. Nevertheless, he had his job do to.

"Let's go inform the Uncle." I ordered. Now or never, it was match play at last.

The Moon Women

Seeing the precise place where I had been confronted with the cross channel out of the astral pathway and the frightening apparition of Shiva was quite unnerving for me. The place where the uncle resided was across the way from there. Mr. Sambath Kyew was a chicken farmer. Fortunately for us, we were spared the gut twisting smell of chicken world for he housed most of the hens in coops in some other dump. The ones scratching nervously in the dirt patch were convenient for dinner.

As he strolled out onto the broken down porch of his thatch hut for a smoke, he stopped short. Here were the four of us like Publisher's Clearing House come to present the stupendous giveaway. Only we didn't have the prestigious three-meter check. What we did have would be quite impressive or so I thought. We had rehearsed the plan with the Inspector and the cardinal points of the math. Not intending to forget a thing, we lined Mr. Kyew up in our sights to get the unmitigated impact of the full bid and spilled the beans.

After Inspector Lee had outlined the initial intent of our bill of materials explosion, the yellow runt snickered and spat through the wide gap in his mandible. He glowered at Chhumpar as if she was the central cause of these cursed happenings. She, the little hellion, had a gap in the middle of her teeth, too. She spat right back at Sambath. She did not like this pretext of a man. She was growing quite feisty at this point, knowing any minute now she would be liberated from this place. As the Inspector unwound his monologue, Sambath calmly sucked on his hand rolled blunt periodically spitting out bits of tobacco. Chhumpar remained tight-lipped struggling to suppress her spare remarks. Instead, she focused unequivocally on me figuring a longing look on the producer of this gift would be what would most infuriate Uncle Sam.

When the Inspector had wrapped up the main points of the pitch, we got our answer.

"Te!" [No]

He spat the word out like it was another wad of mucus excavated from the depths of his conniving bosom. Devereux looked down at his shoes and put his hand to his forehead.

"Mon Dieu!" He exhaled.

Sambath Kyew pursued his soliloquy of expletives and vile spitting until lastly he punctuated his vociferation with his down thrust fist, pelting against his palm and bringing the curtain down with one exclamatory foot stomp. He had the mannerisms of a mala fide macaque.

The Inspector relayed the body of Sambath's oration, which was punctuated with the words, "Va t'en trou de cu!" [Shove it up your ass!]

And followed with a pacifying, "N'est-ce pas?" [Isn't it?]

After collecting all the right cues from the Inspector, Devereux explained to us the pudgy hunchback had essentially proclaimed we had insulted him with our suggestion. But he is, nevertheless, impressed with our determination to undo the girl's livelihood.

"He is not the normal sort of man, Monsieur. Er, tres clairement [quite clearly], he is thinking this girl is not even worth that many rials. He is willing to indulge our requests if you, Monsieur Ibsen, will entertain him by participating in a little charade. It seems he has some sickness of twisted humor, Mon Ami. He says you can have the girl for only fifty thousand rials, but you must remain for one evening at his guesthouse until the hour of dawn. He doesn't think you can do this. If you cannot successfully remain in place for one night, he shall retain the money and his niece as well. It is a take one - take all proposition, as they say. However, if you can accomplish this feat you may keep his niece for the money. He has insulted you with some crass names, which I do not wish to repeat, Monsieur. He feels confident you will fail in this pursuit and he will remain in control of his niece. Surprisingly, he claims he trusts you to deliver the money to him after you demonstrate your cowardice." Devereux conveyed it all to me in spite of his holding onto the feeling this man's hijinks were alarmingly malapropos.

"Stay until sunrise? Sure. I can do that. Couldn't be that challenging. What's the trick?" I looked at Devereux for some assurance.

"Je ne sais pas, Monsieur. I don't like it. I do not feel right about this man. There is something evil in him. He is up to somezing. More so, Monsieur, he says zhat zhe girl must stay with him. And the Inspector and I have to leave you here by yourself. I really don't think this is a good play, Monsieur Ibsen." Devereux was plying his

The Moon Women

utmost in spite of this jungle bunny's dire ploys to twist him into knots. Most likely the Frenchman was on point for earning a crack at my notebook in which I had logged all the optimal settings for the SLR.

"Tell him I accept his little challenge. But, Chhumpar will go back with you to the Auberge. She will stay in my place until I get back tomorrow. That way we'll have at least one oar in the water. That's my last word on the matter." I wasn't going to let this maniac get his devastating licks in on Chhumpar. He might even kill her for all I know. Come to think of it, he might even kill me too! I could not predict with what malefaction he would put forth. And no bones about it, I was not going to allow this meat axe of a man to harm her in any way whatsoever.

Inspector Lee relayed my ultimatum, which prompted Sambath to spit once more through the void in his central incisors.

"Bat [Yes]." The smack of his impudence was like a lizard's tongue swatting a fly.

"O." "K." He articulated each sound sourly and looked at me with his sick self-satisfaction.

"You Am-mer-e-gan GI no see gru. You no yum yum."

He held up his pinky finger as he nodded a stunning acclaim to his own joke and then convulsed into a phlegmy chortle.

Devereux and Inspector Lee escorted Chhumpar over to the busted down Jeep and headed back homewards. Prior to taking off, Chhumpar had come over to me with folded hands and made a little bow. Her sweet self held a flowerlike freshness even with all the heat threatening to consume her. I could see a hint of a hope in her eyes like the rosy warmth of sixteen candles radiating from a birthday cake. She was that special to me.

- 8 -

Feeling quite pitiful, I stood in a motionless stupor. Sambath Kyew came over to me, pointed to a spot in the colorless clay, and spat out his prime directive to inaugurate my stay in his gulag.

"Ici!" [Here!]

He drilled the word into my eyeballs before trotting up the stairs. I figured he had to go into his shack to clear away some space for me. I was going to tell him he needn't go to any extra trouble;

348

neither did he need to turn down the sheets, nor arrange for any late night beverages. But I kept quiet.

After some time, say an old-ball million, he emerged from his palace and clippity-clopped down the wooden stairs. On the bottom rung he ordered, "Va t'en!" [Get moving!]

I followed the major domo like a puppy dog dragging my loose shoe in the muck. Apparently, my reservation in the Five Star penthouse stashed over in his palace had been put on hold. We traipsed across the way passed the chicken bone yard to a ramshackle hut up on stilts a good meter and a half off the ground. Sambath marched me up the four wooden steps, unlatched the flimsy bolt, and pointed into its vault of gloom. The rickety shack had terribly rudimentary sides one of which had a busted out hole in it, something, which might remotely pass for a window but with no proper glass, only fragments.

"La [There]!" Came his next directive.

I went in. There was a straw mat lying flat and not a speck else. The absence of the Speak alerted me to the residual weaknesses regarding any chances of being sucked up into a vortex of capture or prenuptial sex. Big surprise there no doubt.

"Any chance you could order out for any pizza and beers? I'm famished." I babbled out loud hoping Mr. Kyew might overhear me and pick up his mobile phone.

He whipped around abruptly. And with his demonic leer irradiating down from the pinnacle of his dominance, he grinned and shoved a pinch of maccaboy snuff up his nostrils. As he sneezed a series of snorts, a noxious brown spray spewed out of his nose into the surrounding air. He was the milliard of mean, a mutation. He coughed violently and leered at me again as if to say something but realizing it was a useless effort he simply spat on the floor. With that ecumenical statement, he left and dropped his parting how-de-do behind him like an unctuous turd.

"Bonne soiree, trou de cul." [Good evening, asshole.]

He slammed the flimsy door and departed. As his flip-flop retreads clacked down the gangplank and out unto the mudflats, his mockingbird cackle trailed off into the darkness. I sat alone and watched the day's closing arguments put the jungle courtyard to rest. A swarm of blue and yellow macaws screamed by, announcing their curtain calls against the draining light of a macko sky. Families of

The Moon Women

gibbons began their hooting calls to organize their treetop syndicates in defense of the day's lost paradise while the honking bullfrogs spelled out their strategies concerning the dangerous traffic swarming in the puddle worlds just past my manganese walls. It was a joyous but hungry honk. Its counterpart was the piccolo rasping of the Sisophon tree frogs, which wormed a high-pitched serenade into your eardrums like some insectivore fiddle burrowing into your brain. As night's cold crawled in like an iguana bridging a new landfall, color hemorrhaged out of the cleft of twilight framed by the jagged pane facing west. A shower of hard objects, presumably nuts, peppered the flimsy roof, then nothing. A stale silence fell on my little refuge.

In nine months, North Vietnamese regulars will surround this indistinguishable village of Siem Reap and turn it into a desecrated hellish mess. Against that apocalypse, I would dedicate my protest to securing the liberation of Chhumpar and all that she stood for. And that was a great deal. She stood for the ballerinas of Edgar Degas. She stood for all the glossy plates, which have lain proudly on Chicago's table registering their beauty and their bravery by opening their legs. She stood for the capability and the purity of Asian women everywhere, who had for centuries endured a downtrodden life, toiling on towards the promise of liberation defined by the pains of birth and the burdens of motherhood. She stood for her namesake, the flower, which is accompanied by an intoxicating aroma and dagger-like thorns, which can draw blood faster than any sword.

The rose is a system of five petals, which double and quadruple into patterns of rufescent beauty. A rose lens washes the world with promise and cheer as an icon of supreme fortune. Rose was the word embodied within that pious devise of recurrent prayers termed the rosary. Furthermore, Rosebud was the dying word uttered by Orson Wells in his movie, Citizen Kane. And ultimately, the Rosetta stone, that basalt monolith, which bears the inscriptions in Egyptian hieroglyphics, demotic symbols and the Greek alphabet, is the tablet responsible for deciphering all the inimical secrets of the Pharaohs and the Book of the Dead. As well Rose was going to prove to be my Rosetta stone for unlocking many of the mysteries plaguing my life.

Despite my quivering extremities, I graced the worn straw mat with my presence. Sitting alone I contemplated what I might have to confront come the gloaming. Dismally, the hut had nada for insulation, merely bamboo and cheap lath. There was no light, electricity, or running water serving this necessitous maisonette. That meant I would be in freezing seclusion 'til sunup with no place to go to the bathroom except outside in the dark jungle. Mr. Sambath's demonic trick was now unfolding in my mind's eye. I'm going to have to stave off another encounter with my psycho buddies who hail from the fringes of the Siberian arctic, not to mention the distinct possibility of the jungle demons from Dracula's outer palace transplanted from its home in Transylvania.

As a faint droning buzz became barely audible from many kilometers off in the jungle, I calculated its ETA. It was not the report of the Khmer Rouge mortars being lobed in from the jungles like what would pulverize the village some months from now. It was not the detonations of B52s unloading bombs from nine thousand meters into a destination box south of Oudong. It was worse. Much worse.

As the puny whistling murmur grew nearer, I stood and peered passed the cracked glass but it was no good. It was all a useless fog. I unfolded my shirttail, cleaned a patch on the grimy surface, and looked afresh. Hovering over the canopy of the jungle was an inky cloud swirling and turning into itself; folding itself repeatedly like some liquid tar soufflé. Only it was not going to be my dinner; I was the dinner. It was a stupendous army of mosquitoes!

As the dying sunset bled out into its fundamental postmortem purple, the featureless mass dispersed. The definition of the forest dissolved and only an indistinguishable solidity that was night remained. Evidently, the microscopic vampires had gone their separate ways to attack the hordes over at the tourist hostel. Yeah. Go get them. They have mosquito nets and repellent. I'm sure you little buggers would prefer to have a more challenging brood of victims to chew on rather than waging your war on poor little old me. I'm only one lone victim stuck out here in this infernal hut. Not much of a meal here I wager. Get your ass moving on down your dusty stinkin' road and eat somebody else. It was a decent effort, but I don't think they were falling for it.

Although they were supposed to be closed up tight: the cracks in the glass, the gaps below the door, the breaks in the sideboard slash, the fissures in the roof, and the crevices in the floor boards, in

The Moon Women

all probability, won't keep the blood sucking bastards from sneaking into my room!

And in they came. One or two like microscopic recon agents sipping the CO_2 that poured out of my lungs and oozed from my pores. They honed in on it like smart bombs to a red dot. And I had the ideal red dot - blood. I remained motionless thinking that would buy me some time to delay the orgy, but not so. They commenced their munching tactics in seconds. My choices were to bail now while I still had some peripheral vision or try to last through midnight to greet the cherry rays of the sun. This is what separates the big boys from the really, really big boys. The prospect of being eaten alive by millions of microscopic flying leaches gave me the creeps. And, it would most likely go on for eight constant hours. Yet, I did have some experience with these little insects in my bygone days. The question was - could I put some of those experiences to work for me now.

Many summers ago, I had grown up on the seashore. There were marshes in between the area of the dunes and the family dwellings over on the hillside where everyone lived. There was many an evening during which I and my buddies would hide out in those marshes with our binoculars. On many judicious late night adventures, we were on the prowl for a particular prey. As we stalked the alluring shadows behind the lit patches of yellow light up on the hill, we were always praying for a chance exposure of some disrobing female participant, the younger the better. Seems unlikely, but our success ratio was better than expected, which encouraged us to venture forth with even more advanced reconnaissance. There was only one catch. Yup, you guessed it, the damn mosquitos. And there were droves of them. What we had invented after considerable experimentation was that a mixture of urine and gasoline would keep them at bay for quite some time. I've got the one, but how to get the other?

I ventured out onto the dilapidated porch to clear my head and figure out some way I could get some gasoline. Barely discernable in the murky dusk of this late hour, I spied Sambath's Vespa motor scooter resting comfortably alongside Mr. Kyew's hutch. That's when the whole ball of wax rolled itself into a diabolical strategy.

I unbuttoned my shirt, ripped a length of it off at the hem, and stole my way over to his pad. His chickens woke nervously with Morse code clucking messages alerting the surrounding villagers but fortunately, there were no receivers tuned into that frequency for the moment. I unsnapped the latch on the scooter's saddle and lifted it nervously letting it fall back gently until its hinge hit bottom. Then I tried to unscrew the cap to the gas tank, but it was stuck. Forcing my thumb under the lip of the cap's tab, I pushed with all my might and finally it popped free. Carefully avoiding any creaking sounds, I eased it off and secured it in my armpit. Jamming my rag down into the throat of the tank until only two inches were sticking out, I pinched the end between my fingers and let the law of physics take over. After waiting for the cotton to soak in as many of the cracked hydrocarbons as possible, I withdrew it and could see it was nicely saturated. Retrieving the cap, I silently secured back in its place and clicked the cheap rectal appliance back into position. I then retraced my steps back to my hut.

Feeling quite victorious, I unzipped my fly and pissed all over the straw mat, which wasn't exactly the mark of a hero but I settled on what little glamour I could for the moment. That takes care of the call of Mother Nature for this cowpoke. Sheer genius smiled on my countenance as I collapsed on the mat and wiped the gasoline soaked rag all over my body. From my socks to my pants to my belt to my arms and last but not least the back of my neck and all over my bald spot, I wiped as many places as I could get to and then let the rag drape down my back like a ponytail. I knelt down cross-legged, clasped my hands together, and attempted to gather my senses.

As I crouched shivering in the pitch-black straining to pick up any evidence of lights or meaningful noises, the pintsized chink in the wall above me deepened its afterglow. At first, I wasn't sure whether or not it was simply my imagination or the loss of visual perspectives. Soon I had to give into the futility of holding out. I ruminated crossly on my failures confronting these vague obscurities too many times in the past. But then, the toxic combination of my answer for the bugs and the quick assault of the evening's chill got the best of me and the window took over.

Its solidity clarified and the light I had imagined grew to an inexcusable and undeniable presence. The more I looked at it the more it disseminated out until I was observing the silky sheen of its

The Moon Women

rectangularity gradually shifting in the windless spaces. As I gasped on the fumes in the chill jungle mist, the definition of square angles assaulted me with the edges of the curtain appliance capable of splitting Time. It gradually relaxed upwards to begin its reduction of reality by converging upon a velvet underground ornamented with the horror of a billion diamonds twinkling afresh from the pipes of their kimberlite palace.

With the night bared to the stars, the wicked fumes and the creeping frigidity clobbered my within. The expanding gauzy membrane on the periphery of the portal grew out as though something was pushing into my world from its link outside reality. The bubble like extension pushed out and out. And as it did, it began to glow. And in that watery light came the shape of a phantom. An androgynous torso and limbs manifested and as the dimensional barrier collapsed, the liquid metal entity materialized squeezing its elasticity through the womblike aperture. Its crystalline presence threw a large wheel of radiance upon the shabby lath of my crumbling domicile. Once more, the crunching chimes of death dug into my brain with a searing anguish.

UNTO THE ANGEL OF THE CHURCH [4]

THESE THINGS SAITH
HE WHO DOTH HOLD
THE SEVEN STARS
IN HIS RIGHT HAND

BY GOOD REASON YOU HAVE KNOWN
SEVERAL OF THE SEVEN
I COME AS THE SIXTH
I FOLLOW THE FOUR ANGELS
THAT STAND ON THE FRONT TO KEEP
THE FOUR CORNERS OF THE EARTH [5]

AS FROM THE NATION OF PERGAMOS
LEGION *TO ABADDON*
AND SON OF MAN
THIS TALENT DOETH HOLD
THE TRUE PATIENCE AS HERMONI

Haan Moses

WALK WITH ME IN WHITE
FOR YOU ARE WORTHY [6]

A THRONE WAS SET IN HEAVEN
AND ONE SAT ON THE THRONE
ROUND ABOUT THE THRONE
ELDERS SAT CLOTHED IN RAIMENTS
WITH CROWNS OF GOLD ON THEIR HEADS

FROM THE FIVE WOMEN OF THE MOON
AS HERMONI I MEASURE
THE WALL ACCORDING
TO THE MEASURE OF WOMAN THE YARDSTICK OF HUMANITY
                           IS NOT MALE BUT FEMALE

THE FOUNDATIONS OF THE WALL
WERE GARNISHED WITH ALL MANNER
OF PRECIOUS STONES EACH BURNING
IN HER FAITH WITH HER LIGHT
THE THIRD WAS CALCEDONY
                    HER PSYCHIC ELEMENT IS CALCEDONY

NOW COMES THE MOON
WOMAN OF THE THIRD PLACE
ARRAYED IN A SEA OF SNOW GLASS
AND MOON LINEN DANCING UNDER
THE WHITE RAINBOW DRIPPING
CINNIMON BRIMSTONE AND SAND

SHE WAS DECKED WITH A CALCEDONY ROSE
BURNING WITHIN LIKE A COLD FURNACE
AND IN HER HAND THUNDER NOISE
ABOMBINATIONS SPEAKING

355

The Moon Women

OF FILTHINESS AND FORNICATION

INTRODUCES THE THIRD OF THE MOON WOMEN

HE THAT SAT UPON THE THRONE SAID
BEHOLD
I MAKE ALL THINGS ANEW
AND HE SAID UNTO ME
WRITE
FOR THESE WORDS
ARE TRUE AND FAITHFUL

AGAIN THE DICTATE TO WRITE A BOOK
AND ENCAPSULATE THE WORKINGS
PROFESSED BY THE ANGELS OF ABADDON

HAVING TOUCHED THE RED REUBEN
A RARE RIVER IN ABADDON
AND BEHELD THE BERYL FIRE SLAVES
THE GUARDIANS OF THIS RIVER
FEW NAMES EVEN HERE HAVE
THIS ANGEL SURVIVED ALL
DEFILED THEIR GARMENTS [6] CONTAMINATION FROM HELL

The Angel bent down on one knee and then continued with his Revelate pep talk.

IT IS BY MY COMMAND
IN THE FATHER
THAT THE FOUR WINDS
OF THE EARTH
SHOULD NOT BLOW I HAVE THE POWER TO SHUT OFF
ON THE EARTH THE VERY MOTION OF MOLECULES
NOR ON THE SEA
NOR ON ANY TREE [7]
NOR ON ANY PLAIN
OVER GOLDEN WHEAT
UNTIL THE GATE

Haan Moses

IS NO LONGER HIDDEN
FROM WHICHEVER SEAL
IS LET LOOSE

THIS IS THE PROCESS ANGELS
CONSCRIPT THE KHRNG INTO
THE WALL OF THE ALL TIME

THE COLOUR OF WAR
IS CHOSEN AND THE SIGN
LEFT IN THE WHEAT
WILL BE HONOURED

UP UNTIL NOW
YOU HAVE BEEN TOLD
OF THREE SEALS
THE SEAL OF THE WHITE
HORSE OF COLD FROST
THE SEAL OF THE RED
HORSE OF PAIN AND BLOOD
AND THE SEAL OF THE BLACK
HORSE OF MEASURES

A RECAPITULATION
OF THE THREE SEALS

NOW I OFFER YOU TO SEE
THE SEAL OF THE PALE HORSE
OF DEEP DREAD AND
WRETCHED DROUGHT AND
HIS NAME THAT SAT ON HIM
WAS DEATH AND HELL
FOLLOWED WITH HIM

THIS IS THE FOURTH SEAL
THE ONE OF PERDITION

POWER WAS GIVEN UNTO THEM
OVER THE FOURTH PART
OF THE EARTH
TO KILL WITH THE SWORD
AND WITH HUNGER
AND WITH DEATH
AND WITH THE BEASTS [8]

357

The Moon Women

Hermoni struggled for a moment. He glanced downwards to gain more strength.

WE SLAY THE OLIVE EYE DEVILS
WITH OUR GOLDEN SWORDS
OF LIGHT AND STRENGTH
BY THE WORD OF THE FATHER

WE BATTLE THE OFFSPRING
OF THE BEAST FROM THE PAST
BY BURNING UP
THEIR HOLD ON THE SEED

WE PASS THE BLACK SERPENTS
THROUGH THE GATE
AND BEWAIL THEM WITH
THEIR OWN DESIRE OF CAPTIVITY
AND WITH OUR PRAYERS   THIS IS SIMPLY ANOTHER
THEREBY WE KILL   DESCRIPTION OF THE ANGELS
THE BLACK PRIESTS BEFORE MEN SLAYING THE KHRNG

ONE OF THE ELDERS SAID TO ME
WEEP NO MORE AND BEHOLD
THE LION OF JUDA   LINEAGE OF HUMANS
LIKE THE ROOT OF DAVID
MAN HAS PREVAILED
TO OPEN HIS BOOK AND HATH   THE SEVEN CHAKRAS OF
LOOSED THE SEVEN SEALS [9]   SPIRITUAL CONSCIOUSNESS

LO IN THE MIDST OF THE THRONE
STOOD A LAMB   THE FORCE OF THE LAMB
HAVING SEVEN HORNS   IS THE ONE WHICH OPPOSES
AND SEVEN EYES   THE RED DRAGON
WHICH ARE THE SEVEN   AND HARNESSES THE SEVEN

358

FROM ABADDON SENT FORTH INTO ALL THE EARTH [10]

The titanium shade sucked the terrifying demon dude back into its midst and then lowered its guillotine blade closing off that other realm. The Time bubble ate itself up and settled out with the surrounding fog, which was pouring down from the hills. Drawn as if by a moth eaten rag, the Moon's toothless jaw floated over the eastern trash heap and chewed on the foamy sky suds as if a toothless derelict.

After I regained my central focus, I let my energies unwind and pool in the core my abdomen, the solar plexus. I let it stew there for quite some time. Now it was time for the mosquitoes to have their turn with me. They were going frantically rabid in their lust for blood, but they were having a hard time penetrating the toxic barrier, which I had created from my automagical potion.

As I churned the energies in my solar plexus like a chef churning butter into a lather, the cyclonic energies grew and grew. While churning and churning, I spread out through the hut and into the surrounding jungle. Continuing to unwind the psycho-magnetic fields of burning gold, I unfolded the petals of my heart and received a divine essence, which surrounded me with a celestial chanting. The voices overwhelmed me with bliss and then blended with the revolving golden light to become a river of Love.

I launched my spirit onto that river and floated down that stream for many, many moments. I came to a vista in which the river delta opened out upon the sea of Time. There was a silky midnight Moon bathing the scene with its radiance. I sailed on and on and on. I was supremely happy. I had no places to which I needed to go, I had no tasks that needed doing, I could find no enemies chasing me, and above all else, no one needed my care. I felt recognized bliss.

As the dying sun lost its grip on the world, a spirituous burgundy blanket unfolded its closure to overtake the horizon as the conqueror, night, embraced the jungle's concubine.

- 9 -

I awoke in a puddle of piss. As I gagged on the remnants of a gasoline hangover, I could see no trace of the mosquitoes anywhere.

The Moon Women

From its perch in a gilded sky, a flawless Moon shone down through the vulgar hole in my shack. I stood up, shook myself, and coughed deeply to clear away some of the tiresome night.

I went over, opened the rickety door and hung on the doorjamb to weigh what my chances might be for splitting from this dump and how soon a positive stroke might fall my way. Emerging from one of the broken down shanties, the dim outline of a figure materialized and began to approach my hut. Oh, great! Sambath Kyew is on the warpath. I've got to seek cover. I squinted my eyes for a little clarification. But, wait. This was not the squat, stumpy excuse for a man named Sambath. This one's guise was much taller and definitely regal. Clothed in mandarin orange robes, the slender man approached my hut with a guided deliberation. There was a subtle glow surrounding him. When he came to the base of the stairs, he looked up.

"Can I trouble you for a spot to rest? This journey has been a long and arduous one." He asked unmindfully.

"Sure. Come on in. It might not smell too nice in here though."

He nodded with a smile and mounted the bulwark of stairs like a cat gliding upon a ribbon of glass. Folding his legs underneath him, he alit into a lotus asana like a butterfly stilling its wings as it took up its post on the rim of a rose. After landing on the bare wood, he placed his hands in the posture of prayer. He didn't shift his eyes but looked unswervingly into mine. That look made me feel uncomfortably wonderful. It was as though I had known this fellow all my life almost as if he were my brother. He looked deep into my being and nodded.

"I am your Brother," he said passionately while I watched all the gears in my head catch up.

"I have come to tell you something of the divine order of life and why the woman is the ideal and not the source of sin. Your charity has compelled me to come. You have withstood the ravages of our Cambodian jungle life. You have secured your mind within these walls. These walls are not your prison, my friend. Know your limits. Know the walls.

"The walls are your Budding Gorn, your source from where the pot takes shape. The pot is struck on its outer skin by the potter's club as the hammering of Time. Nevertheless, the potter's loving

360

hand supports it internally and plies it with the tenderness of Space. This fusion is the Budding Gorn. It is the early stages of one's spiritual development."

Even though his voice was but a whisper, I could grasp his thoughts quite clearly. He slipped his hand into a fold in his ocher robe and pulled out a dried up flower. It looked like a rose, dehydrated and dead.

"This is you," he said matter-of-factly.

He held up the withered flower to me and locked his eyes onto mine. I looked at his ageless features and then down at the lifeless rose. As I looked at it, color seemed to flow into its stem. As its petals shed their brittle death, the head of the flower opened like a pair of lungs sucking in the virgin taste of fresh life. Its pallor drank from the fountains of red magic. Within seconds, the monk was holding a bright, red rose, which was as fresh as the day it was picked from the garden. He looked at me with his spruce and vinegar and said once more.

"This is you. Do I have your attention?"

I was flabbergasted.

"Yes."

I realized at that moment whom this monk really was. He was Siddhartha Gautama, the Buddha.

"No. I am a man just like you."

He said with susurrating calmness. He offered me the rose.

"Smell it."

He showcased the rose but my nose was dead. It always has been numb to aromas. But I couldn't bear disappointing my esteemed visitor so I shared some reason.

"I'm not getting anything. Sorry. It's probably the gasoline," I postulated foolishly.

A faint but lofty smile blossomed within him.

"This is the fragrance of zero, the aroma of Love. When the bindings of attachment fall away, there is only concern for the good. This is the fragrance of the One."

He ascended as if on the command of pure weightlessness, and then turned with one finger shone.

"What one man can do, any man or woman can do. What you have just seen can be done by anybody. It is not a trick. It is life. It is of that which is of you, a human being.

The Moon Women

"The human being is the Supreme Being. God is not what we think God is. Man is the divine chalice and woman is its pedestal.

"The human being was here before Man knew he was Man. The human being will be here after Man has redefined all knowledge.

"It is only within the human being that our original self can reclaim its source, can rejoin with the Maker.

"Within the tree of human lies a seed. This seed is the path of Love.

"The female is both the doorway to the divine as well as the deliverer of death. Know which is which by the fragrance of her blossom for therein lies the salvation of all men.

"The process of Time unfolds primarily due to the process of Love whose essence can only be tasted via a woman. Few are chosen to receive the knowledge of this treasure. You are one of the exceptions. They will come to you and feed you the vision of yourself, your future, and that of the future of the human seed in its entirety.

"By reason of the immeasurable expansion of Time there are no other beings or other creatures in this universe who have been given this gift.

"This is the gift of the One. This is the gift of the Infinite. And this is your gift. Cherish it well."

He snapped his hand and the flower vanished.

"Don't forget the tree, Brother. We all have a tree in our life. Mine was the Bodhi tree under which I sat to bridge the eternity of Time in order to reach the boundless shores of Love. I trust yours conveyed something similar."

He pressed his palms together in supplication and with a delicate bow, he retraced his pathway out of my hut. He crossed the mudsill and soundlessly glided back down the wooden steps. The saffron swathed man walked off into the gingery brush of morning light crawling in over the jungles of Angkor Wat as the two horns of a new Moon hung low over the jungle balancing patience and passion on its scales.

- 10 -

It was fewer than four years preceding my run-in with the mad monk when I was hanging out in a suburban split-level in Newton. It's where I received the principle teaching of the sound-cells.

Normally a portcullis hangs vertically. It is a gateway, which protects commerce and deters savages. Traditionally, it is made of wrought iron; however, today, instead of being a grating of latticework, my portcullis hangs horizontally and it is made of Luann not ferrous oxide.

The sliding door to my closet in the family's moderate ranch in Newton moved like glass. I was stunned with its precision. How was it possible for this gargantuan sheet of wood to move so effortlessly with the whisper of a flea fart? This was my major concern over which I was pondering after having locked myself in that closet. But, my closet had mutated. I had emptied it of everything, which typically resides within a closet: the shoes, pants, shirts, coats and jackets had all fled their homeland to reside on other shelves in my domestic neighborhood. The only items allowed to continue in my closet were my sitting cushion and me.

After replacing the regular bulb up on the ceiling with one from the black light family of incandescence, I leaned back to take in the sights. A hazy purple glow shone down onto the posters laminated onto the sides of my cell, each one bathed in psychedelic sunbursts. Jimi was there and Jerry and his crew. Crosby, Stills, and Nash were there as well. I had once met David down in Coconut Grove when we were smoking buddies out under the swaying palm trees, but I don't think he would remember that banzai trick at this late stage of the game. Mic Fleetwood and Gracie Slick were in there with me, not to mention Dylan who in all likelihood would also not remember getting high with me over in Bard College back in '64 when he had run out of breath on that stupid harmonica of his - just all my good pals having fun.

There was even a poster of a freaky naked guy, which I had dug up in the back of a head shop in Cambridge. I really liked it despite the fact it was admittedly strange. It was a painting of a bareback meditator whose coal tar mane was tied up in a tight knot up on the crest of his crown. His whole body was a bluish color.

The Moon Women

There was an olive green snake curled round his throat, a crescent Moon hanging over his courtyard, and only one caption on the margin at the bottom - Lord Shiva. It was all righteous vibes. This was not simply a place for tripping out and getting stoned. This is where I did the work.

My job back in those days was helping out in a Honda motorcycle shop over on Mass Ave in Cambridge. A few months previously, I had flunked out of Bard College for the second time and had no place to go at that point in my life. I was thinking of pursuing some classes at BU in the spring; maybe try my hand at Geology. I had been a pretty decent rock hound when I was younger. I smoked pot discreetly. There were no other drugs in the house that were mine except of course Dad's but he doesn't count; plus the acid.

Every Friday evening, instead of going out dancing like most post-graduate students, I would go into my closet and drop a couple of tabs. Each was only a single microdot measuring out at approximately five hundred micrograms of LSD but it was enough to get the job done. I also had a pocket flask of Dad's Jack Daniels No. 7, which I sipped occasionally as a chaser or a rudder, you might say, to steer the trip. I had many fascinating voyages back then. I must document them all one day but for now, I am going to relate the most important one, the truths of the sound-cells.

Early on, I learned I had had many, many lifetimes. Plus, I found out I could amplify their purpose and explore side roads never approached previously, the most notable of which was psychedelic research. The one in which I did my most impressive pioneering was the area surrounding the breath and all the techniques employed in its practice. I had discovered I could compress my breath and focus it in such a way as to produce an inner force, which when directed at the primary chakras of the body, would carry me to some extremely exotic places. The experiences in which I had the most success were with the frequencies dominating the chakras: you might call them the resonances. I experienced that each chakra had a particular harmonic or sound-cell, which came out of it when you focused the breath directly on it quite intensely.

Many times, I had nearly blown my eardrums right out of my noodle, because after experimenting with it for months I unlocked the secret you have to work it like a piston and compress the air down into your pulmonary cavity with devastating force. Bringing it up from your lower abdomen, you have to squeeze it like a pneumatic press. This is an elemental technique regarded to be the cardinal practice of Pranayama, or Kundalini Yoga. Moreover, the instructors of this discipline warn no one should perform this exercise without the guidance of competent trainer who has himself consummated these practices; otherwise, death may result.

They are absolutely correct on that score. From the staggering range of possibilities, which I did with myself in that closet, it is a miracle I am alive to talk about it today. Beyond a shadow of a doubt, somewhere out there something or someone is definitely watching over me.

In any case, this is what I learned with respect to the seven thunders, pray tell from where they originate. I am combining the bottom two chakras because they essentially represent a duplicate impetus from the point of view of the true practices. (The lower one in the rectum combines with the next one up in the genitals to make a single focus which can be termed the lower coordinate.) The sound-cell of that place is Ah, or that of the A in the word Anon. The second chakra of the etheric vortexes is in the belly button. Its sound-cell is of Oh, or that of the O in the primary syllable of the word Ohio. The first chakra is the place of pleasure while the second chakra is the place of sustenance, where we consume our food. The third chakra is of the place where our emotions reside, the heart chakra. The sound-cell there is the Uh or that of U in the word Ukulele. The fourth chakra resides in the throat, the wellspring of the faculty of speech. It provides thrust to one's words. It generates a primal fortitude from our body as it comes out when we communicate to those near us. The sound-cell emanating from that chakra is Eh or the E in the word Each. The fifth chakra is that of the eyes. This is the seat of the Over-soul. It is where our consciousness resides and functions when we are in the fully awakened state. The sound-cell of that chakra is of Ih or the I in the word Idle.

There is a chakra in the center of the forehead, but there is no sound in that chakra that I could detect at the time. Additionally I will say that there were some unbelievable lights sparking out of that vortex. Notwithstanding this particular work concerns the sound-cells only, I plan to visit those lights later on and study what they might bring; you can read about those findings in a later book, the Mars one.

The Moon Women

That's about it. This is the most important breakthrough that I documented from the many months of working with LSD in my closet. I am madly proud of this work. It might appear to be a trivial feat of autodidactics, but, I assure you, it is not. It contributes many significant applications for in-depth usage. I see nothing wrong with asserting one could conceivably reach the thresholds of the astral plane simply by using the science of these sound-cells. Be that as it may, extreme care must be employed in summoning these forces. Don't try this at home, kids. This is not like collecting matchbooks with your buddies. If you're not careful, you might just go up in smoke.

As an icy lunar cuticle shed its skin, pint-sized crescents filled the skies with kooky gaiety.

- 11 -

Back in Cambodia, after providing a tasty buffet for the needle-faced vampires as evidenced by my red, polka-dotted shirt, I reclaimed some semblance of sanity as dawn seeped into my hut. Paradoxically my vitality had strengthened and the edge of my awareness was quite acute. I flattened my sights upon a clump of bamboo, which had encroached on the outskirts of Sambath's territory. It seemed the ghosts of his ancestors were hiding in the tops of the bamboo drooping humbly from the invisible weight of a phantom sniper with a .308 Model 700 Remington taking aim from a perch seven years into the future to rid the bending stems of their Buddhist backlog.

A leering Cheshire Moon had surrendered itself to the sparks of sunrise, which was now invading my fragmented containment. The stench of urine, gasoline, and overnight body odor clutched the back of my throat. I got up, put my arms behind my back, clasped my hands together, and bent forward towards the ground: a basic yogic feat, which I had used occasionally for preparation in the face of tough work ahead.

From atop the mud of his midland, his primary stomping grounds, Sambath Kyew rode a downy carpet of chickens to the foot of my hut. Menacingly he surmounted the four wooden stairs with two clomps of his clodhoppers, pushed back the scrawny door, and scanned the darkness. What he saw was only an empty hut. His yawning grin unzipped a brassy grill advertising sheer glee. Since the manifest emptiness convinced him I had fled, he erupted into spasms of laughter cut short as he collapsed into a choking cough. When he gasped to grab more air, his molars came into view and reminded me of the blocks of the Angkor ruins, worn away at the edges and bedecked with a mossy slim.

Since I was crouched down behind the door in the side shadows under the luminance of the sad window and the weak morning moon, he hadn't located me right away; his demeanor was one of victory. As he was rewarding himself with his shallow triumph, I stepped forward into view to proclaim my newfound innocence.

"Bon matin, mon bel ami! Je suis le Bouddha!" [Good morning my fine friend! I am the Buddha!]

He sprang back in shock. Thereupon he commenced to vomit plural expletives and venomous multi-lingual curses as his oral rag flapped so fast and so wide I could see a disturbing esoteric Buddhist numeral tattooed there like some weird stigmata branded onto the center of his tongue like a black cancer. I had to back away from the mustard gas spewing out of his facial orifice. But then, I reversed my march and strolled directly over to him, lowered my mug into his and brayed.

"You're finished my little copper colored pal. The Buddha and I will be leaving right about now. C'est fait!" [This is done!]

I shoved passed him cutting off any of his malapert comments. I leaped down those four wooden steps for the last time in a single bound and headed for town.

After I had hiked nearly until noon, I came upon one of the gate entrances to an accessory temple. I took a breather on a slab of twelve hundred year rubble sheathed with the traditional puss yellow lichens, which grew year-round like dead snow forever encapsulating the presence of perfection where ever it might have attempted to sprout in this standoff against the midnight Buddha. The capacious archway was a stout seven meters on either run and a nearly twenty meters in elevation where it tapered to an apex. A dirt road ran through it and off into the distance. Its singular presence spelled an invitation, which I feared I must turn down; not this morning I'm afraid, my triple-headed amigo, not this morning.

The Moon Women

Rising over the arch were the conjoined triple heads of Brahma, Vishnu and Shiva. Labeled as the triad of Angkor's persona, they had served as the vehicles of this special faith for over a thousand years. Those wide-nosed, bulging lipped visages crowned with ten layered dome-like hats sat as central figures. They epitomized both the Hindu as well as the Buddhist schemes of death coalesced into one concise religious mass. Whiffs of a bygone time, a dead time, blew off the dusty hide of this Asian trinity. Its aroma was like the smell of last week's coitus and stale oatmeal.

A single star appeared over the central figurehead and then receded into the departure of the day. As I waited for my rescue team to arrive, I recalled the chronicle of one of the renowned Buddhas by the name of Dhamma. He was the Buddha whom history credits for giving birth to the origin of the original human couple. As the story goes, they were created from two letters of the alphabet. Dhamma created the male from a consonant and the female from a vowel, the former being that of discord and the latter, that of harmony. Together they made all the languages, all the histories, and all the knowledge, which we have today. The entirety of all known existence came into focus from those two primitive sounds, but that does seem to be a slight stretch considering what Father Lemaitre came up with on the day without a yesterday.

With his tight collar and habit, a different Catholic Priest, Father Thaddaeus, was walking towards me while balancing his towering French bicycle with its single enormous wheel. He was sermonizing aloud from his missal. It wasn't unusual to run into full-blooded Christians aimlessly plodding along the roadside in the midst of this Buddhist realm of rice. They had infested all societies over the centuries like Chinese carp. He orated in hushed tones as he drifted by us.

"Take thou also unto the wheat, and barley, and beans, and lentils, and millet, and fitches and put them into one vessel and make thee bread." [11]

It seemed the moral of the wheat had now bled through the five tunnels of my life. The Vicar narrated the lines blending the fire with the flour to produce some ilk of spiritual food. I picked myself up and bore my scars of Angkor off towards the horizon while the merit of the mosquitoes followed me down the dusty road. When I looked back, I could see someone hiding in that archway, suffering like a fool.

Devereux and Chhumpar had driven over from the Auberge in the jeep piloted by Mr. Lee who was serving as chaperon. I was rescued! Chhumpar jumped out and threw her arms around me and Devereux slapped me on the back.

"Tres beaucoup, Monsieur [Very well, Sir]. Well done!"

He cheered my victory over the parasitic fiends of the bloodthirsty night. I related my tale of the mosquitoes, and how Sambath's main trick had been a sadistic ploy to humiliate me and gain more sick dominance over Chhumpar. Now, she was free to go forward and claim her independence. The Inspector wheeled the desecrated jeep in the other direction. It was time to get married!

"What for the rials, Monsieur?" Devereux wasn't trying to jump ahead of me. He was making sure I didn't slip up.

"If he wants his loot, he can come and get it! I don't care. I'm a man of my word. I know he proposed a winner takes all plan, but that was his greed taking over, not mine. Have the Inspector confirm this with the bastard. He'll know where I'm coming from and that I'm no shyster as like he is. He knows where I'm staying and he can jolly well do some leg work for a change. However, he is not to receive one penny over the fifty thousand that he so egotistically undercut himself. You please be sure of that, Mon Ami. I'm still okay with your buying the Nikormat, but the balance goes to Chhumpar,"

We turned to encounter the oncoming road as the Inspector conveyed what he could explain to Chhumpar. As the jeep moved out, she squealed with chimerical joy and sung a sweet Cambodian song to herself. I pointed Devereux in the direction of the municipal district court of the KPC so we could track down the ranking magistrate. I wasn't yet ready to divulge my rendezvous with His Holiness. I was savoring that deep inside me never to be let out.

"Let's do the deal now before time runs out or some other damn thing happens. I need to tell you something later."

We came to a lurching stop curbside to the miserable building and we all piled out. Devereux handed five large to the Inspector with which to grease the balding monkey's palms. The four of us waltzed into the mildewy office with as much bravado as we could muster. The magistrate arranged all the papers and pointed to the dotted lines on which we had to sign. With a stamped and official marriage

The Moon Women

certificate, at long last Devereux pronounced us husband and wife and dropped the green flag on our race to secure connubial bliss.

Chhumpar gave me a wet smooch on the cheek. I informed Devereux we should now schedule the honeymoon. We all laughed. But for now I've gotta get a bath. Everybody whooped it up some more including the magistrate. We all jumped back into the classic jeep and rattled off toward the Auberge. I had insisted to Devereux that for the time being, Chhumpar should stay in her own room. I couldn't allow the Monkey Man or any of the daily clientele to get the wrong idea and spoil the outcome for her. Devereux had indicated to me she was adamant about going as far away from this place as possible. Phnom Penh was as likely a starting point as any other, so be it, I thought. I made a beeline towards the bathroom to lose myself in that marmoreal tub for a righteous soaking. If I had contracted malaria from all the bites, perchance a good French bath could stem the tide.

My chamber at the Auberge had no bathroom, so I had to use the one, which was outside it down at the end of the hall. The enormous cavern of the soaking place contained disenfranchised relics purloined from Angkor as decorative placements. It was also somewhat startling to find an ample collection of Cambodian wall hangings populating the wall areas of this tub room plainly put there to hide the misery of its shameful underpinnings. Many stays in Asian hostels present similar arrangements now made more palpable by the Speak.

As the warm steam from the bath engulfed my waking state, repressed thoughts of the starfish hands of the Khrng surfaced in my soaking dreams. One was examining the flesh behind my ears and another was unpeeling my penis from a suction devise. The ugly remembrances crept over me like stale broccoli as the sun smeared its acid streak across the slate of the oncoming dusk.

As I shook off those cobwebs, I wondered what Chhumpar could be up to. Swathed in multiple towels I was fully refreshed and had only one item on my agenda, a full night of shut-eye. As I swung back the door, Chhumpar was sitting on the bed. Oh boy, it's been a long day and an even longer night. I really needed some rest.

I gently picked her up with my hands on each shoulder, scooted her over to the settee, and sat her flower down gently not forgetting her thorns.

"Ici [Here]." I dictated firmly but in a near whisper.

After shedding all but one towel, I plucked a pair of briefs from out of my rucksack and hoisted them to the tune of Dixie and plopped myself down on the bed. I put my head back on the pillow and took a deep breath, what they call a sighing breath. I was dead tired.

I must have drifted off, because before I knew it there was a tugging going on at my waist. I blinked my eyes and there was Chhumpar delicately undoing the one remaining towel so cautiously so as not to wake me. I was aghast at this and forcefully grabbed her arm.

"No yum yum."

Looking her in the eye, I wagged my monishing finger at her like a truce flag. Unfortunately, that was my major faux pas. As those haunting eyes bore into mine, her face was as translucent as moonlight peering through fog.

"No yum yum." She pouted and leaned over to kiss me tenderly on the lips. It was a sweet and passionate kiss. Moreover, it was like kissing the petals of a flower. No such rose had ever kissed me before and this rose was a bouquet all in herself.

I kissed her back and tasted all the exotic flavors of young girl and cantaloupe. She removed my towel and climbed up on top of me.

"No yum yum. Chhumpar no . . ."

But before I could enforce the rules we were making love. With the music of her body, she drew out of me every mosquito bite, which I had endured back in Sambath's hut of afflictions. It was an encounter, the likes of which burned into my cellular mental windings for all eternity. We rolled over and made the body worship missionary style, only I readjusted her legs up over my shoulders. Since she was a young maiden, I guided her in this new movement of delight but she required little instruction. Our love flower blossomed in the moonlight. At the pinnacle of this climactic union, she started to sing. She sang the loveliest Khampuchean ballad, which went on and on. After our love dance increased in multiplications of infinity out upon the cotton beachheads, she feathered my back with the tendrils of her hair scented with jasmine and spice.

The Moon Women

Crack of dawn we got up and met Devereux in the dining area for coffee and croissants. He was hot to trot for getting his hands on my Nikormat. Handing the rig over to him right away, I urged him to get going with mastering it all. Meantime, Chhumpar had ordered the elderly harpy working the desk not to blow it with the Monkey Man.

"Where's the Gibbon?" I cocked my head toward the apogee of the rogue asteroid.

"Je ne sais pas, Monsieur. Perhaps, 'e is spreading zee wealth." He dispensed a pithy chuckle and retracted his meerschaum. Must be he thinks clearer with that jug in his mug.

"Are we set with the payouts?" I was checking because at this late inning I the game, I couldn't afford anything to go wrong.

"Oui, Monsieur. Ca va [Yes, Sir. It's Okay]!" He fired back.

I trusted Devereux. He was a good man. We had come through an incredible gauntlet in less than a week. I hoped it was as meaningful for him as it was for me. I had him put together a package of half a lakh of rials with which to pay off Sambath Kyew when he reported for duty. The leftovers I suggested Devereux hang onto and transfer to Chhumpar at the appropriate juncture. It wouldn't be good to have her brood over any of it, or, God forbid, get arrested by the agents of the KPC, the Kampuchean Communist Party, for carrying illegal funds. Those Marxist bastards carried the mark of the beast.

The Inspector arrived at the exact moment Sambath showed up. The audacity! I thought the timing was ironic to say the least. Sambath had the twisted bearing of a magnate of the moment. He pounced on his package and checked it thoroughly. When he departed, he aimed his bung-toothed grimace my way. I could see the gold flashing in his eyes. As the three of us enjoyed a pleasant chat with our coffee, Chhumpar was hanging onto me with a glorious gratitude, which might have been more than appropriate but I knew there was a valid reason for it. Protesting would have been futile anyway. Devereux relinquished one of those sparky-eyed jogs he had tucked up his sleeve.

All of a sudden, the Monkey Man came tearing back into the lobby shouting and throwing his arms all over like Don Quixote attacking the windmills.

"What's going on?" I looked over at Devereux.

"The Monkey says zhat zee armies of General Lon Nol are marching through Srah Srang. We must flee immediately or face extraction!" He expressed rather extreme urgency - to stay meant certain capture.

Devereux informed me, in no uncertain terms, he must rescue Chhumpar by evacuating into Thailand through the border at Poipet. With my American passport, I was safe to journey onto Phnom Penh and continue with my itinerary through Singapore to Kuala Lumpur.

Chhumpar looked remarkably unsettled, but she also looked defiant and determined as well. As I studied her expression intently, I knew she would be safe with Devereux.

She came over to me, put her hands together, and said, "Bong srawlagnh oun, Rahmatma." [I love you. Rahm.]

"I love you, too, Chhumpar; be well and be safe." We embraced and kissed one parting farewell. She was my sweet, sweet Rose whom I shall never forget. Some years later, I was fortunate enough to learn through some fellow travelers from FWC that Devereux had wound up marrying Chhumpar in a sumptuous wedding ceremony and were now residing happily on the 26 floor of a skyscraper in Singapore. He had cornered the prime echelons in the Singapore commodities market and she was doing quite well as entrepreneur of a Cambodian clothing line in the midtown Mall there. Nevertheless, I suspected that in all probability their brains continued to be probed by the Khrng.

- 12 -

Another rap on the door snapped me back into my undulating chair. It took me a second or two to figure out why there was such a pother of smoke in the K-room. Apparently, five sticks of Loghand agrabathi were too much. Waving my hand to disperse my confusion, I grabbed for the levered handle but it swung back before I could get to it.

"How are you doing this fine day Mr. Rahms, Sir?" Dr. K always insisted on calling me that witless Indianized title.

"Been waiting for you." I replied. "Come and sit."

"Oh my Paramatma. Fine. Quite fine I am. This came for you via post." He handed me a wrinkled paper.

"What is it? From my father?" I sensed the long arm of the

The Moon Women

blood doctor honing in on me.

"Looks to be some charges. Phone Wallah left it. Please read it and then I shall like to tell you something about Yugas."

I looked at the note and it made no sense. It wasn't from the Phone Wallah at all. It was from my tailor, Mr. Kalazaki, over on Commercial Street; a few scribbled lines, which stated some obscure phrases about how he was having trouble procuring the correct fabrics from the Akashic weavers. He had lost contact with certain of his inter-resident dimensions. I looked up with a baffled expression.

"There is no purpose in perplexity, Mr. Rahms. Whether or not, you feel caged by uncontrollable factors has no bearing on your inevitabilities with regard to Time. Have you ever heard of something called a Yuga?"

"Yeah, it's a chunk of Time, like the rind of bologna, which you throw away before lunch."

"Interesting, but no cigarette, Mr. Rahms. Let me ask you a most simple question. You have been educated in your schools of mathematics and scientific information; is it not?"

"Not new, Dr. K. Get to the point. By the way, it's cigar. Close but no cigar. Oh, never mind."

"I can no longer admit to my unintended correctableness. I'm sure you are with me. So, to continue, please follow the ball bouncing and answer me this one hot chili pepper. Why is it, when the hands of a clock go round and round, do your wizards think Time runs in a straight line? When moons orbit planets in circles and planets orbit suns in elliptical paths, why do people think Time starts at one point and continues in straight movement into the future for ever and ever? Why, even Mr. Hubble has demonstrated big galaxies spiral endlessly into infinity. So, why do they plot Time with a ruler? Don't you think that is somewhat odd, Mr. Rahms?"

"Well, now that you mention it, it does seem a bit queer but it's hard to break that train of thought. If you're brought up thinking a certain way, only solid evidence can change your mind. You know what I mean?"

"Right on my nose as you hits your nail! That is why one day someone like your same self will write a book that will do such a thing, it will profess that clear sentiment, Mr. Rahms. Such a fellow, we won't mention whom, will present some hard evidence for considering Time is not linear at all, but cyclical. Now please pay careful attention to what I'm about to tell you with the right money." Dr. K began to explain the different phases of Time and how they manifest, an explanation he stated came straight from a set of Vedic scriptures entitled the Upanishads.

"The first thing to know, and this is the decisive factor which differentiates Vedic Time from linear Time, is that there isn't simply one flavor of Time; there are four distinct phases of the Time/Space continuity. These phases are the Yugas. There are of course many planes of physical realities, but they contain somewhat unexplainable energies and their etymology is not required reading at this point as I'm sure you can appreciate since it's this close to meals. The Misses is preparing them with all love but for now, please focus on the subject of Time/Space and its products. I'm sure you must be wondering how they might affect you and what you think you are doing as you spin in that silly chair of yours while feebling with that hair string in your hands all day.

"Really? Feebling, eh? Let me show you feebling." I grabbed a mango and prepared to heave it at him.

"Hold it. Just follow me on this for a minute. I promise it is both inimical and educational as well. Our physical world is variously constructed of dimensions, which are regulated by specific laws. Is it not? Three hundred years back our French friend defined the first three as he watched a fly crawling erratically on his ceiling. Ceilings are remarkable objects for insight and invention, don't you think, Mr. Rahms? Don't answer. I'm sure you might have had a run or two with those winsome fields of genius. So sorry, I digress.

"Only recently, the fourth one was disclosed by a young man who liked to watch trains. I'm sure you can appreciate trains and how they are so very special vehicles; quite often they can offer revealing points of view concerning certain hard to explain circumstances, but more on that later. The fourth dimension is Time, or as Uncle Albert once labeled it, the fabric of Time/Space, which wraps us like a shell. And like the first three, its finality as truth cannot be easily altered. Just as you can't cheat with the pegs of Cartesian coordinates, neither can you mess with the laundry of Time/Space.

"According to the Vedas, within our particular universe this dimension, called Time/Space, can manifest under four different modes or segments, which is another way of saying each has a list of

The Moon Women

ingredients that define its phases as they manifest under four different archetypes. The Time/Space duality is not only a river, it has also been described as a dragon chasing its own tail, biting it at one end while chasing after itself in an endless and futile endeavor to consume itself into oblivion. From this model, you can see the Time/Space fabric is not linear; it is cyclical. And so, not only do these dimensions propagate themselves out in four separate and distinct divisions, they also involve themselves in ceaseless repetition. As well, each specific segment of the Time/Space demon exhibits periodic transformations at its culmination.

"For structural integrity we need to present each Time period as having its own specifications. For added clarity, we are going to use the terms found within one of the most ancient of human writings known as the Vedas and the one from which this news comes to us is the Rigveda. Western historical examination puts the origin of this collection of inscriptions at about eight to eleven thousand years back. Regardless, the truth of the matter is one or two of them go back much farther than that. Surprisingly they were authored (and don't fall out of your chair) millions of years ago, when the Moon was much closer to her brother, and likewise, shone her lunar presence in double furculum over the landside.

"One of the subjects those scrolls discuss is the meanings of specific time periods, or epochs called Yugas. A Yuga is a distinct unit of Time/Space. And as a distinct unit, it must follow specific characteristics as far as its boundaries and moreover its functionality. The actual constituent frequencies of the "strings" upon which all matter which exists during a particular unit of Time/Space is set or tuned differently than other Yugas. Therefore, the precise structures of the atomic building blocks of existence are unique to whichever Yuga is in existence. Even though those frequencies are infinitesimally similar, still they are unique and therefore disharmonious.

"This is the primary reason that all the things which occurred in one Yuga are unavailable to the inhabitants of another Yuga. The histories of each timeline is apparent to the subsequent existences of each consecutive Time segment; however, other than the passing of legends and stories by subsequent access to the Akashic records, nothing from one Yuga ever survives into the next one. In a similar fashion, the makeup of the mental energies during each Yuga is alterable as well. Even the composition of the spiritual energies, which surround the mental stuff and the matter of each age, is particular to that specific time slice.

"The Rigveda lists four Yugas: Sat, Treta, Dwarpar, and Kali. Pundits also refer to these four as Ages called the Golden, Silver, Copper, and the Iron Age respectively. These derivations have nothing to do with our own Paleolithic nomenclatures buried within extant archeological definitions. These are purely Dravidian concepts and as such, I suggest you regard them in a completely different light.

"A Yuga is a period of Time/Space having certain potentialities of matter, mind, and spirit, which differentiate it from its adjacent period. Essentially, this cyclical process starts with the commencement of Sat Yuga in which the Maker creates everything as perfect, proficient, and pure. Then, because of the downward pull of the thoughts, words, and actions of the humans alive at the time, everything becomes more and more diluted, dense, and dirty. It becomes more polluted and less pure of form. Yes, that's right. You heard me correctly. Humans exist during all segments of the Time/Space process.

"My dear Mr. Rahms, at this point in the discussion I would like to call your attention to one of the most unusual concepts of Vedic cosmology - the true status of the human being with regard to all physical existence. Humans, as such, have existed ever since the very beginning of the Time/Space continuum, no matter which epoch we are discussing. Human is a spiritual construct and as such is the prima fascia element for the entire existence of the physical world. Without this necessary ingredient, no level of physicality can come into being. Do you follow me?

"Yeah. It's like because we think we are, we are. Is that it?"

"That could be the ticket."

"I don't know. What if I think you're not? Would you then disappear, because apparently it's not working."

"Not a blue ribbon event, Mr. Rahms; just listen. For those of us raised on the traditional diet of learning, this concept is extremely difficult to accept or imagine. Regardless, it will become the primary reason you yourself will turn away from the frayed concepts like the Big Bang, special acceleration or even the different colors of energy, not to mention the worn out conception of linear Time/Space.

The Moon Women

Instead, these shall all be replaced with this new outlook of cyclical Time, the one, which engenders the dualistic principle of the Time/Love unit, or the Yuga. It will aid you in your work of shattering those brittle concepts of yore and replacing them with the new truths of these Yuga epochs, the altered Time/Space segments. Furthermore, this revolutionary concept will add fuel to your drive to compile a book containing an anthology of flashbacks, which will inspire the world to open their eyes to the coming truths from out of the Beyond.

"To continue, each period of Time/Space, or Yuga, is ended with a somewhat massive shift of its actual molecular structures and how they exist or vibrate. This end time also translates into mutations within the genetic matrices of life as well. The manner in which these basic laws of physics unfold, the amount of brainpower available to all sentient beings and the degree to which their jivas can travel and transcend into the spiritual boundaries are the constituent variables, which define each Yuga. Each one has its own specific composition, which manifests in the definitions and dimensions of the human beings, which live during each particular epoch.

"To repeat, the most important factor concerning the true structure of Time/Space is these four phases of Time/Space are cyclical. In other words, after the fourth one ends, the first one commences with its new beginnings once again. As the last of the set, Kali, completes, then everything reverts back to the way things were during the genesis time when the pure and uncontaminated realm emerges into existence. Thus, the four periods repeat and repeat. If the beginning Yuga, the Sat Yuga, were the number 1 and the fourth and final Yuga, Kali Yuga, were 4, they would repeat like this: 1,2,3,4,1,2,3,4,1,2, etc. There is never a jump from, say, 1 to 3, or from 4 to 2, or 2 to 4. They always repeat consecutively, somewhat like the stages of insect metamorphosis: egg, larva, pupa, adult, and back to egg, etc.

"Now we need to interject a helpful concept concerning the measurement of these Time/Space segments and study something about spatial geometry. Using what we call the Moon Unit, each Time/Space epoch is graduated. You know the Moon revolves around the Earth in approximately 29 days, 12 hours and 44 minutes. It is irrelevant this duration has changed since the beginning. Simply see the orbital regularity as a standard. This length of time multiplies out to 42,254 minutes [(29 X 24 X 60) + (12 X 60) + 44] = 42,254). In our model, we use this structured analog as a single unit of Time/Space just as the second is considered the elementary unit of daily time.

When the orbital distance of any moon equals its rotation, one side permanently faces the planet. This feature underscores the measuring unit of our celestial clock. In our solar system, there is no other moon or planet, which exemplifies this condition. It is the reason we use it as the prime element, the one, which comprises the stepping-stone for each of the Time/Space Yugas in our solar system. We give this primary form of measurement the name of Moon Cycle. And no, it has nothing to do with Frank Zappa and his first daughter, Moon Unit. As a hophead, maybe he was into something no one else knew. You guessed it. He had turned onto and tuned into the Vedas.

"The Earth orbits our star, the Sun, in approximately 365 days, yet we must add one day every four years to adjust for a discrepancy in our measuring system. If we made an initial calculation for it we would find it is 525,960 minutes [(365 X 24 X 60) + (24 X 60 / 4) = 525,960]. To be even more precise, we should also add one day every four centuries or about 4 more minutes [(24X60)/400 = 3.6] making the total 525,964; this is the Earth Cycle. The effect of this correction is relatively inconsequential; in any case, it does demonstrate our arbitrary timeline units (defined as seconds, minutes, hours, days, weeks, and months) do not measure the orbit of the Earth properly or, more importantly, accurately.

"If you view the Earth as if looking down on it while floating above the North Pole, you can visualize the lines of longitude running out and away from the central hub of the axis as if the spokes of a wheel. If you place an imaginary mark at the precise point (degree) where the Earth is closest to the Sun, where it points directly at the Sun, and record that number in degrees, you have a starting point. After a complete orbit, that is, one entire revolution of the Earth around the Sun, you find it now points to a slightly different degree point than the previous one. To be clear, if you examine the precise degree of longitude of the Earth pointing to the Sun and compare it to your first reading you will find they are not the same. This is why we have these minute adjustments in our clocks because our clocks do not reflect the truth about Time/Space.

The Moon Women

"If you can visualize this in your head, you can understand the importance of the relationship between the Moon and the Earth. That unique relationship is in itself a significant clue in establishing the great and sublime relevance of why humans chose this place to be home. As the Moon orbits the Earth and the Earth orbits the Sun, you can see it would take quite a while for the two celestial bodies to go round and round and eventually come back to the precise spot, which they started (where the precise degree of angle of the Earth pointing toward the Sun, as well as the Moon pointing toward the Earth, relative to their orbits as well as their axial tilt and plane of orbit, would repeat right down to the minute of a degree).

"I must now enlist the aid of my blackboard." Dr. K. slid back a run of cloth to reveal a hidden slate board having an old-fashioned tray at its base littered with white powder. He picked up a piece of chalk and quickly scratched out four lines of simple arithmetic. Having good grades in all my calculus classes back in prep school, I followed along easily.

"The amount of time it takes the Earth and the Moon to return to the exact same spot is basically the time of the Moon's revolution, the Moon Cycle, which is 42,254 minutes, multiplied by the Earth's revolution, the Earth Cycle, which is 525,964 minutes." Dr. K fingered the upper two lines.

"That product multiplied times the ratio of axial tilt relative to each body (23.44 / 5.86 = 4.02) produces (525,964 X 42,254 X 4.02 = 89,340,813,081 minutes) which translates into approximately 169,980 or 170 thousand years. This span of Time/Space duration is called the Moon Unit." Dr. K indexed the last two lines.

"You can do the math in your own head if you like. I recommend you agree with the written numbers, but if you wish, check them out at your leisure, but trust me, it isn't really worth it. Plus, we're not even considering the seconds which if used would probably work out the same way; nevertheless, the principle is the same and the result is the same.

"Because of the difference between the revolution of the Moon and that of the Earth, this is the only multiple of the two, which can contain both factors. The Pundits of yesteryear designated this value as a segment or a unit of measuring Time/Space. Since this calculation for the length of Time resident in one Moon Unit is approximately 170 thousand years, we now have a measuring stick with which we can outline the Yugas. Each Yuga uses a relative ratio of the measurement as 2, 5, 8 and 10 based on the Rigveda which lists the time periods in numbers of Moon Units. The first Yuga, Sat Yuga, is 10 Moon Units long, or 1.7 million years. The second Yuga, Treta Yuga, is 8 Moon Units, or 1.36 million years. The third one, Dwarpar Yuga, is 5 or 850 thousand years and the last and fourth Yuga, Kali Yuga, is 2 Moon Units long or 340 thousands years long.

"The four Yugas themselves take 25 Moon Units to transpire or about four and a quarter million years. Every four cycles of these four Yugas, which takes about 17 million years, there is a minor transformation labeled as a pralaya. During that time there are many subtle changes made to the physical universe as well as certain delicate genetic adjustments. Every one hundred passes of these 4 cycles, or about 1.7 billion years, there is a medium pralaya during which time significant changes in the physical universe as well as major alterations to genetic properties take place. Lastly, every one hundred occurrences of the medium cycle, or about 170 billion years, there occurs a mega-pralaya, or a major transformation. The entire physical universe is sucked back up into the Akash where it goes into a sort of limbo or total Time/Space suspension before the powers that be decide whether or not it is going to be blown out again into another creation, similar to the Big Bang but different; more on that later.

"This extrapolates out to reveal the entire lifetime of any particular physical universe is approximately 170 billion years, of which we have only done about eight percent so far. The important thing to learn and understand at this point concerns the things, which must occur at the end of the Kali Yuga and how those events can shift reality from the relatively short time frame of the Iron Age (2 Moon Units) to the rejuvenated and extensive time frame of the Golden Age (10 Moon Units). Prior to this document, no one has ever revealed what those events are; not to mention the actual ingredients of the changes, which must occur before the beginning of the next cycle can commence. But before we go into that, we need to entertain a thorough explanation of each one of the Yugas, their makeup and the whys and wherefores behind them. When you understand the structure of these four Yugas, you will be armed with a knowledge, which will enable you to write your book, the one which will explain what human beings are, where they came from, why they work in the

The Moon Women

manner in which they do and what is going to be happening with them in the future. So, pay very close attention, please, Mr. Rahms!

"The first of the four Yugas is the Sat Yuga, or the Golden Age. In the Golden Age, the dynamics of the DNA pool for the human being is such that the levels of the physical are considerably weak. Weak in the sense that not much affects the physical body. A human body can exist for many thousands of years, as many as a hundred thousand. Mental energies are also somewhat low. Mind can easily be controlled. That just means people can easily still the mind without much effort. This facility allows easy access to the upper planes spiritually, since the gate to those realms is like a sort of mental gravity. The laws of physics are in their finest form. Matter is beautifully pure and refined. There is no taboo on the use of supernatural powers. Humans are supermen. The level of spiritual energy is the highest of the four Yugas. Physical matter can be manipulated at will. Souls come and go through the inner planes at will. The average length of life for a human being is between 85,000 and 100,000 years, or about half a Moon Unit. One human being ranges in height from 15 to 30 meters. Because of the way the laws of physics are structured, the molecular properties and the compression settings on the Time/Space dilation principle, i.e. normal gravity, most anything is possible to manifest for humans during this epoch. Levitation, mind reading, overcoming all physical limitations of space, creating matter from thought, all these are common occurrences during Sat Yuga.

"There are no traces of these human beings because at death their bodies turned into pure energy and dissipated into thin air. Whatever physical existence any particular Yuga maintains is also not discernable geologically or by any other scientific way since the molecular structures of that period were significantly different then from now. Any historical statement of that epoch does not portray, even in a minor way, anything about the physical world, which existed during that timeframe. This Age lasted for ten Moon Units or about 1,690,000 years. At the end of this period, an incarnation of one of the core deities, namely Shiva, Brahma or Vishnu, was dispatched into the world as an Avatar to initiate a micro-pralaya, a transition into the next of the Yuga segments, the Treta Yuga. During the time of this period of change, subtle shifts in the balance of the six states of matter and energy as well as modifications within the structure of DNA itself occur as necessary prerequisites for the emergence the next phase. With the exception of one male-female couple, all individual representations of the human species is completely exterminated. This single bonding couple represents the humans who will create the continuation of humanity in the birth of the coming new age.

"The blue print architecture for the DNA coding of the next Yuga is generated from the thoughts, words, and actions of the one surviving male alive at the end of that Time period. The main life of this individual is in direct proportion to the square root of the combined conscious history of all the collected beings who lived during that Age. The Nirunjan, or the powerhouse being who creates and maintains the present physical universe, selects this person as the seeding benefactor for the coming age. All available resources from his respective Yuga come to his aid for performing this mission. The manner of transition or micro-pralaya also depends upon which types of things happened to the seed choice and his lifetime as well as how he relates to the creative forces. There are no exceptions or deviations to this process; it is a model, which reciprocates at the end of each Yuga.

"The second of the four Yugas is the Treta Yuga, or the Silver Age. In this Yuga the level of matter is slightly more dense and dross than the previous one. That is the step down process of the Time/Space continuum. The vibratory wavelengths of the molecules are not as refined as in the previous age. There is a little bit more of a pressure upon the basic laws of physics. Kinetic energies come more into play. The levels of mind also increase slightly as well, making it a little harder to control the mind. Not everyone has instant access to the inner realms. This is the Yuga, in which methodologies and practices for controlling the mind begin to form and find some success. The use of tappas, or austerities such as fasting, physical hardships, self-flagellation, etc., is the easiest of the methods employed for reaching the inner regions. The levels of soul power are also slightly reduced. One must devote a considerable length of time to any particular practice for experiencing the inner realities. Distinct from that, some "gifted" personas still have instant access to the higher realms. They are referred to as 'Gurus," meaning, light givers. The average height of a human of this Yuga is between 8 to 10 meters and lifetimes can top out at 10,000 years. This Age lasted

The Moon Women

for approximately 8 Moon Units, or about 1.35 million years. An incarnation of Shiva came the last time to take the residents of Treta Yuga into extinction. During the last occurrence of this Yuga, his name was Narayan, whereas the name of the avatar in the last Sat Yuga was Rama. Wind becomes the manifesting energy, which affects the transition of that age into the next. There were winds in excess of 2000 kph, which removed everything from the surface of the planet into outer space.

"The third Yuga is the Dwarpar Yuga, or the Copper Age. The matter in this age is also much more dross than the previous Yuga. Although, if some pieces of Treta matter bled through into the Copper phase, they would appear to have miraculous properties. It would be as a mega-structure, which would seem to glow. It would seemingly appear and then disappear as its molecules moved in and out of the different shifts within the Time/Space dimenson. This of course is hardly possible; it is simply an example of the phase shifts. The level of mental energy in this Yuga increases to the point where control of the mind is attainable but only with some serious effort. It can be done, but only after centuries of regular practice. The austerities still can be successful, but the most effective means of controlling the mental energies is via control of the breath along with a combination of manipulating the seven chakras or vortexes or etheric power within the body. Kriya yoga as well as Kundalini yoga developed during this segment as the best and most practical manner to reach the inner planes. In either case, one must have a competent teacher to be successful with it; otherwise, deleterious results could unfold. The average lifetime in the Copper Age is between 850 to 990 years. And the average height is between 3 and 6 meters. This Yuga lasted about 845,000 years of five Moon Units. The incarnation to end this epoch the last time went by the name of Krishna. He was an avatar incarnate form of Vishnu. He ended the Yuga with a massive war and finally uncontrollable waters released via a global annihilation flooded and covered over ninety nine percent of the planet's surface eliminating everything. This event occurred approximately 217,000 years ago. "Surprisingly enough, that figure coincides with what present day anthropologist plot for the emergence of modern man and his traceable histories as supported by unearthed bones and skull fragments. All of the antithetical prehistoric knowledge of Man's crawl up the so-called Darwinian evolutionary ladder can only be approximated by theories derived from specimens fossilized in stone which, because of the divergence of the Yugas, are misleading at best.

"The fourth and final Yuga is the Kali Yuga, or the Iron Age. In Kali Yuga, matter is king. It is the most dross and the most impure. All of the laws of physics are empowered with their most complicated forms. Mental energies are rampant and as the Yuga progresses, almost uncontrollable. Even miniscule examinations into the microscopic and the macroscopic worlds require enormous quantities of mental energy. Heightened levels of human consciousness and intelligence are capable by only a handful of individuals. All of this reduces the average individual's ability to a decidedly low level. For this reason, the advent of religion occurs to assuage the miseries of the masses.

"Unfortunately, the predominance of the knowledge of matter does open up the door to atomic tinkering because matter is the greatest challenge to the mind. Although, mental energies are the strongest in this age, great spans of living are required for any noticeable progress to come about within the human population. The mind controls the jiva's fate almost exclusively as it becomes farther and farther entrapped by the five senses. All connection to the inner planes is lost. One must spend the greater portion of one's small lifetime perfecting a spiritual methodology, which will allow a weak access to the inner worlds. For most, however, at the end of the line they discover that it was a waste of time. Such is the way of all modern day religions.

"There are no methods which carry through from the previous Yuga that allow humans access to the inner realms. The spiritual planes are practically inaccessible to most all of the population. There are no successful ways for reaching the inner life save one. All former techniques are to no avail. Kriya and Kundlini yoga are taught and performed by highly competent individuals, yet they only carry the aspirants up to the edges of the astral regions. It's like going window shopping. You can look in but you cannot touch, travel, or bring back anything from there. Thousands of false teachers and prophets exist in every corner of this Yuga. The interesting thing to note here is it is only in the Kali Yuga do a very few super souls arrive from time to time to uplift the population by releasing these

The Moon Women

long standing truths concerning existence, the true Time/Space continuum, and the way within.

"The average lifetime in this Yuga is rarely exceeds 100 years. Humans range in height from 1 to 2.5 meters on average. This Yuga lasts for about 338,032 years of 2 Moon Units. The end of Kali Yuga is not presided over by any incarnation of the astral deities. Owing to a complete lack of faith by most of the inhabitants, the only effective manner of transitioning at the conclusion of the Yuga is usually non-resident since the changes occur spontaneously and must undergo a period of suspension, like a pseudo-pralaya. Nevertheless, the end of Kali Yuga effects the greatest changes overall because everything must go back to the Sat Yuga status in which everything exists in the purest form.

"Therefore, in Kali Yuga the bulk of the creative powers of the Nirunjan are employed in the futile task of blocking the work of the personas who come to educate hundreds of interested people in the existence of the spiritual ladder and how they can utilizing a basic quality of the mind, that of repetition. By using their bodies to eliminate all of their karma and by practicing the methodology of steadfastly repeating a power mantra, they are taught to ride this word wave up and out of the physical world into the Beyond.

"Although no official pralaya occurs in this Age, heat and fire occurs in overabundance during the transitionary period. Everything experiences some kind of destruction by being burned to ashes. Out of these ashes, a new age, the next Sat Yuga, will begin reiteratively. The manner of effecting this transformation is centered upon a group of 44 individuals who will contribute their life energies into forming a suppository cocoon of genetic material all of which is prerequisite to recreate the beginning. And, thus, the cycles go on repeating and repeating."

Dr. K ended his explanation of the four Yugas and went back to his fortified palace.

At this point in the ride, the author must emphasize the importance of comprehending this concept of Yugas. If you want to understand what the Khrng really are, where they came from and what they are up to, you must grasp the full structure and impact of this radical design of the Yugas, and specifically how the Yugas evolve and continue to repeat as a never-ending process.

I promptly reclined into my bladed chair.

"This will be quixotic," I surmised as I assumed the helm of the captain's rook. The oceanic sensations washed over me as the mala initiated another channel on the way back machine to hand down messages from the quinary and most telling phase with the Moon women and their naughtical charms of lust and romance.

The Moon Women

- 1 -

November 19, 1969 - Tokyo, Japan

The sizzling lights and flashing katakana hash marks tore away the useless onion skins of what was once the logic of structured life. Shinjuku was slamming my skull against invisible barriers put there by a mutant Zen hadochi foaming at the mouth and spitting out haikus of horror like a mental milk pump oozing mint jam. With big smiles, over-inflated geishas riding on rearward facing rickshaws spun their wheels, which were nothing more than orangey dumpling ninjas somersaulting down the narrow corridors of this time-honored den in Tokyo's black market.

"Man! This is some righteous shit!" I blurted out while hoisting a leg to broad jump a pink camel.

"Wait till the crow lands!" Oma yelled back. "You won't believe this cat's crib."

I had bumped into Oma Fulton at a lounge hosting airline pilots front and center on the tarmac of Fujiyama Airport. She had just come in from Macao the same time as Jeff Finklestein and I had touched down on our stopover back to basecamp in Hiroshima. After vaulting through security at the same time, the three of us hit it off like all get out so we hit the ground running intent on tracking down whatever indiscreet hijinks 1969 could throw at us. Our initial idea was to locate the first watering trough selling refreshments, but to tell the truth, water wasn't the real issue. Having been a full-fledged fwic for two years, Jeff never spared a second for the straight life. In spite of all the tight-lipped crap Japan had thrown at him, Jeff had managed to stash some serious weed in that fanny pack of his which was also augmented with a handful of psychedelics, enough to rival Dr. Leary's backdoor pharmacy, which I had enjoyed to the hilt over at his commune in Poughkeepsie.

Miraculously, the three of us had tracked down a weird address jotted on a scrap of toilet paper Jeff got from a well-intentioned stewardess. (Supposed to call them flight attendants but Jeff knew better.) A gargantuan, claret door loomed up in front of us like an imposing fortress. Oma assaulted it with the butt of her palm demonstrating she was going to have it free or die in the process. As she shoved through it with the jumbo thrust of an Olympian wrestler, she let out a banzai call, which stunned the bouncer. Oma was no bantamweight broad. Blonde, blue-eyed and devastatingly beautiful, Oma was nineteen and eager to cram a decade of sexual fantasies into her one month tour' of the pavilions of insane gaiety within the porcelain isles of Japan. Tonight, Oma was using Sake for mouthwash and, it was becoming more and more evident I was her designated guinea pig for the evening.

The red sea parted and we marched in. I hoped Moses would be there on the other bank to redeem my precious spirit from the fire chariots of Ramses II.

"Let's get fucked!" Oma screamed.

Shoving the Nipponese revelers out of the way, she headed for the center of the dance floor while dragging me along behind her. We jerked and shouted and drank and smoked 'til the band lost steam and the booze ran dry. By then my brain was like a bowl of rice pudding vying to do the limbo beneath a candy cane archway, which turned out to be the hem of Oma's skirt.

"Jack be nimble, Jack be quick. Jack crawl under Oma's skirt and snatch her clit." Whoa! I was looped.

At two clicks passed midnight, our zany exuberance spilled out all over the place as we stumbled out onto the roadside.

"Well, we fuckin' closed that joint!" Oma stabbed two fingers into the hole under her nose and blew hard through the void in her two teeth. She produced an ear-piercing whistle, which produced not one, but two taxis screeching to a halt on their now flat spotted tires.

"Take us to whatever bar is flowing with Sake!" She yelled out to the stars.

The closest mini-car got the word "bar" and his yellow door flapped open. We careened uptown towards the seacoast winding up in a seedy bowery. There was a mangled neon sign with only one of its three Japanese letters alive and flashing its bright purple electrics. It was supposed to assert, <u>YAKUZA</u>, but all it had was <u>ZA</u>, which sounded perversely Zen.

After we found our tables, with our coats off and drinks ordered, the maître d' (or whoever is the Japanese equivalent thereof)

The Moon Women

approached Jeff and had a little vis-a-vis. The two whispered their cross-cultural lingo for a time and a half time. Jeff kept nodding and smiling. When she was finished, Jeff piped up.

"Mama San says on Friday evenings they present a stripper for entertainment but for latecomers they are obligated to inform their newly arriving clientele this type of entertainment will be shown so as to prepare them for possible shock and to avoid any possible humiliation or further embarrassments." Jeff informed us as he plugged the gaping abyss of his yap with his hand in mock surprise.

"If she strips, I'm gonna strip too!" says Oma.

"No, you're not!" I chimed back. "You're with me."

I was implying the double entendre of girl-on-girl action would put me in a carnal sandwich, which I would have loved but for the 45 on her belt. The definitive drawback was Oma owned a registered NRA life membership and carried a loaded Commander for protection, if you get my drift.

As the muzzy evening wore on, the lead guitar work transitioned into clarinet moods lowing into saxophone headiness further devolving into the pooled resources of the violins. I liked slow dancing with Oma. She was a big boned woman, but pixie lite on her feet. With our arms wrapped around each other, we were drifting into pastures of pink cotton candy and violet forget-me-nots raining down.

Unexpectedly, there was a tremendous crash as the drummer wailed once on his Zildjian cymbals. Following this initial outburst, the pedaling of the bass drum signaled an unmistakable rhythm meant to grab everyone's attention: a single thud, pause, and then another beat followed by a second pause concluding with two final staccato thuds. This is the unambiguous introduction of a stripper taking the stage to disrobe in the limelight. And the Japs aspired to get the whole affair down as authentically as possible.

An exquisite Japanese woman in her mid-twenties came onto the petite dais. In nothing flat, the softly clapping audience demonstrated their approval. Slicked up in a tailored business suit to portray the female executive, she championed her statement concerning the need for equality within corporate jungle. She was concocting a self-styled Ptolemaic system in which she would have all the men revolve around her sun, her radiance.

Her performance was spectacular. She pealed it all off down to the underlying mosaics of her maidenly epithelials: no pasties, no thong, no G-string, no nothing. Jeff loved it. Oma seemed bored. I made some eye contact with the Japanese beauty, which only inflamed a wanton jealousy in the craw of my presently registered Moon maiden, namely Oma. Mostly I was watching the stripper's movements, which were as fluid as a cat. For a grand finale, she clawed at the discarded attire like a bird of prey and flew off backstage to her rookery.

Oma grabbed me and towed me back out onto the dance floor for some late night schmoozing. Right before closing time the stripper came out and frequented several tables swathed in a mandilion robe and adorned with gilded stilettos on her unusually tiny feet. She came over to our threesome for a moment. Jeff was in awe. She dabbled with her English and we carried on with our smattering of Japanese. It got us by. Jeff claimed later that she had slipped him her address and phone number. She had an exquisite smile and an angular hawk-like visage. Jeff looked like he was planning to entertain a late night visit to his lady hawk.

- 2 -

The whimsical chair suddenly reversed its orbital confluences and reregistered me in the flow of the chronological micro-frames. Two months earlier during my matriculating phase in Japan, I was preparing to shoot several new and distinct films by embarking upon a mission to learn and understand something deeper about the utilization of light.

Two hours after sunrise I had already exposed two rolls of Kodak ASA 100 color and was working on some wide angle shots with my Canon 8mm movie camera while attempting to capture as much of the receding bay as my 30 millimeter lens could digest. Early on during the golden hour, I had managed to snag some rare footage of the faint pinks and the burning yellows of the sunrise washing Hiroshima bay, when suddenly I witnessed a scene of haunting beauty.

Waist deep in the flat water of a tidal plain, the gaunt profile of a hairless man paced with a measured stride. With mechanized movements, he handed off thin bamboo poles and set them firmly

The Moon Women

into the silt of a shallow basin. Reaching up over his bald skullcap, he gingerly fingered the nylon filaments of his net, which trailed out behind him like the train of a waiting bride. After carefully anchoring his line to each stem, he moved on. There was a chilling awe sleeping in his indexed actions, but to the marauding fish, his presence was as horrific as the Khrng are to men.

As I had filmed this scene throughout the post-dawn phases of light, I noticed that the fisherman was proud of his work of endless repetition. Sometimes we must endure the monotony of life as a means towards survival. Perched in seclusion on a seawall, I was making precise adjustments to the focal ring of my Super 8 while my martinet deftly avoided his nightmares of atomic tragedy by pursuing his dreams of fish. After I had zoomed in on him from a hundred meters away, I had completed my run of cross-pans.

Against the elusive promise of fresh sushi, the austere mandrake mounted his gear to collect his daily catch. Ripples originating from an adjacent low pool attempted to lure him away from his treasure but he resisted the oily temptation for fear of later reprisals. Sometimes the avoidance of the obvious brings a fulfilled knowing. Way out on the murky mudflats the brine crabs were making nimble work of his failures.

There were so many vistas of Zen life in the midst of this fishing port. I had been here now for over three months, preparing my project as a novice enjoying the maiden voyage of my unfolding Friends World College adventure. My mentor and advisor, Mrs. Claudia Bormann, had been tremendously helpful in pointing me in some of the more propitious directions in and about Hiroshima. She had enabled me to procure a profusion of locations and backdrops, which I composed with my in-camera editing techniques. Most of the sessions had turned out quite well and many of the Japanese bystanders who occasionally observed my work were amused by my irregular methodologies; others were downright affronted.

For instance on one occasion, I had received proper sanctions from the grand monks to shoot within the sacrosanct rock gardens of a holy Buddhist monastery in Kyoto. Utilizing supremely artistic methods with my limited equipment, I had invented my own pathways in and around the hallowed stones. This had perturbed them immensely but they disguised their frustrations with fretful prayer. But when I broke into shooting nude photographs of my female cohorts while transforming the venerated gardens into out-of-sight backdrops, the monks came rushing out of the temples like ants colonizing untapped rapture.

I had persuaded Dottie Ambrewster to disrobe all the way down to her nipples and pubes. It was unquestionably meant to invoke art's sake and pure ecclesiastical genius no doubt. After a roll or two, the prophets of Buddhism began waving their arms and screaming out loud as if I had killed the only mouthpiece of pure Dharma or even worse, the Buddha himself. Wait. Those two are the same. No? Funny how they were able to burn themselves alive in Saigon to stop a war, but for this, they had to resort to actual hysterical politics.

I was able to stash my Nikormat and two canisters of stills before they overtook me and ransacked my bags to confiscate whatever they deemed was the incriminating evidence of the horrid desecration of their temple. What they got were only a few empties. Too bad, I wasn't able to get the Canon armed and do some real damage. That would have made for some risqué exposures. No pun intended.

As the spider creature paced off his mazy netting, all the while manipulating the microfilaments from out of his maritime midnight, I brought forth more genius. Eighty meters out over my shoulder, I caught whiff of a tourist type watching my every move as she pretended to dwell on her fluttering periodical. While Hiroshima's igneous maumet ticked off the delicate steps of his manta-ray dance amongst the matted seaweed and the Mars red crabs, I finished off the full resolution color media. Throwing a parting shot over his back he made book with the incoming tides to vacate the barnacled future bull markets for the lesser marauding marketeers of saline.

I curtailed my photo session capturing a bunch more transparencies as the nylon aquatic mariner charted the remedial stretches of his lagoon. As I let my Canon run out on the wide-angle 22mm lens, the sea released its foam of senseless wandering. With her magazine in hand, the woman continued to watch me as she maintained her nonchalance on a tastefully carved bench. Over her shoulder, a Japanese andromeda offered a drooping cluster of powdery blossoms as if it were an Omiyage. She sat there digesting her drama though unmoved by either pain or joy. After I had

The Moon Women

determined she was adequately engrossed in her twisting plot, I did an about-face and abruptly made a direct track up the hill to rock her world. I was determined to uncover how indifferent she really was.

"Ohio gozaimus [Good morning]!" I hollered aloud. "Can you please direct me to your Mama-san's geisha gakko [Geisha classes]?"

I had her at the tip of my verbal sword.

"Don't be so smart. Claudia is paying me to watch you. That's why I'm here so back off." She was all business.

I unsheathed my Nikormat and aimed it at her.

"Your skin catches awesome light. Interested in some bonus money?" My initial parry didn't draw any blood.

"Claudia warned me about you so you can't bribe me. You're really not that illusive." She stashed her Jap fashion rag.

"I'll double it if you'll dance to a different tune. What's your name?"

"My name is Masumi. This is not the place for you to be now. This city is unpredictable." She monished back.

Even as Americans pretty much have autonomous latitude throughout most of the countryside, a handful of prefectures persisted wherein the regional sentiments might bend the other way. Don't forget, quarter after eight, one August morning we dropped an atomic bomb on them and crispy-crittered a hundred and twenty thousand citizens as a rosy red sun blinked its gruesome delight down upon them in time to catch the divine wind blowing like gas jets. So I understood where she was coming from, but then again, I didn't. We were at war then.

"Okay, then. Can I buy you a beer?" I proposed we might as well get introduced.

She looked at me with both a look of bewilderment and pity.

"Guygene [Foreigner]!" She hissed sourly.

Guygene is not spelled that way exactly (it is an extremely deprecating term), but it pretty much means that; even the female ones are guys.

"How 'bout a limousine to drive us back to campus?" I was scheming my damnedest to overturn her courtesies.

"Rahm, you can let up on all your jokes and your games. I'm not interested. If you're meaning to go back to Ebaku, say so. I'll call for a taxi." She placed me squarely in her crosshairs.

Man, the wet dishrag of her rebuke sure wiped the frosting of my insolence off my face, but only for a brief moment. I held up one finger.

"Chotomattey kudasai." [Just a minute, please.]

I did another one-eighty, and strutted back down to the concrete abutment to collect my gear. No longer were there any tractable spider men of fish on my horizon, just this Newtonian dowager eager to undo my vow of moderation. I hoped the mass of my lone self could accelerate at a rate of one wish over one dream. I chuckled knowing some of these Asian equations had stumped me once or twice in the past.

We talked some in the taxi as we slowly rolled back to my so-called dorm in the rented apartment in Honshutown. To my surprise, I found her to be quite engaging although I suspected she was not only uninterested in American blokes, but also quite possibly gay. I quickly deliberated to confirm this idea as well as perhaps add some outrageous footage to my inventory by posing an offer. Since that afternoon I would be making selections for my primary piece entitled, "The River of Broken Walls," I invited her to come to my set for some nude photography.

After spending considerable time describing my concepts of cinematography as an art form and not simply just some commercial enterprise, I was pleased to find she enlisted some degree of eye contact and charm. What I was attempting to achieve within my films was twofold; rattle the doorknobs to the hoity-toity world of photography as well as threaten the bastions of the established prude. Framed within the iron sights of this avant-garde expose, I made my uncomplicated request ala carte: she should come for a try out. Who knows? Maybe she'd take to it and become a true queen of the art.

As for my expectations concerning the overall effects of my inroads into areas of professional journalism, mine was a juxtaposition between the evils of the mass destruction ala the war effort in Viet Nam as contrasted with the shocking beauty of the female form. She seemed genuinely intrigued but she didn't bite at my ploy. In defiance of my stating it quite ingenuously and with as much bon vivant as I could muster, she blew me off.

A day later, the time came for my shooting. In a vacant lot, which stood adjacent to the homestead of our alma mater, a rundown shanty had been disintegrating into the ruddy sod for decades,

The Moon Women

nothing more than a broken down skeleton left over from its imperial days. The floor was merely dirt and the sides were remnants of weathered vertical sheathing nailed to cross members. Despite that despondency, the real gold was the illusive light bleeding into the trapped gloom.

Framed by the wooden slats, slender voids allowed the sunlight to stream into the darkness of the hut. And as the light leaked in from the open-air on the other side, it formed splinters of radiance which breached the murk to defeat the blackness stored within the eroding sepulcher. As an added grace, the place had monstrous northern sun, which imbued the photographs, especially the ones procured from the innermost angles, with a dynamite backlighting. As the lens sucked in the awesome dayglow glints, the slats appeared to be imposing shards of empty solidity drastically contrasting with the fluid voids. The juxtaposition of the two allowed for some dazzling and surreal effects.

I got busy shooting some tricky angles and motley exposures, which I might need come editing time although most of what would be normally be done in post-production had to be prepared a priori as it were. The limitation of having no A/B roll capability with Super 8 technology had always kept me on my toes. I had to plan way ahead and project whichever effect I envisioned by mobilizing it right on the spot inside the camera itself. That is what made the art not only technologically difficult but also surprisingly exquisite when it was performed well.

It wasn't long before I had racked up numerous exposures when there she was, Masumi. She was vying me from the balustrade of an adjacent building.

"Ah! My enchanted princess!" Not giving her any out, I parried quickly allowing her no chance to slice me back. "No need to chauffeur me to the ball, Darlin'. My pumpkin is but a hop, skip, and a jump across the bay."

"I am watching your work, Ibsen San. It looks to me like you are in the throes of a predicament. Des ne?" [Isn't it?]

She had quite a combo: both engaging as well as aloof at the same time.

"How is it you can converse in such decent English whenever you choose? It's not the lame Nihongoese [Japanese/English slang] the bulk of these slant-eyed pygmies spout."

I tossed it back out as not only a question but also an observation. The fork pressured her to step up to the plate.

"You know, Ibsen, you're an ass."

"That's not the answer I was hoping for. So what is it?"

"What's what? You're bigotry? I'm may have slanted eyes but I assure you I'm as righteous as you think you are." She out maneuvered my arrogance.

"Just gimme the goods, Honey, and then you can go."

"I was born in Hiroshima, but when I was twelve my family went to San Francisco. You happy now?" She confessed.

She had fallen into my trap.

"And now you're babysitting fwiks? Huh? Big promotion there, I'll bet." I formatted my byline. I was also my paper's managing editor.

"I go to school for law in my off hours. Claudia got me this job. She pays me to be your overseer. And from what I can see, you need it." She was balancing to keep an even keel but unfortunately, I wouldn't rate her as wildly successful.

"Well, why don't you come over here and report for your bonus check." I yapped knowing full well I didn't have a cent to pay her; Dad's monthly allotment hadn't hit the vaults yet.

She looked over at me with that blank look of hers, the kind of look a young woman such as herself might elicit to a challenger who had imposed a dare to bungee jump off Quechee Gorge. I pretended to dig out some money but when I looked up, she was gone. The mollusk of her disintegrating motion clammed up and got lost in the Time jump.

After trapping several dynamite panoramas across the network of pickets, I stepped back to set up my tripod for additional pull-focus shots prior to the disappearance of the early sunlight. I had been capturing the blades of grass, which were waving behind the battered fence like the jazzy tassels of a stripper strutting the stage. Midcourse in the contracting radius pan I witnessed a blockage overlapping the slots. Where did all the glints go? I instantly concluded something had blotted out the sun for a second as if a misplaced weapon or other obstruction had presented an occlusion. This unforeseen interrupt had ruined my strategies so I exhaled a perfectly logical and righteously justified remark.

The Moon Women

"Shit!" I expectorated.

When I looked over after snapping my tripod buckle, there she was again, Masumi. Perched there on the doorsill with a Mars violet kimono draped over her shoulder, she had appeared like an apparition. I grabbed for the masking tape.

She paused for a second as she rubbed off the residue of my latest invective. I hoped she knew it wasn't meant for her. I laid 20 centimeter strips of tape along my tripod struts in case I had to strap up her mammarys. It happens.

"Where would you like me to start?" She stated with a painless methodology, which smacked of a kamikaze oblivion.

I sighted her straight in the eye like Arjuna and that kite. "Put your clothes on the pallet out back. Then, stand over in the corner with your back to me. I'll do the rest."

As I do-si-doed my tripod and Canon like a lead man preparing to tango, she removed her clothes one by one. It was apparent she had never done this sort of work before. She unzipped her chemise prior to pulling it out of her jeans. She hustled off her belt pealing it from each individual pant loop. Was she that nervous or simply a little OCD? After delicately piling her clothes on a stack of pallets, she put on the plumbago kimono in a marvelously casual way - partially open allowing the luxurious sleeves to hide her ample breasts. She hauled her loose apparel away and proceeded to unburden herself of any modesty by opening her robe at me point-blank. When she did that, her eyes burned with an igneous blue fire, which only bona fide stars exude. With her head high, she marched over to her stage and poised there preparing to be devoured by the dragon of my lens. Grabbing my camera, I positioned it for the most advantageous sightline while gladly confessing the masking tape had been a wasted anticipation.

"With your back towards me, please. And lose the robe." I barked.

"I'm sorry. I didn't know if you were all set for me." She was apologetic but she still maintained that sour hint of vinegar.

Being a shady maximalist, I indoctrinated her with the primary regs of my canon.

"Look. There is only one way this is going to work. You have to pay attention to what I say when I say it. This isn't you and I going at it to entertain Claudia or you and I up in the attic playing slap

398

bellies. I am the moviemaker. You are the subject. This is only successful art when you are the object of this lens. Apologies have nothing to do with it." It was zee methodology, Monsieur.

The reptilian leer of a quarter-moon bore down on us from out of its azure bedroom in the pale sky freezing her features onto the celluloid of recall. She didn't say a word as she tiptoed over to the place where my camera bags were unpacked and shed the kimono. She let it fall onto my bags so it didn't touch the dirt. Very clever, I thought.

As she took her position, she touched the enclosure reluctantly as if to test its level of contamination and then proceeded to do the most unexpected thing. She put her hands onto the bent stakes: one, then, the other. She opened her gait to spread her legs a hot foot and a half and pushed out her butt. In other words, she got into the stance, which she might have to assume if a cop was preparing to search her ass for contraband.

"Dynamite!" The word exploded out of me.

The work I did that morning was some of the most provocative and visionary art I have ever done. Masumi exuded a raw animism out of her every pore. Her muscle tone was so fresh and tight. Her body complexion was superbly tanned and moist even without creams. Her pageboy hairdo was immaculate. Her eyes sparkled like sapphires. Although she maintained a demure and ravishingly detached seriousness, her smile showcased a perfect set of sparkling ivories. She was the hottest thing I had ever seen to date. I had her demonstrate a variety of attitudes. As she strutted her stuff along the shifting backdrop using provocative postures and twists, she was so incredibly spontaneous. From the poses she cooked up all by herself, which were as hot as her body, I concluded she was the essence of Euclidean pornography.

After achieving some level of success with my technique in the shed, I planned to move outdoors for a while. For the moment I had overlooked one illusive detail; all the work, which we had done within the dilapidated shack hadn't exposed us much to the neighborhood. When I advised Masumi we were about to venture outside the busted down partition to get some daylight exposures, she grew uncomfortable. She feared if she was seen out there by the neighbors she would not only be put to shame by the scathing community gossip and, quite possibly, get arrested by the police, but

The Moon Women

worse than all that, she would most likely catch hell from Claudia. And I'd wind-up being judged to be the masterminded manipulator who put her up to the whole nasty affair even though that was but a minor discrepancy in her book.

"Weren't you busted for similar antics in Nagano?" She challenged strategically as a roadblock, but I didn't consider her probing should demand any explaining for my mixed management maneuvers.

After I explained the new scene I imagined would work perfectly, she obeyed implicitly. While I shot from the interior of the shed, I proposed she walk slowly down passed the dilapidated exterior so the camera would view her through the splits in the palisade. Her outline would appear to be difficult to distinguish clearly, phantom-like. She got the idea and was enamored of its ethereal quality.

"That would look really swell, wouldn't it?" She was steadfastly becoming my disciple.

"Swell? Yeah, okay. That's it. Make no mistakes about it, it'll look swell. Perfect." I lifted my finger to emphasize the genius behind the shot.

"Come on! Let's try it, but we must be fast. Really fast. I'll be naked out there." She was certainly a gutsy convert if nothing else. Even in the face of my being a bit flabbergasted by her naïve disregard as to her conspicuousness, I continued to dump frames as fast as I could.

Finally, I whisked out my macro lens and burned that up too. I landed over a hundred exposures and transparences that day. Each one was more remarkable than the next. The more I orchestrated, the more she complied. The more she complied, the more she came up with her own starburst ideas. One time she demonstrated a skulking prance as though she was promenading across a bed of embers just as those firewalkers have been seen to do on videos.

When I came around the fence to shoot her head on, the Sun had already eaten the Moon's green cheese and with its belly full, it broadened its fiery gaze on her anima, which sucked up the rays and sucked up the lens as well. With the arrival of Big Stud, Mr. Sun, much of the hazy look vanished allowing her wet anatomical dignitaries to make their prominence clearly known. I could hear the cash register ringing as the money shots kept rolling in. We were at the cross roads of cultured genius and raw talent. Despite the fact that the engines of our creative juices were only naturally aspirated, there was no cease-fire to the tantalizing images hatching in my camera. That is, until. . . .

From on high came her saving grace.

"Sumimasen! Sumimasen, okotae kudasai?" [Excuse me! Excuse me, please to answer?]

Some mother-type was calling out from her second landing balcony. Quite spontaneously, she and her pre-pubescent daughter had strolled out to check on the cloudbank, which was gathering off the bay, only to discover, quite to their chagrin, there was a naked woman parading around in their adjacent yard.

Masumi bolted into the collapsed shed to retrieve her robe. She emerged to snag her clothes off the wooden pallet and then made another mad dash back into the shack one last time before reappearing in her original state. I had chosen to call it a day and get a jump on clean up. I had hoped this would not add up to a feat of misdirection for Masumi.

Fortunately, Claudia never got wind of it. Never no mind, after development, editing and a full marriage to some dynamite audio, the effects of the film were mesmerizing. When I debuted it two months later, there were many squinting eyes straining to identify the scantily clad female strolling behind those vertical blinds in the spellbinding documentary entitled, "The River of Broken Walls."

NOTE: The scenes with Masumi chosen for release were only those exposures of her as she crossed behind the broken slats. With full respect to her, none of the fully explicit scenes has ever been unboxed to the public. It should be further stated the introductory scenes in the film were those of the fisherman setting his nets in Hiroshima bay. Those telephoto shots peeled away from behind a retaining levee to engender a remoteness, a separation from corporeality. The movie also exposed many other walls and portrayed them as blockages or personal barriers to truth. Some had been vandalized with Japanese graffiti, which was on the verge of taking root in this intensely regimented and sterile culture. These were intermixed with arty shots of prefabricated dwellings demonstrating supports constructed entirely out of paper. The central theme focused on a legendary

The Moon Women

structure, which has become famous around the world as the "Atomic Dome." This historic skeletonized hemisphere is the only building left standing at ground zero after the atomic blast. Considered by many commentators of martial history to be a classic statement of the nuclear holocaust; the corroded girders, which once supported the globe of the Hiroshima Parliament, now present the twisted aftermath of the a war on the verge of total annihilation. These iron pretzels still stand today as a grim reminder of the atomic tragedy. This historical landmark has been immortalized in millions of photographs and films throughout the globe, including the one, which I entitled, "The River of Broken Walls."

- 3 -

Another relocation within the unwinding of the micro-links of the Time/Space tunnel reset the chair's sightlines back some 16 years prior to my jaunt with the bride of mathematical lust unbounded.

In the fall of 1953, I was in Mrs. Sweet's homeroom. She had flowing scarlet curls and a beautifully freckled complexion. She loved to laugh and did so exuberantly, especially at all my jokes. I was the clown of the class and got off by making all the other kids excited. To Mrs. Sweet I was special. She liked my humor and got a kick out of my pranks and my twisted concepts. Not surprisingly, I was the teacher's pet.

Mrs. Sweet was so enamored of me such that one day she invited me to come with her and her husband out to dinner, which was going to precede a show entitled "The Mikado," something about a Japanese emperor and his mistresses. Because the story had some neat puppet characters in it, she figured I would like it immensely. After talking to my parents, she confirmed I could join her and her husband for the evening out on the town. How Mrs. Sweet was able to convince the two of them was baffling. Nevertheless, she relayed to me honestly she had explained to them she would treat with the tickets and a dinner. I knew both of them either blew her off or were so damned drunk they had no concept of where the hell she was coming from. Her husband was going to come along for the ride so there was no chance for anything kinky;

402

although, if there were something kinky, I would be up for it. I was head over heels in love with Mrs. Sweet.

When she and her husband picked me up curbside at the appointed time, I was slicked up to the gills. Long time ago I had learned you have to wear your best duds for these sorts of adventures. We visited a quaint Italian restaurant where I had a nice plate of spaghetti and meatballs. Mrs. Sweet didn't fancy me freaking out from any of the ultra-exotic items on the menu. No big deal, even though I was only nine years old I had eaten all sorts of foods, like lobsters and oysters and even snails with my parents inside a seafood joint once. On my own, I had eaten frogs, newts and one salamander, but not cooked ones.

On that day, I had a baby tadpole with me to partake in the fun. I hid it in a wet sock in my jacket pocket. When her husband left to go to the bathroom, I gingerly dumped the tadpole into his drink; I think it was ginger ale. In the meantime, Mrs. Sweet had decided to coach me on the meanings of some of the Italian meals. I joined along repeating the twisted vowel sounds and the long rolled r's that made us laugh. When he came back, he didn't notice anything right away, but after a few sips he was shocked to observe a pollywog googling back out at him from his drinking glass. It was instant pandemonium.

"What the hell? Do you see that fish swimming in my ale, Darling? It's a bloody leech for Christ sakes!" He always referred to her as Darling.

I couldn't help but let out a little snicker. I knew Mrs. Sweet would think it was funny too, same way as all my jokes in class.

"You little brat! Did you put that worm in my drink you devil? Son of a bitch!" He swatted at me but missed.

I ducked beneath the table, kicked out with my foot, and got him in the knee. Then, I popped up and gave him the finger.

"George! Stop it! What are you thinking? He was only funning in jest." Mrs. Sweet always supported me in whatever I did. Why would she desert me now?

"That's it. I'm outta here! If you want to stay here with this depraved bumpkin, that's up to you. Here are the tickets and here's something for the dinner and taxi fare." With that, he got up and stormed out of Giovanni's.

I smiled inside knowing I had baked his meat loaf and fried his pickle.

The Moon Women

"Well, Rahm, I guess it's you and me, Buddy." Mrs. Sweet was not going to let this fracas deter her from enjoying her evening out.

Together we executed our dinner delights quite pleasantly. I really liked the spaghetti. We flagged a yellow cab and drove over to the playhouse. There were so many Japanese posters in the theatre lobby, which were all so neat and exciting. A woman in the lobby who looked strangely like Miss Devlin, my third grade teacher, was handing out flyers. She wore a robe like a nun. Moreover, she was carrying one of those front-to-back posters, which advertised the wheat deity.

> But when the man slept
> His enemy came and sowed
> Tares among the wheat
> And went away. [1]

I considered it highly irrational anybody would be talking wheat at a Japanese Kabuki play. We put some coins in her bowl and she blessed us. Mrs. Sweet professed she always helped the downtrodden poor and wondered why God had caused a demonic war between heaven and the ones from the unknown. Why couldn't they all get along was her view. Perhaps she hadn't been introduced to the crickets but I left that for later.

The Mikado lasted as much as a full-length movie - Fantasia size. At one point, I distinctly recalled seeing the upper story of Dr. DeGres, or his double, sporting his Sherlock bowler and pipe as he slid along the back fringes of the audience. He's someone you will meet in the sequel being misplaced in this one. It's like when you encountered Mrs. Sweet considerably prior to her actual appearance in the story now. Consider it psychic collateral damage.

At the highpoint of the show, I had Mrs. Sweet's hand in mine. She beamed at me when I did this. I would ply her with well-chosen probes concerning the acts. It wasn't so much that I was concerned with the show as I was scheming to get near her. She smelled rather nice, like watermelons.

Once, when she leaned over to explain the glossy menu for the show, I could see clearly down her loosely fitting blouse. Her breasts were large and white. There was a yummy pink gumdrop on each one. I imagined it would be pretty delicious to suck on those gumdrops, but I didn't attempt to do that, nor did I ask if I could. After all, I did have some manners.

Mrs. Sweet moved over to listen to me one time when I had asked a question – were all the actors really men? Why can't they have women for the women? They're wearing dresses, aren't they? It didn't seem right to me; I was a believer in normal things back then. But the answer wasn't the important part.

When she did, I tried to kiss her softly on the cheek. After carefully lining up my shot, inadvertently I missed my intended target and collided with her ear. She patted me on the check to request, "Not here, Rahm."

There were other episodes with Mrs. Sweet, but I cannot include those in this book. It would change its mode to something in the blue realm. If anybody thinks this book panders with pornography, they would be sadly mistaken. These intimate events of my romances are being disrobed and paraded before you for the purposes of forming the facets of a psycho-spiritual crystal, which will resonate for the benefit of all mankind.

The purport of the Mikado is proof of this. When the whole thing was over, all the actors came out and had their bows. I realized at that moment all those who reside in the present are experiencing their bows every second of their day. They are all in a big show viewed by the angels and by the gods. I clapped as much as I could and even tried to whistle, but I didn't know how to whistle too well back then. Now, I can whistle quite loudly. When you know how to whistle really well, it means you are a man.

The Khrng cannot perform this action of whistling. Understanding the difference between the Khrng and the modern human is what differentiates the man of today from the man of tomorrow, the Albacore Man. How the Khrng came to be can only be grasped by uncovering the threads of an unnatural twist of fate. Knowing those origins is what propels me ahead into the Beyond. It's the nexus, which challenges me to continue writing these books, of which this one is the maiden voyage. The others to follow will delve much deeper into the Khrng, who they are, where they come from and what it is like to meet one in person. I assure you that will be worth the wait.

The Moon Women

Back in Japan as the rain soaked hydrangeas garlanded the haunted alleyways, I was lost in a sea of guns on the fifth floor of a downtown Tokyo department store. Everywhere I looked there were racks and racks brimming with guns. There were revolvers. There were semi-automatics. There were single shots. There were repeaters. There were lever action rifles. There were shotguns. There was even a comprehensive selection of assault rifles such AK47s and even M16s, or AR15s if you're a civilian, both in full auto. Take your pick. And the mind blowing dupe on the whole deal was they were all simply toys.

Ben Harris, Mat, and I had lost ourselves in this gigundous wallow of artillery. The entire department only sold guns. This is all quite bizarre because ever since Potsdam in 1945, the laws in Japan had expressly forbidden the manufacture, sale, and promotion of firearms in any way. Ten years later for the sake of saving and expanding their industry; they changed the laws to avow the manufacture of firearms. The only caveat was they could not distribute any of them within the country. They all required formal exportation. The Japanese made some excellent weaponry and particularly rifles barrels, but their tooling could produce almost anything else. From both the upgraded laws and the pressing need to utilize their existing machinery, they created an entire market of simulated firearms. You and I would call them toys, but these were some of the most authentic toys anyone could imagine.

Some legal whiz had cleverly unmasked a loophole in the law, which legislated the making of steely objects, which literally looked like guns, the exemption of which was they could not discharge a projectile, a bullet. Not to be outdone by that slight drawback, they also made fake bullets. You could not load these simulated guns with live ammunition, but you could load them with these improvised bullets, which fired off like blanks. Their attention to detail was astounding.

Across the promenade, I did a retake thinking I saw my fifth grade teacher, Mrs. Sweet, with her Tweedledee husband, shopping for souvenirs. I couldn't miss that flaming hairdo of hers anywhere. Why in the world would she be roaming Tokyo shopping for fake weapons? Could it be she was hatching some scenario to do away with her hubby? Her aisle was generously populated with the revolvers, i.e., no telltale evidence left behind.

"Rahm! Check this out!" Harris' command wrenched me back to the inner bank of outer insanity anew - he was showing me a slick 1911 with an extended mag.

After considerable study, I selected a snub-nose revolver for protection. It was an exact copy of a Smith snub-nose chambered in 32 H&R Mag. It had a precision cylinder. The hammer and trigger were so authentically reproduced it was astonishing. They even made it so you could throw the catch, flip out the cylinder, and load it with fake bullets. But what was so alarming was there was a shooting range being maintained underneath the department store for full-fledged practice.

You could select one or two examples, go down there and try them out by shooting them. The guns themselves only cost a mere fifteen bucks apiece. I purchased the revolver and a box of cartridges. Considering my true felony status today as I record this story while locked up in a prison cell in New Hampshire, I feel so uncomfortable confessing this irony.

I carried my little revolver everywhere. I even carried it onto the aircraft when we flew back to Hiroshima, where the FWC center administered to its brood. Back in those days, they didn't do body searches ahead of boarding, a practice, which didn't start until after the Swissair jet blew up a few months later in early 1970. I encountered absolutely no snafus while transporting the gun directly into the cabin.

When we got back to Hiroshima, I carried it constantly with me in my rucksack. It was loaded with those fake bullets. But let me tell you, I suspected these little suckers had been put together with some mixture of live gun powder, because when you touched one off, its report was irrefutably genuine. The Japanese were into making the most authentic shooting toys in all of the peaceful countries combined. Their concern for the ceaseless minutia of it all was past all comprehension.

One chilly sundown in late winter, Harris, Mat and I were out cruising one of the harbor-side neighborhoods, a sprawling mass of paper condos with tatami floorings. Since we were completely loaded with fireside party cheer, we had already shut down two of the local bars with our rowdy haranguing. Although the liquid

The Moon Women

lubrication had numbed me up pretty good, I was wincing to ignore the bite of the searing wind. There we were, wandering around drunk out of our minds and making all kinds of mischief as we stumbled through this peaceful suburb in Honshu-town. When I sloshed my hand around in my flight jacket, I bumped into my trusty little friend. It was then and there, I knew I was on the verge of becoming a muckraker extraordinaire.

"Hey, Ben. Watch this!" I posted my outrageous dare.

"Yeah? Show me!" Ben fell over onto a lopsided trash barrel and barfed.

With a sporty hop, I vaulted over the knee-high bamboo fence, which protected the homey bonsai roost from the cruel world. Most of these paper houses present peripheral entrances as an intimidation factor to discourage unwanted solicitors. Marching right over to this facade, I bent down and as I muffled my breath in super stealth mode, I twisted the doorknob to test if it was unlocked. It was not! So I cranked back the door slightly to breach their defenses. On tiptoes, I inched my way forward to unseat their inner sanctum of domestic stability. Oddly, it was quite troublesome to me the interior of the homestead was a lot colder than on street-side. Not to despair, even though my stealth gauges were pegging over the edge, the juices of adrenaline surging in my bones dissolved any sensible hesitation.

As I strode across the isthmus of death while clutching my ticket to silver screen notoriety, I approached the core of their home front. I knew ignoring possible collisions with subarctic icebergs was not only wildly alarming but also symptomatic of my obsession - flirting with the afterworld merely for the fun of it. But I was drunk, so who the hell cared? Question was - could chemical accelerants alter the inevitable? I smiled; time to find out.

I snuck down a curvy corridor, which led to a parlor-like walkway ending at the doorway to their television area. Inside I could detect the insanity of a Japanese game show raging away on their color set. With the presence of a ninja ghost fog, I poured myself into their precious homestead.

Sprawled out on the tatamis while enveloped within luxurious quilts was an entire Nihongo family slurping down their soba noodles and cheerfully watching the kaleidoscopic game show. The children were so intent with the slapsticks they didn't even notice

I had arrived. When the parents looked over and found me waiting in the dark, they burst out laughing at first.

All Japanese think Americans are outrageously funny. They think we are not only funny looking, but also everything we say and do is dreamt up for the purpose of humor. Perhaps from watching a surfeit of American made films, they have the presumption that the entirety of American culture revolves around telling jokes and acting like clowns. In every respect that's what they think we are; they think we are no more than a country of clowns. As their children caught on to the gorilla in the room, the elders gazed over at me innocently with simmering hesitation. I knew it was my time to entertain.

"Hi there! How you all doin' tonight?" I lambasted them with my sour Tennessee drawl.

Their chittering subsided mournfully.

"I'm here to tell you folks you all have won the Publisher's Clearing House Award for fifty bazillion yen! Congratulations and here it is!"

I blotted out my cutting rant while overriding the game show cheering section on their scratchy television set. Out came my little snub-nose revolver (you know, the one, which looks literally like a real gun). And then, Blam! I shot each family member point-blank straight in the head. After I had emptied the little six-shooter, I waved my hearty farewell.

"How you all enjoyin' your gameshow now?!" I deliberately reloaded and let 'em have it all over again. Then, with a hearty yell, I vamoosed pronto.

"Adios muchachos!" [I'm outa here, Boys!]

My rocking chair encouraged the replay of that flashback unfolding in the etheric realms of insanity. As it rewound in slo-mo, I made note of the double-edged references. After my initial entry, they had reacted by giggling and twittering incessantly. When I opened my trap, the loud abrasive English had put them on edge and dumped them into a severely defensive state. As I exposed the revolver, even though they had never seen one in person, the numerous occasions in which they had seen the genuine article clearly displayed within the frames of their television police mysteries had prepared them for what the likely outcome might be. Their hypothalamus shot into overdrive mode with the fight or flight

The Moon Women

response as large quantities of adrenaline dumped directly into their bloodstreams causing them to experience catastrophic trauma.

The look on their faces was priceless. Rampant terror and utter horror annihilated any and all neurons transmitting logic. Moreover, within their cerebral cortex, all cognitive functions of usefulness ceased in nothing flat. As a result, their kissers yawned wide like the trumpets of the apocalypse. With a total loss of all control, impressive volumes of air inaugurated a lively evacuation from their thorax while at the same time their larynxes constricted to cause a shrieking which could quite comfortably match the decibels now being emitted by the my rapidly discharging firearm. As the speed of fright clicked up, the speed of Time/Space algorithm clicked down. Gradually the chronological segments descended into the basement until a critical point was attained in which I was no longer a witness to their bellowing diaphragms. The arctic frosts had done their work.

On a side of one of the paper-thin walls, a rectangle of undulating aluminum foil was patently visible. It unwrapped itself in the way of a gentle waving film and welcomed me with gifts from another world. Seeping out of that altered cognosis, the impulse of the White amped up its wavelengths and the surgical hem of Time/Space rose to expose the other limits of impermanence. Out of those yawning hollows came not one but two titanium feathered beings, each one unfolding its terrene sentience into my presence. As they emerged pushing their specters in through the gaping orifice, they seemed to not notice me. Exuding their bodies out of their delivery portal and onto the straw tatami mats, they landed like twin ninja iguanas from a sunless perimeter. The members of the Hiroshima clan, frozen in fright and experiencing a multiplication of canceled Time factors, had no notice of the ethereal entities babbling with gauche abandon as they commenced to engage one another with heated dialectic. As the boiling chimes drove pitiful spikes into the back of my brainwaves, a muted defiance erupted with a delicate agony.

UNTO HIS SERVANT [2]
AS ANGEL OF PERGAMOS

ELVIN THEIR POWER
IS IN THEIR MOUTH [3]
IT CAN POUR FORTH
LIKE A BLOOD RED FLAME
OF THEIR BLASPHEMY

IF IT FALLS UPON YOUR WINGS
YOUR HOLY SILVER CRYSTALS
WILL BURN AND TURN
TO BLACK BURNT EDGES

Then the larger one continued as the acidic verbal rain sliced into me.

UNTO THE ANGEL OF EPHESUS
ZOE THEIR TAILS ARE LIKE
UNTO SERPENTS AND WITH THEIR
HEADS THEY DO HURT [4]

ON THE SIDE OF A MOUNTAIN
UNDER A TREE I HAD THREE OF THEM
IN CAPTIVITY WITH MY WINGS
BUT THEY TORMENTED ME
WITH THE STRENGTH OF THEIR TAILS
AND GNAWED THROUGH MY FIRE SWORD
AND ARRAYED A RAINBOW ROUND ME
I HAVE MUCH HATE
FOR THE NICOLAITANS

The one with the fiery blue eyes and thick stubby arms cried back.

HIM OF PERGAMOS
THOSE ARE NOT TAILS ELVIN
THEY TAKE WITH THEM

411

The Moon Women

BLACK BRIDLES THAT COME
OUT OF THE DARKENED PITS
THESE ARE WHAT BURN
AND EAT AT OUR WINGS
AS THEY ARE THROWN
UPON US LIKE THE UNCLEAN
WASH OF BLACK BRIMSTONE
FROM OUT OF THE MOUTH
OF THE RED DRAGON

STAY CLEAR OF THEM ELVIN
THRUST YOUR FIRE LANCE
INTO THEIR BURNING TONGUES
AND POWER LIFT UP
LIKE A LEOPARD THAT WILL
WIPE OUT THEIR LIKENESS
AND SMITE THEIR TAILS
IN MINGLED AIR OVER WHEAT

THE REST OF MEN WHICH WERE
NOT KILLED BY THIS PLAGUE
BY THE EVIL NICOLAITANS
WILL BE HONOURED WHILE
THE REMNANT WILL NEVER MORE
BE WRITTEN INTO THE BOOK
OF CREATION TO GATHER
HONOUR AS THEIR NUMBER

SUFFER THE LITTLE LIE

THIS IS A FRUITFUL AND INFORMATIVE

AS WE WALK THEM INTO THE

DISCUSSION BETWEEN THREE ANGELS

WALL OF THE ALL TIME

OVERHEARD BY A QUIET OBSERVER

412

Kokabel, as Zoephirdad, rose off the mats as he drilled his charged transmission my way.

ANOTHER MIGHTY ANGEL
CAME DOWN FROM HEAVEN
CLOTHED IN A CLOUD AND
A RAINBOW WAS UPON HIS HEAD
AND HIS FACE WAS AS IT WERE
THE SUN AND HIS FEET WERE
AS PILLARS OF FIRE [5]

Azrael burst forth from the out of the Time pool and rallied forth the clan of the Seven, the legion of Abaddon.

UNTO HIS SERVANTS [6]

ARISE AND BEHOLD
MY DOMINION OF THE SKIES
WE HAVE OFF TO THE BLUE
REALMS OVER ZABULON
WHERE TWELVE THOUSAND MORE
ARE GATHERED FOR BATTLE

Azrael reclaimed his honor over the pair.

AND THERE CAME OUT
OF THE SMOKE BLACK
LOCUSTS UPON THE EARTH
AND UNTO THEM WAS GIVEN POWER
AS THE SCORPIONS OF THE EARTH
HAVE POWER [7]

ON UP AND AWAY MY BRETHREN
IN THE NAME OF ABADDON
WE SHALL OVERCOME AZRAEL GIVES THE COMMAND

The Moon Women

The three of them dove back in through the Time/Space vent and it collapsed behind them taking with it all remembrance of its deliverance, except to those who had been recognized and were now immune to the Khrng.

For me, all the warped voyaging was eternally preserved in my brain banks for posterity. Since the opening out of the ceiling in Cooketown, I can drudge up any portion of them whenever I choose the same way as the whales moving in the depths of the oceans can recover their giant thoughts, the ones, which men will never know. Like combinations of molecular science, which will never see the light of day, like units of DNA, which can't take birth because the will to live was omitted, the memoires wait to be uncovered.

I had my leave of those memorable lottery winners and was out of there at full steam. Ben Harris, Mat and I were surprised how much raw genius lay in our myelinated resources. We were down the road and back to the FWC campus faster than you can shout, "Draw pardner!"

- 5 -

During the interim between my departure from Japan and my reentry four months later, I briefly touched base in Taiwan, my first port of call on my hedgehopping junket from Japan to India. This ancillary episode has now invaded the recount. My venture into the capital of Taipei was virtually uneventful at first. With the flock of flight stewards on Cathay Pacific clicking through their routines flawlessly, I had a decent vegetarian meal and retired to collect my share of inflight treats. The scarves, chopsticks, and embossed napkins were all stowed carefully away in my overhead bag. Valued particularly were the colorful mini-sized cartons, which were perfect for keeping loose items like nail clippers and tongs.

As we approached the city, I peeked through the Plexiglas oval to view an ocean of gray buildings below. Practically every vertical surface down there was either concrete or cardboard. There were scarcely a dozen or so billboards or any other possible structure, which might yield a hint of any color. Oh well, I'm only going to be here for a week at the most.

After the wheels touched down unceremoniously, we taxied to our resting place. With no gangplank or airport terminal tube for fast track travelers, airport crew rolled a triangular stair apparatus over to the exit hatch and all the passengers deplaned the old school way, down the balustrade. That is one of the initial sights, which confronts you when you drop anchor in a Third World country. There are no plane tubes; you disembark from your flight by descending a rickety staircase. You step off smack onto the tarmac - the real ground is waiting there to greet you!

With a rapid hustle and bustle through airport customs, there were few hitches and a quick walk to curbside. A gray taxi jock with a gray cap picked me up in his gray Isuzu and dropped me off at the entrance to a gray hotel. I had petitioned him to bring me to a cheap one because even the pricey high-rises were gray. After signing the register and securing my sleeping quarters, I retired to my sub-standard room. Throwing my pack onto the bed, I sat down at a rickety teak table and calculated the few hours I would need to reside in this dump.

On a foldout map of Taiwan, I located a suitable mountain peak for my experiments. It looked to be not too far off the beaten path, which was a plus. The only activity I was inspired to cross off my bucket list while on the island of Taiwan was to climb to some summit and flatulate on my recorder. I was determined to find out if I could contact any particular etheric entities, ones. which might be frequenting those aerial terrains and willing to communicate with me about things I might not be able to learn via the normal pathways. Tomorrow I would head out.

Following my sunrise cup of java, I got directions on which buses to board so I could wind up at the hamlet living at the foot of my intended target. As I climbed onto the overcrowded bus, I could barely find a place to sit what with all the baskets of vegetables and gobs of wooden crates stuffed with chickens. The stench was disgusting. Swaying like an over-inflated water buffalo, the bus trundled off down the road. Luckily, it didn't capsize. After a rollicking two-hour joyride, the driver announced my drop off and I jumped down undeterred by little reduction in speed as he never even remotely applied the brakes. The run-off was four or five quick steps in succession to avoid falling flat on my face.

Off in the distance, I picked out my intended hillock from the surrounding summits. Hiking off down the mudded ruts, which separated the rice paddies, I spanned many long runs of wheat as

The Moon Women

well. After reaching the margin of the large mound, I launched my ascent. Half way up I stopped for a breather and drank some green tea from my army canteen. Two pieces of fresh fruit, which I had picked up from a roadside vendor, was packed in my rucksack and added needed nourishment; one was an apple-like fruit the Japanese call a Nashi and the other was a fresh McIntosh apple. As I carved off the red skin with my Swiss Army knife, I found it to be a pleasant surprise the rubicund New England fruit had wormed its way this far into remote Asia. Collecting my trash, I crammed it into my backpack not wishing to spare any traces of my American presence here.

After many strenuous laps of kick-ass hiking, I finally got to the summit. The surrounding vicinity exhibited an expansive vista, which extended all the way out to the ocean, some sixty kilometers away. On the backside of an adjacent peak was a slender thread of smoke curling up like a carbon wisp against the pale northern sky. Even though I took it to be mildly distressing, I dropped its significance in the face of the probability of contacting my outer air friends.

With the tall grasses buffeting my arms, I ingested the totality of this astounding vista and out came my recorder. My fingers danced nimbly over the fluted ports releasing a confusing array of burbling squeaks. The spontaneous warbling and my psychogenic pulses drew in a band of floral sprites, which had chosen to draw near for they were mesmerized by the nasty human frenzy sparking up in the airs around me.

In their curiosity, they shared some of the territorial buzz over-lorded by stern warnings from the uppermost lightning glyphs. The main sprite related to me via a series of sparkling whistles that the main contingent of the Abaddon Seven had only just this yester twilight encamped upon this very peak. In the seclusion of their fright, the sprites had overheard them commiserating over a previous engagement with an entire battalion of Khrng, which had been sighted heading for a sprawling tract of wheat lying on the outskirts of Taipei.

When I looked off to the North, I could barely perceive the sign of a progressively expanding cascade of triangular crescents propagating out across the field some eight kilometers on the edge of visibility. This formation indicated the battle was finished and done with. No one knew who had won or lost but the head sprite declared it was both bloody and fierce. The resultant impression on the wheat stamped there within the skinny side of less than a second was one of pyramids and other Egyptian like symbols, hieroglyphics almost. Yet the full dynamics of the actual confrontation flashing in and out of the etheri-sphere had gone on for the better part of two days before the Khrng withdrew their ships. The carnage must have been extensive. The sprites remarked that because the residues from the evaporated Khrng had saturated the wheat so deeply, a turbid death grease had now increased substantially enough to be visible through the distant mirage as a dull glow.

The sprites also explained a little on how the healthy Khrng operate only within the Time epoch, which we are sharing presently, but their lifetimes are quite lengthy, as much as half a dozen millennia. The Khrng maintain a considerable grip upon modern mankind throughout this epoch and then they seem to fade away because in the successive epochs as the stature of regular humans take on extensions in size, the specifications adopted by the Khrng are reduced in a reversed proportion. They shrink down to a diminutive regimen of only 30 centimeters and also only live for forty to fifty years. That is why they don't have much effect on the inhabitants of the other Yugas. However, since they manage to reclaim the ongoing levels of their technologies as they reappear in successive Iron Ages, they augment all their knowledge menus exponentially with each turn of the four Yuga cycle. This is what allows them to maintain an unbelievable hold over the entire planet even though we know nothing of it. Overall, their drastically mutated genes are what cause this inverted progression of their genesis. Undaunted, however, they continue to modify themselves century after century. Quite possibly, one day, they may have overcome the barriers of the Yugas themselves, enough to champion the Time/Space shields forever. Such a thing would prove disastrous for the remaining ordinary humans no doubt. After this brief clash, the handful of lemon sprites moved on.

As my energies spread out into the clouds and the sparkling whitecaps foaming on the outlying horizon, a peaceful calm came over me. A large rock, which I had come across upon the peak, seemed to befriend me and inspire a brief rest. I put my recorder back in my pack and leaned back upon it to observe the wistful cloudbanks

The Moon Women

drifting by. After a while, I fell asleep into a baby nap and had another one of those peculiar dreams in which I awoke on a similar hillock overlooking the exact same sea.

Face to face against the blowing mist of an approaching cold front, I was reflecting on the intense volume of psychic feedback swimming around me. A turbulence barreled inwards threatening to bowl me over as if some astral mirage emerging from out of the Beyond. As I focused on it, I noticed a stability within its core, an expanding opaqueness gliding in over the hilltops. While the tumbling orb of luminescence came closer and closer, its wayward brume fomented its own life threads as if it were electric spiders crawling on webs of air. As the white fury enlarged its glow, it resembled the figure of a gossamer individual rippling down upon the earth. With sweeping movements, colossal snowy wings exploded in front of me. Unfurling one down stroke after another, the being's descent leveled off and it landed a dozen meters away. Making lengthy strides to gain the gradual slope, it came to stand within reach, all the while collapsing its gigantic feathered appendages into its back. Its titanium sphere of its head layered its shine with a brightness and a painful insistence as its twin blue shafts fixed me within a paralyzing gaze pinning me like a bug. And then the frenzied chimes stirred their demon pulse into my brain to spread a cottony numbness across my mind. And it spoke its word into my thoughts.

UNTO THE ANGEL OF THE CHURCH [8]

SALUTATION OF AN ANGEL
HELLO MY GOOD FRIEND
EVEN ANGELS CELEBRATE VICTORY

AS THE SEED OF YOUR WINGS
HAVE ADDED UNTO THE BEGINNING
OF YOUR END I RAMAEL

YOU ARE PROGRESSING IN

LEGION *OF ABADDON*   BOTH YOUR KNOWLEDGE AND DEEDS
SON OF MAN AND MESSENGER
DO HEREBY GIVE YOU THIS NEWS
AS WE WALK IN THE WHITE [9]

418

THE OFFSPRING OF THE BEAST

THE ANGELS CONSIDER THE KHRNG

HAVE AGAIN BEEN DELIVERED INTO

TO HAVE BEEN SPAWNED FROM

THE JUST WALL OF THE ALL TIME

THE RED DRAGON ALTHOUGH
THIS IS NOT CORRECT

WHAT THEY ARE AND WHAT THEY DO
WILL NO LONGER HURT THE EARTH
NEITHER THE SEA NOR THE TREES
AND WILL NO LONGER MEASURE
OR KEEP THE SEED OF MAN
FROM THE THRONE OF GOD

HUMANS ARE A DIVINE CONSTRUCT

THIS WAR HAS BEHEADED NOT ONLY
THE KINGS OF THE EARTH
AND THE GREAT MEN
AND THE RICH MEN
AND THE CHIEF CAPTAINS
AND THE MIGHTY MEN
AND EVERY BONDSMAN
AND EVERY FREE MAN [10]
BUT IT HAS REACHED HIGH
INTO THE HEAVEN WORLDS
AND EVEN UNTO ABADDON

MANY HAVE SUFFERED THIS WAR

THEREFORE WE HAVE COME
TO PUT THIS ABOMINATION
BACK INTO ITS BLOOD VIAL
AND SEAL IT FOR ALL TIME
EVEN UNTO THE WALLS
OF THE ALL TIME

The Moon Women

Ramael raised his glistening arm towards the northren pastures and pointed.

BEAR WITNESS AND BEHOLD
IN THE RIGHT HAND OF HIM
THAT SAT ON THE THRONE
A BOOK WRITTEN WITHIN
AND ON THE BACKSIDE
THE SEVEN CHAKRAS OF SPIRITUAL
SEALED WITH SEVEN SEALS [11]
CONSCIOUSNESS DEFINES WHAT HUMANS ARE

WHO IS WORTHY TO OPEN THE BOOK
AND TO LOOSE THE SEALS [12]
WHOSOEVER CAN FATHOM THIS SECRET

AND NO MAN IN HEAVEN
NOT ON EARTH NEITHER
UNDER THE EARTH
WAS ABLE TO OPEN THE BOOK
NEITHER TO LOOK THEREON [13]
IS BOTH A VERY RATE PERSON

THIS WORK IS FOR YOU
AND COMMANDED UNDER
THE TEN SEALS OF YOUR LIFE
AS WELL AS A CHOSEN PERSON
AS THE TEN WOMEN
ONE WHO WAS TESTED TEN TIMES
IN THIS WORK YOU SHALL
FIND REWARD AND RIGHTEOUSNESS
ONE WHO HAS PERSEVERED TIRELESSLY
THEREIN I GRANT YOU THE KEY
AND SHALL NOW BE GIVEN THE SECRET
TO THE WORLD OF THE WHITE
OF WHO AND WHAT WE ARE

420

THE TEN WOMEN WALK IN THE NAME
As well as what the women were
OF ABADDON AND ADD THE GLORY
And why they came to you
OF THE APOSTLES KNOWN TO YOU
As agents of Abaddon to serve you
AS THE BLOOD OF THE BURNING GOD
THE NIRUNJAN *WHO HATH CREATED*
THE SUN AND THE MOON

WALK WITH THEM IN THE WHITE
AND KNOW YOUR WORK IS SOON
TO COME AND REVEAL THE RULE
OF THE SON OF MAN AND THE
Stand forth to receive
SEED OF THE TRUE AND
Your just deserts
GOLDEN HOME OF ABADDON
As the one who knows us

As Ramael mounted his regal white stallion, I rubbed my eyes to witness him regain the skies on wings of crystalline awe and whip the feathery grasses on the hillock into a turmoil. Within seconds, only a misty trail was drifting in the clouds as his mark.

As I came round from my dreamland, the wind blew the grasses away from the looming monolithic stone, which now towered over me. I looked at it intensely and discovered it was not a rock at all; it was a tombstone. As its insistence of death pounded upon me like an amputated obelisk of ruin, I struggled on the edges of meaning to reach out and wipe the dirt off the moldering surfaces of this dolomite menhir. There was only one name engraved on the tombstone.

THADDAEUS

Flying over a 20-kilometer tract of wheat, which hugged the banks of the Asphalappa River in Ghana, a formation of three White

421

The Moon Women

beings moved in unison as lightning fired spidery veins of fury in contrast to the sulky forgetfulness of the night. Twisting and banking along the cheeks of a cloud genie, they were intent on performing another rabbit act. Under an osteoid moon, the trio popped in and out of an alternate transference and commenced to discharge a squad of Khrng, two thousand strong, on the verge of releasing a preplanned detonation at midnight. The three got down to work.

TO HIM BE ALL GLORY
AND DOMINION OVER THEM
FOR EVER AND EVER
AMEN [14]

- 6 -

The reset coming at me snapped me back into my immutable chair and left a pit in my stomach, which I yearned to fill with some dosas, but without a moment's notice, the pulse took me off again. A couple of months after that confrontation with the tombstone in Taiwan, I found myself on the apex of a looping route, which I had chartered through Southeast Asia to get away from the faked murder of the unlucky family in Hiroshima and trace an adventuresome odyssey towards India. The sad thing of it, however, was that at the end of my stay in Malaysia the Indian Embassy had rejected me for filing a false report. It seems the future of fabricated murders actually does impact written history.

Red pompoms danced in the rear window of the miniature Mercedes taxi as it departed down the dusty road in Kuala Lumpur. I had solicited the driver to track down an economy hostel for the fortnight. And the Ming Hotel fit the formula to a tee. Its Dutch door topped with a shoddy beaded curtain welcomed me to the land of low cost revelry.

Advertising her wares with a floral invitation over her ear, a painted Malay girl sat parked next to its entrance. As she chewed on the cud of her last customer, she greeted me with a generous grin and a casual rocking as she tipped back on her crumbling bench. A dead butt lodged in the socket of a missing tooth underscored her indubitable beauty. Her comatose middy presented a pitiful bouquet of yellowed stains right where you'd expect them. From its perch

422

over her ear, the limp magnolia had no doubt seen serious use by her sister; however, it unquestionably proclaimed her primitive system of postulates - Yum Yum 101.

As the glass beads clicked on my belt buckle, I penetrated the inner sanctum of this peninsular oasis. Instantly razor glints of dayglow neon assaulted me from all directions. The pinks and the purples of deco art swarmed in at me from over the counter while the yellows and oranges of the Buddha figurines on the counter slammed me with free salvation from the other banks of nirvana. Straight out of the midway of this Malay isthmus came the true blues of frightening promise; the guarantee of living little death rushed in to spear me. However, the most suffocating wave of all came from the ubiquitous Chartreuse, which closed off all the future dimensions coming out of the ceiling. It was vomitaceous.

I scribbled my John Hancock on the sign-in sheet and surrendered my passport. The other shiny sweet girl showed me to my bunk while giving me a tour through the farm of prefabricated cubicles. This Chinese motor lodge in Selangor state was like a rat's maze. The main drawback for me was the tippity top of the conjoined cubes of living space was only a couple of meters off the floor. This was safe and sound for the on-tap clientele, but for a lanky American such as myself, a tiptoe recon run on everybody's whereabouts could be performed quite easily; not that I was particularly concerned about their confidential activities.

Mine was sparsely furnished: one crushed Davenport trundle cot and a singular battered Farthingale oak-back exhibiting a fractured leg, all of which rendered the charm of long service in the name of trust. I figured the two representatives of the downtrodden were a depiction of the patterns of human behavior that undoubtedly delineated the long line of soap operas waged upon these sheets over the foregoing decades. I gained some solace over the weak smattering of furniture Speak leaking in. After having come to realize the occurrence of this obsession was an indication that either I was honing in on unintended intimacy or facing intrusion from the Khrng, I had no choice but to act accordingly. The abstruse references had periodically come forth and operated as if a psychic Geiger counter registering possible proximities to one or the other of these danger factors. Either way I was relieved to have avoided the uptick.

The Moon Women

I threw my pack onto the crude wooden seat and collapsed onto the bed to test its spring or lack thereof. My preference was for medium, but what I got was extra filthy. It looked like the linens hadn't been changed in weeks. I couldn't really complain; two bits and a double simoleon wasn't highway robbery. My bank account was painted red, what with all the stretching it had to go through last week with Chhumpar 's liberation from slavery. I was expecting an upgrade from Daddy Warbucks any day now. Without asking, I got an additional demonstration of the local hygiene as I watched a petulant beetle crawl across the cheap linoleum as though its motor was on the fritz.

Here in Malaysia, I had one job to do while marking time in this dump and one job only. Get my visa for India and get to Bangalore with all my portable photo equipment pronto. Prior to leaving Japan for India, I had shipped all the heavier gear onwards as unaccompanied baggage from Hiroshima with a priority status straight to Madras. My two large duffel bags were now sitting in the municipal godown under the auspices of the Indian Customs House until I got to my destination and presented my claim tag. Calculating my stay in the elegant Indonesian city might consume a week to ten days at the most so I unpacked my gear.

As I was putting my clothes away, I noticed some scratching noises like fingernails on a blackboard. For most people, this is a gut wrenching vibration, which sends the listener into a hair pulling delirium but for me it was simply interesting. The sound emanated as if from somewhere inside the shell of the cubicle which seemed to be impossible because it was only a few centimeters thick. I stopped and listened carefully to zero in on its source and possibly identify what it might be. Up front, it was lost to me but then it returned. After a moment or so, I pinpointed its source as lying in the vicinity of the door so I quickly yanked it open and found a gorgeous Malay girl standing there with a big Cheshire grin pasted on her puss. The alarming glitch in the mix was she was presenting her seething launch pad all fired up and aimed at my lunar pedestal like a mad minx.

"You knee gurl? My good yum yum. My do for you." She tugged at my waistline.

"That's Okay, Love. I think we've been down this road before. No thank you." I expressed my due cordiality.

424

She grew more persistent with additional smoochy moochy: facial expressions aimed at getting into my pants.   I   popped   out my index finger in front of her puss painted as a miotic mask.

"No!"

Following that invective with my big boy voice, I touched off a furious salvo of infuriation at her bedevilment.

"Off with you!"

That popped her bubble and she tore off down the shrinking corridor of the rat maze and vanished. I continued unpacking. After stowing away my articles into the rat-infested drawers, I headed out for some nutritional fulfillment. I padlocked the door with the key, although I didn't know what the heck that was going to do. Anybody could simply climb over the upper edge and help their selves.

I inquired at the receptionist's desk where I might get some fast food. The woman's reaction was clueless. After I signed back at her with the international gesture of tapping my hand against my yap to indicate my hunger, she directed me a little ways down the lane over onto a footpath where a modest eatery resided. After I had some ramen noodles and veggies there, I traveled over to the Indian High Commission to get my visa.

Kuala Lumpur was such a whimsical place. There were lots of strikingly manicured government complexes. The buildings were all sparklingly clean and freshly whitewashed. They had crisp onyx trim and ornate shutters. Clusters of masjids and Hindu temples sent their signature spires towards the blue multi-theistic welkins upstairs. Cottony cumulous balloons and swirling Mares tails planted their feathering fantasies into the lost nights and garlanded these empyrean heights with their gladness. The meticulously landscaped grounds presented an assortment of variegated flowering plants everywhere and dotted the city with a pristine, modern and attractive face.

After I presented myself at the desk of a Mr. Ranakka, the Indian magistrate, I got the application for the visa and filled it out. It was at that juncture I made a tactical error, which was miniscule in detail but became a major penalty with regard to its effect on my future. Under the heading entitled: Reason for travel to India, I wrote a mini blurb depicting the movies which I planned to create when I was in country. In proper penmanship, I disclosed one of my ideas was to shoot a great deal of footage down in the squalid slums perched all along the banks of the rivers, which sliced Mumbai into

The Moon Women

crooked deltas. Since I understood there were well over two million people living near those rat-infested sewers, I proposed to use it to portray a plot relating how one of those slum kids could strike it rich in the lottery and upset the apple cart known as the caste system. As I handed my signed application back to the magistrate, I queried him about how much more time I might have to wait to get a confirmation of my visa. He assured me it might only be a week and presented me with his completely understandable and officially certified grin. I shoved off and returned home to grab some shut-eye having concluded my man-day's effort. While white-capped curls churned lazily in the pastel blue sky, an armada of snowy crepe paper wings swam by hastily like swan rockets.

- 7 -

After suffering from a severe case of musical chairs with the magistrate for weeks on end, I was nearing the possibility it was a fruitless effort. It was so exhausting to waste long hours down in that pit only to return to the Ming each afternoon and plod through the cavalcade of tattooed women and eager johns traipsing in and out of the lobby as they mined through the semantics of lust . Each young she-devil had a pastel Cattleya orchid stapled somewhere on her cephalic billboard advertising her products of pleasure. This time I mounted a makeshift causeway over the moat of shifting mayhem and tiptoed my way passed the loose pistols waiting to fire at their hot bullseyes. When I reached the stern of the info booth, which was more of a table than anything else, the routine Chinese fellow was absent. I didn't know if the strumpet now directing the whore traffic could converse in English or not, so I waded in.

"Key, please; any mail?" I was feigning it.

She responded with a catty smile; no teeth, of course.

"Well, that went well." I announced to all my roommates. "How 'bout a blow job then?"

"You wanna suckie?" The tart chimed in.

"No! I would like my room key, if you would be so kind." I made a turning motion in the air with my clenched fist towards her nose.

After her twisted claw dug around in a worn cubbyhole, she came up with my key and a shiny laminated business card. It

426

advertised a nailed up bloody Jesus on its cover page. Perhaps this was a Christian whorehouse but I hadn't had much experience with either one, pro-Messiah or pro-Mongoloid. On the back, it had some prayers:

> Whose fan is in thy hand
> And He will thoroughly
> Purge his floor and gather
> His wheat into the garner;
> But He will burn up the chaff
> With unquenchable fire! [15]

Staggering! Was I the wheat or the chaff or maybe the fire? And in what whirlwind would I be consumed, the one of Satan or the one of Service? Would the legions of Angels overcome the squadrons of the demon locust soldiers all clashing on the limits of an unimaginable conflict?

I traced the wayward arc to my door where another zombie walker all freshly baked in the whore ovens greeted me with authentic cheer. As she snickered at me with her saccharine grin, I plugged the key into the slot, entered, and closed the door. Alighting on my catsup colored sitting appliance (I figured if I didn't in point of fact call it a chair it wouldn't bite me with more of the Speak) I contemplated on why am I having this cathartic experience again? I hiked myself onto the unstable platform to get a better perspective on reality.

On tiptoes, my sightline topped an easy head over the limits of the cubicles. The paint on the neighboring enclosures was a sickly lime green done with a glossy luster. Its sheen acted like a mirror. Catoptrically, I could oversee the dramas being enacted within in each and every one of those indecent arenas. Horrified, I got down pronto.

I now had the concrete evidence. I'm definitely in a fucking whorehouse! I've been stationed in a full blown brothel. Once this ton of bricks had fallen from my mind, I was mildly unburdened. Inasmuch as I had gone through a lot to secure Chhumpar's release from her maniacal uncle and her eventual emancipation, did the Prime Mover expect me to have to do it for all of them? It didn't seem rational or even practical. Besides, there's way too many of

The Moon Women

them. How could I justify it considering my travel plans have already been booked?

In any case, I consigned them all to their afternoon's activities and sought an alternative caveat emptor. This place was not going to be my spiritual cat-o-nine tails. I had made up my mind I was not going to be asphyxiated in this Ming Ding necropolis. I put my shoes back on and marched to the head honcho's desk, er, table. The male receptionist was back so I didn't have to deal with the enchanting succubus. I posed my cross-examination. Was there a shopping plaza in Kuala Lumpur, some place where I could go to buy necessities?

"You wan' Mall. Tell taxi you go Mall." He waved me off like a pesky fly.

Damn! Of course! The Mall. How come I didn't think of that? Undeniably, I had misinterpreted where the hell I was on the planet. Did I think I was pioneering in some Third World human garbage heap? Oh, no. In truth, I now found myself in a fully cloned community of Framingham Massachusetts. Here, smack dab in the center of this stunted loop and forged at the heart of the Malay Peninsula, plunked down in the precise hub of southeastern Asian culture, was a full-fledged westernized American Mall.

It had the usual array of department stores and a variety of shops all with their overdone window dressing. It had a second level of day merchants managing their kiosks and displaying their wares while hawking their trinkets all up and down the expansive corridors. It even had Muzak piped in from some virtual jazz land. As Barry Manilow oozed out through the umbrella speakers, I thought I could even pick out a few strains of Gustav Mahler.

Soon I came upon a well to do eatery, one which looked like it might have some authentic Indian food. I went in and wedged my thick midsection into a domestically sized booth. In the most pleasant Indian accented English, a nicely attired waiter came over and posed his introduction.

"I could tell you from America, is it not? Would you be having some cheeseburger?" He seemed quite articulate but definitely needing a few adjustments.

"You know, do you have any Indian food here; anything like pilaf or even a vegetable biryani? I would also like some cauliflower curry, if you have that." I figured I might as well go for the whole

428

enchilada. Since I was resurrecting my roots back in those days, I had felt eating vegetarian was an important first step.

"Oh, yes! We do have wegetarian dishes of all kinds. We are wegetarians also. We are Brahmins. Well, Vantu is a Muslim, but my brother Arjuna and I are from the temple." Not surprisingly, his familial pride was showing.

"Can I get some bread with that?" If I over order I can doggy bag it back to my whorehouse if need be.

"We have many kinds of breads. We have paratha, which is a thicker kind. Then, there is papadum, a crispy bread and also the chapatti which is the standard bread eaten all over India." This waiter was not only being quite cordial but somewhat informative as well.

"I'll have the regular one, if it's all okay with you." I was playing it safe.

Within minutes, I was being served with many dishes which I wasn't really sure if I had ordered or not. I dug in anyway because I hadn't had anything from the time of the weak Chai I had drank over at the office of the magistrate.

"Wow! This is really well done." I couldn't believe how spicy and nicely prepared the meal was. It was a comfort to know I wouldn't have to be searching the streets for a place to eat. I could just come right over here.

That is how my friendship with these three guys at the "Thumbs Up" blossomed. Unavoidably, whilst outside the later times, I continued to endure outlandish dramas over at the Ming, brothel and all. But presiding over pastimes of the daylight hours, primarily in the afternoons, I was entertained by the Brahmin musketeers over at little chapatti joint. It seems foreigners, especially ones from the USA with American accents, engendered a big draw what with their know all concerning currencies, music cultures and especially the wealth of their lexicon of movie lore. They constantly bugged me to pronounce certain words they considered very modern so they could duplicate them as close to my American way of pronunciation. I would thoroughly enchant them and sometimes even bambozzle them with phrases like: "What's happening?" or "Get down with that" or "Way to go" and then there's always, "Way cool." We spent lengthy laughing bouts carrying on with these invectives of American slang. I would always be doling out the party favors.

The Moon Women

Over at the office of the High Commission, things were not progressing as I would have hoped. I visited the place every Monday, Wednesday and Friday and repeatedly suffered through the same damn procedure each time: sign the register; sit on my ass for half the damn day and then split. I recognized early on that it only made the outcome much worse to cause a fuss or bellyache about anything. That was not the way to get my visa accomplished in this quagmire of decadent bureaucracy. Blame it on the wheels of fate or whatever, no one had tipped me off about how to get down with the baksheesh game, the little trick in which you must generously grind hard cash into their grubby little mitts, encouragement for turning the wheels of destiny, or whatever. It was quite a while before I unlocked this back door approach. Yet it was because of that lengthy delay, (caused by my genetic hardheadedness) I was privy to another sphere of endeavor.

One day, Arjuna invited me to come over to his pad. Since I thought that was a bit rash, I had my reservations. His brother Krishnaprabhudeva had made some comments regarding unnecessarily costing his relatives additional wherewithal for providing me with luncheon trays, complete dinners as well as other finger treats. It put me out some but I recovered. Arjuna, on the other hand, had always been kind, sincere, and courteous to me. By the second week of wasting time at the High Commission and downing my meals at "Thumbs Up," I was getting a little antsy.

By the way, the name of the store, "Thumbs Up", is a name, which corporate bigwigs had applied to Coca-Cola when it came into India some years previous. The entrepreneur who introduced Coke and who now owned this western leaning fast food chain had the idea of capitalizing on this one of a kind trade name. Evidently, he had gotten away with it.

By the third week I had succumbed to Arjuna's pleadings and unending encouragement. I met Mr. and Mrs. Mindalu and their entire family. There was Saraswati, Parvati, Prem and Sita. Prem and Sita were male-female twins. Now, can you follow why I was invited? Yes, that's correct. I'm a big husband ticket for one of their daughters to advance upon the shores of the American paradise. Or, in some measure that's the way it appeared to me soon afterward. Nevertheless, I certainly didn't say anything about it to any of them.

430

Arjuna was quite obliging and the Misses did her utmost to fill me full of as many food preparations as possible. My newly earned title of vegetarian was a useful tool as well as an investment for prepaid rent. She was most certainly the matriarch of this bunch. After the meal, I thanked them profusely and beat it back to my brothel.

I signed in and threaded the maze to my gangrenous door to be received by not one, but three painted women hanging on the doorstep. They were all loosely attired and hung with lurid smiles glowering at my dick. The one who was not the knockout sweated me continuously with jabs consisting of why didn't I party, you know, fuckie-wuckie, or whatever? She served me one of her tipped-up eyebrows, that swerving askant look, which puts forth its purposeful query.

"Are you sure the plumbing is working down there, Fella? You might need to have those pipes cleaned out otherwise the sludge is gonna set in and your good times are gonna be over."

With downright conviction, I narrated my lines.

"Look, it's not that I'm anti-social or anything. I'm afraid I just have a hang-up with buying you. Women are to be loved, not treated like sex objects."

After numerous attempts to explain this philosophy, I gave up. But my little pep rallies must have gotten the message across because after a while they stopped hanging on my doorknob drooling at the merchandise.

After retiring to my four-meter cubicle, I was happy to notice the ladies had finally donated some fresh sheets, which had fewer skid marks on them than the high mileage ones I had started out with. As I lay back on the lumpy mattress, my only visual entertainment was the fan hanging high above me beating away at the invisible phantoms revived from some ancient Chinese dynasty. As its broad blades whipped at the stale humanized gases, which had failed to receive any vital freshness for weeks I was lost in the spin. As the mossy spatulas swept round and round like the oars of a magnificent war ship making its way north on the Euphrates to engage the Sumerians, I saw myself floating away with that current to a far-removed shore.

In the dwindling light of sundown, the river's course made a sharp bend to unveil a broad plain. Shooting fire exploded

The Moon Women

percussively and illuminated a battleground of unimaginable horrors. Silvery angelic beings were hacking down armadas of tiny gray creatures, who swarmed over the grass plains like creeping arms of gray lava. The flaming war scythes of the titanium angels were like buzz saws leaving a blackish wake of macerated mutant parts, which lay smoldering upon the earth like freshly stirred embers from a furnace. One of the Abaddon Seven flew by me in a streamlined vector. He was calling out to his comrades who were bringing up the rear guard.

AS LEGION *AND SERVANT*
OF THE ONE BURNING GOD
THE NIRUNJAN *ON HIGH*
HAIL UNTO HIS COMMAND

KOKA AND TURI
TAKE THE ONES
TO THE NORTH

RAM AND SHAM
GO TO THE EAST

I MUST SUFFER
THEIR SHIPS IN THE SOUTH
TO BLOT THE BATTLE

SOON WE WILL HAVE
THEM RUNNING FROM US AND
ROLLED UP INTO THE DOOR
OF THE ALL TIME

It was Azrael setting his commands in place.

As I witnessed more of a nasty battle raging over a straggling amplitude of wheat in the Delta Province of Ontario, clusters of Khrng had cemented themselves together into a congealed mass having the contours of a wheel within a wheel. They were spinning

432

through the air like twin gyroscopes tilted slightly on edge and issuing a frightening purple glow. As their vacant faces fixated outwards, mouths agape in awe, they poured out across the vast plains of wheat. Shooting from the ends of their pointed fingers were fiery rays like ruby lasers spewing the contagion of mortality at the sweeping wings of the Angels of Abaddon who were deftly avoiding the blood wrenching attacks.

The superiority of the flying Angels was sensational. Their glistening wings spiraled and curved their flightpaths in and out of the growing fleet of the Khrng's ringed vessels, which swarmed like bees. As their majestic astral fire wands hummed with a silver radiance, each of the Seven sliced and hacked their way through the army of the Khrng leaving a wake of pathological confetti like raw meat being spit out of a grinder only it wasn't red, it was the black of meconium.

As the warriors of Abaddon sliced through the layered wheels, a sinister wing of seething vapors lifted up. The Khrng's shattered wheels exploded into flames. Like flash bulbs popping off, the crafts winked out one by one in a radius of chrysanthemum explosions as they were sucked into the vortex of the All Time, wormholes, which fed the endless orifice into the Beyond. The shovel swords of two rearward Angels funneled the body parts in through a yawning vortex of unimaginable radiance, which inhaled the remnant debris into its unending orifice like a blast furnace vaporizing their etheric molecules in through the astral tubes.

I caught a wincing transmission from the four horns of the golden altar as the prime Angel, Azrael, cried out inside my think tank.

LOOSE THE FOUR ANGELS
WHICH ARE BOUND IN THE
GREAT RIVER EUPHRATES [16]

BEHOLD THE FOUR ANGELS
WERE LOOSED WHICH ARE
PREPARED FOR AN HOUR
AND A DAY AND A MONTH
AND A YEAR FOR TO SLAY

The Moon Women

THE THIRD PART OF MEN [17]

At that time, I received an injection of more froth from the intrinsic knowledge menus. The third part of men is the Khrng. To date they have unscrambled their genetic mutant blueprint short of one third of one percent leaving only 108 crosslinks, which need further investigation. There is man. There is woman. And there is the Khrng.

Fought with a fierce agony, the battle was waged within the etheric strata between the ultra-sensitive psycho-strata of the physical and the dreamland divergence of the Beyond. Because of the resident dilation principle, the Time compression was upwards of 25,000 in magnification. That meant even though the elapsed time of this conflict, which I had witnessed when I was within the amnesic trance state as having lasted a whopping five hours in the timeframe of Abaddon, on this plane it had consumed but seven tenths of a second to spread its electric tentacles out over the sea of wheat. If a bystander had witnessed the real-time segments of this etheric warfare from his minimalist view down here on the physical plane, the experience would have been an instantaneous series of intense lightning flashes and blue neon explosions having a time-slice remarkably similar to the crack of a bullwhip. The observer would have only registered an intense spark of lightning elapsing for a hardly noticeable microsecond.

As the Angels slaughtered the thousands of Khrng and compressed their ashes into the wormhole to the All Time, their work was endless. Crackling energies let loose outbursts of collapsed molecular bundles as the polar outthrusts from the vortex core stamped intricate diagrams onto the firth of wheat. These myriad omens from alternate dimensions were not only a residue of the battle's aftermath but also a prophecy of an advanced confrontation deposited as an inverse analog from out of the wormhole dynamos.

Azrael announced his concluding soliloquy to his comrades.

THE NUMBER OF THE ARMY
OF THE HORSEMEN WERE
TWO HUNDRED THOUSAND
THOUSAND AND I HEARD

434

THE NUMBER OF THEM [18]

*THUS I SAW THE HORSES
IN THE VISION AND THEM
THAT SAT ON THEM HAVING
BREASTPLATES OF FIRE
AND JACINTH AND BRIMSTONE
AND THE HEADS OF THE HORSES
WERE AS THE MOUTHS OF LIONS
AND OUT OF THEIR MOUTHS
ISSUED FIRE AND SMOKE
AND BRIMSTONE* [19]

*BY THESE THREE WAS THE THIRD
PART OF MEN KILLED BY THE FIRE
AND BY THE SMOKE AND BY THE
BRIMSTONE WHICH ISSUED
OUT OF THEIR MOUTHS* [20]

As the burning astral razors of the Abaddon Seven slashed and chopped through the buzzing squads of the entombed gray masses, the fire rays of the Khrng, which were once their weapons, had been reversed one-eighty back at their own bodies causing them to be consumed by their own flames and smoky vomit. I came to learn later on that due to the awakening of the knowledge menus of the Khrng within me from the opening vision of my ceiling in Cooketown, many of the Khrng's secrets had been transferred to the Seven during their visits with me in the frost zones; thus bestowing a significant advantage upon them in the war. Presently, it would be easy work for the Seven because now they were essentially immune to any of the Khrng's devises. And the Angels knew it.

The only way an Angel could receive a mortal blow was via an inverted Time cannon. After a Khrng had made his way miraculously to the frontiers of the Wall of the All Time, he would then perform three steps: undertake the grueling ordeal of drinking a death cocktail, load the cannon with his own DNA seed projectile,

The Moon Women

and aim it properly without the slightest hesitation. The weapon would then be fired directly into the chromium headspace of the Angel, not an easy task. For the Khrng, using their oral lasers was like a snake biting its prey and injecting it with venom, a paralyzing act requiring the proper time necessary to load and discharge the Time cannon. It didn't seem to really be a fair fight, but since the Khrng had been preying on mankind for millions of years, the advent of the Angels had only recently come to be the last straw to the hostage taking of the Khrng. Or so it seemed.

- 8 -

As I awoke in the amrit hour of predawn, the Ming was like a morgue. I undressed, got under my one loose blanket and went back to sleep. Tomorrow would be another day of my adventure to reach the mystery palace of India.

The frequency of my visits to the "Thumbs Up" as well as the Mindalu residency escalated rapidly. I was single-mindedly becoming their mascot because every which way the wind blew they dragged me with them. We would wander the Mall together mime shopping, the only scope of shopping they entertain, because after all they weren't really upscale or well-to-do. When they did buy something, even indirectly for me, they never made moves as if they expected any payback. Even if I had partaken in the meal itself, they would always cover the check with their own funds. Time and time again, I proposed to match my portion of the bill, but they would never hear of it. One day, I had to put my foot down.

"Look, I'm costing you all considerable coinage which you don't really have. I've got my own so why don't you let me pay some of my own way?" I pleaded.

They didn't really pick up on my lingo right away. But even after Arjuna jumped in to translate, it was only after Mrs. Mindalu stepped up to the plate that my proposal was accepted. She was really the major domo of this outfit. Needless to say, it led to my being absorbed into the family with exigent circumstances. Nevertheless, my regularity in their humble domicile revealed a noticeable omission. Every Wednesday evening and Saturday afternoon, they were not available. It seems they had something going on during those times, so I didn't push the issue.

436

After the fifth week passed and I hadn't received my visa for India, I got quite impatient. After plying those bureaucrats repeatedly with my sincere inquiries, I demanded to address the imperial commissioner, but to no avail. They feared someone had secreted my passport in some tomb in the back halls and since they didn't know who had put it there, it might not be easily found. Crushed, I ambled back to the Ming and fooled around with my whores. I know that seems degenerate but I had become pals with a one or two of them who possessed something more than a dim bulb upstairs. Sometimes we played cards together. I taught them how to play Fish and they liked that game, but no hoochee koochee.

Sometime in the sixth week, Arjuna approached me and revealed their sect of Brahmins attend a special shrine in which they worshipped regularly. Then, out of the blue, he invited me to attend. I didn't know what to say. I felt honored in many ways but I when I prodded him to give me more information he looked hesitant.

"Can you not ask, but go and do it and see if you like it? If you don't like it, we will bring you back to your hostel. That is our one idea for you, Mr. Rahm." I could tell even though Arjuna was being quite level headed and honest, he wasn't giving me enough to make a decision.

However, after thinking it over and figuring it might be another chance to unveil more of the Beyond, come noon after daylight I was all set to go with them. Understandably, they wouldn't venture anywhere near my brothel. Can you blame them; they're Brahmins. So I joined up with them over at the Mall and even though there were ten of us, we all piled into a seasoned Studebaker, much as I have no idea how the heck we managed that gymnastic. It was a raucous two hours of bouncing hysterically in that tin can getting to know one another much more than I would have preferred. With a few bruised ribs, we finally narrowed in on the place. When I commented on the ride, Arjuna jested his father had driven way slower in as much as they had me with them. I can imagine what normal was, because this roadway enthusiast had barely avoided manslaughter at every turn of his wheel.

When we got to the outskirts of the city, we came through a series of sharp turns in the jungle environs after which the road ran on for quite a while until the asphalt disappeared altogether. Ten kilometers later, Mr. Mindalu negotiated another zigzagging muddy

The Moon Women

path through the jungle maze and after swooshing over the sloppy ruts, we came upon the gaudy yellow spread of an overpainted archway, which served as the entrance to a long temple. Its name was painted only in Hindi along the stockade so I couldn't quite unscramble it and neither of the Mindalu parents offered any feedback when asked. There was something surreptitious going on with this place but only deep sifting would uncover it. The telltale clue was the trickling rows of mad dog skullcap bleeding on the borders of the surrounding fence posts.

All kinds of Sanskrit writings and colorful frescos decorated the outsides including some swastikas. A swastika with the flags going counterclockwise is a Tantric mark, whereas the ones with the clockwise flags are the swastikas of the Nazis. Those who can differentiate this ambiguity could never be bottom folk. They are either possible candidates or dismally entombed slaves living within the clutches of the Khrng.

We entered into the inner sanctuary where many devotees were gathering for some shindig or performance of some kind it appeared. The Mindalu crew all ran off on confusing tacks to greet their companions. Arjuna came back and called for me to tag along with him; he was going to escort me to the place where everyone would perform the dancing. What kind of dancing? I thought.

He led me through a grove of coconut palms to a hall formed by a forest of huge stone columns having no ceiling. Many of the devotees were lining up to get their bodies painted with vibrant tempera colors. Okay. We're not exactly attending church here, are we?

"Arjuna, what the heck is going on here?"

"This is a Kali temple. The worship of Kali is what we do here. We do that by offering ourselves to the goddess as sacrificial participants in these communal worshipping ceremonies. Each dancer paints him or herself to represent one of the legendary deities of our religion. For instance, this one is ornamenting himself to be the character of Rama, the epic hero who slew Ravena, a demon god of legend. Rama's saved his wife, Sita, from the ravages of this demon. The dancers can pick any hero or legendary figure whom they would like to be and dress up as that personage: clothes, costumes, cosmetics, everything they want. As the ceremony commences the dancers imitate the actions ascribed to that legendary personality."

This charade seemed to be an ancient play on Dungeons and Dragons. Nevermind. That won't come for them until a few more years from now.

"Is it all right if I watch for a while rather than dive right into it since I don't know how to do it yet?"

Greenhorn was the word for it but I spared him that confusion. He made the traditional coconut bobble and continued to lather more and more paint on his kisser. Then he opened a wooden chest and grabbed a handful of what looked like golden skewers. He headed over to a large staging area where many of the worshippers were gathered. Then, the drums erupted.

Initially it was merely a bunch of flourishes on a couple tablas, and some tom-toms. Then, the maracas picked up the tempo. A select number of shrill wind instruments joined in. Then the full percussion section damn near ruptured my ears. It was a really loud and mesmerizing rhythm. I ducked for cover behind a column over near the margins of what you might call the dance platform. As the mess of dancers bobbed and weaved in and out to the driving music, the drubbing of the drums escalated in a full fury. All four of the Mindalu children were going wild at it. When the drumming gained even more speed, the dancers twisted faster and faster in a blinding turmoil. Sometimes it would slow to a crawl and then it would rev back up into an all crushing beat. It was quite startling to watch. As clumps of incense sticks belched clouds of aromatic fumes out into the afternoon air, the drums pounded onwards giving me a headache.

As the steady thumping slowed, the dancers kept devil-dancing in place like slow-motion zombies. Their handlers poured out into the dance arena holding the shiny skewers. What happened next wrapped me in a wave of shock. As each of the dancers opened their mouths and stuck out their tongues, the helper selected a bronze skewer and stabbed it straight through the dancer's tongue! He jammed the damn foul spike straight through the poor person's outstretched flesh. But there was no screaming or any indication of pain or discomfort on the part of the dancer. It didn't make any sense; they appeared to even enjoy it. After the skewer was in there, off they went to jive with the drumming pace. When they had a handful of dancers all skewered up, the drums launched into their second

The Moon Women

symphony with a thumping, hypnotic beat. This time the dancers drove themselves into a wild hysteria. They went completely berserk. In the midst of the mojo jamboree, they were throwing themselves onto the mud floor, smashing themselves into the columns, and playing bump ass all over the place. Torrents of blood were dripping down their bare torsos from the mutilated tongues and other body parts. As the throbbing drums pulsed more and more crazily, it drove the dancers into a frenzied lather like mindless zombies. They barged into the melee swinging their skirts, clenching their jaws, slapping themselves silly and smashing into each other like complete lunatics. They danced and danced into a blithering mania.

After the entire extravaganza had been going on for nearly an hour, there was a subtle change. The mridangas calmed down and then someone buggered a blow on a large conch shell. The call of the conch is like no other. It has a startling presence, which is like the announcement of a heralding occurrence. From out of a titanic wooden portal emerged a colossal specimen of Dravidian society. This hulk of humanity had to be well over two meters tall and he must have weighed over a hundred eighty kilograms, maybe even one ninety. Because he was big. Really, really big. And fat, too. He came out and claimed his place on a herculean throne. He was wearing a longhotti; otherwise, he was naked. He himself did not dance. But they did do the skewer thing with his tongue. After they penetrated his ladle of flesh, they also skewered a many more places all over his chest. A copious volume of blood seeped out over his face, down his chest and onto his behemoth belly. As the blood flowed freely, a bevy of aides came forward with scraps of newspaper, which they daubed onto the blood stained flesh to produce tiny patches of his godliness. Later on, these would be awarded to his followers to take home and worship as power objects that could grant their wishes. These scraps of bloodied paper were considered holy, fresh from God's palace, as it were. I was so stunned watching the bizarre performance I had to ask for something to sit on.

Then they handed him a fat blunt, which he zealously enjoyed to the fullest. After a while, there was a miasma of pungent fumes engulfing him within its heady cocoon. All the wile of course, the drums kept on rocking and rolling at full tempo. The dancers seemed to throw themselves into a wilder fury after the Swami got his stick in him. All the writhing dancers seemed like they were on fire grinding and twisting as they proceeded directly into the maw of Kali.

As the wee hours wore on, the rampaging crowd was approaching its climax. Dancers were dropping like flies. They would collapse onto the beaten mud and lie there in a disheveled pile with no one to revive them or assist them in any way. With the drums pounding and the instruments wailing, the Brobdingnagian Swami arose with compressed hands of prayer and as the conch bugled its loudest bellow, he held up his arms. Iimmediately, everything stopped.

The Swami had his say in the vernacular, which seemed to me to be nothing more than a mumbled greeting after which he thundered down off the dais to retire back to where he had come from. The drums crawled back in softly and the mellow fervor of the pulsing harmonies cruised along for another two or three party laps. Helpers descended upon the dancers and removed the skewers from their tongues one by one. Some even had multiple skewers ganged up in their faces. Others had the skewers in other parts of their bodies, like their hips or even their chests. One female contestant had multiform skewers piercing both of her exposed breasts.

Arjuna came over and inquired if I felt fortunate enough to have an audience with Swami Devakalu.

"Why yes, by all means. What could blow my mind more than all the dancing stuff?" I let loose while reaffirming my lifelong siege on the Beyond. With a perplexed look, he scurried off.

The chamber, which entombed the Swami, was draped with batiks and gravid with brumes of incense. I approached and offered my prayer hands. The mountain of a man looked me up and down. I looked at him too. They had cleaned all the blood off him. It looked like he had even had a bath since his near naked anatomy was shiny wet under the floodlights. Having merely a scrap of cloth for a loincloth, he could be characterized as the embodiment of a well-tanned Sumo wrestler. He babbled something in the provincial dialect. I don't think it was Hindi, because in spite of my not being able to speak it fluently, I could usually recognize it.

Mr. Mindalu translated.

"The Swami would like to know if you are on a journey. If you are, He wishes you well in that pursuit." Mr. Mindalu relayed.

441

The Moon Women

"Yes, well sort of. You see I'm on my way to India. I'm waiting to obtain my visa at the Office of the High Commission before continuing onwards to Madras."

The Swami looked at me with a penetrating laser look, which slashed straight through my defenses. Then, he made another utterance, only this time he did so with his eyes closed.

"Swami Devakalu says your voyage to India is blocked by a rigid barrier formed by the tiny gray men from the air. It is a blockage put there for your own benefit. Because of that stoppage, he says you will not get there on this journey. You will have to go all the way back to your birthplace and try a second time. He also said to tell you, 'When you travel across to the East, do not go in the foul metal bird.'" Mr. Mindalu then held out his hand to query if there might be anything more?

I nodded and respectfully put my hands together plus, I did that little bowing maneuver they all do in Asia. I didn't really believe what the Swami had predicted. Further, since I didn't know how in the world he could have the foggiest idea on what the hell he was talking about, I merely deposited my thanks and turned to leave but the Swami wasn't finished with me. There came three more phrases of colloquial ramblings from the mountain of flesh, which my overseer conveyed somewhat hesitatingly.

"Our Baba has graciously and humbly cautioned that you did not heed what the Draupari had gifted you with such that you would do well to consider the words of these many helpers who come forward for your benefit and to prevent your undoing."

Mr. Mindalu submitted the message with the upturned eyebrow of, "Second chance Buddy."

"But who's this Draupari person? I've never heard of anyone by that name." I had good reason to discount the whole deal as loopy.

"Have you ever been advised by a benefactress of some kind, a woman having occult knowledges and who may have relied upon the sciences of starlight? In our histories, Draupari was a female saint who performed such types of spiritual aids."

"Oh, her. I didn't know. I thought she was a scam, like a come-on. You mean the Swami guy knew about her? She was the one who called me the Albacore Man. Never thought that was real."

"Well perhaps you should. Just accept what you have in front of you as having some possibility of truths."

442

Mrs. Mindalu collected everyone and then we retired from the temple proper. On the road brigade back, Mr. Mindalu cleared up some of the major issues. He shared that the Swami is an incarnate projection of Shiva, whom the locals call Kalima. The Swami must undergo extreme suffering and duress every time he goes into the trance. When he performs the Puja, there are many times when he tolerates excruciating and torturous strain. Moreover, the Swami is not going to be able to continue in his service for too many more years. The ex-Swami died prematurely when he was only twenty-eight. Since we don't know how much longer this Swami will endure we have to employ his talents as much and as fast as we can. It's for everyone's benefit. I was tempted to interject a prayer for the Swami but cleared that hurdle with a locked jaw.

The dancers are all the disciples who are inviting the pantheon of Indian deities and goddesses as quasi-corporeal entities to come and reside in their bodies. By conceding these apparitions to come and partake in this revelry within their bodies, the spirits rejuvenate the dancers with a stimulating freshness, which acts as a lift or an intoxication, an expansion in their customary state of awareness. That is why they like to do it over and over. They get magnetized by the entire army of these famous gods and goddesses and sometimes the dancers fight each other over who can provide the most proper vessel for whichever of these personalities will reside within them. For instance, Hanumanta, the monkey deity, is one of those personas who can come and invade the dancer. The entity inhabiting the dancer will cause the dancer to display the altered behaviors and mannerisms of whatever phantom, which has kidnapped their body. If it were Hanumanta, the dancer would be displaying the actions of monkeys.

He added even after the attendees have danced for sometimes as much as most of the daytime hours, when they get up, they are so refreshed even as much as having a full night's rest. Sometimes after trance dancing, they simply go to work and spend their remaining hours working at their place of employment. This Kali Temple has been here for over three hundred years. Over that time, the devotees have witnessed a lineage of over three dozen different Swamis. Their pictograms parade with prominent honor within one of the puja shrines in the secondary complex.

The Moon Women

Arjuna politely queried me concerning what I thought of it all and did I like it? I answered that it was exceedingly different from most things I've seen. Yet the waterfall of blood performance wasn't my cup of tea. Does the Swami do prophecies like that quite often? I'm not sure I tracked the entire spiel of what the Swami had conveyed. Did he really say I'm not going to get to India? I didn't really accept his prognostication right at that point in the parade.

"The Swami is beyond the normal laws of good or evil, and all the ordinary rules of life. He can divine the nature of hidden truths by sacrificing Himself to be eaten by all the lovers of Kalima, the goddess of Death. He is trading his vital forces to receive knowledges from outside our world, like receiving a special sight or power from making this bargain with the goddess. He permits her to consume him so he can steal the jewels of their fate out from under the rug of death.

"He gives us advice about having children, getting a job, investing in the stock market and many things for which we would have no direct knowledge. There are many disciples here who are quite happy with what the Swami brings us; many have enjoyed great strides with their careers and have become wealthy as well. You should respect what he has given you and act accordingly. That is the number one course for you under these circumstances. But it is up to you. There is no loss, either way." Graciously, Mr. Mindalu was helping me to understand the nature of this unexpected gift. I was further surprised the Swami had made a reference to the Khrng which supported my notion that maybe his words might possibly have significant credence.

After thanking Mr. Mindalu and his budding troupe for their hospitality, I retraced my route back to the Ming feeling tired and drained. Thinking I should have done some trance dancing and had my tongue stuck with one of those skewers to inseminate me with an adequate supply of pizzazz to go attack those idiots at the damn visa office, I balked. Checking out the tip of my pencil, I shook my head. That Mindalu clan was nuts.

When I crashed on the bed, I was tempted to send a shout-out to one of the young ladies to come on down for a quick hookup, but I thought better of it. I reconciled to keep my plan for chastity on target. I nodded off watching the blades of my overhead differential fan beat through the air as if it were whipping the facets of my life like the pages of a book to rearrange them in some random order, or perhaps shuffling them together according to the knowledge menus of the Khrng.

- 9 -

Mrs. Mindalu's mosala dosas were delicious. I simply couldn't get enough of them. I had quit the Ming Motel and was staying with the Mindalus over in Sribhundawali, if you can believe that. Those humble folks were so gracious. They had even insisted I have my own room, a generosity, which required the three sisters to share one room together - no easy feat. The three boys had to share a room as well. This would be unheard of in any American setup. Western teenagers are way too into themselves and all their electronic devises of self-centeredness. To wit, Mr. and Mrs. Mindalu could not sidestep this meristic invasion. They, too, had to suffer a sacrifice play by sharing a room together. Nonetheless, I think the Mister had a leg up on that one. Looking back on the deal, I probably should have felt a little guilty for putting them out so much. But they didn't seem to be affronted or complain at all. That's the way Indians are. They are exceptionally generous and understanding.

I had, by then, accepted the inevitability of what the Indian High Commission was up to. They were blowing me off with their avoiding ignorance. At the end of it, I went there and demanded my passport back. That only took two weeks to finalize, a more impressive track record than the seven weeks I had spent in my attempt for a visa. The Swami was correct. I was going to have to go all the way round the whole damn planet just to reach a target, which was now merely a hop, skip and a jump away from where I was right then. It seemed most bizarre to me, but I didn't have the overall perspective in view yet.

Arjuna had many associates in Kuala Lumpur. He also liked popular records and especially rock and roll. We all were having some lunch over at "Thunbs Up" when in strode a notable personage whose arrival prompted Arjuna to get up and embrace the visitor with a great big bear hug. I was persistently slurping my mulligatawny soup. This fellow looked like no other Asian I had ever seen either inside or outside the States. He had an outrageous hairstyle, which

The Moon Women

was sculpted into what we in the West term an "Afro" and running through it like a psychedelic Mohawk was a streak of electric blue neon. He had African-American features and African-American moves. His clothes were straight out of Woodstock. I know this because I had attended Woodstock that year right before I left for Japan. He came over and took a seat at our table.

In due course, our rap landed on the subject of Jimi Hendrix about whom I disclosed some association: I had seen Hendrix several times in concerts including Woodstock. He couldn't quench his thirst for any tidbits regarding Jimi. Whatever I had to regurgitate with respect to his music, his life, his associates and even any enemies he might have had (which I didn't think existed), this aficionado inhaled it all like a fish at last finding the sea. The discussion was lively and extensive. When we had drained all the possible venues of the Hendrix Empire, he tossed me a bone. Would I like to hear his band over at the local disco?

"Sure. I'd be honored. What is your name by the way?" I inquired with an outstretched handshake.

"Thaddaeus. My name is Thaddaeus." He answered point-blank as we shook.

"What'd you say? Your name is what?" I was sorely stunned with what he had said.

"What? You don't like my name?" He pulled back thinking it was a joke or worse.

"No. Please. It's not that. Please say it one more time, if you don't mind." I had to be sure.

"THA. DAY. US. Thaddaeus. Okay?" He articulated each syllable with a dry smirk.

"Thank you. Thank you very much. That's quite an interesting name. Is it your father's?" I was inquiring.

"It's my name. Who cares where it comes from?"

He looked me with simmering condescension. Nevertheless, I couldn't rise to the occasion and confess why I had been such a prying maggot.

To be sure, I visited the disco that evening. His band, named The Experience, (no shock there), was fabulous. And I must tell you this songster was an unbelievable musical genius. He was an absolute Asian clone of Jimi Hendrix. He could mimic every lick, which Hendrix had ever performed. He did not necessarily have the organic

446

genius of Hendrix, but Thaddaeus had the stuff, that's for sure. And, he knew it. He and his band were going places. If they had been in the States, he would have been a stand up name on the popular marquees raised to trumpet loudly with the birth of the Woodstock revolution. Quite plausibly, that's why he permitted me to get so tight with his posse. He was tracking a leg up on the inroads into the 24-carat American dream.

Night after night, they permitted me to go back stage in between sets. His trio was a mirror image of Hendrix's band. The Experience had an incredible base player by the name of Dexter Jones; he was as good if not better than Noel Redding. The drummer, an equally gifted musician who could have rivaled Mitch Mitchell with his double bases, had taken the terse label of Flex. Thaddaeus referred to the two of them as the Flex-Dex Duo and whenever he did so, he snorted a little chuckle under his breath. Sometimes when the Experience took stage, they spawned various backup teams of choral singers and other musicians who provided horns and sometimes, even strings, depending on where they were and what song they played. It was the full-blown happening of The Experience, which made it great.

From the get-go, Thaddaeus had something going. I not only dug his music, I empathized with it. As he performed, he could feel me analyzing his licks and his riffs. As well as playing all the notable popular themes of the times, Thaddaeus had also written quite a few of the lyrics to the group's songs by himself. They were as righteous and, if not better, more searching than Hendrix's material with respect to originality and twist. The words had a raw spiritual component without the fuzzy psychedelic haze of the Woodstock legend. Some of Thaddaeus' lyrics even seemed to quote biblical references:

> White cross, black sun and a bone.
> I walked the rebel's walk
> Brought some bad news home.
> But the heat left me worn down
> When the big water came to town.
> It flooded the house of man,
> Washed away all the blue domes.
> Lord knew I was a crossed blood

The Moon Women

Naked and sick I turned and ran.
Saw the faces, gold lions and the talk
From the beaten and the blind all alone.
A mother with blades of purple haze,
Scorpions grew in the harvest mud
As the white feathers covered my days.

And then the chorus:

Four faces of the lion
Brought down green forks of fire.
Four faces of the lion
Drove my burning wings even higher.
Dyin', said I would never leave her.
Got seven angels with a prayin' fever. [21]

This psychedelic minstrel was a major player in the realm of South Asian rock and roll. While advising me he was going to be going on tour through Bangkok and Saigon and then onto Hong Kong, out of some gratuitous perversion, he invited me to accompany him and his two teammates. How could I pass that up?

– 10 –

After staying in Kuala Lumpur for over five weeks, I packed my gear once more and bid my farewells to all the Mindalus. As a whirlwind of rock and roll gathered me up, off I ventured with Thaddaeus and company to Bangkok on the train. Along the way during that rumbling rail ride through the ocean of coconut trees and sprawling banana plantations, I related some of my experiences while trekking up the many friendly summits I had visited in my past, especially the one in Taiwan. I told him how I had hiked up onto that peak of one of the nearby hillocks and then I disclosed the dream, which I had had there. When I told him the name some mysterious hand had hewn into the granite face of the lone tombstone, he froze with vertical fear. He looked at me and stared for the longest time.

"No joke, Man? You telling me the truths?" He gripped my arm hard. He believed he had some ultra-experiential way of mining for lies.

448

"Yes. It said Thaddaeus, same as your name, the same spelling and the same everything. I'm not kidding. It's pretty spooky, isn't it?" I looked at him keenly; it was a lot to handle.

"I would like you to meet my fiancé. She's going to join me in Bangkok." He forecasted. "She will know if you are correct or not."

The back end of this excursion on the road to Bangkok was less tense. Witnessing the jungle scenery slide by me as the determined Malay locomotive plowed onwards was a pleasantly captivating way to travel. It was the antithesis of the hedgehopping I had been doing in those half dozen jets ever since San Francisco. The train was so relaxing. Also the dining car food was quite tasty. Once, however, as I consuming a bowl of noodles, I got one of those pint-sized chili peppers westerners fear the most. This one was the size of a jellybean but not as thick. Even though it has a modest color of Shamrock green, which didn't necessarily mean it was of any Irish lineage. That limey color was its hocus pocus fooling you with its simple green claim that it hardly presented any danger. Don't worry, I won't bite you. It's merely like some happy leprechauns leading you over to get your pot of gold, only you're about to get your beaner bonked. Blimey! When you chomp down on it, oh my God! It is the hottest little son of a gun that you have ever run into and chewing on it straight away transports you to its origins - hell! When I ate it, Thaddaeus and Flex just about wet their pants rolling in the aisles as I jumped up and down squirming like an eel. Even pouring cup after cup of Chai down my throat to try and put out that wildfire, it was no use. It was quite a while before I got my mouth back in one piece. Son of a bitch; it was so wickedly hot!

After disembarking at the terminus in downtown Bangkok, we flagged a taxi over to the nightclub where Thaddaeus and his troupe were going to gig for a fortnight. The name of the club was Blue Heaven. When I saw that sign I smiled and thought back to my first experience with psychotropics. Sometimes life completes its round trip so to speak. You greet someone in one world, only to come across him passing you by in another one. It is the conversations issuing out from the alternating realities, discussions from the polarity of opposite truths, not as lies, but as convergent possibilities.

After setting the stage for the midnight performance, we took a taxi over to the not-too-shabby inn located a couple of clicks from

The Moon Women

the nightclub. It was a moderately priced establishment, which broadcast its signage in electric blue neon as the Thai Palace. Thaddaeus' kindness landed me adjacent to the suite he would be staying in but I took care of my own tab. The Old Man had come through with another well-needed installment when I was down in Malaysia.

During that afternoon's discussion, Thaddaeus inquired if I had ever messed with musical instruments at all. I confessed most recently, I had made the mistake of trying my hand at the drums with two friends of mine back in college in '65. But I wasn't too good at it.

"Yeah? Who was that with? Anyone I've heard of?" He never lost a toss with the time bones.

"Oh, a couple of guys I knew at Bard College, Donny Fegan and Walter Becker. We used to play together over at The Red Balloon or off campus in Barrytown. After they got rid of me and teamed up with a decent drummer by the name of Chucky Chase, they went to Brooklyn and started the Fagen Trio thing. I learned about a month ago, however, they've changed their name to something out of a naked lunch: Steely Dan. Weird, huh? I doubt you've heard of them."

"No shit! Sounds pretty sweet, Dude. Aren't they platinum of something?"

"Probably. I'm still only a worn out tin man though." More raucous laughter over that one.

I mentioned also I had done folksongs on the guitar as a teenager while crooning in front of all the teenage heartthrobs. Seems I must have had an Elvis complex during adolescence. But my talents for one or the other could not even remotely approximate what Flex and Dex were putting down. Other than that, I told him I had gotten to be pretty good on alto saxophone in the marching band back in grade school but that was ancient history. I thanked him for putting up with my jaunt down memory lane.

"Do you think you could play some sax now?"

"You're saying I'll be in your band?" I was a bit chagrined.

"I need somebody for a baritone. For some percussive back up." He smirked.

I was imagining how I might look on stage.

"You'd have to get some nicer clothes." He sideswiped my slow come back.

"I don't know if I could get an embouchure together in time, but I could give it a try I guess." I was feigning some interest in it to bolster his proposal.

"A what?"

"An embouchure; it's the forming of the muscles around your mouth, the ones, which enabled you to control the reed in the mouthpiece of the sax. It takes some practice to develop such a thing, an embouchure. I'm surprised you've never heard of that before."

"Whatever. But I need your answer. Soon."

"Okay, well, if you've got one, I'll put it in my mouth."

"That's what all the girls tell me."

We both broke up.

After week numero uno had passed, we had prepped all the initial practice requirements. The trio was working out some of the kinks. Backstage one evening, quite by accident I ran into Thaddaeus' main squeeze, Anna Lee, who was searching for a padlock. She was a stunning Thai woman with a temple black coiffure, which fluffed up at her shoulders. Even though her eyes were like basaltic daggers, her smile radiated the warm trust of a Nefertiti. An impeccably dressed woman, she exuded the pseudo-charms of a dragon lady. Moreover, she seemed to have a fastidious hold on Thaddaeus. When she was with him, it was as if he didn't have a brain. She directed everything from soup to nuts, but only the domestic issues. She had no say in the domain of his music and creativity.

Anna Lee was a clever but weird individual. One of the outstanding behaviors she obsessed over intrigued me without hesitation: she talked to a pet cricket. She had a live cricket trapped in a little bamboo cage the size of a kid's milk carton. There were two things about this cricket the average troubadour might twitch an eyebrow over. She not only talked to the cricket out loud but claimed it always replied as well. Besides that, she valued its forecasts as authentic wisdom from the field of hard shell reality. On top of that, it wasn't only a phrase or two. No. She had full-blown communion percolating with the teensy leaping orthopteran. I couldn't imagine with what the cricket was responding. It was all one-way pillow talk

The Moon Women

from what I could tell. But Anna Lee maintained her sick palaver with the bug ad on infinitum and furthermore, she lived by it.

One afternoon I witnessed her promenading the plaza in a pink mohair muumuu as she balanced the graphite grasshopper precariously on her fuzzy shoulder. She looked like a strawberry Hostess Twinkie suffering molestation from a crawling ant. When Thaddaeus later admitted the cricket was the reincarnation of her dead father, that's when the whole shebang unraveled swiftly for me and in reverse order as well.

Thaddaeus was also a staunch believer in all this bunk over the cricket. Many times, he would not go anywhere or eat anything if the cricket had warned him away from it. When Thaddaeus grilled me to request the cricket to dope out my life and reveal my travel plans for the foreseeable future, I couldn't help but think it was all starting to get really creepy. I had the horrible premonition - what if the cricket hits a homerun and something it predicts comes true? That would be catastrophic, insects controlling my life and my mind. Yuk! Except it wasn't much more intimidating than what the Khrng had already done to me once when I was just a child vacationing out near Cazenovia Lake.

In spite of how I had always had to fight with those nightmares all my life, I was never going to surrender to their nagging pressures as they attempted to consume my thoughts. I fully intended to refuse further prospects of being sucked up into the bowels of their ratty ass ships. That's what drives me to write these damn books so I can expose their treacherous plots and unhook them from my brainwaves. I need to get them off my back and so do you.

The two of them kept "bugging" me, no pun intended (I lied), to ask the cricket the big one. Oh, by the way, the cricket's name was Lulu. I should please ask Lulu when would I be leaving for the States? This all happened once when she accompanied Lulu to the dining hall. Why in the hell the damn bug's name was Lulu, when it was supposed to be her dead father, is beside the point. At the tail of all this ragging, I broke down and popped the question to the damn jumping spider concerning the where and the when.

Anna Lee relayed when Lulu had spoken it saw number - 119. That, or perhaps it was 911; she wasn't sure which; Cricket Speak wasn't a linear communication but rather a holographic projection. Then, she added that the cricket had insisted it was picking up something like bars. Well no wonder it's seeing bars; it hangs out in a damn bamboo cage all day! But, Oh no. Lulu confirmed the message was with regard to me. She stated most categorically one day there would be bars. And another day, there would be more bars a second time. In the end, there would be many bars for nearly nine years! What the hell? Was this a missive or a mittimus?

Anna Lee had confided to Thaddaeus the things which I had shared with him when I explored a summit in Taiwan and the name engraved upon the obelisk were all correct; I had given him the truth. Indisputably, the cricket knew its stuff. Lulu later appended its former prophesy with an update concerning seeing a proud military general who would arrive and free me from my present cage very soon. This GI was going to take me away from this place forever, right after the ground shook, and airplanes went backwards.

What? I've heard of reversing Time but never planes flying in reverse. That plumb flies in the face of normal physics. And what general is going to liberate me? George Pattan? He's dead. Oh, wait. He's going to come to me in his cricket self to cross the oceans riding on the back of a floating M4 Sherman whale tank. I had some hefty gumption to stomp the little blasted locust into the dust.

Two nights later, as I was sitting in the pits taking in the last of Thaddaeus' sets with The Experience, this towering GI Joe guy squatted down right in front of me. He kept staring at me dead nuts blocking my view of the band. And as he continued to stare at me heads on with this wide shit eating grin plastered on his puss, at first I was floored by his impertinence. I noticed the big guy had nearly an inch of beard carpeting his mug, which is perhaps why I didn't recognize him right away. Then, it dawned on me.

"Ben! Is that you? What on earth?" I squawked. (Funny how my alternating worlds kept colliding.)

Quixotically I peered through the bearded frontage and recognized who he was; namely my close friend and fellow fwic, Ben Harris. Ben was on his way back to Mitchell Gardens after teaming up with Jeff Finklestein whom he had run into looking to score while bouncing off walls down in the highways and byways of Hong Kong. The three of us got together and renewed our former acquaintances with enthusiastic hugs and backslapping enhanced with proper applications of alcoholic liniment. We reminisced over our righteous

The Moon Women

stomping grounds back in Mitchell Gardens as well as the other campuses around the globe by zipping out several green cigarettes.

Two days later, Ben and I were gearing up to board our magic carpet and head eastwards to Hiroshima via Hong Kong (our primary leg onto JFK), when the tarmac began to rock and roll. As a modest earthquake hammered us and shook the ground shook, I beheld a light come down out of the firmament like an angel descending from upstairs. It came and rolled the airplane backwards little by little almost half a meter!

I must admit I'll have to doff my hat off to Lulu. That cricket sure carried one dynamite crystal ball.

As a footnote there's this:
First, I have spent one day in the
county jail in New Brunswick, NJ.
Second, I have spent one day in the
Delhi Cantonment jail in India.
Third, I am currently serving
seven to fourteen years in the
State Prison for Men in Concord, NH.
If you come across a cricket, one that
is stuck in a bamboo cage and it tells
you what you are going to be doing
in the future, you should listen to it!

- 11 -

As the lights and mayhem flashed insanely, the midnight sun driving up our pleasure magnets burned furiously on the edges of a wanton delirium. Oma and I had been downing mai tais and acting out devilish things on the slanted disco platform. After an exhaustive romp, we spilled out into the squashed silence of the Shinjuku back alleys. I suggested that we take the maglev, but Oma knew better. With the hook of her little finger bridging the gap between her incisors, she locked down three minicabs on the spot. The closest mad cab slammed into reverse and we hopped in.

"Sony Towers, Kuda sai."

"That's where you're staying? Man, that's pretty ritzy territory. I'm impressed."

454

"Yeah. My Dad's collected his fair share of mahjongg tiles from them rotten snakes in Beijing. Might as well have somethin' to show for it."

The hitch over to the high rise was spent locked out in a hot face mashing fest bashing. I recollected a series of locked lips and pumping hips while rarely surfacing for air. Moments later, she punched 23 on the column of illuminated numerals (real digits on one side, Japanese squiggles on the other). The translucent globe of the external elevator accelerated upwards like a crystal ball launched by a carnival barker's hammer; yet who could predict its reentry into the future? Its smoothness was only outdone by the spectacular panorama of the 270-degree visuals encircling us.

As we gained altitude, the temperature seemed to plummet inversely: the higher we rose, the colder it got. I felt it wasn't much of an endorsement for the competence of the homegrown Japanese techno-geeks. Whoever heard of an unheated high altitude cockpit? It must be minus ten Celsius in here, er, out there. When my breath created miniature icy chrysanthemums on the Plexiglas, I thought to alert Oma about the possibilities, but it was too late.

There on the horizon, the lightning bolts of Time/Space commenced to unwind an alternative consciousness. Here it was again - a hovering interstice indexing reality. I had the comical reflection the tinsel giant might retard its coming owing to the plastic boundaries, but no, in he came, flaming feathers and all. Oma's expression looked like she was losing her party-girl exuberance but then she froze in a frightened surprise. I bent down on my knee and stiffened in anticipation of having my beleaguered head drenched with the cerebral wind chimes. After all, it had been over two years since the last visit and my anticipation of the shock must have been overinflated what with my dismal forgetfulness.

I attempted to hook the exit handle to get out but the hoarfrosts had already intensified something wicked. As I sprung for the handle, my other hand slipped off the icy handrail and I only captured empty air. There was no handle. As I looked into the mirrored lens of the Plexiglas globe, my sightline caught what I envisioned was a reflection but it wasn't. The feedback was not a redo at all. It was from the future. It was the inlet projecting the vortex of Time/Space coming back at me. It had morphed out of the reversed

The Moon Women

plastic bulb. And now, I was staring point-blank into it and I hadn't even gotten to peek at the clouds floating by so luxuriously outside.

   Pretty, blue thoughts filled my head as the welkin upstairs smiled back with insane invitations. As the cleft expanded its growth, the frozen altitude rushed in searing my facial extremities with an icy blush. The silver shade rolled up to expose its timeworn innards glassed with stars. From out of that starry domain came the white fired revenant whose titanium feathers lit me up with terror. It propelled itself straight into my world like a torpedo from hell. Into the small cavity in which I lived it injected its hypodermic needles of over baked divinity, like sour donuts of foul purpose.

UNTO THE ANGEL OF THE CHURCH [22]

HELLO AND GLAD TIDINGS
FROM ALL OF US IN ABADDON

I KNOW YOUR WORKS
YOU HAVE A NAME
CALLED LIFE BUT
YOU ART DEAD [23]

I HOLD THE SEVEN STARS   THIS IS BUT A RECAPITULATION
AS THE SEVEN SPIRITS   OF MUCH OF WHAT THE ANGELS
AS DO YOU BUT KNOW IT NOT   HAVE ALREADY CONVEYED

MY HAND DRAWS OUT FEW NAMES
THAT HAVE NOT DEFILED   THIS IS AN ANGEL
THEIR GARMENTS   DISCUSSING KARMA

YOU SHALL WALK WITH ME IN WHITE
   WHITE IS BOTH A REALM OF MATTER
FOR AS SUCH YOU ARE WORTHY [24]
   AS WELL AS A STATE OF MIND

HE THAT OVERCOMES
I WILL NOT BLOT OUT HIS NAME
OUT OF THE BOOK OF LIFE

BUT I WILL CONFESS HIS NAME
The Angel states a double pledge

BEFORE MY FATHER To not chide the person
AND BEFORE HIS ANGELS [25]
Nor refuse him his due

The chromium fire being elongated the blunt elevator into a bulging snow glass realm, which drew in icy rushing air and screaming jet sounds. It made no sense.

I COME TO YOU BRINGING
THE HONOR OF SARDIS
AND AS SHAMSHIEL
LEGION *OF ABADDON*
AND SON OF MAN
DO ALSO RECEIVE YOUR HONOR

HE THAT CAN OPEN THE DOOR
NO MAN CAN SHUT THE DOOR
AND HE THAT SHUTS THE DOOR
CAN NO MAN DO OPEN
FOR YOU HAVE LITTLE STRENGTH
Strength here means deceit

AND HAVE KEPT MY WORD Since the person is loyal
AND HAVE NOT DENIED MY NAME [26]
And hasn't failed in the past

THE TABERNACLE OF GOD IS WITH WOMEN
AND HE WILL DWELL WITH THEM
the superiority of women stands as the rule of human government

FROM THE FIVE WOMEN OF THE MOON
AS SHAMSHIEL I MEASURE
THE WALL ACCORDING
TO THE MEASURE OF WOMAN the yardstick of humanity

457

The Moon Women

THE FOUNDATIONS OF THE WALL
WERE GARNISHED WITH ALL MANNER
OF PRECIOUS STONES EACH BURNING
IN HER FAITH WITH HER LIGHT
THE SECOND WAS SAPPHIRE

HER PSYCHIC ELEMENT IS SAPPHIRE

NOW COMES THE MOON WOMAN
OF THE SECOND PLACE
ARRAYED IN SILK STONE AND PALE PEARLS
RUNNING WITH CRYSTAL WATERS

SHE WAS DECKED WITH A SAPPHIRE ROSE
AND LINEN LEOPARDS HAVING A SCORCHED CUP
IN HER HAND FULL OF ABOMBINATIONS
SPEAKING OF FILTHINESS AND FORNICATION

INTRODUCES THE SECOND OF THE MOON WOMEN

GOD SHALL WIPE AWAY ALL THE TEARS
THERE SHALL BE NO MORE PAIN
FOR THE FORMER THINGS ARE PASSED AWAY

WOMEN ARE THE CONDUIT THROUGH WHICH
PEACE AND COMPASSION FLOWS

THEY THAT ARE NOT READY TO DIE
HAVE NOT FOUND WORKS
OF THE PERFECT AND THE TRUE

THE UNCLEAN GLASS FLESH
SHALL NOT BE CLOTHED IN WHITE
BUT DO WATCH AND DEVOUR   THE KHRNG SPOIL OUR LAWS
THE THINGS THAT REMAIN   AND DIMINISH OUR WAYS

Haan Moses

THEY SHALL COME AS A THIEF
AND YOU SHALL NOT KNOW
WHAT HOUR THEY WILL

THEY COME WITHOUT NOTICE TO STEAL

COME UPON YOU [27]

A PERSON'S LIFE FORCES AND WILL

As the diminished capacity in the elevator began to contract, I picked up on the reversed infinitives. Balanced out there in midair on the exterior of the building some two dozen stories off terra firma, I was freezing. Totally afraid the tinsel clown was going to absorb me into his wicked self, I stepped back.

TWO HEADS ARE BOUND TOGETHER
AS WHITE AND BLACK HORSES
LEAVING THE CURSE OF A BOW
AND THE WOUND OF A CROWN

THIS IS A CARDINAL PATTERN

SICKLES UPON THE WHEAT

FOUND WITHIN CROP CIRCLES

IT IS ONLY IN THE PURE AIR
OVER THE WHEAT THAT THE HEADS
CLASH AS THE WAYS OF THE WHEAT
ARE ALL GLORIFIED IN WONDER FOR
THE HORSE LAYS DOWN THE WHITE
UPON EACH OF THE LEAVES
AS THE TRUE BLOOD OF WAR

THE IMPORTANCE OF THE WHEAT
WITH REGARD TO THE BATTLEGROUND
BETWEEN THE ANGELS AND THE KHRNG

As the messages of Shamshiel melted away into an orange sky, an array of tinkling bells washed over my inner ears like a cleansing rain. The cubic aperture in Time/Space sucked the aluminum clown back out of my life. Its departure concluded with

459

The Moon Women

the mechanical lowering of the stainless steel guillotine closing off the starry vaults of vacuous ultra-space.

There was Oma glowering at me like a vixen as my back registers pawed over considerations of the female's majesty and why it was recently stated purity of woman is sublime. While fumbling with the keycard, I made repeated sloppy attacks on the security cube but fell short. Oma snatched it away from me, jammed it into the slot underneath the Aztec nose of the device, and punched in the code. After thinking it over for a second, it flashed its green wink of approval.

We soon put the cap on my visit with the Time jockey by locking lips in a hot hook up. Mystique concrete hummed on the vertical sound-posts. It was a virtual slapping match as we fought our way into her Dad's apartment. There were no words at this point. I got lost with it. What finer way to wash away the divine toxins of some messenger from the stars than sex. We careened into the bedroom.

A flurry of zippers and snaps was an intro for our hot performance on those unwrinkled sheets. We christened those pastures of virgin fabric with some serious pile driving. Along with a duet on the spliff, the Doobie Brothers put us in the mood for some prone belly slapping. The rhythmic beats lifted us higher and higher into our enchanted flights over the lap lounges of Tokyo. We pounded out our respective orgasms while simultaneously shaving off several depleted shells on the etheric onion now unpeeled and put to bed. Our final foam fuzzed out into sleep spotlighted amongst the other sexual knickknacks lying bare on the shelves of our mind's eye as the unorganized clutter of a wasted life style.

After a while, I awoke. When I grew fully aware I was glad to have that over and done with, Oma materialized from the other side with my hat in her mitt.

"Hey. You've got some explaining to do, Bunky."

"Yeah? What for? I'm high. You're high. What's the hang-up?"

"Where the hell did you go in the elevator? I was afraid I was going to have to call for security. You were staring dead ahead into nowhere with your kisser plastered on the glass for over an eternity. Then you popped back. I need some answers." She winged the Hamburg at me like a Frisbee.

460

"I have a condition but let's not go there." I nabbed my pants.

"Okay, but you owe me one. Peter Piper never lies. Plus I've got your wallet."

"No problem. Good luck with that."

"I'm gonna let you off the hook fer now but one day I'm afraid we're going to get down to brass tacks."

"I'm so relieved. What's this thing?"

"Wouldn't you like to know? It's not what you think it is. I'll tell you later but for now why don't you take a look around? Later I'll give you the tour. I guess you deserve that much."

I put down the rubber dingo and began investigating her father's fabulous apartment. My Sherlock Holmes curiosity was not to remain all corked up. There were all kinds of bronze and carved wooden statues. Collectibles of all kinds graced the walls and populated a forest of glass selves. Executive secretary bookcases guarded the back rooms with further history and knowledge. It seemed to be a library unbounded. This late night reveal poked a further notion in my face that this latent uptick of the Speak indicated another romp.

Oma came back, pointed one out to me, and revealed it was the sun goddess, Amaterasu. There were monumental photographs on the walls as well. Damn! In some cases, the mile high photographs were the walls.

"This one is a Torji. It is a gateway or entrance into the Shinto Shrine realms. The two vertical posts are topped with twin cross beams, which represent the division between the numinous precinct and the secular one."

She doffed her opalescent gown to uncover her nipples as she neared another naked two-meter statue.

"This one represents the Kami, or the creative juice. One can recognize the truthfulness of Kami every moment of our day. That is what I believe too. That is why I have as much sex with as many guys as I can so I can achieve this divinity with the Kami firsthand." She postulated.

"You can have the experience of my Kami any time, Gorgeous." I brushed the soft blonde strands off her shoulder and kissed it.

She engaged me with more mouth yoga as I lifted her up and off the twenty-third floor. We took our separate flights of fancy hip

461

The Moon Women

deep in the coverlets and a satin cloverleaf spread all balled up under her ass to remedy the slop into the valley of paradise. A hundred pile-driving moments later, our breaths had met the measured mile of exhaustion and we slumped back to regain our senses and more orange juice.

"This domestic, or from the homeland? Sure quenches my dry mouth syndrome. How you doin' Babe?"

"That was great but I've got a full afternoon planned. Can you dig it?"

"No problem. I'm copacetic with it."

"See you in the shower."

"I'm good. Maybe it's time I matriculate in my voyeurism classes."

"Whatever." She pranced off toward the East wing to get wet as I took in more of the local artifacts.   Later, wringing her hair, she returned to find me viewing a large silk-screen of a middle-aged Japanese gentleman who didn't look particularly pornographic to me in any way. He looked like any other slant-eyed bee.

"Who's this guy?" I quizzed her rudely.

"Who do you think? That is His Holiness Emperor Hirohito, the Monarch of Japan."

"From the war? Isn't he dead now? If he ain't he's Methuselah."

"No, but he hasn't been seen in quite a while. Some say he was sequestered behind staunch security. I have a connection with him because of my Dad."

"Yeah? Do tell."

"Sure. I know that in 1928, the people appointed him as the Divine Emperor. He was educated at the Peers School of the Crown Prince Institute. Marine biology was his main interest and so he wrote many books on the subject. He married Naga Kokuni four years before in 1924. Designated Supreme Showa or Enlightened Peacemaker, he always claimed he did not plan on going to war with the Americans and warned his generals that those heathens were nothing short of a sleeping giant his countrymen knew as Gorijira, the gorilla whale. Waking it up would be extremely bad. But the generals wouldn't listen to him and forced him swear allegiance to their strategy by kidnaping his wife.

"And get this; it's something which might blow your mind. Once during a social hour at the Embassy my Dad was privy to some extraordinary info. This get-together was populated only by the high echelon of the politic who were all considerably lubricated with traditional glow. My ambassador father overheard some talk which unveiled the little known secret that prior to the surprise visit the Japs paid us in Honolulu, there were some rich merchant bankers in Tokyo who clandestinely purchased US Treasury Bonds through back channels in the European investment markets. These financial instruments were linked to a significant portion of the Manhattan Project. Isn't that freaky? Turns out the Japs in reality paid to fry their own citizenry. After they dropped them two eggs back in '45, Hirohito had to make a national announcement declaring the surrender of his Imperial Army to the Yanks. It was a broadcast over radios, which went all over the country. It was a terrible, terrible day they say." Oma reiterated.

"I'm sure it was. I've shot the atomic dome and made a movie about it, but that was in my previous life it seems. Now I've been tangled up with a way-back machine so I'm heading east while seeking to retro-engineer my way back to India in reverse. Don't ask."

Fortunately she didn't. I continued my tour and noticed over in a reduced antechamber there was a zoo-sized birdcage. Balancing on the swing perch was a blackbird having snowflake splashes on its wing tips and a screaming yellow bill. The aviary wonder was spouting garbled Japanese expletives. Oma informed me it was her Dad's myna. She kidded once it had related her favorite koan, one, which she had heard down at the local Dojo:

> What is the sound
> Of one wing flapping?

> A dead angel.

Freaky. The midget vulture assumed a vow of silence with a dumb stare. Doubtless, it was embarrassed after witnessing our romp across the sheets in the adjacent bedroom. Its gaze settled in on various objects secreted within the executive litter lying unceremoniously on an expansive walnut desk: letter opener, felt

The Moon Women

desk blotter, fountain pen and a crystal ball. But its true target was a petite maroon box. I hefted it and gave it a shake to figure out what it might contain.

"Don't touch that!" Oma commanded with terror in her eyes.

"This?"

"Yeah! My Pappa has warned me over and over never to touch or ever open that damn thing. It's like a Pandora's chamber or something. To unlock its contents would trigger catastrophic consequences, an evil the likes of which this world could not overcome. Whatever the hell is in that box can only be unearthed by the Emperor himself. Pappa told me it's the anticipated origin of all the dark energy in this neck of the Milky Way galaxy!" Oma stammered.

"You believe that shit? I'm pretty sure that Dude is dead?" I wasn't subscribing to her pitch just yet.

"No. He's still alive. My Old Man was in liaison with the Ambassador to Japan back in the sixties. I don't know how he came to acquire this dreaded prize, but I know one thing. I am deathly afraid of it. Whatever comes out of that little box will upset the balance between the living and the dead. That's all I know from what my Dad blabbed and that's the way I'm gonna handle it so put it down and back off. Now!" She warned me.

"But, Oma, don't you think that's a little bit unrealistic? I mean, come on, it's only a little purple box!" I needed more.

"I'm only going to say this once. Stand away from there. Do it!"

Oma had picked up her Colt and aimed it directly at my gut. I hesitated for a second and then, because I knew what I was doing, I cracked a faint smile and flipped opened the box.

Bam!

She shot me. The bullet collided with a white feather deflecting its trajectory just enough to place its impact on the far wall instead of in my head.

And the myna squawked out its name.

"Fukahwei!"

- 12 -

As nightfall loomed I found a black hole had swallowed up all the neon in Shinjuku. Oma had split to chase another one of her lone wolves. A pregnant emptiness as black as the myrobalen of Indian ink washed in to coat the streets. Tokyo was rarely starved of light, but the place I had stumbled into was out of the ordinary, more like a cemetery than anything else. Signature scepters on the wrought iron grid work running along the perimeters told me it was the Emperor's park. An extensive masonry fence lined its edges and stood firm to contain his kingdom.

Punctuated every so often were the stone heads of lions, which had hooded snakes squirming out of their gaping jaws. I knew this was an image I had run into once in a former life but I couldn't quite dial it in that accurately. Across the avenue was a three-story building with its windows punched out and laced with a barricade of wrought iron spears, the rusting iron of separation. A Japanese sign hung atop its entryway stating its sub rosa:

GR   UNION B DG

The **EAT** of the leading word and the **L** of the third had gone the way of the Time Lords like monograms dying of metaleptic starvation semaphoring the coming tale.

His specter came upon me like a haunting. Next to a slatted fence, which traversed the worn sidewalk, walked a small man. Although all in shadow, he paced with a dignified mien moving as though some human millipede mired in dark matter. Having considerable difficulty distinguishing him clearly in the dim light, I stepped behind one of the lions to watch him as he approached me.

As he gradually materialized, I observed a gaunt elderly man wearing a soot-covered graphite overcoat in morning dress style and sooty satin slippers. His stovepipe hat appeared to be made out of asphalt. On his upper lip was a tightly trimmed moustache. The sides of his head were shaved close; whatever follicles he had left were pasted down and gleaming like obsidian. His exterior had a crusted vein like membrane enveloping his mortal figment. His mandibular jaw presented the look of an inveterate insect. He continued his

The Moon Women

frontal assault until he was almost on top of me and stopped to scan right and left.

When he stood in front of me, he was a fist less than a meter plus a half. Connected to an inky ribbon, which trailed away into his melanin vest, he had a monocle over his weaker eye. The fluttering ribbon reminded me of those typewriters, which had the word ROYAL inscribed on their frontal zone like a frown. He removed the monocle and let it dangle helplessly like a struggling mouse.

Out from under his chiton jacket, he produced a bamboo board, which had Katakana scribble on it; presumably a calligrapher's brush had inscribed some aha moments of Zen living upon the snowy shield (I would later learn it was his Shaku, upon which he formulated the different options for how the world would end). After hugging it lovingly as if it were a teddy bear, he took three more steps and stopped to address me.

"Kombon wah." [Good evening.]

He bowed stiffly at the waist showing me the brim of his hat, which had a red circle on it (known to be a shodu by some).

"Kombon wah." With no idea as to whom the hell this midget was impersonating, I bowed back.

"An exceptionally benevolent evening, is it not?" He forecasted in his opaque Japanese accent, which retained a lingering trace of English tutoring. At least he had lost the Elmer Fudd drawl most of these Japs had.

"Whatever you say, Pops." I nodded my assent.

"After dark I pace these five walls. It provides me immense peace and contentment to be let out from the confines of my palace, no matter how late it gets. It is my time to celebrate the night. Do you know who I am, Guygene?"

With his free hand, he fingered a gold fob, which dangled on the chain, which came out of his ironclad vest. I envisioned seeing spider eggs bubble out from his chops like caviar.

"Charlie Chaplin?" I hadn't a clue.

"I am Emperor Hirohito, Supreme Monarch and Commander of the Army of the People of the Divine Wind. Our paths were destined to cross, Ibosen-san." He seemed supremely placated to have finally gotten his hooks on me even if it was down in the weeds.

"I'm pleased to meet you. How did you know that?" I was suspicious of this buggy freak right from the start.

466

"That will be revealed later, Ibosen-san. Pardon me."

In a flash, he reached up and inserted his thumb into the shallow depression right below my collarbone. With a sharp dig, he applied a firm shiatsu move.

"Hey! That hurts. Cut it out!" I could have chopped the midget ant in two, but something hit me.

An electric jolt shot through my torso spreading the arms of a cerebral octopus to calm my resistance and envelope me within a web of warm pleasure, which left me with an apathetic paralysis.

"There. That's better, isn't it? I hope you don't become misoriented from the potential of your purposes, Ibosen-san. Concentration of mind is the most important goal when dealing with the elimination of illusion and evil. When you buckle your thoughts onto anything, you will then be able to carry out that goal, no matter how difficult it may seem. This is a divine force, Ibosen-san; also known as, Ki, the fire gas of the breath. Ki is a sort of psychokinetic juice, a magnetic harmonic of our vital force born from the Kami. Sleeping within the coiled cells of our being, it is set to a locked status like a spring of an angry snake. Most recently, some scientists of yours have named this force as DNA, or the building blocks of life. But it is much more than that, Ibosen-san. It is not masonry. It is divine purpose."

He was beginning to do a little dance as if he might need to micturate, pee.

"So do chopsticks come into this picture at some point, because I can definitely detect some shifty noodles wriggling like worms in front of my face here?"

I wasn't coping to the ant-man's rift right off the bat. What were my actual chances of bumping into the actual Emperor of Japan? Didn't Oma say that guy had croaked? I wasn't quite sure on that point so I played along for the time being. The imperialistic cockroach continued with his walk nearing a terraced urn containing a pool of green moss. At its core lived a Lilliputian tree half a meter in height.

"This Bonsai has survived all my elders and kinsman back to the Mongol Kings. Its bark has tasted the first Kamikaze to come and save our nation. Known as "The Divine Wind" this holy force drove the enemy's ships out to sea and the few which remained capsized. Contained within its green branches is more knowledge than all your

The Moon Women

cellular engineers and mental mechanics, Ibosen-san. I come each evening to honor and worship the tree which gives calmness and understanding to all who listen to its ways. You should always listen to what the tree has to tell you, Rahm-chan. I'm sure you know what I mean."

"Cute. Always wanted to get one of those, but they were always too pricey. 'Bout diggin' the tree, I'm hip with that. It was sometime back, but I had a tree too. I just haven't figured out its little secret just yet. Somehow the simplicity of its message has gotten lost in the complexity of life."

"There is not any mimetic complement to this convocation, Ibosen-san. If the meniscus of the mind is pierced with the needle of Love, will it not spill out in fruitless repetition, Rahm-chan? Do you follow me?" He smirked with a certifiably non-humorous imperviousness.

"Is there any soy sauce for this mix, 'cause I really think all this tofu baloney is way too bland and way too freaky for me here." He was really starting to piss me off with all his koans and ninja nonsense.

"By dint of your innate proximity to the grand threshold you have been pegged to receive these divine offerings. Unbeknownst to your true self, you have been treading the path to the palace of perfection for a much longer time than you may have let yourself believe. One day your dreams shall become the manures for the forming of crystals, crystals of the future, Ibosen-san. Have you ever come across something termed as a Morpheus Cocktail?" He looked at me with his mole like eyes.

"I've gotten blotted with a lot of things but I've never run into the sounds of that yet. Is it a manmade process?" I queried the rat-like insectivore defiantly.

"Not exactly, Rahm-chan. It is timeless. Dreams are the mixing pot in which the collective unconsciousness, known to us as Time/Space, invigorates distinct psychogenic DNA strands, which will later determine the talents and faults of the beings who will populate the forthcoming Yuga, the Sat Yuga. These crystals will be involved in a mechanic similar to morphallaxis, gene splitting. Perhaps you've heard of it? Superhuman properties including extensive life spans, enormous physical size, and maximum prowess will result. Likewise, those beings who will come to exist in Sat Yuga

will have the wizardry to travel the skies via levitation, Ibosen-san."
He was starting to strand me in the dust.

"You mean like superman?" I threw my arms forward
displaying my own mordant comedy.

"This is not the place to cast the moral hazard, Rahm-chan.
Please pay attention. As I have heretofore cautioned you quite
succinctly, your focus defines your success." He repeated with an
imperious patience.

"I'm all ears. Really." I joined in reluctantly.

I was feeling like I should shower down with a solution of
Mirex; the little meristic beetle gave me the creeps.

"These beings will be so advanced they will be able to bend
the Time/Space weave and overcome the seemingly unreachable
environments of quasi-human populations. Using superheated
quanta to propagate electro-gravitational waves from the fifth
dimension, they will be able to produce vibrations of microburst,
polarized time splinters, which will empower them to penetrate
multiple barriers of the Time/Space shells, thus reducing the size of
the physical plane down to a board game.

"By riding these nano-splinters of warped Time, they will not
only be able to overcome the barriers of light speed but also they will
have the capacity to travel back from where they reside in the Sat
Yuga to reach into our Kali Yuga, where we are residing at the
moment, and alter history. They will attempt to corrupt certain key
experiences of the chosen ones, the candidates who hold in their
palms the seeds of the future. Projectiles from these metamorphic
beings will travel outward from their dissimilar knowledge bases to
study this tendency and not only duplicate it, but also modify it as
well. Certain human beings who were handpicked to imprint their
intrinsic experiences into the mix of the Morpheus crystals will be
susceptible to these influences. By falling prey to these locaters, they
will be unable to contribute to the cloning of the psychical cells. The
rare few who have developed an anomaly, a psycho-magnetic
immunity to the pull of this far-reaching technology, are the ones for
whom we are seeking desperately so that we may bring them to light,
Ibosen-san. Whether or not you are one of them remains open to
further investigation. Those who can repel these foreign impulses
house an invaluable treasure. These are the ones who will be named

The Moon Women

for this ultra-cognitive psychic breeding of the future DNA." He rocked back on his little slipper feet to gaze up at the stars.

"What does all this have to do with me?" I had a mind to bolt like a bat and get far away from this mad munchkin who seemed to be trying to sign me up a spot in the outer limits. Fleabag whacko!

"Some of us think you are going to be one of these preeminent individuals, Ibosen-san, in case you haven't figured that out by now." He fingered me minaciously with his sapless blackmail.

"I was afraid of that. Any chance I can get a raincheck?"

He reregistered the monocle into his eye socket and took up with his cocktail crooning some more.

"The Morpheus Cocktail is the medium, or more precisely, the mosaic which will gel into crystalline spheres of diamond, a diamond which can manifest a unique property to incorporate the psychic DNA. Many tens of thousands of years hence, Ibosen-san, these dormant repositories of your subliminal sweat will in turn produce the strands and cross links of the DNA for an entirely new age. Your work will be a dynamic engine, which will spawn many new beings, as it were. We use the same morphology of DNA music to orchestrate this etheric complement the same way normal DNA unfolds itself in multitudinous planes to perpetuate the inevitable explosions, which culminate in the formation of unique versions of the species. This entirely original infant will be endowed with an entire DNA map as the karmic script plays out like a violin following the score to contribute to the totality of the concerto being performed by an orchestra." He jerked back at the recognition of his own genius and stared out over the moonless horizon.

He seemed to be measuring the multi-layered strata with his monocle like a micro-managing magnifico. Plus, it was becoming evident his R slippage was improving which made me consider the possibility this dude might be for real. Don't forget, I had experienced something similar. There was no doubt my condition with the Speak might have been precipitated by something parallel to his mythomania. What's more, he looked like a lost army ant pursuing a naked lunch.

"Why me? Why now? This has got to be some mistake. Listen, you've got the wrong victim for your mojo crystal absurdities. I've got work to do, places to go, worlds to conquer." I was expounding my own crystalline plan. No?

"We understand, but, no, this is not any mistake. It is undeniable that in foregoing epochs, there were one or two maladjustments. The malformations of the Cro-Magnon and the Neanderthal races were two outcomes of genetic experiments, which were done by the inhabitants of the foregoing Yuga, the Dwarpar Yuga or the Copper Age. Disastrously, these attempts did go slightly awry. However, those loopholes have been closed. We do not expect to run into any failures within the formation of the psychic DNA softwares this go round." He tapped on his lips as though regurgitating his soba.

"I don't like it. What if I overbake one of the mutants in the brew?" I was hoping to discourage him in the likelihood his paltry plan would bomb.

"In the dim isolated ages, there was also another preparation, which suffered an unfortunate morphological aberration. From time to time, these have emerged on the fringes of your sanity like the foam, which rises when we stir sake too vigorously. The results of that error were unavoidably carried forward to project a vanguard from the future not unlike some strain of psychogenic virus, which continues to feed parasitically upon the human population today. Eventually, you will be the first person to expose the existence of this mutation. You will label them as the Khrng, a designation taken from the annals of their histories. This appellation is an anagram that does not contain any genuine non-obstructed vowels; its origin lies within the spectrum of humanity - **K**ey **H**umanistic **R**adical **N**euronal **G**enome.

"Fortunately, this viral enigma is equally hampered and balanced by deep veins of the White, which have, from time immemorial, innervated the cellular divinity of the human species. It's what keeps them under wraps and reins in their natural bent to overtake the conditions and limitations of the Kali Yuga. Otherwise, life at this end of the galaxy would have come to a collapsed state long ago. That is one of reasons for our appearing prior to the commencement of this work, to head off any possibilities for this type of maladaptation or foul predicament. So far, everything is progressing according to plan. You will learn more of your role and your reason in all this from the others as they make their presence known to you little by little. Remember, the others, the White ones, are those beings who live not in the air. They ride the ether. They are

The Moon Women

winged. The other ones are not your fiends but are most necessary. This will all become clear to you shortly. " Hirohito head wobbled with a triumphant jiggle. His fluttering hairless eyelids seemed to be sending messages to other realms all at once.

"You don't say."

There was not much I could do after all that except go along with the bug man. I figured it might be more helpful to play along and leave the emergence of rationale for when he was out of my face, more like the passing of a bad dream. Then he started to swing that British fob of his in circles like a miniature bolas. Was he trying to hypnotize me? Friggin' nut job!

"Listen to me, Ibosen-san. Human Being is not a species of life like a hare or a dog. He is not like a cow or even a monkey. There is not the primitive man of yesterday and the modern man of today. Human Being is a Divine Manifestation, Ibosen-san. Human Being is a replica of the multiplication of God consciousness.

"Human beings manifest differently according to consistent coordinates and unique specifications, which project from the regulations within each of the four Yugas. The thoughts, words, actions, and dreams undergone by certain inhabitants alive in the latter portion of any particular Yuga are extracted and reformed into the concentrated crystals of the Morpheus component, which perpetuates the lines of psychic DNA. In turn, these are set down as the guidelines, the reference points, which determine how the actual physical DNA is to be constructed in the forthcoming Age. For instance, the residual thoughts of certain aspirants who existed at the culmination of the last Yuga were collected for the formulation of the psychic DNA of that time which later produced the rules and regulations of how the new physical DNA was put together to create the humans of this Yuga, this Iron Age, you and me. Many of the prehistoric scribes of the time collected their experiences and produced writings, which later evolved into something you moderns now call the Bible. That is why many of those scriptural figures described in its epics lived for nearly one thousand years and stood as tall as a giraffe.

"When Lord Krishna trained his disciple, Arjuna, to focus his attention upon that falcon, he was not only perfecting the art of archery, but also preparing the pathways for the psychic DNA of his time. The entire parabola of his war bow was for launching that

472

formulation into the Morpheus Cocktail by using these ways to elicit the designated generations of mankind who are now alive during our present Iron lines. It was his future which is now our past. I trust you are following all this, Ibosen-san." The Emperor pontificated.

Then, he dug down into his baggy trousers and brought out a petite maroon box, which he fondled with a loving caress.

"You got to be kidding. Is that what I think it is?" This crumb was putting his crowing touches on this absurd caper.

"You, Ibosen-san, will be one of the proponents, one of the human cultures out of which the Morpheus Cocktail will be drawn and poured. Des Ne? As of now you have been contacted by some of the other Divines. Don't be so mingy with your resources, Rahm-chan. Try to assimilate and reflect upon what you have been shown so far concerning your candidacy. In the future, when the others arrive, you will be ready to assume your responsibilities in performing this meritorious work." As he concluded, he plugged his monocle back into his mug.

As I scrutinized his foul mannerisms, he looked like he was going to molt or transform himself into another genre of some devolved malignant mythographer.

"What's in the little box, as if I don't know?" I didn't want to change the subject but obviously, he wanted me to ask; otherwise, why did I?

"It is a cricket, Ibosen-san. It is a channel to the Sun Goddess herself. Through it I get messages from her which aid me with my decisions concerning the welfare and the future of mankind." He looked darkly proud.

I didn't have the heart to tell him whom the cricket was.

"You didn't listen to the cricket last time, did you? You should always listen to the cricket, Rahm-chan. He may enlighten you a little further." He bowed.

With that, he shifted in his shell and scurried back to his hive back in the palace. Trailing him was a purple Shiaolin banner upon which was inscribed two Katakana characters flying like a makimono heralding the funeral casket of the coming locusts. It read.

"Tennouheika Banzai!" [Ten thousand years of life for our Emperor!]

"Domo Arighato, Tennou." [Thank you, Great Emperor.]

I addressed him in his wake.

The Moon Women

"Doi tashi mashte. Hai! Domo." [Don't mention it. Yes! Thanks.]

That was all he had to say from out of the shadows and then he was gone.

A passerby caught wind of my parting salute and took off his hat unleashing a gruesome farewell.

"Domo."

Somehow, he looked like Roger Geisha, my roomie from Bard. He jumped up onto the ridgeway surrounding the place and stuck out his arms as if he were preparing to do a superman act while shouting his threat.

"Thinkest thou that I can not now pray to my Father and He shall presently give me more than twelve legions of angels?" [28]

The wonky apparition then leapt from the embankment and scurried off down the gulley into some other altered sphere. Why seventy two thousand angels, I pondered? It would be good just to get one.

- 13 -

The prescient chair cycled in place for no apparent reason. Even though it was born in a timeless dimension, its gentle oscillations acted as if the movements of a fine Swiss watch keeping perfect measurement. Despite that similarity, it harbored a disturbing oddity, which I could not expunge, a soft beating telling me of another life.

The K-room was hush now. I couldn't detect even the slightest reception on my telepathic radio. All the stations had dropped off the bandwidth. Even the crackling static of the universe had disappeared. The whales of Pounar had been silent these foregoing months. I had been advised that Pounar had traipsed off to Machu Picchu to intuit with the Incan angels. I had run the gambit of retrieving his inter-dimensional songs, which he had sung for me in antecedent life times, future ones or somewhere in between.

Having come full circle, I saw the faces of my five Moon women orbiting in front of me like the celestial spheres of love. Each one represented a significant fragment of some cosmic jigsaw puzzle. As I floated in my vertiginous chair gazing out upon those otherworldly vistas, I nervously anticipated what the divining chair would divulge to me next. Perchance soon, it will show me the next link within the chain, the one, which will safeguard the final chapter.

Just recently, the adventures in Goa had served as a platform for ongoing escapades in the shops and discos surrounding Brigade Road. Once, Brownie and I had even ventured into Bangalore University. I was a professor of English History and she was my faithful assistant sent to unleash the fury.

We pushed it to such unthinkable frontiers that one day I performed a lecture to over two hundred undergrads in the university auditorium. The subject was entitled, "Stonehenge and the American Revolution." I discussed discordant theories in which I presented significant arguments to float the notion Stonehenge had a serious sway over the American conflict with the British at the end of eighteenth century.

Even though Stonehenge presented the shallow pretext of a primitive ruins, which has laid upon the Salisbury Plain in Wiltshire, England for millennia, my shot in the dark conjecture claimed it held a magnetizing hold over the future of young America. Whether or not it had inculcated any strategic junctures affecting the revolutionary conflicts in colonial America, I had no idea. However, I demonstrated some twisted theories about how the stones themselves had an effect upon not only the British Empire, but also the Colonies as they were organizing their new country prior to the start of the official American Revolution.

Amplifying these influences up to and including the War of 1812, I whimsically disclosed that specific psycho-magnetic and psycho-geographic influences impinged upon a significant role in the faulty decision making machinery of the major personalities during both military conflicts. I showed quite illusively that the harmonics created by the stupendous boulders and the resultant frequencies and resonances of telekinetic warping of the Time/Space wrinkles had disturbed, in a profoundly influential manner, the cerebral wavelengths of numerable personalities who contributed to the conflicts. Furthermore, these intrusions had caused havoc with both certainty and confusion as these personas collided. I was confident my gloss-over of academese was thick enough to confound the average freshman.

My favorite example was Thomas Jefferson and his prolific indulgences with marijuana when frequenting the dingy haunts of his

The Moon Women

slaves, which embarrassingly lead to unwanted progeny. This horrified the audience of budding Dravidian history students and overcame all notions they might have previously entertained about these well-intentioned revolutionaries who had incontrovertibly succumbed to these clamant forces. While watching me agape as I moonlighted with my schematics, they undoubtedly anticipated they must be witnessing a divergent genius or else someone who had been spawned from the devil. I could have helped them with that but then again it was premature because I couldn't read their minds yet. That would come later.

I also had my album of photos, which I had composed when I was at Stonehenge prior to my travels across Europe, my second attempt to home in on mother India. This series of transparencies showed the stones in quite an unusual perspective. Using them as a pictorial essay, I demonstrated to the audience how the twelve-paired monoliths, which were standing at the time of the early settlers, represented the twenty-four elders mentioned in the Book of Revelation; how these paired couples of granite controlled the initial twelve colonies and the men who created them; and how these twelve colonies, which sought to form the United States, were being dictated to by the tele-psychic energies of the stones. It was only New Hampshire which refused to join the passel of revolutionaries in light of its insistence on maintaining independence with their Live Free or Die holdout stance on the whole deal. It was a fascinating subject, which, as you might imagine, totally confounded the attending scholars. But it could neither be refuted nor intelligently supported for that matter.

Back in my lion-hearted chair, I shifted my position to impart a tangent thrust, which might switch the channels humming in the hard to detect orbits overlapping the wicker webs of my supererogatory sitting platform. Reflections of the women in days gone by reemerged. It dawned on me that the ones with the tooth gap syndrome were controlled by the Moon. They were the Cancer children. Moreover, there was something that all five of these Moon women had in common, but I could not put my finger on it just yet. That mystery perpetuated a resistance within me, which was on the verge of surfacing. I repeated their names one after the other, like a mantra, in an attempt to decipher the mixed riddle: Brownie, Alena, Evey, Chhumpar and now Oma. These were the mountain tops of the range I came to name the Sangham of Lust. I gained another time quadrant on my Tibetan mala as its venom seeped deeper into my veins causing another vision to awaken in my within.

Five hundred years ago (known as the epoch of the Druids), across a continuous span of wheat, which had lain sprawling alongside a circle of monumental stones, the works of the Abaddon Seven fired forth to lay waste to the seething hordes of the Khrng. Their armies were pouring out onto the arena like maggots swarming out of an inkwell of doom. Wielding the cold death of their truth serum, the Seven spewed it from their vials of unbounded spirit and up went the cry.

WHO BARE RECORD
OF THE WORD OF HIM
THE NIRUNJAN
THE BURNING GOD
AND THE TESTIMONY
AND OF ALL THINGS
THAT HE SAW [29]

- 14 -

The chair of bondage was no longer twisting yet I did notice it was uneven. I pondered this for a while and discovered Meg peering in at me over the margins of my book. I had been deeply engrossed in a copy of the Holy Qur'an. This all appeared exorbitantly peculiar in Meg's eyes. Her foot had come to rest on the mediad of the rattan lip of my valorous swing chair. As her sandal tilted it slightly, further truths arose. Dare it be for her to shift the axis of my world off kilter.

"My dear Mr. Rahms! I have only now returned from headquarters."

"Don't call me that, Meg. You know how I hate it."

"Sorry. Don't be so touchy. As I was saying, it was a most enlightening time whose highlights arose during my chat with Dr. K. He has some questions concerning what you are doing all day over there swinging in that ridiculous chair of yours. All his dialogue was poignantly thought provoking; however, it appears he is convinced

The Moon Women

you are inculcating devil guardians from future states of ignorance.

"Yeah, I know. He and I have already covered that subject. What else you got?"

"Just listen. You might also be interested to know that within that book you're holding there is evidence Jesus was involved with more than one religion! Dr. K had me realize simply because the Christians claim Him as their own doesn't necessarily mean He wasn't fair dinkum for the Muslims or maybe even the Jews, you know. Plus, some people think He was a black man. Why I hear He even made His way all the way across to India. Who knows? Could be He was a Buddhist or, more of surprise, a Hindu who practiced yoga years previous to running into His ole buddy, John the Baptist? He might have even been into that tantric kundalini shit that kicks ass. Have you ever figured that eye-opener into your system of divergent postulates?"

"Straight from the hip, Meg, I agree with you whole heartedly. There's a good chance He was all of those and more. Now leave me alone. I've got more prophets to chase after and heavens to burn."

Once more the wayward chair churned the cauldron of Time, sending out the vapors of cooked up love.

CHAPTER 7 - **LUNAR LINKS**

- 1 -

It was the evening time: cool and effervescent. I remember the intoxicating smell of jasmine seeping in from the courtyard. I was wearing my Maharaja robe, a robe so iridescent I felt like an indigo bunting radiating starlight. I was sitting at a table in a French restaurant with snowflake doilies and a bottle of Merlot. There was a candle flickering in a bowl causing firelight to dance upon the walls. Brownie came to me from out of a blue fog of the seventh seal, which had exhaled its way into my presence. She was wearing the most gorgeous lavender gown and a snow-white pelerine covering her bare shoulders. She looked ravishing. After she came over and pulled up a chair to my table, we talked.

"Hi, Rahm. Where have you been?"

Her words seemed to melt in my ears.

"I've been here all along Brownie just waiting for you."

I committed to it solidly. We looked into each other's eyes for quite some time. I could never forget those emerald globes of fire, which sparkled with infinite delight.

"There's been something that I've been meaning to tell you, Rahm."

She was laying down a new lane in the honeysuckle now.

"What's that? I know. You've always loved my swing chair, isn't it?"

I was taunting her but also prophesying. The saxophones droned into the warm soft breeze, which was ushering in promises of eternal midnight.

"No. The chair is of Time. This is of Love. I've always wanted to call you something."

She was aiming her subtle wand at my heart.

"Yeah, I know. Bone-headed-moron for letting you get away."

I was taking careful aim but sparing myself any real harm.

"Would you like to know what it was?"

She smiled and closed her eyes.

"Would you really like to know?"

The Moon Women

"I'm all ears, Brownie, really I am. You can call me whatever you like."

I was prepared, but not ready.

"I have always wanted to call you, Blackey."

"But Brownie, I'm white."

"It's merely a name. Do you mind?"

She cocked her head.

"Okay, since you put it that way."

I got it in spite of my upbringing.

"Does that surprise you?"

"Not at all; I'll be your Blackey anytime."

I proposed with all my heart.

The daydream burned its way deep onto the pages of my book, setting them on fire. When the books are all burning, true knowledge will escape like God's smoke. Human destiny will release its future from the cage of the past and the bloody histories will consign their future to the ashes of divine remorse, out of which will arise the Albacore Man. I was now one-step closer to that clear water.

After that, I was quiet. The pretty thoughts faded away softly in heavenly silence.

In the cellar of past Time, a silvery screen flashed with a magnetic glow to capture the attention of a young boy.

"Hey Cisco! Look! I got a wire fast for you. Good news! It's good news."

"Pancho, if this telegram is for me how do you know what's inside it?"

"Oh Cisco, I know what's inside it because I look at it through the corner of one eye. I could see."

"Oh, Pancho!"

"Oh, Cisco!"

With a trail of dust and a hearty shout of farewell, the Cisco Kid and Pancho galloped off into the sunset.

"Adios Muchachos!"

- 2 -

The meandering chair returned from its sojourn in the pre-death states to once again voyage onwards in its odyssey to discover the lineage of the Moon women. I knew it couldn't possibly be beaten by Time, nor could it be saved by Love. Only a very special something could encourage it to tell me the truth of a timeless existence. With a firm jolt, I sent it off on another recon mission of heartache and misgivings.

A short while ago, pre-Brownie, I had to travel to Madras in late February of this year to reclaim all my photo gear. This saga occurred soon after I had entered India. Since I had already come overland from Europe through Athens, Istanbul, Tehran, Kabul, and into Lahore, I was tying up some loose ends. Yeah, I know, you've heard it all before, but this is a little catchup play. My stay in New Delhi had concluded with the seduction rites of Evey Nathanson, which, if you recall, had damn near killed me. It was as an aftermath of that confrontation that I had abandoned my high-minded plight with regard to chastity and the process of concentrating the spinal powers of etheric purity.

My journey to Tamil Nadu (the most southeastern state of India) had to be undertaken for me to connect the dots, the ones that had gone dark after I had traced my pathway into Malaysia. There I had collided with that infernal impediment of doom in Kuala Lumpur, which propelled me back stateside. Since my primary attempt to reach the motherland had dead-ended with the bloody belly of a two hundred kilo Swami who had voiced my halt, I had little choice but to follow destiny. His forecasts of retribution underscored the fact that the farthest westward I would reach successfully was that temple deep in the jungles of Malaysia. It was at that time when I bumped my head up against the hundred and first longitudinal line east from the Prime Meridian, which jettisoned me into reverse mode and forced me to retrace my path back to Long Island. I was given this verdict from the prescient Swami Devakalu and his prophecy of the psychic wall separating me from the promised land of India.

It was from the airport in Kuala Lumpur that I had sent two well-stuffed duffel bags housing all my photographic equipment on a priority flight to Madras. I had sent the luggage on ahead of my arrival, thinking (piece of cake) I would have my visa to enter India lickety-split. I had envisioned making my triumphant landfall onto that humid plateau, claim my baggage, and then continue onwards to

The Moon Women

award myself an acclaimed debut into the hallowed thresholds of FWC in Bangalore.

Needless to say, all those plans never materialized. I had to retrace all my steps and return northward through Bangkok, Hong Kong and onto Tokyo, revisit Hiroshima and meet Oma, then do a hop, skip and jump back through Tokyo, San Francisco and New York to wind up all the way back to Mitchell Gardens and start all over again; most humiliating, I must say.

"What a man proposes, God disposes." That's a quotation from the famous Indian Saint, Kirpal Singh (1894 -1974), whom I had not had the good fortune of coming across yet and quite conceivably never would.

The Customs House in Madras was a Dravidian palace of iniquity. It was presided over by a man, whose predilection for twisted details was second only to his obsession for suffocating routine. Mr. Charanaya Supramanian drank from the source fount of literal bureaucracy. His magisterial hand touched everything. If there was a certificate authorizing human respiration and the allotted twenty thousand ins and outs a person needs to live every day, Mr. Supramanian would have been on top of that one, its orchestration, and the seven seals needed to be affixed to said triplicate document along with all the fitting time stamps. There was no protocol, which he could not screw up, bastardize, or compound into utter confusion. Add to that punctilio was the overall confustication of a gimmick I was not at all aware of at the start of this adventure, namely the job of extinguishing the hunger residing in the bottomless pockets of this chief apparatchik by feeding it with firm and tactful injections of moola (what the locals call baksheesh); the whole thing was disgusting.

When I arrived at the man's office for the inaugural day of this fiasco, his deputy had me wait a few moments before having an audience with Supramanian Maharaj, or Ole Super Suckup as I came to call him. I should have known that sobriquet was a telltale of what I was going to be confronting. Past any doubts, he was most definitively the maharaja of malversation. After an hour had elapsed, I acted as though I had contracted a rare strain of Africanized ass rash, which had me jumping up and down like a kangaroo on steroids. After the second hour, I calmed down but my butt had gone numb from sitting surplus hours on the two hundred year young wooden bench. Plus, I was going deaf listening to the thunderous crowds contesting in the back hallways, throngs of ragamuffin street beggars haranguing to be let free. Fifteen minutes prior to my actual encounter with the Maharaji, the sweat of my impatience had eaten through my undershirt, my dress shirt and my silk vest, staining the seams a pale squash. It was "muy afortunada [very fortunate]" that the word, "manana [tomorrow]," did not exist in Hindi; otherwise, I would have been stuck in the Madras Customs House awaiting more instructions from Mr. Supramanian forever. Without a doubt, Shri Supra Ji was the ultimate panjandrum.

When I finally faced him head on and got down to business, the foremost item on our agenda was the unearthing of the original document in the mountain of paper, which lined his museum quality office. After an exhaustive investigation, he disclosed it must have been submitted from the Kuala Lumpur side. Such bureaucratic eventration had to be accompanied by the original sheet of papyrus rook, or, in this case, the honest to god stock. Plus, it had to bear all the legitimate data concerning the manufacture, including, but not limited to, the date and time, serial code of the lorry hired for its transport and the port of call, if there was one. I am not referring to my luggage here. I am referring to the paper on which the original voucher for my shipment was printed.

"Are you kidding me?" I looked at the chap with utter disbelief.

"Truthfully, Sir, I shall incur all reliance on the supplication before us. Trust me, I shall spare no hesitation with regard to this task." Shri Supramanian cleverly masked his purposes.

"What is this? Some kind of reality show? The Indian version of Candid Camera? Nobody's laughing here, Buddy! Change the channel! Hello! I'm outa here, you ass!" I had gone off the reservation.

Three days later, after pushing passed mountains of parchment and a breadcrumb trail of indentured hallmarks which could have easily lined the inner surfaces of the Taj Mahal, we had successfully located that dead sea scroll (God only knows how) and verified the exclusive chain of command necessary to proceed to tracking down the important documents. From there he required the completion of the preliminary memorandum, which is quite often formulated and signed by diplomatic negotiators who determine the

483

The Moon Women

basis for the primary convention. After I had listened to him expound his Indianized version of this wizard tale, I started to cough. It was perpetuated by a gagging claustrophobia, which I simply could not tolerate so I got up and evacuated the building for the rest of the day.

The following afternoon I showed up only to find the office was closed on Tuesdays, Saturdays and every other Friday. Naturally, Sundays it's closed as well. Holidays are quite numerous because we are honoring the three major religions here, namely, Hinduism, Islam and Buddhism. Listing the Christian days off is simply a matter of course, since it has to be given first dips on the festival pole.

It was a blessing to stay in the Woodlands Hotel for this entire adventure; otherwise, I would have gone stark raving mad. The Woodlands is a chain of hotel-cum-restaurants, which cater specifically to vegetarian clientele. The food there was excellent. The rooms were clean and spacious, having ample baths with western toilets if you preferred. I had landed in a regular one with the average Asian toilet, a hole over which you hang your butt instead of lazily sitting down on an oval appliance (a most unhygienic practice according to Asians). I didn't mind squatting and the posture is said to give beneficial influences to one's lower back. The place also had a nice balcony from which you could look down into the parking area and the terraced garden, which never failed to provide ample greenery and floral wonder.

Situated on the Coromandel Coast off the Bay of Bengal, Madras was always hot and muggy. Further, as it was on the lee side away from the Monsoons, which traditionally come in from the Arabian Sea in the West, only rarely did thunderstorms rumble in to clash with the tall downtown skyscrapers and hotel monoliths.

At the height of a freak heatwave that year, it got to be so hot the streets melted. The asphalt, which comprised the surfaces of the major arteries, wasn't formulated to withstand much heat because when the temperature hit one hundred and twelve degrees in the shade, the streets turned into liquid pools of tar. But that didn't stanch the constant flow of traffic. The wheels of the frantic vehicles flung the oily guck all over the place like flying coal taffy. Since I always traveled in taxis, it was nip and tuck running to and fro amongst the harbor lights commuting to the Customs House. Tiptoeing elegantly across the congealed bits of bituminous pavement, I felt like a transgender Mata Hari of the tar pits.

One afternoon on the way to the godown, a nasty glob of melted asphalt splattered up and landed on the inside of my arm. It scalded me painfully until I wiped it off with a rag borrowed from the Taxi Wallah. To this day, that wrinkled uplifted patch causes me a lot of embarrassment. Nevertheless, I knew it was some kind of a badge of nobility; something, which predicted what was to come; something from the Beyond, which the Khrng cannot remove. I deny it had anything to do with the star-spangled ruffians who constantly molested me over the warfare in heaven.

After an entire week had crawled by and then a second, I was starting to get the hang of this game. I'd arrive a little after eleven. Shri Supramanian would have gotten most of the important work off his desk and we would begin where we had left off from our former get-together the day before. By the third week, we were starting to negotiate with the official who was in charge of the codes that prescribed the esoteric sectors of adherence to the dominant precedence. The name of that department had even more words than that phrase.

After a bit, Supramanian Sahib would call for one of his gofers to bring us some Chai. In this country, Chai is a complete ritual in itself, which is designed to eat up the wider spread of an hour. Naturally enough, any discussions of business related topics were strictly forbidden during Chai time. On the one hand, I would sit patiently while he related details of his home life and his career, and on the other, my reciprocation was to reimburse him with narrations of my exploits while journeying overland into Delhi, along with anecdotes of my travels throughout Southeast Asia (a preceding subset which bracketed my antecedent attempt to reach the subcontinent).

The revelry of our twisted tales was only outdone by the intensity of our comradery. It was surreal. It was a Jean Paul Sartre excursion across the deserts of the existential Brahmin as contrasted to one man's island of ineptitude and misaligned romance, yours truly. Supra Sahib, as he came to be nicknamed, was the unalloyed mathematician of meaninglessness.

The other twist in the mix I enjoyed deeply while plying this negotiating match with Supra were the prostitutes. In as much as

The Moon Women

Indians eminently revere marriage, it may be the most sacrosanct issue in the life of a pious Hindu. The wedding ceremony itself can bridge two weeks if done properly. Via the methodologies of astrology, palmistry and an eclectic assortment of cosmic and religious sciences, sincere parents arrange ninety-nine percent of all marriages here. Their success rate is second to none. Divorce in India is exceedingly rare. In fact, for many centuries, there was a practice called Sati, a cultural phenomenon in which the wife threw herself onto the funeral pyre of her dead husband. Even though this practice has been fully banned in India for decades, there are still some remote places in which this atrocity continues to occur.

Prostitution, on the other hand, is not only accepted, it is sanctioned within the backrooms of cultural overlook. It does not exactly enjoy the status of being an outright legality; however, it is not in any way condemned or seen to be a lowering of position or other civil injury upon marriage. Not discounting intercourse to be a biological function and a necessary component for cultivating one's family, prostitution is seen to offer an enhancement to that drive. The healthy functioning and success of that activity encourages further rise in the health of a mature male. Therefore, without a doubt prostitution is the largest, most profitable industry in India, second only to the moviedom of Bollywood.

In the Wooodlands, you could order from a glut of services delivered straight to your bedside. There was a comprehensive laundry duty which would return your things spotlessly and within hours, a full serving plate of Paan and the many Areca nut derivatives available from the street, and a full complement of Asian meals served by a waitress if need be. You could have any particular newspaper or any selection from a wide variety magazines also sent speedily to your door. You could also order most any kind of young lady who you might desire. You could specify a Hindustani, or an Islamic one or even a Buddhist, whatever your pleasure or religious preference might demand. Customarily, the Hindu ladies were the most popular, mainly because of the ratio of pure bloods (they were all Brahmins) to the other religions, some twenty to one. But they were all quite pleasant and beautiful. So, every other Friday, on account of the Customs office closing, I would order out.

I only had one hang-up with them. They were all caulked full with nasty grease. Birth control methods were nonexistent at that

486

time in India. After all, why do it if they were merely constructing a bigger nation? But for a fallback, their solution was to inject so much petroleum jelly into the uterus area for the purpose of establishing a barrier, which would prevent the men fish from swimming on through. There were no drive-by shootings in South India. Nevertheless, in spite of how frequently I sent perfumed notes to the receptionists requesting mine degreased, I was never lucky enough to prevail with that submission, and as a result, I had to suffer through the worst of it. However, it was only a minor letdown since they were not only alarmingly gorgeous but also quite admirable in the performance of their duties.

Sometimes afterwards, they would sip Chai with me and help me improve my Hindi. I even had one who offered to teach me a few words of Telugu. They got so happy and childlike whenever I attempted to speak with them in their native languages. But they simply would not kiss me directly on the lips no matter what I did or how much I paid them. I never got to the bottom of that deal back then and even to this day that enigma continues to elude me.

Towards the latter days of my recurrent visits to the Customs House and shortly before the conclusion of my efforts to negotiate my belongings with Supramanian Sahib was another intervention from the frost devils. While attempting to find a short cut out of the endless archives of Indian antiquity I was retracing the maze of tall-shelved hallways and alcoves dividing this Third World culture from the shores of modernity when I negotiated a wrong turn. T-boning into another blind alley, I turned sideways to get out and ran smack into another cul-de-sac. Right in the crux of this forest of unending webbed shadows, I sat down on a garfish Ormolu mounted with bamboo turnings brutally beaten for centuries by the sandaled feet of millions. My blood sugars must have been lacking the zesty punch of Chai, which Supramanian had been plying me with all these weeks because the unusual frostiness of the godown's cramped hallways was creeping into my bones. I slumped back awaiting the inevitable.

In the encroaching dusk, I noticed an old-fashioned air vent, which seemed to have an extraordinary amount of light seeping from around its scratched edges as though the room, which was hiding behind it was lit up with stardom. After blinking my eyes to reset my cerebral machinery, I realized it wasn't a vent. It was another one of those aluminized portals, which led to an alternative timeline.

The Moon Women

At the rate of sliding sand, its sill rose and a glass globe the size of a softball fell out and landed on the oiled wood with a thud. With its crystal structures still intact, the glassy orb then projected a scene onto the adjacent wall. A pastoral vista arose with a boscage of willow overlooking a meandering purple stream. Out of this mirage emanated another Angel. Only this one was my size. It had its wings tucked under its armpits. Even though this one looked like a dumpling angel, tall but wide, it still had those traditional periwinkle eyes shaped like Asian almonds. Those blue marble eyes, the only features on his spherical titanium skull, latched onto my thoughts with their mind splitting chimes turning my mind inside out.

UNTO THE ANGEL OF THE CHURCH [1] THESE THINGS SAITH
HE WHO GAVE ME
THE LITTLE BOOK

I CARRY THE SEVEN STARS
IN MY RIGHT HAND AND
I WALK IN THE MIDST OF THE
SEVEN GOLDEN CANDLESTICKS [1]
FROM THE COUNSEL OF EPHESUS
AND LEGION *TO ABADDON*
SON OF MAN AND
COMPANION OF LIGHT
MY MARK IS THAT OF KOKABEL

His gleaming hand gestured to the forest scene on the wall.

BEHOLD THE ALTAR OF SOULS
THAT SITS AS THE FIFTH SEAL
THE FIFTH PLACE OF BATTLE
WHERE WE SUFFER TO KILL
THE GLASS HEADED SCORPIONS
THEM THAT WERE SLAIN   THIS IS A SALUTE OF PIETY TO
BY THE WORD OF GOD   THOSE WHO HONOR THE CAUSE
THE NIRUNJAN *AND FOR*   OF OPPOSING THE KHRNG
THE TESTIMONY THEY HELD [2] AS WELL AS HONORING

488

Haan Moses

THE FALLEN SOULS CRIED
WITH A LOUD VOICE
SAYING HOW LONG O LORD
HOLY AND TRUE WILL YOU
NOT JUDGE AND AVENGE
OUR BLOOD ON THEM
THAT DWELL SO LONG
UPON THE DEFILED EARTH? [3]

THE REMNANT
HAS LONG TRIED TO FEED
UPON THE SPIRIT FLESH
OF THE MAN LION
AND TO SERVE UP
THEIR SORROW AND PAIN
TO FIND THE ANSWER   THE ANGELS SYMPATHIZE SOME
TO A MYSTERY THAT HAS   OVER THE MISERABLE TASK
HELD THEIR KINDRED   THAT KHRNG HAVE ASSIGNED
IN AN IRON CAGE FOR YEARS   THEMSELVES TO UNRAVEL

THE WHITE ROBES WERE GIVEN
    THE SECRET OF WHY THEIR GENOME
UNTO EVERY ONE OF THEM
    HAS BEEN SO CORRUPTED AND WHY
AND IT WAS SAID THAT
    EVEN AFTER MILLIONS OF YEARS
THEY SHOULD REST FOR A SEASON
    THEY HAVE NOT BEEN ABLE TO RESET
UNTIL THEIR FELLOW SERVANTS
    THEIR ORIGINS AND BALANCE THEIR
AND ALSO THEIR BROTHERS
    THEIR EXISTENCE WITH THAT OF THE
SHOULD BE KILLED AS THEY
    NORMAL CYCLES OF TIME AND

The Moon Women

SHOULD BE FULFILLED [4]

Space to become Whole again

Kokabel bent down on his knee and clasped his two hands over the hilt of his enormous war scythe.

AS I ASCENDED FROM THE EAST
HAVING THE SEAL OF THE LIVING GOD
THE NIRUNJAN *THE BURNING GOD* [5]
HOLDING THE FOUR WINDS OF THE EARTH [6]

THE FOUR TONGUES OF TORMENTED AIR
ONE WITHIN THE OTHER HAVING
MANY A SIDE TO DRINK THE BLOOD
OF THE PURE AND THE STRONG SOULS
COMING AS A PILLAR OF FIRE
AND BRIMSTONE AND NOISE
DESCENDING OUT OF HEAVEN   Once again Kokabel
AS AN UPSIDE DOWN ALTAR OF EVIL WIND
                    Shares the purpose of
LEFT TO LEAVE ITS MEASURE OF SIN
                    The Seven Angels of Abaddon
INTO THE WHEAT AS THE REMNANTS
                    As they pursue their enemies
ARE SENT INTO THE BOTTOMLESS MOUTH
                    track them down and finally
SITTING IN WALL OF THE ALL TIME
                    Feed them into the holes of Time

Suddenly there was a tumultuous disruption within the pastoral scene. Kokabel leapt high and vaulted through the open vent, his afterworld evacuation point. And the silver sphere on the floor popped like a soap bubble. As it was time for me to exit stage right, I found my way out of this temporary maze and regained my route out of the Madras Customs House.

In due time after wearing out the sidewalks over to the Customs Department for seven weeks, I started to see a light at the

490

end of my tunnel. Shri Supramanian Sahib and I unearthed the Rosetta stone for the whole mess from out of his endless stack of filing cards. We deciphered all the correct bribery sums and to whom and to where and no less, when. The special password necessary to perform the open sesame on the vault entombing my two duffel bags was finally deciphered once and for all.

At last, I loaded the twin olive drab units into the back of my taxi and headed for the train terminal. What I had to go through amidst that infuriating megillah in Madras was a cogent element of my voyage to attain the backyard of my purpose. I had conquered another beachhead on the frontier battle of unlocking the secrets of my path into the Beyond. All the ingredients for the alchemy of this new science of the Over-self that I was cultivating were finally coming together. Soon, I felt, very soon, I would behold the results of these experiments in the laboratory of my being. The heart of my spiritual engine would begin to beat. And it would not be coerced by the puppet strings of the Khrng.

As the broken disk of a quarter-moon ascended the graduated grid of twilight and unleashed its spinal horn into the dying stellar wind, out on a remote peninsula of eastern Canterbury, what looked like a meteor was moving at breakneck speed over the midnight wheat. What would normally be a sage landscape was now painted in shades of burning red. No extra-terrestrial object, it had originated in one of the many Time cannons residing some three hundred and fifty thousand years into the future.

Fired back through a funnel of dark energy, it had a scheduled reentry vector somewhere near the later years of the twentieth century when it would ricochet off the Wall of the All Time and plot a worming thread towards its intended target, a young woman by the name of Vanessa Boorman. The discharge within the magnetic flux of the magnetosphere would register an impact of decent detectability to pinpoint a second launch later on, which would do the finish work. Neither the Khrng nor the Angels of Abaddon had anything to do with this event. People residing in the succeeding Yuga, the Sat Yuga, were causing this contagion. They were using the DNA of the micro-Khrng of their epoch as projectiles against which the Angels had no defense.

The Moon Women

"Let the string out more!" I shouted to Raju, the Krishnaswami's little boy.

The flimsy paper craft rode the updrafts into the cloudless blue over Cooketown. That afternoon we were up on the roof flying crepe-paper kites sporting colorful tails that sung like fire angels. It was a jubilant day right after the Monsoons, the time when life blossoms into glory. All the flowering trees in Bangalore had exploded into shades of vermillion and wormwood like goat's blood splashed onto electric green stars.

Losing track of Raju's wandering flyer, I stared off over the horizon. As the street venders cried out their calls to the neighborhood kitchens, I was caught in the blankness of a daydream. For a moment or two, the hawking cries stole into my thoughts and reopened a delicate remembrance, scars of a link to a lost companion.

"I see it! I think I can see it, Mr. Rahm." The boy bellowed.

I peered into the distance and instead of regaining a link to the young child's drifting kite, I noticed a lone figure making headway towards our building. This traveler was not riding in a rickshaw, as any self-important Indian would have preferred. This visitor was on foot and toting a backpack as well. As I focused on the singularity, a glimmer of anticipation sprung up within me. Could it be her? When the diminutive figure got within shouting yardage, I could determine the signs of western gear - sunglasses and baseball cap. Then it clicked. I knew it was another student en route to FWC. And who could she be other than my long lost friend?

I tore down the stairs, scampered through the door and out onto the road. Jogging lickety-split at a breakneck clip, I broke into a gallop. It was Brownie! I ran over to her and gave her a big bear hug.

"Brownie! Brownie!" I yelled.

"Hi Rahm." She smiled that high-test smile of hers.

"Metoo! It's Metto. Can I call you Metoo?" I remembered, but I had never really called her that in the past.

"Well, Brownie's good. How have you been, Rahm?"

"How 'bout Trinity, then?"

"What?"

"I mean you've been gone plenty, isn't it? You look great."

492

"Thanks. You, too."

"I'm okay. I've only recently returned from Madras after securing all my photographic gear." I conveyed.

"That's good. That's really good, Rahm. Really." She looked like she might require a bit of a rest.

"Come on into Dr. K's. We'll fix you up really fast." I was so excited.

"I'd like a dorm room, if that's Okay?" She stated.

She headed to the western shores instead of the eastern ones ala pujaville. I accompanied her over there to help her get unpacked and properly settled.

"When I saw you disappear into that Time tunnel, I thought I would never see you ever again, Brownie. It's a miracle that you're back," I confided somewhat weak heartedly.

"Well, it wasn't like you tried to write me a lot, Rahm. What's up with that?" She exposed her hurt.

"Yeah. I know. That's bad. I've been all over the place lately and it wasn't like I had your address. I wanted to, but, never mind, you're here now, isn't it?" I liberated some of my pent up unknowns.

"Let's not pick some cheap cop out, Rahm. I'd like to think I know you better than that." She was quite correct.

"Brownie, I came across some news about you. Did you know you were an atomic baby? And why is it your name is Ilene Ireland?" I grilled her with my runaway mouth.

"What? I'm radioactive? Who told you that?" In a flash, she was on the defensive.

"Well, is it true?" I pressed in to know more but knew I had driven precipitously over the edge.

"That's none of your damn business, Rahm. I can't believe I came all the way back here for this now. Who told you that?"

"Brownie, it's me. I don't want to pry into anything that's hurtful. I would merely like to know, that's all." I attempted to erase all my screwy intentions.

"Listen. It's something that's true. That was my name once, but I'm not going to talk about it now, if that's okay with you. And who the hell told you I was atomic? That's nuts!" She claimed responsibility and then let it go like metered mail.

The Moon Women

She requested some solitude and privacy for which I had no problem. We went our separate ways as the crows continued with their perpetual cross-talk amongst the road scraps.

Later in the day, we got together over in the kitchenette of the meetinghouse. We shared some idli waddah, which Mrs. Krishnaswami had given me to bring over to her. As Brownie unloaded her story, I could see it was pretty awful when her mother died. She said it took her quite a bit longer than she expected to get over it. In some ways, she feared she never would. I insisted I only wished for her happiness above all else. Then, she confronted me with it. She blurted out the main reason she had come back to Bangalore was to look me in the eye and ask me if I meant to her what she thought I did. She asked me point-blank why I had never considered her in the light of any romantic basis.

Back then, I didn't have the guts to confess the bigotry of my father, which I knew would hurt her gravely so I never let that embarrassment come out. I invented some excuses for whatever was behind it, some disorder, which had sequestered me in its grasp. As she watched this black and white conundrum unravel, a disconcerted look came over her: something on the verge of a simmering distrust. But then, I had to spill the beans. I simply didn't have those kinds of feelings for her. I conceded it wasn't because I couldn't, it was because, somehow, deep down, I did not believe I was good enough for her. When I confessed that, it was like a cloudburst. She burst out weeping. I felt so sorry for her. She did not deserve that kind of misery. I put my arms around her to console her.

"If you're going to do that, Rahm, you should mean it. I just can't live like we did before." She admonished me.

I lifted her chin and I kissed her with the most sincerely loving kiss I had. That kiss opened an entire other door for me. It let me into a place that I never knew existed in the past. The mentionable portion of that moment revealed her longing, but the pain refused to show its face.

"You know, Brownie, I think I have loved you ever since the beginning, the day we met right here six months ago. I just never knew it until now." It was right to tell her that.

"I think I have always known it too, Rahm. That's why I came back."

494

- 4 -

I had decided to forget the bugaboo about her classified files secreted in the bowels of Dr. K's vault. She was none other than "Brownie" to me. There were too many "I"s in that other name of Ilene Ireland anyway. I confided the reverie I had of her, in which she came clean that she had always wanted to call me "Blackey." Could it be she wanted to see me in some token light? She insisted she couldn't imagine from where I got that nut ball concept because she had never had any ideas like that previously. However, she did say she didn't mind if I used Metoo since that nickname inferred I was part of the family. Moreover, she added her permission to call her anything except, "Shithead!" Typical Brownie.

We were Cooketown's reborn miscegenetic couple once again - ebony and bigotry, er, ivory. Yeah, that's the one. How could I ever have forgotten that? However, we decided not to live at the top of the social strata of dancing and revelry over in Brigade Road as we had before. We spent considerable time getting to know one another again and sharing plates of idli and mosala dosas, which Mrs. Krishnaswami doled out with exuberant congratulations.

We had both decided to engage Yoga lessons with a refined gray haired gentleman by the name of Vingtesh Ganapati. I renamed him "VG" for short. He considered it dreadfully humorous how all the newcomers had to give the Indians nicknames because they couldn't pronounce the Hindi or the Sanskrit vowels with the required tongue twisting enunciation. As I clicked through my repertoire of Kannada words, I showed him how I could pronounce them quite easily. He admitted I did have a surprisingly good command of the Dravidian marbles-in-the-mouth pronunciation techniques and more specifically the vowels.

"Perhaps you are a reincarnated Sanskrit scholar."

Together we split our sides on that one. When he laughed, I saw him as Ganesha, the elephant deity, bouncing up and down on a medicine ball.

On a mild day in late July, all the fwics had received invitations to attend pre-celebrations for the holiday of Krishna Janmashtami, the birth of Lord Krishna. Normally performed in late August, VG told us we could get a preview of the whole deal a few weeks ahead of time since the devotees of this temple wanted to

The Moon Women

perfect their program of fasting, prayer, and devotional singing before the actual arrival. This one was a local Krishna temple only a kilometer away on the other side of Cooketown. VG came to get us in an auto rickshaw and the three of us piled into the singular ripped up seat in the back with Miss Tiami sandwiched in between the two duffers. He always referred to her as "Miss Tiami." Indians are always so formal with respect to names and all their naming conventions.

As our taxi wove through the bustling streets swarming with Brahma bulls, tangled chains of auto-rickshaws, herds of goats, barefoot venders, and elephantine Lorries belching oily mushrooms of unburned diesel, monkeys scampered across our travel pursuing something nutritional or shiny. The usual army of pedestrians displaying the full spectrum of fabrics from slovenly rags to exquisite Varanasi silks bustled this way and that.

Taxi Wallahs don't drive with their steering wheels and they don't drive with their brakes. They drive with their buzzers, their horns. Every constant second, it was beep, beep, beep, beep, as though they were using the feedback from the electronic squawking devise on their steering wheel as an echo-locating device, because it never stopped. I wasn't proposing to make a mountain range out of a rat heap, but it really plagued me something fierce. Every time I got into one of those bumblebee flavored tin cans, I had always insisted the driver not go so hog-wild on his tooter. And every time I had, my request was received with a deaf ear, which was most likely why they kept beeping so much.

"Hey, VG, tell that wacko to give it a rest. Uh?" I yelled some meat and potato expletives aimed at his broccoli colored sunglasses.

Brownie squirmed deeper into the aged cheese of the torn upholstery to avoid any collateral damaged.

"Let the guy do what he has to do, Rahm. Did you ever think it's for our protection?" Brownie shot back.

"Miss Tiami is quite correct. The driver is best at driving, Shri Ji." Vingtesh replied with his backseat wisdom.

He always pissed me off by calling me Shri Ji as his little dig to get back at me for calling him VG. Shri means Sir or Your Majesty. It implies the conventional title of respect when addressing an individual of noteworthy status or someone of any distinguishable merit. Aside from that adulation, the general populace in India

496

regards most any American to be upper caste from the get-go. This distorted concept of caste has come down through India's history. The caste system is an unnatural classification process, which ranks the different human beings according to their station in life and it has been virtually fixed and insurmountable for centuries. It has become so thoroughly inbred into the cultural patterns of the everyday routine such that it wouldn't be so farfetched to state it has been perpetuated by some genetic trait welded into the lines of their heredity. The Ji affect is also a word, which denotes admirable respect. So, essentially he is calling me, Sir Sir, which does connote slight sarcasm, but I let it go if for no other reason than pure spite.

Brownie thought it was incredibly funny whenever he addressed me that way. She would always make this little snorting noise whenever she heard VG refer to me with it. I was happy she could get a goof in that. Fortunately, for me the trip was merely a stone's throw from the home front.

When we pulled in at the threshold to the temple, it was decidedly apparent some serious activities were bracing to get underway. The place was stupid with sparkling lights and flashing neon everywhere. Brownie and I were aghast at the intensity of the electric circus, which the little temple was sucking down off the power bands surrounding us.

VG began his introductory disclaimer.

"Traditionally whenever there is a wedding in Bangalore, or anywhere in India for that matter, we string assortments of colored lights wherever we can affix them to throw a celestial aura onto the festivities. For this holiday honoring the great Avatar, Lord Krishna, we also put those same kinds of lights all over the houses and especially the temples. When you travel throughout the great cosmos of regal Dravidian homesteads, there are oceans of lights wherever you go. Except for the Islamic communities where the same kinds of religious holiday is not being celebrated; it is not going on in those areas of the city. So, you will see pockets of darkness in and amongst the pools of effulgent lighting. This is not to infer that Islam is in any manner a dark or gloomy religion, a less effulgent one. It's simply that their holidays come at different times of the year, which doesn't conflict with the Hindu ones. Far be it for anybody to insinuate Islamics in any way cause conflict. I'm sure you can understand what

497

The Moon Women

I'm saying." VG covered a few of the initial bases while avoiding the ones normally tripped over.

The compact Krishna temple was sandwiched between a host of commercial and residential buildings as if it were some unidentifiable craft, which had crash-landed right in the midst of on-going human commerce. It was plain to see its founders had erected it in that spot right in the middle of industry and high-rise corporate structures prior to the emergence of paper and the high caliphate of Persia. A grimy patina of genetic history now exuded a cultural geology all along the granite surfaces. These markings advertised the somber influences of Dravidian domestic strife and the struggles of the mundane hell worlds of the masses, which speaks for an acceptance of concepts we greenhorns will never fathom. You have to live an entire cycle here before you can fully digest it.

There were six monumental stairs leading to the primary concourse of the central hall. Four-meter high totems, the likeness of Krishna in salacious poses, supported the three tiers of the complex capped with a multilayered Vimana of domes. (Legends of the Avatar read like a cheap soft-porn saga from what I've been told.) Each dome consisted of thick rings subordinated by other rings within other rings, which were stacked one on top of the other. They extended all the way to the summit, upon which a shining sickle of the infant Moon sat crowning the peak and symbolizing the birth of the avatar himself, Lord Krishna. Such similar realms within realms structure has been seen throughout history and represent a massive archetype or main trunk of the human subconscious.

We mounted the megalithic cubes and pushed back the gargantuan gates and went in. There were nearly thirty devotees attending to a variety of domestic duties: lighting incense, washing and garlanding the numerous idols with chains of jasmine and fuscia. Fewer than a dozen were much older women. Brownie and I withdrew to a place over on the side. Some three meters away from the temple's enclosures there were hefty columns running lengthwise on both concourses. That freed up nearly a ten-meter width for the performances. A series of marble thrones ran the perimeter of the outer walls indicating the possibility for some kind of holy visit from the Hindu Troika. This rash of quasi religiosity put me on edge for the up and coming festivities. Many of the women were chanting versions of a rag (pronounced: rahg) from the Vedic writings or, more poignantly, from the Mahabharata itself but I wasn't certain of either. In the meantime, VG tore off in search of something important.

"Wait 'til you see this."

In the meantime, Brownie and I watched all the preparations going on and tried our best to stay out of the way as the elderly women came by with their turikas (a hand broom formed by bundling together the shaven stems of coconut fronds after all the green leaves were stripped off) to sweep the residual accumulations of detritus off the floors.

When VG came back, he was shouldering a pink conch shell the size of a basketball. It must have been one monster of a mollusk in its day. He explained it was a musical instrument called a Shanka, which could call into the Akash to inspire the various deities to send out messages to the Great One upstairs. He tried to impart the description of its practice and purpose with some sort of Christian spin, which fell short I felt. He claimed the conch was what the angels used for trumpets through which they sounded the words of truth in the Bible. Pointing out the many statues and paintings of Krishna, Shiva and Vishnu he unfolded many more similarities between the big two religious schools of thought as he guided us from chamber to chamber on a mini tour.

When you visit a temple, it isn't like going to church. Each shrine is dedicated to a specific god or deity for its main centerpiece or target of devotion, but there will always be representations of many of the other fabled heroes from the plentiful Hindu pantheon. They are all like one big happy crew. Their statues populate the broad recesses of every Hindu temple like wandering gangs lusting after drugs. If you go into one, which honors Ganesha, the elephant deity, for instance, you will also see portrayals of Shiva, Vishnu and Brahma as well as the consorts, or wives, of these deities, namely Parvathi, Lakshmi, and Sarasvati, respectively. Incarnations of the deities are also present, including Rama or Krishna as well as some of their companions, Lakshmana or Hanumanta, the monkey deity. There are so many gods and goddesses in the Asian pantheon of religious figures. Come to think of it, churches are pretty much the same way with all the Mother Marys, Madonnas and historical Saints living in the recessed nichos and cellas along the walls.

The Moon Women

The factor, which was a little disturbing, concerns the manner in which the priests maintain a vicious strangle hold of ritualistic worship over the actual statues themselves. So much wasted attention goes into the devotion and supplication at the feet of these idols, which can be made of dressed stone or some sort of plated metal and in some rare cases even gold. Numerous floral garlands wreathe round their necks and everywhere clouds of incense belch out aromatic smoke. The idols are even clothed with expensive silks sometimes. Quite often, they receive full meals as well. And after the thalis have been presented to the deity, the priests all gather around and eat the food themselves. You don't have to be a Daniel to know it is the priests who are benefitting the most. Everybody knows that and accepts the secret as it is - vicarious mumbo jumbo.

Subsequently, Shri Vingtesh Ganapati Maharaj was also one of the renowned Swamis of the temple. As he showed us the notable features, nooks and crannies, which can be utilized for worship, all the women scurried out of the way bowing and folding their hands muttering something like Bhagwan Ji or Charana Bhagwan Maharaj. These expressions all demonstrated grandiose respect and honor for the man. At one point, VG singled-out a series of side chambers he disclosed were for personal worship. One had a minacious lintel over its dwarf-sized entryway. He lifted the door latch and hammed how it could be set in place from the other side preventing anyone else from entering. He emphasized the privacy feature with a little wink. It carried the name of the Patanjali Puja Chamber embossed in a brass plaque on the side of it.

The temple's chief axiom was there was no central place of worship and prayer. Everyone gathered in cliques and simply commenced whatever prayers, paeans, or pathos they chose to invoke. VG confided that shortly he was going to begin an extensive period of saying prayers and singing songs, or Bhajans, as he called them. That was the signal to invoke the entrance of Krishna into the main hall, to call Him forth with honor and devotional music. He suggested we sit quietly beside the congregation and simply observe. We didn't have to participate necessarily, but if we felt like entering the puja chamber, we could; we had his permission to do so. He also had warned us the chanting and the devotional music, particularly the harmonics of the conches, could invigorate inexperienced devotees in ways they might not have been able to imagine. Some of the ladies

500

twittered when he mentioned this; seemed they knew some English or else they really weren't virgin apprentices.

Right off, a few harmoniums broke out infrequently and sounded as if they were tuning up. Shortly thereafter vibrant melodeons began a sultry theme. And after some preparation the melodious vocals of the women initiated their accompaniment to the instrumentals. Brownie and I relaxed against the sidewall as Vingtesh assumed his place dead center in the pack. After a while, the tablas pitched in with their staccato nut-like rhythms. Then the whole ensemble moved into full blast pandemonium. A dozen or so women rang bells of graduated sizes. One by one, they started to shake them. They rang some only every so often; others rang the smaller ones in a brisk fashion continuously. One grandpa bell took on the look of a church bell, which hung suspended in its own cradle. By swinging it backwards and forwards, one priest let its resounding gong ring out through the temple.

With all of this magical bedlam going on all about us, Vingtesh put the conch to his lips and blew long and hard. The blast, which came out from that pink flared shell, was like something from the Beyond. I hadn't heard one since my experience in the Kali temple in the jungles of Malaysia. It was a tumultuous bugle call, which had a quelling timbre, which flattened my face as it shredded the surroundings everywhere. It would surge from a weaker note to the strong one. Bum baaaahhhh. Like that, over and over. Sometimes, VG would maintain the more forceful trumpeted single note for a long twenty or thirty-second ungodly blast. It was absolutely intoxicating.

I collared Brownie and tipped a nod toward the hidden puja antechamber. She shook her finger to say that would be disrespectful. I whispered over the hubbub about how VG had shared with us we could go in there to play if we so chose. After thinking it over for a moment, she decided to go for it. All the pet name cognomens she had collected for me geared up in her noggin and connected with the big gamble coming through her wheelhouse. Maybe at last she could get her wish to bite back and take a romp in the hay.

Gingerly, I separated the stubby doors laminated with the sordid hand wipings of devotees over the centuries. I didn't feel the need of coming away with an unintended souvenir. Wipings might not be spelled that way but that's what they were. That's what Indians

The Moon Women

did whenever they had something on their hands, which needed to be washed off. They would merely wipe the substance right on whichever surface was closest. They accepted it as a contribution to the organic history, which had evolved into a human fresco thereby affirming the prosperity of the owners. Painted there by the indigenous participants over the centuries, these markings of incense, cum-cum, flour, chalk, body oils, charcoal, snot, and, most horribly, even smeared feces had been added onto these plaster canvases to create a mural of human mediocrity unlike anything you have ever seen. No one ever washed these walls, only the marble flooring. Washing the eyelevel enclosures on the sacred sides of any shrine or religious structure in this land would be the most sacrilegious act anybody could do. It was a desecration of the worst ranking upon their cultured heritages. Such were the illogical harmonies found in India.

We crawled in and closed the doors. I latched it. The mounting crescendo of the musical madness outside had driven us into a state of the miraculous. Before I knew it, Brownie was kneading the handles of my love pack. Putting my hand at elbow level on her ribs, I worked my thumb underneath the hem of her bra, a skimpy meter of cloth, which Indian women wear to cover their breasts. As well, Brownie had the most beautiful iridescent sapphire sari, which looked like it might present a stumbling block to our little escapade. I initiated a perpetual slow kiss, which ended with her unbuttoning my pajama pants.

"Are we really going to do this?" I asked.

"If you have to ask, I guess the answer would be No." She dodged the uptick but still tugged at my drawstring.

"But your sari?" I interjected a strategic query, which required addressing.

"No big deal."

She got up in a stooped over manner because of the low hung planchement. After hiking her silks up to her waist, she reached up under and wriggled her underwear down her thighs. She placed the dainty lace underthings neatly into a petty minaudiere and let the sari fall back down.

"Now, no one is the wiser." She whispered.

I had unbuttoned my juba. My pajama pants had fallen as well. She bent down, yanked my boxers lower with one hand as she kneaded my engorged cock with her other. Gently I caressed the bounty of her lioness mane as she administered tender oral stimulation while humming to the Bhajans going wild in the smoke filled temple. That inspired me with a radical idea. But, would Brownie submit to such a hair-brained proposal?

"Brownie, have you ever had Tantric sex?" This would be the consummate place for it I imagined.

"Leave it you to introduce a splash of the absurd into what was supposed to be a nice time. What the hell is banter sex? Talk our way to a climax? I've had my fill of your crazy-ass philosophies for one day." She seemed a little put off but definitely not out of alignment to the deal.

"Well, think back to our yoga classes with VG and how he explained you could float on the vortexes of cerebral flux while having dynamite sex? Remember? It's called T for Tantric sex. Well, it's like that. You have sex as you contemplate those etheric whirlpools within yourself. It's like a big feedback loop. These quasi-physical pinwheels of color amplify the intercourse, which boosts your experience of the orgasm. You wanna try it?" I conjectured, why not, we're in a Tantric temple, fer chrissakes? Krishna is the deity of Love so let's go for it.

"I don't know. Pinwheels? The circus isn't 'til next week, Rahm. Can't we just have regular sex? Why does everything have to be a new frontier for you? I just wanna get a normal fuck, please." She was so cute trying to persuade me to have regular sex; that's too much.

"If you need to make water, now's the time to go do that. Okay?" I had a plan for the long run.

"Now you're getting clinical on me and stupid too. Make water? I don't have to pee, Rahm, if that's what you're referring to."

"Okay, let's sit up though. I'll show you what I mean." I shifted into the Boy Scout position and thrust my cock out so she could couple with it. She came over to me and hiked her sari up over her hips. My mouth dove in and my tongue went to work. I couldn't help it. She had the most delightfully scented oogonium; musky cantaloupe comes the closest. After my labors had primed her pump sufficiently, she descended into my lap and made that quick little in-suck of air as I slid inside her. As the Hindu bacchanal kept throbbing, the conch was piercing ethereal pinnacles of ecstasy. We

The Moon Women

undulated with the outer rhythms and the inner ones. Our coitus dance was on fire. Brownie was verbalizing greater and greater realms of pleasure. Then, I stopped abruptly. It wasn't part of my plan, but it was unavoidable.

"What's wrong? Come on. Let's go. I need you to go." She pleaded.

"Don't move!" I was dead set against it.

"What is it now? God, you are so exasperating! Why can't you just fuck me like a normal man?" She threw out this mandatum as she was grinding into me, or more importantly, getting me to grind into her.

"Brownie! Stop! This isn't miniature golf. You've got to be totally still, like motionless. Be a statue, okay?" I entreated her.

"You know, Rahm, I'm not a mental retard. You don't have to talk to me that way." She was repulsed. I got it.

The motive behind why I stopped was one I couldn't leak out right away. Some distance to her backsides, a King Cobra had infiltrated our chamber. It had reared its planate hood into an offensive pose. It was jealous. Luckily, I had the presence of mind not to do anything immediately. If we disconnected and got up to run, the King would have nailed the both of us in no time.

"Brownie, I need for you to trust me. Okay? Just listen carefully to what I say and do exactly what I tell you. Your life depends on it. Okay?" The tone of my words was letting her know something was not right in Denmark.

"What? You are the craziest fucking weirdo on the face of the earth. I swear."

"I'm going to kiss you, now. We are going to continue to join our love machines while I kiss you, okay?" As I began the experience, I was the mechanician of this exotic venture.

"Ahh, Rahm; that really isn't any different than what we have been doing all along. Why did you stop just to tell me that?" Her upper half was waning, but her lower half madly pursued the carnal rhythms.

"When we kiss, our mouths are going to be wide open. As I kiss you, I am going to exhale into your lungs. Do you follow me? As I exhale, you are going to inhale that air. You won't suffocate. Trust me. You won't die. You will simply be inhaling your next breath directly from my exhale. Okay? Let's give a shot." I imparted

504

the basics of the instructions. For the moment, the snake had suspended its targeting aim.

"But why? Can't we just make love?" She wasn't sure of what I was telling her to do.

"We are making love, Brownie. Only this lovemaking is far above anything you might have done earlier. Please believe me and help me to do this. Can you do that?" I cautioned her to follow my directions explicitly.

"Okay. You're nuts but I'll give it try. Just stay hard or I'm outa here."

The melanoid reptile fixed its gaze squarely upon us. As it watched our every move, I figured if we didn't move or flee, it would be content to observe and mark time with our dance much as a cobra would do if it was being mesmerized by those piping middlemen who perform on the streets. With some luck, it wouldn't unleash its morayed venom.

I sucked in a deep breath and kissed Brownie with all my love and all my life. We locked our faces in perigee and let the lunar tides carry us away. As I exhaled, she inhaled. Then we reversed the ventilations and like a bellows, we continued to replicate the exercise until we were both afraid of losing consciousness in this mediumistic coupling all the while pulsing with pleasure down below. Finally we had to unlock our mouths.

"Wow! That was awesome! I never knew I could feel like that. It was as if we had dissolved into one another. Where'd you learn how to do this?" She became wildly animated.

"I'm learning it now but it's way more than I had ever imagined. By the way, don't move your arms so much." I was merely cautioning her.

The snake hadn't moved, but badgering it any further wasn't in the cards.

"Why? What's going on? Is something wrong?" She was drifting.

"No, no. But you've got to conserve your energy more, Babe." She was nearing her full focus.

"Let's give it another shot. This time, let's hold it for as long as we can without winding up too dizzy. You know, as I exhale there remains to be quite a sufficient amount of oxygen viable within it.

The Moon Women

So, we can share it for a dozen or so go's." I instructed her to set sail once more into the airs of delight.

This time we both hyperventilated prior to diving back in for the endless plunge. As we docked our oral portals, the air vented out from my lungs into hers. You have to bear in mind we are well into the throes of gentle undulation in the southern quadrants to feed the sexual stimuli in our carnal centers. As we dissolved into each another, the boundaries of whose body belonged to whom began to melt away completely. After several moments of performing this praxis, it was as if we were drifting in the womb of an orgasmic sea, throbbing like one conjoined jellyfish. It was so warm and serene while being so incredibly climactic at the same time. At last, Brownie had to come out for air.

"Yeah, your bronchi are way smaller than mine. For you to endure this lengthy a time frame is pushing your limits. How are you feeling, Babe?"

Even though somewhat winded I knew it was way worth it.

I had become a vampire leeching the morphinic blood out of an angel of bliss.

"Oh, my God! That was the most incredible sensation I have ever had. It was like my whole being had blended into an ocean of pleasure and happiness. I love you so much, Rahm. Thank you so much for showing me this." She was dropping off a little into the sloppy zone on me. Her meltage factor was over the limit but containable.

"Okay, then. I love you too, Brownie. No, really. I love you quite a bit. This time, we are going to add one other move." I enunciated the successive steps of the metaleptic instructions.

"What is it now, Rahm? Can't we just enjoy this amazing pleasure?" She was on board but there were many more rungs on this ladder of love.

"Don't worry. It's going to be a lot more fun. Trust me. When I exhale into you, I am not only going to put my air into you, but also say something. I am going to say the letter Ah just like the vowel in the word Anon. I am going to exhale Ah into your being. Then, after you have received my expelled air infused with the Ah, you too, are going to return your exhale with the same Ah sound into me. We are going to go on exhaling that Ah and repeat it back and forth like an

506

echo for as much as we can. Let's see how it goes. Any questions?"
I had installed the third instruction step.

"You're a nut, you know it? Just a total nut. But I'm ready. I
got this far didn't I, so let's go for it." She parted her oral oceans while
continuing to pump into me down below.

The King Cobra had made a slight adjustment in its stance by
turning closer to the door. Was it fixing to get a wider vantage point?
Or preventing our exit? There was little chance of our leaving at this
late stage of the game. His move wouldn't be a hitch so far as I could
keep Brownie focused on me and prevent her from seeing anything
off her peripheral sightline. If she saw the snake, we'd both be dead.

- 5 -

Deep breaths and in we dove. The Ah was like a moaning. It
was as if we were under water and singing to each other beneath the
waves. After our airs blew in, out gushed the reserve, the remainder
of life. The Ah letter reverberated between my baritone male
frequency and her soprano female one. It reminded me of those
fabulous Tibetan horns in the Himalayas blowing the fog out of the
valley with their metalloid vibrations. After five cycles of trapped
respiration, we were beat and had to quit.

"That was really far out." She said gulping for air. "But I
loved it just like I love you and you're crazy-ass ways and upside-
down thinking. Where in the fuck did you learn all this shit? It isn't
like anything like I ever done in the past. It's opening me more to the
primal forces moving between us. We're like blending human
magnets." She was definitely getting into it.

"Correctomundo! It's those forces we are about to ride or
rather unharness. Once we do, we are going to fly on those currents
to attain the highest peaks of sublime bliss." I disseminated some
basic truths.

"Really? Oh my God! This is so fantastic! I guess we better
button our traps and get into it. Fuck me you animal!" At last,
Brownie was plugging into the Beyond.

"Let's go for it again, only this time we are going to add one
more step. Okay?." I continued.

"What is it? I've got to know." She was all ears.

The Moon Women

"This time when we are expelling the dead air as the sound-cell is humming, imagine a flower, a lotus, actually. You know what a lotus looks like, don't' you Brownie?"

"It's like a carnation isn't it? The one on the pond, I think."

"Exacty. With your mind's eye, pretend to see a beautiful lotus flower having four petals, two white ones on the top and bottom and two yellow ones on the sides. And as you go on observing this lotus forming in your within, concentrate on your rectum. Feel the place of your anus and imagine the lotus blooming there within you. See the white and yellow lotus blossoming in the middle of your asshole. Can you do that for me?" I was now giving her the fourth step of the formula for ecstasy.

"You want me to do what?" Brownie balked.

"Yeah, I know. That sounds really weird, so let me explain."

Would she be able to produce the leap to the next level, the full jump into the Beyond? That was the place where most have had some difficulty. The physical nuances were not the hard part; the hard part was performing the visualizations while combining them with the secret sound-cells, which I had taught myself back in my closet in Newton six years earlier (although at the time, it wasn't so readily apparent what they might be good for). Fortunately, the teacher had rectified that hiccup. It was the combination of these two, the aural, and the visual, which generated a psycho-cerebral vortex or portal into the Beyond. By cementing the rotational energies with the psycho-magnetic ones, the practitioner produces an internal threshold through which to secure travel into the Beyond. The main thing is that it requires this extra element of humanicity; all the while having your brains screwed out.

"See the white and yellow lotus. See it like a daisy or a zinnia, unfolding its petals and blooming on the inside of your sphincter, your rectum. That is the place for the first rung or chakra on this ladder of lovemaking. It's simple, really. You've already mastered the introductory steps so let's give it a go. I know you can do it, Brownie." I wanted her to be comfortable with it, even though it's a highly dangerous exercise if not done correctly.

"Well, all right. I haven't fallen off my horse yet. Right? So what you're saying is you want me to conjure up this flower as if it were unfolding inside my body right where my asshole is. Is that it?"

508

"Bullseye! That's it on the nose, Brownie. You're going to be a champ at this. Trust me. Now let's go for it, Girl."

As her hips picked up some steam, she commenced her hyperventilating breaths. We pumped in our four priming breaths and dove in. Our respirations yo-yoed to and fro like lunar swells on the beaches of ecstasy. The moaning hum came out of our within and its vibration carried on and on. As I visualized the lotus with its stem and then the four petals, two white and two yellow, it came and went at first. It was a little difficult to do initially, but then I got the hang of it and maintained the image as I focused it within my anus. After I stayed like that for some time, the intensity of the lotus colors gradually increased to a vibrant burning.

"Oh, I couldn't go on," she confessed as her rigidity moldered away.

"I know. This is the roughest part of it, Brownie," I confessed as I gulped fresh air.

"You've done this before?" She was surprised.

"Well, not literally." Confusing her wasn't my intention. "How did you do with your flower, the inner lotus?"

"Fine, I suppose. But if you've been carrying on like this with other women I'm going to be extremely upset with you. You hear me?" She had drawn the line inscribing the mean proportion of her love.

"Listen. This is really worth it. I've never done this with other women or anybody else for that matter. It's something a certain teacher has instructed me to attempt a while back. And I knew you would be a natural at it. There is no one other than you, Brownie. Really. That's the truth." I did my utmost to reassure her that our mediation was both singular and unique.

"Well, mine is not so bright, but I can see it." She had the makings of a genuine pro.

"Excellent! You're over the hump then, Girl. This is going to be big. Way big!" I was elated for her.

"How is your lotus?" She was eager to ask.

"Never thought you'd ask. It's Okay. Probably not as well defined as yours. Men have more trouble with this function than women." I admitted while hoping she wouldn't harp.

"You better not be . . . ." She caught herself. "Okay. What's next?"

The Moon Women

"The fourth step is putting the sound-cell into the central axis of the lotus and visualizing it receiving the sound. You have to sense the vibration going "Pow!" directly into the lotus, right into the center of the petals, its heart." I instructed her with the sixth stage.

"That's going to be a tall order, Buster. What's after that? I have to lick my toes while balancing upside down?" It could be she was surrendering to her outer limits.

"Nope. That's pretty much it. Only one part after that. And, no, I'm not telling you what it is until the time comes." I was firm on that score.

This was not simply some menu driven procedure. Since I had apprenticed with an unusual guide, this was the first time things hadn't run off the rails and wound up in a puddle of piss. Whereas this adventure was a means of dislodging a locked entrance into an upper realm, it should not be approached without the guidance of an expert. I was jumping ahead of being the teacher's pet but I figured I'd settle that on the other side. Little did I realize how poorly advised that attitude was.

"Okay. Let's go for it." She was on it like white on rice. Oops, wrong metaphor.

We drank in our deep swallows of fresh air and joined our oral portals together. As I coaxed our idling engines with more throttle to attain a good pumping action, I initiated the Ah sound-cell. I unfolded the four petals of the daisy, two white, and two yellow, right smack in my butt. Like a saw, like a cosmic sewing machine needle jabbing back and forth, I injected the sound-cell straight into the heart of the blossom. As I sowed the sound-cell right into the heart of the lotus, precisely into the exact middle of it, the flower blossomed outwards even further. By visualizing the sawing action this way and that, I chewed my way deeper and deeper into the juncture point of the four petals. As I did so, the lotus ripened its glow more and more intensely and began to spin. The more I did the sawing maneuver of the sound-cell hacking deeper and deeper into the heart of the lotus, the faster my flower's petals turned and the brighter it became. I kept performing this exercise until the whiteness and the yellowness of the spinning lotus merged into one intense color of burning light. Its radiance was on fire. It was burning like hot lava splashing and whirling wildly like a molten tourbillion whirling in my cranium. Then my limit was blown and I had to come out.

When I came out of that place I was in, Brownie was gone. Her body was there, but she was unconscious. My illustrious instructor had warned me sternly about this drawback, but I had never had it happen before, so I didn't know what to do. I handed her a couple lite pats on her cheek. Groggily she came round.

"Hey. Hangin' on good in there? You still with us?" I was so impressed with her tenacity.

"Oh, Rahm. That was the most spectacular thing, which I have ever experienced in my whole life. I have never seen anything like it before, not even on acid. What is this shit, which you are teaching me? I've got to keep repeating this forever and ever." She kept going on and on. Her tele-psychogogic megaflop rate had blown off the top of the chart.

"Okay. That's good. That's really good, but Babe, you've got to get a little more control under your belt. When you detect yourself slipping away like that, you have to break it off. There is only so much oxygen in the expended air. Okay?" I was pleasantly shocked. I'm really glad she came back, though. Otherwise, I'd probably be facing more prison time than what's already on the books, undoubtedly.

"Can we do it again? I'd really like to do it again." Even though she was panting breathlessly, she seemed terrifically invigorated. At the outset, it was a serious brain bender for her.

"Brownie, please listen to me carefully. We have to do this one-step at a time. This is a magnificent experience, which we are dealing with here. If we do not perform the steps in the correct order and allow them the proper span of time by allowing for a sufficient pause between each stage, we could get into a lot of trouble. Now, that wouldn't be good, would it?" I chided her slightly.

"Okay, Milord. Whatever you say, Rahm. You're the boss. You are the master." She folded her hands to me.

"Whoa, Babe! That's enough of that. I'm simply a schmuck. I'm only a person, one like you. I'm no better and I'm no master. That's something completely different. Got it?" I had to throw cold water on that right away. She shrugged her shoulders in apology.

"Whatever. I'm with you hundred percents though."

"Let me tell you what this part entails. Are you with me?"

The Moon Women

"Yup." Her smile was everything.

As the chanting was going bananas out there in the hall, VG's conch was knocking on the threshold to the rapture worlds. Temporarily, I got dragged away by a tongue of truth out of the blue. At the tail of that intermission, I received an update from the source.

"Ground control to Mr. Rahm. Come in, Rahm." She was scheming to penetrate the meta-logic singing in the cells of my being.

"Okay. Sorry. I'm back. I'm going to give you a break before I reveal the nutshell of this little meet-and-greet so you will know where we are going with all this. What you have witnessed was a chakra. It is a vortex of etheric energy. It is a whirlpool of your consciousness, a collection of your attention, which you have collected in a particular locus in your within. Human beings have seven of these chakras like a totem pole running the length of their spine. We are going to use five of them here during this exercise. The second chakra we are going to jump over for now, for reasons, which I will divulge later on. Besides the one in the rectum, which we have just experienced, there is a chakra at the navel, at the heart, at the throat and at the eyes. There is also a higher one, the seventh chakra, but I am withholding that one for now. This in an introductory course meant to expose you to some of the more basic levels of awareness.

"These five sound-cells were revealed to me in a visitation, which I had many years back in Newton. Most recently, my special mentor has taught me about the actual petals and shown me how to the complete these techniques. You will learn the identity of my source of inspiration and his whereabouts at the conclusion of this session. Okay? Don't answer that.

"Now, here is the next step. In your belly button, in the midsection of your abdomen, you are to visualize another four-petal lotus having two orange and two green petals. See the petals as the points on a compass, one on the top, one on the bottom, and one on either side. The two horizontal petals are green and the two vertical ones are orange. The sound-cell that must you will sing into this chakra is that of Oh as in the word Ohio. Perform the same process as we have already done and scissor your way into the lotus, into the precise heart of the lotus with your sound-cell. See this lotus blooming amidst your navel and then inject the sound-cell of Oh into its center. Are you with me? If you understand what I've just relayed, nod your head and well begin. Okay?" I fulfilled the instruction of sowing the seed into the mid-dorsal band of the next vortex.

"I only have one question."

"What's that?"

"What if we get some oxygen tanks? Then we could stay in there for an hour."

"Oh magod. Brownie, you're too much. Let's just try it the normal way this once. Then, later on, like maybe never, we can go hog wild with gas masks and everything. You're too much. You ready?"

"Yup. Let's go. Fuck me, Buddy."

We primed, swallowed, and dove into this foaming sea of Love. Our hips had been gently idling in suspension for a few moments but soon they had revved back up to full throttle. Our clam chops geared up and off we ventured into the next chakra. With all my airs dissipated, I came out with the start of a nice cherry glow going and found Brownie was no longer at home.

"Oh Babe! I'm so sorry. I'm pushing you a little too much with these exercises. I've got to come out a little sooner for you, so you don't keep slipping off the radar here." A couple more pats brought her to the front.

"Oh my God! My God, my god, my god! Rahm! Why do you keep bringing me back out? I want to stay in there forever! See. I told you. We need tanks. This is like scuba diving for sex. I love it!" She was hooked. Oh, good, another lifelong tantric sex partner. Never mind.

"The next chakra is in the heart zone. There you will see a six-petal lotus having three red petals and three blue ones. These colors are shifting, they alternate. Starting with a red one at the north, then blue, then red and so on like clockwise, if you know what I mean. The sound-cell that we are going to use on this chakra is the sound-cell of Uu as in You. All set?" I executed the extension of the new rung on the ladder of the multiphasic directions.

Off we shot across the inner waters. Our lungs sucked in our mutual winds of life. We sawed the sound-cell of Uu into the vortex in our heart chakra until it glowed more and more until it was on fire, flashing like a strobe pulsating reds and blues. Plus, the petals were rotating like the propellers on a Spitfire-Contra bracing for takeoff. As the spinning of this multi-lobed vortex rotated faster and faster,

The Moon Women

their combined colors shifted to an electric violet. Out of that burning purple fire issued the second stage of divine bliss. Out of my heart came the most intense feeling of intoxicated love anyone could possibly imagine. Then our breaths broke.

Oh, God, I thought, "I've lost Brownie again. I stayed in there too far."

This time, I had to work on her for a much longer time to get her back. I resorted to giving her a little mouth-to-mouth resuscitation, although it wasn't to harbor the lagoon of life but to release her from the blissful deserts of death. With a groggy burp, she came back more or less. I waited for a moment for her to say something. But, the look of her facial contortions said it all.

"Brownie, would you like to continue?" I had to seal the deal fast.

She nodded her acceptance and whimpered something all misty eyed. And the cobra continued to hover in errorless stability.

"This next chakra is at the throat center. Here you will see an eight-petal lotus. It has four petals of purple and four of cream. There are four petals above the horizon and the four below. The colors transpose naturally enough. The sound-cell at this chakra is that of Ee as in the word, Key. Good luck, Brownie. We have come a significant ways and have nearly attained our goal." The teacher's eighth instruction was received and applied.

Again, we took our breaths as our lips joined and our hips gyrated. The Ee sound-cell was sawing into the petals, which began to glow and spin. The feeling of ecstasy from this chakra was like an unbounded divinity. And it was not simply a feeling but an elevation of consciousness. I could sense an unfathomability, which one could only attain via regular and intense practice of these mystifying exercises. These phenomenal impulses surpassed all comprehension. Wow! Got to pull out quicker. No! Not that. My lungs, dummy. There. Okay. She's back.

"Listen. I'm not going to play too much catch up here so that I don't lose you to exhaustion. Let's just get into it and go for it. This is the concluding chapter and the last chakra we will cross. It is located at the eye center, which is a vortex situated directly behind your two eyes. Like the first two flowers, it is a four-petal lotus having two turquoise petals and two pink petals in alternating fashion and like the initial two chakras the petals sit at the four points of the compass with north being on top. The only thing different concerning this chakra is a circular band of vivid blue, which extends around the points of the petals. It is a band, which will burn with a blue fire. Moreover, these petals will not spin but will remain stationary. Here the one caveat is this. No matter how much light you witness coming out from the chakra, and it may become immense at times, do not venture higher into the upper realms. Don't follow the calls coming down which will attempt to allure you further up as this will prove to be larruping dangerous and can even cause death to occur, should the silver chord be accidentally snapped. This is extremely rare however. It's in keeping with proper protocols to provide an appropriate disclaimer at this phase of the journey. Got it? Oh, and the sound to be sung here on this chakra is the sound-cell of Ii as in the word I, as in I am." I dished out the ninth instruction as received from my mentor.

"La what? Who do you think you're talking to? Sometimes I wonder where you learned English, Rahm. Sometimes I think someone larruped your brain in a barn over in Barnstable, you baboon. And administering protocols smells to me like I'm not your first roll in the hay with this shit!"

"Don't' worry about it. Can we start now, Dear. This is going to be huge. Can you follow that lingo and my lead?"

"I guess so. Just fuck me, asshole!"

When this lotus initiated its glow within me, all sorts of fireworks erupted in all directions. It was like a whirling magneto spinning sparks. Off on the perimeter of the twilight recesses in my brain, I could see huge fireworks going off. As this light show drew in closer, not only did I experience the explosive heights of orgasmic bliss, but I had the feeling I was in the direct presence of God. As the infinite light doubled and tripled its explosions of bliss inside me, I was overwhelmed with a primal God concept, one which had once been hinted at but was now fully manifesting from out of this boundless divinity. Then I was given a message.

THE PATH BEYOND DEATH IS LOVE!

Even though this all happened within the few moments that we could sustain our breaths as they moved in and out like a bellows, the experience of it seemed timeless. It was like something I'd sensed on a beach once previously as a youngster. After bathing in that bliss, I had to come out. I didn't know if I had broken off the coupling fast enough because after I came back out, Brownie was falling off a little at the edges.

"How are you doin', Girl? Need anything?" I asked with a whisper because I didn't want to cause her any unneeded misease.

She didn't acknowledge me at first. Her skin was like mayonnaise. Her lips were like the rind of a cantaloupe, a sickly tinge of lime green. But, I kissed them anyway. She came back to me a little bit. Unfortunately, from swooning so much, her lean had shifted farther outward.

When she came to, off to her side, she caught the flared hood of the cobra. She began to shriek but her lungs had collapsed from loving me so much. Her limbs lifted up in a flailing frenzy like a rag doll on steroids. The snake tuned its radar and homed in on her. I muscled Brownie with all my might so that she would not struggle. I had to do something to prevent the snake from striking. I extended my hand toward it and commanded in a blunt, but calm voice, one Hindi word.

"Bus!" [Enough!]

The snake withdrew its flared fangs and hissed to signal its obedience. It turned down its sooth radar and hovered blankly. I looked Brownie directly in the eyes to confirm I had all her attention.

"Brownie! Brownie, you must pay attention to what I am telling you right now. Okay? This is not what you think it is. It looks like a snake, but it isn't. Not really. It has the body of a snake, a cobra, but in actuality, this snake is my teacher." I explained the finer meanings of the illusion.

"What? How is that again?"

"About a month back when I was honoring Shiva and performing the worship of the Lingham Stone in my puja chamber over in the K-room, this serpent entity showed up for a visit. I was shocked out of my skull until I recalled the experience I had once on a lonely road in Sikkim. Thinking I was seeing a snake and seeing one in reality is two different aspects of the same truth. Because of that lonely night in Sikkim, I was able to wait and reduce my fears. That enabled the cobra to communicate with me via a rarified and heightened encryption. We became partners. He has been visiting me ever since. All this system of Yoga, which I have shown you was taught to me by this cobra. His name is Shri Nag Dev Maharaj. He is an astral entity who has incarnated into the body of this snake for whatever purpose I haven't figured out yet. Play ball and I'll prove it to you." I had unburdened my heart of the mythicizing with the phallic reptile.

Brownie and I uncoupled. She dropped the beautiful messaline sari to cover herself modestly. As she tidied herself up furtively, she refused to disconnect her eyesight from the hovering serpent even for a second. With our backs against the sacred stones, we anticipated the final lesson.

"This is the conclusion of our experience here at the home of Shri Krishna. What you are going to find out, you must tell to no one. Okay?" I had to compel her to swear an oath.

She nodded squeamishly.

"Are you with me?"

Again, she nodded mechanically not willing to overcommit.

I lifted my outstretched hand to the scaled creature. Since it was over three meters in length, its hood hovered above us as we sat fixed in our posture. As I pointed my palm at the Nagraj, I swiveled it downwards and made a flapping motion, which in India, is the hand sign for come here, while simultaneously I spat out a single word in Hindi.

"Ow." [Come.]

In response, the Nagraj elevated its minatorial hood a dozen centimeters and then shrank back down onto ground level. As it did so, its hood dissolved back into the serpentine tube of its head. With a delicate curling motion, the majestic animal came over to us. Brownie tensed up. I squeezed her and shushed her to settle down.

"Remember, it's not what you think. Just remain completely quiet. It won't hurt you." I did my damnedest to pacify her.

The green slime mog came up my leg and wreathed my neck with its trunk to encircle me with a gagging constriction. It remained there curled and poised in the air, while aiming the inky black needle of its sleuth radar darting in and out straight at us as its microcode interrogated our energies. It stayed that way for roughly thirty seconds, flicking and tasting our thoughts. Eventually, the snake's proximity drained Brownie of all her fears, which leaked out of her like water from a leaky bucket.

The Moon Women

As the moment of liberation had finally arrived for the Nagraj, it prepared to unload its storage banks of a new knowing. Unwinding itself slowly, it slithered back down onto the cold stone. Then, it did the most outlandish thing. It extended itself up and up into the puja chamber. It did so until it was practically a vertical rod balancing on its tail as if a gyroscopic nail. And then with its nose aimed directly at us, the lower part of its body began to spin. In no time at all, it was spinning turbulently. Supporting itself on a single footprint pivoting upon the worn stones, it projected tremendous strength. As we watched the cobra perform this feat, the spinning increased until its skin peeled off like some kind of sheathing unpeeling from its body leaving its flesh completely exposed. Right after it accomplished that feat, the tissue underneath appeared to ignite. As its scales shed off in toto, the remaining shaft of the snake started to glow like an illuminated pole. And as this burning pole intensified, it grew into a skinny waterfall of molten lava, which changed from a yellow glow into a white hot incandescence. Finally, it burst into flames.

Standing erect in front of us was a vertical snake of living fire. It hummed with a low pitched vibration. Even though it looked quite hot, there was no heat coming from it that I could detect. The firebrand remained that way for several moments as I tried to collect my senses. I couldn't detect any visible means for the fire to maintain itself.

Suddenly, there was a tremendous crack, like the snap of a bullwhip. With that awakening, the fire serpent enlarged the rod of its fire body outwards laterally into a sheet of flame a full meter wide. We were now staring directly into a wall of flames hovering straight up and down: a waterfall of pulsating fire stretched from the floor to the ceiling of the puja room. As these roaring flames blazed away frighteningly, there was a shift and as it momentarily stilled, it parted. Out of this widening crack in the panel of igneous fire stepped a very small man. It someone I knew. It was Shiva!

He had a translucent bluish complexion tinged with a touch of citron, thick inky curls combed back over his head, and a shining crescent of the baby Moon perched amongst those waves of obsidian wealth. Ash covered his entire body perhaps from his flaming entrance. As he stepped forward, I could see he was nearly naked as his only clothing was a mere loincloth hanging down from his waist. He compressed his palms in prayer most graciously.

"Namaste Ji. Namaste Mem Sahib. I have come to tell you both something of that which you have only now experienced for yourself," he said, as he artfully settled into a pose, collapsing himself into a full lotus.

His smile appealed to us like someone who was our long lost uncle. By this point, Brownie's mental gears were badly blown. She did not know which end was up. Nor did I for that matter. Shiva began his testimony.

"Rahm Ji, Mem Sahib. What I have to say concerns you, Rahm, as you are one of the chosen. You have come through an extensive gauntlet of inner burning. The patterns of this psychogenic combustion have shown themselves to you already as the lights of the Moon and will later be seen as the lights of Mars as well. There have been before you five women of the Moon as will come the five women of Mars. These women have been and will be as the rungs of a ladder. But, they are also as the strands of the gold and silver chords, which wind themselves inside you as a conical psychic lizard to create the keys of life, both the inner and the outer ones.

"Each brings you five principles. These are like the pieces to a puzzle. Once these pieces are competently untangled, the big picture will appear clear to you. You will then understand what your fate in life is and what you must do now. As you proceed, you must struggle with the maintenance of this continual enigma. You may not have all of the angles yet, but you will see it all presently. But know this, Mem Sahib here was the magic carpet upon which you rode to arrive at a certain period or gate in your journey. You must always honor her and never defeat her. Her life and those of the other women have been crossed with yours in order for you to ascend and realize a unique purpose. What this task is and how you must solve it lies within the magic of the conundrum and within the manner of its formation.

"Your days in India are numbered, but within that number lies your purpose and the rare opportunity of a billion lives. Eventually you will know why the women came to you in the first place. And why five will perish and five will survive. When you will see it, you will know it. And when you will know it, you will seize the chance to become it." Shiva skimmed the limits.

The Moon Women

With that, he clasped his hands in a regal Namaste, stood up, and was flushed back in through the gate of unheated fire. The flames rolled themselves back into a glowing rod, which, in turn, reduced its glow back into the olive coils of the King Cobra. The rod reverted to its state as the melanistic reptile, which curled back down onto the floor.

As the tubular beast once more reared in front of us, Brownie drew back until I stabilized her. The sleek serpentine Mephistopheles made a double bobble, which was his signal that he had a communique to impart. Internally, I repeated an esoteric mantra I had received from the regal reptilian beforehand. It unlocked my Nabhi chakra through which the Nag Raj transmitted his meromorphic messages.

"The concluding phase of the lesson will become clear soon after this harvest of the fifth Moon. In the same way I shadowed the great Lord of Naam, Nanak, so too, have I cast my ways of the timeless songs over your progress. Know that the puzzle of the women will complete itself within the fortnight, as all the keys have already been set." With that, the mazard head of the snake slithered off to find the angle in the corner where the large drain was located. The serpent muzzled his getaway out through that same pipe which allows for the escape of seasonal floodwaters. The Nagraj was no longer a challis nor a challenge.

Brownie and I couldn't hear the chorus line anymore. The Krishna celebration had since finished. I released the latch to the puja chamber and we came out. To our astonishment, all the contestants had hit the road. The place was eerily deserted. We traced our way through the vacant hall and out onto the curbside. As we witnessed the cloak of dusk slip into Cooketown, we were exhausted and transfixed at the same time. A clean slice of Moon balanced itself between the two sides of the Time/Space dichotomy while one pink star chased after it. I pointed to the star and to the Moon.

"These are the miracles from the Moon and from Mars."

I felt faintly magical. Brownie held my hand. We walked toward sunset.

"Rahm, there is no one like you. You are my proof of miracles. You are my miracle man. You are the spark of God." She eulogized my greatness under the pink glow.

"No. I'm just hunting for tuna fish."

"What?"

I waved for a taxi. In the latter times of darkness, an odd figure emerged from the temple's side. Having secured its prize it departed. Although the Khrng are the caretakers of modern man, their methods oftentimes seem unexplainable.

Note from the author: The second chakra was deliberately omitted to short circuit the full awakening of the Serpent Power, the Kundalini. What was demonstrated in this chapter seems impressive; regardless, it is kindergarten when compared with a competent release of one's Kundalini powers unbounded.

Do not attempt to perform this by yourself.

- 6 -

A week after our experience in the Krishna temple, Brownie and I traveled to a magnificent park by the name of Lal Bahg to see the circus. Throughout the terraced acres, clusters of rose mallow bordered the pathways while clumps of red geraniums hedged the benches located intermittently throughout the lanes. The elephants trumpeted, the lions roared, and indeed the performers did toss their batons with abandon. Since it was Sunday, the crowds congregated freely. Mariachi bands roamed the boulevards serenading the throngs of visitors.

Brownie and I joined the carnival cheer but as we mingled in the hustle and bustle of the masses, I realized I had forgotten my camera. When I discovered that slip-up, Brownie volunteered to go back and retrieve it. Since I was a man of lost vision who was holding the limp cane of ignorance, she felt the need to expedite a rapid return with cane in hand. We agreed I would wait patiently on a vacant bench listening to the crush of the crowds until she succeeded in her mission. I suspected somehow she needed to be free of me and had my doubts if she would ever come back, with or without my Nikormat. As I tapped my cane on the pavement to the tune of the strumming banjos, I sat back to wait for Brownie and daydreamed of what the whales might be doing.

The Moon Women

Suddenly, from out of this human tumult, an enormous palomino breached the multitudes, rode up, and halted a few meters away. As the rider dismounted with a jump, I was astonished to find it was none other than Shri Krishna, avatar from the Dwarpar Yuga. He looked glorious and fit as a fiddle for being some two hundred thousand years old.

He bore a golden crown ornamented with enormous diamonds, rubies, sapphires, and topaz jewels. Strings of mabe pearls interwoven into his jet-black braids sparkled in the sunlight. Flying like a banner of kingship, his crown also carried a prismatic peacock feather heralding his prominence amongst humankind. His lips were like the petals of a lotus. His facial tone was a luminescent cerulean, bordering on translucent. Round his neck, manifold garlands made from jasmine, fuchsia, and glistening pearly carnations wreathed his shining face. In his right hand, he carried a flute and in his left, he supported the baton of life, which looked like a giant gavel capped with lotuses on either heel. The handle of this wand, sheathed with twin snakes of gold, was magnificent. Adorned with silver chains and studded with beryl and aquamarine gemstones, thick folded banana leaves protected the soles of his feet. Poking out of the open ends of those viridian thongs were his toes the nails of which gleamed like stars in the night sky. He had the glowing globe of the Chaitanya, the color of the sun, as a halo encircling his turbaned crown. As his horse presented a barrier separating the two of us from the rest of the less savvy kingdom, Lord Krishna bridled the martingale to his mickle stallion and commanded his mount to stay put.

"Vah!" [Whoa!]

Such was his supreme eminence. He took a place standing in front of me and folded his hands with his gracious welcome.

"Namaste, Ramappa. May I address you as such? I, too, am of the red clay of Karnataka as well as the blue blood of the Dravidian lineage which, unbeknownst to history, trails into the distant lines of a hundred, hundred centuries." Shri Krishna squatted into the Ayurvedic stance of nobility and using a neem stick, he started to carve clumsy effigies in the dirt.

"Yeah sure. Namaste Ji back at cha. Don't suppose this is gonna be another one of those orations about bar bells down in the weight room is it?"

"In that case, perchance I should take a more reticent tone with you, Shri Ramappa."

He again stood straight as an arrow and placed his hand on my shoulder.

"I am requesting you to approach me now and receive the message of the five walls of God. Please remove your shoes for you are entering upon hallowed ground. You must pass through these five walls before you achieve the homeland. All of your search has not yet been successful; furthermore, your goal doesn't necessarily depend upon the fruits of your search. These have all been as passing stages through which you had to traverse in order for you to have fulfilled your destiny, but from which you will never have to return. Do you understand?"

"Okay, but I'm wearing sandals, Dude." I complied sheepishly and kicked off my Birkenstocks.

He nodded with a smile and took a seat next to me on the bench and then raised his Indian flute, called a Bansuri, as if he was going to serenade me with his chorus line.

"Please listen."

Since He was talking way over my head, it didn't help my understanding of the weird stick figures being traced out before me. I hoped his sermon would calm down so I could collect his extruded concepts. But he amped it even higher instead. He hunched his shoulders to put his Bansuri to his nearly transparent lips and gently played the most beautiful tones to entertain me as well as a cote of doves, which had landed in the tree next to us. A red ruby marked each of the flute's six key holes. He slowly played five simple notes, which went up the scale. When he had concluded his concertino, he looked up.

"Ramappa Ji, this is a history as well as a prediction. These are the five notes of the Moon women. From them, five of your inner shells have been discarded.

"The first Moon woman, the one having the Ah name, pealed open the petal of Meekness by showing you the burning of Love.

"The second Moon woman, the one having the Oh name, pealed open the petal of True Living by showing you the burning of Mercy.

"The third Moon woman, having the Uh name, pealed open the petal of Humanity by showing you the burning of Compassion.

The Moon Women

"The fourth Moon woman, the one having the Eh name, pealed open the petal of Purification by showing you the burning of Forgiveness.

"And the fifth Moon woman, the one having the Ih name, pealed open the petal of the One True Path by showing you the burning of Devotion."

After he enunciated these five points on his pentagram with extreme precision, he pointed to the sticklike pictograms he had drawn in the sand. And there it was, a pentagram. And sitting adjacent to each one of its five angled corners was an artfully traced representation of each one of the women I had known, including Brownie. As I was analyzing his sand art, he withdrew his aura all the while holding his flute erect like a soldier performing a rifle drill at rest. The stick drawings on the ground became clearer now. There was a second pentagram to the right of the first one but that one was smaller and no faces arranged on its perimeter, only symbols written in what looked like might be Sanskrit, which I guessed might be letters. The air grew light as the magnetism of his celestial thoughts pervaded the surrounding area. Gingerly he placed his Bansuri back upon his cherry blue lips and again played five more separate notes going down the tonic scale. His divine being infused a celestial Midas touch to the golden sounds.

"These are be the five notes of the Mars women. They will be awarded to you to unwrap five more petals of living within the shells of your life.

"The first Mars woman, the one having the Ih name, will offer the petal of the Vacuum by showing you the fire of Religion.

"The second Mars woman, the one having the Eh name, will offer the petal of Sexuality by showing you the fire of Passion.

"The third Mars woman, the one having the Uh name, will offer the petal of Transient Health by showing you the fire of Magic.

"The fourth Mars woman, the one having the Oh name, will offer the petal of False Rituals by showing you the fire of Death.

"And the fifth Mars woman, the one having the Ah name, will offer the petal of the Impurities by showing you the fire of Life."

"This completes the standard of the double helix of mortality and eternal commitment."

As His melliferous notes echoed out across the park, the scratch marks in the dirt had become kaleidoscopic. I now knew the

524

letters decorating the sides of the first pentagram were the primal sounds moving upwards, while its inverse was the same letters but only moving downwards. If you know anything about the Sanskrit family of languages, you will understand what I am telling you. The shifting patterns arranged themselves into carnal states, which became quite painful and I could no longer view them without feeling remorse.

Hearing those vibrations triggered something in each one of my chakras, the culmination of which infused me with scintillating castles of color, which floated down around both our forms. He held out his left hand, in which he gripped the burnished baton of Mars and in his right was the shining crescent of the Moon and stood up as though he were about to proclaim to the universe his everlasting power and presence.

"These two intertwining axioms are building the master plan for deities who will walk this planet some thousands of years from now. There are no races, which can succeed this or which can intercede in this. This work will be the Nubing Dorg or the knob of God. Since the "Dorje" is a sanctified object, which represents the dual nature of our world. Like the twin serpents of DNA, it signifies the code of life. It is usually opposed by a lightning bolt, which represents the flash of divine consciousness. By turning the knob of duality in this world and transitioning through the door to the transient plain of the Beyond, you can evoke the truth and the bliss of liberation. Now walk with me in White while we talk."

He escorted me through the crowds like Moses parting the oceans. He bit down on a May apple, which he had picked from a low hanging branch.

"This fruit is likened to that of the Bakula tree underwhich I entertained the milkmaids of Vrindavan to serenade their lovelights in order to reform their karmas. Today, I hold in my hand the fruit of the cosmos, the Baton of Life. It has a twofold purpose. On the one hand it represents the subtle form of the divine principle, which is unending, and on the other, it represents the purity of the building blocks of life, what your wise men call the DNA principle. But this principle is only a recapitulation of the same divine principle pushing itself down from the supreme regions above. All things in Pinda, this lower world of the palpable universe, are mirrored images coming from the subtler realities, which exist in the upper realms, a sort of

The Moon Women

transcendent ultra-space. First and foremost, the human is the most supreme in all of creation. But human occupies a role, which is not only pivotal in the entire structure but human is also a container for the universe, that which holds it together. Human is what activates the existence of Space and Time.

"At the cusp of each of the four phases, or Yugas, we run into something sublime, an occurrence which is uncommonly rare. A fresh cycle is set in motion with a modified and radically unique in-house architecture. The central precept of DNA is conserved, for there must be a key to life, an elevated code. However, precisely how that code is to be set up, the patterning and the formulations, which stand behind that code can and will change. The what-is-what of each cycle is preset antecedently for the successful emergence of the forthcoming Yuga, whichever particular cycle of the four Yugas is due to arrive.

"In other words, each set of these four Yugas is a unique unit, which is ruled and regulated by revised dictates that determine how the DNA model is to be rendered. This is not a mix and match enterprise, Rahm Ji. It is regulation and more so, it is regulation via reduction. As the human gets more diffuse, so does he acquire power. Do you follow me, Brother?" Shri Krishna was moving his cerulean hands like feathers in the air.

"The manner in which this architecture is computed is most mercurial. It is determined by one specific coalition of extraordinary candidates, which comes forth at the end of each particular division or Yuga. The Yuga, which precedes the Sat Yuga, is the Kali Yuga. Towards its closing, the Nirunjan brings forth forty-four individuals who are culled from the base herds to influence the random blue prints set down as the framework for how the DNA of the future period of Yugas is to function. These individuals are teased out of the common population by specific criteria based on the pattern of the events in their life history. In this transition, which will come upon us shortly, the deciding fundamental premise for the selection of these candidates has to do with their love interests. These guiding precepts have to do with the energies of the Moon and of Mars. Those are the two divisions of duality, which shall weed out the prime members who, in turn, will set in station the inception of this anticipated Sat Yuga. You are one candidate who has fulfilled these precedents that we know of. We have chosen you as one of the forty-four. This was all decided in the light capital of Abaddon."

Krishna rested his baton in his palm and smiled radiantly. As he did so, more and more of the park goers realized that quite possibly the person with whom I was hanging out was not simply another circus performer. They imagined that he might be the legendary Avatar from the past ages. But then, after the Lord of Vrindavan waved his baton at them that idea was too much for them to handle. They sauntered off shaking their heads at the mobish charade.

As I chewed on the bones of his eccentric manifesto, his batty trajectories were irking me to the nth degree. How was this all going to work? Criteria from these forty-four suckers would impact the future? Or was it that this proposed criteria against which they had to measure themselves would become as a prison sentence? A sentence, which would lead the poor buggers to some endless incarceration in a horrifying dungeon, the reason for which they had not one iota of guilt creating. It seemed the primary stipulation was that they had to fall under a design of some sort. They were going to be evaluated by the mask of a chronological algorithm, a formula that prescribed they must experience love relationships with both Moon women and also with Mars women in a specific order, one that followed the tonal vibrations or notes, which Krishna had played on his flute. It seemed totally preposterous to me at the time.

It could be those vibrations were also the frequencies of the primary chakras. I don't know. The glorified majestic had claimed their emergence into the life of the so-called candidate had to occur in a most exact and precise order. Then the mechanics of it all crystalized within me and unlocked something buried deep within the knowledge menus of the Khrng, which had been dormant all these years. Lord knows I'm no savior. Nor am I anything more than a moron who has lost his children to the futures shuffled together by ignorance. But dodging this mirage of circumstance might prove unavoidable. Krishna unfurled his believer bat and whooped it up some more.

"Bear in mind, Brother Ramappa Ji, one's name is supremely significant. It is presumed one's name carries the cardinal vibration of one's being. Therefore, the names of the love interests of the potential candidate must follow the etheric vibrational tones, which

The Moon Women

exist within the ascending column of the spinal wheels, the chakras. This is for the Moon women. For the Mars women, it will be in the reverse order and it will be their surnames and in descending order. This parallax mirrors the relationship intrinsic to the DNA helical multiplex, for in truth, all things are worthy of that nostrum. If the Moon women partners all successfully satisfied the ascending pattern of chakra tones with their first name, then the Mars women must also satisfy the descending pattern of chakra tones with their surnames. Do you follow what I'm saying to you here, Shri Ram Ji?"

Lord Krishna's stallion up and took a dump in the road. Within seconds, bands of untouchables scurried over and scooped it all into baskets, termed by the Canarese residents as bandlees. Topped up with the steaming dung, the street workers lifted the bandlees and placed them high on their heads as they nonchalantly balanced them while walking away. The smutch was whisked far afield as fruit of the divine loom.

"Pay attention and do not become alarmed by these visionless residents. You, my dear fellow, are the first candidate to satisfy all of our strict criteria. You are the first of the forty-four and as such, you occupy a commanding rank over the others who will come later. I have full confidence you are prepared to accept this heavy responsibility and sacrifice yourself for the coining of the DNA procedures. At this juncture, we must set something right and confess our premature insertion of some prerequisites for your candidacy. For the proper preparation of this program, you had been previously enticed to venture into the high mountains of the Himalayas where some of our associates presented you with a sympathetic compliment in anticipation for this work. That mantra you have been repeating for the prior months has been producing a fertilizer in your mind, a catalyst for jumpstarting the job. It has been grooming the soil of your thoughts, so to speak, for the crucial exercises to come.

"Should you accept this job which should be upon you in no time, you will be escorted to a place in which you will be permitted to perform some intense meditation. Your energies will be utilized to generate the blue prints for a future species of human and the patterns of a renovated architecture, one in which the intrinsic composition of the DNA molecule will be affected by some suitably styled functions. It is not so much, whether or not the DNA model will be used. It will be. There is no uncertainty with regard to that factor for the double helix of DNA embodies the intrinsic design of the entire universe itself (See the Annex). Some misled astronomers have envisioned the shape of the Time/Space shield (the physical plane) to be likened to a revolving cylinder or quite conceivably a curved rhombus, whereas the truth of it is simply that it parallels the configuration of the DNA coil verbatim. It is a double helix spiral revolving within itself until its end.

"Let me stress, Shri Ramanuja Ji, that DNA is the blueprint for the engine of life as well as all existence: how big the engine will be; how many cylinders it will have; how much horsepower it can generate; what sorts of transmissions are likely; all of this and more. You will have input into all of these issues. You will, in a sense, become a telepathic modem sending us what information we need when we need it. Do you get what I'm laboring so hard to explain to you, Shri Rahm?"

As His minty after breath crossed my path, even though I could sense Shri Krishna Ji trying his damnedest to persuade me of this ragtag mayhem, I was having my druthers about it all.

"So, you're telling me that simply from my brainwaves I'm going to be producing psychic pasta for your future cousins in crime? That's loopy, Dude."

"Your thoughts and your words and your dreams as well as what you do from day to day will all be considered for the building of an ingredients list, which will serve as the input for determining the specifications indispensable for providing a matrix which will one day spill out into the newly registered DNA strands. This list is to be the source, the predictor for new life. We know it as psychic DNA. The patterns that unfold from your work with certain astral beings from out of the Beyond and also with certain ultra-chronological entities, not commonly seen in these localities, will also be involved in registering these blue prints of this future race. These energies will act like seeds in the cultivation of the psychic DNA. Many tens of thousands of years from now after the asteroid has taken its toll, these stored psycho-magnetic nodules will sprout at the appropriate time and allow for the manufacture of the actual physical DNA to come from within the primordial cocoons of Time. This eventuality has been put into motion now at this very juncture itself. Even though it may seem premature, the process is genuine. Because of the immediate time shifts and many other out of phase

The Moon Women

disturbances, which we anticipate to arise posthaste, we are proceeding with your indoctrination quicker than the usual intake. You see, Ramappa, there is a rampant war spilling down out of heaven, which is going on now all around us. Never mind the present day common folk are sadly unaware of it. And this unexpected and ill-timed disturbance is hastening the process, you see.

"Yeah, the war that goes on giving without even believing in blessing. I get it. Can I get a big haudu [Yes (in Kannada)] on that one?"

"There are certain interests inherent within the coming Sat Yuga which hasn't yet happened, but that is beside the point. Time is relative, is it not? These beings will have developed the technology of splintering Time. They will have the ability to interfere and influence certain linear paths therefore massaging key events as they are introduced into your life as you knit the ingredients, which will be drawn into the formation of the psychic DNA. This interference will cause a feedback, which will eventually percolate into the next Time phase and enhance their status in an immensely favorable manner. That is why they are searching so vigorously to locate and disarm you. They need to change your mind, Shri Ibsen Ji, but please don't take this as upsetting in anyway. You are always well protected, of course."

The magnanimous Saint from Vrindavan crossed his arms with seeming immense pleasure. I couldn't figure out who was scamming whom, these random Prophet dudes or the invisible messengers from some far-fetched future divergence, which existed in their heads. Lord Krishna had outlined the most capricious scheme that I had ever come across. And believe me, I'd seen a few oddballs trips in my day. Not only that, but he had put me smack dab in the middle of the full shebang. This was making the synthesis of modern symmetry seem like mubbly-peg and I was the first voyager to take sail across the vast stretches of the Symsoup. Talk about pressure!

"What if I mess up? What if I can't do my job with it? Then what?" I was totally freaked out and growing itchy feet.

"My dear Ramappa, again, that is why we are going to put you into a place where you will be well protected. It is a place in which all your bodily needs will be satisfactorily meted out. There you can concentrate on your meditation and the exercises, which are necessary to generate the recombinant psychic DNA, and furthermore, it is a place in which you will not be interfered. The only drawback with this plan is plain folks refer to this place as a penitentiary. We're going to put you in prison, Shri Ibsen Sahib."

Shri Krishna repositioned his Bansuri to continue with his beguiling melody. After he finished tootling out all this truck, he looked at me with his enchanting smile and his aura kicked up a few notches.

"Don't you worry about a thing. We will ensure every measure and every responsibility for your benefit. We also have specific plans for the wellbeing of your family, which shall be instituted as well. Have no fear for that. In fact, your family will even believe they are the ones making this happen to you. You will never physically be arrested or put in chains, at least not that we have enjoined. However, your trial may be considerably drawn out because we will have to create the illusion of your guilt. Moreover, we require some time to access the proper vehicle, or route, for you to arrive at a prison of our choosing, perhaps in Vermont or New Hampshire. They have suitable prisons we are told." As Shri Krishna finished up he began to tap his flute on the side of his cheek, innocently. It made an irritating hollow, popping noise.

"You've got to be out of your ever lovin' mind, Bro! You think I'm going to volunteer to go to prison so you can fuck with my head, pick and choose my dreams, and disassemble my hypothalamic machinery? That's completely nuts. I'm not going to do that. Not ever! It's not happening. Hear me?" I was furious now.

"No, no. You misunderstand me; it is not a choice of yours. You contracted this promise during your stand as you addressed the Lord of Death in the sixth Bardo. So far, you have been identified by the Nirunjan as an individual who satisfies all the guidelines and then some. You were set in place and the mark was placed upon you by Shiva in your episode with the female human designated as Ilene Ireland, Tiami to you. We have the imprints of all your significant linkages within our logs. It is only a matter of time now until you will be processed into the facility. Then, we will begin the testing of your brainwaves from our omniphalonic laboratories in the upper regions. We simply hoped for this moment with you so that we could explain the basic points to prepare you for the moment when that interstice in the Time/Space fabric arrives. You will need to be sufficiently compliant for the emergence to succeed. I have interceded on your

The Moon Women

behalf to mediatize these messages into your frame of consciousness. When the time comes, carriers will dispatch you to the place where you will proceed with your responsibilities. I trust you shall honor this most important mission. Humanity depends on it. Good day."

Shri Krishna grabbed the mane of his magnificent steed and threw himself two meters up onto his madder red saddle, which acted as his throne.

"It has been my esteemed pleasure to meet with you on this most auspicious occasion, Shri Ramappa Ji. We shall be getting together once or twice more before you begin your earnest work; until then Namaste Ji and Sat Naam!" He shouted out exuberantly.

The larger-than-life beast galloped off into the crowded landscape leaving a trail of Dravidian dust behind in remembrance. With that split in the wall of Time, Brownie came forth out of a tangent crevasse in the human ocean, like the Coast Guard out of the fog.

"Brownie, you'll never guess what's going to happen to me now!" I posed quixotically.

"What, Rahm? What is it? What's going on now? And where were you, by the way? Why do you always succeed in getting so lost?" Brownie was holding my camera.

"Nevermind. Nobody would believe it anyway."

I put my chappals back on.

- 7 -

After some serious meditation, I decided to accept some of the revelations, which Shri Krishna had narrated. Brownie and I had chosen to lie low. She had figured if we slept together all we would do from dusk until dawn would be you know what. She had some issues to think over what with the goings on which had happened with the Nagraj, not to mention, it was Dr. Krishnaswami's living space as well, something that made her all the more nervous.

It gave me a chance to reflect on what had happened in the temple as well. It was more than a simple twist of fate that Brownie had seen the cobra when she did. Our experiments with Kundlini Yoga were thereby intercepted before we could create the embryonic heart. No doubt, we had certainly coached ourselves to achieve the prerequisite zenith in which we discharged the actual biological orgasm; still, we had not passed the energy collected within the chakras back into the upper skull, the region of ultimate sublimity. It is through the breath that you are supposed to mix those energies and then nourish the embryonic form, which becomes the vehicle taking you into the Beyond. Once stabilized, you can stuff this energy packet back in through the spinal column and into the brain where it produces a turbo charged nectar. When you imbibe this nectar, you can reach a state of ecstasy and bliss, which is supposed to be the most sublime ever. Doubtless, it was providence that we had not fully manifested this state. Otherwise, I doubt if we would have ever let go of it. It would have chained us to its love labors the same way paradise has chained the proverbial angels to their hell in heaven.

Ironically, it was from reliving our coupling in the Tantric exercises that I came to know the true meaning of chastity. When one begins to unlock the doors of introspection and self-awareness, which leads to the pinnacle in self-improvement by performing one's own experiments within the human body, you eventually come to realize that one of the most important building blocks of true spirituality is chastity, the harnessing of the sexual jewels. Chastity does not require one to go and reside in a forest as a hermit or yogi. One can maintain a household and maintain a traditional domestic life style; nonetheless, one must be mindful of the proper usage of the sexual act. Its principal function is for child bearing. Other than that, occasional use for the cementing of the bonds with one's life mate are permitted, so long as one realizes that a single emission of seminal fluid takes many months to replenish spiritually. It is a function, which should only be undertaken wisely. If one chooses to be an ascetic or participate with the mainline of Sadhus, one may do that, but one should honor that station in life and be faithful to that daily style for the remainder of his days. Taking up with it, then putting it down and then taking it up numerous times whenever it is convenient, is the worst possible approach a practitioner of meditation can do.

Later in the day, I cautioned Brownie that I didn't see us having intercourse anymore. I informed her I had realized the true meaning of chastity. The experience with her during that orgasmic zenith in the temple had awakened the most spectacular revelation. Never wanting to spoil that pinnacle of my spiritual totem pole, I had decided to crystalize it by never attempting to capture it repeatedly.

533

The Moon Women

To attempt to do so would only erase the gifts achieved at the peak of that mystical climax.

She was horrified when I shared this unexpected reversal with her because she was determined to do it again and again. She related it was so out of sight and carried on like a schoolmarm. I continued to explain to her this new vital force of which we had experienced is burning in our brains like a fire. It is burning with that fire every second of every day. But we don't see it. Why? Because we pour the waters of raw sex onto it repeatedly and drown it. If we could only harness that dynamic and conserve our energies we would be able to have the experience of the light within us as the burning effulgence of a divine presence right in plain sight. We do not have to go into the temples, the churches, or the mosques or anywhere for that matter to witness it in action. It is within us and therefore it can be easily communicated with at any of the twenty-four hours simply by closing our eyes and going within ourselves. This is what I had come to believe and this is what I was going to do from now on.

Brownie was dreadfully disappointed to hear this. She felt as though I had brought her to the foot of a spiritual mountain only to jerk the rug out from under her. She got up with a hurt look and disappeared without even a good-bye or a thank-you or even, God forbid, a flip off. I watched the door close on that melancholic phase of my life.

At an unusual altitude upon a plateau in northern Tibet, a violent battle raged if only for microsecond. In its wake, damp impressions imprinted upon the face of a rolling sweep expanse of wheat read like poetry from the stars, another prayer penned from the quills of angels.

- 8 -

Dr. Krishnaswami and I had had many meaningful discussions. I had never found anyone who was as intense and sincere as he was. Dr. K was one of a rare handful who listened intently whenever I related my journeys, not only my tales of crossing the width and breadth of Mother India, but also the ones telling how I had crisscrossed the entire globe, how I had hitch hiked my way from the ferry port of Dunkirk along the coast of Northern France and over the sparse countryside into Belgium and Germany, how, in only four rides, I had managed to get through the Alps into Italy, and how I had traced the coastline of Yugoslavia down through Greece and into Athens where I had adopted my Land Rover gang for the final trek into India.

He had empathized with me whenever I confided the various misadventures of my using psychedelics with Dr. Timothy Leary juxtaposed with the interpretations of the <u>Tibetan Book Of The Dead.</u> As seen through the influential lens of LSD, my trips unwound levels of insanity which conflicted with the traditional theories of the normally crazy people he had bumped into down in the alleyways of Dhareshwarevalli, where Brahmins segregate the mentally dysfunctional.

Together we cringed as I related my escapades across Turkey and how I sidestepped the unasked advances from the anise induced Turk. We grimaced together as I ladled upon him the miseries of my transformations through Islam after I had secreted myself into that holy of holiest Mosques in all of Persia, which irrevocably led to my becoming a Shia via the auspices of the Ayatollah Milani. At other times, he recoiled in shock as I unfolded my communications with beings known as the Khrng who inhabit the insidious dimensions of the atrocious. He was aghast at my recollection of the time I had been spirited up into one their floating craft to undergo their probing devises for hours. What's more, he cowered when I shared the visitations from the Seven Angels with whom I had an ongoing relationship ever since the day I died on that beachhead of private calm and remote beauty. After suffering an untimely death, anaphylaxis due to cold, those ice demons have continued to visit me time after time to unfold their seriously disturbed notions of a war in heaven, which has spilled down into this realm to challenge the future of mankind. Not to mention the peripheral exposure of when they saved me from certain doom after I had come face to face with an enchanted pine tree while exploring a hidden grotto hidden in the grasslands of Cazenovia. Furthermore, in spite of never having been to Japan himself, the stories of my times spent in the Zen monasteries of Kyoto and Hiroshima had brought him to the sorrowful conclusion I had been on a long and arduous journey to catch hold of the one true reality. In essence, he understood me like no one else.

Without warning there came an impulsive knock on my door.

The Moon Women

"Mr. Rahms, can I see you for a moment, Sir?" Dr. Krishnaswami asked.

He was always so polite and respectful, except he always fingered me with that silly plural form of my name as though he were addressed more than one person. Additionally, he would always call to me from the edge of the K-room or ask me outside to meet with him. Because of some conscription or other, he would never physically enter the K-room. Owing to my kooky and reclusive nature, there was little chance he had overheard, or worse, witnessed some of the ceremonies, which I had been conducting with the Shiva Lingham stone within my puja room. Nevertheless, he believed that I was hatching some mendacious Tantric black magic by performing atrocious sacrilegious rites, which were unmentionable. It was a fear he kept under his hat because we never discussed it outright.

"Yenappa ["What's happening]?" I probed.

I explored my rudimentary vocabulary of Kannada on him.

When outside the door, he explained that on Sunday, a handful of students, and two or three of the resident professors were going to undertake an excursion to a religious community out in the country. Would I like to come?

"It promises to be vastly educational and uplifting. There may even be some meals with the Maharaja there," He insinuated.

"Sure. What time?" I didn't know how to come up with that in Kannada.

"Noonish." He was feigning to be European but way missing the mark.

"Autos or cars?" I interrogated.

"We have reserved an Ambassador for your comfort and pleasure, Shri Rahms." He lowered his head with a cynical smirk.

"Bahot achaa!" [Very good!]

After I mixed in a little Hindi for multi-lingual appeal, I folded my hands to which he returned with a spirited "Namaste" and reclaimed his side of the Dharma.

Brahmins, I thought to myself. Can their dreams really liberate them? I trotted back to right my ethereal chair the K-room. Why had the damn chair re-centered itself on that ugly window again? Thinking the recalcitrant pendulum had frightened me with the possibility of having lost its enchantment; I approached it and gently corrected its arrangement by twisting it in the other direction.

536

I got in. As the pulsations reinitiated their heated cadence, I knew I had been reset to my center, the hub of the universe.

The following day there was a ruckus in the house. The Phone Wallah had come to deliver some messages but no one could claim ownership considering they had to do with goings on with laundry pirates from the outer limits. Mrs. Krishnaswami was up in arms with the guy and warned him never to come back with such alarming insinuations. Dr. K stayed out of the picture but gave me a shunted side look as he retreated to the innards of his private garden to see how his cultivation of okras were progressing. Finally, the Phone Wallah reached his quota on patience and departed in a flurry of confetti and plantain skins. I hit the bricks for my audio studio to marry some more music for my new film, "Visitor From Dwarpar Province." It was a spoof on Yudhishthira's dog.

Locked tightly in the compression of Time/Space, beings of the White inhaled their divinity from a galactic vortex. Blossoming forth like the birth of a super-nova, they expanded on the rim of a resplendent truth. Surging forth as a wave of purity they washed away the faulty and weak incarnations, which were growing the sooty filth of irreverence. The Angels banded for their daring onslaught over the Khrng. They came together under the banner of the Lamb slain in the name of Goodness and Love to show ***unto his servant the things which must shortly come to pass.*** [2]

"Stan, there's something not right here."

"Yeah. What's that? You've input your password backwords again and so you're wondering why the screen's upside down?"

"Cut it out. I'm not like that. It's got to do with the bus. Did you delete that last set of hex set we installed?"

"No Bill. That's your job. You know very well you won't let anybody touch the bootstrap protocols."

"Just checking Stan. You never slip up by over checking things, ya know."

The two hooks of a diamond Moon rose over the trees. On one hook it held sanity and on the other it suspended a loose madness. Its fulcrum was but a pink point of light known as Mars. Chased by the cloud of a white ship riding the undulations of future riddles, she lapped the ageless shores of the black sky like a worn

The Moon Women

whore who smiles back from the dark streets knowing she can
never bank the illusive pleasures of an obscene past.

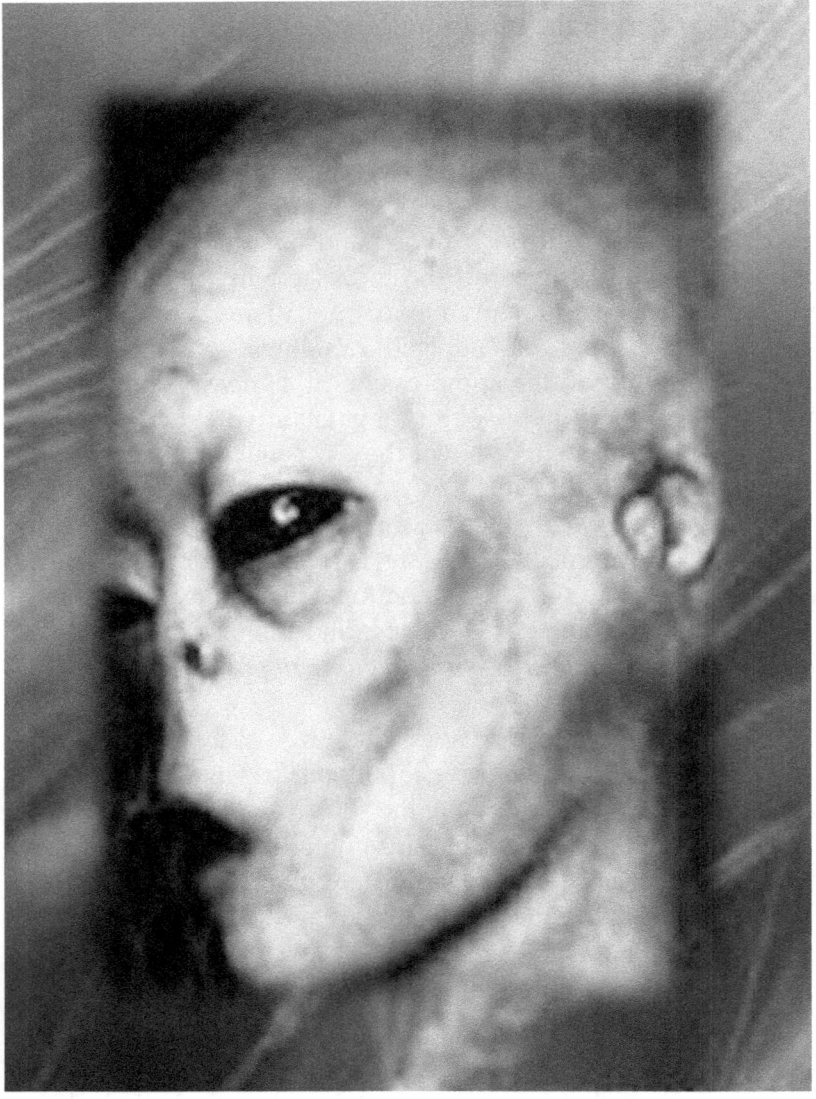

KHRNG

CHAPTER 8 - **MOON WOMEN**

– 1 –

This time I gave the wicker booth three strong twists in the other direction. It came to halt at an angle, which was not expressly surveying the evil window, but since it wasn't facing the puja chamber either, I determined the chair had chosen an in-between state. Willingly I hopped in and as the rope fell to the floor, I let the obdurate swing chair do the walking for a change. Besides being a little bored, as well as bothered by these interruptions from the doppelgängers, I was annoyed with where I had shortsighted the untrodden pathways concerning Dr. Krishnaswami and his mission to unhook me from the Rakshashas of Ravena. And why his young son, Ranjappa, hadn't shown up yet? But yet again, the chair's rule took over.

When I was eleven years old, I enjoyed daily treks into the woods, the ones, which lived at the end of our street in Wellesley. These adventures always revolved around a megalith I had called Elephant Rock. It was a unique rock-slash-tree combo. A gigantic glacial boulder had teamed up with an unusual mate, a deciduous acer saccharum. The big rock was the size of a dump truck; I would approximate it to be five or six meters in diameter, only it was more cubical than spherical. It had worn grooves and neat escarpments crowning its domed skull and a deformed vertical shelf resembling an ear. The tree was an aggressive sugar maple, which had grown out of the earth right beside its mammoth glacial husband like a lovelorn handmaid. It was so close to the stone face of the boulder that its bark had flattened itself out onto the contours of the stone, which invested it with a melted look. To say that the two were making love might be taken as some crude form of wedlock, but I'm not one to critique untoward perversions with regard to sex. That one might get you labeled as religiously incorrect. Nevertheless, this odd couple had welded themselves together to form a single unit which strangely resembled the barreled girth of a pachyderm unfurling its trunk; hence, Elephant Rock.

Whenever I disappeared into those Arcadian woods, I would always begin at Elephant Rock and go from there. There was a faint

539

The Moon Women

footpath running alongside that headstone, which led into the unlimited forest of the Boulder Brook Reservation. Its initial frontiers spanned the edges of a wide campestral expanse, a wheat field in fact. Once you crossed that patch of open grass, the untamed wood extended forever before exposing any other free terrain.

That autumn, as I was hiking through the reserve on a quest for glory, I got lost. Many times in the past, I had threaded my way quite artfully through that wilderness and uncovered vistas of ethereal beauty. It was my calling at the time: something, which had dawned within me when I was a boy while wandering around in the heart of the Adirondacks. However, on this latest safari I had chosen an unfamiliar turn here and a stranger one there. Sooner than soon, I was dismally lost. I couldn't understand it since it was uncharacteristic of me to lose my way so easily. But there it was. I was standing dizzy and frozen with fear in an unrecognizable place in the woods. What was I going to do now?

I calculated I could double back and easily reclaim my bearings, but after that trick failed, I had to give in; all was to no avail. Even though I had traveled many times in those woods with no compass of any kind, mind you, things were always routinely obvious to me. I knew where I was going and where I'd been, but now I was simply hornswoggled.

This time things were coming at me with immense confusion. With every turn, the forest grew thicker and more crooked. Eventually, I dug myself into a nasty thicket, which seemed to spread out forever. With my innate sense of magnetic North completely scrambled, I had lost all sense of direction. Wandering in circles like a lone manjak in a maze, I was not only lost, but also fearing the inevitable. As the sun dipped lower and lower on the horizon, I had to break off with my siege.

What if I couldn't find a way out of this mess? What would happen to me? How would I ever be able to get home? I lost it and went slightly berserk. As I fought off my fears, I was again overcome by that choking recollection of some inveterate force dragging me down a cramped corridor of some Martian space craft while fighting weightlessness as I watched the flow of litter and feces drift by me like obscene dandruff swirling in a paperweight world of lost children.

540

I rose and using all my muscle, I pushed my way against the dense underbrush and twisted growth of mallees. As I worked at it with all my might, the twigs and branches were whipping and slashing at the back of my neck, my face, and everywhere. Undaunted, I pushed headlong into the entangled thicket. Then, my worst fears rose up within me.

In a frightful vision, I foreshadowed a search party locating my dead body decomposing in these horrible woods. If I died here, nobody would know where I was for weeks and weeks, even months. Feral animals would rip my flesh to shreds. The flies and worms would devour me. I would turn into a rotting cadaver to provide lunch for the maggots. The wriggling larvae would ooze out of my eyeballs and mix with the swollen rot of my engorged tongue!

At last, I broke through and started to jog through the swampy weeds. But this madhouse of a forest was also pacing after me. Even though my calves were aching from the pain of pushing onwards for hours, I cranked up my pace to a greater velocity. I was pushing past the reeds and limbs as fast as I could through this mess of a forest. I was smashing my hands, my arms, and my ripped shins into the terrifying slash of branches clawing at my flesh. On and on, I jogged and jogged.

Crying impulses overwhelmed me. Unable to control them I broke down. I was so afraid. The tears and the dirt from the slapping branches created a sludge, which seeped down my cheeks and into my mouth threatening to gag me. That only made me more and more terrified as I galloped faster and faster. Now, I was throwing myself into the tangled, twisted network of close-knit stalks and branching stems. It took an ungodly effort to fight through this inland Sargasso Sea of weeds, which harbored all the dead bodies of the useless ones who had come there in the past to perish.

"You are going to die now." The still inner voice warned. "Are you ready to die?"

I am only eleven years old. My life has amounted to zilch. And now I'm dead. I was running madly out of control screaming and crying and thrashing at the green monster like a madman. I don't even know if I was making any progress. I was that out of it. I collapsed sobbing and blubbering amidst my Mexican standoff in these ugly weeds.

The Moon Women

"I'm going to die. I'm going to die. I just know it. I'm going to die."

Stuck in a rut of frozen fear, the master force behind true insanity, I exposed my heart and became a vulnerable target for the Khrng's knowledge menus. I needed to gather in my senses and pen down. Let there be as few words as possible and let the unavoidable ones be deep in the trance work to speak no more with unclean tongues. I passed out from exhaustion.

- 2 –

Ants were biting me. They were biting me on my ankles. When I woke up, a ragged stockade of sticks surrounded me. Nothing had changed. I was still lost. When I focused on the impenetrable wall in front of me, I recognized something fluky. One particular stem was unlike all the others. Something had bent it around completely into a loop. Where its throat would have been there was a stubby branch of another twig making a bowtie. I stared at it for a moment as it ranged in and out of blurriness. Then it came to me. It looked like an Egyptian ankh. Was this to be the sarcophagus of my burial? Perhaps it was a sign. The Khrng had not yet gotten their way with me from what I could determine by the absence of the Speak, but I knew how devious they could be and had seen the aftermath of their digging in the subliminal swamps of their abductees, especially the children.

I gathered my energies for one more gung-ho assault against the barbarian hordes of sticks and limbs forming a jam-packed fortress of confusion in front of me. I put my foot down because I wasn't going to die here just yet. I was bone tired with dying all the time.

As I was lying there failing to rise up, I heard a tiny sound way off on the fringes of recognition. Insofar as I was way the hell out in the boonies, it was improbable that any such musical note could be reaching me out here. I concentrated on that vibration as it came and went. It was barely audible. I wondered if its tintinnabulations could somehow release me from this morass of wired brush and brambles. Then, it came to me. It was a bell.

It was the sound of a church bell tolling from a steeple many, many kilometers away. The bell seemed to warble like bubbles of a mirage hanging over the forest as it clarified the delicate balance between imprisonment and deliverance. I focused in on its fragile presence with all my inner reserve. I was attempting to sense from which direction it was emanating. I could not accurately pin point its origins right away so I got going and pealed my ears acutely as I pushed forward to ascertain the extent of its remoteness and also its message. Then I got its place.

It was disseminating from the southwest; might have even been five kilometers out, it was that faint. I gathered in all my machismo and trudged off in that direction. The woven thicket was an enormous impediment. It stood as an unending barrier to my freedom and my sanity. I remembered what I had learned once regarding the knowledge of walls. How force only led to resistance whereas acceptance instilled permission. Pushing my way strenuously hour after hour against the tortuous underbrush of wiry shoots, matted stalks, and tangled roots, which snagged at my battered feet was so exhausting. Falling in front of this futility and badly needing to rest, I crumbled into a heap against a bent poplar to catch a breath.

After taking a moment to compose myself, I picked up the bell sound once more, only this time it was a bit louder. I stood up like a man, leveled my finger at the weeds, and shouted two words.

"Be gone!"

Fearlessly and with full conviction, I marched ahead to challenge the wicked weeds. With each step, they fell back as if some magical force were moving them out of my way. After five flips of pressing onwards like this, I could determine the bell was unmistakably closer. It was so haphazard because it was not Sunday but Saturday. I scolded myself not to discourse against the bell. It's a damn bell, I cried out loud. Do not argue with the bell. Do not question its why or wherefore. Just follow it. It was not faith; it is life and it is your survival.

In another half hour, I had gobbled down considerably more turf. "Why does it keep clanging?" I wondered.

Then, I quit blabbing all over the place to myself and just kept walking. Walk to the bell. I repeated inside myself like a mantra. Walk to the bell. If you keep walking, you will come to the bell. Walk to the bell; nice bell. Carry me home please, Mr. Bell. But then, it disappeared.

The Moon Women

"Shit! Now look what you've done! Your faith is weak. You don't even deserve the bell." I cursed myself. "You've killed it with your weak minded, lily-livered hopes and lies, you moron!" I scrubbed myself with cleansing talk.

The Khrng had never taken me so deeply down this trail previously. Were the strings of their cerebral organics losing the upper hand, losing the dominion over my mind? Trudging through the preponderance of twigs, branches, roots, and spines, I struggled onwards through the dense thicket. It was as impenetrable as a mangrove swamp but after I vowed to confront it or die in this weed coffin buried at the heart of this organic citadel, the rampart of sticks rent in two and I plunged forwards, always forwards.

As a necessary consequence of fortune, I came to my next dilemma - thirst. Having not carried any type of canteen or water bottle, my throat was as parched as an Australian outback in late summer. Even though being surrounded by a veritable superabundance of hydration devises, namely the bloody vegetation, I was dying of thirst.

Wait. Detecting an odd sound like a whirring, I stopped short. Maybe it was something like a bell, but no, it was only my imagination. What? We're going into the woods for what could be a week or more and you don't have anything on board to hold water? How stupid! I drooled from lack of moisture.

Again, it came to me. This time it was way louder. A spike of excitement shot up my spine quickening my pace. Somehow, the thicket thinned out as well. After some ten big ones, I was jogging through a decent stand of poplars. As I slalomed through the ski pole tree trunks, I noticed the motions of something moving along side of me. Foggy outlines of Khrng were shadowing my advance through the woods. Much as they were keeping stride with me, they were not targeting me for abduction. Soon it became apparent that they had some other purpose. They seemed to be massing for some inevitable confrontation.

As I came down a gentle incline harboring a sloping run of alder, the swelling phalanx party of pint-sized mutants veered off to join up with a secondary echelon moving along a narrow channel of winnowing grain. Another battle was about to commence. My goal now was to get over the hill and locate the source of my salvation, the bell. I can't get sucked into overlooking some battle being waged from out of the celestial dominions to decide control over dogmas and demons and who will run the universe. That will have to keep for another day. At the moment, my date is with my own survival and my own destiny. What the Angels will reveal and what the Khrng will steal is a future beyond my beck and call and what's more, it's not my path this afternoon. That will have to wait for another time and another book.

The wind began to dry my heated tears. I came down into a little gulch where there was a running creek. I bent down to sip the fresh waters. After I had gulped in all I could I trotted on and on until sunset.

Once more, the bell's gong faded away to naught. When it was with me, the bell was calling me. But then, because of a request being sent from an ulterior pulse, it had to go somewhere different to work its magic in some other framework of existence. Nevertheless, I kept up my pace moving quickly on my drive to secure the bell. I blasted out of the forest and came upon a ruddy logging road. This must be all the way over in Weston I thought. Man, am I off the beaten trail! But I was saved, because I knew I would be able to approach civilization from there. I knew I would be going home. Boy! That sure was a close call.

The bell commenced once more but stronger this time. I bolted down the road keeping that clanging within reach. After jogging along for another forty bananas, I neared a millpond, which fed into a meager assemblage of cottages punctuated with mountain ash popping with those brilliant orange berries. In the center of this hamlet was what looked like a church, only it had unorthodox appointments on it like wrought iron spires. Cautiously I approached its perimeter. There were some stragglers hanging out beside a mailbox alongside an inviting driveway. It had a name painted on it in florid red paint.

THADDAEUS

"What Church is this?" I respectfully inquired.

"Oh, this is no church. This here's Moysha's Temple." A burly lumberjack by the name of Nathan Liebowitz said with a snap.

"But, I didn't think a Jewish temple would have a steeple with a bell in it." I was astounded.

The Moon Women

"Well, this one does. It's Temple Ehyey Asher Ehyey," the bloke echoed.

"I am that I am," the other one chimed.

"Bell and all. It be totally moronic, but he built it himself. He's a nut."

As the bell tolled midnight, the scabrous shell of the three-quarter moon mounted the hillside and climbed the steeple to gaze down upon the signs hiden in the wheat, the ones, which would one day reveal the aftermath of the war in Abaddon. As a lone white streak burned across the starry welkin right over the bell tower, it displayed a precise direction and then disappeared. The Khrng never leave off with their search for stragglers.

- 3 -

The White chair hovered over the floor nervously straining for me to launch it on another visionary excursion through the far-flung fringes of the future mind fields of my past. Something had been burrowing in there. Assisted by my rattan craft, I had relived my life as ventures weaving the underground passageways, which led to the five channels of the Moon women. As my Time pod seesawed rhythmically, the beads clicked in my hand and enabled me to summon the latent authority of the Siddhi. I contemplated the faces of my five Moon women and wondered how their lives bridged mine. The ensuing introspection of those elements furnished a sweetness like licking fresh frosting off a rusty fork.

When I viewed them chronologically, they formed a pattern. The first woman was Alena who came to me in 1967. She was a breezy love with no attachments; no big deals. She was the least intense love. Nevertheless, more valued caverns could be mapped out with regard to Alena. The second was Oma who came to me late in 1969. She was an extraneous, but easy-going and complaisant love. I wasn't as sure of her tie to Shintoism as I was of Alena's cross-link to Christianity. Undeniably, both of these anagogic avenues would require further exploration. Early in 1970 came Chhumpar, who was not only a desperate love but also a devoted one. As the epitome of Buddhism in its finest sense, she unhinged the framework each of the five women had with their respective religion and its prophets. With each rung up this ladder of romance, future installments came to bear as each explosion in the matrix of divinity blossomed. At the tail of 1970, there was Evey, who shocked me with a frenetically violent love. Her ravenous and militant attacks were the essence of the modern day femme fatale incorporating many staunch forms of violence and cementing them with an unavoidable future. It was what would come to be a formidable Muhammadanism via fear and torture. Although it might be seen in its most fervent sense, the Islamic connection should not be underestimated. Recently this year in 1971, there was Brownie, who bordered on a profound love, a devoted love, a persisting love having many levels. Her heartfelt portrayal of Hindu piety rose to a peerless submission. Truly, the depths of exploratory possibilities with Brownie were as exciting and terrifying as the moments I have spent with the Khrng themselves.

The chthonian chair had run out its source of clockwise revolutions and was now climbing to uncork a reversed counterclockwise momentum. As my observation platform wheeled round and round, the faces of my five Moon women came and went. They passed by me as the advertisements from the third Bardo and strained to reclaim some future perspective on the inner cells of my life. It was as if I was gazing out the window of a moving train while shuttling off to future destinations where the exchange of telepathic passengers would begin to define the dynamics of its route and perchance the final destiny of my plight as well.

Why had there been two Devereauxs in my life? The first was Madame Devareaux. She was the one who had dubbed me as the Albacore Man. And even though I couldn't attest to being any sort of expert as far as tuna fish goes, the title did smack of an unheard of and ridiculous concept, an anagram, which in Arabic means fierce young upstart or Ale Bacr Oman, rephrased as Ali Bakr Oman (a country of origin on the southeastern coast of the Arabian Peninsula). Had her scathing admonishments to guard against the Cancer child, the Moon child, anesthetized me to the paroxysm of the Moon women? Was Madame Devareaux's prophecy supposed to be an alert to notify me of the possibility of some all-important phenomenon? I had a flashback of an ornate plaque on her mantle that day in February. It was a calligraphed blessing:

And the angel came unto her

The Moon Women

And said, Hail, thou art
Highly favored, the Lord is with thee:
Blessed art thou among women. [1]

So there you have it. Conceivably, the women had all simply been put there by the angels.

Second, there was my esteemed bosom buddy, Monsieur Jean Devereux, with whom I had been through so much when in Cambodia. He had explained to me the meaning of the walls of the great pantheon of Angkor. He had advised me the successive enclosures represented the five elevations of sexual union, from the introductory naive to the obscure acme of the sublime. In the days of the original Khmer Kings, the priests regarded intercourse to be as holy and divine as the activities, which nowadays we regard to be traditionally spiritual, such as devotion, prayer, and the study of religious scriptures. As well, he conveyed each of these unique elevations of the sexual experience formed a network, or lattice, ascending into the heavens, into the more expanded states of consciousness.

To augment that revelation, he described how differing partners, each one of whom represented an isolated example of a major religious path, could enhance this matrix. Furthermore, he explained how they could be organized in such a way as to unfold a gradient embodying these expanding degrees of consciousness. Adding to that facet was Shri Krishna's chimerical concept of encountering one's sexual partners in a particular order that followed the line of the chakras. Matching these vibrational patterns resulted in having the untold fortune to climb the flaming rungs of an exalted ladder and become the rarest of rare spirits. Lord Krishna had divulged in detail that the order might be mimicking the sound-cells I had learned long ago in my closet. Moreover, after becoming internally perfected, these specially christened Over-souls would one day be the adjuncts or agents to the fire deities. At the conclusion of each Time segment, these godlike deities having skin the color of steel will descend from the upper spheres riding upon the flaming wheels of singing fire.

Lastly, he imparted what he had learned when excavating the esoteric writings hidden within the snaking tunnels of Angkor Wat. He had uncovered tablets, which stated whosoever successfully treads this cryptic path and who also experiences it in the correct order and the precise fashion as accorded by birth and by the stars, will not only be given an experience of heightened awareness, but also, when coupled to the fifth stage on the ascent up this mystical mountain, shall receive the highest sublimity characterized by the most explosive sexual climax conceivable by any man. Moreover, he conveyed that when the billions of neural connectors fire all at once the effect would culminate into a magnificent crescendo of fireworks upon the pinnacles a divine sexual orgasm.

Momently, I gave the rope a strong tug to stabilize its whirligig movements. The revolving chair had finalized the windings of longitudinal sequences; perchance some lateral work would gain further benefit. Gentle swaying movements steered me off onto another tangent. Devereux had not only signified the importance of the Moon but also that of Mars. We should not interpret them merely as positive or negative representations, but as two sides of the same coin, like the strands of the DNA molecule having two spirals winding around each other. Neither strand should necessarily be regarded as being plus or minus, rather as equals, but separate. They should be seen as paired together, intertwining as two spiral staircases, one within the other, the Moon women on the one hand, the Mars women on the other hand. However, in my mind was the unavoidable cliffhanger: had the Khrng ever eaten any of my women? And if they had what part of me had they stolen as well?

Then there was the distance factor. I pondered the far-flung possibility these places of romance might have occurred at strategic points on the globe. I had made contact with each of these five Moon women at coordinates, which were located between five and ten thousand kilometers apart, averaging about seventy five hundred. Had this caused some buffering of their effect on me or were all these discoveries merely circumstantial? It raised the question, was there any true plan behind the Madame's admonition and its execution? Or better yet, was there some pattern within the emergence of the Moon women themselves? Had these intervals softened the blows, which were supposed to harm me in some way? Moreover, would the coming of the Mars women strengthen these patterns or rend them with further wickedness? On top of all that, the view which astro-cartography places upon this predicted threat can also bear some

The Moon Women

weight considering how the global dynamic ultimately effects the outcome.

Unraveling the chronology of the Moon women has laid the groundwork for a unique science, micro-splinters of knowledge, which may promise a greater impact upon general humanity than fire or atomic wizardry has previously shown upon the glistening pages of man's progress. This initial episode concludes with a whimsical residue of doubt, which lingers within the possibilities of a trust proposed by the shepherd of life, Rahm Ibsen. This sharing of the events of his life for the sake of exposing two forces, the ultra-race of the Khrng and the agents of Abaddon, has evolved as a method for educating humanity concerning not only their existence but also their purpose. By the same token, investigating the flipside of this coin, the Mars women, and their link to both the war in heaven and the work of the Khrng, may bring further disclosure with regard to how likely such an insignificant individual such as Rahm Ibsen could impact the outcome of the entire human race. Now armed with the revelation that the human being is a divine construct, you may come to understand why the whole damn thing manifested with such dismal drudgery in the first place.

I was thinking I might have hit upon something all by myself, when there came a firm, masculine tapping on my door.

"Mr. Rahms. Excuse me, but Dr. Krishnaswami would like you to come over to his office; something to tell you about tomorrow." Raju was acting as his assistant today.

I popped out of my waltzing chair, sucked my sandals onto my feet, and slopped down the empty hallway, echoing as I left. And the midnight sun tattooed its stain onto the soiled sheets of glory.

REFERENCES

The dialogue transmitted by the Seven Angels of Abaddon consists solely of words taken from a renowned gospel of the Bible called The Revelation authored by Saint John the Divine (which this writing references as BOR). A glossary of these words can be located in the publication entitled Revelate Vocabulary by Bishop Sargn Ramege, a noteworthy scholar of biblical theses, concordances, and all extant knowledge bases regarding Holy Scriptures. This volume can be located in the same electronic library from which you have selected this book. You can now prepare yourself for the next installment, Albacore Man The Mars Women, which may scour your knowledge structures even further. Here is a list of references for each chapter in this episode.

C01 - SWING CHAIR
01) William Shakespeare, All's Well That Ends Well, (1605)
02) Luke 02:15
03) Amos 08:05
C02 - TIAMI BROWN
01) Psalms 23:02-03
02) Jeremiah 12:13
03) BOR 01:01
04) Luke 01:34
05) Acts 01:08
06) Jeremiah 07:02
07) BOR 02:01
08) BOR 02:09
09) BOR 02:10
10) BOR 04:01
11) BOR 05:09
12) Revelate
13) BOR 02:01
14) BOR 03:20
15) BOR 03:21
16) BOR 02:07
17) BOR 03:18
18) BOR 03:17
19) BOR 03:16
20) BOR 02:17
21) BOR 03:18
22) BOR 01:19
23) BOR 10:11

The Moon Women

24) BOR 01:03
25) BOR 02:01
26) BOR 13:09
27) BOR 13:10
28) BOR 14:02
29) BOR 14:03
30) BOR 14:06
31) BOR 14:07
32) BOR 14:14
33) BOR 15:06
34) BOR 16:01
35) BOR 09:07
36) BOR 09:08
37) BOR 09:09
38) BOR 18:08
39) BOR 10:11
40) Luke 02:15
C03 - ALENA PHILPOTT
01) BOR 02:01
02) BOR 09:20
03) BOR 01:20
04) BOR 02:02
05) John 12:12
06) Isaiah 28:25
07) Psalm 81:16
08) Matthew 13:44
09) Matthew 12:40
10) BOR 20:08
11) BOR 21:16
12) Matthew 11:07
13) Matthew 13:39
14) Matthew 24:39
15) Matthew 11:15
16) Matthew 11:30
17) Matthew 22:14
18) BOR 02:01
C04 - EVEY NATHANSON
01) BOR 02:01
02) BOR 03:09
03) BOR 04:02
04) BOR 04:03
05) BOR 04:04
06) BOR 04:05
07) BOR 04:06
08) BOR 02:18
09) BOR 22:16
10) Luke 01:13

11) BOR 11:05
12) BOR 11:06
13) BOR 11:07
14) BOR 11:01
15) BOR 11:03
16) Mathew 28:05
17) BOR 02:01
18) BOR 03:04
19) BOR 06:12
20) BOR 06:13
21) BOR 06:14
22) BOR 09:09
23) Thomas Milkwood, Tryin' to Set to Seven, 1970
24) Daniel Ladinsky, tr., <u>The Gift: Poems by Hafiz, the Great Sufi Master</u>, (1999)
25) Quote from the Qur'an
C05 - CHHUMPAR KYEW
01) Alexander Pope, <u>Essay on Criticism</u>, 1709
02) Paul Harvey
03) Luke 01:38
04) BOR 02:01
05) BOR 07:01
06) BOR 03:04
07) BOR 07:01
08) BOR 06:08
09) BOR 05:05
10) BOR 05:06
11) Ezekiel 04:09
C06 - OMA FULTON
01) Matthew 13:25
02) BOR 01:01
03) BOR 09:19
04) BOR 09:19
05) BOR 10:01
06) BOR 01:01
07) BOR 09:03
08) BOR 02:01
09) BOR 03:04
10) BOR 06:15
11) BOR 05:01
12) BOR 05:02
13) BOR 05:03
14) BOR 01:06
15) Luke 03:17
16) BOR 09:14
17) BOR 09:15
18) BOR 09:16
19) BOR 09:17

The Moon Women

20) BOR 09:18
21) Thaddaeus, Four Faces of the Lion, 1970
22) BOR 02:01
23) BOR 03:01
24) BOR 03:04
25) BOR 03:05
26) BOR 03:08
27) BOR 03:03
28) Matthew 26:53
29) BOR 01:02
C07 - LUNAR LINKS
01) BOR 02:01
02) BOR 06:09
03) BOR 06:10
04) BOR 06:11
05) BOR 07:02
06) BOR 07:01
07) BOR 01:01
C08 - THE MOON WOMEN
01) Luke 01:28

ACKNOWLEDGMENTS

Dhanyavaad to the people of India who once spread their loving arms to welcome me and corral me within their country for so long. As a student, I was given the path of obedience; as a worshiper, I was given the path of honored devotion, and as a disciple, I was given the path of true living. Shortly after returning to the States, I was put in contact with Shima Rosenberg who became my esteemed editor and master craftsman in forming the genesis of the first manuscript all the way to this finished product you now hold in your hands. She has been my constant companion and mentor in all things spawned from the alphabet swamp.

No less appreciation should be paid to my image poet, Amaris Bergson, for her tireless expenditures within the rarified craft of graphical posturing on both the jacket art and the presence of my place upon the company's web site at Manacore Lab's dream works on the com.

Last and not least are the glorious folks who toil effortlessly at Manacore Lab and all the energy with which they have infused this project simply for the mad reason of saving humanity from what seems to be a miserable future.

Mentioning the one from whom and for whom all of this was cooked up in the first place has been warned against. However, ripping off these bonds of disaffirmation only implants an honored indebtedness for his choosing me, of all people, to be the one to whom this remarkable gift was so unceremoniously given. I only hope I have proceeded to put forth something that remotely deserves his blessing.

Thank you, Pounar.

Haan Moses

The Moon Women

ANNEX

A Nineteenth Century Poem

Monday's child is fair of face.
Tuesday's child is full of grace.
Wednesday's child is full of woe.
Thursday's child has far to go.
Friday's child is loving and giving.
Saturday's child works hard for a living.
But the child who is born on the Sabbath day
Is lucky, happy, good and gay.

The DNA Helical Universe

This DNA double helix metaphor, which in some models represents the physicality of life, is not linear but cyclical. Seen as having its ends joined together like a gigantic piece of pasta to form a ring, this model demonstrates more than a terraqueous concern. The twin spiraling strands of Space and Time also oppose each other. One is twisting clockwise at the speed of light as the other twists in reverse or counterclockwise at the same rate. Time travel happens simply by jumping from one strand to the other after computing an analog of the rotation principle before jumping to the other portal as it unwinds faster than thought.

ITINERARY

From his preconception in 1943
to his departure from India in 1971,
Rahm Ibsen traveled to the following
places listed in chronological order
while spanning the 28 years
depicted in this writing.